'THE FERRERS CONNECTION'

BY

PATRICIA E. WALKER

CHAPTER ONE

MAY, 1747

Culloden: the very name could still send shivers down the spine and put fear into the hearts of men, especially those who had worn the green and white of the Stuarts.

Having landed at Eriskay on the twenty third of July, 1745, Charles Edward Stuart drew the romantic Scots to his side in an attempt to raise the Stuart standard once more. This enterprising attempt, after minor triumphs and even greater set backs, finally came to an end at Culloden.

The Bonnie Prince, who had hoped to surprise Cumberland on that desolate, sleet lashed moor east of Inverness, had witnessed a massacre rather than a battle. True, his brave Highlanders had broken the first English line, but the second had resolutely held their ground and drove them back, before those terrifying dragoons had chased them ignominiously off the field.

For those fugitives still trying to board a ship to France and safety, that fatal day in April, 1746 would live long in the memory, spurring them on to seek the shelter of a country not unsympathetic to their cause with even greater eagerness.

They were no cowards these men, but the horror of that day and its bloody aftermath, was enough to tell them that even now, twelve months later, they would not be treated any better than those poor souls who had been cruelly and viciously struck down on the orders of the King's second son, earning his title 'Butcher Cumberland'. Justice would certainly be denied them and rather than suffer the fate of those who had been slaughtered without mercy, they much preferred the dangers and uncertainties which naturally faced men on the run, but with a price on their heads they could trust no one; having only their wits and their nerves to sustain them.

They knew that the opportunity of raising another army in an attempt to oust the Hanoverians from the throne would never present itself again, but at least they could take solace from knowing that even though they had failed they could look back with pride at their efforts and their handsome young leader, who had filled them with hope and dreams of glory. But with the rebel clans ravaged, their houses burned and their cattle slaughtered, those dreams now lay in ashes. There had been no glory for the vanquished. Only ignominious defeat and the daunting

PATRICIA E. WALKER

Patricia Walker was born in the Black Country and educated at local schools and colleges. An Italian speaker and avid history reader, she has combined her career with visits to world historical sites with her husband, Andrew to places such as Gettysburg, Culloden, Monte Cassino, The Vatican and the Winter Palace in St. Petersburg, and more recently to The Hofburg Palace and Schonbrunn in Vienna as part of her studies about Crown Prince Rudolf.

Apart from History and Travelling, her interests include collection China and Porcelain, the Ballet, Classical Music and watching old black and white movies.

ISBN: 978-1-84944-039-4

British Library Cataloguing in Publication Data.
A catalogue record for this book is available from the British Library.

Published by UKUnpublished

www.ukunpublished.co.uk
info@ukunpublished.co.uk

prospect of saving themselves from capture and death, faced The Pretender's adherents.

There was no romance or spirit of adventure attached to their determined and desperate attempts to escape. For those who did manage to leave the bloodbath of Culloden behind them, the routes to safety were few and fraught with tension and fear. Unable to return to their homes and families; with informants all around them and soldiers searching every cottage and outbuilding, their only hope was to try and reach the coast to board a vessel to take them across to Ireland or France. For the rest, their only hope was to try and cross the border into England, in the misguided belief that their pursuers would not think to look for them in so hostile a country. For those who sought safety via this perilous route most were caught and summarily dealt with; either being cut down in their frantic retreat or hung following what was nothing more than the mockery of a trial.

But miraculously, a handful of Stuart's followers did manage to evade detection and arrest, but the pursuit of these was still ruthlessly and determinedly carried out, their sympathizers in no doubt that it was only a matter of time before they were caught and hung.

But their days of freedom were running out, with no possibility of their leader coming to their rescue by raising another army; whipped and cowed into submission, with no hope of a Stuart revival, their cause was well and truly over. The Hanoverians were too well established to be toppled, and certainly strong enough to fend off a further threat to their dynasty. The flame of the Stuart cause may still burn in some mens' breasts, but it would never be anything more than a flicker.

The romantic aura surrounding the Stuarts still lingered, and in the hearts of many they were the true rulers and had a right to sit on the throne of England. But this belief not only cost money but could ruin reputations; not many were prepared to be stripped of their wealth and dignities, even their lives, on something which could not be totally assured. There were any number of reasons why Stuart's attempt to claim what he believed to be his father's right could fail, and for those who would offer assistance and financial support they needed more than a charming smile and uncertain promises to induce them into giving up everything. If James Edward Stuart, affectionately known as The Old Pretender, had failed thirty years before to take the crown of England, then why should his son's efforts fare any better? Instead, they kept their sympathies to themselves, opening their hearts and minds to only a few like minded and well trusted friends.

The aristocracy, powerful and wealthy landowners as well influential in government, were neither willing nor eager to jeopardize their positions, or to lose their immense wealth and power by aiding and abetting a relict of a past and doomed dynasty, be he never so handsome and charming. For these men it was enough to sit by the fire at night with their friends, reminiscing and recalling past times, longing for the old days, but realistically accepting they were gone for ever.

For those lacking such wisdom as well as heedless of the consequences, they allowed themselves to be governed by their own unequivocal beliefs, eagerly pledging their money as well as their support, truly believing the Stuarts would rise again; their faith and loyalty in their young leader and the veracity of his cause, unwavering.

As for the rest, the weak and ineffectual whose loyalty extended only as far as their personal ambitions, and whose greed and aspirations for power had prompted them into such a venture in the first place, rendering them blind to the dangers of offering their support and allegiance, had no time for such caution. They were considered dangerous by the true believers, their adherence stemming not from loyalty or belief in the Stuart claim to the throne, but from the heady prospect of being promised positions of power and influence when a Stuart would sit on the throne of England once more; positions they would never have achieved under the Hanoverians. Such temptation was too strong to resist, and whilst their enthusiasm may have been slightly tempered by witnessing the downfall of many of their fellow conspirators, they remained undeterred. Avarice and ambition, coupled with the pleasing prospect of what could be, spurred them on, and if they ever gave a thought to eventual arrest and punishment, it was but fleeting. But the arrests and resultant hangings of the convicted had acted as a powerful warning to the cautious amongst them, whose involvement, thus far remaining undetected and given so freely, were becoming increasingly aware that denouncement was coming ever closer. Whatever their dreams may have been of future participation in government and affairs of state, holding unassailable positions of power, this fear instilled in them a strong sense of self-preservation. No one it seemed could be trusted, and in order to keep their dealings a secret they were prepared to protect themselves in any way they could, even going to such lengths as to deliberately point the finger of accusation towards others. Not too difficult a matter when all they had to do was consider whom they disliked or envied the most. They were dangerous times, and for the wrongly accused even more so!

It had been rudely brought home to General Sir John Turville how a proud name could be besmirched unjustly, with little or no hope of restoring its honour. It was difficult to prove innocence where no evidence existed to substantiate it. No one it seemed was above suspicion, especially once the taint of treason had been directed towards them. Their antecedents and connections, however impeccable, could not be relied upon to save them or prevent the inevitable from happening once the seed of doubt had been sown.

It had not taken that visit yesterday morning by His Grace the Duke of Lytton for General Turville to realize that his views were not shared by all. Indeed, he already knew that his opinions, even his tactics, were frowned upon in certain quarters, but he still held to his belief in that there had been enough examples

6

made to give the rest of Stuart's supporters pause for thought! His visitor however, had his own thoughts on the subject leaving him in no doubt that irrespective of how minor or leading a role they had played in the late rebellion or what name they bore, they were not going to be allowed to escape the full penalty of the law. They must therefore, be apprehended at all costs, and no effort was to be spared in ensuring their capture as speedily as possible.

For himself, General Turville envisaged no further threat to the Hanoverian dynasty, and surely now there should be an end to the pursuit for the handful left on the run. After all, they were hardly in a position, financially or physically, to rally themselves into yet another fighting force. But his unwelcome visitor had clearly thought otherwise. Those remaining fugitives had to be sought and punished, if not, then they posed the very real threat of rousing the hopeful once more.

Although outspoken and often brusque, General Turville was a generous and tolerant man, held in the highest regard by all who knew him. To those who had the privilege of calling him friend they knew him to be loyal and steadfast, prepared to stand by his words and actions whatever the consequences. He had little time or patience for men of Lytton's calibre, and to find himself obliged to play host to one whom he neither liked nor trusted was a severe trial, and it was therefore in a mood of considerable misgiving that he received a man whose sole aim in paying him this visit would no doubt turn out to be to someone's detriment.

He had dared to disagree with Lytton, commenting that whilst the French may sympathize with the Jacobite cause they would not be prepared to aid in any way another rebellion and, furthermore, considering the Highland clans had been broken up and their homeland held in an iron grip, the chances of them banding together again were somewhat remote.

For a man of no more than medium height and slight physique, the aura of omnipotence which emanated from His Grace was almost tangible, making one instantly conscious of his presence, and even though he was approaching his sixty fifth year he exuded an energy most younger men envied. To those who had suffered from his unceasing influence, and there were many, he was irreverently known as 'The Weasel'. However apt this sobriquet, one did not deliberately set out to alienate or offend him. It was not only his uncanny ability to discover something which one would much prefer to remain hidden that made one wary, it was his close association with the King, and since he had the ear of the King as well as his trust, the power he wielded was awesome. He knew how to deal with his enemies and those who stood in his way, and his persuasive tongue had only to whisper a word in that royal ear to clear all before him. Regardless of his feelings, General Turville's knew that one did not fly in the face of a man, who, by a few well chosen words in the right quarter, could bring social and professional ruin down on one's head.

From out of his thin and sallow painted face, Lytton's pale grey eyes glittered across the desk at his host, the thin lips parting into the semblance of a smile. He shook his head, the carefully arranged curls of his dove coloured wig responding delicately to the movement. "My very dear Turville," he admonished smoothly, "I fear you do not fully comprehend my meaning." Without waiting for a response, he expanded gently on his theme. "These few stubborn fugitives, if not apprehended and brought to justice, could, I am sure you will agree, threaten the very peace and stability of the realm. His Majesty," he added significantly, "is most conscious of this possibility, and is eager to have peace restored once more."

General Turville did not need to have this scarcely veiled inference explained, its meaning was plain enough. "Everything possible is being done to seek them out, Your Grace," he explained, adding, in perfect truth, "but they are proving very determined and resourceful in their efforts to evade the law."

"Please do not sully my ears by daring to credit them with any kind of ingenuity, my dear Turville," he chided gently, his eyes narrowing. "They escape justice because of those few misguided people who assist them. Find the sympathizers and you will find the perpetrators."

"We are doing all we can," Turville told him, "but finding the sympathizers is not as easy as one would suppose."

"Nevertheless, Turville" he said softly, "you must and *shall* find them."

"Your Grace," Turville said earnestly, "you know as well as I do that men striving to remain free of the law are capable of great inventiveness."

"Indeed!" Lytton dismissed, his penetrating gaze regarding Turville for several moments. "Your explanation for failing to bring these rogues and vagabonds to justice is all very well, Turville," he said provocatively, "but it is results which are needed, not excuses."

General Turville stiffened, his hands clenching on the arms of his chair, saying earnestly, "I have no need to excuse our methods or the poor results we have had from them; no end of obstacles are put in our path. You yourself, Your Grace," he pointed out, not really expecting him to take any notice, "must surely be aware of the difficulties faced when trying to find someone who does not wish to be found."

Lytton inclined his head, but dismissed this as of no consequence. "You will however," he remarked meaningfully, "oblige me in this by increasing your efforts in the future, Turville. While these men remain free the whole of the country is held to ransom."

Turville hardly thought so, but declined from commenting, merely stating they would continue to do everything they could. "It will, of course, take time, Your Grace," he pointed out.

"Time, my dear Turville, is not on our side," meditatively tapping his eye glass against his painted lips. "His Majesty, I need hardly say," he said softly "is most desirous of clearing this land of all traitors."

"Then you may assure His Majesty," Turville told him firmly, not at all pleased by his manner, "that we shall certainly continue to try and do so."

"I deplore the word '*try*', Turville," Lytton told him. "Indeed, it is the very essence of failure."

"Your Grace I ..."

"My dear Turville," he broke in unceremoniously, "I have every faith in you, but you must allow me to say that so far your methods have not been as successful as some would hope for, a mere handful apprehended, no more." He watched the angry colour rise in Turville's face, but disregarding this, continued easily, "There is no need for me to extol your diligence to the majority, they, like me, know you for an honest and energetic man, but things must move along a little quicker, Turville." Sir John, far from pleased at this indirect tribute, if such it was, merely grunted something which his lordship took for granted to mean he had his full agreement. "I knew you would understand," he inclined his head. "*However*" he emphasized, opening his Sevres snuff box with a dexterous flick of one finger, "there *is* one fugitive who continues to elude us; a most desperate fellow in fact!"

"I thought they were all desperate," Turville returned with heavy sarcasm, believing they had finally arrived at the real reason for his unexpected visit. Lytton never wasted time in paying unnecessary calls!

The grey eyes narrowed. "Indeed they are, Turville," he said smoothly, "but this one especially is of particular interest to us."

General Turville raised a questioning eyebrow. "Who is this fugitive?" he asked gruffly, having a pretty shrewd idea to whom he referred.

Flicking a tiny residue of snuff from off the wide cuff of his burgundy satin coat with a heavily laced handkerchief, he looked at General Turville from under heavily veiled lids, his voice deceptively calm. "An extremely dangerous individual, and one whom, or so it would appear, you have made no effort to either seek out or apprehend despite my previous application for you to do so."

The frown which descended onto Turville's face was not lost on his visitor. "I take you to mean Richard Ferrers!"

Turville's friendship with Viscount Easton was of many years duration, and even though their paths had gone diverse ways over the years they had remained firm friends. At no point during their long association had he been given cause to question his friend's loyalty to the King, or that of his only son, Richard. Jasper Ferrers had spent all of his adult life in the service of his King and country, deeply and sincerely attached to both, remaining steadfastly in office long after most of his political allies and opponents had retired. So committed was he to his beliefs that it was inconceivable he had raised a son who held conflicting loyalties; declaring for The Pretender and actively taking part in his attempts to reinstate the Stuarts.

Lytton was fully aware of the connection between Sir John and the Ferrers family and with Jasper Ferrers in particular, and knew that his renewed demands for action would be no better received than they had been before, but as this matter was now of some moment, Tuville's feelings were quite unimportant. "Precisely!" he inclined his head. "I realize, of course, that you are as reluctant to act in this matter as you are to admit his guilt," he smiled, a none too pleasant smile which sent a shiver down Turville's spine, emphasizing his discoloured teeth with macabre clarity. "When last we spoke of this," he reminded him, "you accorded no credence to my claims about his crimes any more than I see you do now, indeed, so emphatic were you of his innocence that none of my earnest representations would alter your opinion. Admittedly," he acknowledged, "you set enquiries in motion but, really, my dear Turville," he shook his head, "they were hardly - well, what shall I say?" he shrugged eloquently, "sufficiently vigorous to yield a response."

Turville swallowed angrily at this smoothly delivered admonition. "As I recall, your Grace," he pointed out, holding onto his temper with an effort, "no news had come to my ears regarding Richard Ferrers' supposed treasonable activities except from yourself, indeed," he nodded, "no rumours were abroad about any traitorous dealings. Furthermore, Your Grace," he impressed, "upon soliciting the reasons for your insistence that I put such enquiries into effect you responded by recommending me to merely do as I was asked without ascertaining why!"

"My dear Turville," His grace warned softly, by no means pleased at this recollection, his eyes narrowing, "be assured that that recommendation is very much alive." Without waiting for General Turville to reply to this rebuke, he queried, raising a sardonic eyebrow, "As for rumours, can you deny that they have abounded the town for many months past?"

"No, Your Grace," he conceded "I cannot. But I have no time to listen to hearsay and gossip put about by scandalmongers whose sole aim appears to be nothing more than making mischief about a man whose name needs no defending!" he bit out.

"My dear Turville," he pointed out with dangerous calm, "there is no suggestion that Lord Easton was a turn-coat, but the evidence against his son is overwhelming. Indeed" he added inexorably, "not only was he misguided enough to offer support to The Pretender, but he even went so far as to actually leak information to him. I daresay," he mused, his eyes watchful, "that he had gleaned much from his father, and decided to use it himself."

"Your Grace!" Turville exclaimed forcefully, disgust showing on his craggy face. "I protest against these accusations. There must be some mistake!"

The grey eyes flickered. "Richard Ferrers is a traitor," he remarked unequivocally, "a circumstance I have already made abundantly clear. No, no, my dear Turville" he shook his head, "the evidence is irrefutable!"

"Your Grace!" Turville protested again. "This denouncement is unjust. I have known Lord Easton for many years, and whilst I know little of his son, I'd take my dying oath he is no traitor!"

"So you have said before, and whilst I bow to your superior knowledge of the family," Lytton replied superciliously, the raised eyebrows haughtily offensive, "the facts of the case are indisputable."

"What facts?" Turville demanded, his face mirroring not only his disbelief but also his contempt.

Once again however, he was presented with nothing more than Lytton's own words, for which he fully expected him to be satisfied. Turville was very far from satisfied and dared to suggest that these so-called facts be shown to him, upon which his visitor cried, "My dear Turville, are you actually *doubting* my word?" He saw the bushy eyebrows snap together and the full lips compress as Turville considered what he had been told, but try as he did he could not accept that his old friend's son had declared for Charles Edward Stuart. "I do realize," Lytton offered with spurious sympathy, "that it is quite distressing to receive such unpleasant tidings, but I do assure you that my information is beyond dispute."

"Your Grace I …"

"No, no, my dear Turville," Lytton cut in. "Naturally, I appreciate the delicacy of the situation, not to mention your feelings upon the matter, and whilst I understand your very natural reserve to act in this affair, you must realize that Richard Ferrers must be caught and brought to justice." Without giving General Turville time to speak, he went on, "As you know the family, I thought you the most proper person to approach in this matter. If this young man is to be apprehended then who better to instigate his capture than yourself. After all," he nodded, "how could he refuse to listen to a man his father had called friend and one, moreover, with wisdom enough to make him see the error of his ways."

General Turville took a deep breath, exclaiming incredulously, "I fail to see that any words of mine will have much of an impact upon a young man who has never laid eyes on me above two or three times in his life!"

"Then you must put forward every endeavour in ensuring that they *do* impact upon him," Lytton suggested ominously.

"And if I refuse?" Turville asked abruptly, attempting to keep a hold on his temper.

The thin lips pursed. "I really do not think that that would be a very good idea," Lytton advised thoughtfully, shaking his head, "especially when one considers your connection with the family."

"Are you daring to suggest that I too have Jacobite sympathies?" he shot at him, staring hard at his obnoxious visitor's painted face, fighting the impulse to send him hurtling through the door.

"My very dear Turville," Lytton sighed, "you pain me, truly you do. I assure you I have harboured no such thoughts regarding your loyalties; merely, I was hoping that in this *very* lamentable affair you would be the most proper person to locate our misguided young friend and, hopefully, persuade him to see that by his continued, but entirely fruitless efforts to evade the consequences of his behaviour, he is merely making his situation infinitely worse."

Turville was not fooled by this, but however much it went against the grain, he had to tread carefully. His reputation as well as his military record were so far unsullied and, as for his loyalties, these surely went without saying, but Lytton was a dangerous man and one, moreover, who could not only make mischief but would have no compunction in doing so in order to achieve his own ends. He meant every word he had said in that he refused to believe the son of his old friend had been involved in treason. He could not substantiate this belief, indeed, the very idea that he needed to was so repugnant to him that it sickened him, but Lytton was perfectly serious in his intentions, and this being so it was going to be no easy matter to disabuse his mind of Ferrers' guilt. How to prove him innocent of the charge of treason however, remained to be seen but, in the meantime, Lytton was patiently waiting for him to confirm that he would seek out Richard Ferrers without any undue loss of time.

Jasper Algernon Fortescue Ferrers, the fifth Viscount Easton, a man of the highest integrity and rigid principles, had, at no time prior to his fatal heart attack almost twelve months ago when the stories regarding his son's alleged activities were beginning to be spread, divulged any worries he may have had over his son, nor, for that matter, so much as intimated that Richard was giving him cause for grave concern. He was convinced that had his old friend felt the least anxiety over his son's political leanings he would have apprised him of it, but there had been nothing to suggest when they had last met that Richard was causing him any unease whatsoever. He could only hazard a guess as to how these rumours had begun about Ferrers' involvement in treason, but he was no nearer to believing them now than he had ever been, and not even Lytton's assurances of the veracity of his crimes would make him change his mind, and certainly the results of his enquiries had not been sufficient to take them any further. It was a pity that this hateful little man sitting opposite him, who appeared to take a perverse delight in the tragedy of others, had become involved in something which he would have much preferred to have dealt with alone, assuming, of course, that there was any credence to it in the first place, which he doubted.

It had been to Turville's deep regret that he had not been able to pay his respects at the funeral, but his duties had unfortunately kept him in town, preventing him from attending the service at Jasper's home in Sussex. If Lytton was to be believed he had been a broken man, his heart attack brought on by the knowledge that his only son was on the run in an attempt to evade capture and ultimately death for his treasonable activities.

To openly accuse Lytton of harbouring ulterior motives was dangerous, but Turville could not just sit back and allow the son of an old and noble house to be hounded and strung up from the nearest gallows without first discovering the truth. One did not question a man of Lytton's standing, but since he appeared to be far from forthcoming with the truth, it was therefore going to take all his tact and patience to sift it out. If all he had been told so far, assuming it were true, was not bad enough, according to Lytton, Richard Ferrers, following his flight from Culloden, if, indeed, he had taken part in that bloodbath, had taken to smuggling in order to escape detection and arrest and was even now conducting his illicit activities off the Sussex coast.

It was becoming increasingly clear to Turville that there was more to this affair than he had been told, and that Richard Ferrers was being sought for an entirely different reason to the one glibly put forward. If Ferrers' capture was as vitally important as Lytton maintained, then why had he so readily accepted his own earlier findings in that there was insufficient facts to make a case of treason, instead of insisting that efforts were made to put a vigorous search into operation as he was now doing? And, which was equally as inexplicable, why had it taken all this time for Lytton to advance any further demands about curtailing this young man's alleged activities by bringing about his apprehension?   The more he considered it, the more sinister it seemed. Surely a Jacobite, and one, moreover, who obviously had been in a position to leak information, would have been sought long since! But when he pointed this fact out to Lytton, his response was one of mournful resignation.

"Ineptitude is something I deplore, Turville. It creates chaos where there should be none. A little time; a little patience, and the task is done to a nicety," he looked significantly across at his unenthusiastic host. "Bungling is abhorrent to me;" he said smoothly, "indeed, it is quite beyond my comprehension," he let out an anguished sigh. "It seems I am surrounded by fools, were it otherwise," he opined, "this Ferrers character would not now be at large, creating all manner of difficulties." General Turville, wishing he would get to the point; found all this flowing eloquence too much for his patience. Trust Lytton to go all the way round to say a few simple words! "We were led to believe," Lytton explained on a deep sigh, "that following his departure to the Continent to join Stuart, he later accompanied him back to England whereupon he eventually fell at Culloden," he let out another deep sigh. "I was, I need hardly say, surprised to hear this, as I would suppose trying to identify one mangled corpse among hundreds to be no easy task. You see Turville," he sighed mournfully, "this is what results from the inept handling of a situation which is really quite simple."

Far from happy with this explanation, General Turville questioned it further. His Grace, by no means pleased at this, said curtly "All you need concern yourself with is that this young man is still alive and must be caught!"

Sir John leaned back in his seat, not for the first time wondering what His Majesty saw in this obnoxious little man to like or trust. "I can only suggest," he offered, "that supposing all of this to be true, he is most probably in France by now."

"No, no, my dear Turville," Lytton shook his head, none too pleased to find that his host still harboured doubts. "I have it on excellent authority that our young friend is still in England."

"England is a big place, Your Grace," Turville reminded him. "Besides, I do not have sufficient men at my disposal to search every town and village in the hope of catching sight of him."

Lytton's eyes narrowed. "There is no need to search the whole of England, Turville," he reprimanded, "and even if there were," he pointed out, "you would be expected to do your duty."

"Are you calling my devotion to duty into question, Your Grace?" Turville demanded heatedly, his bushy eyebrows snapping together and his colour rather high.

"By no means," he replied, an inflection of surprise in his thin voice. "I cannot imagine why you should think I might be. I am merely pointing out to you," he told him smoothly, "that His Majesty, who continually and ceaselessly works for the benefit and welfare of his realm, would certainly expect no less from the rest of us." Turville was by no means placated by this, but the warning, subtly delivered though it was, was unmistakable. Satisfied with the effect his words had had upon him, Lytton went on in the same smooth voice. "I understand that our young friend, not content with committing treason, has now embarked on illicit trading; in truth," he sighed, "it would appear with comparative ease," shaking his head mournfully. T'would seem there is no end to his folly!"

"Your Grace …!" Turville started forward.

"No, no Turville," Lytton shook his head, waving a languid hand, "I must beg your full indulgence in this matter. Unfortunately," he sighed, "he has, I believe, been enjoying considerable licence of late off the Sussex coast. So much so," he nodded, "that he has become a public menace."

"Then surely you would be better seeking the assistance of the Land Guard officer for the area," Turville suggested. "He would, I am sure, be more familiar with smuggling ways than I or my men. His chances of catching Ferrers would surely be far greater than ours."

"If I did not know you better, my dear Turville," Lytton purred silkily, "I could almost think that you are deliberately trying to impede the course of justice."

"By no means, Your Grace," he assured him, "but it seems to me that these Excisemen are better able to deal with those who trade illicitly than the army."

"You may, of course, be right" Lytton conceded, "but their experience in apprehending traitors is somewhat limited. Besides, I would much prefer our young friend to be dealt with quietly. I see no point in alerting the interested to our little affairs." General Turville pursed his lips, feeling decidedly uneasy at the connotations which could be drawn from this statement. Lytton eyed him speculatively for several moments, explaining at length, "His home, Ferrers Court, as you well know," inclining his head, "is situated on the outskirts of a place called Little Turton a few miles inland from Cuckmere Valley where, I understand, the trade is rife. Needless to say," he went on easily, "the searches which have been conducted in the house of late have proved quite fruitless; doubtless he has had warning of them and escaped in time."

"You are certain he has been hiding there?" Turville asked, unable to believe that he would be such a fool, supposing of course, Richard Ferrers was indeed guilty as charged.

"Oh, quite certain," he nodded. "It would be beyond the realms of probability to think otherwise, don't you agree?"

"Frankly Your Grace, I don't," Turville told him unequivocally. "I cannot see a man in his position taking such a risk and, more to the point, placing his sister in jeopardy."

Lytton seemed to give this due consideration, regarding him thoughtfully from out of those all seeing eyes. "There may be something in what you say Turville, but somehow I cannot see a devoted sister refusing him aid," he paused, considering his painted fingernails. "I understand Miss Ferrers, who I believe was extremely attached to her father and presently enjoys the companionship of his widowed sister, is quite indulgent towards him. I can, of course, only speculate how matters stand with the inheritance, but it seems that for the moment at least, she holds full sway at Ferrers Court."

"You seem to know a great deal about the current state of affairs, Your Grace," Sir John commented, wishing to God he would come to the point and stop talking in riddles. If he had something to say, then why the devil didn't he come out and say it, instead of making a damned mystery of it all! "If, as you say, her father's death was brought about by his disappointment and humiliation over his son's involvement with Stuart, and she was particularly close to her father, what makes you think she would assist him? Unless, of course," he pointed out, "you believe her to hold the same alleged sympathies as her brother but, even supposing she does, what makes you think she knows his whereabouts? She could, after all, be in complete ignorance of them as well as his alleged involvement in smuggling."

Ignoring this very reasonable point of view, Lytton chided gently, "My dear Turville, we are talking about a small community where, it would seem, everyone looks out for everyone else. You will find you can safely wager a considerable sum on the chance that if Ferrers did not enlighten his sister to the fact that he was in the locality, someone else did." He pursed his lips before offering suggestively, "A servant, perhaps? Probably one who has for long enjoyed those special privileges usually reserved for old family retainers," again he scrutinized his fingernails. "In fact," he remarked with smooth deliberation, "I believe that there *is* one such individual in the Ferrers household who has a special fondness for our young friend and would, if my understanding of the matter is correct, be only too prepared to help him. Who knows," he observed innocently, "Ferrers may well have been in contact with him. Naturally," he shrugged, "once knowing he was in the vicinity, what could be more natural than to apprise his concerned young mistress of it, who, I have no doubt at all, would clearly come to her brother's aid."

"Even supposing such a scenario to be true," Turville remarked disdainfully, "I hardly think it likely that he would inform against his young master, even to his sister, especially if, as you say, he holds him in such affection. In fact," he pointed out, "there *is* one such at Ferrers Court who does undoubtedly hold Richard Ferrers in considerable affection; one who has been with the family all his life. From all I have ever seen of him," taking immense satisfaction from the look of chagrin which briefly crossed Lytton's face, "I cannot see him informing against him."

Lytton eyed him steadily, saying at length, "One cannot rule out any possibility. Besides," he added disparagingly, "I doubt his loyalty and affection would take precedence in the face of certain inducements."

"You mean bribery!" Turville bit out disgustedly.

"Such a *sordid* word!" Lytton shuddered. "But yes," he nodded, "if that is what it will take to find Ferrers."

"And his sister," Turville urged, "are you asking me to believe that she would tell us any more than she has divulged already? Assuming, of course, that your suppositions are correct."

"She must be made to realize the futility of her refusal," Lytton said quietly, telling Turville more than any words could have that her sex and station were not to act as a deterrent for retribution. "Of course," he acknowledged, "I realize that she may not be any too eager to engage in discussion about such a delicate matter, any more than she has so far, indeed," he shrugged, "her reluctance to do so to date does not fill me with any optimism that a confession is imminent, but I am sure when she has been made fully aware of the situation she is in, she will easily be brought to talk," he smiled thinly. "Indeed, I think perhaps she may be very forthcoming, especially when it is brought home to her that she runs the considerable risk of arrest and imprisonment herself, *which*" he emphasized, "you will make known to her in no uncertain terms." He paused suddenly, an arrested expression entering his cold grey eyes as if an idea had just occurred to him, then spent the next few minutes contemplating it. "You know, Turville," he drawled meditatively, "upon reflection, I think that she may well respond better to the representations of a man she would perhaps regard with less hostility, even tolerance, and, who can say?" he shrugged, "even with eagerness, than to such as ourselves, who, sadly, are no longer likely to hold any powers of persuasion over a young and beautiful woman." Turville was aghast at such a suggestion, but Lytton gave him no time to respond. "He must of necessity be someone who is reliable and, of course, discreet; so I entirely rely upon you to ensure that the young man chosen to act in this matter is made fully aware of the importance of the task ahead of him and the implications should he fail to conclude this matter satisfactorily," his thin lips parted slightly and his voice, silky smooth though it was, was menacing. "I shall take it very ill should I discover that he has failed or, how shall I put it?" he mused, regarding Turville thoughtfully, "it is quite difficult on occasion to find the right words, do you not agree? Let me see," he half closed his eyes as if seeking enlightenment, then said softly, "ah yes, let us say not accorded the matter the attention it requires. So far," he shrugged, as though there had been no digression, "she has proved most stubborn and uncooperative. Indeed, she has constantly denied any knowledge of her brother's activities or whereabouts."

"Good God, Your Grace!" Turville exclaimed, shocked. "She is, after all, a lady."

"Her station in life is irrelevant," he dismissed. "Sentiment cannot be allowed to cloud the truth," Lytton told him. "She will talk," he nodded, "if she knows what is good for her."

Turville shook his head. "Your Grace," he urged, "if, as you say, all the searches conducted so far have proved unsuccessful, and she consistently claims to have no knowledge of her brother's whereabouts, why should she suddenly succumb to the persuasions of a man she has never laid eyes on before?"

His Grace, by no means pleased at having either his opinion or his advice questioned, said coldly, "You will do everything possible Turville to find this man. No matter what it takes or how disinclined you are to do so."

General Turville saw the implacability in his eyes, and knew he had no alternative but to do as he asked, however reluctantly. "Very well, Your Grace," he nodded, "if you insist," resigned but by no means reconciled.

"I do. He *must* be found," Lytton urged with finality. "He cannot be allowed to roam at will." Then leaning back in his chair with all the air of one who was supremely confident in his own infallibility said, "Having found him, he is to be taken to the garrison at Hampton Regis where he is to be questioned. The garrison commander, Colonel Henderson, you may know him" he asked, raising a pencilled eyebrow, but upon Turville's shake of his head, shrugged, "t'is no matter. However, he happens to be a particular friend of mine and he it was who first alerted me to Ferrers being in the vicinity," he paused, by no means pleased at Turville's apparent lack of eagerness. "Needless to say," he impressed, "I quite approved of the searches he instituted, and although he has found our young friend to be most elusive, I think it only fair to reward his painstaking efforts by granting him the honour of questioning him." He rose stately to his feet signifying the meeting was almost at an end. "Of course," he smiled thinly, looking down into Turville's troubled face which was at the moment exhibiting no sign of enthusiasm for the task ahead, "you will quite understand that once your man has found him the matter, as far as both you and he are concerned, is over," adding with dispassionate unconcern, "nevertheless, one must never forget that with men like Ferrers, one must always look to the possibility that they will attempt to escape or evade arrest." Then with a mournful shake of his head, sighed "Under such circumstances, quite naturally, he would have to be shot."

Turville eyed him aghast. "Your Grace, his rank demands fair treatment!"

"He is a traitor, Turville," Lytton reminded him, "and that fact alone, I am sure you will agree, precludes any special treatment."

Turville shook his head. "Your Grace, I beg you will consider. If Ferrers is indeed a traitor then he must be punished, but he is due a proper trial."

"Your sense of justice does you honour, Turville, but I am afraid when it comes to dealing with traitorous rogues like this, then there can be no room for such sentiments." He pulled on his gloves, slowly and deliberately easing his long thin fingers into the soft leather, his whole attention apparently focused on this simple task, until eventually raising his eyes to Sir John's face. "Ah yes, I knew there was something else I had to mention," he remarked, almost as though it were an afterthought. "How remiss of me," he smiled, "I cannot imagine how I came to forget. Regarding our friend Ferrers, you have precisely one week from today in which to find him. Afterwards," he shrugged dismissively, "I am very much afraid he will have to be 'gazetted'."

Turville rose hurriedly to his feet, the legs of his chair scraping violently on the polished floorboards. "Your Grace!" he exclaimed, shocked. "You cannot mean it!"

"Can I not?" Lytton asked, raising a haughty eyebrow.

"Your Grace," Turville beseeched him, "you cannot treat a man of his rank in such a way."

Lytton considered him meditatively before saying softly, "My very dear Turville, you forget to whom you speak. This man," he reminded him "forfeited his rank and standing in society, not to mention the privileges accompanying them, the moment he declared for The Pretender. Since then he has continuously worked towards depriving His Majesty's government of what rightfully belongs to them. He is a criminal and must be treated and punished like one."

Turville stood behind his desk, his splayed hands resting heavily on top of it. "Your Grace," he urged again, "you know what will happen if he is 'gazetted'!"

"Perfectly," he shrugged dismissively. "So it behoves you, does it not, to find him before that happens."

"Your Grace," Turville forestalled him, his distaste for the task in hand clearly evident on his face, "I must tell you that I have no liking for any of this!"

Lytton eyed him pensively through half closed eyes for some moments, and when he spoke his voice was ominously polite. "So I am aware," he dismissed, "but then," he pointed out, "it is not for you to like or otherwise. Whether you approve or not, you will do what is required or suffer the consequences." His eyes narrowed momentarily as he seemed to consider something. "'The Honourable Richard Ferrers'" he mused at length. "Considering his crimes," he reflected, "that is quite a contradiction in terms, wouldn't you agree?" he disparaged, before sweeping majestically out of the room.

Lytton, having made his views as well as his design perfectly clear, had no intention of allowing anyone to overset his plans. On the contrary, he was determined that no obstacle should be put in the way of achieving his ends, and so confident was he that Turville would do precisely as he was told it never even so much as crossed his mind that he would do anything else, much less question what he had learned and then proceed to undertake investigations of his own. He was perfectly well aware of the unpalatable, not to say impossible, task he had given him, but he had no time to waste on sentiment; sentiment which could so easily undo everything he was striving towards and could also be so easily misunderstood.

CHAPTER TWO

From the window of his room at the rear of the main barrack block overlooking the cobbled courtyard below, General Sir John Turville looked down to watch with barely concealed relief as his departing visitor climbed into his waiting carriage. Not until this noble equipage had disappeared from view did he resume his seat, not at all gratified by the honour just done him.

Furiously angry that Lytton, who was not fit to be mentioned in the same breath as Jasper Ferrers, had dared to suggest, and not for the first time, that a man of such integrity and unquestionable loyalty had raised a son who had turned traitor and that his daughter was fully prepared to support and shield her brother in his treachery. It would take more than the word of someone like Lytton to make him believe that a man of Richard Ferrers' background and upbringing was a traitor, and if it took him a whole lifetime he would prove Lytton wrong. It had come as a severe shock when he had discovered that the name of Ferrers had come under suspicion, and even more so to learn that His Grace had not spared Jasper's daughter from the taint. In truth, it would have given him immense satisfaction to have thrown His Grace the Duke of Lytton through the door, but one did not treat even a man of his evil machinations with such contempt. To do so would be to court disaster and for one whose influence was so far reaching, it would be professionally and socially damning.

Sir John's lips compressed and his pale blue eyes narrowed as he reviewed their recent interview. God knows he was no Jacobite, but he was honest and human enough to admit that he had grown sick to the stomach with the so-called trials and hangings of late. It seemed that no man, or woman, no matter how small a role they had played in the late rebellion, were exempt from the horrors of the rope, as could be seen, if one had the stomach for it, at certain strategic points.

He had been a soldier all his life, accustomed to death and the horror of war, but could only thank God that he had played no part in that slaughter called Culloden, a day which would live long in the memory. To kill a man in battle was one thing; both combatants possessing an equal chance to live or die, but from what he had been able to discover the carnage which had followed on that blood soaked field had been a terrible sight.

He was a staunch supporter of the King and a man who surely had no need to prove either his loyalty or devotion to duty. He knew that treason could not go unpunished, and that the perpetrators of such a crime had to be brought to justice, but he was a fair man and one who could find it in him to spare a thought for those few remaining fugitives who continued to evade the law, especially as Stuart's supporters had been declared outlaws by His Majesty and were therefore to be treated as such. Denied the respect as soldiers, either before or after Culloden, as was customary to an opposing army who had suffered defeat, he was forced to acknowledge that he could not entirely blame them for preferring to remain on the run rather than give themselves up, particularly when he considered the treatment which had been meted out over the last twelve months to their fellow fugitives who had been apprehended. He shuddered at the thought of that never to be forgotten day, and wondered when its repercussions would cease to be felt.

He had put his views to Lytton as openly as he had dared, but one did not willingly confide one's thoughts to a man who could so easily turn them against one and whose power and influence could do one so much damage.

The visit had been totally unexpected, Lytton believing no announcement of his arrival to be in the least necessary, but it had raised questions in his mind to which he could find no answers, and to which His Grace had not been any too eager to provide. Apart from disclosing that it was Colonel Henderson who had alerted him to Richard Ferrers being in Sussex, he had made no attempt to put forward the names of those who had irrefutable proof, instead he had skirted over this vital information as smoothly as he did everything else. Lytton's belief in his own importance was such that he took it for granted that his word alone was sufficient, and corroboration, written or otherwise, was not only unnecessary, but a gross insult. Indeed, the interview had been conducted along the most prevaricating of lines; Lytton being none too forthcoming with all the facts. Be that as it may however, no matter how many times he turned the interview over in his mind, he could not interpret its significance any other way than the way he had. Long after his visitor had left he had sat for some considerable time pondering their conversation in a mood of considerable disquiet. Unless he was very much mistaken the capture and arrest of the remaining Jacobites had been merely a camouflage. It seemed to him that Lytton's sole interest was in the capture and arrest of Richard Ferrers or, better still, his demise, and as quickly as possible. Again, he found himself questioning what his friend's son had done other than harbour rebel sympathies, not that he believed it for a moment, but it must have been something rather serious to necessitate the personal intervention of His Grace the Duke of Lytton but, whatever the truth, he had made his position clear.

He could not believe that Lytton was prepared to go as far as 'gazetting' Ferrers, but since this was clearly his intention, it merely served to reinforce his belief that this young man posed a very real threat to someone. Once Richard Ferrers' name was published in the London Gazette for smuggling activities he had forty days in which to give himself up, after which time he was automatically placed under sentence of death. That was bad enough, but anyone who informed on a 'gazetted' man, effecting an arrest, would receive a reward of five hundred pounds. A man would certainly discover his friends, as few could turn their backs on a sum of money which was a fortune; not in twelve months would they earn anything near it. Surely, not many would put friendship and loyalty before such financial gain! Lytton knew this; proving his determination to seek out Ferrers any way he could! The thought disgusted Turville, but it fired him with an equal determination to seek the truth.

For himself, he was still of the opinion that no fugitive from the law and one, moreover, with a price on his head, would seek the sanctuary of his own home thereby placing his immediate family in jeopardy. A Jacobite Richard Ferrers may be, although he adamantly refused to believe this, but he was certainly no fool, since nothing could more surely guarantee him the hangman's noose than turning up on his own doorstep.

His thoughts were far from easy, his pacing up and down doing little to alleviate his ever growing concerns. Despite Lytton's subtle eloquence, he had not liked the tenor of the conversation he had had with him or the unmistakable threat of the consequences resulting from his failure to apprehend Richard Ferrers. He would certainly put enquiries in motion, indeed, he could do little else; His Grace's wish was almost like a royal command, but his own view was that they would prove entirely fruitless. The very nature of their work made smugglers very cagey and suspicious individuals, assuming, of course, he had indeed turned to smuggling! Not only was evading the law an almost every day occurrence, but they doubtless had friends who would come to their assistance if necessary and hide them should the need arise. Undertaking a search for one of their number was going to be no easy task but, bearing in mind Lytton's unrelenting determination that Ferrers had to be apprehended at all costs, there was really no choice but to delegate an officer to investigate this rather unpalatable affair.

He may wish to God that this business was over with, or, better still, had never begun, but since there was no way he could either ignore the orders Lytton had issued or refuse to act upon them, he knew there was really only one man he could trust for such a delicate mission as this.

Major Gideon Neville, second son of Sir Matthew Neville, Baronet, had held a commission in the London and Southern Regiment of Fusiliers since leaving Oxford some years previously. At twenty nine years of age he had graduated to his present rank from merit and not due to any influence or favour on his father's part, earning him the reputation of being an excellent officer, well liked and respected by his men. It was a pity, some said, that he had not been at Culloden with Cumberland when the rebellious Scots had been dealt with once and for all. He would certainly have been there but The Pretender and his newly acquired army had put him out of action only a few months before on that cold January day at Falkirk, when he had been severely wounded thanks to a musket ball in the shoulder. For several months he had played no further part in military activities, but sent home to Wiltshire to regain his health. His recovery had been slow as the ball had lodged deep in his shoulder, tearing through flesh and muscle and causing him to lose a large amount of blood. There had certainly been a time when his anxious parent's had seriously feared for his life, so ill had he been, but gradually he had made a full recovery, eventually returning to duty as personal staff officer to General Sir John Turville.

It was not to be expected that he would remain in ignorance of the full sum of Culloden for long as friends and fellow officers had eagerly brought the news to him, believing that knowing the rebels had been thoroughly beaten would do him the world of good. In fact, it had left him feeling saddened and sick at heart. From all he had discovered, it had been no place for the faint-hearted; the Jacobites not only being comprehensively beaten, but cut down like cattle in their retreat. There had been no mercy or show of respect for an opposing army, who, he learned, had fought bravely enough. They may have been traitors to His Majesty King George II, but their slaughter had surely been enough to damage the reputation of the British army for many a long day.

Fighting a battle was one thing but, having to watch, even to participate, in the butchery which followed, was something he could not contemplate without revulsion and disgust. He was a soldier and proud of the uniform he wore, but from what he had been able to discover, it had been more like a slaughter-house than a battlefield. He was no coward, but he was forced to admit to himself that he was relieved he had taken no part in that day's proceedings, especially the bloody aftermath which, surely, would go down in history as a blot on the integrity and honour of the British soldier.

Traitors they may have been, eagerly desirous of toppling the Hanoverians from the throne and setting up the exiled Stuarts, but their fervour and devotion to their cause had been unwavering, and if their leader had possessed as much tactical knowledge as he had charm, their cause could well have ended in glorious triumph instead of the failed disaster it had been. He could not condone their attempts, but their treatment upon capture was such that he could not accept it as surely right or just. He knew of the title the Duke of Cumberland had been honoured with following Culloden, and whether deserved or not, it was certainly a sad day when a British commander was labelled with a name which surely could do the British army nothing but harm. Butcher Cumberland would not be forgotten in a hurry; certainly not by those across the border!

Having served under General Turville for most of his army career, he knew him to be a good officer and one who supported the men under his command. He had gradually come to know and respect the man beneath the brusque façade and could not help but like what he saw. He was neither a glory seeker nor one to request favours in return for another, but had in fact earned his high rank through loyal and devoted service, his conduct and military skill as well as his integrity, receiving well deserved reward by a series of promotions which had finally resulted in the rank of general.

His role as personal staff officer to General Turville, who, it seemed, had early on taken a liking to his Brigade Major, necessitated regular consultations with him, and upon receiving an order to attend him without delay from a young and nervous subaltern recently appointed to the staff, suffered no misgivings. Following a quick inspection of his appearance, he walked the short distance to his commanding officer's room, where, after a brief tap on the door, he was told to enter.

Despite his suspicions and his lack of enthusiasm for what lay ahead, General Turville had known at once which one of his officers' could be trusted to undertake a task which required no little tact and delicate handling. He still believed that Lytton was playing a very deep game but, for reasons of his own, elected to keep the whole truth of the case to himself. Richard Ferrers may well be involved in the smuggling trade, but he adamantly refused to believe that he was a traitor and had actually taken part in the late rebellion. From all he had ever heard Jasper say of Richard and what he himself had been privileged to see of this young man on the few occasions they had met, he was clearly too much his father's son to embark on insurrection, and could therefore only guess at the reasons for him being hailed a traitor. As for his accuser, whilst he admitted this individual, who clearly preferred to remain in the background, was unknown to him, he evidently had some reason to fear him. He was convinced that Lytton was merely acting in this matter as a very influential go-between, but since he had been extremely reticent to disclose all he knew, electing instead to mellifluously accuse without saying anything definite to the purpose, he could only hazard guesses which proved as frustrating as they were fruitless. He had only Lytton's word that Richard Ferrers had taken to smuggling but, since he had produced nothing to substantiate this accusation, any more than he had that of treason, General Turville felt justified in holding to his own beliefs. This did not mean that he could disregard his instructions, but it certainly cast doubts as to the veracity of what he had been told. If, on the other hand, all he had been led to believe about this young man's treasonable activities were in fact true, then he could quite well understand why Richard Ferrers had taken to illicit trading in order to try and hide himself from his pursuers and the repercussions of the law. This could well be the case, but somehow it seemed to him that if his old friend's son had indeed adopted the fraternity as friends as well as associates, then there must have been a very good reason for him to do so; reasons which did not necessarily include treason.

He could not base his repudiation of Lytton's accusatory statements on personal knowledge of Richard Ferrers, but he found it impossible to accept that Jasper's son had not only turned his back on his King and country, but had in fact gone so far as to leak vital information to the enemy. The very idea was too ludicrous to be taken seriously, especially given his knowledge of the family, which was why he could not rid his mind of the unpalatable thought that someone wanted Richard Ferrers put out of the way and, from the looks of it, as quickly and as quietly as possible. After all, who would question the shooting of a fugitive making his escape from custody? He had no stomach for this kind of dirty work, but it would not do to be seen to be ignoring it. Not only was Major Neville a good officer, but he was blessed with a fair and open mind, and there was no fear of him shooting first and asking questions later.

Despite Lady Turville's entreaties to her husband that he do nothing which could possibly alienate such a powerful and influential man like Lytton, besides there being nothing he could realistically do other than what he had been told, he had nevertheless spent a restless night turning over the problem in his mind. His growing frustration and anger over what he had learned were exacerbated all the more due to the fact that he had been unable to put the problem Lytton had posed him to Major Neville immediately as he had been away from the barracks on other duties. He therefore awoke the following morning agonizingly aware that not only had he lost twenty four precious hours in trying to avert disaster for Richard Ferrers, but that he was no nearer to understanding what Lytton's true motives were for apprehending him. It was therefore in a most formidable mood that he presented himself for duty the following morning, sending a nervous orderly scurrying to inform Major Neville that he was to attend his senior officer immediately, his colour darkening alarmingly as he waited in growing impatience for his personal staff officer to attend him.

Lytton had glibly put forward his reasons for approaching him to act in this matter on the grounds of his friendship with Richard Ferrers' father, but somehow he could not help but think that something more sinister was behind it. His dislike as well as his distrust of Lytton were not without foundation; having witnessed too many ruined reputations through his agency, he was none too eager to take for granted his accusations about Richard Ferrers. Since he was not the kind of man one questioned however, Turville knew it was useless to try and ascertain further details from him, in which case he would have to do what he could to unravel this tangle without any recourse to His Grace. He only hoped that Richard Ferrers would still be alive at the end of it!

Major Neville, unaware of what had gone forward the day before, made his way to his commanding officer's room with no suspicion that he was about to be sent on a man hunt. He was a rather tall young man, whose knee length scarlet coat with white binding and blue lapels, the skirts of which were hooked back to free his legs, exposing his buff waistcoat, showed off his strong, muscular body to admiration, while his breeches, encased in white gaiters to just above the knee, emphasized a fine pair of shapely legs with muscular thighs. He had a handsome, open face with a pair of expressive dark brown eyes which held a great deal of humour, but the firm mouth and determined line of his jaw suggested he was a man who could not be pushed and one, moreover, who held decided opinions of his own. His dark brown hair, usually tied in a small black bow in the nape of his neck, was now concealed by a white pig-tail wig which, however much he would have liked to have dispensed with this one particular part of his uniform, it nevertheless had the affect of accentuating the strength of character clearly visible on his face but, if nothing else, it was certainly preferable to greasing and powdering his hair like the men. He was friendly and generous and never above his company, and General Turville, who had early on recognized his qualities as well as predicted a distinguished and honourable career for him, going so far as to prophesy his attaining a very high rank in the future, had been disappointed and shocked to learn that his young friend was going to sell out. Major Neville, not unaware of such an encomium from a man of rigid principals and very high standards, was both flattered and honoured, but domestic matters had forced the issue.

Being the youngest of the two sons' born to Sir Matthew and Lady Neville, his ambition to embrace a military career had been encouraged and applauded by them, and with Aubrey to succeed to the title on his father's death, there had been no undue cause for concern. No one, least of all himself, had expected his robust elder brother to succumb to illness or that any accident would befall him, and it had therefore come as a tremendous blow when he had been informed just over three months ago, that Aubrey had sustained a broken neck while out riding.

The decision as to whether to remain in regimentals had been taken from him; his duty was clear, but since he was blessed with a strong sense of duty it had not been as painful a decision as his friends had supposed. Naturally, saying goodbye to the career he had always wanted would cause him a pang, but he was aware that his father's precarious state of health, especially since his heart attack, was not going to improve, and whilst his physician exhibited every confidence in that, although he had a weak heart and must refrain from too much exertion or excitement, with care and rest he could live many more years, he was no longer at liberty to make a choice. Being very attached to his father, indeed, he hoped he would live to be a hundred, he knew his position was clear in that he could neither abandon his responsibilities nor leave Billings, his father's man of business, to carry the burden alone. He knew too that there were serious gaps in his education and if he was to eventually step into his father's shoes he knew he owed it to his name to do all he could to carry on where he left off. Being the youngest son he had not been indoctrinated into the management of his father's vast estates, this being Aubrey's sole privilege, but now that circumstances had intervened, he was determined to do all he could to be a good landowner like his father.

General Turville had done all he could to persuade him from making such a momentous decision but, like others before him, he had recognized the determination on his young friend's face, and that once his mind was made up nothing would move him. Having accepted his forthcoming sell-out with deep regret, he supposed he should have expected nothing less from a man whose code of conduct and family honour were as inherent as they were inflexible.

He would certainly miss him as good officers' were hard to find, and could only be thankful that, for the time being at least, he was still in regimentals, as this particular task required the calm good sense of someone like him, and not the quick fire actions of a hot blooded young officer keen to make a name for himself.

"You sent for me, Sir?" Gideon enquired, closing the door behind him; his salute receiving nothing more than a nod of the head.

"I did," he said gruffly, his scowl having lifted upon seeing who had entered. "Come in, m'boy. Sit down."

"Thank you, Sir." Since Gideon was not of a nervous or timid disposition, he was quite unperturbed by his commanding officer's ferocious expression, unlike the orderly who had been sent scurrying to him with orders that he was required to attend General Turville straight away. Gideon, who knew him to be a strict but fair man and one, moreover, who did not condemn or punish out of hand, was not afraid of his occasional outbursts. He was certainly a man who insisted that every soldier under his command, whatever his rank, should not only take his duties seriously but was expected to carry them out with precision and diligence as well as being properly dressed at all times. Slackness and lack of care were not excused by him, but Gideon could not see even the most serious misdemeanour being responsible for such a black mood; but, even so, he would not care to exchange him for another commanding officer. Having pulled out the chair on the opposite side of the knee-hole desk he manoeuvred his sword into a more comfortable position and eased himself onto it, searching the older man's face as he did so for some clue as to the reason why he had not only been summoned to attend him so peremptorily, but what could possibly have occurred to put him in the devil's own humour, but there was none.

Gideon neither flinched nor averted his eyes from the fixed look directed at him from those fierce blue ones, but waited in unruffled calm until General Turville cleared his throat, before asking about his duty yesterday and to take his report. Apart from asking one or two pertinent questions he made no further reference to it, deciding it ranked as quite unimportant when compared with a man's life. It was a moment or two before he spoke, and when he did so it was in a voice which led Gideon to understand that he was goaded beyond endurance.

"Yesterday morning," he informed him, "I was subjected to an interview with none other than His Grace the Duke of Lytton."

"Indeed, Sir! And how was His Grace?" Gideon enquired, needing no further explanation for his commanding officer's mood; knowing his feelings towards His Grace only too well.

General Turville, not deceived by this deceptively polite enquiry, grinned. "Infuriatingly obscure as usual."

A little smile touched Gideon's lips. "May I ask what brought him here, Sir?" "Nothing any good if the truth be known," he snorted, his mouth hardening. "Tell me," he asked abruptly, "do you recall my mentioning a Richard Ferrers to you?"

"Yes, Sir," he nodded, "I remember. You initiated some enquiries regarding his supposed activities. If my memory serves," he said thoughtfully, "you told me how you and his father were good friends and that Lytton had implied his son was involved in treason."

"Well," Turville nodded, "he still implies it! In fact," he informed him, "he does more than that. He states categorically that Richard Ferrers is a traitor and must be caught, indeed," he snorted, "he is looking to me to apprehend him." He was silent for a moment, his eyes looking straight ahead at nothing in particular before focusing on Gideon again. "He refuses to accept that Ferrers could be innocent despite my earnest representations that there must be some mistake. So convinced is he of his guilt," he ground out, "that he has given me no choice in the matter. When I told him I had no liking for any of it he left me in no doubt that I either do everything possible to seek him out or I can face the consequences!"

"That's quite an ultimatum, Sir!" Gideon commented.

"Yes," he sighed, "it is, even so, he expects my full cooperation."

"His Grace is all consideration!" Gideon commented ironically, not at all surprised by these tactics.

General Turville nodded. "His Grace is no fool, he knows that prior to Lord Easton's heart attack almost a year ago he and I were good friends for many years, and now he is prepared to use that friendship in order to apprehend his son." Leaning forward on his elbows, he said, with admirable restraint, "I am reliably informed that Richard declared for The Pretender." Gideon's eyes narrowed slightly, but said nothing. "I am also informed," Turville went on "that Jasper's heart attack was the direct result of his humiliation and embarrassment in knowing that his only son was involved in treason, and who is now on the run, not only trying to evade capture as a traitor but also as a smuggler, since this appears to be his latest venture, according to Lytton. If, in fact, he *has* turned to smuggling," he nodded, "then I can only conclude that it is for a sound reason rather than trying to escape the law for committing treasonable activities. In any event," he shrugged, "Lytton will have it that he has been enjoying far too much licence of late off the Sussex coast, and he wants it stopped."

Gideon looked an enquiry. "I don't quite understand, Sir."

"I am not entirely sure that *I* do," he said grimly, "except to say that I'd stake my life on Jasper's son being as loyal as his father ever was. Unfortunately, all I have is Lytton's word, which" he stated frankly, "is not good enough, at least, not for me it's not, but since he was not very forthcoming with all the facts, I have to rely upon my own knowledge of the family, and that tells me there is something not quite right about the whole affair. I can't rid my mind of the fact that there is more to this business than meets the eye." He sighed heavily. "Having only met Richard on the odd occasion when I visited Ferrers Court, it is unfortunate that I know very little about him. In many ways I suppose it is true to say that he is quite an unknown quantity to me, but from what I was privileged to see of him he struck me as being every inch his father's son. I realize, of course," he acknowledged, "that his politics could be anything, but this I *do* know," he said determinedly, "he's no more a Jacobite than I am!"

Gideon, who knew it would not be the first time that a son from a noble house had trod a different path to his father, eyed his commanding officer thoughtfully before saying, not unsympathetically, "He would not be the first Sir, to go against what he had been brought up to believe most of his life."

"I realize that," Turville agreed reluctantly, "but it is inconceivable to me that Jasper's son is a turn-coat. In fact, the more I consider the matter the more convinced I become that he is totally innocent, and for no reason I can put forward I don't mind admitting to you that I gain the very strong impression that he is being sought because he has become a considerable source of annoyance for someone. Who that someone is and the reasons for hunting him down," he shrugged, "I don't know, but unless my instinct is at fault, and I've never yet found it to be so, whoever it is they want him put out of the way as quickly and as quietly as possible."

Had the accusation come from someone other than His Grace, irrespective of General Turville's firm belief to the contrary, the charge may well carry weight, but Gideon, who by no means liked the idea of judging someone merely on hearsay, and certainly not on the word of a man like His Grace, kept a characteristically open mind as he listened in attentive silence while General Turville recounted his interview in detail. Gideon may not be personally acquainted with Lytton, but he had on more than one occasion acted as escort to His Majesty, who had been accompanied by His Grace, taking part in some ceremonial or other. He was well aware of the unrivalled position he held at court and the influence he carried in the Government; indeed, it would not surprise him to learn that he pulled far more strings than anyone had any idea of. That he was a most dangerous man to cross was common knowledge, to do so would be tantamount to insanity, and since no one was over eager to gainsay him, he continued on his untrammelled course without let or hindrance. Having witnessed more than one fall from grace as a result of his influence, Gideon had long since come to the conclusion that the only safe way round His Grace was to give him an extremely wide berth. Keeping these reflections to himself however, he concentrated on what he was being told, but so surprised was he at what he heard that at the end of General Turville's recital, said "Well Sir, from what you say it does seem as though somebody wants Ferrers dealt with quite desperately, and by any means at their disposal."

General Turville nodded his agreement. "If you were to ask me" he admitted "I'd say it looks as if our young friend has somehow or other managed to become involved in something he was not meant to, and I don't like it, I don't like it at all!" In his frustration he banged his clenched fist down on top of the desk, the glass ink wells jumping in their stands from the force. "Damme!" he exploded, "I've known Jasper Ferrers any time these past forty years, and I'd take my dying oath that his son is no traitor! This heart attack" he scorned, "I'm told it was brought on by his son's traitorous defection; the shame and humiliation to his name! Well, I don't believe any of it. As for the smuggling, that can be easily explained and understood, but if he *is* 'gazetted', they'll put a noose around his neck quicker than anything!"

"Assuming no one informs against him first," Gideon put in.

"Precisely! Five hundred pounds is an awful lot of money; more than enough to turn a friend into an enemy."

Gideon agreed, but although he was quite taken aback at what he had heard, he was not entirely surprised; knowing Lytton he was capable of anything. "There is then, no way of discovering the truth except, of course, from Ferrers himself," he commented, rather wary of relying on the sole word of a man who had brought the downfall of more than one poor unfortunate victim.

General Turville sighed. "All I know is what Lytton was prepared to tell me. According to him Ferrers joined Stuart on the Continent before accompanying him back here. He was, if Lytton is to be believed, at Culloden. They thought him to be dead but, unfortunately for someone," he grimaced, "he showed up in Sussex several months ago. As I have said," he shook his head, "I am not so well acquainted with Richard Ferrers, but knowing his father as well as I did, I cannot see his son betraying his King."

"Forgive me, Sir," Gideon shook his head, a frown creasing his forehead, "but why is His Grace involving himself in this? I am, of course, familiar with his opinions, especially about Jacobite fugitives, but I have never before known him concern himself so particularly."

"I know," Turville nodded. "My own view, and this is for *your* ears only," he emphasized, "is that either someone has petitioned him or he has motives of his own. In either event," he sighed, "it seems that our young friend poses quite a threat, and not necessarily a Jacobite one."

"Well, if what you believe is, indeed, the truth of it, Sir," he nodded, "then it does raise the question as to what other motive there could be."

"I know it!" Turville acknowledged. "I've thought of little else but this since yesterday, and no matter how I look at it, I can make no sense of it." He saw the frown on Gideon's forehead as if he were contemplating something, asking abruptly, "Well?"

Gideon raised his eyes to the belligerent face opposite, but it was several moments before he spoke, turning over something in his mind, saying at length in his quiet way, "Well Sir, as I see it there are only two possible reasons to account for Richard Ferrers being sought so desperately."

"Go on," Turville encouraged.

"Well," Gideon offered, "the first is that he *is* innocent after all, but somehow or other has managed to stumble onto something he was not meant to. The second," he said reasonably, "is that he is, in fact, guilty as charged."

"Is that what you really think?" he demanded.

"The truth, Sir," Gideon shook his head, "is that I'm not entirely sure what to think." He received a hard stare in answer to this, and wished he could offer something more than supposition. "Since you can claim only a limited acquaintance with him and I none at all," he said fair-mindedly, "it seems that all we have to work on is your knowledge of the family and what Lytton was prepared to disclose. All we *do* know, is that His Grace is seeking out Ferrers with a vengeance for which there has to be a reason. If, as could well be the case, he *is* innocent, then I can think of only one reason, which is that he has somehow or other managed to put himself in a position which has rendered him something of a threat to someone."

General Turville looked at him closely. "Are you saying he has managed to acquire certain information?"

"Well, Sir," Gideon shook his head, "assuming he *is* innocent; I fail to see what else it could be."

"What's in your mind precisely?" he demanded, leaning forward on his elbows.

It was some moments before Gideon answered. "Assuming Richard Ferrers *is* in possession of certain information, how did he come by it?" he asked reasonably. "He must have acquired it somehow."

"Go on" Turville urged, his eyes narrowing.

"Well, Sir," Gideon explained, "as I see it, there are four possible reasons to account for Richard Ferrers being in possession of information. The first, and one which I personally believe we can discount," he nodded, "is that Richard Ferrers knows absolutely nothing at all about anything remotely treasonable; he just happened to be in the wrong place at the wrong time and from this unfortunate circumstance someone, who or how I don't know," he shook his head, "believes Ferrers either saw or heard something he was not meant to, to their detriment but, in truth, he did not. Assuming this to be the case, then it explains why he is being sought; they dare not allow him to go free in case he does know something and informs against them."

"There's something in that theory, of course," Turville nodded, "but, like you, I think it most unlikely. For one thing, I gained the very strong impression that whoever it is who wants Ferrers put away, they are not working on speculation, but fact." Without waiting for Gideon to reply to this, he asked, "What are the other three possibilities?"

"Well, Sir," Gideon shrugged, "since Richard Ferrers has not followed his father into politics, it is therefore reasonable to suppose that he does not frequent those circles adorned by his father. It is also reasonable to suppose that he does not have contact with his father's political friends or colleagues, and so the chances of him acquiring information accidentally or otherwise from either of those sources seems rather remote, indeed," he admitted, "I fail to see how he could have."

"And the other two?" Turville pressed, his frown deepening.

"As I have never met Richard Ferrers and you know very little of him," he offered, "we can have no way of knowing who is friends are, let alone their politics. Perhaps one or two of them are in a position where they hear certain things but, even then, we cannot take it for granted that they have said anything to Ferrers. Assuming they have," he said practically, "not only are the reasons for them doing so endless, but I find it hard to believe that whatever information they imparted to him would be of sufficient magnitude to render him such a threat. The problem, of course," he pointed out "is that speculation could quite well lead us in the wrong direction but, unfortunately, we are in a position whereby we cannot afford to discount anything."

"You are right, of course" Turville sighed, his heavy jaws working feverishly. "And the fourth one?" he enquired.

Gideon smiled, showing an excellent set of strong white teeth. "Well, Sir, as far as I can see, it is really the only one which has some merit."

"Indeed!" Turville raised a bushy eyebrow, not unimpressed with Gideon's reasoning.

"Yes, Sir," Gideon nodded.

"Well?" he urged.

"We cannot overlook the possibility that Richard Ferrers was recruited."

This was said so matter of factly that General Turville sat bolt upright in his seat. "Recruited!" he echoed disbelievingly. "You mean a spy?"

"Not that precisely, Sir, no" Gideon smiled.

"What then?"

"Let us suppose," Gideon suggested, "that someone in Government circles knew, or, at least, suspected, that someone was not only offering support to Stuart but was also leaking information to him, but instead of his warnings being taken seriously, they were ignored."

General Turville eyed his personal staff officer with something akin to shock at this calmly uttered statement but, however far-fetched it seemed, it did possess more credibility than anything else. "But that's incredible!" he uttered aghast.

"As I say, Sir," Gideon reminded him, "it is nothing more than conjecture and I may well be wrong, but since nothing else makes any sense we have to consider this possibility. If Richard Ferrers *was* recruited, then the only way I think that could have come about is if this unknown Government official just happened to be an old friend of Lord Easton's or, at least, an acquaintance, and decided that he could trust him enough to confide his concerns to him, and that at some point discussed the matter with him and sought his advice. After all," he acknowledged "Lord Easton must have made a lot of friends during his time in Government."

General Turville nodded. "Yes, he did. He was neither a fool nor a gabster, and his loyalty was unquestionable. So, what are you suggesting precisely?"

"It is, as I say, merely conjecture, but let us assume that such a scenario to be true, and that he did in fact put his concerns to Lord Easton; whether in private or in the presence of Richard we do not know, but what if Lord Easton and his friend turned to Richard to assist them, or, which could well be the case, he volunteered his services." He saw the look of intent interest mixed with astonishment on General Turville's face and continued, "Let us again suppose that during the course of his mission, Richard Ferrers *did* discover something important, possibly even the identity of the real traitor, someone, perhaps, well known to Lytton. If this is in fact how it was," Gideon stated simply, "then it clearly vindicates him of Jacobite tendencies as well as explaining Lytton's reasons for wanting him captured at any price."

"I agree," Turville nodded, after giving this considerable thought, but he was growing more uneasy as he considered the implications of this whole affair. "And if you are right," he pointed out, "it can only mean that the real traitor is someone known to Lytton or, which is more than likely, someone placed too close to the King. But, I must confess," he told him, "even though what you have said makes perfect sense, it *is* pure conjecture and therefore we can still only speculate as to the reasons behind the urgency to find him. I don't mind saying though," he admitted grimly, "the more I consider this whole affair the more determined I am to discover the truth. We *have* to know the truth, Gideon!" he insisted, rising hastily to his feet and taking several frustrated turns around the room.

"I can claim no acquaintance with the Ferrers family any more than I can with the son," Gideon told him quietly, "and my conjectures are based solely upon your knowledge of them but, if I am wrong, then we have to face the unpalatable truth that Richard Ferrers *is* a traitor to his country after all."

General Turville threw him a fierce look, but he was a fair man who realized, no matter how painful, that there was a lot of truth in what Gideon had said. "Yes, I know," he nodded, "that fact does have to be acknowledged I grant you, but you must forgive me if I refuse to believe it."

Gideon was neither insensitive nor unmindful to the feelings of a man who had been forced to face some rather damaging accusations about someone whose father he had held in respect and affection. If his suppositions were in fact true, then Richard Ferrers must be found, not only in order for the truth to be heard, but for his own safety. If, as he was loath to think, he was guilty of treason after all, then he must still be found in order to face his trial. He was not prepared to judge or condemn a man without hearing from his own lips the facts of the case, and certainly not on the sole word of a man like Lytton, who, despite his high rank and privileged position, could not be trusted.

"I realize, of course," Turville owned, returning to his desk and sitting down heavily onto the chair, "that whilst I am looking to you to help clear the name of a man whose father I was proud to call friend, it places you in a most unenviable position. By helping Richard Ferrers we are both of us disregarding His Grace's instructions and, if we are proved to be wrong," he pointed out, "nothing will save us!"

"Well, Sir," Gideon pointed out philosophically, "if we *are* wrong we shall just have to face the consequences when they arise but, His Grace too," he pointed out, "will find himself with awkward questions to answer."

"I can't see that stopping him!" he barked. "Knowing Lytton he will have covered himself at the expense of others. But getting back to Ferrers," he said forcefully, "I cannot and *will* not see a man hang merely because Lytton wants it that way."

"What is it you want me to do precisely, Sir?"

"*You*" he told him, "are to go into Sussex to find him."

"*I* am, Sir?" he repeated, sitting forward a little.

"Yes, *you*," Turville confirmed. "There's no one else I *can* send, at least no one whom I trust enough to deal with this with the tact and discretion it demands."

"I'm honoured Sir, but ..." Gideon began.

"Believe me, Gideon" Turville broke in unceremoniously, looking straight at him, "I smell dirty work in the offing. Lytton said he wants Ferrers apprehended and taken to the garrison at Hampton Regis, where he is to be detained for questioning pending his trial, but I believe he hopes it won't get that far," he admitted. "In fact, I'm sure of it. Why else would he be prepared to 'gazette' him? If my understanding of the matter is correct," he stated, "when you have found him the garrison commander, Colonel Henderson, who, by the way, is a personal friend of Lytton's, is to interrogate him; whereupon your part in the affair is over." An unpleasant look crossed his face and his heavy jaws worked. "He also had the goodness to point out that should Ferrers decide to make a run for it, he is to be shot on sight."

Gideon looked his surprise. *"Very* noble! And did His Grace happen to suggest how we are to effect his capture or, as appears to be the case, his demise?"

Turville gave a sardonic smile. "No, but we have just one week in which to do it, after that" he said grimly, "Ferrers is a sitting duck! However," he told him, "he was kind enough to suggest that we begin by questioning his sister."

"His sister!" Gideon echoed, taken aback at this. "In view of what he confided to you he surely cannot be serious in supposing Miss Ferrers would look upon my arrival as welcoming!"

"I am afraid he is," he told him. "In fact," he nodded, "he looks to you to advise her that her continued denials and open defiance will not be tolerated and that should she persist she will be arrested." He looked a little uncomfortably at Gideon, clearing his throat. "He also feels," he continued uneasily, "that a personable young man such as yourself should have no need to forcibly impress upon her the penalties attached to her continued refutations and defiance but, on the contrary, be able to persuade her to divulge her brother's whereabouts in a way that an older man such as myself, could not."

Gideon's eyes widened at this. "Such faith in my abilities! I am indebted to His Grace!" he said dryly. "Apart from the fact that he can't seriously believe Ferrers would be fool enough to seek shelter with her, he must be optimistic indeed if he believes that she would tell me anything after what she has already undergone, irrespective of how personable and persuasive I am. In her shoes," he admitted frankly, "I would find it almost impossible to trust a red-coat!"

"The last time I saw Jasper's daughter she was still in leading strings, so I can't say what her response is likely to be. I don't profess to understand the workings of Lytton's mind," he admitted, "but he fully expects your efforts to be met with success; and as soon as possible. Oh yes," he added wryly, "I almost forgot. He feels that Ferrers may well have contacted one of the servants at Ferrers Court advising him that he's back in Sussex. He is, unless I mistake the matter," he ground out "of the opinion that this could well be most fortuitous, especially if Miss Ferrers proves uncommunicative."

"I take it," Gideon remarked, "that he knows this for certain."

"Who knows?" Turville shrugged. "Lytton may simply be clutching at straws in his attempts to find Ferrers, but from what I could ascertain it seems very much as though he has been fed this information by someone in a position to know. My money is on Colonel Henderson. After all," he said grimly, "he was the one who conducted those searches."

Gideon shook his head. "He may well, but I fail to see what reason Ferrers would have in seeking shelter under his own roof, with or without his sister's knowledge. He, of all people, would know the precarious position in which he stands, innocent or not, and I doubt he would do anything which could involve her as an accomplice, besides which," he shook his head, "it seems most unlikely she would be prepared to give him any assistance or offer him shelter, especially if, as His Grace suggests, her father's heart attack was the result of her brother's political persuasions!"

General Turville agreed to this. "But we must not forget," he added, "that we have no way of knowing whether Ferrers is aware of his father's death or not, although," he pointed out practically, "if he is in Sussex and so close to his estates, I fail to see how he could be unaware of it." In his frustration he ran a hand through his hair, disarranging his wig, a sure sign he was troubled. "We don't even know if he was actually recruited or not and, if he was, is she aware of it? We can't possibly know for certain the extent of her knowledge or her opinions; for all we know her brother could be guilty as charged and she holds the same sympathies; all we have to work on is what Lytton has seen fit to tell us and our own assumptions. It is up to us to discover the truth. However," he added, "I think you will agree that we must be seen to be doing all we can to bring a fugitive to justice."

"It seems to me, Sir," Gideon suggested at length, having given the matter further thought, "that Ferrers' capture is more important to Lytton than the truth. Whether he holds information or not, the more I think about it the more convinced I am that he is being sought more for someone's personal protection than anything else. The thing is Sir," he pointed out, "that whilst we cannot discount what Lytton says about Ferrers being guilty of treason, so many factors point to him being innocent, and I keep coming back to the question, if he *is* innocent, why is Lytton doing his utmost to apprehend him? *His* involvement is inexplicable."

As if unable to be still, General Turville again stalked over to the window, his massive frame blotting out the light coming into the room, the early morning sun picking out the iron grey of his hair just visible beneath his wig, making him appear all the more formidable. "I'm damned if *I* know, and that's the truth, but tell me Gideon," he asked, "do you believe Richard Ferrers to be guilty or not? I must know what you really think."

"The truth, Sir," he said at length, "is that based on your knowledge of the family and all you have told me, I have to say I believe him to be innocent. However," General Turville spun round to face him at this, but Gideon continued easily, "the thing I find difficult to understand is, if Ferrers *is* guilty of treason, then why not conduct a search for him openly and why the delay, after all, Culloden was thirteen months ago?" He leaned forward slightly, his eyes intent on his commanding officer's craggy face. "*If* he is being sought as a smuggler, then why not let the Excisemen deal with it? No Sir," he shook his head, "it doesn't make sense. There *has* to be more to it than what we have been told, and if we are right in thinking that Ferrers has somehow or other become involved in something serious enough to bring Lytton into it such as discovering the identity of the real traitor, then all the signs point to him being innocent of treason, I can see no grounds for him to act in this matter otherwise and certainly not for reasons of smuggling. Even supposing Ferrers *is* a traitor, why should His Grace become involved when he has not done so in the past?" General Turville nodded and Gideon asked, "And you, Sir; are you still convinced of Ferrers' innocence?"

"*That* Gideon," he told him unequivocally, "goes without saying. Why, I ask myself, would a man with such an impeccable lineage and a father whose whole life had been devoted to his country, suddenly disclose to his world that he is a Jacobite?"

"Unfortunately, it is not too uncommon an occurrence, Sir" Gideon reminded him gently.

"I realize that," Turville acknowledged, gripping the lapels of his coat with two huge paws, "but there's something damned smoky about the whole affair, and before I see that young man hang from the nearest gallows I want to know what the devil makes him so important! And since he is the only one who can tell us, we have to seek him out without any undue loss of time."

Gideon sighed. "Well, Sir, I shall, of course, do all I can to find him but, even supposing I do," he pointed out, "he may not trust me enough to even want to talk to me. If, as you say, his sister has already endured numerous invasions of her home, a circumstance he could easily have got to hear of, it is therefore quite reasonable to suppose that he thinks a very neat little trap is being set for him."

General Turville grunted before barking out, "He may well do, but he must be brought to see that if he doesn't talk to you, then the alternative is either being shot as an escapee from custody or being strung up!"

"Put like that, Sir," Gideon smiled, "I fail to see how he can refuse."

A responsive twitch touched Turville's lips, but he was suddenly serious again. "An unpleasant thought I know, but that is what it comes down to. The more I think about it the more certain I become that Colonel Henderson knows a great deal more about this business than we have any idea of, and unless I miss my guess I would say that this has become a personal crusade for him; although why that should be I cannot tell. I tell you Gideon, there is something devlish underhand going on. Under no circumstances," he impressed, "must Ferrers be taken to Henderson, no matter what you may discover. In fact," he added forcefully, "I am ordering you not to, irrespective of what you find out. With regards to his sister," he warned, "we must tread carefully there. Whatever it is that lies behind her denials, she has already undergone much apparently, and we can't risk alienating her. She may not know her brother's whereabouts, in fact, I doubt she even knows he is at this very moment in Sussex, and even if she is not prepared to aid him herself, she may know people he could go to for help, and if there is the slightest chance of her telling us anything we must do all we can not to estrange her."

"If she is not already," Gideon put in, fully prepared for hostility. "Then, of course, there is always the possibility that she will look upon my arrival as no more welcome than a search party, and who can blame her?" he acknowledged. "However, bearing in mind that there is no one else we can approach, since we don't know Ferrers' friends, there is little choice open to us."

"That's true enough," Turville nodded, "but if she doesn't want to see her brother either shot or hung, she will be well advised to talk to you."

"I rather hope I won't have to remind her of that, Sir," Gideon remarked, "but it may well be that I shall have to take her part way into my confidence in order to discover Ferrers' whereabouts."

Turville nodded. "You must use your own judgement. Nevertheless, it's a damned nasty business no matter which way we go about it."

Gideon agreed. "May I ask what you really think, Sir?"

Turville turned to look at him, his face exhibiting a mixture of emotions. "In truth, Gideon" he confessed, "I believe we are being used for motives we do not yet know, and from what I can make out Richard Ferrers is the only one who can make sense of it."

"I confess, Sir, that that unpalatable thought has occurred to me." Gideon too had risen. "Even so, we must, as you say, be seen to be doing all we can to apprehend a fugitive from justice, but what if all Lytton has said is true and Ferrers is indeed all he stands accused of? As you yourself have already said Sir, we are both of us putting ourselves in an awkward position by not turning him over to Colonel Henderson should I find him. His Grace may find himself in a delicate position, but he will not take kindly to us playing our own game."

Turville agreed to the truth of this. "I accept my feelings are not grounded in fact," he admitted, "but if, as I very much suspect, someone wants this young man put out of the way, then I could not live with my conscience knowing that I helped to do it."

"I feel that way too, Sir," Gideon acknowledged, "but, if we are right, then proving it is not going to be easy. In fact," he shook his head, "I fail to see what proof there *can* be. If Ferrers *has* discovered something, his word alone is going to be no good. We must hope that there is written evidence of some kind to substantiate his findings."

"I know it," Turville replied gloomily, "but, like you, why, I ask myself, if he is a Jacobite, conduct a search so surreptitiously? It makes far more sense Ferrers *not* being a Jacobite."

"Well, if he is not," Gideon said ominously, "and I agree it seems that way, then it can mean only one thing."

Turville did not need to have this statement explained, he knew very well its significance. "Yes," he nodded, "I've thought of that too. Before we can clear Ferrers' name we have to find the real traitor." After several minutes of contemplating the situation into which they had been thrust, he resumed his seat whereupon he pulled several sheets of notepaper towards him. "I shall, out of courtesy, have to write to Colonel Henderson introducing you. He will, of course, unless I am very much mistaken, be aware of what is going forward, no doubt Lytton will already have informed him, but he is to know that you are under *my* orders and not his; answerable only to me." Gideon nodded and Turville continued, "You will naturally have to keep him advised of your enquiries; tell him what tale you will, but under no circumstances are you to make known to him that you have found Ferrers, that is," he added, "if you *do* find him."

"I shall certainly try, Sir" Gideon assured him, "but it may not be an easy matter to fob Colonel Henderson off."

"I should think it damned near impossible!" General Turville frankly admitted. "But on no account must he know anything that could put Ferrers in danger."

"Tell me, Sir," Gideon asked, "you say you mistrust Colonel Henderson; do you suspect him of anything in particular?"

"As things stand at the moment, Gideon," he told him, "I suspect everyone. Lytton told me that it was Henderson who first alerted him to Ferrers being in Sussex and conducting his illicit dealings, and I would stake my reputation on it that it was he who requested Lytton to intervene. I don't pretend to have all the answers, because I don't, but Richard Ferrers is as hot as coals for some reason and I want to know why before we calmly hand him over, and Henderson seems to know a great deal about it!"

Gideon thought so too. "Well, whatever I discover Sir, I shall not hand him over to Colonel Henderson."

"I know you won't, Gideon. Now," he recommended, "I think you had better start making your arrangements. They expect you in Sussex as soon as may be possible, and considering a young man's life is at stake, the sooner the better."

"Very good, Sir" Gideon nodded. "Does anyone else know of my visit, Sir?"

Sir John eyed him sceptically. "Unless Lytton or Henderson have told anyone, no. But then" he nodded darkly, "this matter bears all the hallmarks of dirty dealings, and that being so, we cannot take anything for granted; not even the fact that we have been given a week in which to find Ferrers. Knowing His Grace," he snorted disgustedly, "he is more than capable of inserting his name in the London Gazette way ahead of time."

Gideon nodded, then after a few more words he pocketed the letter Sir John gave him, saluted and left.

CHAPTER THREE

As he made his way home, gracefully reclining against the squabs of his elegant town coach, his face particularly grim, His Grace, pondering his interview with General Turville, came to the regrettable conclusion that he could not claim to be entirely satisfied with its outcome. Admittedly, he had been given Sir John's assurance that he would put forward every effort into apprehending Richard Ferrers, but he was not altogether convinced of this. He had not needed Sir John's parting words to confirm that he had no liking for the task in hand and, being a man blessed with an acute awareness, he had, from the moment he broached the matter, detected the same lack of enthusiasm in his manner as he had previously. Although he knew Turville would ultimately do everything that was required of him, irrespective of personal feelings, he could not quite rid his mind of certain nagging doubts as to the level of his commitment.

There were, of course, any number of people from whom he could have sought assistance to help him track down Richard Ferrers, but the long friendship which had existed between his father and General Turville had been the deciding factor in approaching him in the first place. Not only did it give the matter a certain piquancy, which he owned had been irresistible, but it also provided him with a very convenient scapegoat should anything go wrong, especially when one considered his lenient attitudes towards those who had taken part in the late rebellion! He was perfectly well aware that it was going to be no easy matter for him to track down the only son of a man whom he had admired and respected, nevertheless, he was persuaded that after only a very little thought, Sir John would come to realize that, however distasteful the task, it was not only his duty to seek out an enemy of the King, but would also come to recognize the expediency of doing so.

Sir John may be reluctant but he was no fool, and whatever his private beliefs he would eventually be brought to see that to ignore his directives would be extremely foolhardy. Whilst he acquitted him of deliberately trying to shield a man hailed as a traitor and a fugitive from justice, it could not be taken for granted that he would stress the importance or, indeed, the urgency, attached to the speedy apprehension of Richard Ferrers to his delegated officer. Turville may not relish the idea of running Ferrers to earth but, he felt sure, that after only a very little thought, he would, in the end, do what was required of him, however unwilling or disinclined but, he was by nature an honest man who would doubtless deem it to be his duty as not only an officer and a gentleman but also as a lifelong friend of

Ferrers' father, to delve more deeply into this matter. Under no circumstances could he allow this to happen, to do so would be to open himself up to all manner of gossip and criticism and these were the very things he wished to avoid. A private word in this man's ear therefore, was not only wise but imperative in order to ensure there were no misunderstandings about what was expected of him.

Until Richard Ferrers was in safe custody or, better still, no longer around to create difficulties, then there could be no relaxation in his endeavours to expedite a speedy end to this matter. It was seldom, if ever, he erred in his dealings, but it occurred to him now that whilst he may congratulate himself on the deft way he had handled the interview, by giving Sir John only the bare facts without going into too much detail, and skirting around the edges of the truth in order to avoid divulging names, he could well have raised questions in his mind as to the veracity of what he had been told, and was, therefore, maddeningly brought to realize that it would behove him to tread warily.

When he had laid his plans to effect the arrest of Richard Ferrers they had been calculated to a nicety, and he had foreseen no difficulties, but in view of General Turville's obvious reluctance to accommodate him in this matter, he now saw that there was every likelihood that those plans may have to undergo some modification. That in itself was no great matter, but had others played their part as directed or, better still, have exercised caution in the first place before going headlong into a situation they should have known was destined to end in disaster, then the need for his involvement would never have arisen.

Being a man who liked to know with whom he was dealing, he would have felt much happier to have the identity of the officer Sir John would entrust to deal with this very delicate affair made known to him. It would have afforded him a greater degree of comfort to have been able to take this young man to one side and offer a cautionary word in his ear as to the folly of failing to carry out his expressed orders without deviation, as well as impressing upon him not only the urgency attached in apprehending Richard Ferrers, but also the need for extreme discretion. It went without saying that Turville would choose his envoy very carefully; he would, of necessity, be someone he could trust, and one, moreover, who did not let either his tongue or emotions run away with him.

Discovering the identity of the man whose task it would be to effect the capture of Richard Ferrers would require extreme tact, but it was not beyond his capabilities. He knew he could not trust Henderson to ensure that he was sufficiently acquainted with what was required of him simply because he had already proved what a bungling fool he was. He could only speculate what Sir John would see fit to tell him regarding their interview, but he felt it reasonably safe to assume that he would impart his own doubts and misgivings regarding Richard Ferrers' guilt, and his orders therefore could well countermand his own.

He could think of several capable officers' serving under Sir John's command who would be suitable for such work, but as he had already been forced into showing his hand in this matter he was extremely disinclined to advertise any further interest beyond that which he already had.

It irked Lytton to know that his own position regarding this very sensitive matter was rather awkward to say the least but, being a man of infinite resource and one, moreover, who looked to his own interests, he had no intention of being caught in the middle of this potentially explosive situation.

By the time he was set down outside his house, a rather imposing edifice located in the most fashionable part of town, his very correct and stately butler, having already opened the door in readiness for him to enter, his agile brain had arrived at certain conclusions. Whilst these left him in no doubt that this rather unfortunate affair could still be resolved to the satisfaction of all parties concerned, and to himself in particular, it did mean a slight alteration to his plans which, regrettable though it was, would necessitate a most inconvenient journey into Sussex.

Having languidly handed Parker his hat and cane followed by his gloves without a word of greeting or thanks, his thin lips compressing into an uncompromising line as he considered the exquisite tact and delicacy which would be required to see the end of this matter once and for all, he merely waited patiently until that long-suffering employee had opened the door to the book room at the rear of the hall in order for him to enter. Parker, all too familiar with His Grace, knew something was in the wind; he distrusted that expression, and the look in those cold eyes told him that he was planning something which would in all probability do some poor unfortunate soul no good, but since he knew better than to enquire if all were well, he merely closed the door quietly behind him before resuming his duties.

Leisurely savouring the Madeira in his glass, Lytton sat at his ease in a wing chair by the fire, one leg crossed gracefully over the other, as he again turned his mind to the question of Richard Ferrers. There was no doubt that this enterprising young man was causing all manner of difficulties, not least to himself, albeit indirectly, but with dexterous handling the problem need not reach crisis point, which could well be the case if left to Henderson. Had it not been for his gross stupidity in the first place followed by the eventual mismanagement of what could only be described as a bungling attempt to solve matters, he would not now find himself in a position which he not only disliked, but could, if not carefully managed, rebound on himself. Were it not for the fact that Henderson, in an unguarded moment, could quite possibly let something slip which would inevitably prove to be extremely detrimental to himself, he felt he would be more than justified in letting him and his equally inept confederate settle their own affairs and to extricate themselves as best they could. Whilst they both deserved his contempt as well as being quite unworthy of his continued regard and assistance, he knew he could not shelve this volatile problem as he dare not allow his own involvement in this very regrettable affair, however unwillingly entered into, to become public knowledge, any more than he could allow Henderson to believe that he could blackmail him with impunity.

His eyes narrowed as they stared at the liquid in his glass, his lips compressing into a thin ugly line as he considered the repercussions to himself. At no point did he doubt his ability to settle matters to his satisfaction, and whilst he had not anticipated a journey into Sussex, it was unfortunately a necessary evil if he wished to resolve this matter once and for all. It would be inconvenient, that went without saying, but since he dare not entrust something of such magnitude to that fool Henderson, he realized he had no choice but to make the sacrifice.

He doubted Sir John would drag his feet over this especially now he knew that Ferrers was to be 'gazetted', so it was therefore logical to assume that he would not delay matters any longer than was necessary, indeed, the chances were that Sir John's delegate would be in Sussex before him and conversed with Henderson well before his own arrival. It may be expedient to take this young man to one side for the express purpose of ensuring he knew precisely what was expected of him, but only a moment's thought had been sufficient for him to realize how his own awkward position rendered that quite out of the question, indeed, it could so easily rebound on him. Other measures, therefore, would have to be adopted if he wished to achieve his ends as well as keep his name and reputation unsullied but, even before he had time to yet again regret the origins for his present disadvantageous position, it occurred to him that there was, after all, really no need to advertise any further interest in this affair which would alert the interested to his dealings, especially when he recalled the fact that he had a most convenient tool to do it for him.

Being one who considered every eventuality, he had not overlooked the possibility that Ferrers, who appeared to be a man of infinite resource, may well slip through Henderson's fingers yet again. This would not surprise him, especially if he failed to impress upon Turville's advocate the urgency attached to his capture. Should this in fact be the case, then someone other than Henderson would have to take the blame; and, although it irked him to admit it, even to himself, that should this possibility arise, then he alone was the one responsible for bringing it about. Had it not been for the fact that he had allowed too much wine to loosen his tongue all those years ago when he had made that disastrous confession to Henderson, he would have no qualms in leaving him to his fate. As it was, Henderson was in possession of damaging information, and because he could not be relied upon to keep his tongue when faced with either a crisis or an unlooked for development, he could quite easily allow his emotions to get the better of him when panic set in. Henderson therefore, unworthy though he was, would have to be saved by the skilful adoption of a scapegoat.

He knew as well as anyone that General Turville was no Jacobite and that his loyalty to His Majesty had never been called into question, but should his reluctance to act in this matter of Richard Ferrers ever reach certain ears, then his apparent lack of dedication to seek him out could easily be turned to good account.

He fully appreciated the difficulties Sir John faced in ensuring the capture of those remaining Jacobite fugitives still on the run, but he wondered how it would be viewed in line with the escape of a man who was claimed to be a traitor and whose father he had called friend? Of course, there were very reasonable and practical explanations for this as he knew very well, but with a little embellishment or innocent suggestion, Sir John Turville's future could look extremely bleak indeed!

He experienced no qualms or twinges of conscience as he contemplated this, on the contrary, he looked upon it as not only necessary but expedient. He had no intention of allowing his own name to be bandied about town, especially when he had entered into this business under duress in order to save the reputation of an old friend, a friend, he decided, who really did not deserve either his assistance or continued regard.

Lytton, not unmindful of their long association, was by no means averse to aiding an old friend, after all, favours could always be called in at some point, but it had been apparent to him from the beginning that this particular favour could never be called in as Colonel Henderson knew very well. No more than the next man did he like having a pistol held to his head, but despite his extreme displeasure at finding himself in such an awkward and embarrassing situation, he had to reluctantly acknowledge that his assistance had been suborned with a subtlety of which he himself was a master.

A folly of his youth, long since forgotten, had been resurrected without compunction to ensure his full conformity, and unless he wanted to make the world privy to an indiscretion which, no matter how one looked at it, would be socially damning, he had found himself with little choice but to agree.

Like himself, he had believed his old friend to have forgotten such an ancient incident, and had been somewhat taken aback to discover that far from having forgotten it, he had remembered it and was quite prepared to use it against him.

That neither could expose the other's secret was little solace, but having found himself locked into a set of circumstances from which no amount of anger or self-deprecation at having confided such a momentous piece of intelligence to his friend in the first place all those years ago, would extricate him, he unwillingly accepted the charge laid upon him. Disinclined though he was, he went about the business in his own inimitable style in order to secure a favourable outcome to Henderson's embarrassing problem which, the more he considered it, was equally, if not more, injurious to his future than his own could ever be.

His determination to expend every exertion was not only to safeguard Henderson's reputation and shield his name from adverse criticism and disgrace, but primarily to protect himself. He bitterly resented being held to ransom, and even more to knowing what could result should he fail to bring this matter to a satisfactory conclusion. Not that this was ever in question! He had supreme confidence in his ability to achieve his purpose and was resolved therefore to see the matter through, but he was also equally resolved in his fixed intention of rewarding Henderson handsomely for daring to compromise him in such a way. He knew how to repay a slight or an offence against his person, and even while he was putting plans forward to extricate his soon to be former friend from a most unenviable if self-imposed predicament, he was thinking far ahead to a most exquisite revenge.

For a man who possessed a razor sharp mind and the ability to think and act decisively, it was beyond his comprehension how two of the most incompetent idiots it had ever been his misfortune to encounter, could ever have hoped to succeed in their misguided venture. If this fiasco was ever to be resolved satisfactorily without any fingers being pointed in their direction, then a minor detail, which, in his opinion, should not be necessary after all the effort he had already expended, would require his immediate attention. Strolling over to his desk and easing himself gracefully onto the chair, he leisurely drew several sheets of the finest quality vellum towards him, then, after dipping the nib into the ink pot began the first of his two letters; the pen between his finger and thumb gliding back and forth across the page without a pause. Every word which made up the first half dozen lines in his strong upright hand was calculated to leave the recipient under no illusion that he had incurred his deep displeasure. Having vented a little of his spleen, he then went on to inform him of his latest efforts to relieve him of his difficulties, the outcome being that he would see Sir John's envoy in Sussex within the next few days when, hopefully, he could expect to receive news that their collaboration had proved successful. He concluded by saying that, having already been at considerable pains to offer him every assistance but, alas, to no avail, only to find himself yet again forced to expend unnecessary exertion on his behalf, he hoped that this further attempt on his part to settle matters would now see the end of the affair. The second letter, which consisted of half a dozen lines only, was pithy and to the point, guaranteed to not only inform the addressee that he had incurred His Grace's extreme displeasure, but that failure to hold himself in readiness for his visit on the morrow at ten of the clock precisely, would be to his detriment.

Parker, in answer to the summons on the bell pull, entered the book room some five minutes later considerably out of breath; the back stairs not designed for one of his age and portly figure. "You rang, Your Grace?" he enquired, bowing respectfully.

"Sometime ago," Lytton replied coldly, thrusting the letters into his hand. "I want these delivered immediately."

"Yes, Your Grace" he bowed.

"See that they are," Lytton told him.

Parker, who had no more love for His Grace than any of the other servants, knew the moment he had opened the door to him that something was amiss, and whilst he dared not enquire if all were well, he would nevertheless have given everything he possessed to discover the reason for his master's obvious ill humour. However, by the time Lytton left his house several hours later to join a party of friends at his club, so confident was he of a favourable outcome to his plans that his mood lightened considerably. Not even upon being informed that the letter to Clarges Street had been delivered as requested, but had had to be left in the hands of the recipient's valet as his master was away from home and not expected back until late, had brought so much as a frown to his face. Nevertheless, he had considered it prudent to refrain from informing him that Jem, upon being told he was to journey immediately into Sussex with a letter, was so belligerent at being used more like an errand boy than a groom, argued vociferously before deciding that it would not be in his own interests to refuse, as His Grace was more than capable of casting him off without a recommendation.

General Turville, himself far from happy with his interview, acknowledged the justification of Gideon's observations. Lytton would be far from pleased to know that instead of putting plans into execution for Richard Ferrers' capture and arrest, they were going against his explicit orders. He was not a man who would appreciate his commands being ignored or tampered with, on the contrary, he would take it as a personal affront, and his way of dealing with such insubordination would not only be swift, but merciless. Nevertheless, Sir John had no stomach to see an innocent man hang and, from what he could see of it, that was precisely what Richard Ferrers was.

For his sake as well as that of his honoured parent, he was determined to do all he could to prove him guiltless of the charges which had been laid at his door. Even so, he could not discount Gideon's argument in that, if Richard Ferrers was in actual fact innocent of treason after all, then his word alone would not be sufficient to prove it. Without evidence to substantiate it, then establishing his innocence was going to be almost impossible.

As far as Elizabeth Ferrers was concerned he could make no assessment either way but, even so, he failed to see her as a traitor any more than he could her brother. He could well understand her hostile reaction to the invasion parties which had descended upon Ferrers Court in an attempt to find Richard in hiding there which, he had no doubt, had been conducted without any regard for her dignity or privacy but, on the contrary, executed with a vigour to the point where they had, regrettably, resulted in the unfortunate death of her father. Far from endearing her to the military, such brutal tactics would, he felt sure, achieve nothing other than alienating her, giving birth to a deep-rooted hatred of red-coats which could so easily manifest itself in a ruthless determination to thwart them by any means possible. He could only guess as to whether or not she believed in her brother's innocence but if, as Lytton would have him believe, she was aware of his whereabouts as well as his new found calling and offering him shelter, in addition to refusing to give him up, then not only was she playing a very dangerous game indeed, but placing herself in a most precarious position!

Unfortunately though, everything was nothing more than conjecture. Regardless of what Lytton had let fall, the truth was he had no way of knowing the precise nature of affairs at Ferrers Court or the views held by its inhabitants, much less what kind of a reception Gideon could expect upon his arrival. In fact, the only thing he could claim to knowing with any degree of certainty was that that man of Jasper's, far from being persuaded into accepting money in order to induce him to betray his son, would, unless he was grossly mistaken, much prefer to be arrested himself than give him away. As for Jasper's sister, Clara Winsetton, whom he knew from experience to be a forthright and rather formidable woman, would, unless she had changed dramatically over the years, be more than likely to send them away with a flea in their ear. Sadly, his thinking was not so definite where Elizabeth Ferrers was concerned. It was, to say the least, most unfortunate that he knew nothing about her other than what Lytton had seen fit to tell him but, of one thing he felt absolutely confident, and that was the very real possibility that she may well refuse to grant Gideon an interview let alone reach the point where she trusted him enough to place her brother's life into his hands. Should she refuse to see him, a circumstance he could by no means discount, then where he and Gideon went from there in an attempt to help her brother had him at a loss, because although it was logical to assume that members of the smuggling fraternity had their own means of knowing what was going on, it was useless to suppose that they would willingly identify themselves as such in order for Gideon to speak to them. However, should she decide to speak to Gideon after all, then it was very possible that it could well turn out to be a rather unproductive meeting, because he felt sure that her antagonism towards the military would only intensify when faced with yet another red-coat, impeding any kind of progress or understanding between them. Should this be the way of it, then he could only hope that Gideon would be able to break down her reserve, which, given all that had gone before, must be considerable.

He could not deny that Gideon was a most personable young man with exquisite manners, and had no doubt that he would treat her with the greatest respect and deference, but could not fail to share his distaste at Lytton's suggestion for the best way of dealing with her. There were any number of men under his command who would have no qualms in making up to a young woman in the way

Lytton had intimated, but such behaviour would be repugnant to a man like Gideon, and not for the first time Turville thanked God he was still in regimentals.

Gideon, well aware of the faith and confidence his senior officer had in his ability to carry out such a delicate task, could only hope that he would not disappoint him, because as far as he could see he was about to walk through what was nothing short of a battleground in which there was no clear or safe path. He perfectly understood General Turville's feelings and the implicit belief he had in Richard Ferrers' innocence but, whilst he admitted that this certainly seemed to be the case, for the moment at least, everything was nothing but conjecture. The truth was he had very little, if any, corroborative evidence to substantiate his innocence with which to work, and since he could not rely on Miss Ferrers placing her trust in him as well as having no idea who would turn out to be a friend or foe, he envisaged his investigations to be anything but straightforward. Whether Richard Ferrers was guilty or not, it was imperative that he not only gained the confidence of his sister but conducted himself in such a way that Colonel Henderson would not suspect him of disregarding His Grace's orders by carrying out General Turville's counter ones. He had no taste for dissimulation, but if this young man was indeed innocent then he had to do everything possible to prevent him from climbing the scaffold and, even if he was guilty as charged, then the same still held in doing all he could to protect him from the mockery of a sham trial, or worse, and if all this meant keeping the truth from Colonel Henderson, then he was quite prepared to do so. However resourceful Richard Ferrers may have proved himself to be by so far managing to elude capture, it was surely only a matter of time before he would be caught, especially once his name was inserted in the London Gazette, and no matter how innocent he was Gideon felt fairly certain that he would be given no opportunity to speak in his own defence. The nearer he got to Hampton Regis the more concerned be became, particularly when he considered how little time there was available to him in which to prevent the very worst from happening. He may be a man who kept an open mind but he could not delude himself into believing that his forthcoming task was going to be easy, indeed, he saw himself being faced with all manner of difficulties, but of one thing he could be certain and that was no matter what the outcome of this dilemma the next few days were going to be anything but uneventful.

Arriving in Hampton Regis midway through the afternoon on the day following his departure from London on what clearly was a market day, Gideon's passage through the town was necessarily slow. Navigating his horse up the narrow street leading into the town, a rather steep gradient inclining to the right, he rounded the bend into the main street where, to his surprise, he saw a bustling throng in front of him. Staring in astonishment at the multitude of people spread out before him, he could not help but think that everyone from miles around had descended on the town, and to add to the pandemonium market stalls had been erected on both sides of the street from which all manner of produce was being offered for sale, thereby considerably narrowing the width of the road rendering passage in either direction difficult. Although he could see the garrison located on the left hand side further down the street it nevertheless took him at least fifteen minutes to manoeuvre his way through the heaving crowd, his passage impeded by not only hopeful vendors trying to persuade him to purchase their wares but also having to several times make way for farmers to herd their nervous animals through the busy horde. The sight of a scarlet coat in Hampton Regis may be a common occurrence to which the inhabitants had long since grown accustomed, but Gideon cut a very striking figure as he sat astride his grey mare, resulting in him receiving more than one appreciative look, especially from one dark eyed brunette who clearly was not inexperienced in gaining a man's attention. Her dark eyes flashed up at him suggestively as he past her and her lips parted provocatively, enticing him to stop and engage her in conversation. A smile lit his eyes but as he had no desire to take her up on her unspoken if blatant invitation, he merely doffed his mitre cap followed by a slight inclination of his head before continuing on his way without a backward glance, entering the gatehouse of the garrison just as the clock struck two o'clock.

From his reception by the gatehouse sergeant it was clear his visit was expected and as he waited for someone to come and attend him he unbuckled his cloak bag from the saddle before his horse was led to the stables by a private, whose curiosity was only exceeded by that of his sergeant. He had no intention of imparting any information to either of these inquisitive individuals and therefore adroitly deflected the pointed questions put to him as to the reason for him being here, but was nevertheless rather relieved when a young lieutenant finally arrived to take him to Colonel Henderson's quarters. From the questions the sergeant in particular had put to him he shrewdly suspected that no one knew the reason for his visit, and could only assume that Colonel Henderson did not want it to be known that his failure to apprehend a fugitive from justice had necessitated bringing in some one from outside to do it for him. He knew from experience that in such a confined space as an army garrison news spread like wildfire, but the last thing he wanted was for it to become known that he had come specifically to track down and apprehend Richard Ferrers. He would not put it beyond any one of them to take matters into their own hands by not only trying to make a name for themselves but also proving that they did not need this Major from London to do something they could easily do themselves. Not only that, but he had promised to do all he could to help Richard Ferrers, and to this end therefore he was determined to do just that, irrespective of whether he was innocent or not.

His escort, apart from politely introducing himself, made no effort to enquire into his business, accepting without question that if he wanted him to know he would tell him, and was therefore seemingly content to ignore this very natural query as irrelevant and instead merely commented on the garrison and the surrounding area, unaware of the relief Gideon felt at his lack of curiosity. He listened to his companion's description of the town and castle with great patience, indeed, he was quite impressed at the depth of Lieutenant Beaton's knowledge. He discovered that, like Lewes further down the coast, Hampton Regis was originally a thriving Saxon market town. With the coming of William the Conqueror Sussex was divided into baronies, and, again like Lewes, became one of the main military and administrative centres stretching from the coast to Worth Forest and the Surrey border. William de Warenne, one of William the Conqueror's companions, built his castle in an ideal position, on the highest point of the promontory.

It soon became apparent to Gideon that Lieutenant Beaton, a fresh faced young man with a pleasant and friendly disposition, was a keen historian, and prior to his own arrival had, unfortunately, found no receptive ear into which he could pour his knowledge. No sooner did he learn that this visit of Gideon's was his first, than he took the opportunity to regale him with all the historical background he could possibly want, interspersing his impromptu lecture while escorting him to Colonel Henderson's quarters, by pointing out various landmarks for miles around.

Lieutenant Beaton, seemingly not content with all the information he had already given Gideon, went on to tell him that Hampton Regis castle had been modelled on the same lines as that of Lewes, also built by William de Warenne, both being somewhat unusual in that they had two mounds, one on the south-west and one on the north-east, defended by a bank and dry moat. Gideon replied suitably, putting forward a polite question here and there, only to realize too late that his avid escort had misread his courteous interest for real enthusiasm, and Lieutenant Beaton, taking the rare opportunity offered by what he thought was a like minded individual, eagerly extended his generosity by inviting him to dine with him in his room one evening to discuss in more detail the historical and geographical importance of Hampton Regis. Gideon was left in no doubt as to his companion's all consuming interest in the subject or to his profound knowledge, and tried to disabuse his new friend's mind of its misconception, but was soon brought to see that this was easier said than done.

As he had not the heart to stem this enthusiastic flow he was fortunately spared having to commit himself as they were by now approaching Colonel Henderson's quarters situated in an imposing tower at the foot of a pair of well-worn stone steps at the far end of the bailey. Lieutenant Beaton, his face glowing with excitement, further informed Gideon that the smooth bowling green they were now traversing had been laid over a hundred years ago by the castle's then eccentric owner, but would, in its early days, have been a general meeting place where lords and knights with their ladies would have rubbed shoulders with everyone from the tinker bearing gifts to the blacksmith. As the steps were only wide enough to allow single passage up and down it was necessary to climb them one behind the other, but as Gideon had not really taken in very much of what he had been told, for which the task that lay ahead of him was largely responsible, he was not sorry to take the steps well behind his new found friend, rendering conversation difficult.

He was ushered into a circular room through a door made out of old English oak at least two inches thick. To his surprise it was far more comfortable than he would have supposed. The heavy tapestries lining the walls hid the cold grey stones, and the wide open fireplace presently housing a roaring fire, together with the large faded carpet on the floor, gave the room a warmth he would not have thought possible. It was all so very different to how it must have been centuries ago, when it was no doubt used to house some of the castle's defenders. He had caught a brief glimpse of a door much higher up which obviously gave access to the top of the tower, bearing out Lieutenant Beaton's statement that until a couple of hundred years ago this used to be a gateway and drawbridge, but had long since been bricked up.

The vast collection of paperwork at present covering the desk and the battalion orders and various duty rotas attached to a board on the wall behind, told him that this was clearly the domain of Colonel Henderson's personal staff officer, Major Denham.

After being introduced to Major Denham, Gideon parted company with his young friend on the best of terms, but not before he had promised to show him some of the sights of Hampton Regis. Gideon could all too clearly imagine the sights of antiquity he would doubtless be shown, and whilst this held no real attraction for him, he soon began to realize that this young man's unsurpassed knowledge could come in very useful when tracking down a man whose illicit career naturally rendered him hard to find.

Major Denham, a short and stockily built man in his mid to late forties, bore all the appearance of being a strict disciplinarian, and one who took his military duties very seriously. His eyes, which were of an indeterminate brown, held none of the humour or tolerance which were clearly reflected in Gideon's. He had a high receding forehead, only partly concealed by the white wig he wore and which was tied at the nape of his neck with a small black bow. Having been informed of Gideon's arrival and the reason for it at very short notice by Colonel Henderson, who, unfortunately, had been unable to provide a name or rank since His Grace had not furnished him with this information, had fully expected his personal staff officer to make every effort to not only allocate him quarters but to offer him all the assistance at his command, he had reluctantly ordered the first floor lodging in the gatehouse to be placed at his disposal. In his opinion this man's arrival had not only disrupted his carefully planned duty rotas by having to assign someone to tend him, but it had cast aspersions on their ability to deal with Richard Ferrers themselves. To his way of thinking bringing in an outsider, and from a different regiment to boot, was bound to raise questions as to the integrity and devotion to duty of the men stationed at the garrison. As he was unaware of His Grace the Duke of Lytton's involvement in this matter, he had looked upon Colonel Henderson's reasons for calling in assistance from London as quite unnecessary. What he thought this man could do that they had not was anyone's guess but, by the time he was introduced to him, so convinced was he that it was all a waste of time and a gross insult into the bargain, that he was in no very good frame of mind. His firm mouth, evincing no welcoming smile, bore adequate testimony to his feelings as well as to the fact that he firmly believed in strict discipline with no relaxation of the rules. He firmly disapproved of the kind of fraternization he had witnessed between Gideon and Lieutenant Beaton, looking upon this over-friendliness as bad for discipline. He could only guess as to how things were in London, but he would have this Major Neville know that allowing a junior officer to engage him in a conversation, which he personally considered to be out of keeping with military duties, was something he was not prepared to overlook or tolerate. Unfortunately for him however, as far as Gideon was concerned he had no authority to take him to task, but he would certainly speak to Lieutenant Beaton at the earliest opportunity, in the meantime though, a word of warning in Gideon's ear would not come amiss. He may not be able to impart his feelings as to how he felt at the slur his visit cast on not only himself but the men, but by letting him see that this kind of behaviour was not at all the thing, would at least relieve some of his spleen.

Gideon listened to him without comment, at the end of which he merely shook his head, his ready smile dawning as he said in his quiet way, "The boy meant no harm. He was merely making a stranger welcome."

Gideon may have smiled, but Major Denham was quick to see the look which had entered his eyes, and realized he had allowed his feelings to get the better of him. In an attempt to explain himself, he said in a conciliatory tone, "I realize that. I realize too that things are no doubt conducted very differently in London, but this is a small garrison Major Neville where over-friendliness between the officers and men could easily lead to dereliction of duty."

Gideon's eyes widened in surprise at this, but as Colonel Henderson chose this moment to enter Major Denham's room by a single door to the left of the fireplace, he was not obliged to reply to a statement which he thought rather ridiculous.

Acknowledging the presence of a senior officer, both men stood to attention, whereafter Gideon was formally introduced to him.

From the moment Gideon had set out upon his journey into Sussex he had considered how best to approach this interview with Colonel Henderson. General

Turville had advised using his own judgement in this sad affair, and whilst this was seldom found to be at fault, there was one overriding factor which governed his behaviour and response in this matter. Lytton may be unaware of the conclusions drawn resulting from his interview with General Turville, but he was nevertheless expecting a speedy solution regarding the problem of Richard Ferrers, and would also expect him to carry out his duties with an eagerness he was very far from feeling. He was by no means overjoyed at the prospect of engaging in a man hunt, but since Colonel Henderson and His Grace were determined to put an end to a young man who was making life extremely uncomfortable and both looked to him to ensure it was done, he was fast coming to the conclusion that his task was going to be even more fraught with difficulties than he had initially thought. After deliberating this problem for some considerable time, he had deemed the best way to approach it was to take his lead from Colonel Henderson, with a little dexterous manoeuvring on his part, but from the look on his senior officer's face, it was perfectly clear that apart from viewing his timely arrival as most fortuitous, he also fully expected him to throw himself into this search with gusto, doing everything possible to apprehend a fugitive from justice.

For a man in Colonel Henderson's position Gideon could well understand his feelings of relief, but he also gained the very strong impression that the only thing which rendered his presence acceptable to him was that should anything untoward occur, he would be absolved of all blame. He was quite right. Colonel Henderson would very much like to deal with Richard Ferrers himself, but the whole affair surrounding this young man was far too close to home for comfort. He knew Lytton was right, but nevertheless it went very much against the grain with him to know that his hands were tied, and that he was totally reliant upon a man he did not know to deal with a situation he dare not take any further part in himself, beyond that which would be regarded as his duty. He had already gone as far as he had dared; for some little time now there had been cries of outrage from local dignitaries that he had exceeded his duty where Ferrers' sister was concerned, but he still believed she knew far more than she was divulging.

Her brother's alleged defection may have shocked the local community, but the family was still held in high regard, and since no wind of blame had ever been aimed at Elizabeth Ferrers or her father, the searches he had instituted had been hailed as a disgrace to a young woman who was entirely blameless.

Since local opinion was stacked against him, and his own efforts to secure Richard Ferrers' capture were proving ineffectual, coupled with his rather tenuous position, he had taken the one and only course open to him. A course which by no means pleased the recipient of his confidences and appeals for help.

It had been with great reluctance that he had called upon the services of a man, who, despite their long friendship, was not one to take kindly to threats, no matter how subtle. Were it not for the fact that he was treading on very delicate ground, not to mention the bad feeling his treatment of Elizabeth Ferrers was having on the local community, he would certainly not have done so.

He knew he could depend upon Lytton not to fail him, if only to protect himself, and whilst he had been assured that General Tuville would do precisely as he was told, he wondered if this young man standing to attention in front of him, had any idea of the enormity of what was involved. He doubted it. Robert was no fool. He would know to a nicety how best to go to work on such a delicate affair without the need for any in depth explanations.

He had, of course, heard of Sir John, but to date their paths had never crossed, but from all he had ever heard of him, he was punctilious in his military duties with no breath of scandal or underhand dealings attaching to his name. He could only guess at the tale Robert had told him to induce him to send this Major Neville into Sussex to undertake a job of such magnitude, but whatever it was it had certainly succeeded.

He would have been astonished however, had he known that General Turville, far from accepting Robert's explanation without question, had read between the lines of what he had been told, and even more so that Major Neville was in complete agreement with his commanding officer.

After following Colonel Henderson up the tower's inside and well-worn circular steps to a room immediately above Major Denham's, Gideon handed him his sealed orders from General Turville, and stood to attention while he broke the seal and scanned the dozen or so lines.

Unaware of Gideon's actual orders to withhold any information from him regarding his quarry, he silently hailed his arrival with relief, but could not help regretting the necessity that he had had to relinquish the reins of power in this matter. It was all very well for Robert to admonish him for his previous heavy handling of this affair, but had his quarry's sister not proved so stubborn and recalcitrant he could well be facing a very different situation by now. Nor had he taken kindly to Robert's smooth tongued reproof in that had he not behaved so foolishly to begin with there would never have been the least necessity for any of this in the first place. He had been a fool, of course, he realized that now, but he knew that until Richard Ferrers was laid by the heels he could not afford to be complacent, and looked to Gideon to extricate him from a very embarrassing predicament.

He was a tall man, whose high colour and portly figure were more the results of rich living than what nature had intended. He had a high forehead with a pair of bulbous pale blue eyes which seemed to protrude out of an already prominent forehead. His fish-like face, emphasized all the more by his high-bridged nose and rather loose mouth, held neither firmness nor strength of character. Indeed, Gideon formed the impression that under certain circumstances he could be quite easily influenced and, even, on occasion, bow to a far stronger will than his own.

"Well, Major," he nodded, inviting him to sit down. "I am very pleased to welcome you into Sussex. I was however, informed of your pending arrival," indicating Lytton's letter lying on his desk with a wave of his hand, still smarting from the caustic words he had seen fit to write, and which had been delivered post-haste by the furious Jem, "and it is most opportune," he nodded, "*most* opportune. By the by Major," he offered, "I must congratulate you on your promptness. I had not looked for you for several days." Gideon replied suitably to this and Colonel Henderson went on, "I daresay you don't need me to tell you how important it is to find this Richard Ferrers?"

"No, Sir," Gideon replied.

"He must be caught," Henderson said firmly. "He is a danger and a menace to decent society. He has run riot of late off this stretch of coast which," he nodded vigorously, "is a hanging matter in itself, but it is for his Jacobite involvement he is being sought."

"So I apprehend, Sir," Gideon nodded, not shrinking from the penetrating stare fixed on him. "But, if that is the case, Sir," he felt impelled to ask, "then why 'gazette' him?"

Colonel Henderson's eyes narrowed slightly. "Because, Major," he replied irritably, "we have to use every means at our disposal to catch him, and if 'gazetting' him ensures his capture, then it is more than justified, and I for one have no qualms about doing so."

"I see, Sir" Gideon nodded.

"I don't think you do," Henderson shook his head. "I am sure these smuggling rogues he's tied himself up with won't turn squeamish at the prospect of earning five hundred pounds. Quite the reverse! But you will not need me to tell you that his present activities are equally as malevolent as his Jacobite sympathies," he said forcefully, his face taking on a dull red tinge, making him look more like a landed salmon than ever. "It appears that one venture into illicit dealings is not enough for him," he said severely, "he now feels it necessary to crown his iniquities by turning his hand to smuggling."

"So I believe, Sir," Gideon acknowledged, a little taken aback at his vehemence.

"I am very much afraid, Major Neville," he informed him forcefully, "that you will find Ferrers to be quite a desperate character, and one, moreover, who appears to have neither respect nor consideration for the name he bears or his King. In fact," he nodded, "he has proved himself to be nothing more than a vicious cutthroat!"

"Is that so, indeed, Sir?" Gideon raised an eyebrow, trying to ignore his growing dislike for this man, who seemed determined to paint the worst possible picture.

"Yes, Major, that is so!" he exclaimed, adding belligerently, "and if he thinks his rank can ensure him leniency, then let me tell you he is fair and far off!"

"I see, Sir" Gideon nodded.

Gideon's apparent lack of eagerness for the task ahead of him and his unenthusiastic replies were not at all what Colonel Henderson had hoped for, indeed, he had expected a far more energetic response from a man who wore His Majesty's uniform, and allowed his irritation to show.

Gideon saw the face harden and the lips compress, and remained undaunted by both. Colonel Henderson, desperate for a speedy solution to the difficulties which beset him, not to mention the scandal that would ensue if the truth ever leaked out, decided that Major Neville, for all his punctilio when dealing with a senior officer, appeared to lack the necessary qualities required for the task ahead of him, and wondered how on earth he had ever managed to attain the rank of major without what he called enough 'get up and go'. He would have thought that for a loyal Englishman and a soldier to boot, he would have welcomed the opportunity to rid the world of a traitor, and in view of this would certainly have expected him to exhibit more signs of enthusiasm than he was. His temper was even more exacerbated by the knowledge that no matter how desperate he was to have this matter resolved, if he wished to avoid awkward questions being asked he really had no choice but to accept Major Neville, in spite of his lack of keenness for the matter in hand. Resolutely biting down his annoyance therefore, he decided to push him along a little in the hope that it would fire him with an enthusiasm he did not seem to possess, by venturing to suggest that he begin his enquiries by talking to Elizabeth Ferrers. "Not that I look for any help from *that* quarter," he bit out. "If you were to ask me she is not only in league with her brother, but can lie faster than a dog can trot!"

As Gideon had already drawn his own conclusions as to the type of man Colonel Henderson was, he considered that he did not deserve to have this statement either endorsed or acknowledged. It was becoming increasingly clear to him that Colonel Henderson was not open to discussion on this matter, but since he obviously expected some input from him, he merely asked, "What makes you believe Sir, that she knows the current whereabouts of her brother?"

"It stands to reason she does!" he exclaimed, unable to believe his ears. "Apart from the fact that the two of them have been as thick as thieves since they were children, it goes beyond all reasoning that Ferrers is here in Sussex, only a mile or so from his home, and she knows nothing of it!"

"You do not think, Sir," Gideon suggested, "it could be possible that Ferrers has not informed his sister because he wishes to protect her?"

Colonel Henderson stared incredulously at him as though he could not believe what he had heard, and wondered, not for the first time since making Major Neville's acquaintance, whether he had the stomach for this kind of work. "Major

56

Neville," he sighed, trying to keep his temper, "if you knew them as I do, you would know them both for being the scheming and traitorous rogues they are. Indeed," he shook his head, "it is difficult to know which of them is worse; Ferrers for turning his back on his King and country or his sister for her complicity. As for that aunt of hers," he snorted, "she's no better! She actually had the temerity to tell me that if I had not found her nephew in hiding at Ferrers Court all this time, then I must have windmills in my head to continue looking for him there!"

Gideon's lips twitched, but the feeling this malicious statement engendered in him was enough to tell him that General Turville's instincts were not misplaced. Richard Ferrers could certainly not look for a fair hearing at this man's hands, and that being so he was determined to do all he could to ensure his just treatment irrespective of what he discovered.

Exasperated by Gideon's apparent lack of understanding regarding the seriousness of this matter, Colonel Henderson decided that he needed steering in the right direction as well as being made fully aware of what was expected of him. "Do not allow yourself to be persuaded by sentiment, Major," he said firmly. "I am sure that once you have heard all the facts of the case you will soon be brought to see that Elizabeth Ferrers is as tough as old boots and cannot be trusted!"

At the end of Colonel Henderson's biased account of the affair, Gideon was no nearer liking him than he was before. He still believed that Richard Ferrers would not be stupid enough to run the unnecessary risk of showing himself at his own home without a very good reason for doing so, he of all people would know the risks he would run. From this standpoint therefore he could not quite understand what had brought him into Sussex as so many factors were against it, let alone stepping foot anywhere near Ferrers Court. For one thing, he could not fail to be aware that there must be people here who would be only too willing to inform against him, besides which, every red-coat for miles around were on the watch for him. He found it hard to believe that a man listed as not only a smuggler but a traitor to his King and country, bringing shame and disgrace to an honourable name, would frequent the locality where his family still resided. From what he had been able to ascertain the late Lord Easton had been not only a proud man but an extremely loyal one, and one, moreover, with an impeccable lineage and credentials. It seemed inconceivable therefore that his son, if, indeed, guilty of the charges laid at his door, would go so far as to cause his family further embarrassment by returning to within a couple of miles of his home.

As far as he could see it seemed the only feasible answer to the question as to why Richard Ferrers was back in Sussex, was that he had been recruited after all; most probably with his father's blessing, which would explain why he had returned to the neighbourhood. He could not see Lord Easton denying sanctuary to a son whom he knew to be innocent. If this was in fact the case, then he could only hazard a guess as to whether his sister knew of it or not. Assuming that

Richard Ferrers had learned of his father's death, and he failed to see how it could be otherwise being this close to his estates, then it raised the question as to why he was still in the vicinity instead of making good his escape. If his return home had indeed been to consult with his father only for him to discover that he was dead, then it rendered his position extremely difficult to say the least. Not only would his father's death have deprived him of corroborative evidence necessary to support his innocence but also of a father who was clearly very dear to him. The only logical explanation that he could see to account for Ferrers' continued presence here was that there must be someone or, which seemed more likely, something, which could help clear his name. The fact that he was still in Sussex could only mean that he had so far been unable to gain this vital testimony. In view of this it wasn't difficult to see what his motives were for running illicit cargoes off a stretch of coast so close to home; not only would it afford him much needed protection from his pursuers but it would grant him time to obtain the evidence he so desperately needed. Assuming Elizabeth Ferrers was in ignorance of what he believed to be the truth, and assuming again that Lytton was right in that her father's fatal heart attack had resulted from his son's defection, devoted sister or not, then he could not see his daughter assisting the very person who had brought it about, albeit her own brother. If she did in fact know the truth then she could easily have learned of his return to Sussex and offered him shelter.

Even supposing this to be true then Richard Ferrers, whilst he could count on support from his sister, had regrettably placed them both in a most vulnerable and precarious position. If this was in fact the case, then by trying to protect her brother, Elizabeth Ferrers was playing a most dangerous game; to deliberately throw dust in Colonel Henderson's eyes, even going so far as to make a fool of him, was one thing, but to make a fool of His Grace the Duke of Lytton, was quite another!

He realized of course that all of this was mere conjecture on his part, but try as he did he could think of nothing else which satisfactorily explained why Richard Ferrers was back in Sussex. If his conclusions were found to be wrong after all, then the reason for his continued presence here must therefore stem from other motives as yet unknown.

Colonel Henderson however, appeared to have no doubts whatsoever that Richard Ferrers was receiving aid from his sister. Gideon may not like him, viewing his openly hostile attitude towards Ferrers and his sister as being maliciously biased for reasons he could only guess at, but it only took a matter of moments to see that by voicing his own views, which certainly did not correspond with Colonel Henderson's, would not help him in the least. It was his belief that such a prejudiced and bigoted man did not deserve respect, but the rank he held certainly did, and whatever his personal feelings towards him, he was after all a senior officer. Concluding that it was perhaps wiser to allow him to believe that he was prepared to work closely with him and follow his recommendations, Gideon accepted his explanation of the situation by saying mendaciously that he had not been fully aware of the true facts.

Colonel Henderson, immensely relieved by this reply, sat back in his chair and proceeded to give Gideon the benefit of his advice on how best to deal with the matter. "I realize, of course" he conceded, still far from convinced that Gideon was the right man for the job, "that you will deal with this matter as you see fit, but I would strongly recommend you to take what Elizabeth Ferrers tells you with a pinch of salt. In fact," he urged, "I wouldn't believe a word she tells you!"

"In view of what you have told me, Sir," Gideon said with deceptive meekness, "I shall bear that in mind," wondering what this woman had actually done to set him so resolutely against her.

Accepting this response with a slight feeling of relief, Colonel Henderson further advised that if he were in his shoes he would take along half a dozen or so men with him just to let her see that measures were not going to be relaxed simply because previous searches had not found her brother in hiding at Ferrers Court.

As these tactics had already been tried to no effect, Gideon saw no possible good ensuing by adopting them again, considering that another like venture would kill at a stroke any chance he had of gaining her trust or enlisting her aid, not that accomplishing either of these necessary aims were in any way guaranteed. However, he thanked him for his advice, sweetening his refusal by saying that should his own tactics fail then he would certainly consider his suggestion but, in the first instance, would much rather see what results could be gained by speaking to her alone.

"Very well, Major" he nodded, surprised but not unimpressed by this reasoning. "We shall await the outcome."

Long after his interview with Colonel Henderson was over, Gideon pondered the situation facing him, fast coming to the conclusion that it was going to prove a far more difficult task than he had envisaged. If nothing else, it certainly convinced him that General Turville was right in that someone definitely wanted Richard Ferrers caught very badly, and not simply because of his supposed political persuasions or his present cargo trafficking, but for some other reason as yet unspecified.

He could not quite rid his mind of the fact that Colonel Henderson had a far more personal motive in ensuring Richard Ferrers' capture than he had revealed but, until he found this enterprising young man, who seemed to be the sole cause of so much trouble for someone, everything else was merely speculation and surmise.

To his surprise his quarters proved to be far more comfortable than he had hoped for, consisting of a bedroom and cosy sitting room situated on the top floor of the three storeyed south-east gatehouse. His temporary batman, a cheerful

59

Yorkshireman of long service and indeterminate age, informed him that he could either take his meals in the old banqueting hall with most of the other officers or, like one or two of them, enjoy a very tolerable ordinary at The White Hart further down the street. As it was by now starting to get dusk he could see little point in taking a tour of either his immediate surroundings or the town, besides which, he could quite easily run into Lieutenant Beaton and as he had far too much to think about at the moment, he eschewed both these schemes for his sustenance, taking up Sergeant Taylor's other suggestion that, if he would like, he could bring him a little something to his room. It was not that he disliked his newly found friend, on the contrary, he liked Lieutenant Beaton very well, indeed, he was a most pleasant young man, but he had the very strong feeling that should he run into him then he would have to forgo his plans for this evening.

Having spent some considerable time in studying the map Sergeant Taylor had provided him with, he then set his mind on how best to approach Elizabeth Ferrers. This was, perhaps, the most daunting part of the task facing him especially if, as he had been led to believe, she had been subjected to numerous invasions of her home resulting in the death of her father, then the chances were that her response to his visit could well be hostile. Not that he could blame her for that, but it would make it rather difficult for him to gain her trust, which is what he was going to have to do in order to assist her brother. Whilst he easily discounted Colonel Henderson's biased description of her he was nevertheless shrewd enough to know that even if her reception of him was not hostile, he could nevertheless expect a pretty cold welcome, providing, of course, she decided to receive him at all.

As far as her brother was concerned, he was certainly knee deep in trouble. Colonel Henderson had made his feelings regarding this young man very clear, and nothing would afford him greater satisfaction than to see Richard Ferrers in safe custody. In fact, he would go so far as to say that nothing short of seeing him strung up would do for him. He had seen and heard enough over the last couple of days to realize that the accusation of illicit trafficking could well be nothing more than a fabrication to add weight to the urgent necessity to apprehend him. If Richard Ferrers was indeed participating in this rather hazardous occupation, then he for one had no difficulty in understanding his reasons for doing so. All the same, prolonged association with a group of individuals who could look for little or no sympathy, was only going to exacerbate his problems.

Unfortunately, the excellent dinner put in front of him by Sergeant Taylor, a man he was fast coming to believe could supply one with anything no matter how remote their location, and the warming stimulus of the brandy, which he was convinced had never paid duty, began to take effect. His last conscious recollection before falling into a deep and untroubled sleep was that of a young man who, whether he realized it or not, could not extricate himself from his difficulties without help, and that if he was ever to prove his innocence it was going to be anything but a straightforward matter.

It was at the precise moment Gideon slid into oblivion that the object of his thoughts was busily engaged across the Channel.

CHAPTER FOUR

The Honourable Richard Ferrers, unaware that he had acquired a benefactor, had, for the past hour and more, been kicking his heels at Dieppe with what patience he could muster awaiting the arrival of his French associates for far longer than he had anticipated. For the last half hour or so he had been growing uneasily aware that unless they made haste and showed themselves within the next few minutes in order to allow plenty of time for the goods to be stowed on board, they would miss the tide. To his annoyance, this now made the third time in as many weeks that his Gallic counterparts had arrived late and, unless he grossly mistook the case, he would lay his life that the reason was the same as on the previous two occasions. Pierre's amatory adventures were no concern of his, but when they interfered with the matter in hand then they were very much his concern. It seemed that he was incapable of resisting a pretty face, but why the devil he found it necessary to succumb to temptation when they had a job planned, was beyond him. Attitudes to illicit trading may be more relaxed this side of the Channel but in England such activities were looked upon very differently, and unless he wanted to sail into home waters just as the sun was coming up thereby risking detection, the sooner the cargo was stowed on board so they could weigh anchor, the better. Periodically consulting his watch only served to increase his frustration, resulting in him being assailed with visions of remaining this side of the Channel until tomorrow night. As waiting for the next available tide was not an option, indeed, it would not suit him at all to put to sea in broad daylight let alone attempting to disembark or even lie at anchor until nightfall, should he fail to show himself at Ferrers Court as arranged, he felt reasonably certain that Salmon would work himself up into frenzy of anxiety. He may have entered into this business through the direst necessity but, having done so, as well as accepting the mantle of leader which they had so readily hung upon him, he felt himself honour bound to not only discharge the duty entrusted to him, but to ensure the smooth running of each and every enterprise as well as the safety and welfare of the men. For a man who thought and acted decisively as well as keeping to a schedule, this hanging around, apart from courting disaster and unsettling for the men, was anathema, but it was something he was certainly not prepared to put up with, and so he would have Pierre know, when he decided to show himself!

So far, Captain Waring, the diligent young Riding Officer he had been managing to keep at bay all these months, was by far too intelligent to be hoodwinked for long. Even without a cargo he could not afford to be apprehended especially with his future hanging precariously in the balance, to do so would mean he could say goodbye to any attempts at proving his innocence; Colonel Henderson would see to that. He would not be caught napping a second time! But it was not merely his own safety and future welfare he was thinking of, but that of the men. They may be breaking the law by taking part in illicit trading, but for all that they were decent and honest men who were trying to earn a little extra in order to support their wives and children and for them to be imprisoned would not only be extremely unfair, but would leave their families virtually destitute. For their sake as much as his own, he could not afford to run any unnecessary risks, far better to return to England empty handed than court disaster; after all, they could not be arrested for smuggling if no cargo was found on board, no matter how strong Captain Waring's suspicions! He, of course was another matter! Irrespective of whether any cargo was found or not, he was a man with a price on his head, and Captain Waring would need no suspicions of illicit trading to apprehend him; being hailed a traitor would be all he required to arrest him.

Another quick glance at his watch told him that time was running out, so with characteristic decisiveness elected to get the men on board and make haste for home. It was a pity it had turned out to be a wasted trip, but rather that than delaying matters and risk getting called to 'heave to' by a Revenue cutter with a hoard on board in broad daylight. It was just as he was on the point of calling the men together that the sound of carriers wheels on the cobbles and the impatient snorting of a horse approaching met his ears. Despite the mist which had descended he had no difficulty in making out the carts in the near distance and without waiting for them to pull up alongside him strode purposefully towards them, his frustration finding its natural outlet in immediately demanding to know what the devil had kept them, only to find this ignored by Pierre's cheerful cry of *"Salut mon ami! Comment allez-vous?"*

Goaded beyond endurance, he cried exasperatedly, "Never mind how I am! Damn you Pierre!" he exclaimed, infuriated. "Where the devil have you been?" This may not have been the grammatical French his very expensive tutor had taught him to speak, but it was the kind of language Pierre not only understood but very much appreciated.

A huge grin descended on the face beaming down at him. "Ah, my friend," he shook his head sadly. "I am afraid you do not understand love."

"I might have known there'd be a wench in it!" Richard scorned.

Pierre, a handsome young giant whose open necked shirt and rolled up sleeves exposed a powerful chest and massive biceps, merely laughed good humouredly at this before clambering across the tops of the kegs to vault over the side of the cart. Landing easily in front of Richard he stood towering above him, his massive frame shaking with laughter as he brought a ham-like hand to rest on his shoulder, the force almost knocking him over.

"It's all very well for you to laugh," Richard told him candidly, having to look a long way up into that deceptively cherubic face, "but thanks to you and your bit o' muslin, it's made us devlish late. We'll only just catch the tide as it is!"

"But Richard," Pierre pointed out amusedly, giving his shoulder a shake "the sea is always there! Would you have had me turn by my back on the cosiest armful I've come across in weeks?"

"Yes," Richard replied frankly, "I would. If she's that taken with you," he told him tartly, "she'll wait. Unfortunately, the tide won't!" Pierre let out a hearty guffaw at this, shaking his head wonderingly. "Damn it, man!" Richard pointed out practically. "There'll be time enough for that later. If you can't keep your mind off women long enough to honour your obligations," he warned resolutely, "then you and I will part company! Damn it, Pierre!" he exclaimed, "I can't keep the men hanging about here waiting for you; it's far too dangerous!"

"Ah, the English!" Pierre said sorrowfully. "Always so self-possessed." Richard threw him a scornful look. "You know what your trouble is, my friend?" he asked, giving his shoulder another shake. "You have no sense of romance! It is very sad, I think."

"Not when it interferes with work I haven't," Richard replied forthrightly. "But I'll tell you what *is* sad," he remarked reasonably, eyeing his friend darkly, "being caught by those damned Tidesmen because a certain party can't resist ogling the first pretty wench he sees, which is what will happen if you stand here any longer talking rubbish!"

A deep throated laugh left Pierre's lips. "Very well, my friend," he nodded, "it shall be as you say, but" he warned amusedly, kissing his forefinger and thumb, "when you meet one such as Nicole, you will understand."

"I daresay!" Richard dismissed. "Now though, if you can leave off thinking about your innamorato long enough, it's time we started to help unload these damned carts!"

The only response Richard received to this was a deep throated chuckle, and after a dire warning as to what would befall him if he did not take care, both men then applied themselves to unloading the carts along with their associates. Having had a very shrewd idea as to the reason for Pierre not arriving on time, he had silently cursed his friend for being late. Had it not been for the fact that tonight's consignment was far bigger than usual and would therefore take longer to unload the kegs and packages off the carts and then carry them on board, Richard would not have been so impatient of the delay, but as the minutes ticked by without any sign of him his impatience had steadily increased. But all of this was soon forgotten as he saw Pierre's powerful arms making light and easy work of the task in hand; his huge barrel of a chest effortlessly taking the weight of the casks as they were handed down to him before passing them on to the next man in the chain. For close on a full hour no one spoke or enjoyed a moment's respite until all the commodities had been unloaded and taken on board, beads of perspiration glistening on their foreheads from their exertions, eagerly swallowing the tankards of ale handed them in order to quench their thirst when the job was done. After draining his own tankard Richard then dug a hand into the capacious pocket of his long black overcoat, pulling out a purse full of coins which he handed to Pierre who stuffed it into the pocket of his leather waistcoat without even checking it. With time left only to inform Pierre that word would be got to him about the next run, Richard then waved a hand before striding briskly up the gangplank of 'The Queen of the Sea', shouting to Kit to let go. This apparatus was pulled up and the sails unfurled catching the south westerly wind that would take them across the grey unsettled waters to England. For the first few minutes all was bustle and activity but once the port of Dieppe had been left behind the usual routine of handling the four masted lugger got under way.

Having sailed these waters for more than thirty years, Jim Caites knew the tides and currents by heart, needing neither the moon nor stars to bring his ship and crew safely home. He gave no more thought to the rights and wrongs of his part-time profession any more than the Government did to raising taxation to pay for this war or that. He had a wife and four children to feed and as far as he was concerned that settled the matter. He considered himself as honest and law-abiding as the next man, but he could earn more in one night's run than in a month or more from his legal trade, and all he knew was that it did more good in his pocket than the Government's. He had no need to be told what would happen to him should he ever be caught, but since the benefits far out-weighed the risks, he considered it well worth it.

Having ensured that all the goods were safely stowed, Richard joined his confederate at the helm, a man whom he had known and respected for as long as he could remember. He may not have been bred to this kind of life, but he had taken to it easily enough; if nothing else if gave him something to do. He had a gift for organization and order and during the time he had been participating in his new career the profits had increased considerably. But it was not only his ability to enlarge the financial benefits of their enterprise that made the men hold him in such high esteem, or the fact that he was a gentleman, but because he was loyal and steadfast and totally dependable. If he were not, then all his charm and charisma would have meant nothing. He was very much his father's son; looking after his people and ensuring they were well provided for, and the consensus of opinion was that it was about time the good Lord bestowed some good fortune on him and reinstated him to his title and dignities.

But it was not only his title and dignities he wanted restored, but the right to resume paying his addresses to the woman whom he had been forbidden to see. Pierre had said he did not understand love. He was quite wrong; he understood it only too well, and the pain this knowledge brought was almost too much for him to bear. No one looking at him would ever have guessed he was very much in love, had been in fact for far longer than even he had realized, and although the lady returned his feelings, her father had strictly forbidden them to see one another.

Jane Trench, whom he had known since childhood, was the only daughter of Sir Arthur and Lady Trench whose red bricked manor house, set in the middle of an isolated piece of Ferrers land to the north of the estate, had long since been gifted over to the family for services rendered to the second Viscount Easton. He and her two brothers had run tame in each others houses but, being five years older than his sister and her best friend, he had found their company an intrusion, but although he had finally relented where Elizabeth was concerned and allowed her to tag along, he had adamantly excluded Jane from their adventures. At eight years of age, to her mother's profound regret, Jane had been a mischievous tomboy prepared to undergo any ordeal or suffer any cut and tumble if only Richard would yield to her pleadings to let her join in. A resolute no had been the only answer she had received but, whilst she had assumed the appearance of accepting his decree, it had been to his frustration to find, a short time later, that she had followed them regardless; her dress torn and stained from brushing through the brambles and undergrowth in order to keep up with them.   Her mother had, of course, put a summary end to these activities, stating that whilst it was not for her to dictate the conduct of Lady Ferrers by allowing Elizabeth to get up to all manner of waywardness, for herself she was not going to permit her daughter to trample around the neighbourhood looking like an urchin, and if this was the kind of thing that happened whenever she went out with Richard and his sister, then it was best if she kept her distance from them. She was perfectly aware of the infatuation her daughter had for Richard, but it would not do to either ignore or indulge it, after all, the child was only eight years old and no doubt she would outgrow it in time, providing, of course, she did not associate with them any more than was absolutely necessary.   Upon witnessing her daughter's downcast face upon hearing this, her heart softened sufficiently to enable her to point out gently that whilst she had nothing against either of them, indeed, they were quite delightful children, she did think that these boisterous games they continually indulged in were hardly guaranteed to provide a good grounding for a young girl desirous of entering society. Tears and sniffles had been the response to this dictum as she had dragged one reluctant step after another to her room where, her mother had told her, she would remain until such time that she could behave herself in a manner which would not bring condemnation down on their heads. This deluge of misery may not have lasted for long but, even so, when she eventually closed her eyes and gave herself up to exhausted sleep, it was like her little heart was broken. From then on she only saw him intermittently, and then in the company of her mother, who heaved a sigh of relief when Richard eventually left The Court to go to Eton.   The next few years had been the longest she had ever known, not even being allowed to visit her friend when her brother happened to be at home on vacation, having to glean what information she could from Elizabeth. She did not set eyes on Richard again until her twelfth birthday when he accompanied his sister to give her a present of some sugared sweetmeats, the sight of him so unexpected that she felt quite overpowered by his presence, her burgeoning but immature emotions rendering her almost tongue-tied. Richard, to her mamma's relief, made no mention of how she used to follow him around, indeed, his impeccable manners were all that she could have wished for but, even so, she recognized the glow in her daughter's soft pansy brown eyes, telling her more than any words could have that she had far from forgotten her traipsing around in his wake. It was therefore with immense relief when Lady Trench heard from Richard's own lips that he was commencing a tour of Europe in company with a professor friend of his father's within days of this visit, and would be entering Oxford immediately upon his return to England. Stifling a sob at this news Jane stole a glance at him from under her lashes, only to drop them quickly when he unexpectedly chose this moment to look at her, his warm and comforting smile the only ray of sunshine on her otherwise dull horizon.

She may have been too young to understand her feelings much less the meaning of love and all it signified, but she did know that she was only happy when he was around, indeed, she was utterly desolate without him. It was then that her tiny heart gave a sickening thud when, without warning, she remembered that at no point during their friendship had he ever even said that he liked her; this painful reminder bringing forth another stifled sob. Her eyes dropped instinctively, afraid to let anyone see that the very thought of not seeing him again for another three or four years was too much for one of her tender age to bear, especially when it was more than possible that when they did meet again, he could well have met someone else. A gently worded nudge from her mother telling her that Elizabeth and her brother were about to take their leave suddenly broke into her tangled thoughts, but try as she did she could find no words to say to the tall seventeen year old young man looking thoughtfully down at her. She saw the frown descend on her mother's forehead at what she considered to be a fit of sullenness, but although she was able to say a few words to her friend, it had been quite impossible for her to do more than smile at Richard; her sadness over knowing she was not to see him again for a very long time too much for her to endure. A sharp rebuke for her appalling manners tripped off her mother's tongue when their guests had left, leaving her sad and miserable and with an overwhelming desire to cry her heart out. In the days and months ahead, her only solace was when her mother permitted her to visit her friend or, failing this, whenever Elizabeth either walked or rode over to The Manor to spend a little time with her; eagerly drinking in the news she innocently provided as to her brother's whereabouts and activities. Her illicit forays onto Ferrers land to see if she could catch sight of Richard out riding on the occasions when she knew he would be at home, was the only pleasure to brighten her existence; disappointment enveloping her when she did not see him. But as the months turned into years with no sign of him she had finally begun to accept the painful realization that Richard could not really like her after all; if he did, then surely he would have visited her parents just once during his vacations in order for him to see her. It was just as she had reluctantly come to accept this heartbreaking fact that he took her quite by surprise one afternoon, descending on the household in company with his sister, having arrived home for a short break from Oxford prior to taking his final examinations. Having spent the entire morning tramping out and about searching for one of the stable kittens which had, unfortunately, decided to investigate its surroundings, she eventually returned to the house triumphantly flushed from her successful search. Much to her mother's dismay, nothing it seemed would serve to curb her daughter's hoydenish ways, but the sight of her entering the house with her warm chestnut hair disarrayed, her old cotton dress stained and torn and her boots liberally splashed with mud, made her close her eyes on an anguished sigh of despair. No longer a tomboy of eight years of age with a front tooth missing or a tongue-tied twelve year old girl but an aspiring beauty of almost seventeen, despite some vestiges of awkwardness still in her manner as well as her dishevelled appearance, Richard looked at her as though he were seeing her for the first time. Overcome with mortification at coming face to face with Richard after all this long time looking the way she did, rendered her incapable of saying anything coherent, her disjointed words of welcome and apologies for her appearance causing the colour to flood her cheeks. Uncomfortably aware of her mother's disapproving eye on her, she tried her best to steady her nerves and respond to Richard's promptings about how he had done precisely the same thing, guaranteed to set her at her ease but, whilst she managed to reply with some semblance of calm, at no point could she bring herself to meet his eye. Torn between wishing he would go away so he would not see her looking like and this but dreading his departure at the same time, only served to exacerbate her inner turmoil, but once having finally said a reluctant but barely audible goodbye, she ran up the stairs to her room, from which vantage point she could see Richard and his sister ride away. Not until they had disappeared from sight did she leave the window to sink down onto her bed, the tears rolling down her cheeks as she thought that this would most probably be the last time she would ever see him.

Exasperated beyond measure with her daughter's peculiar behaviour whenever Richard came to call, it was not until this last visit that Lady Trench began to wonder whether her childish infatuation for her best friend's brother had, indeed, grown into something more enduring. She had no qualms or reservations about a connection with the Ferrers family, after all, they were as wealthy as their lineage was long and distinguished and no mamma worth her salt could possibly overlook these necessary attributes. Even so, she would much prefer her daughter to see a little of the world and other men before setting her heart on one in particular before she had had the opportunity to look about her a little. She did not think that Richard held any deep affection for her other than a natural fondness for his sister's dearest friend, because although he had looked rather closely at her, she herself had not detected anything to raise false hopes. Should it transpire that Richard did, indeed, feel something deeper then she for one would have no objection to put forward about such a match taking place and, in all probability, Sir Arthur would not either. However, her own feeling was that it would be foolhardy to settle her daughter's future on the one and only personable young man ever to come in her way, and sought in her mind how best to approach her husband in order to gain his permission to send Jane to London sooner than originally planned to spend sometime with his sister, a middle-aged widow who, having successfully married off all her four daughters, fortunately enjoyed a good understanding with her niece, insisting she come and stay with her when she was a little older. Should nothing arise from this visit after all in the way of suitable candidates for her hand, then she would at least acquire a little town polish, something she herself seemed unable to achieve despite her strenuous efforts to do so; these accomplishments would, if nothing else, render her suitable to become the future Viscountess Ferrers, assuming, of course, that Richard did in fact feel something for Jane after all. Refusing to allow her mind to dwell on the possibility that there was every likelihood that Richard Ferrers had no deeper feelings for Jane other than liking, she went in search of her husband.

And so, within less than a month of seeing Richard, Jane found herself seated beside her mother in their comfortable coach on the way to London for an indeterminate stay. It was not that she minded leaving her home which distressed her, but the fact that she could well miss the opportunity of seeing Richard whenever he returned to Ferrers Court. Her mother, who had a pretty shrewd idea what was in her mind, was determined to channel her thoughts into other directions by pointing out all the advantages of living in London. She described in exhaustive detail the treats in store for her, including attending all the ton parties, alfresco breakfasts and a hundred other things that was customary for young ladies of her social standing but only providing, that was, she behaved herself and did everything her aunt told her. Had her mother known that she looked forward to meeting Elizabeth when she later arrived in town to stay with her Aunt Clara far more than she was in going to any ton party, she would have felt totally justified in boxing her ears but, as she was in happy ignorance of this, she continued with her theme until the coach pulled up outside her sister-in-law's house.

Had Jane the slightest idea that Aunt Matty had been taken fully into her mamma's confidence, she would have been acutely embarrassed, but not by a word or gesture did she communicate to her niece that she knew about her feelings for a young man whose sister was her dearest friend. She had only ever met Aunt Matty when she had come to stay with her parent's, but she had taken to her immediately; her tall and imposing figure hiding the generous nature and warm heart which made her an easy confidante, enabling her to look forward to the London scheme with more pleasure than she otherwise would have. At first it had been a strange and frightening experience to find herself in such a huge and alien place like London, but as she possessed a lively disposition natural for one of her age as well as an intelligent mind, she soon became accustomed to her new life.

Having for a long time wanted to take her sister-in-law to task about her lack of understanding and sympathy as to how to treat a young girl like Jane, Aunt Matty had kept her tongue with difficulty, realizing that she would not only resent such an invasion into what she considered to be her sole responsibility but could well refuse to send her daughter to her for the season. But in one respect she was determined to have her way and, therefore, by dint of half veiled suggestions and intimations she had persuaded her sister-in-law to wisely leave her to superintend her niece's wardrobe, and since she herself was always most fashionably and impeccably dressed, Lady Trench had been quite happy to agree with this arrangement. Jane, who really was a most engaging child, never shone to advantage in her mother's company, indeed, her many endearing qualities, although not immediately discernible, were very evident to those who took the time to look for them. She was, therefore, determined to allow her niece to grow and develop in her own particular soil and to encourage these hidden depths to appear in order to expose her true personality and, thanks to her gentle tutelage, born out years of experience in dealing with her own daughters, she gradually reaped the rewards of her sowing. Her clothes, chosen with the same meticulous care and thought as had gone into fashioning her hair into a style which was far more becoming and modish than she was accustomed to, accompanied with encouragement and affectionate coaxing from her aunt, all saw her eventual emergence from the chrysalis which had concealed so much, allowing her to participate in the many pleasures and entertainments on offer with a confidence she had not known before. She would have been less than human if she had not enjoyed her first London season, which, after only a few weeks, was proving to be a great success and, if her enjoyment was marred by not being at home in the expectation of seeing Richard, she took consolation from knowing that when they did meet again, he would hopefully begin to look upon her in a very different light. If her aunt saw nothing to wonder at in her obvious enjoyment of all the receptions, routs and balls she attended she would nevertheless have been surprised to learn that at the back of her mind there was always the vision of someone she had long come to realize she could not live without; a young man whom her aunt had come to believe as being no longer in her thoughts. It had been impossible for her to continually ply Elizabeth with questions whenever they met at a party or a ball or visited one another and useless too to expect her mamma to write to her with news of Richard so, instead, hoped that good fortune would smile on her by finding a way of bringing them together.   To all intents and purposes her life in London with her aunt was happy, which, relatively speaking, was true, but whether she was sitting quietly setting a stitch at her embroidery or dancing with a most exceptional young man to whom she had been introduced, never very far away was the image of a tall, dark haired young man with humorous blue eyes and a mouth that could, without any warning, smile in that crooked way which made her heart jump.

For a young lady to receive two most eligible offers of marriage in her first season could not be deemed anything other than a great success, the fact that the lady had politely refused them did not detract from this. If her aunt wondered as to the reason why her niece had not accepted them, she wisely refrained from asking but, as she waved her goodbye the morning of her return home, upon seeing the sparkle in those huge brown eyes and the tinge of colour in her cheeks, she shrewdly drew her own conclusions.

Regrettably, her hope of seeing Richard was not to be realized, being informed by her mamma during the course of dinner her first evening home, in a rare attempt at diplomacy, that Richard was presently away from The Court and not due to return for some considerable time. She hid her disappointment extremely well, something she would have found impossible to do a year earlier when she was an awkward seventeen year old, but whilst she made no mention of him or alerted her parent's to the fact that her heart was heavy with misery at not seeing him, it nevertheless took every ounce of strength she possessed to stop herself from riding over to The Court on the off-chance he had come home unexpectedly.   It also took every ounce of strength she possessed to prevent herself from thinking what she would do if the very worst were to happen; her sleep rendered hideous at the thought of Richard introducing his prospective bride to her, taking no solace from the fact that Elizabeth had at no time even intimated at such a thing; even so, the very thought made her heart ache with an unbearable pain.   The only relief was an invitation to stay with friends for several weeks at their home in Hertfordshire and, whilst this may have put physical distance between her and Ferrers Court, it failed to have the same impact mentally or emotionally.

It was therefore with relief that she eventually returned to Aunt Matty for her second season, which, after only a couple of weeks, was proving just as successful as the first and, if that sharp eyed lady noticed a slight shadowing under her eyes or a little less enthusiasm in her manner, she had no difficulty in attributing these to her sister-in-law.   This belief underwent no change when, within a couple of months of her arrival in town, her father had unexpectedly announced that it was time his daughter made a more than ordinarily lengthy stay at The Manor, and this time there would be no visits from home into Hertfordshire or anywhere else.   Not as astute as his good lady, who, despite her lack of understanding in dealing with her daughter, had a sharp-witted head on her shoulders, he had failed to understand why his daughter had turned down two most obliging and eligible offers, stating belligerently, for the umpteenth time until Jane knew it by heart, that if she could not see that proposals of marriage would not continue to be offered her once it became known that she was habitually declining them for no reason he could see, then a spell at home would hopefully bring her to her senses. Besides which, he was not prepared to continually provide funds for her gadding about town for no reason, and therefore looked forward to welcoming her as soon as may be possible.   Upon being informed of this by her aunt, whose faded but shrewd blue eyes had detected a strange light in those huge pansy ones, became alerted to the fact that perhaps her niece had not forgotten a certain young man after all, which would explain her refusal to even consider a proposal of marriage as well as her calm acceptance of her father's decree. She had not, as she considered doing, accompanied Jane to her parent's home, but their parting was not without its tears. She told her niece that she looked forward to her return as soon as possible but as she watched her protégé climb eagerly into the carriage she could not help but wonder if she would ever have her to stay again. Jane had kissed her aunt's powdered and damp cheek, genuinely sorry to be leaving her, but the anticipation of what possibly awaited her at home, happily discounting her father's displeasure, rendered their parting less painful, deliberately pushing the thought that Richard may not love her to the back of her mind.

The memory of seeing her again after so long brought an involuntary gasp from deep within Richard's throat, causing Jim to glance sharply across at him, taking his eyes momentarily off the horizon, but since his young friend would not discuss his innermost thoughts even with him, he refrained from asking any questions.   Having successfully completed his time at Oxford, he had returned home to spend some time with his family. As entering a profession was neither a necessity nor a choice he had spent the next six months either staying with friends or visiting his father when his political obligations had rendered it necessary for him to remain in London. As he had long since lost touch with Jane's brothers, one entering the Home Office and the other the Navy, and she herself was in London staying with her aunt, there had been no need for him to visit The Manor, except on two occasions when prompted by his sister to do so for the sake of courtesy, he had been quite happy at Ferrers Court undertaking responsibilities on his father's behalf for the governance of the estate he would one day inherit.

He had received the news of Jane's stay with her aunt equally enough, but Elizabeth had been quick to notice the slight frown which had descended on his forehead when he was told that it was going to be a lengthy visit. He may have made no further mention of it, but it was growing increasingly evident to his sister that he was beginning to make a point of scanning every item of correspondence which arrived, not quite able to hide his eagerness by asking a little too nonchalantly if she had received a letter from her. He found it incredibly hard to believe that on his visits to town to stay with his father or when he called to see Elizabeth at Aunt Clara's, he had never once run across her, and although he was conscious of feeling disappointed, he had decided against visiting her at her aunt's house, believing that she would be far too taken up with her many engagements to be at home to receive him. Not only that, but there was every possibility that she had outgrown her feelings for him, a circumstance he had been well aware of, and whilst he would not for the world have embarrassed her by teasing her about them, he had not then taken them seriously. He had heard enough from Elizabeth about the sights and amusements in town to keep a young lady entertained to be too optimistic in thinking that Jane would return to Sussex any sooner than she had to and was, therefore, taken quite by surprise one afternoon when arriving back home from a ride around the estate with his father's agent to be met by Elizabeth in the hall to be told that they had a visitor. Staying only long enough to drop his gloves and riding whip onto a table in the hall he strode into the sitting room totally unprepared for what met his eyes, causing him to stop dead in his tracks.

Gone was the mischievous eight year old little girl with a missing front tooth and a mane of tousled and unruly hair that no amount of combing could coax into order and who had followed him around almost continually, taking absolutely no notice of his demands for her to go away but following him as soon as his back was turned. At almost thirteen he remembered a rather gauche and ungainly young girl, who, to his surprise, was emerging from her childhood chrysalis; and at nearly seventeen, still with a mop of untidy hair and torn dress from her trampling across the fields in search of a lost kitten, but clearly bearing all signs of growing into a beauty, had had such a profound affect on him at the time that he had almost reeled. But as he had stood looking at her in the sitting room at Ferrers Court it struck him that without him realizing it Jane had been an indispensable part of his life and that the sensations he had experienced when he had last seen her as a twenty one year old had always been there, hovering beneath the surface of his consciousness, and which now threatened to overwhelm him. It had been impossible at the time for him to say anything; apart from the fact that he was unsure of what his feelings actually represented, he doubted his father would have welcomed the news that his son's affections were leaning towards a girl not quite out of the schoolroom. But even though he had managed to somehow shrug off such a startling discovery, attributing it to nothing more than being taken by surprise at seeing her so grown up, he had never forgotten her. During the time they had been apart, no matter what adventures he had embarked on, she had never been far from his thoughts, but it was not until he learned of her stay in town and the inevitable offers of marriage which would be made to her, did the true significance of his feelings hit him. Jealousy, accompanied by an acute pain at the thought of her even so much as contemplating matrimony with another, had rendered him prey to all manner of unwanted visions; sternly having to take himself to task in order to prevent him from making a dash to the Metropolis to see her and prevent the very worst from happening. He had admirably hid his delight upon discovering from his sister that Jane had communicated her refusal of those two offers of marriage in her letters, but it was only to be expected that at some point there would be one proposal she would not decline, and this thought was almost too much to bear. Once she returned to town he failed to see how any man would not want to offer for her hand especially now when he considered that she had grown into the most beautiful and desirable woman he had ever seen. Gone were the unruly curls and the gap where she had lost that first front tooth, to be replaced by thick and luxuriant warm chestnut hair that was fashionably dressed with a length of blue ribbon threaded through it with a set of perfectly matched even white teeth that glinted when she smiled. Her straight little nose was just as he remembered it as were those dark brown eyes, huge and expressive, giving away so much of what she was feeling, and her mouth, full and generous and quick to smile, was now decidedly kissable. As a thirteen year old adolescent he had looked upon her as a kind of comrade in arms, a like-minded spirit who had thought nothing of participating in all their rough and tumble games, enduring all her stumbles and cuts and bruises, even the loss of a front tooth, in happy and contented silence, whilst he in turn protected and shielded her as he had his own sister. There had been times when he had not welcomed her joining in their adventures but, as she could not be cajoled or coerced into going away, she had been allowed to tag along until her mamma had forbidden any more forays of exploration. But at no time during this idyllic period in their young lives had he looked upon her as anything other than his sister's best friend, but now, looking bemusedly at her, just weeks short of her nineteenth birthday and he just twenty four, his heart was captivated by this young woman who had been his childhood friend, finally able to recognize those earlier feelings for what they really were.

In true Ferrers tradition, he had been educated at home prior to going to Eton, no expense being spared on providing the very best tutors, before his trip to the Continent then entering Oxford upon his return. But despite a rigorous timetable and strict discipline, rigidly enforced by his tutors as well as his father, there had always been enough leisure time to embark on all the mischief that was natural to one of his age.

His time at Oxford had been a happy and productive one, eventually leaving that establishment of learning with a well earned degree. Had some of his former tutors known that his studying had been interspersed with over-spending his allowance as well as embarking on one or two amorous interludes, they would seriously have doubted his acquiring anything remotely resembling a degree at all. But his father, inordinately proud of his only son, by no means frowned upon these extra-curriculum activities, regarding such things as perfectly normal in a young man. His teachers, had they have known, may have described such behaviour as wayward but he had grown up to be reliable and steadfast, and one who had acquired the reputation as being totally dependable. He was by nature open and friendly, but there was that in his face which showed a determination and strength of will, indicating that once his mind was made up nothing would change it. But his experiences, however reprehensible his tutors may have thought them, had certainly given him a self-assurance and confidence which had been lacking as an awkward thirteen year old.   He was not promiscuous by nature or inclination, but neither was he without experience, but as he took several halting steps towards her, it seemed to him that he could well have been a veritable novice, so inadequate did he feel, in truth, as he stared across at her he experienced such an overwhelming sense of joy that he inwardly reeled.

"Hello, Richard" she smiled, holding out her hand to him. "I am not surprised you stare!" she laughed when he made no effort to speak or approach her. "I know it has been a long time since we last met, but have I changed that much?" It was not merely her time in London under Aunt Matty's aegis, giving her the poise and self-assurance her mother had tried in vain to instil into her, but also the fact that she was wearing the very latest fashion, portraying a figure of elegant sophistication which was so very different to how the young man bemusedly watching her remembered.   Having quickly pulled himself together he smiled, replying suitably to this as he took several steps towards her, taking hold of her hand and raising it to his lips, her fingers trembling slightly in his. He found it difficult to believe that this beautiful and graceful young woman was indeed the tomboy friend of his childhood, but as he searched her faced and looked into her eyes brimming with laughter, he saw again that mischievous eight year old, and his heart, which he knew to his painful cost had been susceptible to her for far longer than even he had realized, was now well and truly lost.

Their eyes held for several moments during which time both saw what neither had ever spoken of but could no longer hide. A smile leapt into those intense blue eyes as he read the recognition in those brown ones, her heart jumping in her breast, an organ which had been lost to him for as long as she could remember and now she could let him know it, overjoyed to discover that Richard had, at long last, begun to look upon her in the way she had always hoped he would.

Both of them having arrived at certain conclusions, it was only to be expected that at first they were a little nervous of each other, their conversation somewhat uneasy and disjointed. Elizabeth, who had long been of the opinion that her friend was in love with Richard, decided that they would do very much better without her, so removing herself to a sofa at the far end of the room, watched in contented silence as the couple exchanged reminiscences as well as recounting their experiences since they had last met. It was not to be wondered at that neither of them noticed the time and it was therefore something of a surprise when the chiming of the French enamel clock on the mantelpiece struck the half hour, Jane's face echoing her disbelief at how quickly the time had passed, saying with a reluctance she could not quite hide that it was time she left, but not before a meeting was arranged between them for the following day. It was to be the first of several over the next few weeks.

Lady Trench, whose suspicions were now confirmed, was by no means displeased at the understanding which appeared to be growing between the young couple, conveniently overlooking her daughter's unwillingness to accept those two offers of marriage but, even so, she was not going to allow her to ride unaccompanied around the countryside with a young man, no matter how well they knew him, declaring that Jane's groom ride at a discreet distance behind them. However irksome Richard found this, he accepted it well enough, but had to wait almost three weeks before the opportunity of privacy presented itself.

Due to a brief absence from home by his father, business had unexpectedly intervened rendering it impossible for Richard to escort her home after a glorious day spent together, but walked with her to the stables where her groom was waiting. It had been another beautiful day, the slight breeze softly rustling in the trees of the shrubbery with the sun's rays filtering through the branches to dance on the ground beneath their feet. With her hand resting lightly within his arm they walked leisurely along the path, time as unimportant as words were unnecessary, content just being together; their nervousness of one another having by now disappeared.

As neither of them could quite believe this was happening, both had to continually pinch themselves to ensure they were not dreaming but, as they walked side by side in companionable silence, each with their own thoughts, it was as though the last few years had never been. Suddenly a little laugh escaped her lips causing Richard to stop and look down at her, his eyes smiling into hers. "What is it?" he asked.

"I was just wondering," she mused curiously, "since when has the shrubbery been on the way to the stables? I have never known it so."

"Since now," he smiled a little ruefully.

She raised a questioning eyebrow at this. "I see. I take it you have a reason for this detour?"

"I do," he said firmly, an odd inflexion in his voice. "The thing is," he smiled, "I wished you didn't have to go quite yet. I want to talk to you, and going directly to the stables will not give me sufficient time to say all I wish to."

Her heart gave a little jump at this, but managed with credible calmness, if a little breathlessly, "That is not what you used to say."

"Isn't it? What had I used to say?" he asked quietly, looking down into her slightly flushed face, taking her one small hand in his.

"That you wished I would go away," she told him.

"No!" he cried. "Did I?"

She nodded. "And when I didn't, you pulled my hair."

"I'm sorry," he said contritely, stroking her luxurious curls with one unsteady forefinger. "Did it hurt?"

"Only a very little," she assured him.

"Lord!" he exclaimed. "What a brute I was! It was a wonder you put up with me! Is that why your mamma forbid you to join us?"

"No," she shook her head, her eyes smiling. "Although," she conceded, "she *was* genuinely appalled at the thought of her daughter roaming around the countryside looking like an urchin. Useless to tell her I didn't mind." He smiled abstractedly at this, his mind conjuring up visions of her as an engaging eight year old. "But I think the last straw was when I tumbled into the house after traipsing all over searching for that kitten, looking as though nobody owned me. Do you remember? It was the afternoon you and Elizabeth paid us a visit."

He nodded, his eyes softening perceptibly as they looked down at her, his voice suddenly deep and vibrant. "How could I possibly forget the day I fell in love with you?"

Her eyes widened at this and her heart, always susceptible where he was concerned, began to beat uncomfortably fast; an overwhelming joy enveloping her. "You *do* love me!" she cried faintly, thrilled at having him confirm what she had seen in his eyes, her fingers convulsing in his hand.

"With all my heart!" he told her, his grip on her hand tightening.

"But you never …!"

"Said anything!" he supplied. "What could I have said?" he asked practically. "Like Elizabeth, you were just emerging from the schoolroom! You had seen nothing of the world or other men; I had no right to deprive you of that privilege. Besides," he added truthfully, "I wasn't entirely certain it was love I felt. How could I know that it was not merely the shock of seeing you looking so grown up or simply a natural awareness for one of my age. It was not until Elizabeth told me about your visit to London and those offers for your hand that I realized I *did* love you. I have gone on realizing it," he grimaced, "and that I have in fact loved you all my life without being aware of it!"

"But couldn't you see how I felt about you?" she asked urgently, instinctively resting the palm of her free hand against his cheek.

Waiting only until he had removed her hand to plant a kiss on its soft palm, did he say "I admit there were times when I wondered if you did, but then I dismissed it as ludicrous. At best," he shook his head, "I thought it was merely a childhood infatuation which would eventually fade and die."

"Oh, Richard!" she cried, her eyes revealing all she felt. "Don't you know that I have been in love with you ever since I was eight years old? Oh, I know at that age I was far too young to understand my feelings," she explained, "but one thing I *did* know, and that was I was utterly desolate without you, and only happy when you were with me, and as time passed I knew beyond any doubt that I loved you and would never love anyone else!"

So far he had managed to strenuously resist the overwhelming urge to take her in his arms and kiss her but, upon hearing this heartfelt declaration, suddenly found himself unable to ignore the irresistible temptation any longer and finally succumbed to his inclinations by pulling her roughly against him in order for him to thoroughly kiss her. Had Lady Trench been privileged to have witnessed this passionate scene she would instantly have demanded to know if such behaviour had formed part of the education she had received whilst in her aunt's care, but since her abandoned daughter had no thought for anything or anyone except the man who was crushing her to him, she did not allow her mind to dwell on what her mamma's reaction would be. Richard too, seemed to have forgotten the urgent business awaiting him as he eagerly demolished her defences with his kisses, enjoying the taste and touch of her too much to want to release her just yet, and when he did eventually liberate her lips from the captivity of his he continued to hold her against him, burying his face in the soft curls of her hair, agonizingly expressing his need of her.

"Oh, Richard!" she cried between tears and laughter, when he finally relaxed his hold on her to look down into her glowing eyes, his hands cupping her flushed face, "I have waited all my life for this moment!"

His own colour was a little high, but managed to say, with more steadiness than he would have thought possible under the circumstances, "It certainly seems we have gone the long way round to arrive at it!"

"Yes," she replied breathlessly, "I know."

"Is that why your mamma sent you to London to stay with your aunt?" he asked gently when he had recovered his breath a little, his thumb rhythmically stroking the softness of her cheek.

"Partly. You see," she explained tremulously, "she thought it was about time I received a little town polish." His eyes widened at this, and she smiled. "I understand it is an essential requirement for any young lady on the verge of entering society.

"Is that what you wanted," he asked "to enter society?"

"No," she shook her head, "not particularly. You see," she said a little awkwardly, "I think mamma had come to realize that my schoolgirl feelings for you had grown into love, and thought it wise to send me to Aunt Matty in order for me to look about me a little in case I had mistaken my heart."

"Which you clearly had not, for if you had," he pointed out tenderly, brushing a wayward strand of hair from her face, "you would not have turned down those two most obliging offers of marriage, and we would not be here now."

"Oh, Richard!" she cried on a deep sigh. "How could I possibly accept an offer of marriage from anyone when my heart belonged to another?" her voice failing her as she saw the look in his eyes, surrendering her lips wholeheartedly to his fervent demands.

Sir Arthur, who trusted his wife's judgement implicitly, had been content to allow Jane to be governed in all things by her mother, deeming her the most proper person to oversee their daughter's upbringing and education, never once interfering in Albinia's management. Quite properly, she had consulted him when necessary as to the best direction to take concerning their daughter's welfare, and had, on several occasions, acquainted him as to her partiality for Richard Ferrers' company, something which neither alarmed nor concerned him, seeing nothing surprising in a young girl's infatuation for her best friend's brother, considering it as perfectly natural and something she would grow out of in time. At no point therefore, had he been given cause to either question Albinia's dealings or doubt her word, and whilst he had no reason to complain about the results of her strict supervision, he had nevertheless been relieved to see that Jane's tomboyish behaviour had been brought to an end during her time with his sister. Of course, he would have been less than human had he not felt some annoyance over her refusal to accept those offers for her hand in marriage and from men whom he knew to be from impeccable and unexceptional families. He was not averse to a connection with the Ferrers family, but it could not be denied that the heir to a dukedom or, indeed, an earldom, held out far better prospects than a Viscountcy and for the first time in his dealings with his daughter, he was as vexed as he could be upon discovering from her mother that her feelings for Richard, far from dying a death, had grown into something deeper as well as being the reason for those refusals. However, honesty compelled him to admit that he had never seen Jane happier or in greater beauty than over the last few weeks, for which, according to Albinia, being almost constantly in Richard's company was responsible, a circumstance which made her close her eyes on an anguished sigh, especially when she considered what she had so unceremoniously thrown away. Even so, Sir Arthur saw little to be gained by packing Jane off back to London in the hope that she would meet another eligible suitor, particularly as it appeared she had set both her heart and mind on Richard Ferrers, and since he did not want to be estranged from his only daughter by keeping her as far away as possible from the only man who would ever capture her heart, he agreed to see Richard the following morning.

Having been given his father's blessing as well as Sir Arthur's permission for him to pay his addresses to his daughter, it was therefore with unconcealed pleasure that he courted Jane in form. For several months nothing had occurred to either mar their courtship or to disprove their feelings for one another, in fact, things were progressing between them so well that her father, who had been living in hourly expectation of being asked by Richard for his consent to ask for Jane's hand in marriage for weeks past, had no hesitation in giving it when Richard finally plucked up the courage to approach him.   Nothing now it seemed could stand in the way of the happy couple's future, and as Jane began to formulate ideas for the day she had come to believe would never arrive, she had absolutely no reason to suppose that just over the horizon a storm cloud was gathering in the form of Sir Matthew Mayhew, a man who would change the course of future events and kill at a stroke all her newly found joy.

Sir Arthur may have shown wisdom when dealing with his daughter's matrimonial circumstances, but when it came to upholding and honouring the name he bore, he was a man as blinkered as he was proud, and one who, upon learning of Richard's treachery, had declared him unfit to marry his daughter, taking at face value the charge of treason laid at his door.   He could not pretend to be anything other than deeply shocked upon learning of his perfidy, such damaging allegations turning him almost overnight from a most likeable and personable young man into a traitorous villain.   He loved his daughter, of course, that went without saying, but even so he was a father who fully expected her to respect his wishes, and although she had eventually submitted to his decree about ceasing all contact with the inhabitants of Ferrers Court, and with Richard Ferrers in particular, he had nevertheless detected something in her demeanour which alerted him to the unwelcome suspicion that far from forgetting him, her feelings had in no way undergone a change.   He had hoped that Richard Ferrers' treasonable iniquities would bring his daughter to her senses, but it had become increasingly clear to him that far from being repulsed by his crimes, her feelings for him, far from dying a natural death upon discovering the truth, had remained steadfast.

He had easily acquitted Jasper Ferrers of holding Jacobite sympathies but, even so, it had been impossible for him to maintain relations with the family under the circumstances, and therefore terminated all contact between the two households.   Like everyone else in the vicinity he knew of the searches which had been set in motion at Ferrers Court, and whilst he had held some sympathy for Jasper and his daughter, he had known no hesitation in withholding his support from the man he had known for many years, obdurately maintaining a discreet distance, charging his wife and daughter to do likewise.   Not even upon learning that Jasper had suffered a fatal heart attack did he relent his rigid stance, and whilst it had been the last thing he had expected, having severed all contact with the family, apart from a note of sympathy to Elizabeth Ferrers, his pride would not now permit him to renege on his decision by paying her a visit of condolence.   It was therefore in this resolute frame of mind that he refused to attend the funeral and strictly prohibited his wife and daughter from doing so either.

Jane's docility may have mislead her mother into believing that she had finally recovered from her feelings of affection for Richard but her father, for once far more astute than his wife, had seen beneath the surface of her passivity and was determined to eradicate him from her mind, especially now that he had heard the rumours that Richard Ferrers was back in Sussex. He had seriously toyed with the idea of packing Jane off back to London to her Aunt Matty, but something told him that this would not answer, because even if she consented to go, which he doubted, he held out little hope of her remaining there for very long and if she did decide to stay he placed no reliance upon her accepting an offer of marriage from a suitor far more eligible than Richard Ferrers had proved to be. He would not go so far as to say that Jane would deliberately seek him out, he hoped she had far too much delicacy of principle than that, but he would not put it beyond this young man to try and make contact with her and coerce her into a clandestine meeting. At all costs he had to prevent this from happening and therefore set his mind to the task of averting such an occurrence, the very thought spurring his determination to keep them apart. Like everyone else in the vicinity, Sir Arthur was well aware of Salmon's fervent loyalty to the Ferrers family and to Jasper's only son in particular, and that should Richard take it into his head to contact anyone at Ferrers Court, it would be this unswerving stalwart. He easily dismissed writing to Elizabeth Ferrers on the grounds that, like her father, she was totally innocent of any participation in her brother's crimes and that he, to do him justice, would not do anything to place her in jeopardy. It was with the utmost confidence therefore that he wrote to Richard Ferrers via this old retainer, knowing perfectly well that at some point his young master would be bound to be in touch with him.

He had not erred in his assumption. Sir Arthur's note, coming hard on the heels of Richard learning of his father death, his reaction to its contents was all that insensate man could have wished for. Having been handed the sealed letter from Sir Arthur's personal groom, a crony with whom he often shared a tankard, Salmon had had a pretty shrewd idea of its contents, and although he failed to see any future for the star-crossed lovers, because as far as he could see as matters stood it was going to be impossible for Richard to prove his innocence, he nevertheless dreaded passing it on to him. As predicted, Richard's initial reaction was to visit Sir Arthur straightaway, but the mood he was in he was more than likely to make bad infinitely worse, and it had therefore taken every ounce of persuasion at Salmon's command to dissuade him from such a course.

Frustration and despair enveloped him; so much so that he crushed the expensive sheet of vellum in one white and slender hand, vowing that no matter what it took he would prove to Sir Arthur and the rest of the world that he was no traitor. But as time past this fervent resolve was no nearer being fulfilled than it had ever been, and the overwhelming sense of hopelessness which engulfed him refused to be shaken off.   With Sir Matthew and his father dead; the woman he loved lost to him; his sister in a frenzy of anxiety about his safety and the evidence which would prove his innocence well out of his reach, smuggling run goods had been as good a way as any to not only stave off boredom, but also to help him forget his mounting problems.

From the moment Sir Matthew had broached the reason for his visit to his father, he had known no hesitation in taking up the challenge such a dilemma had thrown in his way. He could not have endured the thought that his country was in danger any more than he could have ignored it, and whilst he was not blinded to the risks and dangers he would face, he knew he had to do all he could to prevent the very worst from happening. Regrettably, there had been little time to prepare Jane for his impending absence, and whilst she had been understandably distressed at being parted from him for an unspecified period of time, she had not bombarded him questions he could not possibly answer, accepting his word on trust. He had thought her father had too, but that was before the news of his supposed treason had spread.   But he had by no means given up hope of marrying Jane! She was in his thoughts day and night, and no matter how long it took he would win her back; not that he ever doubted her love for him, but her father would do his utmost to keep them away from each other, and the very thought of never seeing her again tore him apart.   For himself, he would face any danger to see her just once, and although he had toyed with the idea of sending her word to meet him, he knew he could not; to do so would not only mean forcing her to lie to her father to account for her leaving the house, but it would be a most ungentlemanly act, as abhorrent to him as it was totally out of character.

Then there was his sister. Even though the truth had been kept from her and Salmon had been strictly charged not to divulge it, she had stood by him; her faith and trust in him implicit and the very thought of what she and his father had been subjected to on his behalf was more than he could bear, but he promised himself that sooner or later the debt would be paid in full!

"They wos late agen tonight," stated Jim matter of factly, breaking in on these not very edifying thoughts, looking across at the aquiline profile, quick to notice the sombre look in those alert blue eyes which he was not quite able to hide.

"Yes," Richard nodded absently.

"Wot's the excuse this time?" he demanded, his weather-beaten face showing slight signs of annoyance.

Richard shrugged. "The usual."

"Hm," snorted Jim. "Frenchies! Yer dearsn't depend on 'em!"

Richard laughed, showing an excellent set of strong white teeth. "Perhaps not, but what they lack in reliability you must confess they make up for in excellent cognac."

"I dessay they do," he acknowledged reluctantly, "but when they're late it puts the men on the fidgets."

"They'll be alright when they're paid," he shrugged, casting a quick glance behind him.

"An' wot about you?" Jim asked, casting a glance up at him.

"What about me?" he enquired, shrugging.

"Yer neva teks a penny from the runs," he remarked. "Don't yer think it's about time yer did?"

"That's not why I do it, Jim" he told him, shaking his head. "I thought you knew that."

"I *do* know it," he nodded, "but if the money keeps the men sweet, wot keeps you?" he asked reasonably.

A strange light entered his eyes, bright and glistening as he fixed them on Jim. "The thought that one day I shall take up my rightful place in the world again."

"We all wonts that fer yer," Jim told him, wishing there was something he could do to hasten this wish, "but that could be sometime yet and if that red-coat catches yer agen," he nodded, "'e'll 'ave yer cockin' up yer toes faster than yer can blink!"

He knew Jim was referring to Colonel Henderson and instinctively his hands clenched into purposeful fists. "Very probably," he conceded, "but I shall ensure I do not go alone. I have a score to settle there," he nodded, "and if it's the last thing I ever do I shall conclude my affairs with him!"

Having known Richard Ferrers since he was a boy, Jim did not doubt it. As a youngster he had been an engaging rascal, haunting his boatyard and getting up to all manner of mischief, resulting in him having his breeches dusted for his efforts, but he had grown up into a decent and honest young man whose father he knew had been inordinately proud of him. It had therefore come as a terrible shock when he had learned of the trouble he was in and that he was being hailed and sought as a traitor, but knowing him as he did, in fact, anyone who knew the family, refused to believe it. Like everyone else roundabout, he knew of the search parties which had converged on Ferrers Court and the indignities his sister and father had suffered, bringing about his untimely death. For months now the whole area, from Hastings to Brighton and Beachy Head to Uckfield, were swarming with soldiers on the look out for him, and he could only think it nothing short of a miracle that he had so far managed to evade them, never mind arriving safely on his doorstep one night seeking shelter.

He for one did not need Richard Ferrers' assurances that he was innocent of treason any more than he needed written evidence to prove it. His explanation to account for the sequence of events which had brought him to where he was now, including his brief incarceration at Hampton Regis garrison, was enough for him, as it was for the rest of them. What did he care for kings and thrones and such? It made no odds anyway; you still paid your dues! He and his cronies had been happy to shelter Richard Ferrers for as long as it took him to obtain the evidence needed to prove his innocence, and even though he had known of their nocturnal trips across the Channel at no time had it been their intention to include him in their illicit activities. His involvement in the beginning had been merely to escape detection when news came of a pending search in the area for him until gradually it had become a regular occurrence, going out with them every time there was no moon. It had soon become clear that Richard Ferrers had a head for business, and his knowledge and love of boats and the sea were valuable assets in his new found calling, but Jim knew as well as the rest of them that this was no life for such as him. It may help to prevent boredom from setting in as well as giving him much needed protection from the red-coats, but the sooner Richard Ferrers placed his hands on whatever it was he so desperately needed to clear his name, the better it would be for him.

It was common knowledge that Sir Arthur had deemed the betrothal between Richard and his daughter as null and void and that he had forbidden any contact with the Ferrers family, and whilst it would have given Jim tremendous satisfaction to have set this short-sighted man to rights, he knew he could not; in fact, it had been made abundantly clear to him that the least said about it the better. The disgraced sixth Viscount Easton, as reticent to discuss his private affairs as he was his dealings with Colonel Henderson, may not have told Jim everything, and certainly not about Henderson's iniquities, but anyone but a fool could see that he had a score to settle in that quarter and not simply because he treated his home and sister in what could only be described as a shameful fashion. He and his band of red-coats had run tame at The Court for months now in the hope of catching his young friend in hiding there, but just one look at that determined face was sufficient to tell him that should he ever be fortunate enough to come upon Colonel Henderson again, then it would go very much the worse for him.

As one was naturally taciturn and the other in no mood for talking, being tied up with his own thoughts, conversation between them gradually ceased, one being quite at ease with the other without the need for words but, eventually, Richard's keen blue eyes saw what they had been looking out for. In the distance, he could see the unmistakable outline of the white chalk cliffs of the Seven Sisters, and just to the right of them, at the entrance to Cuckmere Valley, shone a dim light. "Over there!" he cried, pointing in the direction he was looking at.

"Yer know," Jim told him with something close to pride, "yer the best spotsman I've ever 'ad!"

Richard laughed, then lighting the lamp held it aloft; its beam flickering on the water, reaching out to the eager group waiting patiently on the beach.

Apart from the occasional neighing of one or other of the dozen or so ponies huddled together some distance to the rear, the only sound to break the night's dark stillness was the rhythmic lapping of the water on the shingle.

By now, some of the men were showing signs that their nerves were slightly on the fret as Jim's lugger should have been here by now. The Preventive Officer may have been given false information about the destination of tonight's run sending him several miles further along the coast but, even so, it was dangerous to linger any longer than was absolutely necessary. They were expecting a bigger cargo than usual tonight which would not only take longer to land but also to load onto the ponies. Despite the fact that Tom Langney had been on the look out for 'The Queen of the Sea' for almost the past half hour or more, as yet there was no sign of her. Sam Miller, who appeared to be the leader of the group waiting anxiously on the beach, proud to be a land smuggler, slowly pulled out a battered looking telescope from his capacious coat pocket extending it as far as it would go before putting it to his eye, scanning the darkened horizon. For the life of him he could not understand why they had not yet arrived, especially as Richard Ferrers was such a stickler for keeping to a schedule.

Next to him he heard one or two of the men begin to mutter and prophesy disaster if they did not show themselves soon but, just as he was on the point of recommending them to keep silent and have patience, he spotted the faint outline of the sails in the distance, recognizing 'The Queen of the Sea' immediately. "There she is, Tom!" he cried.

Tom Langney needed no telling but straightaway lighted the spout lamp which he then held in the crook of his left arm to begin covering and uncovering the light, signalling all was clear.

Closer and closer came 'The Queen of the Sea' until she eventually weighed anchor several hundred yards out. Almost immediately two small boats were lowered into the water followed by kegs and packages being let down into them by secured ropes. Soon the men on shore were wading chest deep into the sea helping to haul the boats onto the shingle, whereupon they swiftly and silently removed the kegs and parcels, arranging them in piles on the beach. For almost an hour the little boats went back and forth until all the goods were safely on shore, leaving no time for conversation. The ponies, sensing activity, began to neigh and shuffle, pulling at their tethers but, eventually, they were brought to order and harnessed so the kegs and packages of all shapes and sizes could be secured.

In the darkness the men worked quickly and efficiently until the last boatload was seen safely on shore whereupon Richard alighted, leaving the other man to row back to the lugger. Tall and long limbed, Richard Ferrers exhibited the graceful agility of a cat as he jumped onto the shingle and strode towards the group, his keen eyes scanning all around him. Sam Miller, a giant of a man, walked towards him, his frown deepening as he said in a gruff voice, "Thought sumthin' 'ad 'appened to yer; yer very late."

"I know," came the reply, the cultured voice in stark contrast to Sam's, "but

Pierre was delayed; we only just managed to catch the tide."

"Seems to me," he nodded darkly, "that this Pierre's mekking 'abit o' bein' late."

"Yes, I know," he agreed. "This is the third time we have had to wait for him."

"They've bin on the fret," Sam told him, jerking his thumb in the direction of the group quickly dispersing the hoard.

"There's been no trouble, has there?" he asked quickly.

"No," Sam shrugged, "but yer knows wot they are."

"Yes, I do," he nodded, "but they're good men." He then strode over to the group and after a brief word with them he checked the ponies were alright, and turned back to Sam. "Everything appears alright. You know what to do Sam; take them to Harriers Farm. Ben will be waiting. I'll meet you in the usual place tomorrow night."

He nodded. "Wot are you goin' ter do now?"

Richard smiled, a most charming and attractive smile and one which had won him many hearts. "I've business at home."

"'Ome!" he exclaimed, thunderstruck. "Are yer mad guvna? The red-coats 'ave bin swarmin' about the place like flies!"

A dangerous light lit the blue eyes and the well shaped lips thinned. "I know Sam," he nodded, "but they haven't been there now for over a week, besides" he said matter of factly, "I must see Salmon."

"Then wait a few days at least," Sam urged. "They may not 'ave bin there for days, but there's no tellin'; they could be lyin' in wait for yer."

"They could," he smiled, "but you seem to forget; I know my way in and out of The Court without being seen."

"You'll cum a croppa' one of these days, you mark my words!" Sam warned.

Richard laughed. "Very probably, but I have not come this far to be beaten now."

"Cernal 'Enderson wud luv nothin' more than to see yer 'ang!" Sam told him bluntly.

Again those eyes narrowed, but the voice was perfectly calm. "I daresay, but he'll have to catch me first."

"'E *did* catch yer," Sam reminded him. "An' 'e'll do it agen too."

"I escaped, didn't I?" he demanded.

"Yer may not be so lucky next time," he was told.

By now the pack ponies were being led away, and after a quick word with Tom Langney, Richard turned back to Sam. "Don't forget, tomorrow night at the usual place."

Sam nodded knowing it was useless to remonstrate further with him about visiting The Court tonight. As he watched his young friend stride away to where a gleaming black stallion had been brought up he wondered how much longer this young man could go on escaping the law. He did not need to be told that Master Richard was innocent of treason; he knew him and that was enough. He was too much like his father! There wasn't a man here, no, nor anywhere, that wouldn't walk through fire for him. He knew Colonel Henderson would like nothing more than to apprehend him, and although he disliked this particular red-coat intensely, he realized that it was only a matter of time before he eventually caught his quarry. His distrust of Colonel Henderson was such that he would not put it beyond him to have The Court watched day and night, in fact, it was just the kind of despicable thing he would do. It was all very well for Master Richard to say that he knew his way in and out of his home without being seen, he may well, but Henderson was not only sneaky but desperate enough to do anything; so much so that he fully expected any day to hear that he had been arrested or, God forbid, Miss Ferrers, in an attempt to bring her brother out into the open!

In Sam's unqualified opinion, as far as free trading went Master Richard, like Jim Caites and the others, risked his life every time he crossed the Channel! But you wouldn't find him turning tail when things got a little too hot in order to save his own skin; no! He would stand with the rest of them until the danger was over. Nor you wouldn't see him refusing to get his hands dirty or picking and choosing what he would or would not do, he rolled his sleeves up just the same as everyone else. No matter which way you looked at it it had to be said that Richard Ferrers was as good a man as any who ever run goods but, the truth was, he was not bred to the life and although he run the same risks as the rest of them, his heart was not in it. Why, he wouldn't even take a penny for his efforts, despite the fact that he earned his share. It was a great pity he was in the position he was, and if there was anything he could do to help hasten his reinstatement then he would, but since Richard Ferrers was rather reticent to divulge who or what stood in the way of this, then apart from keeping his eye on him there seemed to be nothing he could practically do for him. The only saving grace as far as he could see was that as long as Salmon was around he would take care of him. That did not mean to say that even such a stalwart as he could prevent him from doing something foolhardy when he had set his mind to it, but at least he would be able to temper his more madcap starts.

Richard Ferrers, trotting along at a sedate pace following the river as it meandered through the flat expanse of the Cuckmere Valley, eerily silent and mysterious in the dark stillness, was also pondering his predicament. He had known from the beginning what risks he would be running should he decide to go ahead with Sir Matthew's proposal, but he had accepted the challenge regardless, never for one moment suspecting the personal misfortunes which would come upon him following his participation in the events of the past eighteen months or so. Were it not for these he would say he had no regrets about involving himself in something of such magnitude but, in one respect, guilt hung heavily on his conscience when he considered that all his efforts, far from bringing the guilty party to book, had merely resulted in him ending up being a man on the run with a price on his head, bringing the name he bore into disrepute by having the mantle of traitor hung around his neck. Not even the knowledge that his father had been a party to the truth from the beginning and defended him through all the indignities imposed upon him could rid him of the pain which was his constant companion. Salmon had told him he was not to blame himself for his father's heart attack, that he had gone to his grave inordinately proud of his only son, but he knew only too well that had he not taken such a hazardous task upon himself his father would be alive still, and the desolation this thought engendered was almost too much to bear.

Salmon, whose sage advice had more than once over recent months prevented him from doing something precipitate, was beginning to grow uncomfortably aware that it was becoming increasingly more difficult to hold his young master in check, a man who lacked neither courage nor determination, and it was this knowledge which made him uneasy; living in almost hourly dread of discovering that he had made a spontaneous and reckless attempt to try and place his hands on the evidence which would prove his innocence and unveil the real perpetrator. But no more than Richard could he come up with a serviceable plan that would not only serve the purpose but also prevent him from being apprehended in the process; at all costs he could not allow himself to be found with that vital information on his person. Richard, who needed no reminding of Salmon's fierce loyalty to the Ferrers family and to himself in particular, may, on occasion, regard his concerns as unwarranted, deeming his fears to be the product of an over active imagination, but he knew there was no other man whom he relied on more than Salmon, indeed, his faith and trust in him were unshakeable, as was the very deep affection he had for him. But despite his frustration when cautioned to have a care, knowing that his henchman had his best interests at heart, he had to acknowledge that in one thing at least Salmon was right, and that was his future prospects, no matter how optimistically viewed, looked none too rosy.

He knew he need have no fear of any of his confederates informing against him, especially having known all of them since boyhood. Tom Langney, the blacksmith at Little Turton; Sam Miller, a tenant farmer on his father's estate, Jim Caites, boat builder from Seaford, Ben Harrier and the rest, all of whom were honest men suffering under the burden of the high rates of taxation. He knew that should any of them be caught they would be treated as criminals instead of decent men trying to provide for their families. As for himself, he could not put forward poverty as an excuse for his involvement in what was after all illicit dealings, but even though he ran goods for sport and not profit this would not prevent him from hanging at the nearest gallows. But although running goods under the noses of the Preventive Officers was keeping boredom at bay, he was honest enough to admit that he was tired of living this kind of life. In his more despondent moments he envisaged dodging the law for the rest of his life, especially if he could not put his hands on the evidence which would clear his name of treason. Although at first glance it would seem to be a simple enough exercise to retrieve it, the truth was very different, as he knew only too well. He was perfectly aware of the seriousness of his dilemma, and certainly no one wanted his reinstatement more than he did but, unless a miracle occurred, offering him the means of taking possession of the verification which would prove his innocence, then there was nothing he could do but continue evading the authorities and staving off frustration and boredom in the only way he could.

Having followed the river for over a mile he urged his mount up the grassy incline which would take him out of the valley onto a straight for some little way before veering to the right heading towards Friston, the safest, if not the quickest way, to reach his home. Nothing occurred to mar his progress through the sleeping village, where, at the end of the main street, he came upon a crossroads, the lettering on the weather beaten sign having long since been obliterated. Paying no heed to the right hand pointer for East Dean he veered left into the narrow lane in the direction of Alfriston, where, having arrived unmolested to within a quarter of a mile of the village he coaxed his horse through a narrow gap in the right hand hedge, only the sheep, whose rest was disturbed by the soft thud of his horse's hooves on the grass, showing any curiosity as to his steady progress up the verdant slope. Upon reaching the top he looked momentarily down into the quiet village below before urging his horse forward, his ears going back as he settled into a good gallop over the downland until, after just over a mile or so, he was eased into a canter as the village of Little Turton came into view. Slackening the pace to a trot until he reached the most gentle way down the sharp gradient he carefully guided his mount the length of the hazardous descent, his words of encouragement steadying the highly bred animal as he negotiated the trail to flat ground below, resuming a steady trot across the grazing land until he came to the lane encircling the village. Adroitly avoiding the many potholes, he eventually managed to reach the dirt track which was a natural extension leading from the lane although seldom used, when, just over half a mile further on, he saw the stone wall which encircled the park and grounds of Ferrers Court. He had made no idle boast when he had told Sam that he knew his way in and out of his home without being seen, and therefore had no fear of being caught should Colonel Henderson have left several men on the watch for him. He had known since childhood of the secret passageway that had been constructed during the reign of Mary I in order to aid members of his family escape religious persecution. His father had only spoken of it to him once, and having strictly forbidden him to enter it because it was reputedly unsafe, recalled fondly of being soundly beaten for disobeying him by playing in it as a child. For reasons unknown to him it had never been closed off but, in those far off happy childhood days, he had never thought that one day in the future it would provide the same lifeline for him; once again coming to the aid of the Ferrers family.

Familiarity with the area meant that he did not need the moon to show him the way home, and as he was not of a nervous or timid disposition being abroad at night in almost total darkness held no fears for him, and the sound of an animal scurrying in the undergrowth or crossing his path caused him no concern, any more than the occasional hooting of an owl. As nothing else broke the night's stillness he continued on his way until eventually he dismounted and led his horse as he followed the stone boundary wall for some little way until at last he came to the spot where he veered off the narrow dirt track and headed down into a shallow gully at the side of the road, manoeuvring carefully between the dense growth of trees and bushes until he was on the soft flat. Having led his horse to a sheltered thicket about fifty yards away he then tethered him to a bush, stroking the silken neck of this magnificent animal before turning and walking to where several bushes of evergreen intermingling contentedly with ferns were growing several feet away. Pausing only briefly to look hurriedly around him, he knelt down and quickly dragged the foliage to one side exposing a weather-beaten wooden covering which was completely secreted underneath. Wasting no time he promptly lifted the cover and stepped down into the darkness by way of a makeshift ladder, picking up a lamp which was always left there and lighting it with his tinderbox before lowering the covering and descending further into the dark narrow passage. Over the years part of the brickwork had crumbled and broken away leaving the earth exposed so nature could come into her own again; the clawing fingers of the tree roots resisting his attempts to move them out of the way, while the ghostly threads of cobwebs overhead dared him to disturb them yet again. The ground beneath his feet was soft and moist, the musty dank atmosphere invading his nostrils as he strode doggedly on for almost a quarter of a mile. This was not the first time he had used this passage as a means of entry and egress over the past twelve months but he still marvelled at how well preserved it was and could only regret the fact that he had no leisure in which to study it more closely.

Salmon had not been any too pleased when he had been told to expect him tonight, earnestly remonstrating that he leave it awhile. It was not that he objected to waiting up until all hours of the morning but because he knew just how risky it was, especially so soon after all those searches. He had no fear that Henderson's men would discover the trap door cleverly hidden under the stone flagged floor of the cellar immediately beneath the huge kitchens, but so intense was his dislike of him that he believed him to be capable of any treachery.

In the dim light from the lamp Richard could see that he was only feet away from the ladder, although he knew that no one, not even his sister, knew of the existence of the tunnel he had nevertheless devised a tap that only he and Salmon would recognize. Extinguishing the lamp and placing it carefully down on a makeshift ledge to his left he then climbed a few rungs of the ladder before tapping on the trap door to find it was opened almost at once as Salmon had been waiting for him for well over an hour. As he had spent most of this time in imagining his young master to be in all manner of difficulties, if not arrested, he had worried himself into such a nervous state that when he finally looked down into the face looking up at him cheerfully smiling, he delivered himself of an angry tirade. However much this may have considerably relieved his feelings it was destined to be short-lived. "You've been out, Sir!" he accused, the tangy salt smell unmistakable.

"Of course I've been out!" he said in a fierce whisper as Salmon helped him out of the passage. "Where do you think I've been?" he demanded as he dusted himself off.

"You never said a word to me about going out tonight!" he expostulated.

"Stop fussing," he cried. "I didn't tell you because I knew how it would be! Anyway," he shrugged, "I'm here alright ain't I?"

"Now Master Richard ..." he began.

"I know that voice," he smiled, helping himself to the food and wine Salmon had ready for him, "you always call me Master Richard when you're about to rake me down. Well, let's have it and get it over with," he invited genially.

"I don't know what you're talking about," Salmon sniffed, pouring him out another glass of wine.

"The devil you don't!" he grinned.

"It seems to me," Salmon said awfully, "that I'm wasting my breath."

"Never mind talking that rubbish to me!" he exclaimed. "Everyone in bed?"

"Hours ago," he nodded. "Where *you* should be," he told him, jerking his thumb significantly upwards, "not hiding out like some criminal!"

"How are they?" he asked, ignoring this.

"Your aunt is well Sir, and your sister," he told him, brushing the dust and sand off his tricorne, "apart from worrying over you, is none so bad."

A frown creased his forehead. "Tell her she mustn't worry and that I'm perfectly well."

Salmon looked at his young master meaningfully. "How can I tell her that Sir without telling her the truth?" he asked reasonably.

"You can improvise, can't you!" he demanded.

"No Sir, I *can't*," he told him firmly, pardonably incensed.

"Why not?" he wanted to know.

"Because, Sir," he pointed out, "she won't be taken in by a tale that anyone but a fool could see was a lie!"

"Well, you'll have to think of something," he advised. "Now, about Michael," he asked urgently, keeping an ear open for any sound from above stairs, "any news there?"

"No, Sir, I'm afraid not," he told him aware that this was not what he wanted to hear. "It's just as difficult for me to go to him as it is for him to come here; assuming, of course," he added significantly "that he knows of your predicament and wants to help."

Ignoring the latter part of this speech, Richard told him firmly "Then you'll just have to find a way of getting a message to him somehow."

"That's all very well," Salmon sniffed, "but how do you propose I do that?"

"*Must* I think of everything?" Richard demanded frustrated.

"Well, Sir," Salmon sighed patiently, "since I can't go to him and he can't come to me without the devil of a stir ..."

"Very well Salmon, you've made your point," he said irritably.

"I'm sorry, Sir" Salmon apologized, feeling as though he had let him down.

"No," Ferrers shook his head immediately remorseful, gripping his shoulder, "I'm the one who should be sorry. Egad, what a damned mess!" he cried, beginning to pace up and down the confined space of the cellar.

"Begging your pardon, Sir," Salmon said slowly, eyeing him closely, "but what makes you think that he *would* help you?" Ferrers spun round at this. "You must not forget Sir that he is a red-coat now!"

"What's that got to do with anything?" he asked in a fierce whisper.

"Well, Sir," he offered, "you've not laid eyes on one another since I don't know when. For all you know he could have changed."

"Damn it man, we were the best of friends!" he exclaimed. "Why, he came here often!"

"I am aware of that, Sir," Salmon acknowledged, "and a nice lad he was too. Thing is though," he pointed out fair-mindedly, "he's a grown man now, and a soldier to boot. Could be his ideas have changed to what they used to be. 'Sides," he added practically, "he's been at the garrison long enough to learn of your predicament," he paused uncomfortably as if trying to find the right words. "Surely Sir, if he was still your friend he would have found a way of coming to see us, or try to find a way of helping you."

Richard ran an exasperated hand through his hair refusing to believe that his old friend had changed to such an extent that he would fail to help him. "Damn it, Salmon!" he exclaimed, "if he was going to turn tail on me he would have done so before now!" Salmon acknowledged the truth of this, but hoped for Richard's sake that he was not misplaced in his friend's loyalty. "I'm not," he shook his head. "I'd stake my life on that!" He took another turn about the cellar as if by doing so it would release his pent up frustration. "We find out that he's been stationed at the garrison for several months, yet he may as well be garrisoned on the moon. He can't get his hands on those letters for me because we can't get to see him to tell him about them or where they are. But I've got to get my hands on them Salmon" he declared, "I've just *got* to."

"We'll get them, Sir," he promised. "Never fear."

"Yes, but how?" he asked, tossing off the remainder of the wine in his glass.

"I'm not sure, Sir," he said truthfully dropping his head. "But we'll think of something."

"Well, I hope it's soon," he stated matter of factly, "because much more of this and I'll be dangling from a rope in Hampton Regis market place!"

"Never say so!" Salmon exclaimed, his eyes flying to the taut features opposite him. "You must not say that Sir, you must not even think it."

"Well," he shrugged, his eyes suddenly alight, "if I can't get word to Michael or it turns out that he *is* more of a soldier than a friend, the only alternative is that I'll have to get them myself!"

Salmon was alarmed; he knew that voice only too well, and the look in those blue eyes warned him that he meant it. "Master Richard," he pleaded, almost tearfully, "I beg you won't. It's far too dangerous. They'll pick you up straightaway. They won't give you the chance to say anything and then where will you be? You may not be so lucky next time in escaping."

"Well, I can't be any worse off than I am now!" he exclaimed belligerently.

"I beg you wait Sir, just a little while longer," Salmon urged. "Promise me you won't do anything stupid. Think of your sister. If anything happened to you she would never bear it!"

Richard was thinking of her. She did not know the truth but, even so, she had never doubted his innocence, standing loyally by him as well as coping with Colonel Henderson and suffering the indignity of those numerous searches. He knew Salmon was right. They would pick him up straightaway; every soldier was on the look out for him, even now he could not be entirely certain whether there were any soldiers hiding in the grounds just waiting for him to show his face.

"Please, Sir," Salmon urged again. "Don't do anything yet, only wait."

"Wait for what?" he demanded. "A miracle? No, Salmon," he shook his head, "miracles don't happen, or, if they do, not to me."

"Promise me, Sir," he begged again, "*promise* me that you won't go anywhere near Hampton Regis."

Richard gave his promise but, Salmon, who knew him better than anyone, could not see this assurance lasting for much longer. His master was on the fret, and no wonder. He was a wanted man with a price on his head and anyone found aiding and abetting him were breaking the law, and to make things worse he was not only conscious of his sister's predicament but also of his own helplessness in being unable to help her; added to which, there was Miss Trench! He knew he had made no attempt to convey a message to her or tried to see her, but her father's decree was rendering his frustration worse, especially as Sir Arthur could quite easily send her back to London and, should he do so, then the chances were she would be as good as lost to him; her father would not allow another offer of marriage to be turned down. He wondered what his late lordship would advise if he were alive and, not for the first time, wished that things could have been very different. For himself, he would go through hell and high water for the Ferrers family, but he was as unable to resolve matters as his master was, and if Richard could not go anywhere near Hampton Regis then neither could he. He was known to be a Ferrers stalwart and that he would die rather than betray any one of them but, as he shut the trap door on his young master following his re-entry into the passageway, he could only hope and pray that he would not do anything foolish as well as not placing too much reliance upon an old school-friend.

CHAPTER FIVE

Michael Beaton's friendship with Richard Ferrers had begun at Eton, and although their paths had gone diverse ways over the past few years he nevertheless had very pleasant memories of the times he had spent at Ferrers Court and remembered Lord Easton very well. He only had vague recollections of his sister but, if memory served him correctly, Richard had always spoken very affectionately of her. He had always hankered after a pair of colours, and thanks to a wealthy and most indulgent father, had eventually achieved his ambition. It had been the purest chance that he had been posted to the garrison at Hampton Regis but, whatever hopes he may have had about visiting his old friend, were soon put to flight when he discovered Richard's difficulties. Knowing him as well as he did he found it inconceivable that he had turned traitor by declaring for Stuart. It would have been impossible for him to remain in ignorance of Richard's arrest and ultimate escape and whilst he kept his reflections as well as his association with him to himself, he was nevertheless glad that his old friend, temporarily at least, had extricated himself from such a difficult situation.

He knew only too well that every soldier in the garrison would love to make a name for himself by apprehending such a desperate character as Richard Ferrers. Even those he called friend were not loath to announce how much they would dearly love to be the one responsible for his arrest. He was not ashamed of his friendship with Richard but, if he was going to help him, then advertising this friendship would not serve his purpose.

He had considered how he could possibly assist his friend, but nothing feasible had come to mind. He had not been a member of any of the search parties that had invaded Ferrers Court, for which he was heartily relieved, but even to attempt a solitary visit there to see his sister had had to be discounted from one cause or another.

And now, if things were not bad enough for Richard, along comes Major Neville whose sole intention apparently was to seek him out at all costs. He liked the Major very much, indeed, he had taken to him immediately, but nevertheless he had seen the strength and determination on his face and knew that nothing would deter him from his purpose once his mind was made up. It was not until Major Denham had later taken him to task for fraternizing with a fellow officer did he get to know the reason for his visit; in fact, Major Denham had volunteered the information without a moment's hesitation. "So you see, Lieutenant," he nodded, "Major Neville is going to be far too busy hunting down Ferrers to find time for your history lessons." For some reason this information had been like a douse of cold water. Major Neville bore all the signs of being a decent and honest man, but this news had placed a different complexion on things altogether. After only a little consideration he had deemed it wise not to apprise Major Neville of the fact that he now knew the reason for him being here or that he and Richard Ferrers were friends. He did not think he would hold it against him, but he may enlist his aid because of it, and whilst he had no wish to alienate him, neither had he the wish nor the desire to assist him in hunting down a man he was proud to call friend.

It was much too late now to regret the friendly way he had greeted Major Neville or the invitation he had offered him, but he could and must ensure that from now on a discreet distance was kept between them. He may not be in a position to do anything positive to help his friend, but he certainly was not going to participate in assisting to bring about his downfall. With this resolution in mind he set himself the task of trying, for the umpteenth time, to hit on a way to help Richard Ferrers.

Had Colonel Henderson the least idea that one of his junior officers was closely associated with the man who was currently posing a danger to his peace of mind, he would have had no hesitation in dealing with such a potential threat. Unlike most senior officers he had scant knowledge of the men under his command, much preferring to leave the day to day business of running the garrison to Major Denham, a man in whom he had complete faith. This faith however, did not encompass confiding his innermost thoughts to him or anything connected with his private affairs, but it was certainly true to say that he reposed enough confidence in him to make some believe that Major Denham and not he was in fact the commanding officer.

Whatever Major Denham's thoughts about his senior officer no one knew, he was far too much the professional soldier to allow them to show, but the truth was that whilst he respected Colonel Henderson's rank, he had nothing but contempt for the man. In all the years he had served in the army he had never before known a commanding officer shelve his duties so easily. Not until the advent of Richard Ferrers had he known him expend so much intense energy as he was now doing over the apprehension of this young man. That Richard Ferrers posed a real threat was not in question, what *was* in question was this sudden devotion to duty which, no matter how he tried, found quite inexplicable. He supposed he should be thankful that he was rousing himself at last and behaving in a way a colonel should, even so his unexpected venture into military duties coupled with the arrival of Major Neville, not only roused his curiosity but increased his scepticism as to his motives.

Colonel Henderson had no intention of enlightening him. Indeed, he could not, to do so would be to undermine everything he was striving for. Already he felt himself to be drowning under the pressures of trying to save himself from disgrace and ruin and if he wanted to come out of this mess unscathed then it behoved him to not only keep silent but to increase his efforts to rid himself of his problem. He was still far from happy that matters had been taken out of his hands, but if this Major Neville could do the trick by putting an end to Richard Ferrers once and for all, then he for one would not care how he did it. He only hoped that whatever he did it would be soon, because he doubted his ability to keep up this pretence for much longer, placing no reliance in his overstretched nerves holding together or on keeping Major Denham in ignorance of the truth. His staff officer was far too astute to fool for long, and should he ever so much as suspect then he could say goodbye to everything he was aiming for, perhaps even his life!

Having spent a night in untroubled sleep, Gideon awoke early the next morning to find the sun streaming in through the open window and the sound of a drill sergeant's voice raised above the thudding of marching boots. While Sergeant Taylor filled his bath and prepared his shaving water, he leaned out of the window to watch the group of hapless individuals being put through their paces, evoking memories of doing precisely the same thing. He had no regrets about his military career, but he was honest enough to admit that he was rather relieved to know that never again would he be called upon to rise from a warm bed at an ungodly hour to perform a set of disciplines.

Despite rising early, followed by a substantial breakfast provided by Sergeant Taylor, it was unfortunately well after half past eleven before he was able to set out for Ferrers Court; for this, two reasons were responsible. The first being that his meeting with Colonel Henderson had had to be delayed for at least an hour due to an unfortunate occurrence the night before, necessitating the disciplining of an unlucky private found drunk on duty, and the other by his seeking out Lieutenant Beaton for directions or a more up to date map of the area than the one Sergeant Taylor had provided him with. Eventually however, he managed to escape from his unexpectedly lengthy interview with Colonel Henderson, his reiterated advice still ringing in his ears, but the meeting with his young friend had been a far cry from the one yesterday and his attitude so very different to his eager excitement. He had certainly provided Gideon with a more serviceable map, but there was definitely a lack of friendliness in his manner and, unless Gideon was mistaken, he had the feeling that he was keeping him at arms length. He wondered whether Major Denham had warned him to keep his dealings with himself to a strictly professional level, but his attempt to enquire if this were indeed the case, was merely met with a careless shrug of the shoulders and the eagerly offered excuse that he had made rather a night of it with some of his friends. Apart from the fact that Gideon saw no signs to substantiate that he had imbibed too much the night before, considered this reply just a little too glib but, as he had other important things on his mind, accepted it easily enough. There would be time later to ponder the unexpected change in Lieutenant Beaton's manner, now though, he could spare no more time on something which was most probably nothing very serious; finally setting out on his journey at least two hours later than he had intended, wondering what kind of a reception he could expect to receive or if, which was more than likely, Elizabeth Ferrers would refuse to see him.

Glad to be able to have the opportunity of seeing a part of the country he had not so far visited, he thoroughly enjoyed his ride through the Sussex countryside. He was not disappointed with what he saw, and could not help noting, as he skirted his way round fields and rode down lanes banked by sweet smelling hedgerows, that it was the perfect landscape for smugglers to hide and confound their pursuers.

For almost half a mile away, one could easily pick out the tall twisted chimneys of Ferrers Court, situated in its own neat parkland just to the north of Little Turton. The original Medieval manor house, which had been raised to the ground by fire, had been re-built during the reign of Edward VI and replaced with the beautiful mellow Tudor mansion of grey stone, whose mullion windows glowed warm and inviting in the early afternoon sun; a proud and emotional sight for any Ferrers, who regarded every inch of the place as sacrosanct.

The ancient horse chestnuts, planted by the first Ferrers in the fifteenth century and which had miraculously escaped the fire, had grown and matured, standing tall and erect on either side of the broad avenue leading from the north front entrance. In the distance, Gideon could see the herd of fallow deer which were the direct descendants of their Tudor forebears. No longer hunted for sport or food, the herd had grown in number and the late Lord Easton, who had been a good landowner, had insisted the annual cull be as humane as possible.

It was virtually impossible to believe that anything as remotely exciting as harbouring Jacobite fugitives or smugglers took place within ten miles of this peaceful and tranquil scene, but Gideon, by no means convinced that brother and sister were in collusion against the law, kept a characteristically open mind. He still believed that Richard Ferrers must have had an extremely good reason for returning to Sussex, and whilst he was unsure of what Elizabeth Ferrers may know, he felt that Colonel Henderson's heavy-handed tactics were not the answer if he wished to discover the truth. Apart from the fact that he did not approve or advocate these kind of methods, he was not entirely surprised to learn that far from encouraging Elizabeth Ferrers to tell him anything, they had instead merely resulted in her total lack of cooperation.

He naturally discounted more than half of what Colonel Henderson had told him but, even so, it was going to take a great deal of tact and persuasion to induce Elizabeth Ferrers to talk to him. In truth, he would not blame her if she even refused to see him, after all, it was no pleasant thing to constantly find one's home and privacy invaded, not to mention the tragic results which had ensued from it.

It was inconceivable to him that His Grace and Colonel Henderson would be prepared to move heaven and earth to find a man, albeit a traitor, with such fierce determination unless they had good cause. Not even the most prolific smuggler or disloyal of men could warrant such a calculated effort to seek him out, but until he had spoken to Elizabeth Ferrers or, better still, her brother, then everything else was meaningless.

He could only guess what the outcome of all of this would be but he was firmly resolved in sparing no exertion into discovering the truth and protecting Richard Ferrers from the combined forces of Lytton and Colonel Henderson. Whether Richard Ferrers was guilty or not he was determined not to hand him over to the two men whose ruthless methods to seek him out would ensure his life ended on the gallows without even the pretence of a trial. He was still of the opinion however, that a man in Richard Ferrers' position would not be fool enough to seek sanctuary under his own roof. Colonel Henderson had been proud to admit instigating those searches at Ferrers Court in the hope of finding his quarry in hiding there, and would, if necessary, be more than prepared to renew them with vigour. He himself was not at all surprised to learn that far from skulking behind his sister's skirts, he had been nowhere in sight. Being an active member of a group of individuals who seemed to know everything that was going on around them, with eyes behind every tree and bush, and on his home ground, he could quite easily be informed of a pending search and moved to a place of safety with ample time to spare. This was, of course, perfectly feasible, but somehow he could not see him jeopardizing his sister's safety by looking first to his own. Whatever Richard Ferrers may or may not be he had at least been born a gentleman and, irrespective of what Lytton or Colonel Henderson may choose to think, he could not see him turning his back on this merely in order to save himself.

Even supposing Elizabeth Ferrers held the same sympathies as her brother, there was no saying she would welcome him at Ferrers Court especially if she regarded him as the one responsible for her father's death.

So many questions remained unanswered, not the least being why His Grace was putting forward every endeavour into finding him. True, Lytton's views on traitors and law-breakers in general were public knowledge, but not even his strongly held opinions totally explained away the urgency to rid the world of Richard Ferrers, even going so far as to 'gazette' him to ensure it. If, as General Turville believed, Lytton had motives of his own, then he for one failed to see what they could be other than as a measure to protect someone whose identity could not be divulged, but that he and Colonel Henderson were working in collusion in this matter was in no doubt.   From all he had ascertained so far all the signs pointed to Richard Ferrers being innocent of the charge of treason but, even supposing this to be true, then it in no way solved his difficulties, especially as he had compounded his seemingly untenable position by apparently turning to smuggling. If he was innocent after all, and had in fact been secretly recruited for the purpose of discovering the identity of the real Jacobite conspirator as he and General Turville seemed to think, then it would go a long way to explaining why he was being sought so desperately and by any means available. The questions were endless and for the moment unanswerable but, as speculation all too often led one in the wrong direction, he saw little point in indulging this fruitless practice any further.

But as he rode his fine grey mare along the shaded avenue, he found himself for the moment more intent on admiring his surroundings too much to spare a thought for escaped Jacobites and illicit traders.

He would never have believed it to be possible that he could actually feel such an affinity for a place other than his own home in Wiltshire and, whilst he would never wish to live anywhere else other than Burroughs Croft, the ancestral home of the Neville family for centuries, he had no difficulty in understanding why the Ferrers family were inordinately proud of their home.

Colonel Henderson's suggestion that he take a handful of men with him had been quickly but politely rejected. He saw no point in alienating the household further by yet another military deputation. Nothing would more surely set up their backs by arriving on the doorstep with armed men at his back. No! If he was to discover anything he firmly believed that a solitary visit would reap far more rewards. Of course, there was no saying that he would be received with open arms, if at all, but it would certainly be looked upon more favourably than the tactics adopted so far.

The arrival of yet another scarlet coated young man, and at such an hour, for it wanted only twenty minutes to two o'clock, was regarded by Salmon as not only unwelcome but most inopportune, as his young mistress had, only twenty minutes before, retired to her room with a severe headache. Besides, there had been enough soldiers in the house already to set up a barracks, without any more descending upon them and was, therefore, quite ready, if not entirely able, to send this latest representative of the military to the right-about.

He had been prepared for imperative demands, even brusque orders, but the polite, softly spoken apology for this unannounced and unforgivably late visit, threw him off his guard, so much so, that before he realized what he was doing said that he would enquire if Miss Elizabeth would see him.

"Under no circumstances will I have her disturbed," Gideon told him, his smile denting Salmon's armour even more. "Please to tell her that if she is indisposed, I shall be happy to return at her convenience."

Not used to such politeness or consideration from the military, he was at first incredulous, rendering him rather bereft of speech but, eventually, he managed to pull himself together and, with the faintly uttered promise that he would enquire if she would spare him a few moments, left him standing in the

100

lofty entrance hall while he climbed the wide oaken staircase to her room.

Gideon had to wait almost twenty minutes before Salmon returned to inform him that Miss Elizabeth would see him if he would not mind waiting a little longer, to which Gideon said he did not. Following Salmon out of the entrance hall and into the great hall which, were it at all possible, he would have liked to have stayed awhile and studied it in more detail but, Salmon, either because he wanted this man off the premises as soon as may be possible or because he himself was so used to the place he took no notice of it, he merely sniffed, "This way, Major." Gideon followed him the full length of the great hall, the three long windows to his left letting in the afternoon sun, its rays forging a path across the top of the long oak table picking out not only the portraits on the opposite wall but also, just above the huge stone fireplace, to where the Ferrers coat of arms hung proudly, the family motto 'A Duty to Serve', emblazoned in vermilion on a carved scroll. Salmon, giving him no time to fully appreciate his surroundings, opened an oak door at the other end of the hall leading onto a stone-flagged hallway where, just a little way down to the right, was the sitting room, usually used by the family, saying stiffly, "Through here, Major." "Thank you," Gideon smiled.

"Miss Elizabeth will be with you directly," he told him grudgingly.

"Thank you," Gideon smiled again. "It is most kind of her."

Salmon eyed him with a nice mix of surprise and suspicion but, since this unexpected visitor seemed to be neither impatient nor impolite, indeed, he believed him to be a real gentleman, and he knew a gentleman when he saw one, felt his mistress need have no fear of being treated uncivilly. Upon his rather unsteady exit, for he could not quite believe that at long last Colonel Henderson had been brought to see that his mistress was a lady and should be treated as one, Gideon took appraising stock of his surroundings.

Salmon may have described it as a sitting room but he found himself in a surprisingly spacious apartment which he could see at a glance was clearly used by the ladies of the house; the pieces of embroidery and various ladies monthly periodicals scattered here and there giving it an inviting and informal feel. It was an unexpectedly high pitched room, his attention caught by the white plastered ceiling which was delicately but intricately carved with Tudor roses and the arms of the Ferrers family. On the far south facing wall were long windows giving excellent views to the rear of the house, drawing the eye to the lawns and park beyond while the south-east facing window gave one tantalizing glimpses of a walled garden in the distance. He was pleasantly surprised to see that the original oak panels had not been removed; unfortunately, so many of these beautiful old houses had been stripped of their antiquities to accommodate more modern tastes but, this room, as with the entrance hall and the great hall, had been left untouched. The furniture was a finely balanced mix of different styles, representing every generation of the Ferrers family. It did not take much to see that everything associated with Ferrers Court denoted wealth and influence, but it held a warmth which told him that it was also a home. In the centre of the room was a round rosewood table, on top of which rested a vase of yellow roses, their delicate perfume filling the air, bringing the late spring sunshine into the house. He supposed there must be a rose garden somewhere, but the grounds were vast and like so many of these houses had hidden herb and rose gardens to surprise and delight the visitor. With the exception of clusters of spring flowers dotted here and there the front aspect of the house, impressive to say the least, was intensified by the expanse of luscious green lawns on either side of the avenue.

He knew very little about Elizabeth Ferrers other than what Lytton had divulged to General Turville and, of course, Colonel Henderson's rather biased description of her. He could only wonder what she looked like; but, if the Restoration lady in the portrait over the fireplace was anything to go by, most probably a family forebear, then she was, indeed, beautiful, but no amount of imagining could quite prepare him for the vision which eventually burst upon him; his interest in the house and garden instantly forgotten as he turned to face her. She was of no more than medium height, in fact, she barely reached his shoulders, with a good figure and skin resembling fine porcelain. Her hair was free of powder or adornment of any kind other than a length of blue ribbon threaded intricately through the thick dark curls, which danced with every movement of her head. She had a narrow forehead and a perfect little nose which in profile was classically straight; her mouth bordered on the wilful, but it was decidedly kissable, and Gideon, rather taken aback at the sight of her, found himself momentarily forgetful of his manners.

Her deep sapphire blue eyes showed neither annoyance nor frustration at his arrival, but they looked straight at him with frank appraisal. "Major Neville?" she enquired, her well shaped eyebrows raised slightly.

"At your service, Miss Ferrers," he bowed, in a voice which he knew must be his own.

"How do you do," she smiled, dismissing a reluctant Salmon with a nod of her head before floating towards him in a rustle of stiff blue skirts. "I'm Elizabeth Ferrers. I apologize for keeping you waiting."

"It's no matter," he shook his head, taking the small white hand she held out to him and raising it to his lips. "I had not meant to disturb you," he apologized, quickly regaining control of himself. "I would not for the world have intruded had I known you were feeling unwell."

"Your concern is most touching, Major," she smiled, showing a perfect set of pearl white teeth, "but it is nothing but a migraine. I believe I stayed too long in the sun cutting flowers." He glanced briefly across at the freshly cut roses on the table and her eyes followed his glance. "My mother," she explained, "was used to say that it was a shame to cut something which was intended to be outdoors only to bring inside," she smiled, "but I'm afraid I can't resist; they look so beautiful." He returned a suitable reply, and she said, "I understand you wish to see me."

"Yes, Miss Ferrers, I do," he nodded, conscious of wishing they could have met under different circumstances.

"In that case," she offered, "shall we be seated, Major?"

"Thank you, Miss Ferrers," he inclined his head, sitting down in the chair she indicated with the wave of one white hand.

After making herself comfortable opposite him, she asked, "How may I help you, Major?"

It was several moments before he spoke, and when he did so he felt the words stick in his throat. "In truth, Miss Ferrers," he replied reluctantly, "I am here to try and establish the whereabouts of your brother, Richard Ferrers."

"Yes, I thought perhaps you were," she acknowledged without rancour. After eyeing him closely for some moments, she said "I haven't seen you before Major Neville; I take it that you have not long been in Sussex?"

"No," Gideon replied. "I arrived only yesterday."

"I see," she nodded. "So Colonel Henderson has brought in reinforcements, as he?" she stated provocatively.

"I must tell you, Miss Ferrers," Gideon pointed out, "that I am here, not under the orders of Colonel Henderson, but those of General Sir John Turville in London."

She raised her eyebrows at this. "It seems desperation knows no bounds!"

"It is not how it appears, Miss Ferrers" Gideon told her.

"Then how is it, Major?" she asked.

"In truth," Gideon explained at length, "your brother's dilemma has come to the notice of General Turville, who, I understand, was a close friend of your father's, from none other than His Grace the Duke of Lytton, who, we believe, was approached by Colonel Henderson to assist him in the apprehension of your brother."

"I thought the name Turville sounded familiar," she nodded, "but you must realize Major, that I never really knew my father's friends," she smiled. "However, I must tell you that I am not generally considered to be obtuse," she told him, not unkindly, "but I am afraid you will have to explain a little more clearly. I have, of course, heard of His Grace, indeed, I can recollect my father speaking of him on more than one occasion, but I do not entirely understand what he has to do with my brother."

It had struck Gideon at the outset that she was by no means lacking in intelligence, nor did she strike him as being a woman who was prone to fits of the vapours or afraid of facing the truth, and he therefore decided that to fob her off with some tale would be to insult her, besides which, he doubted she would believe him. Nevertheless, deciding that it would perhaps be better if one or two aspects of her brother's alleged career were kept from her, gave her a slightly edited version of his interview with General Turville. She may not have succumbed to palpitations, but she was certainly shocked at his disclosure, although this was slightly tempered by the relief of knowing that someone other than herself and the inhabitants of Ferrers Court believed in Richard's innocence, but not until he had come to the end of his recital did she put a question. "You say His Grace is quite prepared to 'gazette' Richard? Pray, what does that mean precisely?" Its meaning did indeed horrify her, but the sparkle in her eyes revealed her anger, prompting her to say, "They *dare* to call my brother a traitor! Do they call 'gazetting' him *honourable*?"

He was not unsympathetic, but his reply was delivered in that calm way which General Turville placed so much reliance in. "I cannot take it upon myself to answer that, but I do know they are perfectly serious in their efforts to find your brother, and if 'gazetting' him will effect an arrest, they will have no compunction in doing so. It is imperative therefore," he told her earnestly, "that I find him without any undue loss of time."

She eyed him steadily. "I had no idea my brother was back in Sussex until Colonel Henderson took pleasure in informing me of it. You must know, Major," she pointed out, her face becomingly flushed, "that not only did he have the goodness to point out that my brother is a vicious traitor, but that he has also deliberately contrived to deprive His Majesty's Government of import duty due to his illicit dealings; and as such he is fully justified in seeking him out by any means at his disposal, just as if he were a common felon!" She looked straight at him, lifting her chin defiantly. "Colonel Henderson" she told him with feeling, her eyes sparkling, "left me in no doubt that law-breakers and Jacobite fugitives, my brother in particular, will not be allowed to escape the law. However," she commented, not unreasonably, "in view of what you have told me I am somewhat surprised he has allowed you to visit without an armed escort at your back!"

He smiled. "He certainly tried to persuade me, but as this has already been tried to no avail I saw little point in attempting it again. Besides which," he added sincerely, "they are tactics of which I do not approve. In truth, Miss Ferrers," he confessed, "although I have to keep him informed of developments, I do not take my orders from him. Indeed, General Turville has given me full authority to act in this matter as I see fit."

She looked impressed, saying amusedly, "Am I to understand, Major, that you would *dare* to override Colonel Henderson; a senior officer?"

"I am afraid that is so, Miss Ferrers," he smiled ruefully, "but, providing he does not know it, we may yet come out of this unscathed."

"I certainly hope so," she nodded. "But you must know as well as I do that he is determined to seek out my brother at all costs, indeed, this house has been ransacked from the attics to the cellar on numerous occasions in case my brother is in hiding here. Indeed," she confessed, "I do believe there is not a single nook or cranny which has not been subjected to the most intense scrutiny."

"I regret to confess, Miss Ferrers" Gideon expressed unhappily, "that I was aware of it. I take it, then," he said tentatively, "that you have no idea where your brother may be found?"

"None whatsoever, Major. In truth, Sir," she told him, "I have not set eyes on Richard since he walked out of this house over fifteen months ago."

"And you have not heard from him in all that time?" he enquired.

"No," she shook her head, "not once. To be honest with you, Major, Colonel Henderson has never shown the least inclination to listen to my representations, and he has made it quite clear that I have known all along about Richard being in the vicinity. Indeed," she shrugged, "I doubt he would believe me even if I signed an Affidavit!"

"I realize this is all very distressing for you, Miss Ferrers" Gideon said quietly, becoming increasingly aware of the alien sensations she was evoking within him.

"Yes, it *is* most distressing Major," she told him candidly, "but whilst I can readily believe Richard has taken to smuggling, I have never believed him to be a Jacobite," she paused and he made no effort to rush her or to interpose, quite happy to wait for her to continue. "I do not expect you to understand this Major, but whilst turning his hand to smuggling would appeal to the adventurous, even romantic, side of his nature, he is not the type of man to turn traitor. No doubt you think that stems from bias," she smiled, "but I know it to be the truth." It was a moment before she spoke again. "At no point did Richard ever indicate anything to suggest he had Jacobite sympathies. We have always been very close and had he held such views I would have known. If he did confess to my father that he was intending to declare for Stuart it was never divulged to me; at no point did my father ever discuss with me any of what passed between them before Richard left." She looked defiantly at him. "Even *had* Richard told me himself that he was a Jacobite I would not have believed it! Naturally, when I discovered the circumstances of my brother's hasty departure I was very much shocked. My father refused to discuss it with me, merely stating that I need not worry my head over Richard." Her eyes clouded momentarily, and Gideon knew a moment's impulse to take her in his arms, but as this was out of the question he tried to banish this pleasing picture from his mind. "I loved my father very much, Major," she told him, her voice quivering slightly, "and know that a confession of this nature by Richard would have hit him very hard. *Had* Richard indeed have confessed something like this to him I would have expected him to be worn down with the shame of it, or something to at least indicate his humiliation and pain, but there was nothing; it was like a calm acceptance had descended upon him. But I could not believe what I had been told and refused to accept that Richard had turned traitor. Knowing him as I do I was incredulous; it was so unlike him that I knew a mistake must have occurred. When I approached my father on this he adamantly refused to speak of it."

"But surely your father must have known his son was no Jacobite," Gideon offered.

"One would have thought so," she nodded, "especially when one considers that my father was an intelligent man and one, moreover, who was regarded by all who knew him as having wisdom and understanding, but whenever I tried to reason with my father and plead with him to believe that Richard was no traitor, that he could not possibly hold Jacobite sympathies, he demanded to be told the reason for my belief. I had none," she shrugged, "except my instincts, but my father was a proud man Major, and one who had served his King and country loyally all his life; he expected no less from his son, which" she pointed out, "makes his behaviour about the whole affair even more inexplicable. Had Richard turned traitor I find it inconceivable that my father would have accepted it with such complacency. I know my brother better than most, and I would stake my life that he is no Jacobite!" she swallowed. "The last time I set eyes on him was when he was leaving the house with nothing but a portmanteau. According to Salmon," she pointed out, "who, I might add, is not prone to exaggeration or telling lies, Richard and my father had had the most dreadful argument, which I found very strange Major, especially when I consider the enormity of what Richard was proposing to do and what he now stands accused of. I would have thought that they would have been arguing continually. Certainly I never witnessed any such disagreements." There was a moment's pause before she explained, "I had been out riding and did not return until it was over; I don't know what passed between them precisely, as I have said my father never discussed it with me, but within minutes of my return Richard came striding down the stairs with his portmanteau. When I asked him where he was going he merely shook his head and told me not to worry. I urged him to tell me what was happening but he would not, all he would say was that his departure was for the best and no doubt my father would tell me everything. He did not, of course, but then I did not expect him to; in fact, it was Salmon who told me the truth. My father merely notified me that my brother would no longer be living here and he would be greatly obliged if I would refrain from discussing it. When I tried to ask him what had happened or even try and talk to him about it, he refused. I have not seen Richard since." She had no idea why she had told him all of this, as far as she could see there was absolutely no reason whatsoever to trust him, all she knew was that her instincts told her she could. Her clear blue eyes searched Gideon's face, but gleaned very little from the closed expression which had descended upon it.

In fact, Gideon was now more than ever convinced that he and General Turville were right in that Richard Ferrers was no Jacobite. The more he considered it the more likely it seemed that he had merely been enacting a role, which only served to reinforce his belief that Richard Ferrers had been recruited and with his father's knowledge and approval. He could only assume that Salmon, a man whom he had no difficulty in believing to be close-lipped, had been privy to the truth, and had therefore played his part in keeping the whole of it from her. He may not entirely agree with withholding the truth from her but, if his assumptions as to their reasons for doing were so correct, then he could quite well understand it.

"What reasons do you think your brother could have had for behaving the way he did?" he asked gently, refraining from imparting his views.

She shook her head. "I don't know! That is what makes it all so hard for me to understand. What I *do* know is that I am terribly afraid for him."

"There is no need," he smiled, impulsively leaning forward to cover the cold hand which lay limply on the arm of the sofa with his warm one. "I promise I will do all I can to help him."

"But what of Colonel Henderson?" she demanded. "He is determined to find Richard at all costs."

"I know," Gideon nodded, smiling reassuringly at her, "but I have no intention of assisting him in that aim nor of handing your brother over to him when I do find him."

"You may have no choice, Major" she pointed out.

"I hate to contradict you, Miss Ferrers" Gideon smiled, "but I have every choice. Do not forget, I am not under his orders."

"Perhaps not," she shook her head, "but he can compel you to hand Richard over to him. He is not a man to give up on something easily."

"Nor am I," Gideon assured her quietly. "Should I find him, Colonel Henderson will never come to hear of it from me."

"But how *can* you find him?" she asked, raising a questioning eyebrow. "If Colonel Henderson has not managed to do so with a whole battalion at his back, how can one man alone succeed where he has failed?"

"From what I have been able to ascertain, Miss Ferrers," he told her, his eyes taking in every inch of her exquisite face which was at the moment very much flushed, "apart from the fact that you have been subjected to the most unforgivable treatment by Colonel Henderson, his attempts so far have not only been calculated to bring failure upon him, but also the well deserved condemnation of General Turville and myself."

She had neither missed nor misinterpreted that look which had entered his eyes just now; she had not enjoyed a successful London season with three proposals of marriage to her credit for nothing. Had it not been for Richard's circumstances and the untimely death of her father, last year would have seen her in the throes of another season, enjoying the many attentions a beautiful woman could expect to receive. At twenty years of age she was young enough to miss the excitement of balls and dancing, and whilst her aunt had tried to persuade her that a visit to London for yet another season, participating in only the most select and discreet forms of entertainment would be quite acceptable, she could not bring herself to do so. For one thing, it was too soon after her father's death; she had not yet come to live comfortably without him, and for another, while Richard's future remained uncertain she would much rather remain at Ferrers Court.

It came as something of a surprise to her to discover that she was not averse to this man sitting opposite her, on the contrary, she liked him very much. She supposed she should not allow herself to get too fond of him or, indeed, to accept what he was saying as the truth or even that he meant it. For all she knew it could well be just another tactic to try and get her to betray her brother; how could she be certain that he was not working hand in glove with Colonel Henderson and that this little display of kindness and understanding was not just another clever ploy to trap her?

"What is it?" he asked, when he saw her bite her bottom lip. She shook her head. "Do you think I don't mean what I say? That I shall turn your brother over to Colonel Henderson?"

Her colour deepened, realizing how accurately he had read her thoughts, and she turned her face a little away.

"Miss Ferrers," he said gently, "I realize you must have doubts as to my sincerity, but I have given you my word that I will not turn your brother over to Colonel Henderson irrespective of what I discover."

She swallowed, then biting her lip again, said contritely "I'm sorry. I did think that."

He leaned forward a little in his seat. "Miss Ferrers, I know well how you have been treated and the tragic loss of your father as a result, for which I can only express my regret but, even though I need to find your brother, I am not working in collusion with Colonel Henderson. I give you my word," he said earnestly, "that you have no reason to fear me."

Her dark blue eyes searched his face and knew instantly that her initial instincts had not erred. She recalled what Salmon had said to her when he had come to tell her that Major Neville was desirous of a few moments of her time, and if there was one man she knew she could rely on totally, it was Salmon.

"Miss Ferrers," he urged, "if you know of your brother's whereabouts, I beg you tell me. If General Turville and I are right in that your brother is innocent, then he must be found and his innocence proven."

She clasped her hands together in her lap, her eyes reflecting her concern. "But I can't tell you where he is Major, I don't know!"

Gideon hesitated before saying urgently, "Miss Ferrers, it is vital that I find your brother, for more reasons than we yet know he is being sought with a vengeance, and I have to know why. If His Grace does 'gazette' him for smuggling activities, then he will not only be facing the law for allegedly taking part in the late rebellion, but he will be at risk from his friends; five hundred pounds is a lot of money and there are not many who would put friendship before that."

"I know you are right, Major," she acknowledged, rising hastily to her feet, agitatedly clasping and unclasping her slender hands, "but I can't help you. I have no idea where he could possibly be."

"Do you know of anyone who would be willing to give him shelter?" he pressed, also rising.

"I daresay there are any number of people who would be willing to help him, but since they are no doubt involved in the trade themselves, I am afraid I have no idea who they could be. You must know, Major," she smiled in spite of her anguish, "smugglers do not readily advertise their calling."

"No, which is most unfortunate," he said ruefully, his eyes twinkling.

"It is certainly most unfortunate for us," she pointed out practically, "especially as they appear to be the only ones who could possibly tell us where Richard is."

"Miss Ferrers," he assured her, "I accept your word that you do not know where your brother is to be found, but if there is the slightest chance that word could be got to him that I wish to see him, I need hardly say that not only would I be most obliged, but you would be serving him a very great turn."

"I don't know how word can be got to him, Major," she said earnestly, "indeed, I wish I did."

Having been received far better than he had ever expected as well as discovering for himself the true circumstances prevalent at Ferrers Court, he felt he could not trespass upon her time or generosity any longer. He was not unmindful of her feelings and all she had endured over the last twelve months, and recognized at once her distress as well as her valiant attempts to hide her anguish, so instead of plying her with further questions, which she was clearly in no position to answer, he prepared to take his leave of her adding, as he bowed gracefully over her hand, "You know, you are nothing like what I have been led to believe."

"And just how did Colonel Henderson describe me?" she asked, her eyes suddenly alight with amusement. His lips twitched in response to this, and she smiled, her curls dancing, "It's all right, Major Neville, I can well imagine what he told you. The truth is," she told him without any rancour, "Colonel Henderson and I do not get along. In fact," she confessed, "we dislike one another intensely. He is rude, arrogant and self-opinionated. He refuses to believe that I am telling him the truth when I say that I have no knowledge of my brother's whereabouts." As this description fitted him perfectly, Gideon's lips parted into an involuntary smile, and she responded easily to it, having been very much aware from the beginning just how attractive it was. "I have shown him every observance, even when the house has been virtually demolished brick by brick I have made no demur, but it has all been to no avail. He refuses to accept my word. He threatens me with all manner of dire consequences if I do not give my brother up to him, and despite my assurances that I have not seen Richard since he walked out of here, he refuses to believe me. You must know," she told him, "that Colonel Henderson has spared me nothing. Not content with tearing Richard's character to shreds, he even went so far as to try and convince me that he fought alongside Charles Stuart at Culloden." Her clear blue eyes looked directly up into his, not quite hostile but with a definite challenge. "I wonder why you never mentioned that to me, Major?"

"Because I don't believe it any more than you or General Turville," he told her truthfully. "I saw little point in distressing you further with something that has no basis in fact but, on the contrary, is nothing more than a piece of manufactured evidence clearly calculated to discredit your brother even more."

"Well," she nodded, after giving this considerable thought, "I meant it when I told him I did not believe any of it. I never shall! I love my brother very much, Major, but whilst he may have many faults," she conceded, "treasonable intentions are not ranked amongst them, and if it takes me my whole life long I shall prove his innocence."

"Will you allow me to prove it for you?" he asked gently, taking hold of her hand again. He sensed a slight hesitation. "Miss Ferrers, I give you my word," he told her unequivocally, "the only deceit I am guilty of practising is that of withholding the truth from Colonel Henderson." He saw that kissable mouth compress and the fear and uncertainty enter those intense blue eyes and, whilst he could not blame her for being fearful, he knew, if she did not, that without her trust and support then her brother was lost indeed. "Miss Ferrers," he told her genuinely, "I realize how difficult it is for you to place your trust in a red-coat but, indeed, if I am to help your brother, then you must do so." Reassuringly squeezing her fingers which still lay in his, he smiled down at her, his eyes looking directly into her hesitant ones. "I give you my word that neither you nor your brother will come to any harm through me. Upon my honour you will not."

Something she could not quite define told her he was telling the truth and that she need have no fears about reposing her faith in him, and impulsively her slender fingers quivered in his, revealing more than she knew to the man whose heart she had captivated.

"Major Neville," she breathed eagerly, her instinct exonerating him of any duplicity, "if you could, indeed, prove my brother's innocence, I shall be eternally in your debt."

He raised her trembling fingers to his lips, saying without any pretence, "I shall deem it an honour to serve you in any way I can."

She knew he meant it, and immediately felt the need to apologize again for doubting him, for she did indeed feel a little embarrassed. He responded in a way that was neither calculated nor contrived but, on the contrary, an innate part of him, but which did her pulse rate no good at all. "My dear Miss Ferrers," he assured her, his eyes looking straight into hers, "your doubts are perfectly understandable, indeed, it is natural you should question my intentions but, although I shall do my utmost to assist Richard, I meant what I said in that if I can serve his sister, I shall consider it an honour."

This was no flowery speech designed to win her over or to deceive. She had seen at the outset that he was a gentleman and one, moreover, who had not only breeding but an inherent courtesy. His good manners were neither forced nor a practised art, on the contrary, they were perfectly natural to him. He was certainly the kind of man her father would have approved of, indeed, she did herself. Like her father she was a good judge of character, and saw something in him which had been lacking in those three aspirants to her hand. Her aunt had thrown up her hands in despair when she had told her that she had turned down their very obliging offers, but she could not marry where she did not love. "And what has love got to do with marriage?" her aunt had demanded. She had not replied to this, all she knew was that she could not marry a man simply for money or position, she already had these, and had no desire to leave a happy home with a father who was in no hurry to see her married out of hand. She knew, in fact, had known from first setting eyes on Major Neville, that she liked him. He was certainly good looking, but that did not wholly account for her being so strongly attracted to him, and on so short an acquaintance, but there was something about this man she liked, and knew she would like to get to know him better, but realized that whilst things remained so uncertain and Richard was being sought as a traitor, it would not do to become too fond of him. She could not help but wonder though how it would have been to have met him under different circumstances and, for one insane moment, allowed her mind to consider this pleasing prospect. Suddenly she became aware of those dark brown eyes fixed on her and blushed, stammering "You are most kind, Major."

"Not at all, Miss Ferrers," he bowed.

Feeling suddenly a little shy, she offered unsteadily "I swear I have told you the truth, but you must understand Major, that even though I hold no Jacobite sympathies and do not believe Richard does either, he *is* my brother, and I shall never turn my back on him."

He nodded acceptance of this. "And I swear to you I mean neither you nor your brother any harm."

She nodded. "I believe you mean that, Major."

"I do," he said simply. He paused slightly, before venturing, "Would it be an inconvenience if I called again?"

Although she told herself that her sole aim in receiving Major Neville again at Ferrers Court would be merely to acquire further news of her brother, she was honest enough to admit that she would very much like to see him again for reasons her heart, behaving very strangely all of a sudden, knew only too well. "My aunt and I," she told him as calmly as she could, "are seldom to be found away from home. We shall be pleased to welcome you whenever you choose to call."

Having thanked her for her generosity, apologized once more for intruding on her privacy, he bowed over her hand again before taking his reluctant leave but, as he rode away, he was conscious of an immense feeling of relief in that Colonel Henderson had not overrode him at the last minute by ordering him to take an escort with him, which would have served no purpose and certainly would have ruined any chance of her opening up to him in the way she had. He had seen at the outset that she was still grieving for her father, and although he had lightly touched upon it, had refrained from discussing it in any detail but, from what he could see, she in no way blamed her brother for it. He had no doubt she was telling him the truth when she had said that she had no idea where Richard was to be found, or that he had been smuggling off this stretch of coast for several months until Colonel Henderson had apprised her of it.

She clearly loved her brother, and whilst she would most probably give him aid should he ask for it and jeopardize her own safety, she was not blinded to the enormity of what he stood accused of. Sibling ties were strong, and as he rode away from Ferrers Court he asked himself how he would have felt had he ever been asked to betray Aubrey, and was honest enough to admit that he did not think he could.

Having met Elizabeth Ferrers he could see all too clearly why Colonel Henderson had taken her in dislike; she was neither a coward nor a fool and it came as no surprise to him that to a woman of her spirit his provocative actions had brought him nothing but failure and disappointment. He had spent only a short time in her company, but she had given him no cause to doubt either her integrity or sincerity and instinctively knew that she had not lied to him as well as that her brother was completely innocent of the charges laid at his door. He was determined to do all he could to protect Richard Ferrers from the forces bearing down upon him, his only fear being that these forces could well converge on Elizabeth Ferrers instead in an attempt to draw her brother out into the open. At all costs he must ensure this did not happen, and was firmly resolved to protect her with every means in his power.

He was an intelligent man and one, moreover, who had had no difficulty in reading between the lines of Colonel Henderson's vitriolic description of Elizabeth Ferrers. He could see how her hostility would not only exacerbate his temper but would increase his feelings of desperation in settling this matter of her brother once and for all, fuelling his hatred towards her. His biased account of his dealings with her and his reception at Ferrers Court had been the outpourings of a man goaded beyond endurance as well as one being made to look not just a little foolish by a young woman whom he found could not be threatened into betraying her brother. These bullying tactics were not what Gideon was used to, indeed, he thoroughly deprecated such crude and brutal methods and therefore had no hesitation in regarding Elizabeth Ferrers' feelings as perfectly justifiable.

He may have discounted most of what Colonel Henderson had told him about Richard Ferrers' sister but, nevertheless, he had fully prepared himself, if not for outright enmity, then certainly for a very cold reception.   What Colonel Henderson's embittered description of her had not prepared him for was that The Honourable Elizabeth Ferrers was the most beautiful woman he had ever seen in his life.

So beautiful in fact, she had quite taken his breath away and his heart, usually a most reliable organ, had leapt at the sight of her. There had, of course, been a number of beautiful women with whom he had enjoyed a pleasurable interlude but, whilst he could not claim to having been in love with any of them, or they with him, both parties concerned had certainly enjoyed the liaison for as long as it had lasted, eventually parting on the best of terms with no remorse or recriminations of any kind. He had certainly spent more than one pleasurable hour in their company but, even though there had been passion and amusement enough to satisfy a man's natural needs, there had been no thoughts of love or marriage on either side.   But, however alluring these charmers were, his heart had remained unaffected, so much so that at no time had it ever so much as crossed his mind that he wanted more from the relationship than what was on offer or that he wanted to spend the rest of his life with whoever it was currently enjoying his patronage. From the moment he had met Elizabeth Ferrers he had intuitively known that at long last he had met the woman with whom he did indeed want to spend the rest of his life, rendering his past affairs as empty and meaningless. He could put forward no reason for this except an immediate but inexplicable awareness of an invisible force springing to life between them; something he had never before experienced and for which he could find no rational explanation. He was no inexperienced youth but a grown man not unused to amatory adventures, but from the moment of first setting eyes on her he had experienced such an emotional upheaval that he almost reeled, rendering him totally inadequate to the occasion. He would never know how he had pulled himself together to enable him to conduct his interview with her but, somehow, he had managed to bring his emotions sufficiently under control to prevent her from being alerted to the fact that he had, at long last, found the woman for whom he had been searching all his life.

Despite her understandable wariness and distrust of red-coats, there had been no attempts to deceive him or to dissimulate, on the contrary, there had been an openness in her manner that was as inherent as it was guileless. No one could possibly question her loyalty or steadfastness any more than they could her determination and strength of character but, beneath those traits and exquisite features, there was a vulnerability about her which not all her spirited efforts could hide but, for all that, he had seen another Elizabeth Ferrers lying just beneath the surface. He had detected a sense of humour which was as infectious as it was irresistible and, lurking somewhere in the depths of those deep sapphire blue eyes he had caught an elusive but tantalizing glimpse of the intensely passionate creature he believed her to be, and that was the woman he yearned to know. During the time he had spent in her company he had more than once found himself obliged to strenuously fight his very natural impulses but, difficult though this had been, he had somehow managed to ignore the temptation to take her in his arms and kiss away her fears. Not for the first time during the last hour or so he wished he had made her acquaintance under more happier circumstances but, no matter what the outcome of her brother's difficulties, he was resolved in that, having at last found the woman he knew perfectly well he could not live without, he was not going to let her slip away.

He had never really given much consideration to marriage, after all, his choice of bride and the consequences attaching to it were not as important as they would have been to Aubrey as the eldest son and, this being so, he had never really thought about the woman to whom he would eventually endow his name.   He had, of course, known the background from which she would hail the same as he knew what type of person she would be but, at no time, had he been able to put a face to her. Until now! He would not have believed it to be possible that one could fall in love at first sight, but so it had been. He knew beyond doubt that Elizabeth Ferrers was the only woman with whom he wanted to share his life and, just the thought that this could not be, was too painful to be contemplated. With Aubrey's untimely death it meant that his marriage would now assume the importance his had and, whilst he knew his parent's would welcome with open arms the woman he had chosen to be his wife, he knew too that he owed it to his name to marry a woman who would be regarded as acceptable. In the eyes of society and the world in which he and his family moved, Elizabeth Ferrers was certainly acceptable. Despite her brother's current difficulties, her birth and antecedents were impeccable, apart from which she was the most adorable creature he had ever seen. He was certain his heart had not mislead him when it told him that she was not wholly indifferent to him and, no matter what the future held for Richard Ferrers, he was determined to win the heart of the woman without whom his life would no longer have any purpose.

As for the lady herself she, too, had come to similar conclusions about him. When Salmon had informed her that yet another red-coat had arrived on the doorstep requesting a moment or two of her time, she had known a moment's irritation and seriously contemplated refusing to come downstairs but, upon that stalwart tactfully informing her that, not only had he no soldiers in tow but had come alone as well as assuring her that he was by no means like the others they had had in the house, and that he would take his dying oath that this one was a gentleman, she paused to consider. On the one hand she was heartily sick of being asked the same questions over and over again, and equally sick of the house being ransacked, on the other of course, to openly show her annoyance could easily make them believe that she did in fact have something to hide after all, namely, her brother!

She had been pleasantly surprised by Major Neville however, so much so that she had no difficulty in arriving at the same opinion as Salmon. Appreciative of his kindness and understanding, which had been sadly lacking in the others she had entertained; and, not forgetting that he believed in Richard's innocence, which they certainly did not, she had found it easy to speak openly to him. It had made an agreeable change to be spoken to in a way that was not only polite and courteous but as though no suspicion of blame attached to her in that she was harbouring a fugitive from justice.

It was not simply because he was good looking or that he had impeccable manners which drew her irresistibly to him; her time in London more than proved that. There had been any number of eligible gentlemen to whom she had been introduced who possessed a handsome face, in fact, quite a number of them were by far better looking but then, none of them had looked or smiled at her in just *such* a way as Major Neville had. Their manners too had been exceptional, indeed, there had been nothing in their behaviour to make her dislike them; their lips had no more than brushed her fingers, but the touch had not left her skin tingling well after they had gone!

Salmon's old eyes had been quick to detect the mutual attraction between the two of them and prophesied disaster, but only to himself. Having known both Master Richard and Miss Elizabeth since they were in their cradles, he took liberties which would not have been tolerated in any of the other servants and, when, later that afternoon, she asked him for his opinion of Major Neville, he said bluntly "You wouldn't take any notice of it if I told you."

"You really are most provoking, Salmon!" she admonished. "If it weren't for the fact that you have been here for years and years, I would dismiss you!"

The only affect this had on him was to cause a deep throated chuckle to escape him. "No, Mistress," he chided, "you couldn't do it. 'Sides, what would you do without me?"

"I daresay a great deal better!" the smile in her eyes at variance with the tart reply.

He said something in the broadest of Sussex, to which she was taking absolutely no notice, which, considering the thought that had suddenly occurred to her, was not surprising. What did surprise her was that she had not thought of it before Major Neville's visit earlier. "Salmon, *you* don't by any chance know of my brother's whereabouts, do you?"

Salmon looked wary. *"Me*, Mistress?"

"Yes, *you*," she nodded, walking towards him, her eyes intent on his face. "Now, don't lie to me," she told him as firmly as she could, trying to banish from her mind the affection they all had for this man who could proudly boast of being the only servant to have been born on the estate. "I won't be cross," she promised, "but I have to know."

"I've *never* heard the like!" he exclaimed, shocked. "And what do you think *I* know of smugglers, or free traders, I should say?"

Her eyes gleamed. "So you *do* know," she pounced. Realizing his mistake he tried to make a recover, but to no avail. "You *must* know, Salmon" she said eagerly. "I never knew they were called free traders; neither Colonel Henderson nor Major Neville called them that. I suppose Richard told you so?" His hasty attempt to retreat to his own quarters was instantly thwarted. "No you don't. And don't think you can fob me off!" she warned him. "You know more about my brother than you're letting on, and I want to know."

"It was nothing but a slip of the tongue," he extemporized, swallowing uncomfortably.

"Indeed!" she nodded, her face becomingly flushed. "You said it without the slightest hesitation," she accused as severely as she could. "Richard could always twist you round his little finger and it appears he has done so again. *Now*," she demanded, *"where* is my brother?"

Salmon looked his indecision. The whole truth had been kept from her for her own safety and, he for one, did not mean to tell her, that was for Master Richard now that his father was dead, but the look on her face told him that she was very far from satisfied with his reply and would have the truth out of him. He knew his young master was in the worst kind of trouble and needed help, but he had given his word to him that he would say nothing to his sister about him being back in Sussex, or his latest exploits, and since he was not a man to go back on his word he was ready to face instant dismissal rather than betray him.

She saw the mutinous look settle on his wrinkled face and knew that no amount of cajoling would move him. The only course open to her therefore, was to tell him the truth. He had proved a good friend to both of them over the years but Richard seemed to possess the knack of getting this stubborn Sussex man to do anything he wanted. Perhaps if he knew the real danger her brother stood in he would relent sufficiently to tell her where she could find him. She was not wrong.

Having digested what she told him, he said slowly "They *wouldn't*!"

"Yes, Major Neville told me," she confirmed, "and I had no reason to doubt he was speaking the truth."

"To do *that* to Master Richard!" he shook his head.

"So please, Salmon" she urged, "you must tell me where my brother is. Major Neville needs to talk to him."

Salmon seemed to consider this, saying at length "I don't know where he lies up Mistress, but when I need to see him I can get word to him. There's a place we usually meet."

"Where is this place?" she asked eagerly, laying a persuasive hand on his arm.

But he would not be moved. "Master Richard would flay me alive. He straitly forbids me to tell you anything."

"But surely you can see how important it is that Major Neville sees him!" she told him, frustrated.

"I don't see any such thing, Mistress," he told her with a shake of his head. "'Sides," he explained, "Master Richard don't want you involved in his affairs."

"How can I not be involved in them?" she demanded. Receiving no answer to this, she tried again. "Salmon, Richard must be told in what case he stands. Major Neville had no cause to lie about it."

"Daresay he didn't," he shrugged, "but I don't take my orders from Major Neville!"

She came as close to losing her temper with him as she ever had but, since he would not be moved, she was forced to reply sharply, "No you don't, but you take *my* orders."

A smile crept into his faded brown eyes at this. "Ay, you're my mistress right enough; follow you to the last ditch I would," he admitted, "but I can't have you visiting a place where all the skaff and raff haunt."

She hesitated, her brain racing ahead and decided on a compromise. "If I promise not to set foot inside this place, at least tell me where it is."

He eyed his young mistress with caution. "If you don't want to go inside the place," he asked warily, "why do you want to know?"

"Listen to me Salmon," she pleaded. "You don't need me to tell you that I have never believed Richard to be a Jacobite any more than you, nor for that matter does Major Neville *or* his commanding officer, but the Major needs to talk to him. He means him no harm, he gave me his word and I believe him." Seeing that more was required she explained, "Listen to me, Salmon. Major Neville's commanding officer, Sir John Turville, was an old friend of my father's, you *must* know of him; he visited here often. He and the Major only want to help Richard, they believe him to be innocent." Trying to read the expression on his face, she persevered, "Only tell me where you meet Richard and I'll engage to inform Major Neville."

Salmon hesitated. It was true that Sir John Turville had been a regular visitor here and that Lord Easton had always held him in high regard; it was also true that Major Neville struck him as being an honest young man and one who

117

could be relied on to keep his word but, before he did anything, he would have to speak to Master Richard. After all, it was his life that was at stake!

Since no persuasion of hers would move him from this stance she had no choice but to accept it. She knew he was only thinking of her brother's safety, but it left her anxious and fearful. According to Major Neville he had less than a week to find her brother and discover the truth, but every tick of the clock passing resolutely by, even the few hours Salmon was away meeting her brother, seemed like his life ebbing away.

For a man in Richard's perilous position the rewarding sum of five hundred pounds was a fortune to people who could not even imagine such a figure. Friendship she knew would come a poor second to such temptation, and the thought that Richard was standing precariously between betrayal and death was something she found impossible to bear.

It was over three hours later when Salmon finally returned from his errand and one look at his face was sufficient to tell her that his meeting with Richard had not been an amicable one. It was some time before she could speak to him alone as her Aunt Clara seemed oddly reluctant to retire but, after tactfully persuading her that she looked fagged to death, she finally bid her niece goodnight, but not before warning her not to stay up all night. When she was at last at liberty to speak to Salmon she was unable to gather from the impassioned outpourings, delivered in the broadest of Sussex, a habit he had when he was put out, whether her brother had been more annoyed over her knowing his current trade and whereabouts, or that his family retainer had tried to persuade him to meet Major Neville.

"*However*," he concluded, "he did finally agree to meet the Major, *but*" he emphasized, "he must come alone."

Thankful that he had begun to speak in plain English again, she nodded, asking "Where?"

Salmon heaved a deep sigh, between the pair of them he would end up either dead or imprisoned but, carrying out his orders, said bravely "I'm only to tell you that Mistress providing you don't go anywhere near the place yourself. Master Richard strictly charged me to tell you that if ever you go so much as a mile near it, he'll tear me limb from limb!"

Despite her anxiety a smiled played at the corners of her mouth. "I promise."

Salmon eyed her closely, but as he had never known her go back on her word he appeared satisfied. "The only problem now," he pointed out, after divulging the venue, "is how you are going to let the Major know. If you go into Hampton Regis to see him you'll be bound to cause talk, and that is something we *don't* want!"

"No, indeed" she shook her head, a frown creasing her forehead. "I daren't run the risk of Colonel Henderson getting wind of it."

Salmon agreed to this but, as it turned out, the problem fortunately solved itself.

CHAPTER SIX

Immediately after leaving her aunt's room the following morning, wearing a very becoming riding habit the same deep shade of blue as her eyes with the most dashing hat adorned with a curled white feather, which, said her aunt, must have cost a pretty penny, Elizabeth Ferrers mounted her chestnut mare and rode out of the stable yard just as the clock was striking ten o'clock.

As much as she loved her brother and wanted to help him, she experienced a slight feeling of vexation; Richard had certainly not granted her much time in which to notify Major Neville that he would meet him this evening. How on earth he expected her to inform him of it at so short a notice, she had no idea! Major Neville may have said that he had the intention of visiting her again, but that may not be for several days, by which time it would be too late, and there was no guarantee that Richard would be in any frame of mind to arrange another meeting. He of all people should know that she could hardly show herself at the garrison demanding to see him without kicking up a dust; any more than Salmon could, the chances were they would be arrested on sight and then the fat would be in the fire!

Once clear of the stable yard she headed towards Copse Rise, a densely wooded area to the north-east of the park which had always been a favourite place since childhood. The sun, filtering through the branches of the trees heavy with blossom and brushing her hat as she passed, only seemed to enhance its magic. Beneath her horse's hooves the springy grass, liberally interspersed with clusters of late spring flowers and still covered in early morning dew, glistened in the bright sunlight, momentarily distracting her from the cares which beset her and Richard. Eventually emerging from the trees she cantered towards the grey stone boundary wall of the park until she came to an old wooden door that was no longer used except by herself, which would lead her to the lane. Pulling out a key from her pocket she leaned forward in the saddle and opened it, her mare sensing that on the other side lay a good long gallop; tossing her head impatiently while her mistress paused to lock it behind her. She patted the silken neck before lightly easing off the reins to trot along the lane that would lead her past Little Turton towards Alfriston and East Dean, little realizing that she was following virtually the same route Richard had taken the night before last. From East Dean it was only a matter of three or four miles to Cuckmere Valley, where the white chalk cliffs met the turbulent expanse of the English Channel. Not until she was clear of the village did she spur her horse on, swiftly covering the ground as she sped across the open stretch of downland where she could see the river down in the valley below. As if intuitively knowing their destination her mare needed no steering or words of instruction as to their direction, instinctively knowing the point on the headland where they veered off to descend into the valley, negotiating the decline with a sure footedness that came from long experience, her ears going back immediately she was given her head. Following the silver thread of water glistening in the sun's rays as it meandered on its way between the cliffs on the left and the luscious green slopes to her right where sheep were contentedly grazing she met no one on her ride, for which she was thankful. Usually, she was happy to stop and pass the time of day with various tenants or acquaintances of her father but, this morning, she was in no mood for conversation, especially as it appeared her brother's difficulties were beginning to overtake them. It had been bad enough before but, now she knew for certain how matters stood, it seemed that there was no time to sit and wait and see. But her worries were for the moment forgotten as she gave her horse full rein, enjoying the feel of the wind on her face and the sense of freedom and exhilaration being here gave her, only slowing her pace as the river petered out to meet the sea, reluctantly bringing her mare to a halt. Dismounting, she folded the skirt of her habit over her arm as she walked onto the shingle, crunching beneath her boots, to stand looking out at the swirling mass in front of her. How long she had been standing there she did not know, but it was not until she heard the sound of a horse neighing somewhere behind that she became aware she was no longer alone. Having for so long looked upon this particular spot as peculiarly her own she was not at all certain whether to welcome an intruder who clearly sought to share it with her but, upon seeing who was approaching, the frown lifted from her forehead and a smile lit her eyes. She was conscious of an odd sensation in the pit of her stomach and in spite of herself she could not prevent the breath from catching in her throat; the fortuity of his arrival momentarily escaping her. She could not believe that a man whom she had never laid eyes on before yesterday, especially a red-coat, could have such a profound affect on her, so much so, that should he disappear from her life as suddenly as he had entered it, she would feel quite bereft. She saw him dismount then remove his mitre cap and gloves which he attached to the saddle, before walking towards her. "Are you following me, Major?" she smiled when he eventually came up to her, relieved to feel some of the betraying colour receding from her cheeks.

"Not at all, Miss Ferrers," he shook his head, delighted to have come upon her, taking her oustretched hand and raising it to his lips. "I happened to be out riding; finding my way around, when I caught sight of you."

She smiled up at him. "So you thought you would take the opportunity of questioning me further, or do you believe I am here on my brother's behalf; sending him a signal perhaps?"

"By no means, Miss Ferrers" he assured her good humouredly. "No such thought entered my head. I may not be overly familiar with smuggling ways but, even *I* know, they do not land their cargoes in broad daylight!"

She laughed at this. "Does this mean then that I am acquitted of harbouring a fugitive from justice or being in league with smugglers?"

"You mistake me, Miss Ferrers" he bowed. "I never laid those charges at your door."

No, he had not, but again that persistent voice of caution raised its head. What did she really know of this man who seemed to be taking a definite hold of her heart? "No," she conceded, making a valiant effort to ignore the promptings of this very tender organ, "but Colonel Henderson has."

He nodded. "Yes, but as I am not one of his adherents, I see little point in discussing it further. When we spoke yesterday" he reminded her, "you told me you had not seen or heard anything of your brother. I had no reason to doubt your word then, any more than I do now."

"That's gallantly spoken, Major" she smiled up at him, not averse to his company.

"It's the truth, Miss Ferrers," he impressed.

"I want to believe it," she told him in that candid way he was becoming used to, "but, please, try to understand my hesitancy in reposing any trust in you."

"You may safely do so, however," he assured her, not offended by this statement. He took a step nearer to her, his eyes never leaving hers. "I told you yesterday that I am not working in collusion with Colonel Henderson, and that neither you nor your brother have anything to fear from me."

"Do we not?" she asked, raising a questioning eyebrow, even though she knew that her practical and cautious mind had really lost the battle against her heart, and although she could not have said why she believed and trusted him, she only knew that she did.

"I give you my word," he told her solemnly.

She turned away from him, her eyes suddenly dark and sombre as they looked out at the ever growing turbulence in front of her, the waves as restless and unsure as herself. It was several moments before she spoke and when she did Gideon heard the unsteady note which had crept into her voice. "You must forgive my seeming ingratitude at your desire to help Richard, Major, but my brother's life is very precious to me." She swung round to face him, the wind whipping up the feather in her hat as she did so. "My experience of the military," she explained, "which you must allow to be prodigious, has not exactly inspired me with any desire to repose my trust in its representatives."

"I thought you had declared me innocent of entertaining any ulterior motive," he said quietly. She blushed slightly, but made no answer. "Miss Ferrers," he urged, "I know how important Richard's life is to you but, should it transpire that he is indeed guilty of treason after all, then I promise you I intend to ensure that he receives a fair trial. In any event," he promised, "I mean to do everything I can to help him, which does not mean handing him over to either Colonel Henderson or His Grace."

Her clear gaze searched his face, but she could detect no dissimulation. "Yes," she nodded, "I believe you mean that, but we cannot discount Colonel Henderson!" she shook her head. "We cannot pretend that he is anything other than hostile; Richard will not meet with just treatment at his hands!"

He could not deny it. "No," he shook his head, "but I shall do my possible to ensure that he does not fall into his hands."

She nodded her acknowledgement of this and, as he looked down into her face, suddenly troubled and anxious, he waited patiently for her to unburden herself of whatever it was that was clearly worrying her. "I must confess that coming upon you this morning is most fortuitous," she smiled uncertainly up at him, biting her bottom lip. "You see," she told him a little awkwardly, "I have been striving ever since yesterday evening how best to get a message to you. You must know," she explained, "that neither I nor Salmon can visit the garrison to speak to you."

As he had already exonerated her of any deceit or pretence, he had a pretty shrewd idea that following his visit yesterday afternoon she had gleaned news of her brother's whereabouts, most probably from Salmon, and was now trying to find a way of how best to tell him as well as convince him of her ignorance of any previous contact. He knew her to be open and candid but, in her present state of indecision, she glanced helplessly about her in several directions as if seeking inspiration, but only succeeded in looking adorably confused and, when she eventually stole a glance up at him from under her lashes, her colour just a little heightened, it took all his efforts to strenuously suppress the desire to take her in his arms and kiss her but, managing to ignore the impulse, said, with more calmness than he felt, "Is there something you wish to say to me, Miss Ferrers?"

Without knowing why, this softly uttered enquiry only seemed to make her confession all the more difficult but, telling herself that if Richard's affairs were to be settled and as speedily as possible, then the sooner she told him the better, so, taking a deep and resolute breath, said, a little awkwardly, "Well, yes, actually there is." Realizing how her disclosure could be interpreted she felt the colour in her cheeks deepen and quickly lowered her eyes from his intense study. "Well, you see ..." she faltered, "I ..."

"Is it so bad you cannot tell me?" he asked gently, putting an end to her discomfiture.

"Not *bad* precisely," she shook her head, looking fleetingly up at him.

"I'm relieved to hear it," he said amusingly, smiling reassuringly down at her. "Yes, well, you see" she swallowed, dropping her head, "it is just that I discovered something after you had left yesterday," then looking straight up into his face to see what reaction her words had had on him, said in a rush, "the thing

123

is, it appears that Salmon has been in the habit of meeting Richard since he came into Sussex."

Gideon was not surprised by this information, in fact, he had counted on it. It went against all probability that an old and trusted family retainer, and one who clearly had his master's interests at heart, should not have received news of him. From what he had been privilged to see of Salmon, he would say that far from being bribed into disclosing his whereabouts as Lytton seemed to think, he was more than likely to do his utmost to shield him irrespective of the consequences to himself.

"I did not know of this until after you had left yesterday when I questioned him," she told him earnestly. "I really have been most stupid!" she shook her head. "It never occurred to me that he would know where Richard is, but I should have guessed; Richard could always get round him. Naturally, he was rather reluctant to say anything at first," she confessed, "but, eventually, he told me of his meetings with him."

Gideon listened to her recounting the conversation she had had with Salmon without any surprise, saying at the end of it, "Certainly I shall meet with your brother, just tell me where and when."

She bit her lip, an irresistible gesture he had already become very receptive to. "Before I do so," she said uncomfortably, "Richard made it perfectly clear you must go alone."

"Of course," he assured her, no intention of doing otherwise.

"I have been pondering ever since how to get a message to you," she explained, "especially as Richard has not granted me much time to arrange it; it is impossible for either Salmon or myself to visit Hampton Regis asking to see you."

"I quite understand, Miss Ferrers" he inclined his head. "For either of you to visit the garrison requesting to see me would have immediately aroused suspicion."

She agreed to it. "Richard told Salmon to tell you that he will meet you tonight about eight o'clock at an inn called *'The Moonshadow'*. You will find it at Westbourne, about three miles to the north-east of Little Turton."

He nodded. "I'll find it."

She hesitated, not a little embarrassed. "Major Neville, I *swear* to you I had no knowledge of this prior to yesterday."

"I believe you," he stated simply, the smile in his eyes causing her to catch her breath. "But *you* must believe *me*" he said firmly, "when I tell you that under no circumstances must you take it into your head to visit this inn, or to try and make contact with your brother. To do so," he told her reluctantly, "could place him in grave danger." He paused only long enough for her to digest this. "Colonel Henderson is very suspicious of you and, even though I am not in his confidence, I would not be at all surprised to discover that he could well be putting a watch on you. I am sure if your brother were here he would tell you the same."

"Yes, he would" she agreed. "Indeed, he rounded on poor Salmon dreadfully when he knew he had told me. In fact," she admitted, "he told Salmon he would flay him if ever I tried to make contact with him while matters stood so uncertain."

"Then you must do as he and I request," Gideon insisted gently. "To do otherwise could be dangerous, for both of you. If, as we believe, your brother is innocent of the charge of treason, then it must be proven but, until then, you and he *must* remain apart."

She assented to this and, after extracting his promise that he would come and see her to tell her how the meeting went and all about her brother, she asked "Do you really think I am being watched, Major?"

"As I have said," Gideon reminded her, "I am not in Colonel Henderson's confidence, but he would like nothing better than to catch the two of you together. In fact," he pointed out, "he would give a year's pay to apprehend the pair of you."

She glanced cautiously all around her, but the landscape, as Gideon knew very well, would afford little or no hiding place for any watchful eyes. She shuddered at the thought of being spied upon. "Well, let them spy," she bravely, "I have nothing to hide!"

"I am very much afraid that you do, Miss Ferrers" Gideon pointed out reasonably. "Whether or not we believe your brother to be innocent, in the eyes of the law he is a wanted man and, for someone like Colonel Henderson, who has sought him for months, his arrest would be a real feather in his cap, and if he could catch you aiding and abetting your brother into the bargain, so much the better."

"But surely he can't still seriously believe that Richard has been in the habit of visiting Ferrers Court?" she exclaimed.

"Oh, but he does," Gideon told her. "He is firmly convinced that you know far more than you are revealing, and if the only way he can catch you in league with your brother is by having you watched, then I would not at all put it beyond him." Again she glanced around her. "Do not be alarmed, Miss Ferrers," he assured her, "I have seen nothing to corroborate my theory; I merely warn you of what Colonel Henderson is capable of." She nodded. "It is imperative," he told her, "that you do not make any attempt to see your brother; your safety as well as his, lies in you both remaining apart."

"Yes," she agreed, "you are right, I know you are. It is simply that I worry over him. He is so impulsive and heedless of danger that he is more than capable of doing something which could place him in even more trouble."

"I have no wish to cause you further distress, Miss Ferrers," Gideon pointed out gently, "but I fail to see how much more trouble he can be in. His involvement in smuggling, perhaps only to alleviate boredom, has nevertheless compounded his problems."

A frown creased her forehead. "Tell me the truth, Major; even if you can prove Richard innocent of treason, will he still have to face charges of smuggling?"

He shook his head. "I can't tell yet, but I think it best if we deal with one accusation at a time."

She nodded, then turned away from him to look out at the troubled sea beyond as if mentally debating something, before saying tentatively, "I think there is something else you ought to know, Major."

"Do I need to sit down?" he asked amusingly, "because if I do," he smiled, looking about him wonderingly, "it is going to be a little difficult given our present surroundings."

She laughed at that, not impervious to his sense of humour. "No, I promise you it is nothing very dreadful."

"In that case," he smiled, "I am all ears, Miss Ferrers."

For reasons her heart was beginning to know only too well it was going to prove increasingly difficult to resist this man who had entered her life less than twenty four hours ago but, somehow, she managed to ignore this unexpectedly unreliable organ by haltingly telling him of Richard's betrothal to Jane Trench and her father's subsequent negation of it. "So you see, Major" she explained, "when you asked me yesterday if there was anyone to whom Richard would apply for help, I purposely refrained from telling you about Jane. It was not that I was being deliberately obstructive you understand," she told him truthfully, "but, apart from the fact that I cannot see my brother doing anything to place her in an awkward position by attempting to see her behind her father's back, or persuading her into hiding him, Sir Arthur has strictly forbidden her to have any contact with us at The Court, indeed," she told him sadly, "he has detached himself and his household completely from us. This, and his refusal to honour the engagement," she said regretfully, "has, as one would expect, been common knowledge for some time, which is the reason why I believe Colonel Henderson has never found it necessary to interview either Jane or her father. So you see," she insisted, "I saw little point in mentioning it."

"I quite understand, Miss Ferrers" Gideon replied whole-heartedly, not insensitive to the burden she had been carrying.

"You do?" she questioned warily, having fully expected him to challenge it.

"Of course," he nodded.

She regarded him closely for a moment or two, saying at length "Thank you, Major. You are most kind."

"Not at all, Miss Ferrers" he inclined his head.

"And Jane?" she asked eagerly. "You won't …?"

"No, Miss Ferrers," he assured her, "I won't. In view of what you have told me, I too see very little to be gained by questioning her on something she clearly knows nothing about."

Although her father had made no mention of Sir Arthur distancing himself, he had nevertheless been terribly hurt by his shunning; and, whilst she had wanted to take up the cudgels on his behalf for such treatment, she had managed to refrain from doing so, especially when she had read the letter which Jane had had smuggled in to her by means of Sir Arthur's head groom, a particular crony of Salmon. Jane, already enduring much at being parted from Richard, did not deserve to be subjected to the ordeal of being asked questions either by Colonel Henderson or the Major and, because she had no desire to cause her dearest friend any further distress, was extremely relieved upon hearing Gideon's promise. It was not simply because she was unused to solicitude from the military or that this was not the answer she had expected, but because the man standing next to her, whilst so very different to what she knew of red coats, was looking at her in such a way that made her heart beat uncomfortably fast. There was an expression in his eyes she could not mistake and, although it struck a responsive chord somewhere deep inside her, she was momentarily a little overcome and, in order to not only compose herself but to hide her innermost feelings, turned away to look out at the grey unruly waters. "Richard and I haunted this place when we were children," she told him unsteadily, gaining time to recover her poise. "Poor Salmon would threaten us with life and limb if we came here again without him or a groom. He was afraid one or the other of us would stumble and hurt ourselves! But I do so love it here," she confessed. "If ever I have a dilemma and need to think it through or simply to be alone, I always come here. Have you ever seen anything more beautiful, Major?" she asked, not looking at him.

Although he was fully aware of her concerns over Richard and the bitter feelings she had for the military, which did nothing to endear him to Colonel Henderson and his treatment of her, he instinctively knew that her present discomfiture had nothing to do with either of these things and could only hope it signified that she was not entirely impervious to him. "No," he said in a deep voice, but he was not looking out across the sea but at her. "I can't say that I have." The wind, which was blowing her dark curls provocatively around her slightly flushed and glowing face, gave her a radiance which was reflected in the sparkle of her eyes, rendering him acutely aware of his ever-increasing responsiveness to her and his urgent need to relieve her of her troubles.

"I am told," she could not resist teasing, having by now recovered her composure, "I can't recall by whom," she smiled mischievously round at him, "that this is one of the places where they land their cargoes at night."

"I have been told precisely the same thing," he nodded, his eyes smiling down at her.

She laughed. "Sometimes I wish I were a man; you seem to have far more excitement than us women."

"I am very glad you are not however," Gideon said between amusement and relief. "Imagine what a fix that would place *me* in!"

She raised her eyes quickly to his, her breath suddenly constricted in her lungs at the unmistakable look she saw in those dark brown depths, substantiating his words. She felt suddenly shy and gauche and looked hurriedly away deeming it best to steer the conversation into other, and far more safer, channels. "Whether or not it is true about their landing cargoes here," she said unsteadily, "I don't know. What I *do* know is that I shall miss it when I leave Ferrers Court."

"You're leaving here!" he repeated, surprised.

"Well, not quite yet," she smiled thankfully, more in control of herself now. "I shall have to one day though, especially if my cousin succeeds to the title." She saw the frown crease his forehead. "You see," she explained, "whatever the truth about Richard, only days before he died my father summoned Pritchard, his legal man, and his nephew William, to Ferrers Court when, I understand from Pritchard, it was agreed between the three of them that the title would not pass automatically to William upon my father's death, but only when Richard's affairs had been settled."

"But that can't suit your cousin, surely!" Gideon exclaimed.

"No," she smiled ruefully. "That's the point, it doesn't; especially when one considers that in the eyes of the law Richard's supposed treason means that he has forfeited everything." Gideon nodded. "The last time my cousin visited here, about two weeks ago, he was perfectly amiable," she informed him, "but no matter how he couched it, it was clear that he wanted matters settled as soon as may be possible. He told me his visit was primarily to ascertain if he could be of any assistance during what he termed a most disagreeable time, but I believe it was really to see what news there was of Richard. I could tell him nothing, of course, but it is obvious that he is looking for a speedy solution and, if Richard's arrest could spur things along, so much the better." She glanced sideways up at him. "I gained the impression that he had come to regret making that promise to my father and even more to signing the document Pritchard had had drawn up to that effect." Gideon looked a little taken aback at this. "I suppose one really cannot blame him for that," she admitted, "but should William ever take hold of the reins at Ferrers Court, it would be extremely difficult for me to see him in Richard's place."

"I can imagine," Gideon sympathized.

"You see Major, my father was an extremely wealthy man, and despite my portion on marriage and my quarterly allowance, whoever inherits the title and estates, they will enjoy enormous wealth, which is why I believe William to be growing impatient."

Gideon did not doubt it. "Does your cousin possess money of his own?"

"A mere competence, no more," she shook her head. "You see, my grandfather left my Uncle Lawrence, he being my father's younger brother, very well provided for, but he was rather partial to games of chance; dice I believe," she shook her head, not quite certain on this point. "He worked his way through his money quite rapidly. My cousin's money is inherited from his mother, nothing to turn one's nose up at, of course, but nothing compared to the Ferrers estate. Unfortunately however," she confided, "it appears that my cousin has inherited his father's taste for gaming, and whilst I cannot say whether he can comfortably afford to fund this pastime or not, I would imagine coming into what he believes to be his inheritance cannot come soon enough. You look troubled, Major" she remarked. "Is something wrong?"

"No," he shook his head, "not wrong precisely; it's just that I find it hard to understand why he made such a promise to your father, much less sign an agreement to that fact."

"I know," she nodded. "But I must confess that when I learned of it I was too relieved to give it much consideration but, since my father's death, I have often wondered why he did so. However reluctant I am to acknowledge William as head of the Ferrers family, in the eyes of the law that is precisely what he is."

"I can, of course, understand your father's reasons for wanting your cousin to make such a promise," he told her, "but for a man to sign a legal document virtually renouncing his claim doesn't make any sense."

"No, it doesn't," she agreed fair-mindedly, "and try as I do I can't explain it at all, although" she pointed out "it has to be acknowledged that William has no strength of character. Indeed, I have often gained the impression that he would much prefer to adopt the line of least resistance than bring condemnation down on his head. Oh, he's perfectly amiable," she assured him, "but he does have a tendency to bow to a far stronger will than his own. In fairness to him however, he never shone to advantage in my father's presence, nor Richard's for that matter, so it could well be that when faced with my father *and* Pritchard, two people whose determination and strength of will were far stronger than his own, he felt himself to be quite overborn."

They had by this time begun to make their way back, walking slowly to where their horses were happily munching on a tuft of grass. "But didn't your cousin consult his own legal man before signing such a document?"

A frown creased her forehead. "Well, I don't think he could have, do you? Had he have done so I am quite sure that he would have been advised not to sign such a document. Even had he have consulted someone after signing it I am quite sure it could have been overturned on the grounds of having no substance in law." She considered a moment. "I have not discussed it with him but, the more I think about it, the more certain I am that he never consulted anyone; had he have done so," she said truthfully, "I have no doubt we would have heard about it and he would now be residing at The Court as the sixth Viscount Easton."

He nodded agreement to this, before asking gently "But should it transpire that your cousin does inherit, where will you go?"

"Oh, I daresay to London with Aunt Clara," she managed airily, but he was not fooled. It would cost her a pang to leave her home for such a reason. "She is a widow you know," she explained. "She and Sir Thomas were not blessed with children, but she does not repine, at least," she considered "not outwardly; she never mentions it, but I believe that is the reason why she has taken to the two of us the way she has. She adores Richard; but then, everyone does so. He is almost five years older than I," she told him, "but as with Salmon, he can get her to do anything he wants. He has only to smile at her and she gives in immediately," she smiled. "You may be thinking Major, that a man who stands accused of treason and then follows it up by turning to smuggling, would turn people against him; but that is not so, except for Sir Arthur, of course. Aunt Clara especially, I am sure, would see herself imprisoned before she gave him up; not that she knows where he is, you understand," she smiled mischievously. "I have not told her about Salmon's meetings with him, once she knew that the poor man would get no peace until he told her where Richard could be found. You have not met her yet," she stated, "but she is delightful. She has an imposing house in town, which she insists of having maintained by an army of servants who have hardly set eyes on her in almost twelve months." He could not help laughing at this description. "She loves to know what's going forward and enjoys nothing more than a good gossip. She does have quite a sharp tongue on occasion however, and does not hesitate to speak her mind, which is why William does not like her. She has several times given him some home truths which he has resented but never challenged, but she has the kindest heart of anyone I know. She is as different to my father as anyone could be, but somehow they always managed to rub along together exceptionally well."

"You are right," he agreed, "she does sound delightful. I hope to have the pleasure of making her acquaintance."

"I think you will like her," she nodded. "But then, you see," she acknowledged, "I am more than a little biased." He looked a question. "After my mother died following a short illness," she explained, "while Richard was still up at Oxford, my father, who had adored her, was totally desolate, but Aunt Clara knew no hesitation in coming here to take care of us," she smiled at the memory. "It was due to her bullying and coaxing and sheer persistence that my father resumed his political life and that we all of us continued as before just as my mother would have wished us to; including taking me to London for my first season."

"I'm sorry," he said earnestly, resisting the impulse to hold her close.

"I don't know what I would have done without her," she confessed, "especially when my father died," summoning up a smile. "By then, sadly, she had lost Uncle Thomas but, putting her own grief to one side, she once again came back here to take care of me. Indeed," she admitted, "I could not imagine my life without her. If it had not been for her and Salmon I would have felt truly lost and certainly I could not have faced the worry of Richard's difficulties as well as all that was to come."

"It must have been hard for you," he looked down at her, his eyes clouding.

"Yes, it was," she nodded, not daring to look up at him. "Oh, I know what people think, and, indeed, they are partly right, but it was not only Richard's so-called treason and expulsion, it was other things too."

"What things?" he pressed gently, wishing he could take her away from all of this.

She sighed. "Oh, the fact that he was required to go to London to endorse his loyalty to the King for one thing. That hurt him very much, Major" she told him, a hard note creeping into her voice. "For a man like my father, who had served his country well during his lifetime, it was impossible for him to bear such a slight with equanimity. Then, later," she explained, "Colonel Henderson began the first of his searches for Richard. Despite my father's insistence that he was not here and he had not laid eyes on him in over twelve months, made no difference," she swallowed. "Colonel Henderson told my father that if he did not allow him and his men access to the house and grounds, they would be forced to gain entry by any means at their disposal."

Gideon swallowed a rare surge of anger, but his voice was perfectly controlled. "They had no authority to do so."

"So my father pointed out, but it made no difference." They had reached their horses by now and, taking the opportunity to allow herself a few moments to regain her composure, stroked the silken neck of her horse. "For months they haunted the house and grounds, even going so far as to inform us that if we did not give Richard up voluntarily, they would be forced to take my father into custody for harbouring a vicious traitor. My father remained resolute, indeed" she grimaced, "he would have been hard put to have told them anything. They refused to believe him. But the strain was beginning to tell on my father," she told him, "after weeks of searches and seeing the house turned upside down, he suffered a heart attack. It had all proved too much for him. It left him weak and too ill to leave his room; the doctor advised quiet and rest, but still the searches and questions continued. It was then that he summoned Pritchard and William to him." Her anger bubbled up. "Even now, almost twelve months after my father's death, he continues to hound us! Perhaps now Major, you will understand my animosity towards Colonel Henderson and why I would never inform him of Richard's whereabouts."

"I had no need to hear your explanation, Miss Ferrers" he told her sincerely, "to understand your feelings."

"Thank you, Major" she said in a quiet voice. "But I must acknowledge that when Salmon told me of the arrival of yet another red-coat, I was in two minds whether to see you or not."

"I am very glad you did, however," he smiled, not unmindful of how his visit would have distressed her.

"I was," she admitted, "agreeably surprised in you Major Neville. I had not expected you to be so understanding or prepared to help Richard."

"I have no stomach to see an innocent man hang, Miss Ferrers" he told her as he cupped his hands and hoisted her up into the saddle.

Colonel Henderson had already exceeded his authority in dealing with the Ferrers family and Gideon could easily understand her feelings. It was becoming increasingly clear to him that Colonel Henderson, as General Turville had construed, knew a great deal more about this affair than even they had guessed. His treatment of the family, and of Elizabeth Ferrers in particular, had bordered on harassment, and even if it meant facing a Court of Honour, he was determined to keep Richard Ferrers as far away from Colonel Henderson as he possibly could. Where Lytton fitted into all of this was, as yet, unclear, but that Colonel Henderson had sought his aid in dealing with Richard Ferrers was in no doubt. They were after all old friends, and certainly Lytton was in a position to give him every possible assistance, that being so, he knew he was up against a formidable foe; His Grace never forgave those who worked against him!

Seeing the troubled look on Gideon's face, Elizabeth smiled down at him. "I am afraid we are causing you a great deal of trouble, Major" she apologized.

"Not at all, Miss Ferrers" he assured her, smiling back at her. "I was merely contemplating my forthcoming meeting with your brother."

She did not think this was the reason for his abstraction, but accepted his explanation without comment, refusing to allow him to escort her home.

Her mare, not having ridden off all her energy, was still fresh and enthusiastic for a good run, tossing her head impatiently as she felt Elizabeth get on her back, snorting her eagerness to be gone. Leaning forward a little, she extended her left hand while holding the rein with the other, saying earnestly, "You have been most kind, Major. Indeed," she smiled, "until you came along I saw no hope for Richard."

Never taking his eyes off her, he took hold of the hand extended to him, brushing her fingers with a feather light touch of his lips. "I shall do all I can to help your brother," he assured her, adding, with indisputable sincerity, "I give you my word Miss Ferrers, that neither of you have cause to either fear or doubt me."

Although her eyes held his unflinchingly, it was in a somewhat breathless and husky voice that she said, "You have it quite wrong, Major; I do not fear or doubt you; now. On the contrary," she told him, taking comfort as well as pleasure from the grip of his fingers encircling hers, "my faith is such that I am reposing my whole trust and dependence in you. Indeed," she smiled, "I know both Richard and I may safely do so."

"Thank you, Miss Ferrers," he inclined his head, unable to resist kissing her fingers once more before releasing her hand, the warmth of his lips penetrating the leather of her gloves, leaving her skin burning long afterwards, detaining her only long enough to renew his promise to let her know the outcome of his meeting with her brother.

"I shall look forward to hearing all about it," she smiled shyly, recognizing the unmistakable look in his eyes. "Please to tell Richard that we miss him and long to have him home again."

"You may be sure of it, Miss Ferrers" Gideon promised.

"I must go now," she said hurriedly, feeling the colour flood her cheeks, "or I shall have Salmon fretting!"

After patting the silken neck of her mare with the hand he had just released she adjusted the bridle slightly before giving her a gentle nudge to trot off, but it was not long until she gave her her head to break into a canter to which she readily responded. Unfortunately, the ground was all too soon eaten up beneath her hooves, horse and rider disappointed when the long stretch of Cuckmere Valley began to narrow as it gradually fused with the fertile hillsides comprising the downs, and forced into slackening their pace in order to allow them to ascend the slight incline which would eventually lead them onto the road homeward. Having seen her ride away Gideon mounted his grey mare and turned her to the left, trotting up a verdant hillside which would take him in the direction of Seaford, riding along the top of the ridge where he kept her in view from his high vantage point which looked down into the valley. Elizabeth, pulling her mare up just long enough to adjust her skirts, briefly turned in the saddle, her heart almost stopping at the unexpected but thrilling sight of Gideon sitting astride his horse looking down at her, igniting a frisson of excitement which ran deliciously through her; her reaction to such a powerful and alien stimulus causing her to uncharacteristically jerk the bridle. She saw him doff his hat and bow low over the saddle, firmly convinced that he could see her flaming cheeks even at this distance, then raising a far from steady hand to wave back at him, turned her mare in the direction of home, ignoring the temptation to stay where she was until he had gone. She knew perfectly well that should Salmon or her aunt see her they would not be fooled; the glow in her cheeks and the sparkle in her eyes had little or nothing to do with worrying over Richard's difficulties and even less to do with her morning's ride.

Her unexpected meeting with Major Neville had been nothing if not timely, because had she not have come upon him then she had no idea how she could possibly have got word to him about meeting Richard tonight. She could, of course, have sent a message to the garrison with a groom, but she felt reasonably certain that in order to get past the guards on the gatehouse entrance, he would have not only had to inform them where he was from, but also to disclose his errand, and the chances were that he may not even have been allowed to speak to the Major, but could well have been taken directly to Colonel Henderson for questioning. Should this have happened then nothing could have saved Richard, because there would be no way Colonel Henderson would allow such an opportunity as this to pass in which to apprehend him. The thought made her shiver but, even though she had momentarily managed to avert disaster from descending upon him, she realized just how powerless she actually was to help him. Keeping her brother safe long enough to prove his innocence was paramount, but since there was very little if anything she could personally do to ensure this, her hopes were now all on the Major, the thought of whom brought the colour back into her cheeks and the luminosity into her eyes.

Entering the stable yard half an hour later to find Salmon restlessly on the watch for her, was enough to tell her just how long she had been away and instantly apologized for worrying him.

"I was afraid something had happened," he told her anxiously, imagining all manner of disasters having befallen her. "You've been gone awhile."

Waiting only until he had assisted her to dismount and handed her mare into the care of a groom, did she say contritely, "I'm sorry Salmon, I did not mean to worry you or be out so long, but I was unavoidably detained."

Suddenly his eyes opened to their fullest extent as a thought flashed into his mind. "Never tell me you've been to the garrison!" he cried, horrified.

"No," she shook her head, surprised at this. "Why should you think so?"

"Because it's the kind of thing you would do!" he told her frankly, relieved to see her back in one piece. "But if you've not been into Hampton Regis" he demanded, "where have you been?   And don't say nowhere," he nodded, "because I can tell from the look on your face that you've been playing off your tricks!"

She laughed. "Well, I have not."

"Having known you from the cradle," he told her, his voice a nice mix of pride and anxiety, "I can tell when you look as though you've been up to some waywardness!"

"And how do I look?" she asked mischievously, realizing too late her tactical error.

"Full of fun and gig!" he replied promptly. "Something's happened on your ride; what was it?" he asked suspiciously, taking full advantage of his position.

"Nothing," she shrugged, adding airily, "I ran across the Major, that's all." Upon hearing this she saw the shrewd look which entered his eyes as they searched her flushed face, and knew instantly what he was thinking, and felt her colour deepen. The old eyes narrowed even more, needing no further explanation.   "I see," he said with slow deliberation.

Avoiding his close scrutiny by looking down to examine the toe of her boot, said casually "Yes. It was most fortunate, don't you think?"

"Yes," he nodded, "*most* fortunate."

She moved her foot from side to side before tapping it with her riding whip, saying with studied indifference, "He was familiarizing himself with the neighbourhood, and as we have been striving how to get word to him I thought it was an opportunity not to be missed. Indeed," she shrugged, "it would have been stupid not to have taken advantage of it, especially as he is quite prepared to meet Richard this evening."

He raised an enquiring eyebrow at this, not deceived by her nonchalance. "Oh! That accounts for it then."

"Accounts for what?" she asked warily, darting a quick look at him from under her lashes.

"For you being gone awhile, Mistress," he replied innocently.

She was not fooled by this, knowing perfectly well what he meant, indeed, she would have to be blind not to notice the way he was looking at her, and that he did not believe for one moment that either her ride or the fact that she had arranged the meeting between her brother and the Major were the cause of her radiant appearance.   Feeling something was required of her she smiled, saying encouragingly, "It is what we wanted after all, isn't it?"

The moment he had laid eyes on her he knew something had happened; just one look at her face had been enough to tell him that no matter how much she enjoyed her ride, no canter would have had quite such an affect on her.   He was as proud of her as if she were his own daughter, and loved her as much as he did her brother, both of whom meant more to him than anything else but, at the mention of the Major, a man whom he may own to have taken a liking, he nevertheless considered it was early days to be placing their reliance in him, and told her so outright.

Upon hearing this, her brows drew together, conceding, "I realize that, but what else are we to do, Salmon? Richard cannot remain outside of the law for ever, and since our own hands are tied and no one else is prepared to try and do anything to help him, we have no choice but to rely on the Major." She saw his lips compress and a frown descend onto his wrinkled forehead as he pondered this, knowing precisely what was going through his mind.   "Salmon," she said earnestly, laying a reassuring hand on his arm "I know we have no reason to trust the military, indeed, they have done too much against us but, whilst I accept that we have not known the Major long, less than twenty four hours, in fact, I really do believe we can trust him and that he means Richard no harm."

"Well," he offered, after giving it some thought and rubbing his chin reflectively, "he *is* a gentleman, I'll say that for him; saw it the first time I laid eyes on him and, from my brief talk with him yesterday when I showed him out, I'd take my dying oath he's a man of his word but, as for anything else Mistress," he shook his head, "I'd rather we wait and see what tonight brings!"

"So you *do* like him?" she smiled confidently.

"Yes, I do," he nodded, adding knowingly, "but not it seems as much as you!" She blushed, but did not deny it. "Yes I do, very much."

"I thought so," he sighed. "Suspicioned it when I saw the two of you together yesterday."

She bit her bottom lip, not at all sure whether to be glad or not that this vigilant overseer saw so much. "Well," she shrugged carelessly, disregarding this last utterance, "as you say, we shall just have to wait and see."

"Yes, we will" heaving a sigh. "Not that it's in any doubt!"

"What's in no doubt?" she demanded.

"That he's very taken with you too!" he told her straightforwardly.

"I thought we were speaking of the Major and the outcome of his meeting with Richard tonight!" she reminded him.

"I *am* speaking of the Major," he told her unabashed. "Like I say, he's very taken with you."

She may not have been displeased to hear this, but to her chagrin the colour deepened even more in her cheeks and the sparkle in her eyes intensified, confirming Salmon's opinion as to why she had been so long away. She looked directly at him but, in her embarrassment, words failed her, then, turning on her heel, strode into the house, leaving him to follow behind, sadly shaking his head.

CHAPTER SEVEN

William Ferrers, arriving home at his lodgings in Clarges Street at an advanced hour of the evening after spending another fruitless day at the races in the hope of bolstering his fast dwindling resources, recognized the handwriting on the letter immediately it was handed to him by his man, Whitney. He should have known that Lytton would not let him escape so easily and, it was with a rather unsteady hand, that he eventually opened his letter. It contained six lines only written in a strong upright hand, staring up at him from the finest quality vellum, their meaning unequivocal, leaving him in no doubt that he had incurred His Grace's extreme displeasure, for which he would require immediate explanation. If he wished to see this matter through to a satisfactory conclusion therefore, he must not, in future, disregard his instructions so casually. To this end then, he would do himself the honour of visiting him at his lodging the following morning at ten of the clock precisely.

Only now, when it was too late, did William Ferrers realize the enormity of what he had done and the repercussions which had followed in its wake. It was pointless telling himself that he had allowed his dreams and ambitions to get the better of him, somehow it did not make him feel any better.

It was true that he had never liked his cousin, indeed, he had always been extremely jealous of Richard; it was not only the title which would be his on his father's death that he coveted but also the huge fortune which went with it, not to mention vast estates in Kent and Sussex. It had always been a thorn in his flesh to know that Richard was everything he himself was not nor ever could be and, whilst he was not a man given over to self-analysis, he had to admit that had he have possessed even a modicum of resolution and followed Lytton's directives, all of this could now be his. Unfortunately, he had not possessed that resolution nor, for that matter, any foresight; had he have done so, he would have seen at the outset that the venture he had heedlessly embarked on was bound to end in disaster. It was not until now, when matters seemed beyond unravelling, that he could admit to himself that through his own reckless behaviour and his envy of Richard, he had placed himself in a position which, should it ever leak out, would be certain to ensure him a place on the scaffold. His Grace, who, apart from holding ineptitude and stupidity in the greatest contempt, did not suffer fools gladly but had, for reasons best known to himself, shown a marked degree of magnanimity in attempting to extricate him and his accomplice from the consequences of their actions.

Just as Gideon was wondering what kind of a reception he would receive upon his arrival in Sussex, so too was William Ferrers mentally steeling himself for his forthcoming meeting with Lytton. He knew his credit with him to be almost spent but, no matter how much he dreaded another encounter with him, there was no way it could be avoided especially if he was ever going to extricate himself from the insurmountable difficulties which beset him. He knew the interview would not be pleasant, indeed, he could expect a pretty disagreeable time, and this thought alone made him blench. His Grace's mellifluous tongue, as he knew to his cost, was deceiving. In a few well chosen words Lytton could render one extremely uncomfortable, immediately putting one on the defensive and, he could not deny, that he had a lot to be defensive about having already gone against his instructions which, if he were honest, had been perfectly calculated to bring him about.

His Grace could, if he so wished, leave him and his co-conspirator to their fate, but his letter had not indicated this which meant that they were being given one final opportunity to rid themselves of an embarrassing predicament. Not being a man to consider anyone other than himself, it had never once occurred to him to question the reason for Lytton's involvement in his affairs, or his continued benevolence in assisting him and his accomplice to bring this delicate situation to a satisfactory conclusion without there being the devil of a stir. Instead, he had accepted it without question and certainly with relief.

It was not to be expected that a man being sought as a traitor could be kept secret for long, indeed, once his name had been besmirched it was surprising how quickly the news spread. Within no time at all it seemed the name of Richard Ferrers was on everyone's lips and, although it was not in his interests to publicly defend him, he had, by cleverly worded denials or disclaimers, set the seal on his cousin's fate, Providence coming to his aid when the already disgraced future sixth viscount took to illicit trading.

Lord Easton, of whom he had always stood in considerable awe and dread, had even, on his deathbed, seemed to have the power to make him do precisely as he wished. By not only getting him to hold his claim until Richard's affairs were settled, but also by signing that document, it had been all that was needed to seal his own fate. Faced with Pritchard's strong sense of loyalty and devotion to the Ferrers family and his uncle's earnest desire to do everything possible for his only son, he had found it impossible, when faced with their joint determination, to assert his right to his uncle's title and dignities.

It was, of course, too late for self-recrimination but, although he may tell himself as well as all his acquaintance that it had been out of loyalty to the head of his family, he knew it was no such thing. Lytton had been scathingly contemptuous at his total lack of moral fibre and he could still feel the lash of that smoothly eloquent tongue. He visibly winced when he recollected the meeting which had followed when yet again he had had to account for his failure to carry out the most simple of instructions. It did little to his lacerated feelings to know that his co-conspirator had fared no better at his hands, or that between them they had allowed a delicately balanced situation to become a potentially dangerous one.

Upon hearing a vehicle come to a halt outside his lodgings, he knew before even looking down onto the street to see the immaculate person of His Grace alighting from his coach, that it was he. For one insane moment he thought to have his man, Whitney, deny him but, almost immediately, he realized that this would not answer. For one thing, his circumstances were such that he could not possibly extricate himself from them without assistance and, for another, Lytton was not fool enough to believe that he was still away from home, especially as he had had his return to town verified by Whitney. He knew that if he was to make a recover and without any adverse repercussions or public scandal, he would have to face him at some point and, he supposed, that now was as good a time as any. Besides, he could not afford to waste another moment, his affairs having already reached crisis point.

It was too late now to wish he had not acted so recklessly to begin with and then commit the further folly of going against Lytton's orders to liberate him from his own heedlessness, not to mention providing him with the means to take his cousin's place. Had he have had any resolution he knew he could well now be facing a very different future indeed.

Not even in his wildest periods of optimism could he claim to have been the most popular visitor to Ferrers Court; with the exception of Elizabeth, who had endeavoured to make up for the cold reception he had received from her father and brother, his visits had been tolerated rather than enjoyed. His Grace's suggestion that he ingratiate himself with Elizabeth for the sole purpose of locating Richard had come to nothing, as he knew it would. On his last visit she had been her usual polite and courteous self, treating him with the utmost friendliness, but no persuasion of his had managed to glean even the smallest snippet of information. In truth, he could not see her ever confiding anything to him about her brother's whereabouts and, even when he had tried to commiserate with her over the difficult time she had had of late, it had brought forth no confession. He was not entirely surprised at this, she and Richard had always been extremely close, more like best friends than brother and sister, and not even the most optimistic of people could see her doing anything which would harm Richard.

She may not know the whole truth about her brother's current activities, but he felt it reasonable to assume that she knew more than she was saying, but how to get her to open up to him he had no idea. His efforts to wheedle the truth out of her had failed as they had with Aunt Clara, and his tentative questions to Salmon had fared no better. A more resolute man than himself, or, at least, one with more adroitness, would have easily found a way of getting Elizabeth to confide in him or, to at least voice her concerns about her brother, but since he apparently lacked the necessary qualities to achieve this, he had no very clear idea of what to do next. If he thought for one moment that by waiving his rights to the title until his cousin's affairs were settled one way or the other, would render her susceptible to his carefully practised charms, he was mistaken. Elizabeth may have welcomed such news with barely disguised relief, but it did not make her want to confide in him any more than she ever had. Whilst he could not prove that she knew of her brother's whereabouts, he found it went beyond all probability to believe that she did not, but any further attempt on his part to press the matter would merely result in Elizabeth shutting him out completely. His efforts to follow Lytton's instructions had regrettably come to nothing, and was, therefore, at a loss to know what step he should take next. All he did know was that as long as his cousin remained at large, the danger to himself and his associate grew. It was also true that the longer it took to apprehend Richard the longer he had to wait to get his hands on what he had come to regard as his inheritance.

Unlike his father, who never seemed to worry about anything other than his own pleasure and the means to fund it, he had always keenly felt the disparity between their respective sides of the family. Lord Easton, who had had nothing but contempt for his younger brother, had firmly believed that Lawrence had wasted not only his time and energy by indulging in a frivolous lifestyle which was destined to ruin him, but also his capacity to spend his inheritance as fast as he could at the gaming tables. In fairness to his father however, he had never gone cap in hand to his brother, somehow managing to steer clear of that necessity as well as the tipstaffs by either enjoying an unexpected run of luck at the tables or seeing an outsider pass the winning post against all the odds. His predilection for all games of chance had, therefore, rendered it impossible for him to do anything more than to provide sufficient funds for his son's education; William's inheritance had therefore been only the portion, respectable but by no means handsome or, indeed, adequate, left to him by his mother. The only legacy his father had left him was his propensity for all games of chance and spending far above his means.

He may not want to meet Lytton, but necessity dictated that he had no choice but to do so. To see him again with the same cry on his lips and to witness that look of utter contempt on his face, filled him with dread, and not for the first time wished he had never entered into this business.

William Ferrers may bitterly regret that promise to his dying uncle but, being a naturally weak man who invariably gave in to a far stronger will than his own, he had lacked the courage to do anything else. He had convinced himself that he had merely acted out of sympathy for a dying man who was trying to salvage something for his only son, at least, this was the glib reason he offered his friends and acquaintances in response to their questions about his inheritance. The truth was that when faced with the combined forces of his uncle's legal man, determined to serve his client to the very end, and his uncle's unexpected request, he had quaked at the thought of doing anything other than what was asked of him, even though he knew in law the title and estates were legally his since Richard's treasonable activities had automatically rendered him disinherited.

Not only had Richard made his own situation worse by embarking on illicit trading but, his uncle had, at a stroke, done the same to him. Legally he should now be the sixth Viscount Easton enjoying all the wealth and privileges that accompanied it but, instead, he was plain Mr. William Ferrers with a lodging in Clarges Street, and barely a shilling in his purse to call his own. The fact that he had shown neither strength of character nor resolution in asserting his rights made little difference, certainly it was something he had much rather not dwell on. The inheritance he had received from his late mother had long since disappeared, for which, like his father before him, playing piquet for inordinately high stakes and dice were largely responsible. He was therefore reliant on his winnings to maintain himself but, since this precarious and intermittent source of income was barely sufficient to support his daily needs, let alone funding the lifestyle he not only enjoyed but believed was his by right, the time had come for drastic measures.

He had, for some little while, been forced to pledge his credit all over town and, although at first his tailor and bootmaker, along with other tradesmen who enjoyed his patronage, were prepared to accept further orders for coats, breeches and other indispensable items necessary to a gentleman's needs, the moment had finally come when they wanted settlement of their accounts. To his dismay, it seemed they had all conspired against him at the same time by demanding immediate payment in full, or, failing this, a considerable sum to reduce the balance owing but, if he thought that his future change in circumstances would stay their hand, he was mistaken. It was common knowledge that his cousin was being sought as a traitor but it was also common knowledge that he had waived aside his automatic rights to the inheritance and, whilst no wind of blame had been attached to him regarding his political persuasions, it nevertheless rendered him a poor viability where tradesmen were concerned. It was true that creditors were quite prepared to allow their accounts to mount up with no payment to reduce the balance, but he had completely failed to realize that this was only the case where the gentleman concerned had unquestionable future prospects and not for a man whose inheritance was anything but a foregone conclusion. Word it seemed had spread about that promise to his uncle, and he bitterly regretted it and his credit around town had suffered because of it. It appeared that not only had Richard made his own position untenable but had rendered his cousin extremely uncomfortable and, for one horrifying moment, it seemed there was more likelihood of him being clapped up for debt instead of becoming sixth Viscount Easton!

Whatever the outcome of this most disagreeable state of affairs, it had been made abundantly clear to him that his creditors would much prefer their accounts to be settled. At this moment he had a drawer stuffed full with unpaid bills and final demands, and since his future prospects were having no affect in placating them, he had no idea of how they were going to be defrayed.

His luck at the tables had been quite out for months, rising a loser time after time, resorting to punting on tick, with no hope of honouring the vowels he had so recklessly handed out. Already he had been politely refused in some clubs unless he had the money to lay on the table, infuriating and embarrassing him at the same time when it had been made clear that his vowels would not be accepted. Despair was fast creeping upon him, especially when he thought of the vast sum he had lost a few nights ago. He had covered the debt with a promise of honouring it within a few days, stating he merely needed time to apply for funds. The recipient of his promissory notes, far too intoxicated to have anything other than a vague idea who had presented them to him, had politely inclined his head, assuring him in a slurred voice that he was prepared to wait a few days for settlement but, even as he emerged from the house, he knew that he had no hope of covering this debt of honour. If he thought that the early morning air would clear his head and help him find a way out of his difficulties, he was mistaken. All it did was to increase his fear and the daunting prospect that he faced public disgrace and utter ruin, his father's edict coming forcefully to mind, 'Pay an' play m'boy, pay an' play'. His situation was indeed desperate, and it made him realize more than ever what a fool he had been to give his uncle such an insane pledge, but how to extricate himself from it he did not know. All he did know was that he could no longer live off his future expectations, if, indeed, he had any, as he had thought, and since there was no one to whom he could apply for relief, the future seemed bleak indeed. Sleep had brought him no counsel or comfort, but it had brought him that letter from Lytton! Unfortunately, it had also brought him yet another, if far from polite, reminder from his tailor.

His Grace, exquisitely attired in salmon pink and pale blue satin, paused on the threshold of the small sitting room and scanned his surroundings through his eye glass, finally bringing it to rest dismissively on his nervous host. One look at that thin, painted face was enough to tell Ferrers that he had incurred his deep displeasure; his expression a nice mix of intolerance and boredom and such was his air of condescension that William Ferrers swallowed convulsively, the lace at his throat suddenly a little too tight. He was no match for Lytton or, indeed, anyone with a stronger will than his own and, right now, if it were at all possible, he would have made a bolt for the door. As this was out of the question he could do nothing but wait with as much courage and fortitude as he could muster while His Grace, contemptuously silent, tiptoed further into the room, the high heels of his shoes tapping like a death knell on the polished floorboards. As if determined to keep him hanging on his nerves awhile longer, Lytton, after languidly retrieving a lace handkerchief from his pocket, began flicking imaginary dust from the chair which stood next to the table with such slow deliberation that Ferrers began to feel quite sick. To one in his over charged state of nerves it seemed a very long time before Lytton appeared satisfied that the chair had been dusted to his satisfaction, finally sinking gracefully onto it, unhurriedly crossing one shell pink stockinged leg over the other, deliberately taking his time to return the handkerchief to his pocket.

"Y-Your Grace!" Ferrers stammered, feeling something was required of him. "This is *indeed* an honour," colouring slightly as he moved awkwardly forward to hold out an unsteady hand, only to find it pointedly ignored by his guest. Never at his best in Lytton's company, that haughty air did nothing to lessen his nervousness, on the contrary it made him feel even more overwrought than ever.

"For you, perhaps" he inclined his head. "For me," he shrugged, "it is a *great* inconvenience." Lytton's whole demeanour may have been that of infinite tedium but those keen and alert eyes of his missed very little; including the reminder from Ferrers' tailor which he had forgotten to put away and was still lying on the table. Resting his arm along the edge of it he slowly and rhythmically began to strum his long white fingers on the polished top, his ruby signet ring glittering in the sunlight streaming in through the window. "You look decidedly uncomfortable, Ferrers" he remarked. "For one who is allegedly honoured by my visit, I find that hard to understand."

Ferrers swallowed, his palms beginning to sweat. "No such thing, Your Grace," he replied unsteadily. "You mistake the case!"

Lytton eyed him calculatingly. "You know, Ferrers" he sighed at length, "you really are becoming rather tiresome; one might almost say as tiresome as your cousin. Although," he smiled thinly, "it appears that he at least has *some* sense."

"Your Grace I ..." he began, stung by this offensive comparison.

"Please" he begged, waving a languid hand, "enact me no tragedies I beg of you, or offer lame excuses for your inability to do what is required of you!"

"I was not about to, Your Grace," Ferrers shook his head, realizing that trying to defend his actions or, to be more precise, the lack of them, was going to be even more difficult than he had envisaged, unaware that the fear and uncertainty in his pale brown eyes were not lost on his visitor. "I was merely trying to explain to you the circumstances which prevented me from doing what you suggested."

"The only circumstance that I can see," Lytton told him nastily, "is your complete and utter lack of character and resolution."

"Your Grace!" Ferrers exclaimed. "I really must protest!"

Lytton's eyes raked scathingly over him and the red painted lips thinned. "Have a care, Ferrers" he warned softly. "Do not forget to whom you speak," he reminded him ominously, not at all mollified by the tinge of colour which flooded his cheeks at this rebuke. "You appear, do you not" he pointed out, "to be overlooking one pertinent point, which is that you are really in no position to make protestations." He saw the flush in Ferrers' cheeks deepen, then, as if satisfied his censure had gone home, pointedly glanced in the direction of the unpaid tailor's account on the table, picking it up with his thumb and forefinger to cast a fleeting look at the disheartening reckoning by his creditor. "How many more of these do you have?" he asked, letting the account slip from his fingers, "or don't you know?"

"Of course I do!" Ferrers snapped irritably, annoyed to think he had forgotten to put it away. "Too damned many if you must know!"

"I don't," he shrugged, "but you know, Ferrers," he said dispassionately, "you really have only yourself to blame for this predicament. You seem, do you not, to have been living far beyond your means of late! Indeed," he raised a pencilled eyebrow, "for some considerable time."

"Can I help it if they all decide to dun me at once?" he demanded tetchily, grabbing the offending account and stuffing it into his pocket.

"Apparently not," Lytton replied coolly, "any more than you can help being a fool." Ferrers was about to argue this point, but was immediately forestalled. "I hear you dropped two thousand the other night at Dolly Kilpatrick's to Dalmond; that was not very wise of you," he shook his head. "For one thing," he reminded him, "even private gaming hells have rules and people, you know," he smiled, "however vulgar, talk; and, for another, Dalmond will not expect to be kept waiting overlong for the redemption of your vowels." He saw the colour fade from Ferrers' cheeks and added disparagingly, "Only a fool attempts to solve his difficulties by way of the turf or the tables."

"What else was I to do?" Ferrers demanded peevishly, "with every damned tradesman in town dunning me!"

"It is no more than you deserve," Lytton informed him, quite unmoved. "Already I have offered you a way out of your difficulties, twice if my memory has not erred, and yet you have seen fit to disregard me! Really," he shrugged, "you are *quite* undeserving of my continued observance."

He may not like Lytton's tone, in fact, he bitterly resented it but, lacking the courage to do anything about it, he swallowed the angry retort on his lips and, instead, offered, somewhat lamely, "It is not how it appears, Your Grace! I can explain everything."

"Can you?" he asked sceptically. "I wonder?" he mused, tapping his eye glass against his lips. "How *does* one explain ineptitude and stupidity?" his tone an insult. "You know, Ferrers" he sighed, "it astounds even me how you and your equally inept collaborator have come thus far unscathed, let alone how you could have believed for one tiny instant that Stuart's attempt at insurrection would succeed." He eyed his host derisively. "Between you, you have put me to *quite* an inconvenience; and what is my reward for this?" he demanded, raising those pencilled eyebrows, "disobedience and even more stupidity."

"If you would but give me a moment, Your Grace, I can explain everything," Ferrers urged. Lytton eyed him dispassionately, but remained silent. "It is true that I offered support to Stuart," he said nervously, "but I would never have done so had I not been forced into it."

"Please, do not sully my ears with these lame excuses," Lytton begged, his eyes cold and disdainful. "Neither you nor your equally undeserving associate were forced into anything as you would wish me to believe," he pronounced scathingly. "Both you and your imprudent friend, being of the misguided belief that should Stuart succeed you would be showered with honours, offered your support;" his lips curled "honours which you knew would never be forthcoming otherwise." He saw Ferrers flinch, but continued inexorably, "You had neither affection nor loyalty, much less belief, in Stuart. Indeed, had you have done so, I could more easily pardon you. Your *beliefs*, if such one can call them," he disparaged, "extend only as far as the worth you put upon them and, as such, they really are beneath contempt." His lips thinned and his voice took on a most unpleasant note. "When no one believed Mayhew about information being leaked you thought you had escaped detection. What neither of you inept bunglers realized, nor made the least effort to establish, was that Mayhew was a close friend of your uncle's, and turned to him for help." Ferrers swallowed uncomfortably at this scathing attack. "When Stuart failed you thought you were safe, especially as your cousin's unexplained disappearance meant that suspicion was turned in his direction. You were most fortunate there, were you not, when he unwittingly assisted you and was blamed for your treachery!" he scorned. "But then, you discovered his estimable qualities had been put to excellent use by Mayhew and, he had, in fact, acquired the evidence he had been sent to find; evidence which would prove you guilty of treason." Lytton's lips twisted disdainfully. "So you both panicked until you saw a way out of your difficulties by ensuring the guilt was irrevocably transferred onto him, which would mean that not only would he be arrested for treason," he derided, "but automatically disinherited, enabling you to take up the title which you so desperately covet. But you are not quite out of the wood yet, are you?" he raised a pencilled eyebrow, totally unmoved by Ferrers' dilemma, "especially having managed to allow him to escape from custody."

"I had no hand in that!" Ferrers exclaimed, rising hurriedly to his feet.

"*That*, is no saving grace, I assure you," Lytton told him contemptuously. "You're treading dangerous ground, Ferrers," he pointed out in ominous calm, "particularly as your cousin holds in his possession certain letters; letters that could send you and your friend to the gallows." Ferrers swallowed more convulsively than ever, his eyes mirroring his fear. "Of course," Lytton shrugged expressively, "one can only assume that these letters, which your equally inept confederate was foolish enough to write to Stuart, are in a safe place - so safe, in fact, that your cousin cannot as yet place his hands on them to produce them - were it otherwise,

145

you both of you would have faced your trial for treason long since." He paused long enough to allow this to penetrate Ferrers' scared brain. "Your fears however, are that if he does manage this fete, you are both of you condemned. Do not delude yourself into thinking that your cousin's venture into illicit trading will save your necks," he told him unemotionally, "it won't. For a man of his infinite resource and enterprise, it is only a matter of time before he places his hands on those letters and, once they are produced," he said dispassionately, "all will be forgiven him, while you and your equally incompetent friend, will hang from the nearest gallows!"

Ferrers wiped his mouth on his handkerchief, the scared look in his eyes not lost on his visitor. "I thought they would have been destroyed," he offered. "How was I to know that Stuart would have kept them or that they would have come into Richard's hands?"

"It seems to me," Lytton said nastily, "that thinking is something neither of you have been in the habit of doing; were it otherwise, you would not be in this predicament now."

"Damn you!" Ferrers snapped, taking a hasty turn around the room. "I know we have made a mess of things, but …"

"A gross understatement of the case, I assure you, Ferrers!" Lytton exclaimed disparagingly.

"It's all very well for you," Ferrers shot at him, "you are not the one facing perdition!"

"And nor would you be, had you possessed the least resolution," Lytton reminded him, relieved that his own folly which had resulted in Henderson approaching him in the first place, had not been divulged to Ferrers. "I have already attempted to solve your difficulties only to have my assistance disregarded."

"You don't understand," Ferrers told him, holding his head in his agitated hands, disarraying his very expensive wig.

"I understand perfectly," he was told scornfully. "You and Henderson both looked to attain the impossible but never once paused to consider the implications should Stuart fail. Your hopes of high achievement under the Hanoverians were remote, neither of you being possessed with either the required talent to bring you to notice or the ability to go further; so you cast your line into other directions. Your aspirations, Ferrers," he pointed out unpleasantly, "are never going to be fulfilled under *this* or *any* dynasty. Stuart may have been a fool, but not such a fool as to offer either of you positions of power."

"But he promised that when he …"

"Of course he did" Lytton shrugged, "after all, he had to offer *some* inducement to receive aid. Had you not been so obtuse," he pointed out unpleasantly, "you would have realized that."

Ferrers looked peevish, but bit back the angry retort on his lips. "So," he shrugged, "what do we do now?"

His Grace twirled his eye glass on the end of its ribbon, his eyes contemplative as though this was a vital task. It was a moment or two before he looked at his host and, when he did so, his eyes were full of contempt and disdain, rendering Ferrers acutely uncomfortable. "Once I advised you to take up your inheritance without delay, in law, the estate and title are now yours but, for reasons which I still find incomprehensible, you allowed yourself to be persuaded to wait and, worse, you permitted yourself to be coerced into signing a document to that effect. Really, Ferrers," he shook his head, the smile on his painted lips offensive, "I do declare, I have yet to meet two such fools as you and your bungling friend!"

"Your Grace is unjust!" he cried before he could stop himself.

Ferrers soon learned the mistake of addressing him in such a manner. The pale grey eyes narrowed and the red lips thinned into an ugly line. "My dear Ferrers," he said ominously, "you are anything I choose to call you. You *dare* to address me in such terms again and I shall make you rue the day you ever came in my way."

Ferrers blenched. "I'm sorry, I ..."

"Your apologies," he was told scathingly, "are as worthless as your assurances. Indeed," he shook his head, "I marvel at myself for wasting my time on one who is fully deserving of all that befalls him. When I counselled you to ingratiate yourself with your cousin Elizabeth, in the hope she would confide in you in order to discover Richard's whereabouts, what did you do?" he demanded. "Nothing!" Those grey eyes swept over him, before rising to his feet in a rustle of satin. "I confess," he shrugged, "I am at a loss! For one who finds himself in such precarious straits, you are remarkably slow in remedying the situation. Between you, you and Henderson have failed to either bring your cousin to book or to ensure that he is no longer in a position to threaten you. I have already expended considerable time and effort on this matter, but should you flout my instructions again," he warned menacingly, "I shall have no compunction whatsoever in washing my hands of you and leaving you both to your fate."

Unable to bear the thought of what their fate would be, Ferrers promised that he would not again disregard him. "I swear I will do everything you tell me to." "Very well, then," Lytton nodded after a moment's thought. "When did you last visit Ferrers Court?"

"About two weeks ago. Why?"

"I think perhaps it is time you paid another," Lytton suggested.

Ferrers considered this. "Another! On what pretext?"

"No pretext," he shook his head, "merely as a matter of cousinly concern. She may not have confided in you thus far, but who knows what may befall to render her willing to do so now."

147

Ferrers shook his head, eyeing him cautiously. "If she has not already done so, why should she suddenly change her mind?"

"Why?" Lytton repeated, raising an eyebrow, "because I deem it so," he declared, believing this to be sufficient explanation. "She is, of course, unaware of it at this precise moment," he told him smoothly, "but she is about to receive a visitor."

"A visitor?" Ferrers questioned. "What visitor?"

"Someone who, unless I grossly err," he shook his head at such an absurdity, "will force the issue."

After digesting this for a moment or two and coming to the conclusion that he was by no means happy about this unexpected move to settle matters, Ferrers, plucking up all the courage he could muster, demanded to know not only the identity of this unlooked for individual but why he had felt the need to include him in the first place.

Lytton, far from pleased at having his methods called into question, eyed him with barely concealed disdain, taking a moment before stating coldly that since he and his accomplice seemed incapable of dealing with the situation themselves, they were hardly in a position to query any means he cared to adopt to resolve the matter. Ferrers hastily begged pardon but, even so, he could not help feeling apprehensive at the thought of a third party being included in something he much preferred to keep between themselves. "Your cousin," Lytton explained painstakingly, "after enduring numerous searches of her home, which, regrettably, proved too much for her father, has no doubt had her fill of the military. It is, therefore, natural to conclude that being faced with yet another red-coat whose tactics, however different to those of your inept and bungling friend Henderson, will be bound to have the same effect upon her. No doubt by this time your cousin will be only too relieved at your presence - perhaps even," he suggested, "pleased to have the opportunity to unburden herself and, who knows," he raised an eyebrow, "even be glad to shelve the responsibility of her brother."

"A red-coat?" Ferrers repeated surprised.

Lytton inclined his head. "A masterstroke of genius, wouldn't you say?"

The truth was Ferrers was not at all sure what to say but, since his observations and points of view had already been contemptuously dismissed, he deemed it wiser not to comment further on his chosen strategies. As far as his cousin being influenced by a stranger was concerned, and a red-coat at that, he could not help but feel that His Grace was being a little too optimistic but, since he was none too eager to be on the receiving end of that rapier sharp tongue yet again, he merely shook his head. "Are you suggesting that she does indeed know where Richard is?"

Really, he was quite unworthy of his attention! Lytton sighed, not quite able to hide his impatience, but said, with remarkable restraint, "I think that more than probable. I find it hard to believe that he is in Sussex and so close to his estates, yet she knows nothing of it."

Ferrers nodded. "There's something in that," he conceded. "Indeed," he admitted, "I have often wondered whether she was aware of it." He paused momentarily, eyeing his visitor cautiously before pointing out, not unreasonably, "But what makes you think she will tell me anything? She has not so far. The pair of them were always as thick as thieves and she is bound to put her brother first."

Lytton nodded. "Yes, that is quite possible but, do not forget, she has had plenty of time since her father's death to think things over. Of course," he acknowledged, "I can readily understand her reluctance to make a confession to Henderson, whose bungling attempts were doomed to failure as anyone but a fool would have known but, now, it could well be that she is only too willing to have your ear into which she can pour her concerns, especially if this latest representative of the military gives her food for thought."

Again Ferrers pondered what he had been told before asking abruptly, "What else do you know about Richard that I do not?"

"Considering I have never met your cousin and my information is as limited as yours," he replied, an inflexion of surprise in his voice, "I know as much about him as you do. However," he told him indifferently, "I know that for his smuggling activities he is going to be 'gazetted' and, I think, you know what *that* implies," he inclined his head.

Ferrers stared aghast. "I hope to God that never gets out!" he exclaimed.

Lytton looked him over from head to foot with scathing contempt. "The intention is that it should. Why else does one have a man 'gazetted'?"

Ferrers flushed a little at this, but demanded, frustrated, "What the devil made him take to smuggling anyway?"

"If you do not understand that," His Grace remarked coldly, "then you understand nothing."

Unable to find the courage to utter the retort on his lips at such dismissive mockery, he asked "Do you think his cronies will turn tail on him?"

"Who knows?" he shrugged. "One would have thought so. After all, five hundred pounds is a lot money but, then," he sighed, "one never can tell what the vulgar will do, or why they do it; they are really quite unfathomable. In any event," he pointed out reasonably "*you*, at least, must hope and pray they do, but if," he suggested meaningfully, lowering his eyes to scrutinize his painted finger nails, "he was dealt with before that eventuality arose it would save a deal of awkwardness, and you," he nodded, raising his head "would come into your inheritance at last."

William Ferrers did not need to have this inference explained, its meaning was plain enough and, whilst he may have no stomach for such work, honesty compelled him to admit that his options of resolving the issue at hand were somewhat restricted. It was true that he had always enjoyed a fairly good relationship with Elizabeth, but he could not see her relenting and confiding in him any more than she ever had. He had no doubt at all that should this red-coat, whoever he was, prove to be as ruthless in his dealings with her as Colonel Henderson had, then not only would she be more than capable of defending herself as well as ignoring any warnings or threats he may dangle over her head but, he for one, held out very little hope of her looking to him for protection, let alone open her mind to him.   As far as Richard was concerned, he could not deny that he would not be overly sorry to see an end of him but, the subtly suggested alternative for dealing with him, apart from making him fervently hope that he would not be the one to have to bring it about, rendered him acutely uncomfortable. He realized perfectly well that he could not go on living indefinitely on credit or his expectations, which, unfortunately, were by no means certain, but when he finally took possession of the title and everything that went with it he wanted no questions raised as to the legitimacy of his claim or how he had attained it. He knew as well as anyone that no man accused of treason could inherit from his father and, not for the first time, he found himself railing against his stupidity in giving his uncle that promise but, worse than this, was signing that paper Pritchard had presented him with.   If only he had been able to find a way of getting Elizabeth to trust him there would have been no difficulty in passing on his whereabouts to the right quarter, and he could then have left his cousin's demise to the law with no finger of blame pointed in his direction but, resorting to the more distasteful alternative Lytton had delicately intimated, was something he had not even so much as contemplated.

"Since your cousin is proving to be most elusive," Lytton broke into his unpleasant thoughts, "and his sister is no nearer divulging his whereabouts to your accomplice any more than she is in confiding in you, it would appear that other stratagems will have to be employed in order to track him down, especially if you fail again to secure her trust when next you visit her." He eyed Ferrers calculatingly for several moments.   "In fact, I understand that there *is* one at Ferrers Court who probably knows where your misguided cousin may be found."

"What!" he exclaimed. "You mean Salmon?"

"If that is his name, yes. Perhaps he could assist you to locate your troublesome relative."

"Much chance of that!" he cried. "For one thing, he don't like me above half and, for another, if he *does* know where Richard is he would die rather than disclose it!"

"I have no doubt it would require a great deal of tact and persuasion to induce him to divulge such information," Lytton commented, adding smoothly, "but I have yet to meet a man who did not have his price."

William Ferrers eyed his visitor aghast. "What! Well, if you think that," he told him candidly, momentarily forgetting to whom he spoke, "all I can say is that you know nothing about it. *Salmon*, taking bribes!" he scorned. "I wish I may see it!"

"I bow to your superior knowledge of him," Lytton inclined his head, perfectly prepared to overlook Ferrers' temerity in speaking to him so a moment ago. "You must not be thinking that I am unappreciative of the dilemma facing you," he smiled thinly, "I assure you I am but, since your cousin has so far refused to adopt anything like a conciliatory attitude in this matter and, one can, of course, only hazard a guess as to what her reaction will be to the presence of yet another representative of the military," he shrugged exaggeratedly, "one has to face the fact that this man of Richard's may well be the only link you have to him." He saw the scowl descend onto William's face and, although he had no patience with those who made not the least push to help themselves, he was quite prepared to ignore it, since he, as much as his host and partner in treason, wanted to make a quick end of Richard Ferrers, because the longer he remained on the run, the more chance there was of Henderson losing what little wits he had and, therefore, no reliance could be placed on him keeping their dealings to himself. The last thing he wanted was the reason for his involvement in this distasteful affair to be made known, because no one knew better than he how Henderson was by no means capable of holding his tongue or his nerve in a crisis. He saw the frown deepen on William Ferrers' forehead and bit down his irritation, saying, with spurious sympathy, his voice mellifluously smooth, "It is most unfortunate that necessity has a way of compelling us into doing something we would much rather not; but, desperation, my dear Ferrers, requires desperate measures and, I am *very* much afraid," he nodded, "that this is one such occasion when your situation demands you respond to it." He resumed the scrutiny of his painted fingernails, his eyes beneath his heavily veiled lids watchful. "I am not unmindful of how provoking it is to be obliged to approach one who, well - what shall I say?" he smiled, "is a mere servant but, there are times when one does, regrettably, find oneself entirely dependent upon them. This is one such time when you really *must* steel yourself for such a degrading task; unpalatable I know," he nodded, looking mournfully up at William Ferrers, "but, when faced with the alternative you will agree, I am sure, feel it expedient." Removing his Sevres stuff box from his pocket he deftly flicked the lid and delicately took a pinch allowing William Ferrers time to let his flowing eloquence sink in. "Were it not for those letters, the urgency attached to your enterprising cousin's apprehension would not be quite so acute but, regrettably, they have given him the means whereby he does, unhappily, hold your future as well as Henderson's in his hands," he pointed out in a honeyed voice. "Of course, it is no small matter to approach one for whom one has no liking, and a mere servant at that but, the longer view must be considered, indeed, it is imperative it is not ignored and, therefore, I am confident that you will find the right words in which to bring about his change of mind." His Grace, an unparalleled exponent in the art of verbal seduction, was playing on William Ferrers' worst fears with devastating effect; his sinuous and tempting eloquence seeping into his scared brain with a deadly accuracy which was acting on him like a powerful stimulus. Ensuring the seeds he had planted would take root, he pitilessly embroidered his theme, turning the screw with such cruel delicacy that his host was almost beguiled. "Needless to say," he said with specious sincerity, "I am fully conscious of how demeaning it is to be obliged to lower oneself to the level of such as he but, your affairs will not wait upon such niceties. Should your cousin prove herself reticent yet again, then I am sure that a man of your acumen will be easily able to break down any reserve this man may have. I realize, of course," he went on smoothly, "that for men with such exquisite sensibilities as us, recoil from the distasteful necessity of having to embark on such a painful task but, since Henderson has failed to locate your cousin and dispose of him legally and both of you face exposure as well as the gallows should those letters be produced, I fear the time has come when we must aside our personal preferences. It is, I need hardly say," he sighed, "regrettable to own that the unpalatable alternative to your dilemma, however repugnant to one of such discernment as yourself, must be adopted after all."

Unaware that he had been dexterously manoeuvred into a position from which there was no withdrawing, Ferrers, under His Grace's compelling articulacy, had not only pictured a secure future for himself and his confederate but had entirely failed to see that His Grace, to ensure his own self-protection, had skilfully manipulated him into putting a period to his cousin's existence. He owned it would be a tremendous relief to rid himself of all his difficulties, and the thought of what the future held without Richard being around to thwart him by any means at his disposal, was a pleasing prospect. His Grace had spoken no less than the truth when he said that his ever resourceful cousin would put his hands on those letters one way or another; perhaps not today or tomorrow but at some point when he least expected it, exposing him as a traitor; the very thought making him feel sick. Even so, it did not make him feel any easier when he considered what bringing about Richard's demise would entail. It seemed it was to be his hand that would set the seal on his cousin's fate, after all! Should Elizabeth indeed decide, for whatever reason, to divulge her brother's whereabouts to him, or, for that matter, Salmon, he was uncomfortably aware of the unenviable choices which would face him. Of the two, he much preferred the safer option of anonymously informing against him thereby allowing the authorities to either arrest him, or, which was more than likely, shoot him on sight. The second and, by far the less favoured option, was seeking out his cousin and putting a period to his existence himself, the mere thought of which made him inwardly recoil. It was not merely because he lacked the courage and fortitude he readily boasted he possessed to his friends and acquaintances which rendered him totally unable to look Richard in the face and engage him in a fair fight but, also, because his cousin was far too skilful with a pistol and had never been known to miss his shot. As far as attempting to eliminate him at the sword point was concerned, not only had his cousin been taught by the best fencing master in London but he possessed a natural ability in using this viciously cold weapon. The thought of facing his cousin using either of these armaments did nothing to endear him to the scheme, in truth, the very idea made him shiver but, even so, there was no avoiding the fact that should he remove Richard by his own hand he would, out of necessity, have no alternative but to resort to using means which, should it ever become known, could only be described as stealthy and cowardly. Taking Richard unawares or even from behind, would be the only way he could achieve his demise but, it was not something he could contemplate without revulsion. Nevertheless, the plain truth was that only Richard's death would save him from climbing the scaffold as a traitor or entering a debtors prison as a result of being unable to discharge his ever growing mountain of obligations but, since neither of these ends to his fluctuating career held any appeal for him, he was forced to accept that, one way or the other, Richard would have to be disposed of. He was not overly squeamish when it came to witnessing something particularly gruesome but, to actually take part in a brutal act himself was another matter entirely and, just the thought of having to either face his cousin man to man or employing some devious means to deal with him, was something that gave him considerable food for thought. Had it been anyone other than his own cousin there was every possibility he could pluck up the courage to do whatever was necessary, as it was, he was honest enough to admit that he would much rather let someone else do it for him. He and Richard had never been close, his cousin being far too autocratic and top lofty, unlike Elizabeth, who, although proud, had always treated him with civility. It seemed that protecting his interests and claiming what was, in his opinion at least, rightfully his, was proving to be far more problematical than he had had any idea of but, since the time had come when he could no longer shelve the unpalatable task ahead of him and dark clouds were fast gathering over his head, he mentally braced himself for what was to come, devoutly praying that no one would ever know of his involvement in the downfall of his cousin.

Lytton, watching with keen interest the various emotions flit across Ferrers' face as he paced anxiously up and down, knew that no matter how much he lacked the stomach to do what was required of him, he would, no matter how distasteful, ultimately agree, and waited patiently for him to come to a halt in front of him.

"Very well, Your Grace," he nodded, putting him in mind of a scared rabbit, "I'll find my cousin and do whatever is necessary."

"I knew I could rely upon you to see sense," he said approvingly. "And only think," he smiled thinly, "how much more comfortable you will be when you have honoured all your obligations."

"I own I shall find it a relief to clear myself," he admitted, wishing there was another and, by far safer way, of doing it.

"I do not doubt it," Lytton acknowledged, "not to mention the threat of the scaffold receding."

The thought made Ferrers blench but, deciding it best not to think too deeply on this horrifying aspect, heartily agreed. Then, as if suddenly bethinking himself of something, said tentatively, "I hope I have no need to tell Your Grace how much I welcome your assistance but," shaking his head, "I do not quite understand why you are involving yourself in this."

A steely look entered those cold grey eyes and the painted lips thinned. "My dear Ferrers," he said with menacing calm, "there are some things which do not concern you, and this is one of them. Content yourself with knowing that very soon your difficulties will be at an end." Ferrers heard the threat distinctly. "As for you welcoming my sponsorship," he remarked coolly, slowly drawing his gloves over his hands, "you have yet to prove your gratitude by doing what is required of you. By the by," he commented casually, giving Ferrers no opportunity to respond to this rebuke, "I trust I do not have to emphasize the need for discretion. It would not do to alert the interested to my visit here today!"

Ferrers looked a little wary, but nodded comprehendingly. "I understand, Your Grace."

"I do hope so," he was told, the smile not quite reaching those cold eyes. "I should not take it kindly if my visit was commented upon."

"It won't, Your Grace," Ferrers assured him, the very thought of his retribution making him sweat, "I give you my word."

His word was very far from satisfactory and a frown descended onto Lytton's forehead. "That man of yours; can he be trusted?"

"Yes, Your Grace," Ferrers hastily assured him. "He can be as close as a clam when the occasion demands it."

"This had better be one such occasion," Lytton warned, turning towards the door.

"What are you going to do now, Your Grace?" Ferrers demanded, his voice a little high, reflecting his agitation.

Lytton eyed him speculatively for a moment as if debating whether to answer him. "I" he said softly, "am going to repair into Sussex."

"Sussex!" Ferrers echoed.

"A most beautiful county," Lytton smiled.

"Yes, but ..."

"All you need concern yourself with," he was told dismissively, "is that you do not fail a third time. Please, do not render it necessary for me to have to expend any further effort on this matter; my patience will not bear it." On this parting note he swept majestically out of the room leaving Ferrers in a mood bordering on relief and something he could not quite define. Having set his foot on the path towards his salvation, he tried not to allow his mind to dwell on it nor on the consequences should what he had agreed to this morning leak out, much less that it should fail.

CHAPTER EIGHT

Not until Elizabeth Ferrers was lost from Gideon's sight did he make any attempt to ride on. His decision to embark on a reconnaissance of the area was purely to familiarize himself with a locality her brother and his associates not only frequented but knew very well, and not with the intention of deliberately trying to see if he could come upon her, much less in the hope of doing so. It had been quite by chance therefore, that he had happened upon her and, although he was not quite able to believe his good fortune in having done so, considering that Cuckmere Valley was not that far distant from her home, he supposed he should have known that there would be occasions when she would visit this particular spot.

He had no doubt his friends would recommend caution in his dealings with Elizabeth Ferrers, not only because she could easily take advantage of his feelings for her by cleverly exploiting them in the furtherance of her brother's cause but, also, because it was not possible to fall in love on so short an acquaintance. Certainly to date, his amatory experiences, whilst thoroughly enjoyable while they had lasted, had not encompassed love and, consequently, prior to yesterday, he would undoubtedly have agreed with this very reasonable point of view. Now though, having met Elizabeth Ferrers, he had not only proved that it was entirely possible to fall in love at first sight but, more importantly, knew that his feelings for her rendered at a stroke his past affairs as nothing other than empty and meaningless. His head may still spin at the swiftness with which it had happened and in the most unlikely of circumstances too but, from the instant he had set eyes on her, somewhere deep inside him he knew that at long last he had found the woman for whom he had been searching his whole adult life.

He could not blame her for distrusting any man who wore a scarlet coat, after all, her treatment at their hands had been very far from what he would expect of those who wore the King's uniform and, for this reason, her hesitancy to place her trust in him was perfectly understandable. In view of this then, he could only be relieved that she had eventually come to see that by putting her faith in him was the only way she could possibly help her brother and, by promoting a meeting between them this evening, was, if nothing else, certainly a step in the right direction. She may be prepared to do everything which lay within her power to aid her brother but, from what he had seen of her, she was far too honest and forthright to resort to such subterfuge as taking advantage of his feelings, in fact, he would own himself astonished to discover that such a thought had crossed her mind   Setting aside the fact that he was not without experience where the female sex was concerned, he was an excellent judge of character and more than capable of recognizing guile when he saw it and, intuitively knew, that far from considering how best to use him to her own advantage, no such thought had entered her head.

He shrewdly guessed that, despite what must have been a very successful London season, she had never before been in love and, unless he grossly mistook the case, he would say that her feelings for him were very far from detached but, however inexperienced she may be he felt certain that she could not fail to see that he was anything but indifferent to her, as well as recognizing his sincerity regarding her brother.

If nothing else, their conversation this morning had gone a long way to not only reinforcing his belief that she was not wholly impervious to him but that her brother was innocent of treason. Unfortunately, it also confirmed his view that if Richard Ferrers was to be brought home safe, then he could expect to be faced with numerous difficulties and, unless he was very much mistaken her cousin might well turn out to be one of them.

He found it incredibly hard to believe that any man, even one of such a weak character as William Ferrers, would sign away what was legally his merely because it was asked of him. In law the title and estates were his, as Elizabeth Ferrers herself had acknowledged and, whilst he could understand her father making such a stipulation, he nevertheless failed to see how her cousin could possibly have allowed himself to be so easily persuaded. He was convinced that had William Ferrers consulted legal counsel he would have been advised against signing such a document but, as this was apparently not the case, he could well understand Elizabeth Ferrers' comment about him wanting Richard's affairs settled as soon as may be possible. What he did not understand was why William Ferrers had committed himself to such a binding agreement in the first place, especially as it appeared that he was by no means financially secure. When he considered the evidence stacked against Richard Ferrers, whether fabricated or not, all the signs pointed to him being guilty as charged and therefore disinherited. In his opinion, this fact alone should surely have told his cousin that it would take a miracle to extricate Richard from his difficulties in order for him to assume his father's dignities and, this being so, he found his actions incomprehensible. What was even more incomprehensible about him signing such a document was that considering Richard had managed to evade capture all this while, and there was no reason to believe he would not continue to do so, then William must surely know that he could well be waiting to take up his inheritance for some considerable time to come.

Salmon's part in the affair had been expected, in fact, he would have been astonished if he had not known of his young master's movements but, he knew, if

Lytton did not, that a man like Salmon, who was looked upon as virtually one of the family, could not be coerced into informing against him. The idea of trying to either trick or bribe Salmon into divulging Richard Ferrers' whereabouts had never entered his head, not only would such conduct kill at a stroke any hope he had of gaining his trust should it ever be discovered but, the very thought made him recoil in disgust. But his forbearance had born fruit, resulting in a very satisfactory outcome. At least, he had Salmon to thank for arranging the meeting this evening with Richard Ferrers.

As far as his sister was concerned, he had seen enough of her to know that she was innocent of the charges Colonel Henderson laid at her door and that she had not known where her brother was to be found or of Salmon's regular contact with him until yesterday. It was not because he was allowing his feelings for her to cloud his judgement, but because he genuinely believed her to be telling the truth. He was certain that she could not have confided in him the way she had unless she had been innocent and, although she had tried to make light of her uncertain future, there had been no disguising the sadness this thought brought her, or the fact that she had been very much upset by her father's untimely death. But there had been no ambiguity in her opinion of Colonel Henderson or that she held him personally responsible for what happened.

That she loved her brother as well as having absolute faith in his loyalties was unquestionable, and he could only hope that she would not take it into her head to do something to aid him which would make matters infinitely worse than they already were. He also hoped that she would keep her promise and stay away from Richard until such time as his name was cleared and he could once again take up his rightful place in society.

Having lost her from sight, Gideon turned his horse and headed in the direction of Seaford, a few miles further along the coast. He had deliberately kept his destination from her, having a pretty shrewd idea of her reaction at what he was going to do but, if he was to convince Colonel Henderson that he was doing all he could to apprehend Richard Ferrers, then he had to make it appear as though he was doing precisely that. A visit to the Riding Officer for the area therefore, would go a long way to substantiating this.

It had not taken him long to arrive at a fairly accurate assessment of Colonel Henderson's character and temperament and, whilst he knew that he had been faced with no other choice but having to hand over full authority to him in this matter, his pride had taken quite a beating because of it. It was not simply because he was not of equal rank, although this was humiliating enough but, the truth was, he would dearly love to be the one responsible for apprehending Richard Ferrers and not some junior officer brought in specifically for the purpose. Although Colonel Henderson had agreed to go along with his idea of how to deal with this affair, Gideon would not put it beyond him to work behind his back. In fact, he suspected that nothing would give him greater pleasure than to be able to see him removed from any further involvement in this matter.

In the short time he had been here he had seen enough of the coastal terrain to understand why this particular stretch of coast was ideal for landing smuggled goods. It was perfect for such work, especially under the cover of darkness. Their activities may be against the law, but he had to admire the resource of these men. Getting heavy goods up the six hundred foot high cliff would be no easy task and would require organization and ingenuity as well as daring and determination to ensure their cargo reached its destination. Then, of course, there was keeping a watchful eye for Riding Officers and Excise cutters which was why he believed landing the goods here at the entrance to Cuckmere Valley would make far more sense.

It took him almost an hour to reach Seaford, a quiet fishing village bearing all the appearance of being quite removed from illicit trafficking and the harbouring of desperate law-breakers. He had no need to ask the way to the Preventive Office, spotting the small grey stone building almost immediately as he rode into the village. Situated on the cliff top a couple of hundred yards from the edge, he could see at a glance that it would afford the hapless individual in charge an unrestricted view out to sea.

Captain Waring, the hard pressed Riding Officer, soon disabused Gideon's mind of any illusions it may have had about the peace and tranquillity of the area. He was a man of about thirty two years of age and, whilst he could not be described as handsome precisely, he was pleasantly good looking in a quiet, unremarkable sort of way. He was a diligent and earnest young man and one who took his duties very seriously, but it was apparent from the harassed expression on his face that his work was becoming increasingly more difficult and frustrating. Over a tankard of ale inside his rather cramped quarters he was only too eager to pour the difficulties facing him and his colleagues into Gideon's ears, relating the numerous occasions they had been tricked by these people.

"Everyone is involved in the trade, Major," he complained. "You would not believe the lengths they go to to confuse and trick us officials. Even the parson allows church property to be used for the storage of run goods but, when we search the place, there's not a keg to be seen!"

He then went on to recount many such instances of the same nature, bitterly animadverting on the information which they had received only to discover that either it had turned out to be false or the villainous rogues had had word of a search and cleared everything out.

"When we receive news of a pending run," he commented bitterly, "it turns out to be nothing more than a hoax, and the chances are the goods have been landed elsewhere! The night before last, for instance," he nodded, "we had word that a run was due several miles along the coast and, what happened?" he demanded scornfully, "Nothing! Over three hours we kept watch but not a sign of a run did we see! Even those who are not involved in the trade," he complained, "knows those who are but they will not give them away no matter what inducements are offered them."

Gideon sympathized and replied suitably, but his attention was soon caught when Captain Waring advised him of the difficulties Colonel Henderson had also encountered in his efforts to stem the trade. Gideon listened to him with keen interest but, when he asked him if he knew of Richard Ferrers, he sat forward in his seat, his dull grey eyes taking on a sharpness that had not been there before. Certainly he knew Richard Ferrers, or, rather, he had heard of him. He would give a month's pay to get his hands on him, even more so when he considered his treasonable activities but, although he had never actually been caught in the act of running illicit goods, everyone knew that he did so.

"You cannot prove his complicity, then?" Gideon asked.

"No, Major, I cannot!" he said, disheartened. "But what, I ask you, can one expect when his accomplices lie and cover up for him? Even Colonel Henderson, who has been within a hair's breadth of catching him more than once, found he has slipped through his fingers! I consider myself a fair man, Major," he told him matter of factly, "but I would lay you any odds that the other night's run was the work of Ferrers!"

It was obvious to Gideon that Richard Ferrers was held in great respect by his confederates; whether this was due entirely or in part to who he was he was not quite certain but, it gave him some glimmer of hope in that any charges of smuggling brought against him could be argued away easily enough. Clearly, Colonel Henderson had been the one to point Captain Waring in Richard Ferrers' direction in the first place, cleverly linking his name with the smuggling trade in order to gain his help in apprehending him. However, one could not be accused of something without evidence and, if Captain Waring was right, then Richard Ferrers had never actually been found red-handed running cargoes at all!

Colonel Henderson, deeply distrusting of Elizabeth Ferrers, had listened eagerly to Gideon's edited version of his first meeting with her, but remained convinced that his methods were still the best. He informed him in no uncertain terms that the only way she would be brought to tell the truth was by arresting her as an accomplice to her brother's crimes and bringing her in for questioning. It had taken much time and patience on Gideon's part to persuade him that this was not the answer, playing for much needed time by cleverly pointing out that by allowing her to enjoy her freedom she would sooner or later give herself away but, once officially brought in for questioning, she would be on her guard and, thus, any chance of catching her in collusion with her brother would be lost.

Much struck by this point of view, Colonel Henderson, after deliberating this reasoning for several minutes, nodded his full approval of such a plan of action, unaware of the deep sigh of relief which escaped Gideon's lips.

He was to heave another sigh of relief the following afternoon when Colonel Henderson showed his further approval upon learning of his visit to the Riding Officer at Seaford that morning. He may have been a little surprised to learn that his reconnaissance of the area had taken place at what he considered to be a ridiculously early hour but, it was nevertheless rather encouraging to think that he was at last taking this matter more seriously; giving him to hope that it would not now be long before this thorn in his side was caught and hung. Had he have known of Gideon's accidental meeting with Elizabeth Ferrers prior to his visit to Seaford and the gist of their conversation, he would not have been quite so optimistic.

Despite Gideon's relief at Colonel Henderson's reception of his news, blissfully unaware of the understanding which was growing between himself and Elizabeth Ferrers, he received Colonel Henderson's direct question as to what his plans now were with a little caution. It would not do to let him suspect that he was keeping the truth from him so, instead, elected to generalize by saying that he thought it best if he continued to familiarize himself with the locality first, getting to know the haunts of the men who participated in the smuggling trade and working more closely with Captain Waring, which should, hopefully, result in the eventual arrest of the fugitive. Again, Colonel Henderson nodded his approval, fast coming to the conclusion that he had grossly misjudged this young man.

Gideon had scaled the first hurdle in his efforts to protect Richard Ferrers and his sister from Colonel Henderson's private war against them, but he had every reason to believe that he was going to be called upon to be even more mendaciously creative before very long. Of course, without results, Colonel Henderson would not be placated indefinitely but, at least, Gideon now had some idea of how his mind, always suggestible to proposals and ideas, worked, which gave him much needed lee-way in his dealings with him, while at the same time trying to discover the truth about Richard Ferrers in the little time he had available.

Thanks to Lieutenant Beaton's map, he could clearly see that Westbourne was at least three miles to the north-east of Little Turton but, unfortunately, as he was a stranger to the area and unfamiliar with local tracks and shorter routes, he would have to follow the more clearly visible roadway which, unfortunately, would take far longer. He could only hazard a guess as to the condition of the roads leading to it, even at this time of year but, unless something untoward occurred to mar his progress, he had no doubt he would find it easily enough.

Captain Waring, whose sole efforts to stem the trade along this particular stretch of coast had proven to be quite ineffectual, despite his diligence and determination, had meant him seeking a more closer collaboration between himself and the garrison at Hampton Regis. Gideon could quite easily understand his frustration, because although this may be a farming community quite a large number of them supplemented their legitimate, if meagre, income, by assisting the 'Gentlemen', and therefore no inducement this enthusiastic young man could put forward had brought forth dividends. They may not actively smuggle the goods in, but they were not averse to keeping an eye open for Excisemen, or to running the pony trains of cargoes to their various inland destinations; land smugglers, Captain Waring had called them who, notwithstanding his exasperation, had been honest enough to admit that farming on the Downs was a hard life with few rewards and, their illicit sideline apart, they were generally honest men. "Do not take that to mean, Major," he had said earnestly, "that I approve or condone such illicit behaviour; I do not. High taxation or not," he had stated unequivocally, "the law is the law and it must be complied with!" Honest men or not, Gideon felt it reasonably safe to assume that *'The Moonshadow'* would enjoy their custom and, this being so, they would not take kindly to a stranger in their midst, and certainly not one in a scarlet coat.

Since Colonel Henderson did not venture from his quarters unless specifically required to do so, Gideon was therefore able to leave his own without the risk of running into him; the last thing he wanted was to be faced with a barrage of questions which he would rather not have to answer. If the farrier sergeant felt any surprise at seeing Major Neville enter the stables out of uniform and being asked to saddle his horse, he did not show it and, since Gideon saw no necessity in enlightening him as to why he was dressed in a sober brown coat with matching breeches and top boots and with his dark hair tied in a black bow at the nape of his neck, forgoing his white wig, he was able to mount his horse without any awkward questions.

Emerging from the garrison, Gideon turned right out of the gates and made his way up the main street at a sedate pace. Not until he had left the town behind him did he spur his horse to a trot, steering south-west, heading in the direction of Glynde. He calculated it was a good twelve miles to Westbourne and, being a stranger to the area, had allowed himself plenty of time in case of taking a wrong turn, but his unerring sense of direction did not fail him and, eventually, he rode through the village of Alfriston just as the church clock struck the half hour. Taking the road out of Alfriston, which would lead him in a northerly direction to Westbourne, he entirely failed to appreciate the beauty of his surroundings or the delicate perfume of the wild rose bushes intermingling with hawthorns banked on either side of the road; his mind focused totally on the evening ahead. Having been born on his father's country estate in Wiltshire, where he had spent a happy and idyllic childhood with Aubrey, he had a natural love of the countryside but, tonight, his mind was solely on his meeting with Richard Ferrers and not on the beauty of the landscape.

Even supposing Richard Ferrers to be as desperate as Colonel Henderson would have him believe, he was not such a fool that he would resort to harming a man in the service of the King. This being so, no such thoughts of being led into a trap entered his head or even that Ferrers would not show himself, if, for no other reason, than he was bound to be curious as to who he was and the precise nature of his motives.

Westbourne, a typical Downs village, bore all the appearance of a sleepy backwater, nestling comfortably at the foot of the South Downs, yet, beneath this tranquil surface, he had the feeling it was alive with activity and that his progress through the village was being watched by numerous pairs of wary eyes. After passing the forge on the right hand side with the church and parsonage to his left, set a little off the road next to a stagnant duck pond, he rode on past the rows of cottages on either side of the main street leading through the village until he came to 'The Moonshadow', located at the far end on the left hand side of the street. It could clearly lay no claim to being a posting inn and he doubted they did very much trade from passing vehicles but solely reliant upon local custom or the odd traveller having lost his way. It was a low and rambling building built on two storeys, covered overall with a thatched roof. The sash windows were small and well covered from prying eyes and the noise which emanated from within suggested a taproom full of people. Whether they were smugglers or not, they would instantly recognize a stranger in their midst and, since he had no idea what Richard Ferrers looked like and he held out little hope of any one of them telling him if he was already here, he prepared himself for an indefinite and, most probably, hostile wait.

Handing his horse over to the young boy who had emerged from the small stable at the rear of the inn, not altogether surprised at being called out at this hour, he stared wide eyed at Gideon's mare, an animal he had no hesitation in describing as a 'bang up prancer'. After assuring Gideon she would be looked after proper, he grabbed the coin which was tossed at him with a grin, leading the mare into the back yard, leaving Gideon to quickly look around him before striding across the short distance to the inn and lifting the latch of the solid oak door.

It opened with a seering scrape onto a small square step from where an inner door led into the taproom down two deep and well-worn stone steps. He found himself in a surprisingly large room, but the low beamed ceiling and closed windows afforded little or no escape for the pipe fumes and the strong smell of ale hanging heavy in the air, neither of which seemed to be bothering the patrons. Upon his entrance the noise abated almost immediately, every face suddenly turned in his direction, their expressions ranging from surprise to caution. Men in smocks and some in woollen cloth coats with battered tricorne hats, stood or sat with tankards held in their hands staring guardedly across at him but, apart from a natural wariness in their eyes, he was allowed unmolested passage to the counter. The landlord, a burly faced and uncommunicative individual, looked cautiously at the newcomer, then as if deciding he meant none of them any harm or, perhaps, because he had been informed by Richard Ferrers of his visit, cocked his head, which Gideon inferred to mean that he was being asked what he wanted. Since ale seemed to be the popular beverage he asked for the same, quite unprepared for the large tankard of local brew thrust at him, far stronger than that offered him by Captain Waring. After handing the landlord a coin, Gideon looked around the room to see that his presence was still causing something of a stir but, undaunted by their interest as well as the caution in their behaviour, he sauntered across the uneven stone-flagged floor where he sat down on the empty settle by the huge inglenook fire, with nothing to do but await the arrival of Richard Ferrers. He had no need to look around him to know that numerous pairs of wary eyes were still looking in his direction, having a very good idea as to the meaning of their whispered mutterings but, since he appeared to be harmless enough, the noise soon picked up as they resumed their various conversations.

The fire was desultory, the odd flickering flame showing itself occasionally between the gusts of smoke, and Gideon, eyeing its failing efforts to get started, wondered when Richard Ferrers would show himself. It had struck him that he may well be here already but, just as he was on the point of turning round to see if he could possibly recognize him amongst a sea of faces, he felt someone slide onto the seat beside him, immediately followed by a pistol being dug into his ribs.

"Good evening, Major. No, no, do not turn around," he told him just as Gideon was about to look at who had joined him. "You will oblige me by continuing to look straight into the fire."

"Ferrers!" Gideon exclaimed, putting his tankard calmly down on the table.

"At your service, Sir," Richard returned in a pleasant voice. "I am sorry if I startled you and spoiled your enjoyment of Sussex's best ale," he told him humorously, "but I shall not detain you long."

"You are too kind," Gideon inclined his head.

"Not at all, Major," he assured him. "I infinitely regret the necessity for this charade," Richard apologized, "but I feel sure you will understand."

"I do not find a pistol stuck in my ribs conducive to understanding," Gideon told him.

"My apologies Major but, one cannot, after all, be too careful," Richard explained.

"You're damned polite, Sir" Gideon told him.

"Well Sir," he pointed out, his cultured voice full of humour, "whatever my crimes, I *am* a gentleman!"

"So it would seem," Gideon replied cynically, indicating the pistol by a movement of his hand. "It may surprise you to know, Ferrers," Gideon told him, "but I have a strange dislike of conversing with someone when I cannot see their face."

"Once again my apologies, Major," Richard offered, "but until I get to know you better, I feel much safer this way."

"Whether I see your face or not," Gideon informed him truthfully, "you have nothing to fear from me."

"Do I not? Then if that is so, why are you here?" Richard asked reasonably. "Colonel Henderson must be desperate indeed if he has sent you here looking for me."

"Then you do not know?" Gideon asked, under the impression that Salmon would have told him, feeling the renewed pressure of the pistol in his side when he was about to turn his head.

"Know what?" Richard asked sharply.

"I thought your man would have told you," Gideon remarked.

"Told me what?" Richard demanded.

"That I am not here on Colonel Henderson's behalf, but under the direct orders of General Sir John Turville in London," Gideon explained.

"So," Richard mused, "he's called in reinforcements, as he?" unconsciously echoing his sister's thoughts.

"Not in the way you think," Gideon told him.

"Turville?" Richard pondered, turning the name over in his mind. "I seem to know that name."

"You should," Gideon told him, "he and your father were the best of friends."

"Ah yes, I remember now," Richard nodded. "I do seem to recall having met him once or twice."

"Then you should know you can trust him," Gideon said firmly.

"My father was no fool Major, indeed, he was most astute. But tell me," he questioned, "why should I put my trust in someone I've only laid eyes on a couple or three times in my life?"

"I never had the pleasure of knowing your father," Gideon told him, "but I know General Turville, indeed, I have served under him for most of my service and, with the exception of my father, I know of no better or more honest man."

Richard digested this. "Are you saying he believes me to be innocent?"

"Implicitly but, in order to establish your innocence," Gideon explained, "we not only need proof, but your cooperation."

"What makes him so sure I am innocent?" he demanded. "After all, he does not know me."

"He knew your father," Gideon told him, "and that is more than enough to convince him. He held him in great esteem," he assured him.

Richard considered this for a moment before saying circumspectly, "I am, of course, grateful, not to say relieved but, if that is indeed the case Major, how come I am still being sought by Colonel Henderson? He seems to know no bounds in his dealings, in fact, he treats my home and sister with contempt. Is his desperation so great that he disregards not only the law but what is due to my sister?"

"You are right in thinking he is desperate," Gideon acknowledged. "Unless I miss my guess, he would give all he possessed to see you hang. He is already convinced that you and your sister are in league against him in his efforts to bring you to trial. In fact," Gideon told him truthfully, "I would say that if he could dispense with a trial he would. He will stop at nothing to apprehend you."

"My sister knew nothing of my whereabouts until that fool of a man of mine blabbed the whole to her!" Richard exclaimed. "And as far as Colonel Henderson is concerned, I shall repay him handsomely for treating my home and sister with such disdain."

"You will do as seems best to you, Ferrers" Gideon said, "providing, of course, your name can be cleared but, from where I am sitting, you are in no position to do anything."

"And what is more, Major" he pointed out, disregarding this reasoning, "I will not have you upsetting her."

"I have no recollection of upsetting your sister, Sir" Gideon told him calmly.

"But you did visit her yesterday," Richard commented, his tone far from pleased.

"You should be thanking me, Ferrers," Gideon told him, "because if I had not she would not have got the truth out of Salmon and we would not be here now. I am very much afraid, Ferrers" Gideon informed him, "you are in far more danger than you have any idea of and, little though you may relish the thought, I am the only one who can help you."

"Is that so indeed, Major?" Richard mockingly acknowledged.

"That is so," Gideon confirmed.

"You seem to forget, Major," he reminded him, "that being this close to my estates I get to hear things. I know precisely in what case I stand."

"So I gather. Salmon apparently keeps you remarkably well informed."

"Thank God for the misguided!" Richard exclaimed.

"That's as may be, Ferrers" Gideon said sceptically, "but Salmon is in no position to tell you everything."

"For example, Major?" Richard enquired politely.

"For example, Ferrers" Gideon pointed out, "Colonel Henderson has called in reinforcements as you rightly say, but the man leading this renewed attack is none other than His Grace the Duke of Lytton, and he left General Turville in no doubt that if you are not apprehended by me within the space of one week, he is going to 'gazette' you."

Gideon heard the sharp intake of breath beside him and the involuntary jerk of the pistol, clearly indicating his surprise at this disclosure. "The *devil* he will!" he exclaimed slowly.

"You see what I mean, Ferrers" Gideon argued reasonably. "Salmon may be able to keep you informed of domestic and local matters, but he would never know about something of this magnitude."

"Salmon did mention something now I recall," he reflected, "but he was in such a stew that I could not make out the half of what he was saying!" He looked down into the fire, his eyes dark and sombre. "And are you a party to this, Major?" he enquired.

"By no means," he informed him, shaking his head.

"You must forgive me if I appear a little obtuse, Major" Richard mockingly apologized, "but if you are not a party to this, and you are not here on Colonel Henderson's behalf, what *are* you here for, precisely?"

"To try and save you from having your neck stretched," Gideon stated matter of factly.

"A feat indeed!" Richard exclaimed. "And do you really believe that you have the power to prevent the inevitable from happening, Major?"

"Only if you tell me the truth," Gideon told him. "Of course, if you prefer to go to the gallows that is entirely your own affair but, I think before you set your feet any further on that road, you should consider your sister." He felt the renewed dig of the pistol and heard the low voiced curse, but continued inexorably, "She does not believe you are a Jacobite any more than General Turville and I do. That being so," he pointed out, "the question as to why you are being sought so desperately cannot help but obtrude."

A faint flicker of hope burned in Richard's breast at this, but caution made him wary. "How do I know that this is not a cleverly designed trick to see me strung up?" he asked reasonably. "Why should I trust you?"

"Because I have given you my word," Gideon replied candidly, "and also because at this moment in time I am the only friend you have."

A low chuckle of laughter escaped Richard's lips at this. "Look around you Major; I have a room full of friends."

"Very probably," Gideon acknowledged, "but I am afraid they cannot help you in this."

"And *you* can?" Richard mocked.

Gideon nodded. "But as I have already said; only if you tell me the truth."

Richard hesitated. He had never known Salmon mistake his man and, from the looks of it, Major Neville certainly seemed honest enough. God knows he was sick and tired of the life he was leading, but long practise had made him wary, especially of red-coats. "I'm not acquainted with Lytton," Richard told him, "although I have heard of him. He's a dangerous man to cross and not one to be trusted. Do *you* know him?"

"I am not his boon companion, if that is what you are thinking," Gideon told him firmly, "but you are right in that he is dangerous. You must know, as I do, that he is one of the most influential men in the Government and, what is more, he has the ear of the King. He has been brought in by Colonel Henderson in order to curtail your activities Ferrers, or, better still, to make an end of you by any means at their disposal."

His anger and frustration over the treatment his sister had met with and his own inability to come to her aid had not endeared him to the military but, according to Salmon, Major Neville had treated her with the utmost respect and courtesy; so very different to what she had previously encountered. Even so, he was not about to jump blindly into a trap! "Why has Lytton involved himself in this?" he asked abruptly.

"I can only assume," Gideon offered, "it is because he carries much needed weight; weight which Colonel Henderson desperately needs in apprehending you," he shrugged. "I believe they are old friends but, what Lytton's real motive is, I know no more than you."

Richard paused, considering a moment. "Very well, Major, since you seem determined to offer me assistance, though God alone knows why!" he cried, "I'm going to trust you. I'll tell you what you want to know, but not here."

"Where then?" Gideon asked, relieved to feel the pistol removed from his side.

"Do you know Harriers Farm?" he asked. Gideon shook his head. "Take the road from Birling Gap in the direction of West Dean," Ferrers told him. "Once there take the road north out of the village for about two miles, after which you will come to a dirt track on the left hand side of the road. Go down there for about half a mile; you will see a barn in the distance. I shall be in there. Ten o'clock tomorrow night. And come alone, Major."

"You may be sure of it," Gideon said firmly.

"Just one thing, Major" Richard warned, "the reason I agreed to see you here tonight is because Salmon vouched for you and, if there's one man I trust above all others, it's him. I will not take it kindly if you turn tail on us!"

"Apart from having given my word to your sister that neither of you have need to fear me, I am no more a liar than I am an infiltrator trying to bring you out into the open by trickery or deceit," Gideon emphasized, "therefore, you may be sure I won't. But if, as I suspect" he pointed out calmly, "you still have doubts as to my integrity, I can offer you nothing other than my word. Of course," he shrugged, "if that is not good enough then there is nothing more to say to one another!"

"You've said a deal already, Major" Richard told him, not without a touch of humour. "But surely you must realize that my position is somewhat awkward, and my dealings with the military to date are such as not to inspire either confidence or faith in its representatives."

"Yes, I realize that," Gideon nodded, "but whilst I accept you've never laid eyes on me before, you should at least have some good opinion of your father's judgement in choosing his friends.   General Turville adamantly believes in your innocence purely on the grounds that he knew your father and, for that reason, sent me here to find you and discover the truth and, although I have a pretty good idea what that is, in order to get you out of this mire you are in, you have either got to trust me or prepare yourself for a future career of dodging the soldiers as well as the Preventives!"

"Egad!" Richard exclaimed, much struck. "You're very eloquent, Major! Did you never think of entering politics instead of the military?"

"It may interest you to know, Ferrers," Gideon pointed out, firmly suppressing a smile which twitched at the corner of his mouth, "that I have no desire to enter politics any more than I have to see you have your neck stretched and, if my eloquence, as you call it, will convince you that I am here to help you prove your innocence and not climb the scaffold, then I am quite prepared to talk all night!"

"Very well," Richard conceded at length, having turned over in his mind all Gideon had said, "until tomorrow night, Major. By the way," he said in his ear as he stood up, "tell my sister that I am well but, on no account is she to try and find me. I'll only see her when my name is cleared."

"I've already told her ..." but Gideon spoke to the air, Richard had gone; disappearing as suddenly as he had arrived.

He may not have liked having a conversation with a pistol stuck in his ribs but, he was as certain as he could be, that Richard Ferrers was innocent of the charge of treason. He would have much preferred to have looked at the man's face to see for himself whether he was telling the truth or not but, something in that well-bred voice, had told him equally as well. He had not missed that hopeful note when he had learned that two people at least believed him and wanted to help but, believing something was a far cry from proving it.

He had no doubt that Richard Ferrers was on friendly terms with everyone drinking ale in *'The Moonshadow'* but, he wondered if they would let that weigh with them once he had been 'gazetted'? Five hundred pounds was a lot of money and not to be lightly ignored and, honest men or not, he could not see them thinking twice about turning him over to the authorities. He could be wrong, of course, perhaps there was honour among thieves after all, he hoped so for Ferrers' sake but, in either event, he had the very strong feeling that their difficulties were only just beginning. He was convinced that Ferrers was no more a traitor than he was and, therefore, determined to do all he could to help him clear his name. But, even supposing these friends stood by him; they may be willing and able to assist should it come to making a fight of it but, since it was safe to assume that they themselves could not take too much scrutiny regarding their activities or reputations, they were clearly in no position to come forward with character references. This being so, Richard Ferrers would be well advised not to place too much reliance on their assistance.

Salmon, by no means hoodwinked by Elizabeth's casual indifference when he mentioned the Major's prospective visit to inform her of how his meeting with her brother had fared, did not fail to notice how she looked up expectantly from her embroidery every time she heard a noise or footstep approach. Knowing her as well as he did he strongly suspected that she no more had embroidery on her mind than she had of flying to the moon, indeed, he would lay his life that she had not set half a dozen stitches in all the time she had been sitting beneath the branches of the huge oak tree out of the glare of the early afternoon sun. Nor was he fooled by the innocent looks she aimed at him and the nonchalant shrug of her shoulders whenever she caught him watching her. In fact, far from proving her claim that she merely wanted news of her brother, these demonstrations of unconcern only served to reinforce his belief that she was very far from disinclined to seeing Major Neville again on her own account and, when, half an hour later, he witnessed her reaction as she saw him walk towards her accompanied by the Major, he was sure of it.

Her embroidery forgotten, she rose to her feet on a soft rustle of turquoise satin, watching the Major's tall, red-coated figure approach her on legs which seemed oddly unsteady and a dramatic increase in her heart beat. To her chagrin she felt the colour creep into her cheeks as they came up to her, whether this was due to the knowing look on Salmon's face which clearly said 'I told you so' or because the Major was looking at her in a way she found strangely exciting, she would not like to say, and hurriedly averted her eyes from Salmon's meaningful ones to look up at Gideon. Salmon, eyeing the pair of them together, shrewdly guessed which way the wind was blowing and, since his young mistress clearly liked the Major and he himself could find nothing to take exception to, he deemed it wise to keep his own counsel for the time being and, after receiving Gideon's thanks for showing him the way, walked off in the direction of the stables, leaving the two of them together.

"Major!" she smiled up at him, holding out her hand. "How good of you to come all this way to see me, especially on so pleasant a day! I had not expected it to be so warm," she remarked, suddenly feeling a little shy as she saw the look in his eyes, "especially when I recall how cool it was yesterday."

"It is a pleasure, Miss Ferrers" he replied truthfully, bowing over her hand before taking the seat indicated next to her. "But having given my word to come and advise you of how my meeting fared with your brother, it would have been unforgivably rude not to have done so simply because it is uncommonly warm."

"I daresay," she shrugged, as casually as she could manage, very conscious of her heightened colour and the burning of her skin where his lips had lightly touched her fingers, "that being a soldier, you are used to varying weather conditions?"

"Yes," he nodded, "one does become immune but, even had I awoken this morning to find myself besieged in my quarters by three feet of snow, I would have found a way of keeping my promise to come and see you." Something very like a choking sound escaped her lips at this and, sitting forward a little, he asked solicitously, "Are you feeling a little unwell, Miss Ferrers; the heat, perhaps? Would you like me to pour you a glass of lemonade?" indicating the jug and glasses set out on a wicker table.

She shook her head, one dusky ringlet falling over her shoulder. "No, thank you," she said huskily, "it is nothing. I hope," she went on inarticulately, "that I have not put you to any inconvenience, Major?"

"No service I could render you would ever be an inconvenience, Miss Ferrers," he replied in a deep voice, delighting in her adorable confusion.

At this the colour in her cheeks deepened and, lowering her eyes, began straightening an imaginary crease in her skirt, not daring to look at him, saying unsteadily "That is most kind of you, Major."

"Not at all, Miss Ferrers" he told her sincerely. "As I told you upon the occasion of our first meeting," he reminded her in a deep voice, "it is a very great pleasure to serve you, at any time. You must have known, " he said pointedly, "that I was not merely offering you society manners."

Her eyes flew to his, her heart pounding at the look in his while her breath wedged somewhere between her lungs and throat, rendering it necessary for her to take a moment to steady herself. Turning her head a little away, she picked up her basket of silks where it lay beside her on the seat with fingers that were markedly unsteady to place it on the grass beside her with more haste than poise, so that the man sitting calmly watching her had to sternly suppress his very natural inclinations. Having somehow managed to steady herself she brought her head round to look at him, trying desperately hard to ignore the warmth in his eyes as they rested on her. "Yes, I remember," she told him, in a stifled voice, "and, of course, I know you meant it, but ...well...I..." she faltered, then, realizing her reply was becoming rather entangled, said instead, somewhat hurriedly, "but I think you were going to tell me about Richard."

He knew perfectly well that nothing must come between him and trying to settle her brother's affairs but, for a brief moment, he had allowed these to be relegated to the back of his mind while he delightedly observed the affect his words had had on her; her delicious loss of composure momentarily taking his mind off the matter in hand but, at the mention of her brother, the reason he was here resurfaced. "Richard?" he raised an eyebrow. "Oh, yes of course!"

"You... you did see him last night?" she urged, leaning forward a little.

"Well, yes;" he nodded, "in a manner of speaking, that is!"

"I don't understand," she shook her head.

"You see, Miss Ferrers," he explained, "I never saw his face."

"Never saw his face!" she exclaimed, bewildered. "Do you mean he was wearing a mask?"

"As to that, Miss Ferrers" he replied gravely, sternly suppressing the smile hovering on his lips, "I really could not say." She looked a question, her eyes reflecting her bemusement. Leisurely resting his arm along the back of the seat to allow him to sit facing her, he told her about her brother's cautious approach upon his arrival at 'The Mooonshadow' and the use he had made of his pistol.

Her eyes widened in surprise as she stared at him, his own brimming with undisguised amusement at the recollection. "Oh, no!" she exclaimed, putting her fingers over her mouth. "You don't mean it?" He nodded. "Oh, that was too bad of him!"

"Never say so, Miss Ferrers!" he exclaimed in mock horror, succumbing to his keen sense of the ridiculous. "We ought, surely, to be thankful that your brother's spirit is not wholly broken or that his sense of humour has totally deserted him!"

She could not help laughing at this but, pointed out, a little seriously, "You make light of it Major, but, indeed, it must have been most uncomfortable for you!"

"No," he shook his head, "not at all. I own it was not quite what I expected," he offered truthfully, "but, given the provocation he has received, I have to say that, upon reflection, I really cannot blame him. After all," he conceded, "there is no reason that I can see for him to trust me; a man he has never laid eyes on before."

She nodded. "Yes, I know, but he trusts Salmon; we both do," she told him earnestly. "He is devoted to the pair of us; to Richard especially. He is an excellent judge of character Major and, if he had doubted you for a moment, he would never have gone to see Richard to promote a meeting between you."

"Yes," he nodded, "I had gathered as much."

"You see," she explained, "Salmon was born on the estate, as was his father and grandfather, in fact, there's been a Salmon at The Court for ever, indeed," she smiled, "the place would not be the same were it otherwise. He has watched over us both since we were born; my father trusted him implicitly and he would never do anything to harm any one of us. So, you see, Major, although Richard himself has excellent judgement, he trusts Salmon more than any man alive. He *will* come to trust you Major," she assured him, "as I have come to do."

"I don't doubt Salmon's loyalty or devotion, Miss Ferrers" he shook his head, "but I *shall* need Richard's trust if I am to help him."

"Yes, of course," she nodded. "Was Richard able to tell you very much last night?" she enquired, looking intently at him.

When he had finished telling her of their interview the previous evening, she agreed to it that whilst she was certain Richard was right in staying away from his home until his affairs had been settled, she could not refrain from imparting her own views on the inexplicability of male reasoning. "It seems to me that men have such strange notions!" she exclaimed. "Really quite ridiculous!"

Unable to prevent a smile at this very feminine view of things, he reminded her gently, "You seem to have forgotten, Miss Ferrers, that during our conversation yesterday, you promised not to make any attempt to find your brother."

She nodded. "Yes, I know, and I mean to keep that promise, but I am sure he would be far more comfortable here than wherever it is he stays."

"I am quite sure of it," he acknowledged, "but it would be far more dangerous. Your brother is in the right of it. He knows, if you do not, that to approach you or his home the way matters stand at the moment, it would place you both in a most hazardous position."

She digested this for a moment, and Gideon, waiting in contented silence while she seemed to consider for a moment or two, had a fairly good idea what was going through her mind and, when she eventually looked up at him, her face clearly echoing her worries, he knew he was not wrong.

"Can you bring my brother off safe, Major?" she asked hopefully, her candid gaze searching his face.

"Only if he tells me the truth when I see him tonight," he told her truthfully. "Once he does that," he nodded, "I shall certainly do everything I can to help him."

"Do you think he won't tell you the truth?" she asked, surprised at this.

"There is that possibility, yes" he admitted.

"But, why should he not?" she wanted to know.

"There could be several reasons," he told her. "As I mentioned earlier, it is not unreasonable to suppose that he is very far from placing his trust in me."

"But you do believe he is innocent, don't you, Major?" she demanded eagerly.

"From what I have gleaned so far Miss Ferrers, yes" he nodded. "Also, from what you yourself told me at our first meeting, I am quite convinced that your brother's actions stemmed from patriotism rather than treason."

Her face creased in thought before exclaiming suddenly, "Do you mean that Richard is a *spy*?"

He smiled. "I think they prefer the word 'agent', Miss Ferrers," not at all sure he shared her obvious excitement at this prospect.

"But, could he, do you think?" she pressed, unconsciously laying an impulsive hand on his arm as it rested on the back of the seat.

He could feel the touch of her fingers through the sleeve of his coat, and tried hard to ignore it. "I think it very likely."

"So, it could be," she said slowly, thinking it through as she went along, "that Richard has discovered the identity of the real traitor, and they are now trying to prevent him from revealing it."

"That is my view, yes" he conceded, this statement corroborating his first impression of her in that she was by no means lacking in intelligence.

"Where do you meet Richard tonight?" she asked suddenly.

"I think it best if you do not know," he told her frankly, feeling quite bereft now that she had removed her hand.

"Why, do you think I may go there too?" she smiled, her eyes mischievous.

"That possibility has occurred to me," he nodded, sternly suppressing a smile. "But your brother would not like it, *nor*" he emphasized, "for that matter, would I."

"Well, I won't" she promised.

Gideon was conscious of a strong feeling of relief, because despite his feelings for her, he was fast coming to the conclusion that the lady who had taken a hold of his heart had very definite opinions of her own, and was more than capable of doing precisely the opposite to what one wanted her to do. He knew that she would never deliberately do anything to hurt her brother, she loved him too much for that but, even so, he felt it behoved him to reinforce the necessity of keeping her distance from him. "Believe me, Miss Ferrers" he told her earnestly, "whilst I have no desire to distress you further, I do not exaggerate when I say that Colonel Henderson is determined to apprehend your brother by any means in his power and, whilst I cannot say for certain that he is in fact putting a watch on you, to run the risk of attempting to see Richard could only bring misfortune down on both of you. Whilst I can readily understand the need you have to see your brother again," he acknowledged, "at this precise moment in time it could only do harm."

From the moment she had learned of Richard's supposed treachery followed by her shock over the unfortunate death of her father resulting from it, hardly a day had gone by without she strove to find a solution to his difficulties as well as trying to discover a way of absolving him of all blame and wrong doing. Were it not for Salmon and Aunt Clara, her life would indeed have been insupportable, rendering her totally incapable of dealing with Colonel Henderson and his constant invasions of her home and privacy as well as callously disregarding her grief over the death of her father. Having for so long carried the heavy burden of anxiety on her shoulders it was with relief to suddenly find another and, by far more broader, pair, willing to take the responsibility off her as well as knowing that he was not only prepared to help Richard but believed in his innocence. Running parallel to this was the knowledge that at long last she had found a man for whom she felt more than liking and, unless she was grossly at fault, he clearly felt the same. She would have been less than human had she not recognized the look in his eyes every time they rested on her, or felt a thrill running through her whenever he just so much as lightly clasped her fingers. She could not explain it any more than she could prevent her heart from pounding in her breast or the breath stilling in her lungs merely at the sight of him and, whilst she knew that until Richard's affairs were settled, she had no right to indulge her dreams in thinking about this man, she could not rid him either from her heart or her mind. She had borne the anxieties of the last fifteen months with courage and fortitude and, whilst she would continue to do everything in her power to help Richard, there were times when she felt herself to be drowning in despair and, although she had always pulled herself out of the pits of despondency into which she had fallen every now and then, she could not help but wonder how much longer she would be able to do so. But, thanks to this man, who only entered her life two short days ago, she felt relief in that her brother's life as well as her own heart, could be in no better hands. To see that warm and tender look in those brown eyes and to hear his assurances that he would do all he could to help her brother, almost proved too much for her. "I know you are right," she acknowledged, unsteadily, "and I would never do anything to harm Richard; it is just that...well," she faltered, her emotions threatening to overcome her, unaware of how he was struggling against the temptation to take her in his arms and kiss away her fears, "I could not bear anything to happen to him!"

Throwing caution to the wind he leaned forward and took hold of her hand in a reassuring clasp, his eyes looking deep into hers with a warmth and understanding that made her draw in her breath. "Miss Ferrers," he told her gently, looking directly into her eyes, "nothing is going to happen to your brother as long as I am here to prevent it; I promise you. You do believe that, don't you?" he asked urgently.

She nodded. "Yes, I believe that," she said sincerely, returning his look, having to exert every effort to resist the overwhelming urge to throw herself into his arms; arms she instinctively knew would welcome her eagerly. The fluttering of a bird in one of the branches overhead broke the spell she was under, causing her to hurriedly remove her hand from his. "May I offer you some refreshment, Major?" she asked in a suffocated voice. "I really should have done so before. I have clearly forgotten my manners!"

"You are most kind, Miss Ferrers" he replied in a deep voice, knowing precisely how she was feeling, "but it is time I was taking my leave of you."

"Must you leave so soon?" she asked impulsively, wishing he did not have to go quite yet.

"I can think of nothing more agreeable than to accept your invitation," he told her warmly, seeing the colour rush into her cheeks, "but I am afraid I have already trespassed too much upon your time, besides which, there are things I must attend to before I see your brother this evening."

Following his lead she rose to her feet, extending her hand to him. "In that case," she smiled, "I must not detain you. You have been most kind, Major. Thank you for coming to see me and telling me about Richard."

"It has been a pleasure, Miss Ferrers" he said truthfully, bowing over her hand. "If I may call tomorrow," he suggested, "when, hopefully, I can bring you more encouraging news." Upon receiving a breathless "Yes, of course," he reluctantly took his leave of her.

She watched him stride away in the direction of the stables, little realizing the effort his refusal had cost him and that he could have remained with her under that oak tree all afternoon.

He had known no hesitation in giving her his promise to come and visit her tomorrow to inform her how he had progressed with her brother but, he was honest enough to admit, that much more time spent in her company was going to require every ounce of self-restraint he possessed.

Salmon, who had been on the watch for him, no sooner saw him approach than he instructed a groom to bring out the Major's horse and waited for Gideon to come up to him in the stable yard. Taking the reins from the groom, he took a moment or two to check the girth, fully conscious of Salmon standing a little to one side closely regarding him. The corner of his mouth twitched appreciatively but, not until he was satisfied that his saddle was adjusted to his satisfaction, did he say, "Well, have you finished taking my measure yet?"

"Just about I have Sir, yes," he nodded, totally unabashed.

"And?" Gideon prompted.

The old eyes lit up as he looked up into Gideon's face. "Begging your pardon, Major" he grinned, "but I'd say you were what his late lordship would call 'fit to go'!"

Gideon laughed. "I take that as a compliment of no mean order!"

"Ay," Salmon nodded, "as shrewd as he could hold together he was." He shook his head at the memory, then eyeing Gideon fixedly said, "No offence intended, Major."

"None taken," he assured him, climbing into the saddle.

Taking a step towards Gideon, he looked up into his face, his expression a mix of hope and anxiety. "Can you help Master Richard, Major?"

"I shall do everything in my power to help him," he said firmly.

Salmon nodded. "Thank you, Major. It's just ..."

"I know," Gideon smiled sympathetically, "but you leave worrying about Master Richard to me; you just concentrate on taking good care of your mistress." Upon being assured that he need not fret himself over Miss Elizabeth, Gideon trotted out of the stable yard relieved that he had met with this man's unequivocal approval.

Colonel Henderson, unaware of the growing understanding between Major Neville and Miss Ferrers, looked upon Gideon's further visit to Ferrers Court as simply turning the screw. Fast coming to the conclusion that his first impression of Major Neville had been completely wrong, he now considered him to be a rather astute and clever young man. There was clearly more to his thinking than he himself had at first thought, in that a more subtle and gentle approach, and from a good looking and personable young man like Major Neville, would have far more affect on her than any number of searches. Patting Gideon on the shoulder in heart warming approval, suggested that he keep up the good work, especially if, as Gideon had mendaciously led him to believe, she had shown a distinct thawing in her attitude.

Gideon may find dissimulation abhorrent, but there was more than his own feelings to consider; the life of a man was at stake and, for that reason alone, he was quite prepared to keep up the pretence with Colonel Henderson for as long as he possibly could. He was confident that Elizabeth Ferrers would have no objection to fooling Colonel Henderson, in fact, the more he thought about it the more certain he became that she would give it her full approval. However, it would not do any harm to enlighten her of his dealings with Colonel Henderson, as should he ever take it into his head to pay her an unexpected visit, she would not unwittingly undo all he was trying to achieve.

In such good spirits was Colonel Henderson over the progress Gideon appeared to be making, that he cordially invited him to dine with him that evening at half past seven. He may have been in Hampton Regis only a few days, but he had learned that Colonel Henderson, unlike most commanding officers, rarely invited his fellow officers to share his dinner with him. This unlooked for honour held no appeal for him at all but to refuse would not only be discourteous to a senior officer, but would jeopardize the understanding flourishing between them. At all costs he wanted to avoid a rift between himself and Colonel Henderson. He could not claim a liking for the man but, keeping him contented while matters were so unsettled, was paramount. At the same time, if he accepted he had every expectation of it going on for some considerable time and, since Colonel Henderson bore all the appearance of a man who was not indifferent to the odd glass of port, he envisaged the evening stretching out far into the night. There would be no possible way he could reach Harriers Farm in time and, since he was not familiar with the area, he would need to set out in plenty of time to find it. If he missed this opportunity of meeting with Richard Ferrers he may not get another one and, as he was here specifically to find him and discover the truth, he decided that only one option lay before him but, how to decline such an invitation, had him in a quandary. In the event however, it was Colonel Henderson himself who had to apologize to Gideon for cancelling the engagement altogether. Important matters called him away he said, regretfully, but, if Major Neville would do him the honour of dining with him another evening, he would be delighted. Hiding his profound relief admirably, Gideon bowed. "I shall be honoured to accept, Sir." Whatever these important matters were they were certainly most opportune and, if they obtruded in Gideon's mind at all, they were short-lived.

Had he have had the least idea however, that the unexpected arrival into Sussex of His Grace was responsible for Colonel Henderson's sudden cancellation of dinner, he would not have set out for Harriers Farm in quite such a relaxed frame of mind.

Salmon, who had not felt relaxed or enjoyed a moment's peace of mind since this whole thing began, had heard with mixed feelings how the Major's meeting with Richard had fared and about his second meeting with him that evening as he escorted him to the garden where his mistress was sitting. He had nothing against Major Neville, indeed, he seemed to be a decent enough young man who genuinely wanted to help his young master but, his experience of Colonel Henderson and his sledge-hammer tactics, had engendered in him a distrust of anyone who showed even the smallest interest in the mercurial young viscount.

He had known from the first that his mistress had taken a strong liking to Major Neville and, unless he was very much mistaken, which he doubted, it was entirely reciprocated. It was obvious that the Major was a gentleman and knew how to treat a lady; he was as different to Colonel Henderson as a man could be. It wasn't that he did not trust him, in fact, he would take his dying oath that the Major was a man of his word and, if he could bring Master Richard off safe, then all well and good. His worry was that for the life of him he failed to see how he was going to achieve it, much less keep Colonel Henderson at bay whilst doing so.

And if all this were not bad enough His Grace the Duke of Lytton had taken a hand in the affair. He knew his late lordship had had no liking for the King's favourite, and he had been no fool, on the contrary, he had been very astute as well as an excellent judge of character. If Colonel Henderson had seen fit to bring in such a powerful and influential man to aid his attempts to arrest his son, then he for one could not see how the Major could possibly do anything against two such determined adversaries. He had seen enough of Major Neville to know that he was a man who not only played fair but was extremely honourable, indeed, his young mistress clearly placed great store in him and his abilities but, whilst he himself had no doubt that the Major could acquit himself very well under normal circumstances, from what he could see it was going to take all his ingenuity to outwit Colonel Henderson and His Grace.

His real concern however, was that his master would not remain quiet for much longer. It was not only what he had seen and heard the other night that worried him but, for some time now, he had begun to rail against his enforced way of life. He may have extracted his promise to go nowhere near the garrison in an attempt to retrieve those letters himself but, knowing him as well as he did, he could not see it lasting long. His only hope therefore, lay in a man who was really nothing more than a stranger to extricate his young master from the difficulties surrounding him.

He still believed he was doing the right thing in keeping Richard's nocturnal visits a secret as well as his surreptitious mode of entry from his sister, even though it pained him to see her distress. So far, no one knew about that underground passageway or even suspected one existed, not even Miss Elizabeth, who, it had been decided by her father years ago, would be far better off not knowing anything about it and, although he knew he could trust her with such intelligence, he deemed it wiser not to tell her. As for the Major, perhaps it would be as well for the time being to keep it from him too and, as for that rasher of wind William, under no circumstances must he discover it. Richard, he knew, would not be any too pleased to learn that the whole household, particularly his cousin, was aware of his only means of safe entry. Ferrers Court may not be the safest place for him to be at the moment but, as long as that passageway remained a secret, then he could at least be certain of a safe haven for a short time!

CHAPTER NINE

Torn between settling his affairs with all possible speed yet not wishing to alienate or arouse suspicion in his cousin's mind by arriving on the doorstep so soon after his last visit, it was therefore three days after His Grace's departure from Clarges Street that William Ferrers set out on his journey into Sussex. Not only that, but regardless of the contempt Richard had for him he could nevertheless boast a small but long-standing circle of friends, a number of whom he had arranged to see over the next two days. He had no doubt that His Grace would accuse him of having cold feet and thereby delaying his departure deliberately in order to postpone the inevitable with regards to his cousin but, although there was an element of truth in this, for he really had no stomach for putting an end to Richard's life himself, there were nonetheless very practical reasons for the delay in setting out on his journey to Ferrers Court. The truth was that he was none too plump in the pocket at the moment and, whilst His Grace would almost certainly accuse him of latching on to any excuse, the fact was that he was owed small sums of money from some of his friends as a result of several games of cards they had engaged in and which he needed to help defray his travelling expenses. He supposed Lytton would put forward the argument as to what was a few paltry guineas in comparison to the vast fortune which awaited him once his cousin had been dealt with but, without this much needed enrichment to his purse, he was going to find it extremely difficult to make the journey at all. Out of necessity he would have to provide himself with not only outriders to protect him from possible highwayman or other nefarious individuals who may attempt to impede his journey, but there would be at least one change of horses required en route, not to mention partaking of a little refreshment while he waited. As it was out of the question for him to stop at 'The Green Man' in East Grinstead as was his custom due to a well overdue unsettled account, it meant he would be forced to stop for refreshment and a change of horses elsewhere. He had the sneaking suspicion that should he take the risk and pull up at the 'The Green Man' then Povey, usually a most genial landlord, could well demand settlement of the account as well as preferring him to pay for whatever services he may want immediately and, as it was at the moment impossible to defray such a sum, then another posting house it would have to be so, his winnings, however meagre, would be needed if he did not wish to find himself humiliatingly embarrassed.

Whitney, surprised at being told to prepare for an indefinite stay at Ferrers Court, saw at a glance that his employer was not his usual self. He had managed to refrain from listening in at the door but, he would lay his life that something was in the wind, and that His Grace's visit had had a lot to do with this unplanned trip.

He had no objection to taking a bolt out of the Metropolis, as not only had he been fingered as Ferrers' man by disgruntled but hopeful creditors but, also, persistently accosted by an exasperated landlord about the rent. His employer had been skating on very thin ice recently and, the only surprise as far as he could see, was that he had not been clapped up for debt long since. During his five years as his valet-cum-general factotum, he had never yet known the dibs be in tune but, somehow, they had always managed to avoid total financial ruin by a lucky throw of the dice or a turn of the card and, even, but only seldom, a long odds nag beating the field. Lately though, it seemed as if good fortune had turned its back on William Ferrers, so much so, that London was not the most comfortable place to be at present.

His wages more often than not went unpaid, his only monetary reward being a generous purse on the odd occasion his employer had enjoyed a run of rare good luck. If anyone were to ask him why he remained in Ferrers' employment, he would merely shrug his narrow shoulders and say "Why not?" The truth was that his life as a jack-of-all-trades for William Ferrers was far better than he had ever been used to but, he was human and honest enough to admit, but only to himself, that if the question of the Viscountcy could be sorted to his employer's satisfaction, then he could expect a pretty comfortable existence for himself in the future. Whilst he could not say that his employer was the most reliable of men he had ever known, he was certainly the most easy going; provided he was there when needed he seldom found himself rebuked for some oversight or misdemeanour. This casual behaviour therefore, had resulted in a most unusual partnership and, in return for Ferrers' careless and blasé attitude about what was expected from a servant, he was more than prepared to carry out any task he asked of him.

Being a man of no political persuasions himself, it had not mattered to him in the least whether his employer had declared for Stuart or not and, as for his reasons for doing so, they were a matter of complete indifference to him, as were Ferrers' feelings towards his cousin. Nevertheless, Ferrers' involvement with Colonel Henderson and his venture into treasonable activities, had eventually brought him to the notice of His Grace the Duke of Lytton and, although he had had no dealings with him himself, he knew enough about him to realize that he was not the kind of man one either crossed or gainsaid and, unless he much mistook the case, then he would lay his life that more trouble was coming their way.

William Ferrers may be careless in his dealings with Whitney, resulting in his henchman's lack of due deference which would not have been tolerated by anyone else, but he certainly could not afford to dispense with his services. He knew too that not many in Whitney's position would remain in his employer's service with no regular payment but, since he made no complaint and appeared more than content with his lot, then he himself was reasonably happy with the situation. But although he was able to count on Whitney, he could not say the same about his reception at Ferrers Court and, as he sat back against the squabs of his newly acquired but as yet unpaid for coach, he began pondering how he was going to explain this visit so close on the heels of the last one. He felt reasonably certain that his cousin would have no objection and, even if she did, she was far too well-mannered to let him see it. Salmon however, was another matter, so too was Aunt Clara, both of whom had made their feelings towards him abundantly clear. Neither of these individuals he knew would be in the least gratified by his arrival, doing absolutely nothing to make him welcome.

It was all very well for His Grace to suggest that he pump Salmon for information about Richard, even using bribery as a last resort but, what he failed to understand, was that not only did Salmon dislike him and make no effort to hide it, he was much too fond of his cousin to give him away; and no inducement he could offer him would change that. As for Aunt Clara, it seemed her sole aim in life was to render him acutely uncomfortable by any means at her disposal; being especially fond of recounting reminiscences of his father which were deliberately calculated to not only remind him that she had never had any time for her younger brother, but that he resembled him too closely.

Considering the hostile reception he had met with to date, he had therefore fleetingly toyed with the idea of approaching Miss Trench in the hope that she could shed some light on Richard's whereabouts but, almost immediately, discarded this as useless. Although he had heaved a tremendous sigh of relief upon discovering that Sir Arthur had forbidden any connection between his daughter and Richard, he doubted very much that his cousin would secretly involve the woman he loved in his troubles. Even now, he could not help but shudder as he re-lived the moment when he had learned of their betrothal, because not even in his most optimistic moments could he fool himself into believing that their marriage would not produce an heir; relegating him even further down the inheritance ladder. Had this have transpired, then his difficulties would be all the more insoluble than they were now; getting rid of his cousin was problem enough but, to get rid of his son and heir was quite another!

No amount of optimism therefore could dispel the growing unease he felt the nearer he got to Little Turton. He was not such a fool as to believe his unexpected arrival would be anything other than unwelcome, but his affairs were such that he could not allow the inhabitants of Ferrers Court to deter him from his purpose.

He knew that trying to get information out of them about Richard's whereabouts was not going to be easy, in fact, he could foresee any number of obstacles being put in his path but, if this unknown visitor Lytton had spoken of played his part as expected, although what this was precisely he had no very clear idea, then his task may be that much easier. Colonel Henderson's treatment of his cousin may not have met with his full approval but, given her stubborn refusal to divulge information about her brother, he failed to see what else he could have done in the circumstances. He knew that she blamed Henderson for her father's death, and that alone had stiffened her resolve and would continue to do so, but matters had reached a point where consideration for her feelings had to be put on one side.

For the life of him he could not understand what it was about Richard that endeared him to people but, that they were all partisan in the furtherance of his cause, was unquestionable. Hopefully though, Providence would now come to his aid and prevail upon Elizabeth to turn to him for guidance and help in ridding Ferrers Court of yet another red-coat and, perhaps, even persuade her to divulge where Richard was hiding out. Of course, this could not be taken for granted, but Lytton was right when he said that Elizabeth had endured much recently, and it was therefore natural to assume that sooner or later she would come to see that she could no longer deal with this heavy burden alone.

To him it was quite unnatural for a woman to deal with such matters, but experience had taught him that his cousin was made of sterner stuff than most, indeed, she possessed far more strength of character than himself. Had he have but known it, his cousin, far from wanting to turn to him for the guidance he believed she obviously stood in need of, would have much preferred it if he stayed away from Ferrers Court altogether. For her part, she had no intention of either consulting him or of confiding in him about her concerns for her brother, let alone divulging his whereabouts.

Lytton, unsure as to whom General Turville had appointed as his advocate and what he had advised in the way of approaching Elizabeth Ferrers, or, indeed, what he had told him about this lamentable affair in general, had used William Ferrers as an actor would a prop. He had had every intention of seeking out this young man in order for him to have a private word in his ear as to what he expected of him but, after only a little further thought, he had been brought to see that this would not answer. Having already exposed his interest in this affair more than he would have liked, he knew he dare not make any approach to Turville's advocate but, being a man of infinite resource, it had not taken him long to recognize that he had a very useful tool to hand in William Ferrers, which would answer equally as well. Having deliberately manoeuvred him into a position whereby he could not only counteract everything this officer was trying to do, no doubt at Sir John's instigation, but he would be on hand to provide a shoulder on which Elizabeth Ferrers could unburden herself. He felt it rather safe to assume that by now Elizabeth Ferrers had had her fill of the military and, unless William Ferrers was more of a fool than he believed him to be, then the opportunity to take advantage of her vulnerability had never been more favourable. In fact, he had no doubt that Elizabeth Ferrers, saddled with yet another red-coat on her doorstep, could well greet her cousin's arrival at Ferrers Court as not only most fortuitous but, even take benefit from his presence by helping her to deal with the question of her brother.

Had His Grace's unsuspecting puppet the least idea that it was nothing but a clever ploy on his part to not only deflect any adverse repercussions ensuing from the Major's meeting with Elizabeth, but also to make an end of a young man who could render his position extremely uncomfortable or that he was the last person the inhabitants of Ferrers Court wished to see, what little optimism he had about the task ahead of him would have been killed at a stroke.

He could not say that he was looking forward to putting an end to Richard's life either by pulling the trigger himself or at the sword's point, much preferring to inform against him so that someone else did it for him but, as this seemed to be the only way of setting his affairs in order as well as ensuring his activities regarding Stuart never came to light, there was nothing else he could do. Like it or not, there was no alternative especially as Henderson's efforts to apprehend his cousin had proved unsuccessful. It was a thousand pities he had allowed Richard to escape, but was able to take some comfort from knowing that he could not as yet have been able to retrieve that incriminating evidence which would condemn him once and for all. Had he have done so, as His Grace had rightly pointed out, then he would have gone to the gallows long since! The thought made him shiver but, it also had the effect of spurring his determination to make an end of his cousin once and for all, because if he did not, then there was more chance of him being clapped up for debt than becoming the sixth Viscount Easton.

It was useless to suppose that Richard could either be persuaded into destroying that evidence or calmly walking away from his inheritance. For one thing, Richard was inherently honest and it would therefore be impossible for him to turn his back on the truth and allow traitors to evade the law. It would be equally impossible, not to say unthinkable, for him to forgo his right to take up his father's dignities in his favour; for a man of his integrity it would be an act of unspeakable dishonour. In view of this therefore, William Ferrers mentally braced himself for the task ahead, but it was one he was not looking forward to, in fact, it merely reinforced his rather belated belief that he should never have allowed Colonel Henderson to take advantage of his greed and ambitions or to use his jealousy of Richard against him in the first place.

It was all very well for Henderson to advise that they did not see one another for awhile or, at least, until Richard was finally out of the way but, in view of his previous escape from the garrison, it seemed to him that the only way his cousin would ever be laid by the heels was for the two of them to work together.

This in turn then raised the question as to how he would be able to visit Hampton Regis to see him without creating suspicion but, as he could see the chimneys of Ferrers Court come into view, he decided to leave pondering this hurdle until later, for the moment it was all he could do to come up with a fitting reason to account for his unexpected arrival! Useless to suppose that they would think he had a right to visit what was, after all, his own property!

Having said a reluctant goodbye to Major Neville, Elizabeth continued to sit beneath that ancient oak tree for some considerable time contemplating her brother's dilemma, her embroidery forgotten on the grass beside her. She had promised not to try and approach him and she fully intended to keep her word but, she could not deny, that with every tick of the clock her fears for his safety grew. She knew implicitly that Major Neville would do everything in his power to help Richard but, like Salmon, her greatest fear was Colonel Henderson. She neither liked nor trusted him, and knew that he would stop at nothing to hurt Richard and that should he ever discover his hiding place, it would take all the Major's efforts to protect him.

Not for the first time she experienced a feeling of utter frustration knowing that there was absolutely nothing she could do to aid her brother but, should he ever arrive at Ferrers Court, then no power on earth, not even the threat of arrest and imprisonment, would prevent her from offering him shelter.

Alongside her concerns over Richard was another and far more personal one. Considering the predicament in which Richard found himself it struck her as somewhat self-indulgent, perhaps even, a little selfish, to realize that her thoughts and concerns now also incorporated the Major but, try as she did, she could not dismiss him from either her mind or her heart. Until a few short days ago she had not known he even existed, now, she could think of little else but him. It was incredible that a man she had known for so little time should have taken such a hold of her heart but, should anything happen to him, she would feel the loss as deeply as if it were Richard. That he felt the same about her was patently obvious and, although her heart was heavy with worry over Richard, the mere thought of Major Neville made that most unreliable organ jump with joy. It was therefore in a somewhat pensive mood that she slowly made her way back to the house via the stable courtyard, entering through the rear door just as the elegant timepiece in the hall struck three o'clock.

She was already half way up the stairs when the sound of carriage wheels met her ears followed seconds later by the clanging of the bell. Wondering who could possibly be paying them a visit and at such an hour, she half turned and, looking over the balustrade, saw Salmon walk into the hall and look up at her, his expression more eloquent than any words could have been. Her heart thudded painfully but, when Salmon opened the door to reveal her cousin standing on the threshold, she was not entirely sure whether to feel relief or annoyance at his unexpected arrival.

Feeling something was required of her she descended the stairs, trying to school her face into one of welcome, sincerely hoping that the baggage his man was bringing in did not denote a lengthy stay. "William! This is indeed a surprise!" she exclaimed.

"Not too unpleasant I trust, Cousin" William bowed over her hand.

Over his bent head Salmon's eyes briefly met her own troubled ones and, what she read in them, made her heart sink. "Of course not," she smiled. "How could you even think such a thing? I could have wished for a little warning, however."

He raised his eyebrows at this. "If my presence here is …"

"No, no" she offered hastily. "It is merely that I could have ensured everything was ready for you. As it is," she shook her head, "I am afraid we have nothing prepared."

"Oh, I see," he nodded, mollified by this explanation. "I would not for the world wish you to go to any trouble on my behalf, Cousin."

Not daring to look in Salmon's direction, she assured him it was no trouble and, after instructing her overseer to ensure William's man was to be looked after and her cousin's bags were to be deposited in his room, which was to be made ready immediately, she showed him into the small sitting room just to the right of the main front door which was as far removed from the family one as possible. She knew her aunt had long since retired for the afternoon as was her custom but, just in case she had taken it into her head to come downstairs sooner than was expected, the last thing she wanted was the two of them to meet right now; she was in no frame of mind to be in the middle of two people who disliked one another intensely.

"You know," he told her boyishly, the smile not quite reaching his eyes, "I had almost convinced myself that my unannounced arrival may well have inconvenienced you."

"Not at all," she assured him, feeling the lie stick in her throat. "But, tell me, what is it that brings you here so soon since your last visit?"

"Nothing alarming, I assure you" he shook his head. "I merely thought my presence here may in some way assist you during what can only be described as a most distressing time."

She did not think this was the reason, but allowed it to pass. "That was thoughtful of you, thank you" she nodded, hoping this did not presage a lengthy stay but, considering the amount of baggage he had brought with him, she had the awful feeling that it did.

He looked nervous and uncomfortable, more so than usual, reinforcing her belief that he was not telling her the truth. Her aunt, she knew, had never liked him nor, for that matter, had her father or Richard and, as for Salmon - well, he made no secret of the fact that he not only disliked him but mistrusted him into the bargain and was not afraid to let him see it.

He began to play nervously with his eye glass and, although he looked in her direction, his eyes never quite met hers. "You know, Cousin" he offered, choosing his words carefully, "I believe I have been rather remiss in my responsibilities where you are concerned"

"Oh! Why is that?" This was said quite politely but it had the effect of slightly disconcerting him.

"Well," he smiled, feeling as though the lace around his neck was suddenly a little too tight, "I am a quite ashamed to confess that I feel I have left you to carry an impossible burden. I see now that it was very wrong in me to leave you to deal with things as best you may." Apart from a raised eyebrow, Elizabeth made no response to this. "I hope you know that if there is anything I can do to help Richard," he told her awkwardly, clearing his throat, "you have but to name it."

"Thank you," she smiled. "I take it then, you mean to make a long stay with us?"

"Not too long to incommode you," he shook his head, his boyish smile beginning to look more forced, "but long enough to offer you support until my cousin's affairs are settled with the least distress to yourself."

"I see," she nodded, a slight frown creasing her forehead. "Then you were right to bring so much baggage with you." Missing the irony of this statement, William raised a questioning eyebrow as if seeking clarification. "Since Richard's affairs, as you call them," she pointed out as calmly as she could, "have been unsettled for months, and there is every likelihood they will remain so for the foreseeable future, we could be entertaining you for quite sometime!" Giving him no opportunity to respond to this, she continued, "However, in view of your urgently voiced concerns, I must own to some surprise in that this has not prompted you to visit The Court more often in order to relieve your mind of its misgivings!"

He may not possess the sharpest of minds but, there was no mistaking the inference behind the subtlety, causing him to dart a quick look at her, startled by the barely suppressed annoyance he could see lurking beneath the composed surface, causing him to experience a moment of intense discomfort. He supposed he should have known that his cousin would not be taken in so easily but, since he could hardly tell her his true reason for being here, he quickly took refuge in prevarication, laughingly apologizing for putting his own engagements before her worries.

Having a very shrewd idea that her cousin had descended on them merely in order to ascertain how matters stood regarding the unresolved question of the inheritance, it therefore took her a few moments to get her temper under control but, when she eventually spoke, there was no trace of annoyance in her voice. "I realize, of course, that you must honour your obligations, indeed, it would be extremely discourteous to disregard the commitments made to your acquaintance but, unless you have received favourable tidings from Pritchard, your journey into Sussex was quite unnecessary especially as I fail to see what can possibly be done to either prove or disprove Richard's guilt until he is found."

By no means pleased by this equably delivered statement any more than he was to acknowledge the fact that he could not afford to set her back up, especially if he wanted her to confide in him, William bit back the stinging retort which sprung to his lips. It may go very much against the grain with him to adopt a conciliatory attitude but, under the circumstances, he saw no option open to him other than to set himself the task of appeasing her. "I do not need to be told that you believe him to be innocent of the charges laid against him," he smiled tautly, "but, forgive me Cousin" he apologized, "in the eyes of the law he is already pronounced guilty and therefore disinherited."

She controlled her temper with an effort and, when she spoke, her voice was distinctly restrained. "Are you saying that you believe him to be guilty?"

"By no means," he hastened to assure her, "but, you must acknowledge, that his position is most awkward." He paused for a moment as if deliberating his next words. "I realize, of course," he pointed out carefully, "that you would much prefer to see Richard step into your father's shoes than I, but, as matters stand, I cannot help but wonder where it leaves me."

"Is that why you are here," she demanded, unable to hide the accusatory note from creeping into her voice, "to take possession of the title?"

This direct question threw him off balance. How like Elizabeth to come straight to the point! "You wrong me, Cousin," he reproved. "Why," he exclaimed, "I do not even demand an allowance from the estate!" He saw the sparkle in her eyes but managed to continue, with more confidence than he felt. "However, reluctant though I am to be the one, I feel I must point out to you one painful circumstance; in the eyes of the law I am the rightful sixth Viscount Easton, and I am well within my rights to take up my inheritance immediately."

"In that case," she stated heatedly, "one is given to wondering why you do not."

The flash of anger in her eyes made him pause, realizing that he had been too precipitate. "That is easily answered," he told her, making a quick recover. "Having given my word to your father, I could not in all conscience break it."

Had she not been so angry she would have applauded such a glib response on the spur of the moment but, as it was, she wanted nothing more than to hit him. Something of what she felt showed in her eyes and, beneath his delicately painted face, the colour flooded his cheeks, but his affairs were such that he could not allow himself to be dissuaded simply because he may upset or offend his cousin.

Nevertheless, it was obvious that he had angered her and knew he would have to try and recover lost ground as quickly as possible, after all, it was not in his interests to alienate her.

He looked contrite, and apologized. "Forgive me, Cousin, it was not my intention to distress you. I mean Richard no harm, indeed," he smiled, "I have only his interests at heart." Taking a hasty step towards her he took possession of her hands. "If I have said anything at all to make you think that I wish ill on Richard merely in order to step into his shoes, I humbly beg your pardon. It is merely that I cannot allow my position, which you must agree to be somewhat awkward, to continue indefinitely."

She could see the justification of this but, even so, she still mistrusted him as well as his reasons for being here. Withdrawing her hands from his, she smiled up at him, but not without an effort. "I understand you wish matters to be settled as speedily as possible, as I do myself but, I can only repeat, that until Richard is found I fail to see what can be done."

"I am aware of the difficulties attached to Richard's present position," he told her circumspectly, stealing a fleeting glance at her, "and how uncomfortable it must be for you; not knowing from one moment to the next if he is safe or not." He hesitated, saying at length, "It is because of that that you *must* let me help you," he begged. "You cannot be expected to carry such a heavy burden alone."

"But I am not alone," she told him, her smile annoying him.

"You mean Aunt Clara and that man of yours," he nodded. "I daresay they mean well but ..."

"They give me all the support I need," she told him firmly. "Indeed, I need no other."

This was not what he wanted to hear and, yet again, found himself having to swallow the retort on his lips. Annoying her would do no good and, although it irritated him to have to placate her, especially as how the title was his in law, he knew he had no choice if he was to succeed in his purpose of endeavouring to discover where his cousin was. "That may be, but I believe I am better placed to assist you and Richard than they are. If you know where my cousin is to be found, you can tell me" he coaxed, his smile more forced than ever. "I'll go and see him; talk to him."

"And tell him what?" she asked, raising an eyebrow.

"Simply that I will do everything in my power to assist him," he assured her.

She swallowed her irritation. "Even if I knew where Richard could be found," she shrugged, "I fail to see what you could possibly say or do."

The sceptical look she threw at him rendered him acutely uncomfortable but, it also told him that she was no nearer to giving Richard up than she ever was. He had no idea whether she had as yet received a visit from this red-coat Lytton spoke of or not but, as he dare not ask, which would only arouse her suspicions, he was left to feel his way as best he could, which, considering the desperation to settle his ever worsening affairs, his frustration over her stubborn defiance and the thought of having to confess yet another failure to Lytton, rendered him tetchy and irritable, bringing another flush of colour to his cheeks. He could feel his temper rising, made worse by the fact that he could not allow it expression; to do so would only serve to strengthen her hostility and set her even more against him. "I take it then," he stated as calmly as he could, "that you have taken no steps to locate him."

She eyed him in frank astonishment. "Steps? What on earth do you mean?"

"I should have thought my meaning was plain enough" he replied more sharply than he had intended. Realizing too late that he had been far too imprudent in permitting his exasperation to show, attempted to make a quick recover by pointing out, in a far more pacifying tone, "Forgive me my dear, I had not meant to be so ill-mannered by speaking to you in such a way but, surely you must see that Richard's predicament is placing us both in a most awkward, not to say, unenviable position, and the longer he remains at large, the worse it will be," pausing long enough before adding significantly, "but for Richard especially. His venture into smuggling following his treasonable activities, my apologies, Cousin," he amended hastily when he saw her fulminating stare, "his *alleged* treasonable activities, has only served to worsen his situation; and any attempt to prove him innocent of such serious charges is going to be extremely difficult the longer he evades the authorities."

"I have never doubted my brother's innocence!" she told him unequivocally, her eyes flashing. "Nor do I doubt he will be exonerated; and as for taking steps," she shook her head, "in what direction do you propose I take them, since I am not personally acquainted with any member of the smuggling fraternity?"

Unfortunately, his bow at a venture had failed, disappointing, of course, but it had been worth a try nonetheless and, instead, set his mind to another tack in order to draw Richard out into the open. "In that case," he told her, as firmly as he could, "I think we should do everything possible to try and find him by other means. After all," he offered, "his situation must be as uncomfortable for him as it is for us."

"I daresay his situation *is* uncomfortable," she replied sharply, "but since he has made no attempt to approach me and I know of no one who knows where he is, everything else is meaningless, wouldn't you say?"

"Well, not quite" he shook his head, averting his eyes from hers. "As it happens, Cousin, I think there may be a way. In fact," he confessed, darting a wary look in her direction, "I have given this matter some considerable thought, and I believe it is our only way forward."

"And what way is that?" she asked, looking straight at him, her intense blue eyes keenly searching his face. She wondered what he was planning to do, but nothing quite prepared her for his response.

The look in her eyes made what he had to say more difficult but, undeterred, said "I appreciate you will not like it Cousin but, I really do think it is the only thing we *can* do."

"Go on," she nodded, waiting expectantly.

"Well," he smiled nervously, "as I say, I have given it some thought and I believe that I should go and see Colonel Henderson! Talk to him and explain that he has obviously made a mistake where Richard is concerned." The look on her face made him take an involuntary step backwards but, persevering, faltered, "I think, well... what I mean is, Cousin, between the two of us we should surely be able to find Richard and get this confusion sorted out once and for all!"

"*Go and see Colonel Henderson!*" she exclaimed incredulously. "Are you mad?" she demanded.

"Not at all," he sounded affronted. "Indeed, I cannot imagine why you should think I might be."

"Go and see the very man who is not only responsible for my father's death but has hounded us to the point of insanity!" she cried, her face flushed with anger.

He swallowed. "You must see that it is the only thing we *can* do," he explained hastily. "Richard cannot go on indefinitely in this manner and, surely, Colonel Henderson is open to reason."

"Reason!" she rounded on him. "I cannot believe you even suggested such a thing!"

He was just on the point of saying something when the door opened and Salmon walked in, informing his mistress that Mr. William's room was now ready if he would like to go up and change out of his travelling clothes. William most certainly did not want to go up to his room just now but, one look at his cousin, standing stiffly upright with her face angrily flushed and Salmon's innocent expression, not to mention the fact that he was standing with the door open ready, he felt impelled to leave the sitting room. Declining Salmon's escort by saying somewhat irritably that he knew the way, he strode out of the room feeling very much like a schoolboy who was being punished for some misdemeanour, whereupon Salmon immediately shut the door on him.

One look at her stormy face was enough to tell him that their unwelcome visitor had set her back up but, knowing her as well as he did, refrained from commenting, saying instead "Well, that's *him* out of the way for awhile. What's he doing here, Mistress?"

Her eyes still smouldered as she looked at him. "He's trying to discover if I know where Richard is," going on to tell him what had occurred between them.

"Hm!" he shook his head when she had come to the end of her recital.

"You can take that look off your face," she scolded. "I know you think I should have sent him packing, but you must know I could not!"

"I don't know any such thing," he shrugged. "Easiest thing in the world."

She laughed in spite of herself. "I confess it would have given me the greatest satisfaction to have done so, but that is not the answer."

"Then what is?" her stalwart wanted to know. "We can't have him going to Colonel Henderson, goodness only knows what the two of them will cook up together, *nor*" he pointed out firmly, "will it do for him to meet the Major, ten to one he'll put two and two together and come up with five!"

In her surprise at finding William on the doorstep and her subsequent annoyance over his intentions, she had momentarily forgotten about Major Neville but, at the mention of his name, it immediately brought to mind his forthcoming meeting that evening with Richard. "He's promised to come and let me know the outcome tomorrow."

"That's the dandy!" he scoffed. "Discuss Master Richard's affairs with that ferret stuck in the house. He's here for the duration, you mark my words! Why, we won't shift him in under a month!"

"Oh, I do so hope not!" she cried, wringing her hands. "I couldn't bear it Salmon, truly I could not! Under no circumstances must he even suspect that Major Neville is trying to help Richard."

"Well, you just leave that to me and the Major," he advised her. "Between us, I've no doubt we can hoodwink that rasher o' wind upstairs. He's up to no good Mistress," Salmon nodded darkly. "He'd like nothing better than to learn Master Richard's cocked up his toes so he can get his feet under the table here. Why" he scorned, "he already believes it belongs to him. But, never you mind," he told her as she threw him a horrified look, "he ain't master here yet!"

"No," she nodded, "but he could be, sooner than we would like, especially if the Major can't help Richard after all."

"Now, that's enough of that," he admonished. "As long as I've breath in my body he'll never be master here and, as for the Major," he told her, "he'll do the trick, never fear!"

"The mere thought of William here in Richard's place horrifies me!" she confessed. "I couldn't bear to see it."

"And nor you will," he asserted.

She eyed him steadily. "I know my father never trusted him, nor Richard for that matter."

"And with good cause if you ask me," he told her forthrightly.

"I know nothing against him," she admitted, shaking her head, "and yet, I have a terrible feeling that despite his protestations of only wanting to help, he means mischief."

"I'd lay my life he does!" Salmon nodded.

"Salmon!" she exclaimed, resting a hand on his arm, "we must be careful not to let William know anything about Richard!"

"Now, Mistress," he soothed, patting her cold hand, "you leave him to me and the Major, we'll see to him, never you fret."

"But what of Aunt Clara?" she demanded. "She must be told the truth. It is unjust to keep it from her. She would never betray Richard."

"Of course she wouldn't," he agreed.

"I *must* tell her," she said firmly.

"She won't like it Mistress," he shook his head, "to think she's been left out of things. You'd better leave it to me," he advised. "I'll settle things there."

"Oh, Salmon!" she cried. "I know I should not leave it to you but …"

"It'll come better from me," he told her, "especially as I'm the one whose been seeing him. 'Sides," he grinned, "it'll sound more like a confession, which'll please her." She laughed. "Now," he said seriously, "what time did the Major say he was meeting him?"

"Ten o'clock, he said," she told him. "I just hope that Richard will be able to tell him all he needs to know in order to help him clear his name." She took a hasty turn around the room as if by doing so it would release some of her pent-up anxiety. "How on earth I am to get through dinner this evening without letting my cousin know that my mind's elsewhere, I don't know."

"You just forget about Master Richard for tonight," Salmon chided. "No doubt he and Major Neville will sort things out between them."

She hoped so but, as the evening wore on, she could not quite prevent herself from continually looking at the clock, wondering what the outcome of it all would be and, if this were not bad enough, she was on tenterhooks in case her aunt decided to take it into her head to accost William regarding his real motive behind this visit. She did not but, at the earliest opportunity berated her niece for keeping the truth from her about Salmon's contact with Richard, conveniently overlooking the fact that she had not known of it until a couple of days ago. However, her niece, showing proper contrition, eventually won her over but not without that redoubtable lady saying tartly, "But I tell you this, if this precious Major of yours don't do the trick, I'll do it myself!" In no hurry to follow her niece to the sitting room she was still seated at the dinner table ten minutes later when Salmon entered to check the maid had cleared everything away, rather surprised to find her still there.

"My Lady!" he exclaimed.

"Ah, Salmon," she nodded. "Just the man!"

"Is something wrong, My Lady?" he enquired.

"How long is my nephew intending to stay here, do you know?" she asked forthrightly.

"No, My Lady," he shook his head, "although, the Mistress says she wouldn't be surprised to find it was going to be a lengthy stay due to the amount of baggage he has brought with him."

"Hm!" she snorted. "What's he doing here?"

"We believe, My Lady," he sighed, putting the silver tray down on the table, "that he's trying to find out what's happening about Master Richard's affairs."

"Ha!" she cried, banging her hands down on the table. "That don't surprise me! Encroaching upstart! I daresay he's under the hatches again."

"As to that, My Lady," he offered, "I really couldn't say! However, the Mistress tells me that he has the intention of going to see Colonel Henderson in order to discuss his cousin's affairs to see if something can be done to find him and help him out of his difficulties."

"Does he?" she nodded, her eagle eyes glaring at him. "Well, if he thinks he can come here dictating terms, or bringing that rascally bully into the house, he will very soon discover his mistake. He ain't master here yet and, by God" she cried, "he never will be if I have anything to do with it! What," she scoffed, "William help Richard to settle his affairs so he can become the next Viscount; yes," she nodded, "I wish I may see it! I've never known him do anything for anyone other than himself and, unless he's undergone a rapid change of disposition, I'd say he's up to something."

"Rare put the Mistress out, he did," Salmon informed her, "when he told her what he was meaning to do, about going into Hampton Regis; said he had a right to know where he stood regarding the inheritance and matters could not drift on indefinitely."

"I don't wonder she was put out!" she snapped. "Although why she permits him to come here, I don't know!"

"Well, My Lady" he told her quietly, "she says herself that to prevent him could only make matters worse; especially as he could step into the old lord's shoes if Master Richard can't prove his innocence."

She threw him a fiery glance but, she was honest enough to admit, that her niece was probably right. The longer Richard was a wanted man the worse it looked for him and, William, not one to let the grass grow under his feet, would not be slow in taking advantage of it.

"Thing is," Salmon said gloomily, "we must be careful that Mr. William don't grasp the fact that the Major is here to help Master Richard; should he do that and he reports it to Colonel Henderson, goodness knows what will happen."

She nodded. "Yes, that's true enough; he'll stop at nothing to impede his own chances of getting his feet under the table here. About the Major" she asked abruptly, looking directly at him, "you say he's going to do all he can to help

Richard?"

"Yes, My Lady" he confirmed.

"What do we know about him?" she demanded. "You tell me he's not with that scoundrel Henderson and his horde from the garrison."

"No, he's been sent here by Sir John Turville in London, My Lady. He was a friend ..."

"I know who he is," she broke in abruptly, "or, I should do, after forty years!" Rising stately from her chair she looked at Salmon, her eyes narrowing. "What does he have to say for himself, this Major Neville?"

"He told the Mistress straight that he was here under Sir John's orders and not Colonel Henderson's; and, no matter what he discovered, he would not hand Master Richard over to him."

"Hm!" she pursed her lips. "You say this Major Neville and my niece seem to go on together wondrous great?"

"Yes, My Lady," he nodded, "like a house on fire."

"So," she mused, "that's why she's been looking like the cat whose been at the cream, is it! He's a gentleman, you say?" she said thoughtfully, darting a look at him. Salmon nodded. "He's not a ranker playing off the airs of an exquisite?"

"No, My Lady," Salmon shook his head. "The Major is a real gentleman. Saw it the moment I laid eyes on him."

"Well, you should know," she stated candidly, "you lived with one long enough!"

"Yes, My Lady" he replied proudly, "I did. His late lordship was most truly the gentleman. *And,* if I may say so," he told her firmly, "so is the Major."

Pulling her shawl tighter around her, she eyed Salmon closely. "Who are his people? Do you know?"

"He hasn't said, My Lady," he shook his head, "the occasion not arising to require him to do so but, begging your pardon, My Lady," he reminded her, "it's not my place to ask him."

Ignoring this as irrelevant, she half closed her eyes as she contemplated an idea which seemed to have taken possession of her mind. "The only Nevilles I know," she said at length "are from Wiltshire. An old family, good lineage; came over during the Conquest or some such thing! I wonder if this Major is related to Sir Matthew? A nephew perhaps?" She pondered for a moment or two. "Can't think now whether he had one boy or two, not that it matters," she shrugged, "if the connection is there!"

"I really couldn't say, My Lady" Salmon said unhelpfully, picking up the tray where he had placed it on the table.

"If he is," she told him optimistically, "and Elizabeth's taken to him, it may well answer."

"As to that," he warned her, not without a touch of pride, "knowing the

Mistress, whether he's connected or not, she'll go her own way!"

"Yes," she said irritably, not quite able to hide her own pride in her niece. "I only have to think of those offers of marriage she turned down and I could box her ears!" On which tart note she told Salmon he could escort her to the sitting room, ignoring the sigh which escaped his lips as he once again put the tray down on the table.

CHAPTER TEN

Harriers Farm, unfortunately unmarked on Lieutenant Beaton's map, proved to be more difficult to find than Gideon had expected. No less than three times did he take the wrong turning to the designated meeting spot and, by the time he eventually saw the barn in the distance, he could not help but wonder if Richard Ferrers had been deliberately misleading with his directions or had not taken into account that being a stranger to the area, he would not realize that the dirt tracks prior to the one he wanted, led nowhere.

By now the moon was almost at the full and, in its silvery light, he could easily see the barn and a horse tethered to a somewhat rickety fence. In the far distance he could make out a farmhouse to which the barn no doubt belonged and could not help wondering if its occupants were aware of the illicit meeting taking place between himself and Richard Ferrers. No sound broke the silence as he dismounted, tying his grey mare next to the thoroughbred black stallion which looked decidedly out of place in these dilapidated surroundings. After looking cautiously around him he pulled open the one half of the barn door which was already ajar; creaking abnormally loud in the stillness then, pausing only long enough to take another quick look behind him to ensure that he was still alone, entered the dimly lit interior.

In the middle of the floor stood a rather battered wooden keg standing on its end about three feet high, on top of which stood a lamp, its obnoxious fumes filling the air, almost drowning out the sweet scent of the hay. It took several minutes for his nostrils to accustom themselves to the smell and for his eyes to adjust to the dim light, standing on the threshold to gain his bearings before venturing further into the dark space before him. Gradually he began to see more clearly and to make out the sheaves of hay neatly stacked all around him, no evidence remaining from the last illicit run. Although total silence met his ears he sensed he was not alone and, once his eyes had accustomed themselves to the darkness, he glanced around him; no one was in sight but, just as he had begun to think that he was being led into a trap he heard a familiar voice from the dark recesses in front of him. "You are certainly punctual, Major."

"Ferrers?" Gideon asked sharply.

"You are alone?" Richard demanded.

"Yes, quite alone," Gideon confirmed, gradually beginning to make out a shadowy form emerging from the very rear of the barn into the beam of light from the lamp.

"I regret I cannot offer you more comfortable surroundings, Major" Richard apologized, "but, for the time being, these will have to suffice."

"It's no matter," Gideon assured him, in his quiet way. Richard was by now standing within a few feet of him, only the makeshift table separating them, a dark mysterious figure wearing a tricorne pulled low over his forehead with a huge muffler covering the lower half of his face. "Tell me," Gideon asked, not unamused, "do you always keep your face hidden or are you overly fond of charades?"

"Habit, Major" he nodded.

"Do you think you could break it for tonight?" Gideon asked. "I have an aversion to talking to someone I cannot see. I think I told you so last night!"

"So you did, Major" Richard affirmed affably. He seemed to consider Gideon's request for several minutes, then raising a pair of beautifully shaped hands, the light from the lamp picking out a heavy gold signet ring on the little finger of his left hand, removed the black tricorne from his head, revealing his thick dark hair, not quite as dark as his sister's, but neatly tied in a black bow in the nape of his neck. He then proceeded to unfold the muffler, not the usual coarse woollen type used by his associates, but of the finest black lawn. "Happy now, Major?" Richard enquired, not shrinking from Gideon's scrutiny.

He was far taller than his sister, lean and loose limbed, exuding the nimble agility of a cat. He was almost twenty five years of age but looked older and, although he had the same wilful mouth and striking blue eyes, which were equally as searching, the similarity between them was more in facial expressions than actual features. Instead of her classically straight nose his bordered on the aquiline; and, where her chin was softly curved his was squarely determined, the slight cleft emphasizing his decisiveness. He could not be described as handsome precisely but there was something oddly attractive about him and, coupled with that air of excitement and danger which hung about him, Gideon shrewdly guessed the ladies would no doubt find him quite irresistible. Miss Trench obviously did!

"You're not very like your sister," Gideon told him, removing his own hat and gloves and tossing them onto a pile of sheaved hay.

"No," Richard acknowledged. "She is unquestionably the beauty of the family."

"Unquestionably!" Gideon agreed.

"Well," Richard nodded, his white teeth glinting, "at least we agree on something."

"We may agree on a lot more, Ferrers," Gideon remarked, "providing you tell me the truth."

"Ah yes," Richard mused, rather mockingly, "the truth. But, you know Major, there are those who do not wish me to tell the truth."

"I am beginning to believe that," Gideon nodded, "but do not count me among them."

"Why should I not?" Richard asked, raising a questioning eyebrow. "After all, you have been sent here to find me."

"That is true," Gideon admitted, unperturbedly, "but, as I have already made perfectly clear, neither you nor your sister will come to harm through any agency of mine."

"Words come very cheap, Major" Richard pointed out, his eyes watching Gideon's face intently.

"To some men, perhaps" Gideon acknowledged, "but not to me."

"Why should I believe you?" Richard asked.

"Because I have given you my word," Gideon stated simply, testing the strength of several bundles of straw before sitting cautiously down on top of them.

"You think that is sufficient?" Richard asked, taking the opportunity to peer round the door to satisfy himself that no one was outside.

"I told you I came alone," Gideon reminded him.

"I know you did," Richard replied calmly, "but a man in my position cannot be too careful," he pointed out. After ascertaining that he had indeed come alone, not that he really expected anything else, he repeated his previous question as he sat down on an improvised seat comprising bundles of straw opposite to Gideon.

"My word is all you have," Gideon told him matter of factly. "If you can't or won't accept it, then there is nothing more to be said."

Ferrers looked searchingly at him, debating whether this man was indeed telling the truth or merely attempting to trap him into a false sense of security before handing him over to Colonel Henderson. He did not think so, in fact, he was sure of it but, it would not hurt to be cautious. "You seem mighty eager to help me Major, but for the life of me I cannot conceive why! However, before I tell you anything," he said bluntly, "I would like to know precisely what your orders are and where exactly this General of yours fits into all of this."

"As I told you last night," Gideon reminded him, "I have served under General Turville for most of my service, and a more fair and just man I have yet to meet. You should know that better than most; he being a lifelong friend of your father."

Ferrers nodded. "Yes, I know but, as I said, I only met him two or three times in my life," he paused as if considering something. "You say he believes me?"

Gideon nodded. "Without question. When Lytton insisted that you were a vicious traitor who must be caught, he knew something damned ugly was in the wind. As for *my* orders," he told him, "they are really very simple." He paused to take renewed stock of his surroundings. "However," he commented, bringing his gaze back to rest on Richard's face, "I cannot blame you for being cautious, after all" he pointed out, "you know nothing about me." Ferrers eyed him closely. "But I, too, can say the same," he pointed out, "until a short time ago I had never before heard of you."

"I'd lay a monkey you are wishing you never had!" Ferrers grimaced. "Association with me ain't good for the health."

"That remains to be seen," Gideon smiled, "but, if you are as hot as coals as General Turville seems to think, I would rather like to hear your side of the story before I leave you to your own devices - or to those of Colonel Henderson!" he remarked pointedly. "General Turville spoke very highly of your father; which is why when he learned of your difficulties, he refused to believe you guilty of treason."

"And what of my other activities?" Richard questioned, a light entering his blue eyes which left Gideon in no doubt of the affect they would have on people. "Does he believe me innocent of those too?"

"Let us just say," Gideon inclined his head, "that he is keeping an open mind."

"I am beginning to wish that I had known my father's friend better," he grinned. "I am growing to like him more with every passing second."

Gideon made himself more comfortable. "I know you can trust him."

"That's as may be," Richard replied cautiously, "but, I think I will reserve judgement on that for the time being."

"Very well," Gideon shrugged, "as you wish. The day before I spoke to him," he explained, looking straight across at his young friend, "he had received a most unexpected visit from none other than His Grace the Duke of Lytton, who, it appears, seems to want you arrested or, better still," he emphasized, "disposed of with all possible speed." Other than a lift of his eyebrows, Richard made no response to this. "He informed General Turville that you were a most desperate character, a Jacobite fugitive no less turned smuggler, and that no matter what it took you must be apprehended at all costs." He moved uncomfortably on his makeshift seat. "So eager was he to impress upon General Turville the urgency attached to your arrest and the advisability of keeping it as quiet as possible, that he began to wonder more particularly about you, and why it was so vitally important to find you." Gideon paused to see what effect this disclosure had had upon his listener, but no signs of any kind were visible on his face. "Indeed," he went on, "your capture is so imperative that he is quite prepared to use your smuggling activities against you and to 'gazette' you to ensure your arrest."

"And what did your General conclude, Major?" Richard enquired, meditatively chewing on a length of straw, a frown descending onto his forehead.

"Several possibilities sprung to mind," Gideon informed him, "but, since very little time has been granted to us, we saw little point in wasting what little there is by considering something which, after all, is pure speculation."

"Very wise, Major" Richard nodded approvingly, throwing the straw away.

"I am glad you approve," Gideon replied mockingly, "but it does not alter your situation in any way. At the moment," he informed him, "I am managing to keep Colonel Henderson at bay by making him believe that I have no knowledge of your whereabouts and that your sister, although hostile, is now hovering on the brink of confiding the truth to me, under threat of arrest. How long this pretence can be maintained I don't know but, if I were to carry out His Grace's orders to the letter, you would be at Hampton Regis garrison in far more uncomfortable surroundings than those in which you now find yourself."

Richard seemed to consider this. "You must not think that I am unappreciative of your efforts on my behalf Major, I am, but, whilst you and Turville appear to be quite prepared to go against Lytton's orders by carrying out your own, I cannot help but be a little suspicious and wonder why."

Gideon was quite unperturbed by this. "It is really very simple," he shrugged. "If, as they are trying very hard to make us believe, you are indeed a Jacobite, then why should it be necessary to conduct a search for you so surreptitiously? Why not do it out in the open as has happened before?"

"I see your point," Richard acknowledged. "But, if I am not a Jacobite," he asked provocatively, "what then am I?"

"You could be anything," Gideon dismissed. "Of course, the most natural conclusion to arrive at would be that you were employed by someone to seek out the real conspirator," he smiled. "I am not entirely sure whether to use the word 'spy' or 'agent', not that it signifies," he shrugged, "they mean the same thing."

"So I believe," Richard nodded, his eyes narrowing.

"Of course," Gideon told him, "if you were to tell me the truth it would save a considerable amount of time in conjecture, because from what I can see, you have precious little of it."

Richard rose to his feet, striding across the space to the double doors of the barn, peering out into the moonlit night with an intense look on his face. "Is it true what you said," he demanded urgently, "that I am going to be 'gazetted'?"

"I wouldn't lie to you about something like that," Gideon told him firmly.

"No," Richard sighed resignedly, "I don't think you would." He turned to face Gideon, a taut look on his face. "His Grace, *will* he 'gazette' me, do you think, or is it merely talk?"

Gideon could not prevent a smile. "His Grace," he informed him, "never *'merely talks'*, but, considering you have some knowledge of him, I thought you would have known that."

Richard nodded, the frown on his forehead deepening. "My personal knowledge of him is non-existent, I am glad to say, but his reputation goes before him, Major. I understand he is really quite ruthless in his dealings. I recall my father saying that it does not pay to get too close to Lytton or to let him know that you harbour a secret. He will destroy you without mercy!" He paused, saying at length, "I can only hazard a guess as to what he told Turville, but I am no Jacobite; upon my honour, I am not!" Gideon made no attempt to speak. "Oh, it suits them very well to say it, but they have need to fear me, Major, which is why they're doing their utmost to apprehend me, even going so far as to 'gazette' me," he grimaced. "How little they know my friends if they think they can be bought for five hundred pounds!"

"I bow to your superior knowledge of them," Gideon inclined his head, "but, whilst I commend your faith in their friendship and loyalty, it is an enormous sum for men in their position to forgo."

Richard, who had been contemplating the shine on his black leather boots, shot a quick look up at him, his eyes sparkling. "They may run illicit cargoes Major, but they do not turn tail on their friends!"

Gideon again inclined his head. "Very well," he shrugged, "I accept you word on that point. So, tell me," he asked, "how did you become labelled as a Jacobite in the first place?"

It was a moment or two before he answered this question, his intense blue eyes regarding Gideon thoughtfully but, like his sister, something told him he could be trusted. He did not need Salmon to tell him that he was a far cry from the others with whom they had had to deal, he could see that for himself and, upon reflection, he supposed it was a perfectly natural conclusion to arrive at about the fidelity of his associates.

Gideon, not unmindful of how his arrival could be construed, met his searching look unwaveringly, realizing perfectly well what was going through his mind.

"It wasn't that difficult," he shrugged at last. "Were you acquainted with Sir Matthew Mayhew?"

"Not intimately," Gideon shook his head, "but my father was. They were friends of long-standing. *I* only saw him a few times in my life. I believe he died not long ago."

Richard nodded. "Yes. Inflammation of the lungs or something. He and my father were close friends," he explained, resuming his seat opposite Gideon. "Politically they held the same views and opinions. Sometimes he would come and stay here at Ferrers Court or my parent's would stay with him and Lady Mayhew on his estate in Hertfordshire. When Sir Matthew was not committed to remaining in London he would go home to Hertfordshire but, when his wife died, he visited his estates less and less; either remaining in town or spending a few days here with my father."

"Didn't he have a son?" Gideon enquired. "Peter, I believe."

"Yes," Richard nodded. "It seems Sir Matthew was destined to lose those he loved quite early. I was at Eton with Peter and we became great friends, but he died young from some kind of lung disease. Sir Matthew even sent him to Italy in the hope that the mild climate would help him but, I am afraid, it did not serve," his eyes clouded. "Sir Matthew was never quite the same after that and, unfortunately, there was no other son to inherit the title," he shrugged. "I understand some cousin or other inherited."

"My father always spoke very highly of him," Gideon told him quietly, shrewdly suspecting that Ferrers was contemplating his own uncertain inheritance.

"Everyone did so," Richard nodded, "they knew he could be trusted and that he was not a man to engage in loose talk. He was a clever and intelligent man and one, moreover, who was not prone to exaggeration or jumping to conclusions. Which is why," he offered "my father and I took him seriously when he told us about information being leaked to Stuart."

"So, he employed you?" Gideon supplied.

"In a manner of speaking" Richard shrugged, "but, it happened purely by chance." Gideon looked a question. "My part in this," he explained, "came about because I happened to be at The Court one time while Sir Matthew was there. It was after my sister had retired that he confided his concerns to us in that someone was leaking information to Stuart. His attempts to discover the identity of the one responsible had failed but, this was more from no one wanting to accept the unpalatable truth than from any real effort on his part. Sir Matthew told us that he was convinced the real conspirator was someone in a position of considerable trust or, at least, someone in a position to get hold of the information, especially about what military deployments and strength Stuart could expect to be faced with. He was almost in despair and, yours truly," he inclined his head, "suggested that if the real Jacobite sympathizer was to be caught then the search for him would have to be conducted by someone outside the usual official departments, possibly by a much younger man than my father or Sir Matthew or, even, those long established stalwarts in Government. Whoever it was," he explained, "had to be prepared to convince everyone that he held sufficient Jacobite leanings to join The Pretender on the Continent. God knows" he pointed out, "there was more than enough sympathy for him in many quarters but, a much younger man, would stand a better chance of making the pretence more believable in that he was open to new ideas and more likely to be influenced by The Pretender's claim and charm than someone Sir Matthew's age."

"So, you volunteered," Gideon supplied.

Richard grimaced. "In a manner of speaking, yes. Sir Matthew was very influential in the Government but, even though there were pockets of sympathizers scattered about who had already proved themselves ready to welcome Stuart with open arms, as they had with his father thirty years before, certain of its members refused to believe that a leak existed, much preferring the more comfortable theory that Stuart was merely dogged with good luck!" he grimaced again. "So, Sir Matthew decided to instigate a hunt for the traitor on his own and, yours truly," he bowed mockingly, "apart from the fact that my father's friendship played a part in my recruitment, was by no means happy knowing that someone was prepared to work against his King and country, found myself persuading Sir Matthew and my father that I was more than prepared to help seek out the true source of the leak. No doubt," he grinned, "spurred on by too much wine!"

"I thought it was something like that," Gideon nodded. Upon receiving a questioning look from Richard, he smiled. "Having given your dilemma a considerable amount of thought," he informed him, "the only thing that made any sense and, which would account for the ruthless determination to find you, was that you were recruited. However," he remarked, "I must confess I did wonder whether your father knew the truth."

"Of course he did!" Richard exclaimed. "I wouldn't have done it otherwise. I'm not saying he was any too enamoured of the idea, especially when one considers the enormity of what I was taking on and the possible consequences but, he agreed that the leak had to be stopped and the perpetrator brought to justice and, was finally brought to agree that I work with Sir Matthew in this."

"And your sister?" Gideon wanted to know, directing a searching look at him.

"Ah, yes" Richard nodded, "my sister. My father decided that under no circumstances was she to know the truth, not because she could not be trusted, far from it," he shook his head, "but merely to protect her."

"And that story Salmon told her about the row you had had with your father the morning you left?" Gideon enquired.

"Make believe, Major" he grinned.

"You confided the whole to Salmon but, not your sister?" Gideon questioned, taken aback a little.

"Why not?" Richard demanded. "He's more than a servant Major. Salmon's been with the family for ever and my father trusted him implicitly. Nothing would induce him to give any one of us away. Besides," he added, when he saw Gideon was not convinced of the wisdom of this, "there was always the possibility that if something went wrong I would need to contact him."

"I can understand that," Gideon nodded, "but ..."

"There's no 'but' about it," Richard shook his head. "You've seen Salmon, does he strike you as being a gabster?"

"No," Gideon admitted, "far from it but, between you, your sister has suffered all manner of incivilities and worries, being subjected to treatment you yourself condemned."

"And what do you think would have happened had she have known?" he asked. "Probably she would have been bullied to the point where she would have told them the truth."

"I think we are destined to disagree on this, Ferrers," Gideon told him, "so, let me ask you, did you attempt to withdraw your services once you had sobered up?"

Richard shrugged. "I confess it did cross my mind but, I couldn't do it. Like my father, I'm a loyal Englishman, besides" he grinned, "I thought it would be rather exciting."

"Exciting!" Gideon exclaimed. "Do you call being charged with treason and disinherited, exciting?"

"I know," Richard smiled, "but I'm damned glad I didn't shy off!"

Gideon looked keenly at him. "You found the real conspirator?" he asked eagerly. Richard nodded. "Then, who is he?" Gideon urged.

It was several moments before Richard answered him. "Not he, Major" he shook his head. "*They.*"

Gideon's eyes widened. "*They?* How many are we talking about, precisely?"

"Two, to be precise," he nodded rising to his feet, a strange light entering his eyes. "Well, Major?" he raised a questioning eyebrow, as he stood looking down at Gideon's upturned face. "Are you telling me that no one springs to mind?"

Gideon shook his head, his eyes narrowing as he looked up at his young friend but, as he slowly rose to his feet, he was conscious of a sickening sensation springing to life in the pit of his stomach, not daring to believe what was going through his mind.

"You know, Major" Richard told him, "I am surprised that a man of your intelligence and astuteness has not yet guessed." Gradually the significance of these words sunk in and, when the awful realization of their meaning could be seen in those shocked brown depths, Richard confirmed, "Precisely, Major!" A twisted smile touched his lips. "How demoralizing it is for me to learn of my cousin's involvement in treason and, how disillusioning for you to learn the same of Colonel Henderson!"

There was no doubt that Richard was speaking the truth but, the effect his announcement had on Gideon was one of utter disbelief, so much so, that it was several moments before he could fully comprehend what he had been told. It seemed that General Turville's feelings about Colonel Henderson's involvement in this affair were more accurate than either of them had had any idea of but, the realization as to the extent of his participation, filled Gideon with profound shock.

What had motivated either Colonel Henderson or William Ferrers into taking such drastic steps as to not only declaring for Stuart but also leaking information to him, he could only guess at. What was equally as puzzling was

Lytton's involvement in all of this. Lytton may be a long-standing friend of Colonel Henderson but, he easily exonerated him of being a party to treason. Nevertheless, for a man of his strongly held opinions and unequivocal loyalty to the King, helping a traitor would surely be the last thing he would do. For a man of his perspicacity it would be logical to assume that he had either guessed the truth about Colonel Henderson or that he himself had confided it to him, together with his appeals for help but, in either event, it did not explain his reasons for coming to their assistance in helping to find Richard Ferrers. Lytton's participation in this affair therefore, continued to remain inexplicable but, if nothing else it explained why they were moving heaven and earth to find this young man.

"What's the matter, Major?" Richard asked, when Gideon made no reply. "Surprised? Or is it because you find it easier to believe that I am the traitor rather than someone like my cousin and Colonel Henderson?"

Gideon shook his head. "No, I never believed you guilty of that charge but, it *is* true I am finding it hard to believe that a man of Colonel Henderson's standing should have lent himself to the intrigues of treason."

"He would not be the first to offer support," Richard pointed out, "especially if that support were well rewarded."

"Yes, I know" Gideon acknowledged, "but it does not make it any more palatable."

Richard shrugged. "Probably not, but then, one never thinks that a man who wears the King's uniform is capable of embroiling himself in treason."

"Perhaps," Gideon nodded, still reeling from the shock.

"A scarlet coat does not necessarily mean the wearer can be trusted," Richard pointed out.

Gideon eyed him steadily. "No, it does not," he concurred, "but, whilst I too wear a scarlet coat, I hope you have now exonerated *me* of suspect motives."

Richard smiled, his eyes glinting. "Don't worry, Major, we would not be here now if I thought I could not trust you. I have never known Salmon mistake his man!"

Gideon inclined his head. "I am indebted to him. Unless I mistake the case, coming from Salmon that is quite an encomium!"

Richard laughed. "Salmon's no fool, on the contrary, he's as shrewd as he can hold together. I trust his judgement above any man's."

"You are, indeed, fortunate to enjoy the loyalty of such a man," Gideon remarked, who had no difficulty in believing Salmon's complete trustworthiness and devotion to the family. "But, do you think we could now return to the matter in hand? Did you ever suspect your cousin of holding such strong political views?"

"No," Richard shook his head, "and I still do not. For your information Major, I have never felt the least desire to converse with my cousin on any topic and certainly not to the extent of discovering his politics. In fact," he admitted, "my dislike of William is only equalled by his dislike of me." He grimaced. "Do not be thinking however, that I have fabricated any of this. I may not like my cousin, much less trust him but, I would never go so far as to accuse him out of spite!"

"I never suspected you did," Gideon replied, "but he must surely have had some reason for throwing in his lot with Colonel Henderson! No man takes a step of such magnitude on a whim!"

"No, I suppose not but, my feelings for William apart," he explained, "one cannot discount the fact that my cousin has no moral fibre whatsoever; too often he has allowed himself to be led by someone with a far stronger will than his own."

Gideon, still trying to come to terms with Colonel Henderson's complicity, had no difficulty in believing this. "I did gain that impression when your sister told me about him signing that document holding his right to the title in abeyance," he confessed. "Signing away what was legally his until your affairs were settled, made no sense whatsoever."

A wry smile played at the corners of Richard's mouth. "However much it pains me to say it," he admitted "in law, I am guilty as charged and, therefore have forfeited my rights to my father's dignities but, that any man would do what my cousin did is certainly proof of his complete lack of resolution or character, but then," he shrugged, "my father could always wither William with nothing more than a glance. Then, of course, there's Pritchard. He's handled our legal affairs for as long as I can remember and has always had our interests at heart." His eyes clouded momentarily. "Whatever the rights or wrongs of it Major, my father tried to protect me right up to the very end by insisting William sign that document and, Pritchard would have eagerly endorsed it. My cousin, when faced with such opposition, would have had neither the nerve nor the desire to do otherwise."

"That certainly explains a lot," Gideon said slowly, "but not how he came to embroil himself in something as serious as treason. Your sister said nothing to me about him knowing Colonel Henderson."

"She wouldn't," he shrugged, "she doesn't know. Like me, she had no idea they even knew one another. She still does not."

"But, how would he have come to know him in the first place?" Gideon asked, a frown creasing his forehead.

"There was always the title," Richard said sardonically, his lips thinning. "He's always had an eye to the viscountcy and has found it hard to accept that upon my father's death his dignities will fall to me. William is two years older than I but, he has never been able to accept that he is my father's nephew and not his son. One has to remember," he pointed out, "that there was always the possibility that I would predecease my father and, with no other son to inherit, the title would fall to William. He has always been a frequent visitor to The Court, riding around the estate as though it were already his. My father may not have welcomed his

207

visits but, he was wise enough to know that it would be foolish to ban him visiting The Court as one day it could well be his. Unfortunately for my cousin, there was no guarantee that I would die before my father, or that I would die without issue of my own," he looked meaningfully at Gideon. "I say that because I have the feeling my sister has told you about Jane." Gideon nodded in response to this, but made no reply. "In fact," Richard scorned, "he was here only a couple of weeks ago." He smiled irresistibly across at Gideon. "You see what I mean, Major? I know precisely what goes on at my home."

"You are clearly well informed," Gideon stated, his frown deepening, "but it still does not explain how they became acquainted in the first place."

Richard shrugged. "I can't answer that; they could have met at any time, but my cousin has never been one to let opportunity slip."

Gideon seemed to be considering something, saying at length "I understand from your sister that your cousin has a predilection for gaming; do you think that money was his motivation rather than loyalty?"

"Egad!" he exclaimed. "Never doubt it! He never has a feather to fly with. He takes after my uncle in that. William played wily beguiled with the money my Aunt Sophia left him and, if all I here is true," he nodded "his affairs are in a pretty bad way; he's been pledging his credit all over town with no hope of defraying the half of it." He eyed Gideon thoughtfully. "I'd say my cousin has been in a hole for far longer than we have any idea of."

"Financial reasons could explain your cousin's involvement," Gideon acknowledged, "even his jealousy, but not Colonel Henderson's."

"I'm not so sure," Richard said slowly. "From all I hear Henderson's tastes are more than he can adequately afford; he's ambitious too but, he's held the same rank now for a long time with no further promotion or prospects of any. Stuart was grateful for any help and, he would have well rewarded his supporters. Of course," he added, "it also has to be remembered that his grandfather was with Charles I when he raised his standard at Nottingham in 1642 and that his father joined James II in exile in 1688, taking part in the battle at the River Boyne. There is no doubt that the Henderson family hold Stuart sympathies but, whether the same can be said for our friend the Colonel, remains to be seen. From what I have been privileged to see of him," he offered, "I would say he has no sympathies for anyone but himself."

"If he *does* hold them," Gideon pointed out, "then one has to admit he has done remarkably well in the military so far."

Richard raised his head at this. "I hear the powers that be are prepared to overlook quite a lot in certain circumstances."

"You hear an awful lot," Gideon smiled.

"It's kept me alive, Major" Richard told him.

"And it's my job to ensure you remain so," Gideon pointed out. He paused momentarily, eyeing his young friend thoughtfully. "You're sure about all of this?" he questioned, "their involvement with Stuart?" envisaging all manner of pitfalls in attempting to prove it.

"Quite sure," came the unequivocal reply. "There's no doubt that Henderson and my cousin were in league with Stuart."

"Yes, but can you *prove* it?" Gideon asked urgently, his eyes narrowing.

Richard suddenly looked a little shamefaced. "Well, yes and no," he smiled.

"What do you mean?" Gideon demanded. "Either you have proof or you do not. Which is it?"

Richard, seemingly untroubled about the situation he was in, merely picked up another length of straw and began to chew it. After eyeing Gideon speculatively for several moments he said placidly, "Do not be alarmed Major, there is evidence enough to hang them both."

"Where is it?" Gideon asked urgently, unable to share Richard's apparent unconcern, "and, more to the point, *what* is it?"

Considering he was only inches away from the hangman's noose, Gideon would have thought he would be taking his unenviable position a little less casually but, all of a sudden, the smile dawned, putting Gideon very much in mind of his sister. The resemblance between them was not distinct but, that smile was unmistakable.

"Why don't you sit down Major, while I tell you."

The request was irresistible and, in that moment, Gideon had no difficulty in understanding his sister's comments in that his present difficulties, with the exception of Sir Arthur, had made no difference with people or how he had managed to persuade Salmon to keep in touch with him. He could well imagine his illicit accomplices falling into line with whatever he said, he could only hope that his charm and charisma could prevent him from dangling at the end of a rope!

"Despite what you may think, Major" Richard told him, "I am fully aware of the position in which I stand."

"That's something, at least," Gideon inclined his head, reluctantly smiling before taking his advice and resuming his seat.

Richard laughed. "You're mighty cautious Major but, I don't despair of you!"

"And you're a young fool, but never mind that!" Gideon told him. "Tell me about this proof you may or may not have."

Richard shrugged his shoulders and, seating himself down opposite Gideon, explained "It's perfectly simple. Stuart was a man who had grand aspirations but, in order to achieve them, he not only needed money in which to fund an army but men in prominent positions who could help him; feed him vital information, especially regarding what military strengths and deployments he could expect to face. Of course," he remarked, "the ironic thing is that should he have succeeded it would have been his father who mounted the throne, not him. But, I digress," he smiled.

"I am aware of the genealogical implications," Gideon told him, "but I am more interested in your involvement."

Richard grinned. "So is half the world!"

"Well, if you will embark on such escapades as this," Gideon pointed out, not without a touch of humour, "it is hardly surprising."

"That's as may be," he pointed out, "but, in spite of it all, I wouldn't have missed it for anything!" His eyes sparkled at the memory but, only briefly; his father's untimely death and the indignities heaped upon his sister as well his enforced estrangement from Jane, damping any enthusiasm he may have had. "Having gained written support of allegiance and help Stuart set about making plans to arrive in England, before that however, I joined him on the Continent offering my loyalty and support. The Bonnie Prince, despite the fact that the French were prepared to support him if he could begin an insurrection here first, was in urgent need of friends and men he could trust. Incredibly, he believed the tale I told him and took me to his side without a moment's hesitation. He was young and inexperienced and not always discreet. When I asked him what support he could count on in England he was only too happy to tell me. Whether he thought I would turn tail and run if assistance here was uncertain, I don't know but, it didn't take much to get him to tell me the name of the man who had been feeding him information about military deployments here and what strength he was likely to encounter," he paused, throwing his straw away. "I asked to see the letters and he was perfectly happy to oblige, incredible when one considers that I had only been with him a short time and he had no guarantee I could be trusted!" he shrugged. "Colonel Henderson had gone into great detail," he explained, "even naming my cousin as a party to it, all signed by him with a secret mark at the bottom proving they came from him. At the earliest opportunity I retrieved those letters, all six of them. Fortunately for me, affairs kept Stuart too busy to notice their disappearance. When he sailed for Scotland I sailed with him and, after leaving Eriskay, we landed in Moidart on the mainland a couple of days later where I parted company with him on the pretext of approaching certain parties I knew who were sympathetic to his cause, promising to join him as soon as I could. So desperate was he to draw people to his side that he believed me. You know the rest," he shrugged. "Stuart made Lord George Murray his commander of the army and together they began to drum up men to their banner. Then in the September General Sir John Cope suffered that shattering defeat at Prestonpans, Stuart then marched south, reaching Derby at the beginning of December when, for reasons I have never quite understood," he shook his head, "turned and marched back across the border. As you know," he nodded, "it created virtual panic in the city and the Government recalled Cumberland and the army from the Continent. Falkirk was a minor victory for Stuart but Colloden was a different matter altogether. As for me," he inclined his head, "when I left him in Moidart I began to make my way to London by a circuitous route; I knew the tale of my supposed defection would be abroad and I could not take any chances. After about three months I had almost reached London when I heard of Sir Matthew's death. Since no one but the two of us and my father knew the truth I decided to come home to talk it over with him," he paused, his eyes clouding as he thought of him. "He was a wonderful man Major, the best father anyone could have and not one to lose his head in a crisis. I thought if anyone could advise me he could, but I'd only been in Sussex a matter of thirty six hours when I was spotted by some of the soldiers from the garrison at Hampton Regis. I was immediately taken to the prison block and held in a cell for close on half an hour before I was taken to Colonel Henderson for questioning. Even now," he shook his head, "I cannot believe they did not search me first but, luckily for me, they did not. I knew that once I *was* searched those letters would be discovered and confiscated. So," he smiled, "I took the only opportunity I had of hiding them. I had to work pretty quick as you can imagine, but I managed to remove a brick which I saw was already loose in one of the walls near the bottom and had gone quite unnoticed, so I put them in there, where they still are, wrapped in an oilskin," he smiled across at Gideon. "I think I was pretty damned clever! He's been searching all over for them and they're sitting virtually under his nose; have been in fact for twelve months or more!"

"I suppose you *had* to tell him of your discovery in that he was a traitor?" Gideon sighed, not quite sure why he was so surprised at this.

"Of course!" Richard nodded.

"So that explains why he's been searching all over for you," Gideon remarked, eyeing his young friend.

"He was as sick as a horse, I can tell you," Richard commented, not without a touch of satisfaction, "especially when I told him that I could prove his treason. Naturally, he didn't believe me but, eventually, he saw I was telling the truth. When I wouldn't divulge the letters' whereabouts he went off into a tangent, spluttering something about how it would go very much the worse for me if I didn't hand them over and, no doubt, I would be singing a very different tune after a spell in one of the cells. By then it was quite dark," he explained, "and the two young privates' whose job it was to escort me back to the prison block were either eager to see the end of their patrol duty or they were mighty inexperienced, because their grip on me was slight. At the first opportunity I managed to free myself from their hold. I hit the one and sent the other sprawling then ran to the wall and managed to scale it. The cry went up for me but they were too late; I had gone."

Gideon, who had listened to this with interest, eyed his companion with respect. "You have clearly had a rather eventful time of late."

"But worth every minute of it!" he exclaimed satisfyingly. "Of course," he told him seriously, "once he knew about those letters that's when the searches at The Court began, the very next day, in fact, and, of course," he said, suddenly sombre, "they resulted in my father's death. When I escaped from the garrison I knew I could not go home as that would be the first place they would look so I went to see a friend of mine who took me in but, it was not long before I heard of what had happened to my father and, although I could still not go anywhere near The Court," he said with a touch of bitterness, "I decided to get word to Salmon."

Gideon nodded, but somewhere at the back of his mind he had the very strong feeling that there was something Richard was not telling him but, if he was going to help this madcap young man to clear his name, it was imperative that he was totally honest. Upon pointing this fact out to him he found himself on the end of a long and questioning stare.

"You don't miss much, do you?" Richard commented.

"It may interest you to know, Ferrers," he told him firmly, "that I did not attain my rank either through paternal influence or by being half asleep!"

Richard laughed out at that. "Very well, Major," he nodded, "if you must have it!"

"I *must*" Gideon confirmed. "I cannot help you if you do not tell me the whole truth."

Richard nodded. "Very well, I'll tell you."

"Do I need to sit down?" Gideon asked amusedly, recollecting saying precisely the same thing to his sister, both of whom it would appear made the most serious confession seem almost commonplace.

Richard smiled. "No, it's nothing I've done," he promised.

Gideon's eyebrows rose. "I'm relieved to hear it. You have presented me with enough difficulties to overcome as it is!"

Richard laughed. "Nothing like that! It's to do with a friend of mine," he told him. "I discovered quite by chance that he had been stationed at the garrison in Hampton Regis some months ago, and I ..."

"Don't tell me" Gideon shook his head, his eyes alight with amusement, "Lieutenant Michael Beaton?" Richard nodded. "I thought so," Gideon smiled.

"You've met him?" he demanded.

"Yes, I've met him," Gideon acknowledged, "and unless I miss my guess I think you need have no concerns about him helping you." He then went on to tell him about his first meeting with his friend and how he must have since discovered the reason for him being sent here as he had done his utmost to keep him at arms length ever since.

"If that ain't just like him!" Richard exclaimed. "Silly clunch! He probably thinks you're here to see me hang!"

"I think so too," Gideon agreed, "but, even so, I am going to need his help."

"You must not think too badly of him," Richard shook his head. "He's a good friend. I've known him since we were at Eton and he often came to stay at The Court. He can't be stationed at the garrison and not know the position I'm in but, as neither Salmon nor I can get into the place to see him and he can't get to The Court, he doesn't know about those letters, because if he did" he nodded firmly, "he would get them for me."

"Don't let that worry you," Gideon assured him. "I'll speak to him."

"Well," Richard nodded, "I am going to have to rely on you to convince him that you do not have designs on my life!" Gideon acknowledged this with a perfunctory smile but, it soon became obvious to Richard that his benefactor too had something on his mind. "Now it's my turn to think *you* are holding something back," he said thoughtfully.

Gideon eyed him considering for a moment. "Not that, precisely," he shook his head, "but it's something that could be used against you." He paused for a moment, then looking straight across at his young friend said, "They have it you were at Culloden."

"I daresay it suits them to say so," he acknowledged, not entirely surprised by this, "but I was otherwise engaged at the time. Besides," he pointed out, "I told you I left Stuart after leaving Moidart; but, from what I was able to discover, I am damned glad I was not!" His face darkened. "I don't condone what Stuart attempted to do Major and, I would do the same again if I were asked, but those men who fought for him were no cowards, on the contrary, they were brave men, and did not deserve to be cut down and butchered like cattle!"

"I know," Gideon agreed quietly.

"Were you there, Major?" Richard enquired.

Gideon shook his head. "No. I was at home on sick leave. I was wounded in the shoulder at Falkirk."

"I'm sorry," Richard nodded.

"It's no matter," Gideon shrugged. "Although I must confess that, like you, I am glad to say I took no part in it." A sombre expression entered his dark brown eyes. "I realize that for one who wears the King's uniform that is not the attitude one should have but, if all I here is true, it was no place for the faint-hearted."

"The rebellion has done no one any favours, Major" Richard stated simply. "Noble enterprises never do; they always end in disillusionment and disaster."

"Stuart obviously didn't think so," Gideon remarked.

Richard grimaced. "No, but then, no aspiring usurper ever does. They all fall into the same trap in believing that promissory notes of support and financial help will win the day. They don't," he said firmly. "People like Henderson and my cousin offer allegiance because they hope to attain what they could never realistically achieve otherwise. They then straddle the fence in fear and apprehension; afraid their complicity will be discovered if the coup fails and apprehension if it succeeds, because they don't know for certain whether all they have been promised will come to fruition."

"Did you like Stuart?" Gideon asked curiously.

Richard sighed. "I suppose one could not help but like him. He was a most charming and charismatic man; like all the Stuarts. He could win one over with a smile. To his adherents he was a romantic and irresistible figure, but his was a doomed campaign and his weakness lay in not knowing it."

Gideon nodded. "But your campaign, Ferrers," he pointed out, "was certainly successful. My compliments on an excellent piece of work."

Richard offered a mocking bow, his eyes gleaming. "Thank you, Major."

"Now, though" Gideon pointed out practically, "we are left with the task of proving you innocent. You say those letters are still there?"

"As far as I know. You see," Richard apologized ironically, "I can hardly walk into the place and retrieve them."

Gideon eyed him. "Naturally. So if we are to prove you innocent of treason we must get them back into our possession as soon as possible."

"As you say, Major" Richard bowed, his eyes alight with amusement.

Gideon grinned. "Yes, I know, I have stated the obvious. But I have not set foot inside the prison block since my arrival, indeed, there is no reason why I should," he paused for a moment, considering. "I think this is where your friend Beaton comes in. Which cell was it?"

"The second one on the left to the main door."

"Very well," Gideon acknowledged, "I'll look for them, but it will take time and planning."

"I have every confidence in you, Major" Richard smiled.

"I daresay," Gideon frowned, "but you haven't yet told me how you came to take part in your present activities, *which*" he pointed out grimly, "has only served to compound your difficulties as well as to place you in the worst possible light."

Richard shrugged. "What else was there for me to do? With my father and Sir Matthew dead I couldn't report Henderson's complicity any more than I could my cousin's; without those letters who would have believed me? I couldn't go home because there was every chance it was being watched and I couldn't just walk into the garrison and take them."

"So, you joined the fraternity!" Gideon supplied.

"Why not?" Richard shrugged. "I knew quite a few of the men who were involved in the trade, in fact, my father often took possession of a keg or two!"

Ignoring this, Gideon asked, "How involved are you?"

Richard eyed him closely. "Why?"

"I should have thought that was obvious," Gideon told him. "Trying to extricate you from a charge of treason is difficult enough but, to be expected to do the same regarding your illicit cargo trafficking, has it perils! His Grace being only one of them!"

"Egad!" Richard laughed. "I was right, you *are* cautious. However, I see your point. Do not be alarmed, Major," he assured him, "I only go out with them for sport, not profit."

"Sport or not" Gideon commented, "under the law you are committing a felony and, if I am to bring you off unscathed, you would be doing us both a very great service by refraining to participate further."

"Is that an order?" Richard enquired amusedly.

"I am afraid to say that it is," Gideon confirmed. "You are in enough trouble as it is without adding to it, and *if*," he pointed out, "Lytton does 'gazette' you, you will find yourself in a whole lot more. A high honour, Ferrers!" he remarked sardonically.

"Egad! Ain't it, though!" Richard mused, rubbing his nose with a long forefinger.

"You will oblige me, therefore," Gideon told him unequivocally, "by keeping an extremely low profile until I can put my hands on those letters." Richard looked as if he was about to argue the point, but was immediately forestalled. "If you don't have a care for yourself," he pointed out, "have a care for your sister. She is deeply concerned over you and, to see you strung up for smuggling in Hampton Regis market place will not serve her in the least!"

Richard looked closely at him. "You seem to know a great deal about my sister."

Unperturbed by this, Gideon nodded. "Yes, and I intend to know a whole lot more about her when this is over."

"Is that so?" Richard asked quietly.

"That is so," Gideon confirmed, eyeing him squarely. "In the meantime," he pointed out, "I know enough to tell you that she has endured much at Colonel Henderson's hands, which you already know and, despite her earnest entreaties that she knows nothing of your whereabouts or activities, he has pursued her relentlessly." Richard's eyes gleamed, but Gideon, not unused to dealing with hot blooded young men, said practically, "Put out of your head any ideas you may have of seeking retribution. They will serve no purpose. Channel your energies into more practical matters, such as coming out of this unscathed."

Richard considered the face opposite and, like many before him, saw the determination and strength of will lying beneath the even-tempered surface. Nothing would give him greater pleasure than to be able to repay Colonel Henderson for the treatment he had handed out to his sister but, Gideon's reasoning won the day. He would have his revenge when he produced those letters! "As you wish, Major" he inclined his head. "I want more than anything to clear my name."

Gideon nodded. "I realize that," he acknowledged "but your part in this affair is over for the time being. Make no mistake," he promised, "I will engage to find your letters but, it will take time. As for you," he smiled, "there's to be no more nocturnal trips across the Channel, that is not going to help you." Richard, who knew it was true, nodded agreement. "There *is* one thing you haven't told me though," Gideon said calmly, whereupon Richard raised a questioning eyebrow. "Captain Waring told me that he knew of your smuggling activities from Colonel Henderson, yet no one had ever caught you red-handed running goods."

"So?" Richard shrugged.

"So how did Henderson learn of your activities in the first place?" he asked reasonably. "You said yourself you had only been back in Sussex a day or two when you were spotted and taken to the garrison, that being so, you had not then commenced your illicit trading."

"I see your point," Richard nodded, pursing his lips.

"Either someone did see you and reported it to him, or he automatically assumed that that was what you would do in order to hide yourself from your pursuers until you could place your hands on those letters," he explained logically. "If that is, indeed, the case," he grimaced, "then it is the greatest piece of foresight and intuition I have ever encountered; and, quite frankly I don't believe he possess either!" He eyed Richard closely. "Someone must have informed him."

It was several moments before Richard spoke, a light of recognition gradually entering his eyes. "Of course, William!" he said at length. "It must have been he who told Henderson."

"William?" Gideon repeated. "How would he have known?"

"I remember now," he nodded, "his man, Whitney, saw us one night." He saw Gideon raise a questioning eyebrow and explained, "We ran a cargo in one night but, when we arrived at the place to store the goods the Excisemen were swarming around like flies, so we had to take the goods to the inn in East Dean instead; the landlord there is a particular friend of mind as well as sympathetic," he grinned when he saw Gideon's expression. "One of us went on ahead to tell Eli to expect us but, when we arrived, I was told that one of the customers had been too drunk to make his way home but I was not to worry because he had dragged him to a back room. Well," he pulled a face, "he either had an extremely hard head or he was merely foxing, because about ten minutes later while we were hiding the goods the man staggered into the taproom wondering what the devil was going on. It would not have taken much to see what was happening," he shrugged. "but, I saw at a glance it was Whitney, and he recognized me immediately."

"So that explains it," Gideon nodded.

"The little rat!" Richard exclaimed, his eyes glinting.

"Well," Gideon sighed, "it's no use repining, the damage is done. But I meant what I said, Ferrers," he reminded him firmly, "your days of running goods are over."

Richard nodded. "I give you my word," he promised but, as he clasped Gideon's hand, his eyes clouded. "I have only one regret in all of this, and that is that my father died before I could see him. He went to his grave knowing his only son to be hailed a traitor. He never lived for the truth to come out. For that," he exclaimed bitterly, "I shall never forgive myself!"

Gideon returned the clasp, not unsympathetic to his feelings. "Try and take heart from knowing that your father knew the truth, and that his son is a loyal Englishman. I wish I could help you in this but, I cannot; what I *can* do however, is to try and clear your name."

Richard's eyed glowed. "If you can do that Major, I shall be forever in your debt!" he exclaimed fervently.

"And I shall be in yours, if you will endeavour to keep out of trouble," Gideon returned, picking up his hat.

Richard grinned. "I am yours to command, Major," executing an exquisite bow.

"I seriously doubt that," Gideon laughed, putting his hat on. "If you need me," he said, "let Salmon know. By the by," he asked, raising a questioning eyebrow, "does Salmon know about your cousin and Colonel Henderson?"

Ferrers shook his head. "No. He knows I've discovered the identities of the real traitors, but not who they are. I would trust Salmon with my life Major" he told him sincerely, "but, he so hates my cousin and not afraid to let him see it; there could come a time when he allows his feelings to get the better of him. As for Elizabeth," he shook his head, "she knows nothing." He saw the look which crossed Gideon's face and, explained, "I realize you don't agree with that but, it's the only way I can protect her, besides which," he added, "William's visits to The Court must not be accompanied by suspicion, once he guessed they knew the truth he'd shab off quicker than a jack rabbit and, I *want* him Major," he said firmly. "I want them both to pay for what they have done."

"They will, I assure you," Gideon promised. "They will stand their trial for treason."

"Are you going to tell Salmon and my sister the truth?" he asked.

"Yes," Gideon told him unequivocally, "I have to. Events have moved along too far to keep it from them but, I think you know as well as I that I doubt I shall have to impress upon them the need to keep it to themselves."

"There's no need to tell me that," Richard replied. "Although, why the devil I should command their loyalty, beats me!"

"I think you know the answer to that," Gideon smiled. Richard returned the smile a little self-consciously. "And don't forget, Ferrers" Gideon reminded him, "no more escapades."

Richard nodded absent agreement to this but, Gideon, suspecting there was something on his mind asked if anything were wrong. "Not wrong, precisely," he shook his head, "but about my sister, did you mean what you said about getting to know her better?"

Gideon looked straight at him. "Yes, every word."

"You like her that much?"

"Yes, I like her that much," he confirmed. "I also happen to be very much in love with her despite the fact that we have not long met. I'm sorry if that does not meet with your approval, Ferrers" he told him, "but, whilst I appreciate your natural anxieties where she is concerned, I tell you now that I fully intend to marry her with or without your blessing."

Richard knew he would too. He may not have known Major Neville for very long but, he had seen enough of him to realize that he was not a man given over to making false promises, besides which, if what Salmon had told him were true, then Elizabeth was not averse to the Major either, on the contrary, it appeared as though she fully reciprocated his feelings. "It's not that, Major " he confessed, "it's just that - well, she's always been my sister, if you know what I mean?"

"I do," Gideon acknowledged, "and, I daresay, I would feel the same had I a sister. However, I do appreciate your feelings, especially when I consider we only met a little over two days ago. I could, of course," he smiled, "offer you all manner of assurances as to my intentions and credentials but, I think they will keep until your affairs are settled. Suffice it to say," he promised, "she will come to no hurt through me."

Richard nodded, then forestalled him by saying, "By the way Major, should Michael doubt your word about having met me or prove a little unwilling to believe you mean me no harm, just ask him if he ever managed to persuade his father into buying him that bay hunter he had set his heart on."

They parted on the best of terms with Richard reiterating his promise but, Gideon's hopes far exceeded his expectations regarding his young friend's assurances to keep out of trouble and to refrain from taking any further part in his present occupation. He had no difficulty in believing him when he said he did it for sport and not profit. Having made the acquaintance of Richard Ferrers he could well understand his sister's observations in that it appealed to his adventurous spirit. He was certainly a young man who had an abundance of that and, one to whom inactivity and idleness were intolerable; were it otherwise, he would never have put forward a proposal, albeit well intentioned, that would be looked upon favourably by not only Sir Matthew Mayhew but his father also, thereby propelling him headlong into a situation that was far from enviable as well as leaving his future looking extremely bleak to say the least.

He had undertaken the task with eagerness and dexterity and had proved himself worthy of the trust placed in him but, unfortunately, Sir Matthew's untimely death as well as that of his father, had placed him in a most awkward position especially as no one else was party to the transaction. Salmon's word would count for nothing except that of a last ditch attempt by a man who had only his young master's best interests at heart.

Despite his outward show of optimism, Gideon knew it was going to be no easy matter to retrieve those incriminating letters from their hiding place as the prison block was constantly manned. He could not see Richard Ferrers kicking his heels in idle expectation of being extricated from his difficulties for very long and could only hope that the thought of clearing his name would be sufficient inducement to temper the more energetic side of his nature.

Richard Ferrers may have commented about not daring to enter the town himself, let alone the garrison but, he believed he had measured that young man's character accurately enough to be able to say that he would not put it beyond him to make the attempt to retrieve those letters himself without waiting for him to do so. In fact, it would be precisely the kind of thing a young man of his stamp would do and, enjoy doing it; the danger adding a certain piquancy to the task.

He was not at all sure whether he approved of Richard Ferrers informing Colonel Henderson of the existence of proof of his complicity and that of his cousin in the late rebellion or not. The more he thought about it the more inclined he was to believe that the searches conducted at Ferrers Court had been more in the hope of finding such damning evidence rather than Richard Ferrers himself. The fact remained however, that he did know of their existence and, would not rest until they were in his possession and safely destroyed. It must have come as a reeling blow to discover that far from having disposed of them, Stuart had kept them and had been misguided enough to show them to other eyes.

He could well understand Colonel Henderson's and William Ferrers' anxiety in knowing that at any moment they could be revealed as traitors to their King and country and that all which stood between them and exposure was a young man who seemed to be just tantalizingly out of reach. What he could not quite understand though, was how they had managed to obtain the assistance of a man like Lytton, whose views on matters such as this were common knowledge. It was therefore reasonable to assume that Colonel Henderson had not told him the whole truth, in which case His Grace's intervention could be explained easily enough. Nevertheless, a man like Lytton would surely demand to know why a garrison commander with armed men at his back had failed to secure the arrest of one man, who, apparently, was not the only supposed fugitive still on the run. Even taking into account their long-standing friendship, it did not entirely explain Lytton's involvement to his satisfaction, especially when he considered the intention of 'gazetting' Richard Ferrers. It was certainly a drastic step to take but, whether this course of action stemmed from Colonel Henderson or His Grace, remained to be seen.

In either event, Richard Ferrers was treading a very perilous path and, by the time Gideon eventually arrived back at Hampton Regis, his mood was far from positive, indeed, he was apprehensive and fearful. His young friend stood in more danger than he realized and, his mood was not enlivened when he considered that time was not on their side but, on the contrary, in extremely short supply.

The object of Gideon's anxious thoughts, in no hurry to leave his humble sanctuary, remained chewing his length of straw in quiet contemplation long after his benefactor had gone. He was all too aware in what case he stood, and that his future prospects looked extremely bleak but, he was also aware that he could not extricate himself from his difficulties without help.

Smuggling run goods under the noses of the Excisemen was all very well, indeed, it was excellent sport, as well as affording him much needed protection from his pursuers but, the truth was, his heart was not in it. But, more than that, he wanted to clear his name and take up his rightful place in the world where he belonged, not to spend the rest of his life dodging the preventive officers.

It was impossible for him to be in Sussex and not know the state of affairs at Ferrers Court. He knew that his disclosure to Colonel Henderson about those letters proving his participation in the late rebellion with that of his cousin, had been one of the reasons for the constant attacks upon his home and sister, the fact that he had not found either those letters or his quarry had only served to increase his efforts. However, the knowledge that he could not show himself without the evidence he desperately needed to get his hands on to prove his innocence, coupled with his impotency to protect his sister, all served to increase his frustration. The only saving grace as far as he could see, if such one could call it, was that due to Sir Arthur's rigid stance about ceasing all contact with Ferrers Court and his refusal to honour their betrothal, had meant that Jane, at least, had been spared the necessity of undergoing rigorous interviews and answering probing questions. He could only be thankful that Colonel Henderson, irrespective of what he knew to be common knowledge, had not taken it into his head to visit The Manor and interview Sir Arthur in the vain hope that he had somehow managed to persuade Jane to assist him or even offer him shelter without her father's knowledge. Should that have happened then Sir Arthur, whose pride and self-worth even exceeded that of the Ferrers family, were such that he would never forgive such a slight, his innocence would mean nothing and, therefore could not see him sanctioning a marriage between himself and Jane.

When he had received that visit from Salmon he had not known which aspect of it annoyed him the most; the fact that a red-coat wanted to talk to him or that his sister had wheedled the truth out of him. However, it had not taken him long to see that Major Neville, not only coming at just the right time to save him from utter despair but, had appeared as the answer to his prayer.

He had spoken no less than the truth when he told Gideon that he had no regrets about his part in uncovering the identity of the real Jacobite conspirators, save those he had mentioned. He knew he would never forgive himself for the deception his father had been forced to adopt as well as bringing disgrace to an honoured name and, although that outward breach with his father had had his blessing, it pained him to know that his father had not lived to see the truth be told. He knew his father had had no regrets about supporting his son's actions but, even so, it did not help to lessen the pain. But there would be time enough for grief and recrimination. His main concern now was to clear his name but, he knew better than anyone, that that was going to prove to be no simple task.

Colonel Henderson knew of that damning evidence and would stop at nothing until those incriminating letters were in his hands and himself dangling from a rope. He knew too that Colonel Henderson would fight to the last ditch in order to save himself, even at the expense of others. He had made a colossal error in offering aid and allegiance to The Pretender, and was now in the uncomfortable position of having to rid himself of who or whatever could prove his involvement and expose him as a traitor and, if that included his accomplice, so be it. In his attempts to save himself Colonel Henderson would not give a moment's thought to anyone or anything except bringing himself off unscathed. If he had not been quite so angry and frustrated he could almost have felt sorry for William.

Without those letters he could kiss goodbye to proving his innocence and gaining his freedom. Although Major Neville had not struck him as a man given over to making false promises, he would nevertheless be interested to learn how he could possibly search for something under the very noses of the guards on duty. Then, of course, there was always the possibility that the cell in which he had hidden those letters could be occupied, in which case, the task of retrieving them would be well nigh impossible, at least, for the immediate future.

From the moment he had escaped from custody he had tried to hit upon a way of reclaiming those letters from their neat little hiding place but, to no avail. He was no coward and, although he was quite prepared to make the attempt to try and get his hands on them, time and time again Salmon's commonsense had held him back. Every soldier in Hampton Regis knew his face and, even to try and set foot within the town, let alone the garrison, would be to put a rope around his neck; the result being that he had been left to kick his heels in frustrating impotence, relieved only by his nocturnal trips across the Channel. His friends had given him much needed sanctuary but, the time had come to take up his place in society again but, just when he had come to believe that he would be living outside of the law for the rest of his life, Major Neville had arrived in the guise of a saviour to his problem!

CHAPTER ELEVEN

Had William Ferrers the least idea that his cousin was at this very moment divulging the truth to a man who could do him irreparable harm, he would not have closed his eyes all night. As it was, he was far too taken up with Elizabeth's coldness towards him. He realized now that he had been far too precipitate in his dealings with her, especially when it came to mentioning the inheritance. He knew perfectly well that even if Richard were to die from natural causes or the victim of an accident, she would never really accept him as the sixth viscount.

He had no need to be told that every member of the household believed in Richard's innocence and were extremely partisan and, that the slightest inference on his part to the contrary, would be met with horror and contempt. It was all very well for Elizabeth to hold him in such low esteem but, even without his participation in the late uprising, he would still like to know where he stood.

As he prepared himself for bed he realized what a colossal mistake he had made in saying anything about visiting Colonel Henderson in order to discuss Richard's affairs. He should have known that this would have set her back up especially as she regarded him as being entirely responsible for her father's death. There was no getting away from the fact that he had to see Colonel Henderson at some point during his stay and, this had been a perfectly feasible excuse for visiting the garrison, because should he be spotted going there and, knowing his luck, that would be precisely what would happen, she could easily be informed of it. Upon reflection, he thought he would have done better in not being quite so blunt in telling her of his intentions or that it would, perhaps, have been better left unsaid but, he supposed he should have known that no matter how he broached it, it was never going to be acceptable to her. Having made strenuous efforts to placate her, even going so far as to apologize to her over dinner for his lack of sensitivity, it was clear that she was in no mood to receive either his apologies or explanations. Her unwillingness to meet him half way annoyed him and, although it would have afforded him great satisfaction to remind her that he did not need her approval for whatever he chose to do or that her own position at Ferrers Court was none too secure, his courage failed him.

What Elizabeth lacked in inches she certainly made up for in spirit and, although she had the full support of Aunt Clara and Salmon, he knew perfectly well that his cousin could fight her own battles. He had inwardly quailed at the flash of anger she had thrown at him this afternoon, and knew it would be awhile before he would forget it. The fire in those wide blue eyes may have abated but it still smouldered and, any conversation he attempted at dinner, was politely but coldly received. Aunt Clara, when she was not pointedly ignoring him, was doing her utmost to goad him and Salmon, whilst doing nothing he could take exception to, certainly failed to accord him the respect he considered his due.

It was therefore in a mood of considerable peevishness that he bid his relatives goodnight, the only light on his horizon being that Whitney had not long returned from Hampton Regis with the news that his confederate had agreed to meet him the following evening.

"*Why* you don't send him packing, I don't know!" exclaimed her aunt as soon as the door had closed behind her nephew.

"Please, Aunt" she begged, "you know I can't."

"I don't know any such thing," she claimed tartly, throwing her napkin down onto the table with some force. "If ever a man means mischief, it's *him*. I can't abide him; never could. His father was just the same," she said forthrightly, "although I will say one thing about Lawrence, he was not a mealy-mouthed encroaching upstart like his son!"

"What possible reason could I give for asking him to leave?" she asked reasonably.

"There's no 'ask' about it," she stated bluntly, "just tell him to go!"

"Begging your pardon, Mistress," Salmon put in helpfully, "but your Aunt's right. If he could do Master Richard harm, he would."

"What possible harm could he do Richard when he knows no more than us where he is?" she asked judiciously. She saw the look of scorn on both faces. "Very well," she conceded, frustrated, "I admit he does not like Richard and he can't wait to step into his shoes, but to ask him to leave will only make him suspicious. Surely it is far better to have him here where we can keep our eyes on him!"

Her aunt, who clearly found no favour with this reasoning, merely snorted something which her niece understood to mean that if that was the best reason she could come up with then she washed her hands of the whole affair. "You won't shift him in under a month! However," declared that redoubtable lady, pushing her plate away with all the air of one who had tried her best, "if that is what you want, so be it!"

Elizabeth listened to her expound at length on the troubles which beset them and which would continue to befall them, as long as William remained at The Court and Richard skulked in hiding like a common felon. Over her head Elizabeth and Salmon exchanged significant glances but, her aunt, far from soothed by her forthright speech, rounded off her catalogue of grievances by saying that as far as she could see their deliverance appeared to be totally dependent upon a man they had never clapped eyes on before, ending with the pronouncement about doing the trick herself if all else failed. Upon seeing her aunt make no move to accompany her to the sitting room, she left her alone in the dining room to brood sombrely at an invisible point straight ahead of her, with a sinking heart. "Oh dear," she sighed, as she walked through the great hall beside Salmon, "I'm afraid I've upset her."

"She'll come round," he assured her, "never fear."

"What can I do, Salmon?" she demanded. "I don't want William here any more than you or my aunt but, surely you must see how awkward it would be for me to ask him to leave?"

"Well, Mistress" he offered, rubbing his chin, "it's a right pickle and no mistake!"

She could not help laughing at this. "Well, that's one way of putting it I suppose," she nodded, "but it doesn't solve the problem of how to get rid of my cousin without making him suspicious."

"Then there's tomorrow," Salmon reminded her fatalistically.

"Tomorrow! What about tomorrow?" she asked, puzzled.

"The Major's coming to tell you about Master Richard, that's what about tomorrow," he told her.

"Oh, goodness!" she cried, putting a hand to her forehead. "I had completely forgotten."

"Thought you had."

"Under no circumstances must William see Major Neville," she said earnestly. "The last thing we need is for him to start asking probing questions."

"Well," he told her practically, "I fail to see how they won't run across one another. Bound to, but I doubt he'll get much out of the Major."

"No," she shook her head, after giving it some thought. "I think you are right. I can't see Major Neville discussing my brother with William."

"Of course," he put in, "if you got rid of him now ..."

"Oh, for goodness sake, Salmon!" she exclaimed exasperated, thrusting open the sitting room door impatiently. "You know I can't. Please, don't mention it again."

"Very well," he nodded, in the voice of doom.

She was vexed about upsetting her aunt but, however much she regretted her cousin's visit and knew her supporters were right, she was firmly of the opinion that to ask him to leave could probably create more problems than it solved. In truth, she was not at all certain whether to be glad or sorry that William had arrived at this particular point in time, because although having him here at The Court meant that he was not creating mischief elsewhere or, rather, trying to do what he could to find a way of out of the promise he had made to her father, the fact remained that William, far more astute than he was given credit for, would be bound to question the Major's motives should he run across him. Since it was useless to suppose that their paths would not cross, all she could hope for was that

William, impatient to take possession of her father's title and dignities, would not take it into his head to use the Major's visit to his own advantage by offering to join forces with him in an attempt to seek out Richard on the pretext of only wanting to help him resolve his difficulties. She did not think that Major Neville would be taken in by such a ruse, for a man of his intelligence and acuity he would easily see through William's guile but, the fact remained, as long as Richard remained outside of the law and her cousin was presently residing at The Court only waiting for the opportunity to step into his shoes, she could not dismiss her concerns. The recurring question of her cousin as well as how Major Neville was progressing with Richard, tumbled around in her head for some considerable time and, it was not until she had lain awake for several anxious hours, that she finally fell into a fitful sleep.

She awoke the following morning not much refreshed and dreading yet another request from her overseers to send her cousin packing, her only solace being that Major Neville was due to visit. Salmon was neither surprised nor fooled by her nonchalant disclaimer that, apart from wishing to hear further news of her brother as soon as possible, she was merely hoping to speak to Major Neville and forewarn him about her cousin's unexpected arrival and not from any personal desire to see him. Taking advantage of his unassailable position within the household as well as having known her from the day she was born, he informed her that she would be far more convincing if she did not keep glancing at the avenue from whichever vantage point she happened to be at every few minutes.

"Major Neville will not show himself until he's ready," he told her matter of factly, much to her annoyance. "And, since I shall be the one to open the door to him, I can tell him all he needs to know. And *another* thing," he nodded, "should your cousin pose any awkward questions, which I can't see him doing, I am sure the Major will be able to deal with them adequately enough!"

As usual, Salmon had assessed the situation perfectly; but his shrewdness did not meet with approval from his mistress. It was true that she was eager for news of Richard but she was honest enough to admit that she was also desirous of seeing Major Neville again, no matter on what pretext. Annoyingly, Salmon knew it too and could not be brought to believe her feeble attempt to convince him that she did not want him to arrive at Ferrers Court just as William was returning from his ride.

Despite her valiant attempt to shrug off his unspoken suggestion with disdain, the colour which flooded her cheeks told its own tale, resulting in a deep throated chuckle from her aged tormentor. "That's no road to take, Mistress," he shook his head, "leastways, not until Master Richard is safe and, certainly, not until *he's* gone," he scorned, jerking a thumb.

She watched him walk away down the long gallery with his bow-legged gait, knowing he had spoken no less than the truth. She had never trusted William and certainly not enough to confide their difficulties to him now but, although she could not say why she felt this way about him, she only knew she did. She could not base her suspicions on anything definite but, the last thing she wanted, was for him to know that Major Neville was doing everything possible to help Richard, or that he had already met with him on two occasions. When William had mentioned about visiting Colonel Henderson it had not only angered her but alarmed her also. She failed to see what possible good a meeting with him could achieve, especially when she considered how he had behaved so far. Having adamantly refused to believe she was telling him the truth, surely his complete lack of respect in his dealings with her and her father merely went to prove how very far from being a man of reason he was.

As expected, her aunt and Salmon had so far behaved towards William in a manner which would have been amusing had it not been so very embarrassing, necessitating her to step into an uncomfortable breach more than once in the short time he had been here. She was not certain whether her cousin was extremely thick-skinned or blissfully unaware of the barbed arrows aimed at him, in either event, he had brushed through the ordeal of her aunt's sharp tongue and Salmon's silent disapproval with a composure that, in spite of herself, commanded her admiration.

Since Major Neville had not stipulated a time for his visit she had no idea when he would be arriving and, although she would like to keep the two men apart, she was realistic enough to know that this would be really quite impossible, despite her or Salmon's efforts to waylay him before he entered the house. Irrespective of her feelings for William and, not forgetting the weaknesses in his character, unlike Richard, she had always suspected him of being far more astute than he was given credit for.

According to Salmon he had breakfasted quite early, after which he had taken a stroll around the grounds, returning an hour or so later for a little refreshment before having a horse saddled and taking a ride around the estate. She could only hazard a guess as to how long he would be gone and fervently hoped that he and the Major would miss one another, but took some comfort from knowing that Salmon was right in that he would be more than capable of deflecting any pointed questions William may pose.

Deep in her heart she knew she could trust Major Neville and that he was a man of his word. She knew too that Salmon had come to the same conclusion but, having watched over her and Richard from infancy and would give his life for the pair of them, his acceptance of a stranger in their midst had at first been tinged with caution. It had not taken him long however, to conclude that not only was Major Neville a gentleman but had integrity as well as the good manners of a man of breeding, resulting in him placing his faith in someone who was not a Ferrers, had he not have done so, he would never have agreed to arrange a meeting with

Richard in the first place. He seemed to be in no doubt that Major Neville would find a way to bring Richard off safe and, as far as William was concerned, he was equally confident that the Major would know to a nicety how to deal with him. Richard of all people was no fool and, surely, if he had suspected Major Neville's integrity after their first meeting, he would not have suggested a second one?

She may at times find Salmon's over-watchfulness frustrating, but she would be lost without him, indeed, she would not be without him for anything. During the years she and Richard were growing up, he had taken them very much under his wing, becoming almost a surrogate father while their own was away and, upon the death of her mother, he had proved himself a tower of strength. She may, in moments of frustration, tell Salmon that she would do very much better without him but, not only did she have no authority to dismiss him but would never even consider doing so, as he knew very well. Over the past few months, with the exception of Aunt Clara, he had been her only friend and ally, shielding her from the brunt of those distressing searches which had been ruthlessly conducted without any thought for her or her father's feelings or dignity. It therefore spoke volumes for his shrewdness in summing up Major Neville as being a very different type of man to those others who had invaded the house wearing a scarlet coat.

Aunt Clara, who had yet to meet the Major but had heard all about him from Salmon, had taken one look at her niece and knew precisely which way the wind was blowing. Although her first concern was for Richard's safety, if this Major Neville was all that Salmon had led her to believe and her niece was not impervious to him, then she could not see Elizabeth doing any better than tying herself up to him. She also gave it as her opinion that anyone prepared to help her nephew could not be anything other than a decent and honest man and, for her part, she could not wait to make his acquaintance. Still disgruntled at being the last to know about Salmon's regular contact with Richard, her feathers were still very much ruffled, informing him in her direct way that if he had anything about him or harboured the smallest speck of concern for his master as he professed, he would make a push to do something to help him instead of leaving it to a man who, she was totally convinced, had her nephew's interests at heart more than he apparently did. Placing the tea tray down on the table with unnecessary force, Salmon merely grunted something unintelligible to this remark, causing her to admonish him for his clumsiness.

Clara Winsetton was as voluble as Salmon was taciturn but, despite the differences in their station as well as their personalities, there existed between them an unspoken respect one for the other and, Elizabeth, who had witnessed more than one difference of opinion between them, guessed that her overseers rather enjoyed their regular bout of verbal fisticuffs. In fact, she would not be at all surprised to discover that anything remotely resembling politeness from either of them would be regarded with scorn, not to say deep suspicion.

Elizabeth knew perfectly well that her aunt did not for one moment believe that Salmon lacked the concern she had accused him of but, since neither of them were in a position to do anything practical to help Richard, it was natural that they should relieve their pent-up anxieties by sparring with each other.

She had not liked deceiving her aunt and was relieved now she knew the truth but, she fully agreed with Salmon, that to tell her where they met would be a grave mistake. Indeed, she could see it only doing more harm than good, because knowing her aunt as she did, once she was in possession of such information nothing would prevent her from attempting to seek him out and, if Major Neville was right and Colonel Henderson was indeed keeping a close eye on the house, then it would not be long before Richard was discovered and arrested. Her knowledge of Colonel Henderson was such that he would be in no frame of mind to afford her brother a trial, but would seek to see him hang at the very earliest opportunity. The thought made her shiver but, at this moment in time, Richard's life was more important than upsetting her aunt by keeping his current whereabouts from her. There would be time enough later for explanations and apologies, not that she expected her aunt to bear a grudge; she was nothing if not fair and forgiving.

By the time Gideon arrived back at the garrison following his meeting with Richard at Harriers Farm, it was after one o'clock and far too late to track down Lieutenant Beaton, besides which, he was far too tired to engage in a discussion which he instinctively knew would take time. In view of what Richard had told him, it was not hard to understand his friend's sudden change of attitude towards him but, somehow or other, he had to try and convince this young man that his intentions were to try and save Richard Ferrers and not help to see him strung up. He could only hazard a guess as to what Major Denham had seen fit to tell him but, clearly, it had been sufficient to make Lieutenant Beaton extremely wary of him.

Despite the lateness of the hour and the fact that he was by now rather tired he knew there was one task he must do before he retired. Pulling off his gloves and dropping them onto a chair, he sat down at the table which also served as a desk and, pulling several sheets of notepaper towards him, dipped the pen in the Standish and began his report to General Turville. It was concise and to the point, at the end of which, he concluded that whilst there was little doubt Richard Ferrers would be cleared of the charge of treason there still remained the allegations of smuggling to answer but, nevertheless, was hopeful that these could be easily waived aside as no one had ever actually caught him in the act of running goods.

Having met Richard Ferrers it was not difficult to understand what it was about him that endeared him to people and, more than this, why everyone who knew him offered him loyalty and respect. Beneath that steely determination he was certainly a charismatic young man and one blessed with his fair share of charm and, since having made his acquaintance, Gideon was forced to admit that should he be unfortunate enough to be 'gazetted' after all, then the chances were that none of his confederates would take advantage of it as he had at first believed.

As those letters were all that stood between Richard Ferrers and the gallows it was imperative he speak to Lieutenant Beaton as soon as possible but, enquiries into his whereabouts the following morning, brought the unwelcome news that Major Denham had sent him out on a patrol, despite his duties the night before and it was not known when he would return. Since there was nothing Gideon could do until he arrived back at the garrison and he was reluctant to report to Colonel Henderson until he had seen Elizabeth Ferrers, he handed his sealed letter into the capable hands of Sergeant Taylor, who assured him that he knew the very man to ensure it was conveyed to Sir John that very day. Upon asking who this 'very man' was, he was told that his cousin's only son, a trustworthy lad who, by a stroke of good fortune, had only recently been stationed here, could be entrusted with such a mission. In the short time Gideon had been here he had seen enough of Sergeant Taylor to have sufficient faith in him to carry out his orders, and it was therefore with the utmost confidence that he handed him the letter, after which, he ordered his horse to be saddled, hoping he could leave the garrison before being requested to attend his senior officer's quarters.

It was almost two o'clock before he finally arrived at Ferrers Court, correctly interpreting from Salmon's expression as he relieved him of his hat and gloves that something was amiss. By the time Salmon had come to the end of his embittered account about William's unexpected visit and how he had put his mistress's back up, Gideon was more than ever convinced of the wisdom of informing him of the truth. The disclosure that the late Viscount Easton's nephew had become involved in treason not unnaturally came as something of a shock but, when Gideon had finished recounting all he had gleaned from Richard, those old eyes widened, staring at him in total disbelief, rendering him incapable of saying anything for several moments. "I can't believe it, Sir!" he exclaimed, shaking his head. "I knew Master Richard had discovered something but, never this! I've never liked Mr. William I know," he admitted, "much less trusted him but, this is something I never suspicioned! Are you certain there's no mistake?" he asked hopefully, more for the family than himself.

"I'm sorry," Gideon sympathized, "there's no mistake. Richard has irrefutable proof of his complicity in those letters."

"I'm not doubting your word, Major" Salmon assured him, "but, Mr. William, for all his faults, never struck me as being one to involve himself in something like this, being too fond of his own skin, I mean." His eyes narrowed as he considered all he had been told. "Colonel Henderson, too!" he exclaimed bitterly. "When I think of what he put the Mistress and his late lordship through!

Why, it makes my blood boil just to think about it!"

"I know," Gideon nodded, "but Richard and I don't want you to let William know you know any of this."

"But Major N ...!"

"No, Salmon," Gideon said firmly. "On no account must you let him even suspect you know the truth. Once he does, he will be off."

Salmon digested this but, the look on his face, told Gideon that he had no liking for it and, his next words, bitterly delivered, proved how dissatisfied he was. "I don't like it, Major. Why, he's already going about the place as if it's his already."

"Well, I don't like it either," Gideon told him, "but, until I get those letters in my hands, there is very little else we can do."

Again Salmon considered, eyeing Gideon thoughtfully. "The thing is, Sir" he explained, "Master Richard puts great faith in this young man being able to help him, but they have not seen one another in a long time and he may not wish to become involved."

"I think you will find that he will," Gideon assured him. "From what I have seen of this young man, Richard can count himself fortunate to have him as a friend."

"You really think so, Sir?" he asked, his crinkled face brightening.

"I know so, Salmon" he smiled, "so you can stop worrying."

"Master Richard told me those letters will do the trick," he told him, "but, do you really think they will?"

"If they contain such damning information as he has led me to believe," he nodded, "yes, but I'll need time to get my hands on them."

"Very well, Major" Salmon nodded, "I'll keep mum, but it'll go against the grain with me to do it," he admitted. "However, if that's how you both want it, then that's how it'll be."

"Thank you," Gideon smiled. "I knew I could rely on you."

"Are you going to tell the mistress?" Salmon asked.

"Yes, her aunt too." It was clear to Gideon that Salmon was none too enamoured of this but played a successful gambit. "They have to know Salmon. If we are to keep our eyes on William we can only do so if you all know the truth. Richard agrees they should be told."

At the mention of his master's approval, he nodded his own. "Very well, Major."

"How long is he intending to stay, do you think?" Gideon asked.

"Well, Sir" he snorted, "unless I much mistake the case, which I doubt, I'd say he's here for a spell. Got his man, Whitney, here with him too."

"Well, we can't get rid of them, no matter how tempting," Gideon laughed when he saw Salmon's expression. "Just think of it as another step to helping your master."

The bait worked as he knew it would. "Very well, Major" he nodded resignedly, opening the door into the great hall, "it will be as you say. You will find the ladies in the sitting room, if you'd like to go through. I'll give you a nod when he returns, Major."

Clara Winsetton, who, apart from bemoaning those rejected proposals of marriage, had, for a long time, believed her niece needed someone other than herself and Richard and, therefore, deliberately delayed retiring to her room for her afternoon's rest in order to meet the man who had suddenly entered their lives, waiting expectantly for Major Neville's arrival. She was by no means impervious to a personable young man but, upon him entering the sitting room, resplendent in his regimentals, she had no difficulty in understanding why her niece had taken to him. He was certainly handsome, and there was no denying that his face displayed a generosity of spirit as well as understanding that only seemed to enhance his masculinity, beneath which, she glimpsed a sense of humour she owned she found rather attractive. Nevertheless, that well shaped mouth and firm jaw depicted a strength of purpose which told her that once having made up his mind to something he was not the kind of man who would easily abandon it. Having taken one look at them together and the warm greeting they exchanged, she knew she had not erred, and could not see her niece doing better than tying herself up with the Major, especially when she saw the answering response in those dark brown eyes. Entirely satisfied with what she saw she knew that she could not have chosen a better husband for her niece herself and took great delight in watching them exchange pleasantries, regarding this budding romance indulgently. "So, you're this Major Neville I've heard so much about!" she exclaimed affably.

"How do you do, Your Ladyship," Gideon smiled as he bowed over her hand.

"I do very well," she told him, leaning back in her chair, her pale blue eyes raking him over from head to foot. "You're not at all what I expected," she told him in her frank way.

"And what *did* Your Ladyship expect?" Gideon asked, his eyes alight with amusement.

She seemed to consider this for a moment, chiding at length, "You're a handsome rogue, to be sure. But handsome is as handsome does! You find that amusing, Major?" she asked as he burst out laughing.

"My apologies, Your Ladyship," he inclined his head, "but you put me so much in mind of my grandmother; she was used to say very much the same thing to my brother Aubrey and I."

"No doubt the pair of you drove the poor soul into Bedlam!" she told him severely but, the laughter in her eyes, told her niece that she fully approved of the Major.

231

"In truth, Your Ladyship," Gideon confessed, his lips twitching, "she lived to be ninety and, to my recollection, was perfectly sane."

"You surprise me!" she exclaimed. "However, I daresay the truth of it was kept from you," she remarked.

"Your Ladyship could well be right," Gideon told her without a tremor, taking an instant liking to this redoubtable old lady, who, he had no doubt at all, would be more than capable of dealing with a dozen Colonel Hendersons'.

"Where are you from, Major?" she asked abruptly.

"From Wiltshire, Your Ladyship," he told her.

"And there's no need to keep calling me 'Your Ladyship'," she admonished, taking an instant liking to this young man. "Wiltshire, eh!" she mused, looking him over from head to foot. "You're no relation to Sir Matthew by any chance, are you?"

"Why yes, Your L…Ma'am," he bowed, "he is my father."

"Ha!" she cried. "I knew it!"

"What did you know, Ma'am?" he asked.

"You have the look of him. The moment I laid eyes on you I knew that you came from good stock. Why," she told him, prodding him with her cane, "I've known your father any time these past forty years! How is he?"

"Regrettably, Ma'am" he explained, "he has not been in the best of health of late, having suffered a heart attack sometime ago but, I am assured, that provided he rests and does not over exert himself, he should make an excellent recovery and live for many more years."

The next fifteen minutes were spent in enquiring about his mamma, lamenting over Aubrey and general reminiscing, after which, he spent a further ten minutes indulging her humour. If he had expected her to talk at length on the unexpected arrival of William then he was destined to disappointment as she only made a passing reference to him, from which he accurately assessed how little time or liking she had for him. He had no difficulty in believing what Elizabeth had told him in that once her aunt knew where Richard was, despite her age and the distressing pain of arthritis, nothing would keep her from him. He did not think that Salmon, deeply protective of his master though he was, would be able to withstand her forceful pressure in demanding to know her nephew's whereabouts for very long, in fact, he was surprised she had not wheedled it out of him long since.

It was not until she was on the point of leaving him alone with her niece did she mention Richard. As he stood holding the door open for her, she suddenly gripped his arm with her long bony fingers. "Just tell me one thing, Major" she said urgently, "can you bring my nephew off safe?"

"Yes, Ma'am, I believe I can," he told her sincerely.

She nodded. "I don't suppose you are going to tell me how you mean to go about it?"

Gideon shook his head. "I infinitely regret, Ma'am, that I cannot."

She eyed him closely, but accepted this without comment. "Very well, Major but, if you do succeed, I want you to know that I shall be eternally grateful."

He bowed over her hand. "I shall endeavour to make myself worthy of your gratitude, Ma'am."

"Thank you for not telling her of Richard's whereabouts," Elizabeth smiled gratefully when her aunt had left. "Although she knows that Salmon has been meeting him she does not know where but, once she did, I am quite sure she would do her utmost to go to him."

"I don't doubt it. She's a most determined lady but, I own, I like her," his smile making her heart skip a beat.

"I do hope you were not offended by her directness;" she asked, a little unsteadily, "about your family, I mean."

"Not at all," he shook his head. "Why should I be?"

"Well, she can be very forthright at times," she explained.

"I recall you telling me so that day I came upon you," he reminded her.

She looked up at him, a slight frown creasing her forehead. "Is it true what you said," she asked hesitantly, "about selling out?"

"Yes," he confirmed. "I cannot possibly leave my father with an estate he is in no condition to administer."

"No, of course not," she agreed. "Will you mind very much?"

"No," he shook his head, "not very much."

She nodded. "Your home; you say it's in Wiltshire?"

"Yes," he smiled wistfully. "Burroughs Croft. It is not a rambling Tudor house like this," he explained, "but very beautiful, all the same. Perhaps, when Richard's affairs are settled," he suggested, an odd inflexion creeping into his voice, "you will permit me to tell you about it."

It was not what he said precisely but how he said it which brought the flush of colour to her cheeks. "I would like that very much," she managed huskily.

"So would I but, I must warn you, however," he cautioned in a deep voice, "that being inordinately fond of my home, it could take a very long time."

Her eyes flew to his, realizing her error in doing so immediately upon seeing the unconcealed warmth and tenderness in those dark brown depths as they rested on her, causing the breath to still in her lungs. Her heart, by now well and truly lost to him, soared at the implication these words conveyed and, not for the first time since making his acquaintance, found herself experiencing a moment of pure selfishness in that she could so easily forget all about Richard and the difficulties which beset him in the arms of the man facing her, arms she instinctively knew would welcome her eagerly. It was an attractive vision and one she found difficult to dispel; but, after several moments of concentrated mental effort, she eventually relegated such a pleasing prospect to the back of her mind; horrified and not just a little ashamed that she could even allow herself to think of her own feelings while Richard's life hung precariously in the balance. She turned her head away, hoping that he had not seen that brief but silent confirmation of her feelings.

He had seen it and was overjoyed but, like her, was forced to dismiss the ever growing intensity of his feelings in face of far more important issues. He had known almost from the beginning of their acquaintance that she was not indifferent to him but, like the lady who had taken over his heart and was now adorably covered in confusion, he knew that Richard's life must take precedence over everything else and, therefore, tried sternly to suppress the overwhelming need to fold her in his arms.

"You...you did see Richard last night," she managed, trying desperately hard to ignore the fluttering in her stomach his words had evoked.

This question may have brought Gideon back to the matter in hand but, it had in no way brought sufficient enough control over his voice and, consequently, it was little unsteadily that he replied, "Yes, Miss Ferrers."

Mistaking this for something else, she asked anxiously. "Has something happened to him?"

"No, nothing of that nature," he assured her, pulling himself together.

"But, something has occurred," she stated. "I can feel it."

"Richard is not ill, if that is what you mean," he promised her. "Indeed, when I left him last night he was in perfect health, if frustrated."

She heaved a sigh of relief. "I thought that something may have happened to him."

"No, I give you my word," he told her truthfully.

"Was he able to tell you anything?" she asked, feeling a little more comfortable now.

"Yes," he nodded, "he told me quite a lot; in fact, everything I needed to know. I am also informed by Salmon that your cousin is here."

"Yes, he arrived yesterday afternoon," she confirmed. "I wish he were not but I could hardly bar him the house."

"No, of course not" he agreed, "but, in view of what Richard confided to me last night," he told her gently, "his presence here at this moment could not be more inopportune."

Her eyes widened at this. "His presence is always inopportune but, why now particularly?"

General Turville may have great faith in Gideon's tact and diplomacy but, right now, he was very far from knowing how to break such news to her. To tell her that her cousin was involved in treason together with the very man she not only hated but blamed for her father's death was difficult enough but, to tell her that it was they who first pointed the finger of suspicion at her brother in order to save themselves from exposure, bringing about his current difficulties, was not only going to cause her great distress but require all the tact and skill at his command; his love for her and his wish to protect her, making it doubly difficult and, therefore, it was several moments before he spoke.

Elizabeth, seeing the expression which had entered his eyes, intuitively knew that he was not the bearer of good news and, suddenly, her throat felt a little dry and her heart began to beat uncomfortably fast in her breast but, without waiting for him to find the right words in which to tell her, she clenched her hands at her sides, asking, in a voice she knew must be her own, "What did Richard tell you last night? Was it bad news?"

Taking several steps towards her, he said solicitously, "Let us just say, it was not what I expected; in fact, what he disclosed came as quite a shock; which is why," he said gently, "I think it may, perhaps, be better if you were to sit down." She stared up at him, bracing herself for the worst but, after assuring him she was perfectly well standing, he told her of what had passed between them but, no matter how gently he recounted his interview with her brother, she was palpably shocked by what she heard, her eyes staring almost blindly up at him.

"I am afraid," he admitted, "that their identity was as much of a shock to me as it is to you. I realize," he told her quietly, "that this is not what you expected to hear but, at least now, we know with whom we have to deal. Apart from which," he pointed out carefully, having no desire to cause her further anguish, "it explains why William is here now and why Colonel Henderson has been seeking Richard so remorselessly."

She shook her head in mute denial, unable to either question or refute what she had been told, indeed, it would have been quite impossible for her to have done so; so stunned was she that she could not utter one word.

From the moment Richard had disclosed the truth about his cousin and Colonel Henderson, Gideon had known that informing his sister of their complicity, especially after all she had endured, would be a terrible shock to her. In fact, so great was her distress that he longed to take her in his arms and comfort her but, as this was out of the question, there was nothing he could do but watch in frustrating impotence as she struggled to come to terms with his revelation. Her face clearly echoed her disbelief and incredulity as she continued to stare incomprehensibly up at him, her stupefied senses unable to absorb all he had told her, leaving her cold and numb with bewilderment. For several moments she was unable to move or speak but, gradually, the rigidity which had taken over her body began to recede, leaving her trembling and tears forming on the ends of her lashes. A cauldron of emotions raged through her but, superseding them all, was an anger so intense that she clenched her small hands into tight fists at her sides until her knuckles showed white. The tears which she had strenuously tried hard to fight off began falling unheeded down her pale cheeks, her efforts to wipe them away entirely useless; they would not be stemmed. Turning her back on Gideon she walked over to the window where she retrieved a handkerchief from the pocket of her skirt and, after dabbing at her eyes, ruthlessly blew her nose, for once the pleasing view outside going quite unnoticed. She sensed rather than saw him come up to her but, not until she had her emotions reasonably under control did she turn round, staring up at him with such a look of hurt and puzzlement on her face that should her cousin have walked in at this moment he would have known no hesitation in sending him sprawling to the floor.

"I wish I could have spared you," Gideon told her gently, hating to see her like this, "but, you had to know the truth."

She looked intently up at him. *"William and Colonel Henderson!"* she exclaimed, her voice hardly above a whisper and her eyes searching his face for explanations he could not give her. "I can't believe it to be possible!" She shook her head. "When I think of what we have suffered at their hands!" she cried, her eyes swimming afresh. "Richard, my aunt … my …" she could get no further as her emotions overwhelmed her at the thought of her father, covering her face with hands that visibly shook.

Without even thinking what he was doing Gideon wrapped his arms around her and held her close, her body racked with convulsive sobs as she gave vent to her feelings. He felt her fingers grip his shoulders as she clung to him for much needed comfort and support and, although her very nearness was enough to evoke all his masculine needs and desires, to have taken advantage of her distress and vulnerability would have been quite repugnant to him.

Discovering the truth had come as a tremendous shock, as he knew it would but, he shrewdly suspected that her tears and pain were more for the loss of her father than anything else and, therefore, was content to offer her the protection of his arms and to keep her safe from harm. William's involvement naturally hurt but, it was the knowledge that the man she blamed for her father's death and who had hunted her brother relentlessly for months, that had been the cruellest blow of all.

Eventually her tears subsided and her body relaxed but, her erupting emotions had left her limp and drained and in no hurry to move away from the warmth and comfort his nearness gave her. She had no thought for the rights and wrongs of being held in the arms of a man who really was, to all intents and purposes, a stranger, all she knew was that she felt safe and warm held close against him. She felt his lips brush the top of her head and was oddly comforted and, not until several minutes had passed, did she raise her head from where it rested against his chest to look up at him, offering a watery smile. "I'm sorry," she managed, "please, forgive me."

"You have nothing to be sorry for," he soothed, "and certainly there is nothing to forgive. Your feelings are perfectly understandable."

She looked questioningly up at him, her emotions having in no way impaired her beauty. "Perhaps they are," she acknowledged, "but, I am afraid, I have embarrassed you."

"I am not embarrassed," he shook his head, smiling down at her.

"No, but I am," she confessed in a stifled voice. "My behaviour was ..."

"Your behaviour," he broke in, still holding her in his arms, "was no more than I expected."

"You are most kind, Major" she faltered, "but ..."

"You know," he told her, pulling himself a little away from her to enable him to look down into her upturned face, a smile playing at the corners of his mouth, "I wish you would call me Gideon. Major and Major Neville are all very well but, they *are* rather formal and, I had thought, or, at least, I had *hoped*, we had gone beyond that."

It was a moment or two before she spoke, her clear blue eyes reflecting her every emotion. "Gideon," she repeated, her voice not quite steady. "Is...is that your name?" she faltered.

He nodded. "If you say it often enough," he advised amusedly, "you will find it will trip off your tongue without any difficulty."

"I like that name," she told him unsteadily.

"I am so glad," he said with mock relief, "because you see, it is far too late for me to change it."

She gave a shaky little laugh, which is what he had intended. "Well, I shall certainly try to remember to call you Gideon in the future," she promised shyly, "but, if we are to be on first name terms, then you must call me Elizabeth," she told him unsteadily, suddenly conscious of his arms around her.

"I would like that," he smiled, looking closely at her, correctly interpreting the meaning of the fresh tinge of colour in her cheeks and, whilst he could have held her in his arms all day, he resolutely relegated this pleasing image to the back of his mind. "Would you like to sit down?" he asked, with more calmness than he felt.

"Yes, thank you" she smiled gratefully, allowing him to guide her to a sofa.

Apart from an enthusiastic bear hug from Richard and an affectionate embrace from her father, she had never before been held in the arms of a man and, certainly not so close that she could feel his heart beating next to her own. It had been an alien but exhilarating sensation and, as he led her to a Queen Anne sofa resting against the far wall, she found herself feeling quite bereft without them but, as he sat down beside her and clasped her right hand, cold and trembling, she took renewed comfort from the warm strength of his fingers. She looked up at him and swallowed. "Maj - Gideon," she hastily corrected herself, "what you said about William and Colonel Henderson, are you sure?"

"Quite sure," he asserted gently, mentally promising himself the pleasure of seeing these two men receive their just rewards.

She shook her head, still not quite able to take in the enormity of what he had told her. "But, I don't understand."

"I am not entirely sure that I do," he confessed, "but those letters prove their complicity beyond any doubt."

"But, why?" she demanded, bewildered.

"I wish I could offer some kind of explanation for their actions," he shook his head, "but, I cannot. Richard believes that William acted in this matter for financial reasons; he also believes that it was out of jealousy because he could never be certain the title would ever fall to him."

She considered this for a moment or two. "I don't know anything about his financial circumstances," she shook her head, "or, indeed, his politics but, I do know he has a tendency for gambling, so, perhaps Richard is right. When it comes to the title," she shrugged, "although he makes an effort to hide his ambition, he always has coveted it." She looked at Gideon, a question in her eyes. "Are you saying that William deliberately pointed the finger at Richard in order to render him ineligible to step into my father's shoes?"

"That is how it appears, yes" he nodded.

"And Colonel Henderson?"

"According to Richard," he explained, "it seems that his family have always been loyal to the Stuarts. From what he has been able to discover I gather his grandfather was with Charles I when he raised his standard at Nottingham in 1642 and that his father accompanied James II into exile in 1688. How much of this loyalty has rubbed off onto him however, I don't know," he admitted. "It could well be that he holds no feelings for them at all but, entered into this business purely for personal gain and to further his ambitions. The only thing I can't explain, though," he told her, a slight frown creasing his forehead, "is His Grace's involvement."

"You don't think he is a party to treason too, do you?" she asked, her eyes widening.

"No," he shook his head, "on that I would stake my life! Whatever faults His Grace may have, questionable politics is not one of them." He felt her fingers move slightly in his hand and brought his gaze back to rest on her face. "What is it?" he asked gently.

"Those letters! We must get our hands on them," she said earnestly. "They are all that stand between Richard and his freedom!"

"I know," he nodded, squeezing her hand reassuringly. "We shall get them, have no fear."

"I know you will do all you can," she said earnestly, "but, Maj...Gideon," she offered a little awkwardly, his name still rather strange on her lips, "I know my cousin and Colonel Henderson better than you and I have every reason to mistrust them; Colonel Henderson especially." A renewed sparkle lit her eyes. "I can't believe they hunted my brother down like a criminal in order to protect themselves! Are they *such* cowards?"

"No," he shook his head, "I don't think they are, at least, not in the way you mean, but they are certainly desperate and it's that desperation which has driven them to seek out Richard at all costs. Remember," he reminded her, "he holds vital evidence which could see them hang; under no circumstances can they allow those letters to be produced." He smiled encouragingly down at her. "Elizabeth," using her name with far more ease than she did his, "whilst I have no experience of your cousin, I have already gained a pretty fair estimate of Colonel Henderson and, I assure you, there is no need to distress yourself. Have I not already promised that I will help Richard?"

"Yes," she sniffed, her watery smile wringing his heart, "but, when I consider what they are capable of I must confess I do fear. I cannot worry over you as well as Richard."

"There is no need to worry yourself over me, I assure you" he told her, his voice deepening.

"I can't help it," she shook her head, rather helplessly, "if anything were to happen to you I …"

"You'd what?" he pressed, his eyes searching her face.

"I couldn't bear it!" she cried, turning her head a little away.

"I had dared to hope," he said hesitantly, "that it was because you held a fondness for me, as I do for you." The words were out before he could stop them and, almost at once, believed he had been too precipitate but, the movement of her hand in his and the look she threw at him, told him it was not so.

The breath stilled in her lungs but her eyes held his, knowing from the look in those dark brown depths that no words were necessary to confirm this statement. "It…it is more than a fondness, Gideon" she breathed, her voice hardly above a whisper, "much, *much* more."

His heart leapt at this but, the only reply he gave to her confession was to lower his head and kiss her parted lips. It was not a passionate kiss merely an acknowledgement of his feelings but, as he felt her quivering response and the way she seemed to melt into him, the pressure of his lips increased until he evoked a small cry from deep within her throat. The wisdom of what he was doing, particularly while her brother was in the worst kind of trouble, took second place, but only for a moment. "Forgive me," he told her unsteadily when he finally released her, "I had not meant for that to happen, but I cannot regret it."

"Nor I" she smiled tremulously.

He took hold of her hands in a firm clasp. "I had no right to take advantage of you in such a way," he told her truthfully. "It was unpardonable.

Forgive me."

"There is nothing to forgive," she smiled, shaking her head.

"Indeed, there is," he nodded. "I may not be able to prevent myself from falling in love with you, but I had no right to act upon it, especially while your brother's affairs stand so precariously and I cannot yet ask his permission to pay my addresses to you."

Laying the palm of her hand on his cheek she smiled mistily up at him. His reference to her brother did not surprise her, on the contrary, it was just what she would have expected from him. She had known her feelings towards him almost from the moment she had first set eyes on him, and was honest enough to admit that she had wanted him to kiss her ever since. She could not explain why she had fallen in love with him almost at first sight but, it was enough to know her feelings were entirely reciprocated but, the thought of Richard's difficulties brought the worry back into her eyes. "I do not fear Richard's refusal," she told him, "but, I feel you are right." He kissed the palm of her hand before holding it firmly against his chest. "I love you with all my heart," she breathed, "although why that should be on so short an acquaintance, I don't know," she shrugged helplessly, "I can't explain it but, our love for one another must take second place for the time being. Richard's safety, his very life, must come before anything else."

He smiled down at her, raising the hand he held to his lips. "My dearest love," he said softly, "I fell in love with you the first moment I saw you. If you are talking of explanations and reasons, then I have none. All I know," he said hoarsely, "is that I love you and want to spend the rest of my life with you. In fact," he confessed, "I told Richard my intentions towards you last night and, whilst he is in no position at the moment to concentrate his mind on our future together, he was not displeased. As far as his safety is concerned," he pointed out, "it has always been my intention to clear your brother's name, now, though" he smiled disarmingly, "I have even more incentive to do so."

Her skin tingled from the touch of his lips but, although her heart cried out for more, she managed to push her own needs and desires to the back of her mind. "Until we get out hands on those letters," she said resolutely, "nothing else is of any importance. How will you contrive it? Will Richard's friend help?"

"Yes, I have no doubt of that," he assured her. "However," he sighed, "whilst it would seem a simple enough exercise, the truth is I cannot simply walk into the prison block without a perfectly good reason. In my experience these places always have at least two guards on duty, and I cannot see Hampton Regis garrison being any different, then, of course," he inclined his head, "the cells may be occupied. Getting in there without creating suspicion therefore," he told her, "will be a task for Beaton."

"But, you *will* find a way, won't you?" she implored.

"You may be sure of it," he promised, "and as soon as possible."

240

"Yes," she nodded, "I fear we do not have much time."

He was certain of it. Not for the world though, would he confide his own suspicions to her but, the truth was, he placed very little reliance on Lytton's word regarding the time available. He would not put it beyond him to 'gazette' Richard ahead of schedule, after all, it would be in his and Colonel Henderson's interests to do so, not to mention William Ferrers, who would come into the title sooner than anticipated. As matters stood at present, no one would take the word of a traitor turned smuggler against that of two most prominent and respected members of society. Without those letters, Richard Ferrers could do or say nothing in his own defence.

Captain Waring may not be able to put any definite evidence forward to convict Richard Ferrers of smuggling activities, indeed, no one it seemed had ever actually caught him participating red-handed in the trade in any way but, again, the likes of two such men as his ruthless and determined pursuers, would have no difficulty in putting forward a case against him. That it would be detrimental to his name was certain, but no court of law would go against such a powerful alliance and, with the King at his back, His Grace would easily win the day. Those letters then, had to be retrieved; they stood between Richard Ferrers and the hangman's noose and, no matter what it took, he must reclaim them at all costs! He looked down at the bent head next to him in some concern, knowing perfectly well that should anything happen to her brother she would never totally recover from it, especially having already lost her father to the machinations of two men, whose own skins they were prepared to protect at no matter what price! "I know this has come as a terrible shock to you," he told her gently, "and, whilst I would give anything to spare you, both Richard and I felt it wiser to tell you and Salmon the truth, your aunt too, must be told. Your cousin's presence here, whilst unwelcome, is a mixed blessing; on the one hand," he explained, "it could well impede our efforts to help Richard but, on the other, we can at least keep our eyes on him until I can put my hands on those letters."

She looked up at him. "I still can't believe it! It is beyond everything I had imagined. Never did I suspect either of them for a moment. It is too incredible!"

"Yes, it is" he agreed, "but, once those letters are produced Richard will be free and they will stand their trial for treason."

"When I think how Colonel Henderson has hounded us," she cried, "drove my father to his grave and all to protect himself and my cousin from having their crimes exposed!"

"I understand your feelings," he soothed, "but, you must not distress yourself. I promise you they *will* pay for what they have done."

"I never believed Richard to be guilty of treason," she told him fervently, "and as for William, I never even considered him but, now, to learn that he is indeed guilty and all this time ready to blame Richard, makes me so angry," her face becoming as pink as her skirts. "Only wait until I see him!"

"My darling," Gideon cautioned, "under no circumstances must your cousin even suspect that we know the truth. Once he does, there is nothing to prevent him from seeking out Colonel Henderson and telling him the whole. Until we have the evidence in our hands to prove Richard's innocence, neither of them must be approached with this." Although her eyes had taken on a stormy look they had lost that earlier fire and, slowly, she began to see the wisdom of this. "Believe me," he urged, "nothing would give me greater satisfaction than to deal with them right now, but we must put our feelings to one side and think only of Richard."

"Of course, you are right," she acknowledged. "I know you are. I would do nothing to jeopardize Richard's safety but, to see them walking around as though nothing had happened, is more than I can bear!"

"They certainly have a lot to answer for," he agreed, kissing her fingers, "but now is not the time. Only wait until I have those letters safe."

She raised her eyes to his, their entreaty not lost on him. "I have every faith in you but, can you, indeed, get your hands on them?"

"Yes," he nodded, "I can."

"Then Richard will be safe?"

"Richard will be safe," he confirmed softly.

She leaned contentedly against him, feeling his arm encircle her waist. "You say my aunt is to be told?"

"Yes, she has to know the truth. Matters have gone too far to withhold anything from her."

"Then let me do it," she urged, looking up at him. "I can do it so much better as well as choosing the right moment. Even though she has never liked William, it will still come as a shock to her."

"Very well," he conceded, "if that is what you want."

She nodded. "Yes, I think it will be better that way."

From the expression in her eyes, he knew that something was on her mind and, after brushing the top of head with his lips, gently enquired what it was. Upon being asked if Richard would still have to answer charges of smuggling, he was relieved to be able to tell her that as no one had ever actually caught him in the act of running goods, then the chances were that he would not. He felt the relief leave her body and held her closer to him, wanting nothing more than to protect her but, having already discovered her independent streak, he knew she was more than capable of confronting Colonel Henderson with her discovery. If she did that he would be faced with little choice but to arrest her, and who would even begin to believe the accusations of a woman whose brother was listed as a Jacobite fugitive turned smuggler?

But, Elizabeth Ferrers did not want for sense. She would know that to divulge the truth, especially to the men themselves, would only hinder her brother's chances of clearing his name, indeed, it would only serve in putting a noose around his neck without even the pretence of a trial. In fact, he would not put it beyond Colonel Henderson to give instructions that Richard Ferrers was to be shot on sight and, with a man like Lytton to support him, this action would never dared be questioned.

None of these thoughts however, were disclosed to her. Instead, he told her about his deception and how he was mendaciously keeping Colonel Henderson at bay. As expected, she fully agreed with his plan of campaign and praised him for his ingenuity. "Oh, how I wish I were a man!" she exclaimed.

"I seem to recall you voicing that wish before," he smiled, "but, I can only repeat, I am very glad you are not."

She laughed. "Yes, of course, but only think of the excitement in outwitting them!"

He felt it behoved him to point out to her that outwitting them was all very well but, keeping up the pretence, was something entirely different. "However much we may dislike and mistrust them," he told her seriously, "Colonel Henderson is no fool and, sooner or later, he is going to expect a full confession from you."

She considered this, saying at length "Well, he shall have one."

"He will?" Gideon asked warily, wondering what outrageous thoughts were going through his love's mind.

"Yes," she nodded vigorously. "Of course, he cannot be told the truth but, at least, I shall think of something convincing enough to appease him."

"I cannot imagine what," he admitted. "Nothing short of divulging Richard's whereabouts will satisfy him." Her eyes danced, filling him with disquiet. "Before you go any further," he advised gently, "rid your mind of trying to fool him. He is far too clever for that and, what is more," he pointed out seriously, "he is far too desperate to be put off by lies or evasion."

"Yes, but ..." she began.

"No 'buts' my love," Gideon told her firmly. "I tell you only to put you on your guard should he ever take it into his head to pay you a visit without my knowledge. If this turns out to be the case, you will know what line to take but, under no circumstances, are you to make the attempt to even hint about knowing the truth."

"But he won't be fobbed off with prevarication, surely?" she cried, disappointed to learn that she was not going to be granted the opportunity of paying him back in some small measure for all he had done.

Gideon, not unaware of what was in her mind, sympathized but, said firmly "My darling, I pray you consider a moment. Colonel Henderson, after months of searching for your brother, will find it hard to believe you to be suddenly eager to make a confession to him. All you need do is to tell him that although you begin to realize the seriousness of the situation, it is no easy matter to betray your brother."

"Yes," she nodded, having digested this. "You are quite right, but I would dearly love to play him false!"

"I know," he soothed, "but what we have to remember is that your brother's life is far more important than gratifying one's very natural desires." He hesitated before saying carefully, "I know the pain he has caused you and it is unpardonable but, we have to think of Richard. Nothing must come between us in our resolve to settle his affairs."

"Yes," she acknowledged, "that is paramount." A frown descended on her forehead. "How much time do you think we have before we can expect a visit from Colonel Henderson?"

He shook his head. "I wish I could answer that but, the truth is, I do not know. Most probably he won't visit you at all, I daresay it will depend on whether he continues to believe me. Until I get those letters in my hand," he pointed out practically, "I must make him believe me for awhile longer. On no account can either of us take anything for granted."

However much it may irk her to know that Colonel Henderson must be placated until Richard was safe, she had finally been brought to accept the need for such devious actions.

Resisting the impulse to take her back into his arms and kiss her, he contented himself with taking hold of her hand and listening to her highly impractical but very entertaining schemes to pay back her cousin and Colonel Henderson for their deceitful treachery. Just as he was on the point of recommending her not to embark on any of her outrageous plans, the door opened to admit Salmon, informing them in the voice of foreboding that Mr. William had just ridden into the stable courtyard.

"Are you prepared to embark on a little play acting?" he asked amusedly. Her eyes glowed and her answer was just as he expected. "Then let us not forget," he reminded her, "Colonel Henderson believes you are on the point of capitulating and, bearing in mind we now know the truth about him and William, I think it a fair assumption that at the earliest opportunity your cousin will report to him on what he has witnessed between us today." She nodded, but it was obvious she was thinking of something else. "What is it?" he asked.

"Are you hoping that William will betray himself?" she enquired.

"Not that precisely," he shook his head, "but, at least, it will give him some food for thought."

"I hope I don't give myself away!" she exclaimed. "When I think of ..."

"You won't," he smiled, giving her hand a reassuring squeeze. "Just follow my lead."

CHAPTER TWELVE

Having spent a pleasurable few hours riding around what he had no hesitation in regarding as his estate, William Ferrers emerged from the stables with all the air of one who was very much at home in his surroundings, looking forward to the day when all of this would be his, hopefully, not too far distant. Whatever his opinions about his late uncle, he had to admit that he had been a good landowner, all he saw being in very good order.

He liked the idea of being the sixth Viscount Easton, envisaging the day when he would be master at Ferrers Court and, so agreeable was this prospect, that everything else was relegated to the back of his mind, including that agreement he had been fool enough to sign deferring his immediate right to take up his inheritance. So pleasant was this daydream that he was able to allay any qualms he may have had about being culpable in putting an end to his cousin's existence, telling himself that, however regrettable, it was nevertheless very necessary when he considered all he had to gain.

In view of this therefore, it was somewhat annoying to know that Colonel Henderson was unable to see him until half past six this evening and not at the garrison as he had thought but, at *'The Peal of Bells'* in Lewes, just a couple of miles to the west of Hampton Regis. By no means pleased with a venue he firmly believed to be too far distant for his convenience, he had instantly demanded of Whitney why he could not visit him at the garrison, to which his henchman had merely shrugged, explaining that Colonel Henderson had not seen fit to go into any detail with him. This was all very well but, it would mean leaving Ferrers Court well in advance of half past six, something which by no means pleased him.

Elizabeth may have accepted the glib reason he had put forward to account for his absence from the dinner table this evening without question but, even though he was by no means pleased about it, it was nevertheless an unavoidable circumstance and, had it not been for the fact that he was eager to get this matter over with, he would have felt more than justified in not going. But, however much he resented the inconvenience of a ride into Lewes, he was, in spite of everything, in an excellent frame of mind as he entered the house, confident that before too long not only would his financial circumstances be dramatically improved but, also, the risk of exposure as a traitor would be gone for ever.

Tossing his gloves and whip onto a table in the hall, he was just on the point of finding his cousin, certain that although he was still wearing his mud splashed boots and riding coat, she would excuse his appearance, he heard Salmon come up behind him, a man whom he had no hesitation in deeming his enemy. One look at that wizened face was enough to tell him that not only did he regard him as a most unwelcome guest but, should the day ever dawn when he was master here, then it would be a sad day for the Ferrers Family. As it would not be to his advantage to set Salmon's back up he bit down the retort on his lips, consoling himself with the agreeable thought that before too long he would be able to give this defiant and insubordinate individual his marching orders. He cared nothing for the fact that Salmon had been born on the estate and was looked upon as much a part of the family as himself, in fact, he would go so far as to say that the inhabitants of Ferrers Court looked more kindly upon Salmon than they did on him. As far as he was concerned, he regarded Salmon's position within the household as being of no significance whatsoever and, as if to prove this point, he totally ignored that stalwart's attempt to point out to him that his cousin had a visitor and did not wish to be disturbed. Brushing past him without so much as a glance in his direction he strode through the great hall with Salmon's entreaties going over his head, determined to prove to him once and for all that when he was master here, things would be very different.

Throwing open the sitting room door he found his cousin standing with her back to the fireplace in what appeared to be a somewhat disjointed discussion with a man in a scarlet coat. Since he had no reason to suspect that she knew the truth or that her heightened colour was due, in part at least, to her anger over his duplicity, he instantly read this to mean that the Major was causing her distress. Bearing in mind His Grace's instructions, he felt sure that he would have no difficulty in carrying them out as this insufferable intruder, as his cousin's rigid demeanour clearly signified, seemed to be playing right into their hands. "Can I be of assistance, Cousin?" he enquired, closing the door behind him and stepping further into the room.

"William!" she exclaimed, her temper rising at the sight of him. "I had not looked for you for some time. Please, allow me to introduce Major Neville to you." She saw him eye Gideon suspiciously through his eye glass. "He is from the garrison at Hampton Regis. He is here to ascertain the whereabouts of Richard."

"Major," he inclined his head.

"Servant, Ferrers" Gideon bowed slightly.

"Forgive me," William smiled nervously across at Elizabeth, "do I intrude?"

"Not at all," she told him, forcing a smile to her lips, biting down the overwhelming impulse to throw his perfidy at him. "There is nothing I have to say to Major Neville which cannot be said in your presence."

William, not at all sure whether to feel relief or not at this statement, said, as casually as he could, "I see you are a fusilier, Major," hoping he sounded more relaxed than he felt. "I was not aware that any fusiliers were stationed at the garrison; or, are you, perhaps, part of a detachment?"

"No," Gideon inclined his head. "No detachment."

"But, how is it ….?" raising a painted eyebrow.

"I am temporarily quartered there," Gideon informed him.

"Quartered?" William queried.

"Yes," Gideon nodded. "I have come into Sussex under orders to settle this matter of your cousin, and I am to remain here until it is resolved," he told him quietly, summing him up straight away.

"Oh, of course," he nodded. "You're searching for Richard, you say?"

"That is correct, Sir" Gideon inclined his head.

"And what makes you believe my cousin knows where he is?" William demanded, his voice a little high pitched as was always the case when he was nervous. "Do you not think," he asked, believing he was enacting the role of future head of the family with becoming dignity, "that you would, perhaps, be better employed seeking enlightenment elsewhere instead of harassing my cousin?"

"And do *you* not think," Gideon suggested, hugely enjoying himself, "that it is a little strange that Richard Ferrers is in the vicinity, conducting his illicit affairs, and his sister remains in ignorance of it?"

"Major Neville!" he expostulated, "I must say that I do not like your tone!"

"My apologies, Ferrers" Gideon bowed his head, "but this matter has gone beyond good manners."

"So it would seem!" he exclaimed, his pencilled eyebrows rising.

"Considering the situation," Gideon commented, hoping to manoeuvre him into betraying himself, "I would have thought that locating your cousin would be of as much importance to you as it is to me."

William swallowed uncomfortably, still smarting from Elizabeth's verbal attack yesterday. "Well, yes" he conceded, his pale face slightly tinged with colour as he saw his cousin's eyes upon him, "I admit I would like to know where I stand, but I really must protest at the way you are badgering my cousin."

"I have no recollection of having done so," Gideon told him coldly.

"I would remind you, Sir," William pointed out, "that my cousin *is* a lady!"

"I am aware," Gideon bowed, "but I must tell *you* Sir, that no one, whatever their station in life, can hope to hide a fugitive from justice and expect to get away with it.   Miss Ferrers," he said, turning to face her, "you are doing your brother no good service by continuing to shield him."

"How many more times do I have to tell you and Colonel Henderson," Elizabeth argued, her anger at her cousin's treachery assisting her to play the part designated for her, "that I have no idea where my brother is to be found?"

"A circumstance I find difficult to believe," Gideon informed her, "especially when I consider the fact that he has been in the vicinity for many months."

"Are you calling my cousin a liar, Major?" William demanded, taking several steps towards Gideon. "Because, if you are," he told him, "I take leave to tell you, Sir, that I take exception to it; great exception!"

His own perception of his behaviour was that of the future head of the family merely attempting to protect one of its members but, he encountered such a look from Gideon that he inwardly flinched, immediately regretting his hasty outburst. He gained the impression that this red-coat would like nothing better than to send him sprawling but, even though they were of similar height, Major Neville was far more powerfully built and, he instinctively knew, that he would be no match for this man should it ever come to a bout of fisticuffs and quickly offered a faltering apology.

His impression had not been wrong; Gideon did indeed experience an overwhelming impulse to inflict the most dire punishment on him but, two reasons held him back. The first was because to indulge his natural inclinations in a lady's sitting room would have been quite unforgivable and the other because, for the moment at least, it would serve no purpose other than to gratify his own desires for the pain and indignities he and Colonel Henderson had imposed on the Ferrers family. "I had not intended to offend or cause you distress, Miss Ferrers" he apologized, turning his back on William, "but, when last we spoke, you promised to give consideration to my advice. You think you are protecting your brother," he told her, hoping she could hold her temper in check awhile longer, "but, indeed, you are doing him a great disservice, besides which," he pointed out, "this matter is now of some moment."

"I know nothing of the kind!" she replied, resorting to her handkerchief. "It is no easy matter to betray one's brother."

"I realize that," Gideon acknowledged, "but, whilst I take into account your very understandable reticence, I feel I must point out that Colonel Henderson is desirous of a speedy solution to this matter."

"I daresay he is," she replied into the folds of her handkerchief, not daring to look at Gideon, "but I could never live with myself if I said or did anything to hurt him."

"All I ask, Miss Ferrers" he told her reasonably, "is that you give me some indication as to where he may be found. Surely, there is someone you know who would be willing to offer him shelter!"

"And what do you think *I* know of smugglers?" she demanded, borrowing from Salmon's vocabulary.

"Are you seriously suggesting, Major" William broke in heatedly, "that my cousin is in league with these rogues?"

"Not at all," Gideon shook his head, "but this is a small community, after all."

"I don't like your tone, Sir!" William exclaimed. "By God, I don't!" taking a few steps closer to Gideon.

"I would advise you, Ferrers" Gideon said ominously, "to refrain from making comments which can only be construed as an attempt to impede the course of justice."

Elizabeth stifled the laughter bubbling up in the back of her throat, not daring to look at Gideon, while William spluttered something to the effect that it was a pity honest citizens were insulted in their own home by someone who, he had no doubt at all, was not only exceeding his authority but his orders as well. Ignoring this, Gideon turned to Elizabeth, only too aware of how she was just managing to contain not only her laughter but her earnest desire to hurl the truth at her cousin.

"Very well, Miss Ferrers, since you are unable to accommodate my request, I shall leave you now to think over what I have said. I shall return tomorrow when I expect to receive a very favourable response from you." After bowing gracefully over her hand he inclined his head towards William, leaving the room without a backward glance with William's mutterings falling on deaf ears.

Salmon, who had been keeping a watchful eye from the great hall, turned as he heard the door to the sitting room open. It only took a glance at Gideon's face to know what had passed between him and William and, as he walked beside him on their way back to the entrance hall, apologized for his untimely entrance but explained that he had been powerless to stop him. Gideon's graphic comments, music to Salmon's ears, raised him even higher in his esteem but, his instructions following this unflattering description of their unwanted guest, made him stare in surprise. "Well, Major" he shrugged, raking a hand through his grizzled hair, "if that's what you want."

"It is," Gideon nodded. "Give it about ten minutes."

William meanwhile stared at the closed door then back at his cousin, his delicately painted face unhealthily flushed. "It is a good thing I returned when I did," he told her satisfyingly, convinced that it was his presence which had intimidated the Major and ultimately sent him packing, blissfully unaware of the fact that he had not shone to advantage in the encounter. Having firmly persuaded himself that he was more than fitted to be head of the Ferrers family, he had no difficulty in foreseeing an agreeable future for himself as the sixth Viscount Easton but, deciding to keep this pleasing thought to himself, began by delivering a bitter censure as to the types that abound in the army today. "Did you notice, Cousin," he nodded, "how he would not argue with me? Why," he told her, "I came very close to planting him a facer!"

He ran on in this fashion for several more minutes and, Elizabeth, still smouldering with anger at what Gideon had disclosed, was lending only half an ear to his comments. It took every ounce of will power she possessed to keep her tongue, but it would have afforded her tremendous satisfaction to have been able to have thrown the truth at him. She could not, for Richard's sake, but her hands itched to slap that painted face but, just when she thought her resolution would break, she heard the sitting room door open and turning round saw Salmon walk in. She was not entirely sure whether to greet his entrance with relief or not but, one look at his face, made her pause. She could not accuse him of looking conspiratorial precisely but there was an expression in his eyes which told her to be cautious. "Yes Salmon, what is it?" she sighed.

"It's Mrs. Finch," he told her forebodingly.

"What about her?" she enquired, realizing he was trying to convey a message of some kind without William's attention being caught.

"It appears she's had words with cook," he said ominously. "She's desirous of seeing you to settle a disagreement."

In all the years Mrs. Finch had been housekeeper at Ferrers Court there had never been a cross word between them, and she was now convinced that Salmon wanted to get her out of the room without arousing William's suspicions. "Really, Salmon!" she exclaimed, attempting to do justice to her part. "Can't you deal with it?"

"I'm afraid she insists on speaking to you personally," he informed her, his eyes darting to where William was standing looking curiously from one to the other of them.

"Can't it wait?" she asked impatiently.

"Not if you want dinner this evening," he told her in the voice of doom.

"William," she sighed, turning to face him, "would you mind excusing me while I deal with this nonsense?" still struggling with her natural impulses to charge him with his duplicity.

"Not at all," he assured her, convinced that her obvious annoyance was due to Major Neville and not anything he may have said or done, refusing to believe that she still bore a grudge because of his careless remarks yesterday. "In fact," he told her, "while you're dealing with this little affair, I'll go and change into more suitable clothing. It would not do for Aunt Clara to see me in this rigout as well as all my dirt; you know what she is!"

"Yes, indeed," she smiled, gritting her teeth. "You don't want her giving you one of her scolds!"

"Goodness no!" he shuddered exaggeratedly, his boyish grin irritating her. "The mere thought terrifies me!" He followed her out of the sitting room and into the great hall, tactlessly commenting as he did so about certain changes she may consider making.

"I'm afraid I have no desire to make any changes to the hall or, indeed, to anywhere else in the house. Besides," she reminded him, attempting to put him in his place, "it is not for me to initiate any. *That*," she said pointedly, "is for Richard." It was a poor substitute for being unable to speak her mind to him but, at least, it served in some small way to relieve her feelings. He was just about to argue this point when Elizabeth, not waiting to hear his response, walked through the massive oak door which Salmon was holding open ready and entered the entrance hall leaving him to follow in her wake.

She fervently hoped he would not at the last moment take it into his head to accompany her to the kitchens to see for himself what kind of a domestic crisis was taking place. He did not but, it was not until she saw him turn the bend in the stairs which led to his room, that she was able to let out her pent-up breath. "Salmon!" she demanded, hardly above a whisper, taking another quick look up the stairs, "what on earth is going on?"

He jerked his head towards the rear of the hall in answer to this whereupon she instinctively looked in the direction he was indicating but, if she expected him to say anything further by way of explanation, she was mistaken. Threatening him with all manner of dire consequences if he did not stop being mysterious, she gave an indignant toss of her head before hurrying towards the far end of the hall, the click of her heels on the stone flagged floor and the rustle of her stiff skirts drowning out Salmon's low voiced chuckle. Just as she was approaching the door which led to the kitchen quarters, a hand came out and grabbed hold of her arm, drawing her into the dark shadows of a side passage which gave access to the rear of the house and gardens. The next moment two strong arms were around her pulling her against a firm hard body, forcing her head back in order for her to look up. "Gideon!" she cried, surprised. "I thought you had left!"

"Not until I had said goodbye to you," he told her in a deep voice.

"But, what if William should see you?" she demanded anxiously.

"He won't," he shook his head. "Salmon will see to that."

At the mention of her tormentor's name her eyes sparkled. "You're as bad as he is," she told him. "It seems to me that you're no better than Richard; you can both of you twist Salmon round your little finger!"

"You mean you *didn't* want to say goodbye to me?" he asked surprised, his eyes alight with amusement and something else she had no difficulty in defining.

"No...I mean, yes" she hastily amended, "of course, but ..." She got no further as his lips fastened themselves to hers.

She had never been kissed before today and, therefore, had not known what to expect when it happened but, the touch of his lips on hers, warm and seductive, rendered her acutely susceptible to not only his needs and desires but to her own also, awakening her to unknown emotions before today. She could lay no claim to being experienced in these matters but, the woman inside her knew instinctively, that he was holding his passion on a tight rein as well as recognizing that he was no callow youth in the throes of a first love affair; accepting it as perfectly natural that he had enjoyed more than one amatory adventure. Somewhere in the far recesses of her mind ran a jumble of tangled thoughts jostling one another; Richard's dilemma, her aunt's disapproval at such unmaidenly conduct, the arrival of her cousin and a host of other things which demanded her attention and yet, at this moment, all of them seemed rather insignificant. All she knew was that she was in the arms of the man she loved and was in no hurry to leave them, receiving his kisses with as much pleasure as he was giving them. Gradually the pressure of his lips eased until eventually he raised his head to look down into her upturned face, her eyes pools of dark blue that reflected the emotions inside her.

"I remained behind merely in order to assure you that there is not the slightest need to concern yourself over your cousin," he told her hoarsely, "as well as there being not the least occasion to distress yourself over his visit, and not from any desire to make love you, not that I do not want to; I do, so desperately," he assured her in a deep voice. "I promised myself I wouldn't kiss you again until Richard's affairs were settled but, I am afraid my self-control is not as strong as I thought it was."

"Gideon!" she exclaimed, when she had finally recovered her breath, "this is madness!"

"If it is," he told her unsteadily, holding her tight against him, "then I shall take it any day over sanity."

Her quivering response to this made him kiss her again and, therefore, it was several minutes after his lips left hers before she was able to speak. "I love you so much," she cried huskily, raising her eyes to his, trembling at the message she read in them, "and it is because of this that I am afraid for you. I don't trust William," she shook her head, "nor his man, Whitney. If either of them saw us I dread to think what would happen."

He raised her chin with his forefinger, his eyes devouring every exquisite inch of her face. "My darling," he soothed, "I will not let either of them hurt you and, as for me," he shook his head, "there is not the least need to be afraid, I assure you."

"But I can't help it," she said earnestly. "We are dealing with people who will stop at nothing to ensure Richard never tells the truth!"

"Yes," he agreed, "I realize that but, what they do not know, is that we now know the truth and also the whereabouts of those letters."

She bit her bottom lip, her eyes looking anxiously up at him. "Do you think we fooled William with our little charade?"

"For now, yes" he nodded, "but, something tells me that all we have done is manage to buy ourselves twenty four precious hours and no more. Between now and tomorrow when I come here for your supposed answer," he pointed out, "I have to get my hands on those letters! We cannot deceive ourselves into thinking that William won't visit Colonel Henderson; he will, if, for no other reason, than they can't deal with this matter of Richard alone. Colonel Henderson is bound to enquire of your cousin what he witnessed between us here today."

"Oh, dear!" she cried, "I forgot to tell you, you just put me in mind of it. William was talking yesterday about Richard's difficulties and how he would like to do all he could to help him. He said he thought he ought to visit Colonel Henderson to speak to him about Richard and try and reason with him."

"Very clever," he nodded, his eyes narrowing.

"Clever!" she exclaimed.

"Yes," he confirmed, kissing the top of her head. "William has to see him at some point, there's no way he can avoid it but, there is always the possibility that his visit to the garrison may be witnessed and reported back to you. This way," he nodded, "he obviates the necessity of having to lie to you."

She looked up at him. "I think he's *despicable*!"

"Yes, so do I" he agreed, "but, for the time being, we have no alternative but to play along."

"Do you think you *can* put your hands on those letters tonight?" she asked hopefully.

"I *have* to," he told her firmly. "With or without Lieutenant Beaton's help I have to gain entrance to the prison block, even if that means I get myself arrested."

"Oh, Gideon," she exclaimed between tears and laughter, "please do not; we are in enough trouble!"

"It won't come to that," he promised. "Unless I am grossly mistaken, which I doubt, I shall have Lieutenant Beaton with me. I cannot see him failing Richard."

"I was forgetting Michael," she nodded, "but, he wasn't all I forgot," she confessed, looking contrite.

"No?" he asked, looking down at her, his eyes smiling.

"No," she shook her head. "You see," she managed, the colour flooding her cheeks, "well, the thing is," she faltered, "when you kissed me just now nothing else mattered, not even Richard. I'm ashamed to admit it but, I didn't give him very much thought!"

"*Not even Richard?*" he asked in mock surprise, his voice a caress.

"No," she shook her head. "I know it was a dreadful thing to do, relegating my brother and his difficulties to the back of my mind but, it was *entirely* your fault!" she accused defensively.

"*Entirely?*" he questioned, proving his point by taking her back into his arms and kissing her again.

Eagerly folding her arms around his neck she was perfectly happy for him to prove his point but, eventually, she came to her senses telling him that it was dangerous to remain any longer. He reluctantly agreed to this and, allowing her to take hold of his hand, followed her down the passageway to the door leading to the rear of the house. "William is still in his room," she told him, pulling open the door, "fortunately, it's at the front of the house, so he won't see you."

He nodded. "Don't let your cousin worry you too much," he advised gently. "No," she smiled, "I won't."

After assuring her that everything would be all right, he briefly kissed her and left, running down the half dozen well-worn steps to find himself in the rear courtyard. Traversing the lily pond with an innocent looking cupid standing in its centre, he entered the stable block to find his horse ready and Salmon waiting for him. "Be ready to send a message to Richard," he told Salmon as he handed him his hat and gloves.

Salmon nodded knowingly. "I'll be ready whenever you are, Major."

"Make sure you guard your mistress well, Salmon" Gideon warned him.

Salmon eyed him closely. "Expecting trouble are we, Major?"

"If I am right," Gideon nodded, pulling on his gloves, "we can expect it very soon."

Salmon considered this. "Master Richard's in deeper than I thought then."

"Not too deep that he cannot be extricated," Gideon told him, "but disentangling him from the difficulties that surround him may not be as well received in some quarters as it will be here at Ferrers Court."

"Colonel Henderson!" Salmon snorted disgustedly, an unpleasant look crossing his face. "As nasty a piece of work as I've ever clapped eyes on! He'll do harm to Master Richard if he can, and *him*" jerking his thumb towards the house, "sure as check."

"Without a doubt but, we must ensure they do not," Gideon stated firmly.

"Can you help him, Major?" Salmon asked earnestly, his old eyes revealing the affection he had for the late Viscount Easton's only son as they searched Gideon's face.

"Yes, I can" Gideon promised, "but he must have patience and keep out of trouble."

"That's something I've never known him do yet," Salmon said with a mixture of pride and regret.

"If he wants to save his neck," Gideon remarked unequivocally, climbing into the saddle, "he is going to have to."

One look at Gideon's face had been all that was needed for Salmon to see how he and his mistress had spent the last fifteen or twenty minutes, confirming his initial estimation of the attraction which had existed between them from the beginning. He had nothing against Major Neville, on the contrary, he liked him very well but, he would have much preferred to have got Master Richard's problems out of the way before they decided to fall in love. Nevertheless, he was not one to try and fight the inevitable, especially when his young mistress had clearly made up her mind to something and, since she had set this very determined organ as well as her heart on Major Neville, he knew it was useless to remonstrate with her. Even so, if she had to tie herself up with someone he would much rather it be with Major Neville than anyone else, because if anyone were to ask him for his opinion he would have to say that a better man she would not find!

Since Major Neville had not informed him as to how he was going to put his hands on the evidence which would prove Richard's innocence, he was left to draw his own conclusions but, as these were many and varied and he could personally see all manner of pitfalls arising to prevent him from doing so, he could only hope that whatever he had in mind would come off all right. But he had seen enough of Major Neville to know that he was not a man who gave up easily and certainly not because the obstacles seemed insurmountable; if anyone could save Master Richard, then it was he. In the eyes of the law Richard Ferrers was a traitor with a price on his head and, if this were not bad enough, he had added smuggling to his list of crimes, for which he was going to be 'gazetted'. He shook his head over the business, wondering what the outcome of it all would be, because whilst he understood his young master's reasons for taking to illicit trading, embarking on such a crazy exploit had only served to put him in the worst possible light with the authorities.

But, when he met him that evening, drinking a tankard of ale as calm as you please with his cronies in *'The Moonshadow'*, it was obvious that he was very far from despondent, in fact, he held out every hope that he would soon be cleared of the charges laid against him. Salmon, frustrated beyond bearing, demanded to know what made him think so, to which he was carelessly told, "It's all planned out as snug as you please; the Major's going to do the trick for us. All you need do is to look after my sister."

Salmon eyed him warily. It was all very well to say the Major was going to do the trick, he may well, he would certainly give it a good go but, should he fail, then he would not put it beyond this mercurial young man to attempt something himself. He knew that look in those blue eyes too well to feel easy, and could not rid his mind of the worrying thought that that was precisely what he would do. He knew when he was up to something and, unless he missed his mark, he would lay his life that he was already planning some scheme or other should the Major fail. Whatever it was that was in his head it would be bound to lead to trouble. "I've known you from the cradle," he pointed out unnecessarily, "and I tell you straight, that whatever it is that's in your mind, I wish you'd forget it. And *another* thing," he told him bitterly, "it seems to me this precious plan of yours, which I know you're concocting," he nodded, "is going to bring more trouble down on your head. Major Neville told me to expect it any day now." His feelings by no means relieved, he further pointed out, "It comes to something when I, who's helped you out of one scrape after another since you were knee high, that I'm kept in the dark about what you're meaning to do. It would serve both you and the Major right if I disowned the pair of you!"

"Why you cantankerous old fidget!" exclaimed Ferrers, his eyes alight. "If I knew what the Major was planning I'd tell you but, I don't. All I know is that he aims to speak to Michael to see if there's a way of getting into that cursed cell block."

Salmon snorted. "And if there ain't?"

"Then I'll have to think of something myself," he shrugged, taking a pull of his ale.

"That's the dandy!" he exclaimed. "With every red-coat for miles around on the look out for you; you calmly plan to go to the garrison yourself!" banging his tankard down on the table.

"All right!" Ferrers exclaimed frustrated, "it's not going to be easy but, unless you have another plan, *which*," he shot at him, "can get one or the other of us inside that damned place without being seen or coming under suspicion, I'd be mighty glad to hear it, *and*" he added, just as Salmon was about to say something, "as you yourself have pointed out, since I dare not show my face within a mile of the cursed place because I'm known to almost everyone there, seems to be no other choice open to us but to wait and see what the Major can do."

"I daresay," Salmon grunted, by no means pacified, "but if ..."

"And if the Major *can* do the trick without anyone being the wiser," Ferrers commented, "all well and good."

"Ah," Salmon nodded, "that's just it, Sir, suppose the Major *can't* do the trick, what then? Seems to me you'll be as bad burned as scalded. Of course," he remarked, "if you hadn't told Colonel Henderson about those letters in the first place it would have given us a better chance but, since you *had* to go spouting it to him, you've left yourself without a feather to fly with. *If*," he emphasized, taking a pull of ale, "Colonel Henderson hasn't already found them!"

As this disagreeable thought had already occurred to him, Richard looked particularly grim but, since he was of an optimistic nature, he was soon able to shrug it off, assuring his henchman that it seemed most unlikely. "Besides," he dismissed, "he may know I have them safe, but he doesn't know where."

Salmon, far from cheered that the future sixth viscount seemed to have little care for his own safety, deemed it necessary to offer a word of caution but, as this was met with a careless shrug of the shoulders, followed by "Damn you Salmon! You're nothing but an old woman!" he knew that any further warnings were a waste of time.

Nevertheless, he did manage to extract his promise that he would keep his word to Major Neville by refraining from taking any further part in his nocturnal activities but, knowing him as well as he did, he could only guess at how long this abstention would last.

Elizabeth, whose thoughts and concerns now incorporated Gideon as well as her brother, shared Salmon's unease regarding Richard's assurances to remain out of harms way until his affairs were settled.   His temperament was such that he much preferred to be up and doing rather than sit back and allow someone else to do it for him but, since he could not show himself for fear of arrest, necessitating him having to leave the acquisition of those letters to another, his frustration would be all the more exacerbated.   All she could hope for was that further enforced inactivity would not lead him to embark on any more trips across the Channel, because although Gideon had assured her that he had never actually been caught in the act of running smuggled goods, which meant that it would be far more difficult to bring a case against him, it would be just his misfortune for that to happen should he decide to make one last run.   But, when, a few minutes later, she saw Gideon emerge from the stable yard and make his way along the rear pathway towards the south entrance, having ran up the stairs to the short side gallery specifically for that purpose, she found her emotions equally torn between them.   She knew Richard's life depended on those letters and, that he in turn, was depending on Gideon to retrieve them, a man whom she knew would do everything in his power to do so but, as she watched his tall, red-coated figure retreating further into the distance, she failed to see how he could possibly do so without running the risk of being arrested himself and, perhaps, even being charged with complicity in treason.   She could not bear to think of Richard being hung, no matter on what pretext, the very thought bringing a sob to her throat but, nor could she contemplate the same happening to Gideon, the very idea being too horrendous to consider.   Her heart still pounded from the emotions he had aroused within her and her lips still felt a little bruised from the thoroughness with which he had kissed her, and knew that she could not bear to never again experience such exquisite joy. She felt her whole being was in torment over the two men who formed such a major part of her life; unable to face the prospect of a future without Richard, the brother whom she had dearly loved since childhood. But, now, there was another man in her life, a man who evoked a very different kind of love to that she had for her brother; a love which could not be explained or rationalized and, yet, was all consuming, leaving her in no doubt that she could not live without the man who had entered her life only a few short days ago and awakened her to such overwhelming joy.   And, now, as if this agony of apprehension was not enough, along comes William and, with him, the truth about his complicity in treason in company with Colonel Henderson, both of whom would stop at nothing in order to protect themselves from being exposed as traitors and, if that meant getting rid of two men who could denounce them, then so be it. It was then that the sickening realization of the presence of a third party in the form of His Grace the Duke of Lytton, darted into her mind.   Had Colonel Henderson and William not have been experiencing difficulties in apprehending Richard, then he would never have been approached for assistance.   His reasons for coming to the aid of two traitors may be inexplicable but, there was no denying, that he was a man of far more skill and dexterity than her cousin and his accomplice would ever be but, worse than this, was the unlimited power he wielded.   His Grace, always an awe inspiring figure on his own account, was rendered doubly dangerous due to not only his friendship with His Majesty but also being his acknowledged favourite and, therefore, it was reasonable to suppose that he would make no mistakes or errors of judgement in his dealings with her brother.   Richard had been extremely fortunate in escaping from the garrison as well as hiding those letters right under Colonel Henderson's nose but, it was safe to say, that with His Grace now at the helm, albeit hovering discreetly in the background, Richard would find himself facing a very different adversary indeed.   Whatever Lytton's reasons for lending a hand in this business, it was certain that he would have far more success in capturing her brother than Colonel Henderson and William and, the thought of what could well await Richard and Gideon in their attempts to expose the truth, made her all the more fearful.   As she peered through the leaded window to try and catch the very last glimpse of him, she experienced such a feeling of foreboding that she covered her face with hands that visibly shook, unable to bear the thought that her worst fears could be realized and, in her anguish, sent up a silent prayer to keep Richard and Gideon safe and to bring them good fortune in what was to come.

CHAPTER THIRTEEN

Colonel Henderson's mood went from hope to despair the longer those incriminating letters remained out of his reach. Like William Ferrers, he had been shocked to learn that instead of Stuart disposing of them he had kept them but, he had been even more shocked to discover, that they were now in Richard Ferrers' possession, a man who could bring all to ruin. If all this were not bad enough, his quarry had been allowed to escape from custody and was now not only running rampant along the Sussex coast conducting his illicit activities and evading the law but, constituting a real threat to his peace of mind.

Panic may have set in which had brought about those searches at Ferrers Court but, he had managed to retain just enough sanity to realize that wherever Ferrers had those letters hidden they were obviously inaccessible to him, if they were not, then both he and William Ferrers would have faced their trial for treason long since. Surely, no man in his right mind would continue to live outside of the law as Richard Ferrers was now doing when he had such valuable evidence which would exonerate him of treason! He knew perfectly well why this young man had joined the fraternity as well as the reason for his continued stay in Sussex; those letters then, must be somewhere in the vicinity of Ferrers Court but, where, remained a mystery. Those searches had been thorough as well as intense but, so far, they had not come to light; if they had been hidden anywhere in the house then they would have been found. As far as the grounds were concerned they were vast and, although his small army of soldiers had done their best to locate them, they had failed to do so. If memory served him correctly, Richard Ferrers had had nothing on his person when he was searched at the garrison, which could only mean that he must have put them somewhere safe before he was arrested. This enterprising young man had been quick to boast about the evidence in his possession which would prove him as well as his cousin guilty of treason and, although he had not really expected him to divulge the whereabouts of those letters there and then, he had genuinely believed that after spending time in a cell as well as being made aware of the consequences to not only himself but his sister, he would be brought to change his mind. He had certainly not expected him to make good his escape en route back to the prison block, a circumstance which had served to not only inflate his anger but also increase his fear, as once Richard Ferrers was free there was nothing to prevent him from retrieving those letters. The fact that he had not done so could only mean that they were located in a place to which he could not gain easy access but, where, he had not the least idea. As searching the garrison had never so much as crossed his mind, he was of the opinion that until Richard Ferrers was recaptured and in safe custody when he could be questioned more closely, it seemed there was nothing else he could do but live on his nerves awhile longer. His prolonged presence in the vicinity was surely sufficient proof that he had so far failed to retrieve them and, his continued association with the fraternity, was ensuring not only protection from his pursuers but providing the perfect means for him to bide his time until the right moment showed itself to recover those letters. Nothing would disabuse his mind of Elizabeth Ferrers' guilt and complicity. As far as he was concerned not only was she offering her brother shelter but was hand in glove with him and, he would prove it, if it were the last thing he ever did. His treatment of her, perfectly justified in his opinion, had not only set her back up, causing her to dig her heels in but had created ill feeling in the community and he could only hope therefore, that Major Neville would have more success with her than he had. If all he had been led to believe by this young man were true, then it would not be long before Elizabeth Ferrers divulged her brother's whereabouts and, once he was in safe custody, it would only be a matter of time before that damning evidence was reclaimed. It seemed that Major Neville, a handsome and not inexperienced man, was beginning to find favour with her and, if his predictions were correct, then he could expect a pretty favourable outcome before much longer. It appeared that Major Neville's tactics had a lot to recommend them after all, they certainly seemed to be reaping rewards where his had failed.

It had never once occurred to him that Major Neville was playing him false, feeding him manufactured information deliberately calculated to keep him quiet in order to play for precious time. It would have astonished him to know that far from waiting for Elizabeth Ferrers to succumb to the Major's persuasive charm, he had already had one meeting with Richard Ferrers with another one planned for this evening.

He admitted that his first impressions of the Major had not been any too favourable but, he had soon been brought to see that he had wronged him, indeed, he was pleasantly surprised in his ability and depth of understanding. At first he had detected a little reluctance on his part to embark on such a serious affair as this but, once the true circumstances had been thoroughly explained to him, he had shown himself keen and full of ideas. Nevertheless, nothing would alter the fact that he felt very much aggrieved by not having the satisfaction of dealing with Miss Ferrers himself but, as this was out of the question, he had no choice but to accept Major Neville's assistance. However disinclined he was to have to hand over the reins in this matter, he had nonetheless been much struck by this young man's somewhat unorthodox approach to this delicate affair, electing to adopt far more subtle methods in his dealings with Miss Ferrers and, whilst he himself still believed that nothing short of her arrest and imprisonment would answer, he had allowed Major Neville to follow his own inclinations. It had never so much as entered his head that Turville's advocate was guilty of practising deceit; deliberately leading him into blissful ignorance as to what was actually taking place under his very nose as well as raising false hopes in allowing him to believe that his difficulties would soon be at an end. So confident was he of a speedy conclusion to this matter that he had found himself looking forward to dining with Major Neville this evening in order to discuss it in more detail. Unfortunately, that was now going to have to wait, Lytton most certainly would not!

He had recognized the handwriting on the letter immediately it was handed to him by Major Denham, who stated dispassionately that it had been delivered by a waiter from '*The White Hart*' at the far end of the town and that no reply would be necessary. His face may have been a mask of impassivity but his sharp eyes had detected the slight change which had come over his commanding officer's face and, unless he was very much mistaken, he would lay his life that something untoward had occurred. Had he have been privileged a few minutes later to have seen Colonel Henderson break the seal with fingers that were not quite steady, he would have been sure of it.

His Grace, having taken it for granted that he would fall in with his wishes, left him in no doubt that this unplanned visit into Sussex was neither welcome nor of his choosing, and hoped that it would not prove to be a wasted journey by yet more failure. By the time he had finished reading the half dozen or so lines, he was not at all sure whether to be relieved or not at his unexpected arrival in the vicinity but, of one thing he was certain, he was not going to be given the opportunity to decline the invitation.

It had been as a last resort that he had enlisted Robert's aid to help rescue him from his difficulties. That they were self-inflicted mattered not at all in the face of his ever growing fears of exposure as a traitor and, whilst he knew of Robert's unswerving loyalty and devotion to the King, he also knew that he would die to protect the secret he had long kept hidden from the world. Upon reflection, he marvelled at his own temerity in daring to hold this unflattering episode in Lytton's past over his head but, his case had become desperate, and observing the niceties would not release him from the insurmountable problems which beset him.

It would be long, if ever, before he would be able to forget that interview with Lytton. There had been no voice raised in anger, no outward display of temper or righteous wrath, indeed, His Grace had been civility itself but, that noble peer had, in a few well chosen words, not only called into question his intellect but disparagingly condemned his flagrant stupidity. This calmly delivered annihilation, demoralizing enough, had ended in an affronted reminder that not only had he involved him in something which he had neither expected nor welcomed but, had also greatly offended his person, to which he took immense exception.   Nevertheless, Robert had agreed to assist him but, there had been something in his manner which told him that he would remember his audacity. Well, Robert had assisted him but, Richard Ferrers was no nearer being caught now than he ever was and, unless he grossly erred, which he doubted, Robert's visit into Sussex was neither for his health nor because he liked the locality. He would lay his life that Lytton's sole aim in coming into this rural backwater was for no other reason than to discover the current state of affairs and, bearing in mind his barely concealed contempt when he had learned that Richard Ferrers had been allowed to escape from custody, he could well imagine what he would have to say about him still being at large, posing the same problem as before and demanding his involvement yet again.

He was not looking forward to this evening's meeting but, how like Robert to take it into his head to come into Sussex without any prior warning and expect him to fall in with his wishes! He grudgingly acknowledged that he supposed he owed Robert that much at least but, his presence here at such a moment was as unnecessary as it was unwanted. Now Major Neville seemed to have the matter well and truly in hand, he failed to see the need for Lytton's continued participation, indeed, he viewed his unannounced arrival as more of an annoyance than a help. He had not liked the tenor of Robert's letter but then, he had never been one for polite pleasantries when he deemed the situation did not warrant them.

Then, of course, there was William Ferrers, who, for reasons best known to himself, had also taken it into his head to come into Sussex. He failed to see what possible good would ensue from meeting his partner in treason, especially with his cousin on the loose. His presence here now was not only imprudent but extremely dangerous; whatever else Richard Ferrers may be he was no fool and, since he knew that his cousin was involved with him in the late rebellion, he would have thought that keeping their distance from one another was essential. Until this enterprising young man was in safe custody and those letters securely in his own possession, he could not afford to relax for one moment but, with the arrival of William Ferrers, the situation in his view could only worsen. It had been with extreme reluctance therefore, that he had told Ferrers' man to inform his employer that he would see him tomorrow evening at *'The Peal of Bells'* in Lewes. He had no idea what Ferrers hoped to gain from such an interview but, if he refused to see him then, knowing him as well as he did, there was no saying what he might take into his head to do.

It was far too late to regret his actions but, if Stuart had succeeded, he would not now be faced with the probable revelation that he had embarked on treason but, on the contrary, a hero. Unfortunately, Stuart had not succeeded and he was not a hero but, a man fearful of being caught and tried for participating in insurrection. If all this were not bad enough he was faced with the thought that he was totally reliant upon William Ferrers keeping his nerve but, as he was not blessed with his cousin's courage or ability to remain calm in a crisis, he dreaded to think what the outcome of his visit would be.

Out of choice, William Ferrers would never have been included in his plans but, his foremost ambition to be sixth Viscount Easton together with his constant need of money and his deep rooted jealousy of his cousin, had made him indispensable. It had been pure chance that had brought the two men together and, their destinies had been entwined ever since. He was not entirely certain whether to be glad or not that their paths had crossed that evening nearly two years ago but, he could not deny that William Ferrers' dislike and resentment of his cousin, had come in extremely useful by providing a most convenient scapegoat in Richard Ferrers. A casual word here or careless reference there had been all that was required to seal Richard Ferrers' fate and, until this young man had announced that he had those letters which he himself had written to Stuart, he had considered himself reasonably safe. Now though, he could not rest or know a moment's peace of mind until he had them secure. Once again his mind ran over the problem of those letters to which he could find no satisfactory answer, continually arriving at the same point without being any closer to ending this nightmare. It had been a great pity that he had been allowed to escape but, that in itself was no great matter, since he could not show himself without producing that damning correspondence. It followed therefore that he did not carry them on his person, if he did then they would have been discovered when he was arrested, nevertheless, they had to be found and as quickly as possible. Those searches at Ferrers Court had revealed neither the disgraced sixth viscount in hiding there nor those compromising letters, so it was logical to assume that they must be close by, Ferrers would not have returned to Sussex without them.

Since that energetic young man had withheld nothing from him during the brief time he had interviewed him, he knew that as Sir Matthew Mayhew had died while Richard Ferrers was with Stuart, those letters could not possibly have been handed into his care; so, where were they? The thought made him sick with worry. Whilst capturing Richard Ferrers was all very well, indeed, it was not only imperative but it would be a tremendous relief to see him safely in a cell, it did not take long to realize that this would by no means serve his whole purpose. Richard Ferrers of all people knew the damning significance of those letters, after all, wasn't that the reason he was still in Sussex? Should he be caught and tried he could not see him denying their existence; no man would go to the gallows when there was evidence to prove his innocence. Whatever this young man's alleged crimes his rank would ensure he received a trial and, more than this, the authorities would have no choice but to hold the trial in abeyance until those letters were before them; once that happened, there would be no stopping the scandal which followed. Even if he was shot on sight, it did not rid him of his problems as those letters could come to light at any time. He knew he could not afford to abate his efforts until not only this thorn in his flesh had been captured, but that correspondence was in his safekeeping.

If only Major Neville could persuade Elizabeth Ferrers to confide in him, his difficulties could still be surmounted. From what he could gather, Major Neville appeared to be making significant progress with her but, he knew from personal experience that she was not only obstructive but extremely stubborn. Regrettably though, he could not afford to be complacent; he would give the Major a few days grace and, if she was still not forthcoming, then he would have to take measures of his own.

It was unfortunate that he would not be dining with Major Neville after all this evening to discover his progress but, he dared not ignore Robert's summons to visit him at *'The White Hart'*. He supposed he could expect a rather uncomfortable time but, consoled himself with the fact that as long as he held Robert's past misdemeanour over his head, he could still prove extremely useful. Had he have known that Gideon was preparing for his second meeting with Richard Ferrers at Harriers Farm at this very moment, what little optimism he had would have been killed at a stroke.

Waiting for his horse to be saddled and brought round to his quarters to take him the short distance to *'The White Hart'* , he took the opportunity of pouring himself a much needed glass of cognac. To be honest, he was not really looking forward to this evening but, if it were not tonight, then it would be another, and he could only hope that he would be spared another verbal annihilation.

'The White Hart', a three storey Queen Anne Building situated at the far end of the main street, was a busy posting inn which, at this time of an evening, was packed to the rafters with guests who were either partaking of refreshment while waiting for a change of horses or those who had booked a room for the night, resuming their journey next day. As he approached the inn he could see it was a hive of activity, the harassed waiters running back and forth to answer calls from numerous irate and tired travellers, all demanding to be dealt with at once. Being a man who seldom if ever indulged in physical exercise, he had decided to ride the short distance to *'The White Hart'* and, although it had only taken him a few minutes, he was now beginning to wish he had walked instead, because despite his strenuous efforts to call for assistance in stabling his horse his cries for immediate attention went unanswered and, it was therefore, close on ten minutes before he was able to hand the reins into the hands of an out of breath groom. Among the hustle and bustle he had spotted Lytton's elegant travelling coach, bestowed safely under cover out of the way of the elements, his perfectly matched horses in the stall next to it, being tenderly cared for by his own groom. Robert, of course, not only demanded instant service but expected it as his right and would have hired the best private room for himself and his valet, irrespective of who else was

inconvenienced. No common tap room or private parlour for him! *'The White Hart'* could be packed to capacity but the landlord would rather turn out any guest than offend His Grace.

Entering the inn by a side door which led to and from the stables, he walked along the passageway towards the main entrance. Distracted waiters came and went, impeding his passage and brushing past him with laden trays and hasty apologies, only one promising to send for the landlord to attend to him. The noise and laughter emanating from the tap room as well as the coffee room opposite was testament to *'The White Hart's'* popularity, indeed, he knew that some of the officers from the garrison were known to come here for the excellent dinners. He had never dined here himself, but as he stood impatiently waiting to be attended to the aroma of cooking from the kitchen made him realize that he had not eaten since luncheon, and that he was extremely hungry. He had no idea whether Robert would invite him to share his dinner with him or not, he hoped so, it was surely the least he could do for descending upon him without any prior warning, but with Robert one never knew. Having been standing in the middle of the lofty square hall for almost ten minutes, he was just on the point of setting up a cry for the landlord himself, when a tall, thin man dressed all in black came silently and majestically down the stairs, his sunken eyes looking at him dispassionately. "Colonel Henderson?" he enquired impartially.

"Yes," he nodded, "I'm Colonel Henderson."

"His Grace is expecting you, Sir" he informed him. "If you would care to follow me."

By the time they had reached the top of the stairs Colonel Henderson, in no very good humour at having been kept hanging around like a nobody, enquired of his escort how he knew he was here. "His Grace," he told him flatly, "had seen your arrival, Sir."

He sighed frustratedly, but followed the valet across the first floor landing where he tapped on a door at the far end, and without waiting to be told to enter, pushed it open and announced, "Colonel Henderson, Your Grace."

He was ushered into what was clearly the inn's best bedchamber overlooking a small but well kept garden at the side of the hostelry. The roaring fire was most welcome because although May was well advanced offering agreeably warm days, such as today when it had really been quite hot, the evenings were still a little on the chilly side; across the sash window the heavy curtains had been drawn, and in the centre of the sitting room stood a table laden with plate and cutlery. Seated in a winged chair by the fire His Grace, resplendently attired in gold and blue satin, sat at his ease with his legs stretched out before him, one ankle negligently crossing the other. At the sound of his guest being announced, he raised his head but no smile appeared on those thin painted lips or in the cold grey eyes. "Thank you, Benson" he nodded. "You may serve dinner in about ten minutes."

"Very good, Your Grace" Benson bowed, retiring as quietly as he had entered.

"Well, George" Lytton smiled thinly, when his man had left him, "it is good to see you again."

"Robert," he nodded, dropping his hat and gloves onto a chair, unable to share this sentiment. "I had not looked to see you in Sussex so soon after your last visit."

"Indeed!" the pencilled eyebrows rose. "I cannot imagine why you should not, especially having requested my urgent intervention in this matter, and to which my efforts appear to have been entirely wasted." Henderson coloured slightly. "You must agree therefore," he inclined his head "that we have much to discuss, particularly as things have not been progressing well of late."

Henderson eyed him warily. "How do you know things have not been progressing well?" he enquired sharply.

"The same as I do everything else," he was told smoothly. "Unlike you," he remarked disparagingly, "I make it my business to know." He eyed Henderson dispassionately for a moment or two. "Can you deny that Richard Ferrers still roams free," he invited coldly, "conducting his illicit affairs? No," he nodded, "of course you cannot."

Henderson swallowed uncomfortably. "I own he has been somewhat elusive of late," he acknowledged, "but I have now every hope that before many days are out he will be enjoying the sparse comforts of Hampton Regis garrison."

"I see," Lytton inclined his head, putting his wine glass down onto a small side table next to him with painstaking care, "and what, may I ask, leads you to this conclusion?"

Colonel Henderson, watching his friend closely, walked over to the fire and spread his hands out to the warmth, an inherent sense of self-preservation warning him to tread carefully. There was an air of heightened confidence and self-possession in Robert's manner, more so than usual, and unless his instincts were at fault they presaged a real danger to his interests as well as comfort, so much so that he was assailed with the unnerving feeling that what had seemed a foregone conclusion up until now, suddenly appeared to be in doubt. It was several moments before he spoke and to his chagrin was not quite able to hide the reservations in his voice, indicating to Lytton that he was very far from convinced of his assertions. "It would appear" he explained, clearing his throat, "that Major Neville, Turville's representative, has managed to persuade Miss Ferrers into giving her brother up."

Those cold grey eyes widened in surprise. "Indeed!" he exclaimed, "he is to be congratulated!"

Henderson straightened up, looking as uncomfortable as he was beginning to feel, but then he was not the first to do so after a few minutes in Lytton's company. "Tomorrow, the day after at the latest," he told him, swallowing nervously, "I expect to apprehend Richard Ferrers. So you see Robert," he smiled with an assurance he was very far from feeling, "your journey into Sussex was not necessary after all."

Lytton looked up at his old friend thoughtfully, the light from the fire picking out the diamond pin in his lace cravat. "I take it that this Major Neville told you so?" he asked quizzically.

"Yes," he confirmed, his unease growing as he began to wonder what Lytton knew that he did not, "he reports to me regularly, indeed, he holds out every hope of success."

"Marvellous, is it not!" Lytton exclaimed shaking his head in astonishment, "that you, after months of arduous effort, have failed to achieve what he has managed to accomplish within a mere few days!"

He knew that tone of voice only too well and the implications of his words were not lost on him, but made a valiant attempt to conceal his growing apprehension, asking warily, "What are you saying? Do you doubt it?"

"Let us just say," Lytton offered, shrugging eloquently, "I find it quite remarkable that after so long a silence we now find the girl is on the brink of disclosing all!"

The inference attached to these calmly uttered words could not be ignored, indeed, they had such an impact upon Colonel Henderson that he could do no more than stare incredulously down at the delicately painted face regarding him in silent indifference. "Are you saying it is not true?" he managed with credible composure, feeling his legs to be in imminent danger of collapsing under him; his mind racing at the connotations these disturbing words implied.

"No," Lytton said slowly, pursing his thin painted lips, "just a little improbable."

His heart began to beat uncomfortably fast and his lips felt suddenly dry, but worse than this was the sickening acknowledgment that Robert's words held a ring of truth and that all the signs pointed to him having been duped, but it had the immediate affect of putting him on the defensive. Feeling the need to explain himself, although whether this was due wholly or in part to assuage his own doubts or simply to justify his actions to His Grace he was not entirely certain, but when he eventually spoke his voice, which sounded rather lame in his own ears, was far from convincing. "I own when I first met Major Neville I did think he was not entirely suited to the task ahead of him, but I have since been brought to see that I wronged him. His tactics," he confessed, in a further effort to explain himself, "though they differ somewhat from my own, seem to be having a most favourable affect on Miss Ferrers. In fact," he acknowledged, with more zeal than he felt, "I have never found it necessary to question anything he has told me;

accepting it as true."

Lytton's half closed eyes observed him steadily, a cold grey stare that made his guest feel even more uncomfortable, stripping him of every last vestige of calm. "You do not think," he suggested, raising a questioning eyebrow, "that he has been merely placating you?"

Somewhere at the back of his mind hovered the painful realization that that was precisely what he had done, but so eager was he to see the end of this business that he had eagerly accepted everything Major Neville had told him. Now though, when faced with the undeniable truth, he felt physically sick, but managing to retain sufficient control over his escalating fears, repeated feebly, "Placating me! Why should he do so?"

"I should have thought that would need no explaining," Lytton sighed.

It did not, but the mounting panic welling up inside him at Major Neville's palpable deceit and what would almost certainly result from it, began to make him tetchy and irritable, and since he did not perform well under anxiety, his nerves more often than not overriding commonsense, he was goaded into unguarded speech. "Well it does!" he snapped. "Major Neville," he informed him irascibly, "has conducted himself in an exemplary manner, and I have no cause to doubt either his integrity or his word!" This tersely delivered assertion had the immediate affect of allaying his fears as to what had momentarily appeared to be the truth about Major Neville's duplicity, but was in fact nothing more than Lytton trying to create difficulties. It also helped to boost his fast dwindling confidence, but unfortunately this much needed injection to his ever diminishing faith in his unassailable conviction that his troubles would soon be over, was unfortunately only transitory, as His Grace's next words proved.

"Clearly not," Lytton shook his head. "Has it not occurred to you that this imminent capitulation could well be feigned?" he questioned superciliously. "Why," he asked, "after all this time, has Miss Ferrers suddenly decided to tell us where her brother is to be found? Are Major Neville's powers of persuasion so irresistible? No, no my dear George," he shook his head, "I think not."

Henderson, whose legs now seemed quite incapable of bearing his weight any longer, sank heavily onto a chair, his heart thudding so fast that he felt sick. "What are you saying?" he demanded, his breathing becoming a little laboured. "He has been lying to me!"

"That is precisely what I am saying," Lytton told him, rising stately to his feet and walking leisurely over to the dining table. "My dear George," he advised, "think a moment. Turville and Ferrers' father were old friends, indeed, when he learned about Ferrers he found it impossible to accept that his friend's only son was a traitor. So much so," he shrugged, "that he made his feelings to me perfectly clear, going so far as to say that he had no liking for hunting him down."

Something resembling a hunted expression entered Henderson's starting eyes as he stared almost blindly across at Lytton as he joined him at the table, not quite able to dispel the panic as he mentally braced himself for what he sensed was to come. "But if you made it clear to Turville that Ferrers must be caught and he sent this Major Neville here to find him, then why is he lying to me?" he demanded desperately, his heavy jaws working feverishly and his face now as red as it had been white a moment ago. "Are you saying that Turville is playing his own game and Major Neville is a party to it?" frantically trying to stem the rising tide of fear he could feel sweeping over him.

"Well," Lytton shrugged, "it would make sense, would it not? When one considers the long-standing friendship between these two men, what could be more natural than Turville wanting to make sure of Ferrers' guilt before he hands him over to you. He could so easily have told this Major Neville a slightly different tale or," he suggested smoothly, totally indifferent to Henderson's unenviable position, "given him quite different orders to mine."

"Well if you think that," Henderson threw at him, panic momentarily depriving him of his senses, loosing sight of the wisdom of daring to speak to Lytton in such a manner, "why approach Turville in the first place? You should have known that he would not tamely accept your tale!"

Those grey eyes narrowed, and Henderson visibly winced under their cold condemning stare, reminding him to whom he spoke. "You know George," he said at length, his voice cuttingly polite, swinging his eye glass to and fro, "I have expended considerable effort on your behalf, but I am given to wondering whether you are deserving of my endeavours. You *dare* to address me in such terms!" he accused. "*You*, who recklessly embarked on a course of action which, should it ever become known, would see you hang!"

Henderson, feeling himself to be drowning, hastily begged pardon and tried to recover lost ground, but to no avail.

His Grace, deeply offended at having his methods called into question, continued inexorably, "You extort my help and then dare to question my dealings! It would serve you well if I left you and your equally undeserving friend to your own devices!" Henderson looked apprehensively at the painted face opposite, realizing too late that he had spoken out of turn. At all costs he dare not offend the only man who could save him from the gallows! "You ask why I approached Turville," he smiled unpleasantly, "because I know precisely what I am about; and why is that?" he asked, raising a haughty eyebrow, "because, unlike you, I consider a situation from every aspect as well as foresee every eventuality."

"Robert I ..."

"Please do not interrupt," he was told coldly. "I realized that there was always the possibility that Turville would impart his own views as well as his orders to this young man," he continued as though there had been no interruption, "which, naturally, would run counter to my own, and should such be the case and

Ferrers remained at large then a sacrificial lamb on the alter of duty would be required in order to save your *worthless* neck!" Having vented some of his spleen he continued in a much milder tone. "I had no idea who his representative would be, which was a circumstance I could not like, but given the facts of the case I could hardly make a point of attempting to discover his identity, especially when one bears in mind your role in the affair and the measures which you have forced me to adopt." He looked at Henderson's haggard face quite dispassionately, completely unmoved by his plight, but his irritation over his ingratitude still lingered, and could not resist saying nastily, "If this Major Neville has indeed played you false, then clearly he has taken you for the fool you are!"

As the enormity of Lytton's words sunk in Colonel Henderson felt as if the ground was opening up beneath him. If Lytton withdrew his support then he was lost indeed and for one awful moment he experienced such a sense of terror that he could hardly speak. Retrieving a handkerchief from his pocket, he wiped his forehead with a hand that visibly shook before raising his eyes to that cold impartial face, receiving neither a word nor a look of sympathy much less understanding. "You think me ungrateful," he managed, "but I assure you it is not so," he asserted. Receiving no response to this he raised his head, his hands dropping heavily onto the table. "I cannot believe Major Neville has lied to me all this time; leading me to believe that Miss Ferrers is on the point of confessing everything. Why?"

"I thought I had made that obvious," Lytton dismissed. "To gain time in which to discover the truth, of course."

"I can't believe it!" Henderson exclaimed, shaking his head, his face taking on an unhealthy pallor. "You must be mistaken!"

"I could, of course," Lytton acknowledged, "but you must admit that Miss Ferrers' imminent cooperation does stretch probability a little too far."

Yes it did, and he knew it. He could not believe that he could have been so blind as not to have seen it before, but so desperate was he to see the end of this matter that he had grabbed at any straw. Now though, he was back where he started, and dreaded to think what Major Neville had discovered.

Something of this was evident on his face, and Lytton, correctly interpreting his thoughts decided to turn the screw a little tighter. "You have been most remiss, have you not?" he reprimanded. "But then," he pointed out unkindly, "coherent thinking never was your forte, was it?"

Those bulbous blue eyes stared across the laden table at his friend, echoing not only his shock and fear but utter disbelief in that he could have been so stupid and gullible. He reached out a trembling hand to pour himself a much needed glass of wine, drinking it down all at once before saying incredulously, "It never occurred to me to question him," he shook his head. "Indeed, I had no reason to do so."

Lytton sighed. "Considering the position in which you and William Ferrers find yourselves," he remarked pungently, "I would have thought that that would have been a necessity. I would also have thought that the insertion of Richard Ferrers' name in the *Gazette* would be something you yourself would have orchestrated, but instead of taking any steps to do so, you allowed an opportunity to slip through your fingers. Yet again," he pointed out offensively, "you left it to me to do your thinking as well as your deeds for you." Again he scrutinized his painted fingernails. "Unless, of course, you were labouring under the belief that his accomplices, who are of course honest and upright citizens," he commented sarcastically, "would come to you of their own free will!" He eyed his visitor dispassionately. "You seem, do you not" he said coldly, "to have squandered so many opportunities!"

"Yes, I daresay!" he exclaimed irritably, pouring himself another glass of wine, "but you are not facing exposure as a traitor!"

"Nor would you be," Lytton reminded him, recalling the same cry from his confederate's lips, "but really," he shook his head, his lip curling contemptuously, "you have only yourself to blame for being in such a predicament."

"I did what I thought ..."

"You did precisely what others have done," Lytton broke in unceremoniously, "attempted to further your feeble ambitions as well as increase the weight of your purse without any consideration given to the consequences should Stuart fail."

This home truth did nothing to either dispel his growing anxiety or endear him to his host. "I realize now that I was wrong," Henderson admitted gravely, gulping down the remnants in his glass.

"A little late in the day for regrets, do you not think?" came the sardonic reply, calmly sipping his own wine.

"It *can't* be too late!" Henderson cried frantically, his hand trembling so much that he almost spilled his wine. "I won't let it be. Do you think that I am going to allow my name to be sullied and my position taken away from me all because of a man like Richard Ferrers? No, Robert" he said firmly, "I won't!"

"Very fine talking," Lytton grimaced, his tone an insult, "but how are you going to accomplish it when you cannot even ascertain Major Neville's commitment or the extent of his dealings to date?" It astounded him to know that Henderson had come thus far, not only in his military career, but also managing to steer clear of exposure and public condemnation. He could not understand how he had come to make friends with this man in the first place, so unalike were they that it annoyed him to think that he was now saddled with such an inept and incapable individual. "So," he asked sceptically, considering his painted fingernails as if they were of paramount importance, "what do you propose to do now?"

"Speak to Major Neville, of course," he told him, his tone a mixture of

271

defiance and petulance.

Those eyebrows rose in surprise. "And say what?"

"Merely that I wish him to tell me the truth," Henderson replied. "That I know he has been dissembling."

"And what reason will you give for this enquiry?" Lytton asked cynically.

"I shall say that ..." he broke off, realizing that it was going to be no easy matter without divulging the truth.

"Precisely!" His Grace inclined his head. "It is not quite so simple a matter, is it?"

Henderson swallowed. "No, it is not." He rose hurriedly to his feet, the chair legs scraping on the polished floorboards. "What am I to do?" he demanded desperately, rolling an anguished eye in Lytton's direction.

Pouring himself another glass of wine Lytton then took time to savour the rich ruby liquid in his glass before asking at length, "Have you heard from William Ferrers?"

"What? Oh yes, William" he nodded. "I am meeting him tomorrow," he said abstractedly before resuming his seat, his brief pacing around the room doing nothing to calm his nerves. "Although why he needs to show himself now I don't know!"

"He has come into Sussex on my orders," Lytton told him composedly, placing his glass down on the table before raising his eyes to see what affect this had had upon his guest.

"*Your* orders!" he exclaimed, darting a startled look at him.

It had not been Lytton's intention to come into Sussex in order to draw up emergency contingency plans, believing he had already done more than was required of him in this matter, but merely to warn Henderson that his patience would stand no more inefficiency and to acquaint him with his interview with William Ferrers. However, only a very little thought had been enough to caution him about placing too much reliance on William Ferrers' nerve holding out sufficiently to enable him to dispose of his cousin himself.   Considering the position in which he found himself he had been remarkably slow in remedying the situation, and whilst he had not yet come across Richard Ferrers, from all he had ever heard of him, he would go so far as to say that his cousin was no match for a young man who had hitherto managed to run rings round him as well as his accomplice.   He had told General Turville that he was surrounded by fools, a heartfelt sentiment which was as true now as it was then. He was heartily tired of this affair, and therefore decided the time had come to make an end of it once and for all, and not for the first time found himself railing against his own stupidity when he had allowed too much wine to loosen his tongue all those years ago! "Since it appears that neither of you are capable of performing the most simple of tasks," he was told with derision, "I have decided to take a more active part myself;

though not, I hasten to add, from any concern as to whether either of you are hung or not, but since you have seen fit to embroil me in this imbroglio of yours by dint of blackmail, I believe it prudent in me to protect my interests."

"Robert!" Henderson cried, shocked. "You must know I would never ..."

"But yes, George" Lytton nodded, "you would, and you must see that I could not possibly allow that to happen."

Henderson's face became suffused with colour, particularly as Robert had hit the nail on the head. He was placing all his hopes on Lytton coming to his aid, and whilst so far he had honoured his side of the bargain and done everything possible to assist him in his dilemma, his intervention to date had brought Richard Ferrers no nearer to being captured, but was in fact still roaming free and causing all manner of problems. So anxious was he to see the end of this matter, that he admitted to himself that if denouncing Robert would serve his purpose he would do so willingly, especially as he held such a piece of news that would instantly condemn him. "Well if you think that!" he spluttered at this accurate analysis, "I wonder ..."

"I not only think it," Lytton broke in decisively, "but I know it for a fact. So desperate are you to be released from this unenviable predicament that you would not care whom you used. *I* do not intend to be used!" he warned.

"I would never do such a thing!" he cried mendaciously. "You must know I would not. Why, I have known you for years!"

"Time is as meaningless as your promises," Lytton dismissed caustically, denying Benson with an infinitesimal shake of his head as he silently entered the sitting room to serve dinner. "I am tired of listening to excuses about why you or Ferrers have not been able to carry out the most straightforward of tasks, tasks I hasten to add a child could perform, but should either of you fail again," he cautioned, his eyes glinting, "I promise you I shall have no compunction in leaving you inept pair of bunglers to your fate." He saw Henderson was about to say something, but forestalled him. "If you think that my abandonment of your cause would give you leave to attempt to discredit me in any way, then think again," he said unpleasantly. "I do not take kindly when I have threats held over my head, and should you or that equally incapable individual you call a friend dares to imagine for one tiny instant that I shall merely allow you to sully my name and reputation, you quite mistake the matter!"

"Robert," Henderson declared, feeling his every thought was known to this man, "I give you my word that I would never use such a thing against you. You must know I would not have approached you had matters not been desperate."

"It appears they are still in the same case," Lytton remarked sardonically, "were it otherwise we would not be here now. This Major Neville of yours" Lytton mused after giving it a moment's consideration, "unless I grossly err, an absurdity I know," he inclined his head, "could very well be turned to good account."

Since it was becoming increasingly apparent that he was not going to be invited to share Robert's dinner, Colonel Henderson, no matter what trials beset him could still find an appetite, tried to ignore the tantalising aromas which pervaded the air and turned his mind instead to disentangling himself from this never ending nightmare. "In what way?" he asked sharply.

"You said, I think" he pondered, tapping his nose with his quizzing glass, "that he reports to you regularly?" Henderson nodded. "I take it that he is at the moment in the garrison?"

"Yes, or at least," he amended hastily, "he was. He was due to dine with me this evening, but upon receipt of your letter I thought it best to cancel the invitation," he swallowed. "I believe he went to see Miss Ferrers earlier today in order to discover her mind, but as yet I am not aware of how this meeting fared."

Lytton sipped his wine, considering his soon to be former friend over the rim of the glass. It was never easy to know what he was thinking, but Henderson, rendered acutely uncomfortable, found it very difficult to withstand such close scrutiny. "Under no circumstances are you to let him suspect you know the game he is playing," Lytton warned. "You will continue therefore, to receive his reports without question and treat him in exactly the same way as you have to date."

"Yes, of course," Henderson nodded, not daring to disagree even though it would be a severe trial to do as Lytton instructed, in fact, he would go so far as to say that it would be well nigh impossible, but since Robert appeared prepared to continue offering his support he deemed it expedient to do as he asked, "but to what purpose?"

"I could, of course, be quite wrong," Lytton nodded, not really considering this as even a remote possibility, "but we must not overlook the fact that our friend Major Neville and Miss Ferrers may not be quite so averse to one another as we have conjectured."

"What!" Henderson exclaimed, taken aback at this.

"Why not?" Lytton asked reasonably, replenishing his glass. "From what you yourself have told me I would infer that Major Neville is quite a personable young man and, or so I should suppose, not without experience in these matters. As for the lady," he shrugged, "I am reliably informed that she is indeed quite beautiful."

Henderson pursed his lips at this, and his colour rose in indication. Little though he relished the thought of attributing anything remotely complimentary in her favour, honesty compelled him to admit the truth of this, but considering Elizabeth Ferrers' obstructive attitude to date, it went very much against the grain to acknowledge that she possessed any good points at all. Lytton, reading his expression with unerring accuracy, was tired of his friend's inefficiency as well as his ceaseless wallowing in self-pity due to the calamitous consequences resulting from his blunders to date, all of which, in his unchallenged opinion, could so easily have been avoided, deemed it time to put an end to this latest descent into melancholy. Without a doubt, Elizabeth Ferrers had very much ruffled his feathers by thwarting him at every turn, which had clearly brought about his intense animosity towards her, and now, if that were not bad enough, along comes this Major Neville to add to his grievances by not only taking him for the fool he was but also subjecting him to unremitting dissimulation. He had a pretty shrewd idea as to the reasons behind this young man's motives for playing Henderson false, and were it not for the disadvantageous position in which he found himself and the urgent necessity to keep his name untarnished, he could almost applaud the results deriving from the devices adopted by both these individuals. As it was, their handling of him was merely exacerbating his incompetence which in turn could only rebound adversely upon himself, and therefore felt it behoved him to not only terminate this lamentable affair once and for all, but to ensure his own protection.

Experience had taught him to place no reliance on Henderson keeping his word to remain silent as to the reason for his recruitment into this reprehensible affair, especially when he had imbibed a little too much port or cognac or, as seemed to be the case of late, when panic set in. Not for the first time then, he found himself in the intolerable position of having to put forward the rudiments of a plan to extricate Henderson and his equally inept accomplice from the consequences of their actions. The more he considered it the more convinced he became that William Ferrers, who possessed not one iota of courage or determination, could quite well fail in his attempts to deal with his cousin himself, despite his assurances that he would do so. The very idea of aiding traitors to evade punishment for their crimes was so repugnant to him that he bitterly resented having to come to the rescue of two men who deserved neither his assistance nor magnanimity, but, on the contrary, the full penalty of the law, and it was therefore in a voice totally devoid of enthusiasm that he unveiled his scheme to rid themselves permanently of this never-ending nightmare.

Having listened to Lytton's proposal on how to deal with Richard Ferrers once and for all so he was no longer around to create difficulties with an eagerness he had not experienced for some considerable time, Henderson enthusiastically rallied to the scheme. The fluently expressed proposal appeared flawless, but its appeal was soon marred by the knowledge that he would have to be the one to work out the details to ensure its success. He was not saying that it was beyond him, not at all, but it would take a deal of arranging in which to get it all organized, which would, of necessity, require time and planning, after all it would not do to bungle it, but since Lytton was clearly expecting him to expedite this plan immediately, he foresaw all manner of obstacles confronting him. Logistically, it bore all the hallmarks of constituting nothing short of a nightmare as trying to get all the players in the appropriate place at a particular time so the intricacies of the scheme would go according to his arrangements, was going to be no easy undertaking. When he considered the people he was dealing with, all of whom it seemed had minds of their own and more than capable of ruining his carefully contrived design to accomplish such a feat through a variety of reasons, a rather petulant look descended onto his flushed face.

Lytton's all seeing eyes had not missed that gleam of hope in Henderson's bulbous ones as he expanded eloquently on his theme, but neither did they miss the look of peevishness which quickly followed, and understood its meaning perfectly. "You know, George" he sighed, unable to hide his intolerance, "if you and William Ferrers are an example of the men Stuart had around him, I do not wonder he failed in his venture."

Henderson's colour deepened at this smoothly delivered accusation, but however much he resented it as well as those uncharitable denunciations as to his competence, he knew better than to voice it.

"I shall, therefore," Lytton said meaningfully, ignoring his friend's piqued expression, giving him no time to either agree with or argue the point, "expect to receive favourable tidings very soon, but I feel sure," he smiled thinly, "that you will ultimately adopt the right way to go to work on this most delicate matter in order to ensure an agreeable conclusion. And only think," he smiled coldly, "how much better you will feel when you discover that the results of your efforts have come to fruition."

Ignoring this subtle reminder as to what would happen should he fail again, Henderson deemed it wise to let this unflattering utterance pass, and instead took a few moments to consider the proposed scheme for their deliverance more closely. It was unquestionably intricate, and without meticulous care he could see it all going horribly awry, but even so he was eventually brought to admit that Robert had certainly come up with a most ingenious proposition. "You know," he said thoughtfully, having giving it considerable thought, glancing across at Lytton, "I think it may just work,"

Lytton's eyes narrowed at this. "It *will* work," he told him unequivocally, "unless, of course," he offered nastily, "William Ferrers is as big a fool as you!"

"Curse you, Robert!" Henderson exclaimed incensed, growing tired of his vituperative tongue. "Do you always have to be so damned offensive?"

"My dear George," Lytton derisively admonished, his eyes glinting, "since it appears that both you and your ineffectual accomplice are incapable of undertaking the most simple of tasks without them disintegrating into chaos, I deem it a necessity."

"I daresay!" he cried heatedly, "but you know as well as I that things do not always go according to plan!"

"That is unquestionably true where the two of *you* are concerned," he retorted contemptibly, his lip curling. "In truth," he shrugged, "I must own to some surprise to know that you have come thus far unscathed. However," he inclined his head significantly, paying no heed to Henderson's fulminating stare, "considering that you are both of you sailing pretty close to the wind and your future prospects are not looking any too promising, I do not, on this occasion at least," he warned ominously, "expect you to fail again. Indeed," he emphasized awfully, "I feel sure that once you have explained the case to your adherent, he will make an extra special effort to ensure that this is one instance when his endeavours prosper."

Lytton's smoothly sinister eloquence was not lost on him, indeed, he needed no explanation as to his meaning or what would result from yet another failure, and whilst he had no liking for the dismissive treatment he meted out, he felt himself quite incapable of either stemming the flow of his overt insults or refuting the aspersions cast on his competency, so swallowing down the retort which sprang to his lips, said instead, "I shall speak to Ferrers tomorrow."

"Do that," he was told, ringing for Benson to serve dinner. "Make no mistake," he said with dangerous calm, "I shall not take it kindly if this latest venture fails. My patience," he cautioned, "will not endure it."

"It won't fail," Henderson assured him irritably, devoutly trusting that William Ferrers' nerve would hold out, not to mention his own.

"In that case," Lytton nodded dismissively, "I see no reason why I should be troubled with this affair any longer, or see the need for me to animadvert further upon it other than to say that Major Neville and Miss Ferrers will lead us to her brother one way or the other."

Henderson, who had come to the conclusion that Robert was not offering him an invitation to dinner after all and the matter in hand, as far as he was concerned, was no longer open for discussion, rose from his chair and began to collect his hat and gloves. Despite the fact that Lytton had put forward a foolproof move in which to solve his ever growing difficulties, there were naturally a number of points on which he would have liked some clarification, but since his friend had clearly deemed the interview to be at an end and saw no reason for further discourse or elucidation, in fact his whole demeanour was one of infinite boredom, killing at a stroke any desire or, indeed, the courage, of plying him with questions, said instead, "Do you intend making a long stay in Sussex?"

"That depends," he was told enigmatically.

"On what?" he was bold enough to ask.

Lytton eyed him quite dispassionately. "On whether you and your so-called friend are capable of following instructions," he told him ill-naturedly. "You have no objection to that, I trust?" he asked as he saw the irritation on his friend's face.

"No," Henderson shook his head. "None whatsoever." As it was apparent that Lytton had no more to say on the subject, he wished his friend a terse goodnight, not daring to think what would happen if this latest scheme failed, either through their own mistakes or Major Neville's intervention. In either event, he had no doubt at all that the blame for the failure would fall squarely upon his shoulders.

Gideon had no regrets about falling in love with Elizabeth Ferrers, on the contrary he wished he had met her long before and could not imagine his life without her, but he could not deny that this unlooked for aspect rendered an already heavy responsibility into an onerous trust, especially having given her his word that he would do everything possible to save her brother.

Unaware of the plans being laid to ensnare his future brother-in-law as well as the conclusions drawn concerning his dissimulation, he left Ferrers Court, not only with Elizabeth's kisses still burning on his lips, but also with the same thoughts in mind as Salmon. Although Richard Ferrers had given his word to refrain from taking any further part in nocturnal activities, he doubted it would last very long. He acquitted him of taking part in the smuggling trade for personal profit, but he had met many young men of his stamp who found inactivity insupportable, becoming easily bored. Richard Ferrers, a man not given over to idleness, would soon find a purposeless existence begin to pall and boredom setting in. When he had given his word he had meant it, but given all the factors, no reliance could be placed upon him keeping it indefinitely. Regrettably, the same could be said for him keeping his distance from Hampton Regis. Should the recovery of those letters take longer than anticipated, then he would not put it beyond that young man to make the attempt himself, a circumstance of which Salmon was extremely fearful. He had seen enough of Richard Ferrers to know that once he took the idea into his head nothing would deter him, indeed, he could only marvel how Salmon had managed to restrain him thus far. Should this indeed turn out to be the case and he was caught, which was a very real possibility, then no power on earth would save him, and at all costs this eventually must be avoided, his fears for Richard's safety spurring his determination to retrieve the evidence which would prevent him from the hangman's noose as soon as may be possible.

Between His Grace's intention of 'gazetting' him and Richard Ferrers' mercurial temperament, Gideon did not need reminding that time was relentlessly ticking away, and if he was going to prevent this young man from hanging in Hampton Regis market place or being shot on sight as a wanted felon, then he had to get his hands on those incriminating letters tonight.

Somehow or other he had to try and convince Lieutenant Beaton that he was not here to see Richard Ferrers hang but on the contrary to try and save his life. He supposed it was too much to expect Major Denham not to reveal the reason for his visit to Hampton Regis, but having done so he had killed at a stroke the initial signs of trust and friendship there had been on so short an acquaintance, and had therefore made it extremely difficult for him to try and regain either. If what Richard Ferrers had told him were true then he was convinced that once the circumstances had been explained to him and the precise nature of his own involvement, then he could not see him turning his back on his request for assistance in order to help his friend. The truth was that without his assistance he could see no possible means of gaining entry into the prison block, there being no conceivable reason for him to visit the one part of the garrison that somehow or other he had to gain admittance to. At all times there were no fewer than two guards on duty inside and he could not even offer the excuse that he was there in order to speak to one of the inmates, temporarily enjoying its sparse comforts. Should he fail to convince Lieutenant Beaton of the sincerity of his intentions then he was faced with the daunting task of coming up with a feasible plan to gain legitimate entry.   Several ideas sprung to mind only to be discarded almost immediately from one cause or another, the result being that his casual comment to Elizabeth about getting himself arrested, seemed to him to be the only way he could gain admittance to the prison quarters. The problem nagged at him, forcing every other consideration from his mind; nothing at this moment was more important than saving Richard Ferrers' life, and the acquisition of those letters were all that stood in the way of that. It was not only the thought of sending an innocent man to the scaffold that strengthened his determination, but the devastating affect it would have upon his sister, but until he had spoken to Lieutenant Beaton, hopefully having returned from the patrol he had been sent on by the time he returned to the garrison, there was nothing he could do but wait with what patience he could muster.

Whatever he may think about Richard Ferrers informing Colonel Henderson about that damning evidence he had to admire his quick thinking in hiding those letters under the very nose of the man who would stop at nothing to get his hands on them, but it had left him in a quandary as to how he could possibly hope to retrieve them.

It was close on half past six by the time he entered the garrison's precincts and already dusk was beginning to set in, but just as he turned his horse in the direction of the stables who should be turning the corner towards him but Lieutenant Beaton. Immediately setting eyes on a senior officer, Lieutenant Beaton saluted before continuing to walk away towards his own quarters.

"Lieutenant!" Gideon forestalled him. "One moment, if you please."

Lieutenant Beaton stopped dead in his tracks his stomach lurching, having a very good idea of why the Major wanted to talk to him, then turning round he stood to attention and waited for Gideon to dismount and come up to him.

The corners of Gideon's mouth twitched at this very precise military punctilio, but managed to suppress it. "I want to talk to you."

"To me, Sir?" he asked warily.

"Yes, to you," he nodded.

"What about, Sir?" he asked, looking straight ahead of him.

"I think you know what about," Gideon told him meaningfully.

"I...I'm afraid I'm at a loss, Sir" he faltered, glancing briefly up at the determined face in front of him, not at all sure how long he could withstand Major Neville's resolve to speak with him.

"This is no time for prevarication, Beaton" Gideon told him urgently. "I need to talk to you about our mutual friend."

The hazel eyes darted a cautious look into those compelling brown ones, but whilst some doubt still lingered as to his intentions regarding Richard, there was something in them that told him he could be trusted. Nevertheless, his loyalty to his friend held him back. "Indeed, Sir" he replied nervously. "I can't imagine whom you mean."

"Don't be a fool man!" Gideon said earnestly. "I'm not here to see Ferrers strung up but to try and prevent that from happening!" Gideon saw the indecision on his face and pressed home his advantage. "I know Major Denham has been talking to you, but I'm here to try and help Richard, you *must* believe that!" He looked down into the troubled face. "You don't need me to tell you that Richard is in trouble. I've been sent here to try and help him but I can't do it alone. I shall need your help; and I shall need it tonight!"

It was clear to Gideon that Lieutenant Beaton was still debating the issue, but although he was still cautious it was becoming more evident that he knew he was being told the truth.

"I want to believe you," he told him at length, Major Denham's words still hovering in his mind, his uncertainty clearly evident in his eyes, "but I would never forgive myself if anything happened to Richard because of me."

"Do you think that's what I want?" Gideon asked. "Whether you like it or not you and I are the only ones who can help him. Tell me Richard was not wrong in you and that I may rely on you!"

He shot a quick look up at Gideon but he could see nothing in his face to suggest he was either untruthful or setting a trap for him. "You've seen him?" he asked sharply.

"Yes, I've seen Richard," he confirmed. "He told me all about you; how you were at Eton together and the times you spent at Ferrers Court. He also suggested I ask you if your father ever bought you that bay hunter you hankered after!"

Lieutenant Beaton let out a deep sigh. "You would only know that from Richard" he nodded. "You could not possibly have had it from anyone here as I have told no one that I know Richard."

"Does this mean you trust me at last?" Gideon smiled encouragingly. Upon receiving an answering smile and a confirming nod, he exclaimed, "Thank

God!"

"I'm sorry about before," he apologized, "keeping you at a distance I mean, but when Major Denham ..."

"Never mind that," Gideon dismissed. "All that matters is that you believe I am here to help Ferrers and not to see him climb the scaffold."

"Very well, Major" he nodded, "I'll help you in any way I can. What is it you want me to do?"

"Unfortunately," Gideon shook his head, "there is no time to explain anything now, besides" he pointed out, "we can't talk here, we may be seen. Come to my quarters tonight about nine o'clock."

He nodded. "I'll be there," he told him, but felt it behoved him to point out that he was orderly officer for the night, but would come and see him before he commenced his duties.

"Very well," Gideon smiled, "nine o'clock." He sensed his young friend wanted to say something, but just at that moment Major Denham emerged from his tower quarters and began to make his way across the courtyard. He did not think he had seen the two of them together, but it was clear that Lieutenant Beaton did not want it to be seen that he was fraternizing with him, so after renewing his promise to see him at nine o'clock, quickly made his way to his own rooms.

Lieutenant Beaton was by no means averse to helping his friend, indeed, he would like nothing more than to see his troubles resolved, and although he was pleased to know that his initial opinion of Major Neville had not been wrong, he failed to see what he personally could possibly do.

But when he arrived at Gideon's rooms a few minutes past nine o'clock it was to be met with the news that he had been summoned to Colonel Henderson's quarters about half an hour before. Sergeant Taylor, who had his own views about the garrison commander, told him that Major Neville would like him to wait, so making himself comfortable accepted the glass of wine offered, hoping that nothing untoward was going on across the courtyard.

CHAPTER FOURTEEN

Colonel Henderson had known his meeting with Lytton would not be any too comfortable, but he had not expected to be treated with such contempt. It was not his fault that Richard Ferrers had been allowed to escape, and as far as his actions were concerned regarding his dealings with this young man and his family he had no regrets whatsoever, and therefore considered his treatment at Robert's hands to be grossly unfair. It was all very well for him to issue instructions and fully expect them to be carried out, but he was not the one having to execute them in the face of overwhelming odds. Nevertheless, he had to acknowledge that the scheme outlined had a lot to recommend it, and providing William Ferrers played his part in the forthcoming plan to rid themselves once and for all of their problems, then he was perfectly prepared to overlook the verbal annihilation he had suffered yet again.

He had been a little surprised to learn that William Ferrers had come into Sussex on Robert's orders, but since his old friend had only told him what he considered necessary, then he could only construe they had met in London prior to his departure into this rural backwater. Robert's tendency to withhold certain facts may afford him some kind of personal gratification by letting it be seen that he was not only without equal in all things but that he had the right to dictate events without recourse or consultation, but in view of what was at stake a little consideration would not come amiss. Much as he resented Robert's high-handed and dismissive attitude, he nevertheless took no small satisfaction from knowing that his partner in treason would doubtless have received the same treatment as himself.   He may not always like the way Robert spoke to him, indeed, he was greatly offended by it, but it was at least some comfort to know that he was not alone in being on the receiving end of that rapier sharp tongue!

Not for the first time then did he take exception to Robert's manner but there was certainly nothing to take exception to in the idea he had put forward, on the contrary, he liked it very well.   Naturally, its success would largely depend on William Ferrers doing everything that was expected of him, but if he did not want to come face to face with the alternative then he could not see him refusing to play his part, in which case he had every hope of being relieved of his difficulties before many days were out.

Since Richard Ferrers had escaped from lawful custody he had deliberately kept a discreet distance between himself and his cousin believing that no good would come from seeing one another until their quarry had been recaptured and was no longer in a position to make mischief. It was all very well for William Ferrers to write to him urging the necessity that they meet in order to discuss their difficulties and the best way of extricating themselves, but with his cousin on the loose he had considered it to be the height of folly. Lytton's intervention however, had forced the issue; his cunning manipulation ensuring William's presence in the vicinity and whilst he considered the arrival on the scene of both these men as being extremely detrimental to his own peace of mind, in view of the plan put forward he was quite prepared to overlook such a primary consideration. He may have regarded Lytton's sudden and unannounced arrival in Hampton Regis as a great piece of effrontery, implying that he could not deal adequately with the situation himself, but he was now forced to admit that it was perhaps a blessing in disguise. He could not deny that his own efforts to waylay Richard Ferrers had so far proved unsuccessful, and if he were honest he had to admit, however reluctantly, that there was no way he could rid himself of all the worries that surrounded him on his own. When he had informed Whitney that he would meet Ferrers this evening, he had had no idea that Lytton had sought him out and recommended he come into Sussex, much less what would come of a meeting between them.

Robert's carefully expressed proposal as to how an end could be made of the difficulties which beset him and William Ferrers, was not only a masterstroke of genius but extremely audacious, and however much he may resent having to admit it, it was perfectly calculated to bring them about. Regrettably though, it did have one flaw, and that was that Robert, whose sole aim in all his dealings was not only to achieve his objectives but also to protect himself from any adverse repercussions, had therefore run true to form by skilfully planting the seed of an idea into his head subtly allowing it to take root on its own. Not only had this line of approach effectively provided Robert with a vital loophole enabling him to deny any knowledge or involvement should it become known, but had left it to him to take it further by working out the details and putting it into execution.

Had Major Denham been privileged to know what was going forward he would seriously have doubted his commanding officer's ability to plan and execute something of this magnitude, but to do him justice Colonel Henderson could, on occasion, be quite resourceful, especially when it concerned his own welfare. But necessity it seemed had spurred him on, because after only a very little thought the rudiments of Robert's idea were beginning to formulate in his mind, and even though there were still some finer points to be ironed out, he failed to see how it could possibly founder. Sadly though, it would require the input of William Ferrers for its success but bearing in mind how he had so far failed to follow Lytton's instructions, he was forced to own that whilst his participation was essential he was not at all confident in him holding his nerve, and once again shuddered to think of the consequences resulting should they fail.

Then of course, there was always the possibility that Major Neville may thwart their plans either by design or accidental means, and considering his mendacity and cunning so far regarding his dealings with Elizabeth Ferrers, he viewed this young man as posing the biggest threat to the eventual success of their efforts. When he had worked out the details of the scheme he had naturally taken into account the need to get this young man out of the way for long enough to enable him and William Ferrers to execute the task ahead of them, but since then it had been uncomfortably born in on him that getting rid of him temporarily, whilst serving a crucial purpose, would only mean storing up trouble for themselves in the future. He had every reason to suppose that Major Neville, especially taking into account his devious tactics so far, would not stand idly by and allow an innocent man to be hung, and therefore had concentrated his mind on how to deal with such a potentially dangerous eventuality. The same could equally be said of Elizabeth Ferrers. For a woman of her spirit and courage it would be impossible for her to remain silent, and to take for granted that she would not raise a hue and cry at the earliest opportunity following her release, denouncing him and her cousin as abductors and would-be murderers of her brother, would be indulging optimism too far. The thought of denunciation, especially at this juncture, was too horrendous to contemplate, but it certainly served to increase his efforts in coming up with a solution, so much so that within a very little while he believed he had devised a way of obviating this risk.

His method of dealing with Major Neville and Miss Ferrers may not have formed part of Robert's calculations, indeed, nothing so distasteful had even been inferred, but considering the menace they both posed he could see no alternative. He had no doubt that Robert would be far from pleased to learn that something so perilous as murdering a man in the service of the King as well as a woman whose family and connections were impeccable, despite her brother's so-called iniquities, had been committed, albeit in the guise of accidents. He could not see their deaths being reported as anything other than a most unfortunate consequence resulting from Richard Ferrers' dealings, but Robert for one would not be so easily taken in; he would know precisely what had happened and the truth surrounding their demise. That he would let such an incident pass unchallenged was hoping for too much, in fact he would not be at all surprised to find himself being required to give an account of his actions as well as having to undergo yet another comprehensive demolition of his intelligence as well as being viciously accused of flagrant stupidity. This was all very well, but what Robert would fail to make allowance for was the fact that he had adroitly ensured his own protection against any charges or allegations being flung at him, whereas he and William Ferrers had been left open to all manner of accusations. This being so he was faced with little choice but to do all he could to protect their interests, and whilst he could not deny that by making an end of Major Neville and Miss Ferrers was drastic to say the least, as far as he was concerned not only did he look upon it as expedient but nothing short of inspired. Besides which, it would go some way to repaying them both for daring to treat him with such dismissive contempt.

The very thought of Major Neville and his carefully calculated deception as well as his effrontery in daring to treat him with such disdain, made him seethe with anger. Nothing would give him greater pleasure than to be able to take him to task for his underhand dealings with him, but if he and William Ferrers were to emerge from this horrendous nightmare unscathed then he knew he could not. However abhorrent the thought he had little choice but to do as Robert recommended and continue to behave towards Major Neville in exactly the same way as he had thus far, but how he was to accomplish this he had no idea. When he considered the perilous position he was in, made worse by the fact that he had no way of knowing how much Major Neville had either discovered or deduced, and that at any moment the whole thing could explode in his face, filled him with dread. If all this were not bad enough the mere thought of such insufferable conduct being allowed to pass unchallenged was something he found quite intolerable, but more than this was the idea of allowing Major Neville to believe that he had succeeded in duping him.

He could only guess at the reasons behind this subterfuge but undoubtedly his relationship with Miss Ferrers, which clearly was on a far more friendly basis than he had been led to believe, had played a part. His experience of Elizabeth Ferrers, whom he had no hesitation in deeming to be devious and conniving, had obviously played on Major Neville's sympathies. For such a clever woman it would not take her long to realize that the only way she could continue to aid and protect her brother was by using her youth and beauty to their best advantage. He was not excusing Major Neville's deception, but by adopting such restrained tactics in his dealings with her, it had clearly led her to believe that by using her greatest assets and taking advantage of his compassion, was the only certain way of getting him on her side and therefore helping her brother.

He would have been astounded to know that far from being lured into her web of deceit and cunning as well as being blinded to the truth by her calculated charms, Major Neville had fallen headlong into love with her without any tempting on her part. He would have been even more astounded to know that that astute young man had read the situation for precisely what it was well before he had encountered Miss Ferrers, and her explanation of events had merely proved his own theories to be correct.

However much he may distrust Elizabeth Ferrers as well as being firmly of the opinion that she was hand in glove with her brother, he had long since come to the conclusion that Richard Ferrers could not have revealed either his own or his cousin's complicity in treason to her. His experience of her told him that had he have done so she would have acted upon it long since, and whatever his feelings were the name of Ferrers still carried weight, and this being so her claims and allegations would not have been ignored. In such circumstances therefore, both he and William Ferrers would have faced their trial for treason before now or, at least, been questioned as to the veracity of her accusations. If his suppositions were correct about brother and sister, and he was certain they were, then he could only speculate as to the reason why Richard Ferrers had withheld such damning information from her. If his motive for not telling her had its roots in blackmail, deciding to turn a hopeless situation to his own advantage, then surely he would have received some kind of demand by now, but his knowledge of him and the kind of man he was turned this theory on its head, especially when he considered how he had entered into this business in the first place. Whatever else Richard Ferrers may be he was certainly no blackmailer, if he were then the possibilities were endless, but since no requests had been made to extort either money or any other form of currency from him in order to secure his silence as well as his own reinstatement, then he was left with only one conclusion. There could be no doubt that his sole aim in not telling his sister was precisely as Major Neville had construed; he was simply doing all he could to protect her, and therefore the only important thing as far as he was concerned was obtaining those letters in order to clear his name and to bring both himself and William Ferrers to account.

Since he was convinced that his conjecture was correct in that Elizabeth Ferrers knew nothing of his involvement in the late rebellion, and there was no reason for him to suppose that Major Neville should have discovered it, he remained quite confident that he could even now emerge from his difficulties intact.   Had he have suspected that either of them knew the truth or that two meetings had already taken place between Richard Ferrers and Major Neville, he would not have set out for Lewes in such an optimistic frame of mind.

Lewes, a busy market town situated at the foot of the South Downs, boasted a number of excellent inns, but the landlord of 'The Peal of Bells', a most discreet if condescending individual, was in no doubt that he not only served the best ale and spirits for miles around but enjoyed the patronage of several distinguished citizens, Colonel Henderson among them. His red-coated figure was a familiar sight in the town and one who could be seen in Judson's establishment at least twice a week. Judson, recognizing immediately that he was a man who knew a good port or cognac when he tasted one, had a pretty shrewd idea that no questions would be asked about how he had acquired it. He knew too that it was not only because he was assured of a good port or brandy which brought him frequently into Lewes, but a discreet little house at the end of the town. Not that he blamed him for that, after all Mrs. Jaynes was a fine looking woman whose ample charms clearly appealed to the bachelor Colonel rather more than they did to her frequently absent husband. In return for the landlord's silence on such a delicate matter, he was therefore quite prepared to turn a blind eye as to the source of the contents of his cellar, which he knew full well were run goods. But Judson had not acquired either his clientele or reputation, however suspect, by blabbing to all and sundry; discretion was his watchword and when he had told such a valued customer as Colonel Henderson that he had the perfect place for a private meeting he had not exaggerated. The snug little private parlour at the rear of the premises, used only by himself and a few likeminded cronies, was everything that Colonel Henderson could have wished for, being neatly tucked away out of sight of the tap room and the front facing coffee room.

Still smarting from Lytton's verbal attack the night before Colonel Henderson, immediately prior to his meeting with William Ferrers, had sought solace by visiting the lady who, like him, had long enjoyed their illicit assignations, arriving at '*The Peal of Bells*' in a most charitable frame of mind. Having drunk two glasses of Judson's finest cognac while he was waiting for Ferrers he was well on the way to believing that this time they would be successful in their forthcoming efforts, and by the time his confederate was shown into the little parlour he was in an extremely mellow mood. But one look at his accomplice's face was sufficient to kill at a stroke any feelings of well-being he had as it was clear he was not only extremely nervous and on edge but rather excitable into the bargain.

For this, several reasons were responsible. He was still far from pleased that he had been obliged to come all this way to consult with his partner in treason, at a loss to understand why they could not have met at the garrison in Hampton Regis or even at '*The White Hart*', which surely would have been far more convenient for both of them. Not only that, but had Henderson not been so edgy, forbidding any contact between them, then he would not have been subjected to that humiliating interview with His Grace. Surely between the two of them they could have hit upon some way of dealing with his cousin without the further intervention of Lytton, of whom he stood in considerable awe. He was certainly in no hurry to have a repeat performance of that verbal exchange to which he had not shone to advantage, and he could only hope that this meeting with Colonel Henderson would prove fruitful so that they could finally end this nightmare, because he not only doubted his nerve holding out, but also his purse in accommodating any further travelling expenses. Added to this was the knowledge that his cousin was still roaming free, and whilst his position was precarious to say the least, he could nevertheless do them irreparable harm should he ever manage to put his hands on those letters. But more disturbing was the discovery that Elizabeth was actually considering divulging Richard's whereabouts to a man who was virtually a stranger to her. He knew of the treatment she had met with from Henderson and his band of red-coats which had engendered in her a deep rooted hatred and mistrust of anyone wearing a scarlet uniform, but so carried away had be been with his beautific dreams of being master at Ferrers Court, that he had been eager to prove to his cousin as well as himself that he could enact the role of

Viscount Easton equally as well as her father had. It was therefore not until he was on his way to Lewes that the conversation he had witnessed this afternoon began to take on some significance. He would have staked his life that Elizabeth would rather die than give Richard up, especially to a red-coat, but unless he had misunderstood, Major Neville had definitely expected her capitulation. It was not like his cousin to dissemble, which was why he could not even begin to understand what game she was playing, particularly as he could not be entirely certain whether she knew where Richard was or not. Assuming she did know and ultimately decided to reveal his whereabouts heaven only knew what would happen, but of one thing he was fairly sure and that was that he and Colonel Henderson would find themselves with an awful lot of questions to answer.

If this Major Neville was indeed the man His Grace had spoken of, and it seemed safe to say that he was, then he could only speculate as to what his real orders were and what the result of his investigations would reveal. If he was honest he was not at all sure what His Grace expected to happen from this Major Neville's visit to Ferrers Court, but that some effort was required from himself was certain. In truth, he doubted whether he would ever be able to persuade Elizabeth to talk to him about Richard much less confide in him, and as far as Major Neville was concerned, he would have to be a fool not to recognize that he was no dupe who could be hoodwinked any more than he would be easy prey if it came to a bout fisticuffs. All these ills played on his mind especially when he thought that nothing seemed to be going right, ensuring the hangman's noose was getting ever closer, doing nothing to boost his confidence about coming out of this in one piece.

From the look he threw the landlord who had obsequiously bowed him into the little private parlour, it was evident that he lacked his co-conspirator's faith in either his discretion or reliability. Not by a word nor gesture did Judson give him cause to question his trustworthiness, and whilst he never allowed his gaze to rest on him for many seconds, there was something in those dark, almost black sunken eyes, lacklustre and seemingly inoffensive, that made him wary, giving him the very strong impression that they missed very little, indeed, he sensed they were constantly on the watch, and this knowledge alone filled him with caution. "Did we have to meet here?" he demanded urgently when they were alone, not at all convinced that the private parlour of *'The Peal of Bells'* was as private as Colonel Henderson made out. "Anyone could walk in here and see us," he complained peevishly.

"No one is going to walk in," he was told irritably. "I know Judson, he'll make sure we are not disturbed."

Ferrers was far from happy, and upon asking why they could not have met at the garrison or, failing that, *'The White Hart'*, was told that if he were not such a fool he would know the answer to that. Taking instant exception to this he began to argue the point but was immediately interrupted with a frustrated demand to stop behaving like the fool he was and say what he had to and be quick about it as they had far more important matters to discuss other than his personal and, which was most probably the case, imaginary injustices. He was deeply offended by this stating belligerently that they were very far from imaginary, and if they were going to talk of fools then he himself was one, which he must be if he thought for one moment that he was in some way detached from all the problems surrounding them, before hurriedly going on to unburden himself of his cares. He may have felt a little better for gaining a point over his accomplice as well as getting his grievances off his chest, but he was not such a fool that he did not realize that he had by no means solved them.

Colonel Henderson, fully aware that he was plagued with the same concerns, did not need to have them reinforced. He knew perfectly well the threat Richard Ferrers posed and what could happen if he was not dealt with, the same as he knew what would happen if those letters surfaced and were made public. The mere thought of exposure, resulting in an inevitable walk to the scaffold, rendered him as tetchy as his accomplice, whose somewhat stilted account of all that had had happened to him since they had last met fell on deaf ears.

"I don't know how much more of this I can take!" Ferrers exclaimed, a little shrilly. "Not only have I had to endure a severe lecture from His Grace, and in my own lodgings too, but have had to rely on a few paltry guineas to enable me to defray the cost of coming into Sussex. If something is not done soon, I don't know how on earth I will show my face in town again! I have barely nothing in my purse as it is!"

"Never mind that," Henderson bit out.

"Never mind!" Ferrers cried. "It's all very well for you …"

"We have more important things to discuss than your creditors," Henderson cut in harshly, demanding instead to be told of the situation at Ferrers Court.

Ferrers eyed him resentfully, but after debating the issue for several moments decided that if his impecunious circumstances as well as his involvement with Stuart were to be sorted out then they would first have to decide how best to deal with his cousin. Only when Richard was safely out of the way would he be able to breathe more easily as well as enabling him to take up what he believed to be his inheritance, rendering it possible for him to discharge his escalating debts. It was therefore in a mood of considerable petulance that he recounted all that had occurred since his arrival at Ferrers Court, including the treatment handed out to him by his aunt and Salmon, ending his list of grumblings and complaints with an impatient account of what he had witnessed between his cousin and the Major, the latter part of his speech proving to his listener that Robert's suppositions had indeed been right. By the time he had come to the end of his recital he was by no means pleased at having his word called into question about what he had observed between his cousin and Major Neville. "Damn it man!" he exclaimed irritably, "I tell you that my cousin was very much upset by the Major's attitude."

Henderson's eyes narrowed. "Are you saying he was rude to her?"

"No" Ferrers shook his head, "nothing like that. In fact," he admitted, "he was extremely polite; really quite courteous, but it seemed to me that my cousin was beginning to have second thoughts about divulging Richard's whereabouts which did not please the Major at all since he appeared to be expecting a full confession from her."

Colonel Henderson shot him a quick look. "Are you sure?"

"Of course I'm sure," he bit out. "I know what I saw and heard," he told him, "and whilst Major Neville accepted it, albeit reluctantly," he pointed out, shooting a nervous glance at the door to make sure it was still securely closed, "he told her he would call again tomorrow when he expected a more favourable response from her."

"You are quite certain about this?" Henderson asked urgently. "You did not mistake the case?"

Ferrers sighed impatiently. "No!" he exclaimed resentfully, "I did *not* mistake the case. How could I?" he demanded, "when they were standing there right in front of me!"

"So," Henderson mused at length, "it would appear that Robert was right after all. It does look as though they are playing their own game."

William Ferrers knew instantly to whom he referred and immediately demanded an explanation of this vague statement. Those bulbous blue eyes regarded him steadily for several minutes as if contemplating whether or not to tell him about his meeting with Lytton the night before, but it took only a matter of seconds to realize that he had no choice. Robert's proposal for their salvation depended upon the participation of both of them for its success, and whilst he would be glad to see the end of this sorry business once and for all, he could not help but inwardly shudder at the thought of what the outcome would be should anything go wrong. However reluctant he was to admit it, there was no denying that William Ferrers was not the most reliable of men, especially when faced with a crisis, but as the plan required both of them playing their part he could only hope and pray that nothing would go amiss because if it did, then there was every likelihood that William Ferrers could well lose his nerve and bring all to ruin, resulting in both of them climbing the scaffold.

William Ferrers, unaware of Henderson's lack of faith in his abilities, listened incredulously to the edited version of what had taken place the previous evening, but upon learning of the scheme put forward to end their difficulties, he stared in astonishment. He knew His Grace was coming into Sussex, but that he had arrived so soon and formed such an opinion in so short a space of time astounded him, although why this should be he had no idea. His Grace was more than ordinarily astute, indeed, he saw far more than one would like, but he was finding it extremely difficult to believe that his cousin and the Major had been enacting a scene merely for his benefit. He of all people knew of the close bond which existed between brother and sister, and even supposing she knew where he was hiding out he could not see her revealing it. In fact, he would go so far as to say that she would rather be imprisoned than give him up, which made her behaviour this afternoon, particularly her indecision as to whether or not to tell Major Neville his whereabouts, even more inexplicable. Now though, after learning what had occurred between Henderson and His Grace, it would appear that Elizabeth and the Major were indeed working hand in glove to protect Richard after all. If what Henderson had told him was true then it seemed they were more closely aligned than they were letting on and that General Turville was indeed running counter to His Grace's explicit orders. The thought of the hangman's noose, especially since his cousin remained at large, was never far away, but the idea that the Major, his commanding officer and Elizabeth appeared to be joining forces in defence of Richard, the horrific picture of the scaffold resurfaced with a vengeance. He felt physically sick, rendering him even more testy and irritable, and not all his reasoning could dispel the unease growing inside him. He did not perform well under anxiety and it therefore took Colonel Henderson some considerable time to assure him that the scheme His Grace had in mind would settle the matter once and for all. He was not convinced and demanded to know what would happen if this idea of Lytton's failed.

"It won't fail," he was told irascibly. Henderson, whose own nerves were in danger of breaking under the strain, managed to retain sufficient hope of emerging from this debacle unscathed as well as enough clear-headedness to not lose sight of his objective. It took time and patience to instil into William Ferrers' agitated mind the simple fact that the risk of discovery was remote, bearing in mind that Major Neville and his cousin would be taken totally by surprise by their strategy, and that he would see to it Major Denham was out of the way. Gradually, this painstakingly delivered summary began to take root, until eventually Ferrers was able to see the merit of the plan outlined. Colonel Henderson, trying to convince himself as well as his confederate, managed to impress upon him the importance of the venture ahead of them, and that if it failed then it could well be the last chance they would ever have of resolving their difficulties.

"I realize that, damn it!" Ferrers exclaimed frustrated. "But what if Richard doesn't come to his sister's aid? It will all be for nothing and we shall find ourselves worse off than we are now!"

Henderson eyed him closely wondering, not for the first time, how he could have been stupid enough to enlist the help of this man who seemed incapable of understanding anything. "He will," he snapped. "You of all people should know that! Besides, I personally shall see to it that he gets to hear of it. I only have to drop a word in the right ear!" His eyes protruded alarmingly as he stared across the table at Ferrers.

"Whose ear?" he demanded nervously.

"Never you mind," Henderson nodded, re-filling his glass.

"Yes, but ..."

"He *will* come to her aid," he claimed heatedly, trying to convince himself as well as Ferrers. "Why should he not?" he demanded. "They're as thick as thieves after all said."

"All right, so he walks into the trap," Ferrers conceded sceptically, still not convinced, "but what about this Major Neville?" he argued. "Are you seriously expecting me to believe he will fall for a trick like that?"

Henderson eyed him disparagingly. "Refuse a senior officer's invitation?" he scorned. "Major Neville is nothing if not polite!"

Ferrers swallowed, foreseeing all manner of obstacles. "All right," he nodded, still sceptical, "so he accepts your invitation; but what makes you so certain he will partake of a drink with you?" The glowering stare he received at this very practical enquiry was enough to put an end to any further questions he may have had concerning Major Neville's cooperation, but the gloomy look in his eyes remained. "How long will it take this drug to work?" he asked petulantly, his nervous fingers almost spilling his drink as he raised the glass to his lips.

"Within less than ten minutes," Henderson assured him. "And do not worry yourself over Major Denham," he reiterated. "I shall ensure he is away from the garrison. All you need do," he nodded firmly, "is to make sure that Major Neville does not see you arrive."

"That's all very well," Ferrers snapped, "but you can't seriously expect me to carry a lifeless body down a flight of steps and into a waiting carriage and hope it will go unnoticed!" he cried aghast.

"You forget," Henderson reminded him sharply, "it will be getting dusk, and should anyone see you they will merely think that one of my officers' has had a little too much wine." Ferrers began to say something but was unceremoniously interrupted. "We are in this together Ferrers; right to the end. Do not forget that!" Leaning forward with his elbows on the table, he cast a quick glance towards the door before bringing his gaze back to his accomplice. "If you think that this problem of your cousin is going to go away without any effort on our part, then you are an even bigger fool than I took you for!"

Ferrers may not like his tone, but felt incapable of refuting his remarks, even so he retained enough spirit to argue several points further. "What about Elizabeth?" he urged fiercely. "What makes you think she will do as we want?"

"She will," Henderson assured him. "If everything Lytton has said is true, and I have never yet known him be wrong," he admitted grudgingly, "she will move heaven and earth to meet the Major at whatever venue he suggests," devoutly trusting this will indeed be the case as the success of the whole scheme depended largely on this one circumstance.

Ferrers remained cautious. "She may well," he conceded, "but that don't mean she will tell us anything more than she has already."

"I do not expect her to," Henderson surprised him by saying.

Ferrers' mouth dropped open. "You do not expect her to!" he repeated, aghast.

"If you had been listening," he was told disparagingly, "you would have heard me say that abducting your cousin was not in the hope of making her talk, but as bait to bring her brother out into the open. Of course," he shrugged, "*should* she decide to tell us anything all well and good, but whether she does or not just knowing that she has been taken will be enough for Richard Ferrers to effect a rescue."

"Very well," Ferrers acknowledged not very hopefully, his palms beginning to sweat, "even supposing this strategy does bring my cousin out into the open, aren't you forgetting one thing?" he asked, turning round in his seat as he heard someone walk along the passageway. "This letter from Neville to my cousin?"

"What about it?" Henderson shrugged.

"How do you know what his handwriting is like?"

"I don't" he dismissed, "but I do not regard that as an obstacle."

Ferrers looked horror-struck. "Not an obstacle!"

"By no means," Henderson shook his head, "indeed, I see no reason why it should be."

"No reason ..." Ferrers uttered, lost for words.

Henderson sighed. "Whilst I admit to not having seen an example of his handwriting, I think it safe to say that you can lay a rather heavy wager that your cousin has not either." He let this sink in. "You must therefore allow it to be probable that she will accept the letter as coming from Major Neville without question."

Ferrers took time to consider this reasoning, but even though he still harboured doubts he finally came to accept that it was more than likely, but felt it behoved him to point out one more nagging doubt, "But there is just one minor point you seem to have overlooked." Colonel Henderson raised a questioning eyebrow. "If you and His Grace are right in that my cousin and Major Neville are on far more intimate terms than they are letting on, how do you propose to compose such a letter?" he asked reasonably. "How would he address her? You must acknowledge it poses a problem," he argued anxiously.

As this aspect of the case had not occurred to him, Colonel Henderson took refuge in prevarication, commenting instead on the perilous position in which they found themselves, stating that he for one was not going to allow such a trifling matter as that deter him. "I have no intention of failing now," he told him unequivocally, "and if you had any sense neither would you! I do not intend to go to the gallows simply because we cannot agree on his manner of greeting!" he said with finality.

Ferrers was far from satisfied with this, envisaging all manner of problems arising but his attempts to question his confederate's apparent unconcern over what he considered to be a matter of great importance, were brushed aside as being inconsequential. He had no desire to climb the scaffold any more than the next man, but whilst he was prepared to do anything which could prevent this from happening, it seemed to him that there were too many aspects which could go wrong, and by the time they parted company it could not be said that either of them were overly optimistic that the proposed scheme would succeed, neither it seemed having much faith in the other.

As far as William Ferrers was concerned it was not simply because Elizabeth was not fool enough to be enticed out of her home without a good reason for doing so; it was the very strong possibility of once having managed to get her to a venue of their choosing she would not accommodate them by either telling them any more than she had already or prove herself to be a cooperative prisoner, much less a docile one. In addition to this, there was no guarantee that Richard would fall into the trap set for him; daring he may be but a fool he was not! Unless his cousin had changed dramatically over the last few months, then he held out very little hope of him being taken in by a ruse which anyone with only half a mind would see was an ambush. Nor was he by any means pleased to know that Henderson, through what means he had not seen fit to elaborate on, had commandeered the home of a man who would be bound to raise the devil of a hue and cry should he ever discover that in his absence his house had been used for holding a captive, albeit for only a short time. He was not overly familiar with Sir Evelyn Joyce but he knew enough of him to be able to say that should he learn of the illicit use to which Hamstoke House had been put during his visit to town, then he could see no way of keeping a lid on the truth. As far as he could see there were far too many 'if's' for him to feel confident, but like it or not he was stuck with the plan outlined and since he could come up with nothing better to ensure the end of their ever mounting difficulties, he had no choice but to play his part in forthcoming events. Not for nothing had Colonel Henderson withheld his intentions from him regarding the end he had in store for Major Neville and Elizabeth Ferrers, although this clearly could not be kept from him indefinitely, but he had deemed it wise, for the moment at least, to say nothing of the fate which awaited them, because from what he had seen his accomplice's peace of mind not to mention his already overstretched nerves, were already balancing on a very fine line. This was no less than the truth, especially when Ferrers considered that the scheme would leave him far too exposed for his liking, added to which was the very real fear that the whole thing was more than likely to die a death. He realized, of course, that something had to be done to stave off disaster, but he could not help but wonder whether His Grace had taken certain pertinent points into account when he had put forward his proposal for resolving their difficulties, or whether Henderson had either misunderstood or was simply moulding his own ideas into it, but it seemed to him that the success of their strategy rested far too much on luck, and since this commodity had been rather elusive in his life of late, he did not place much faith in it.

Colonel Henderson, anxious for a speedy solution to the problems besetting him, arrived back at the garrison in a most uncertain frame of mind. William Ferrers' participation in the forthcoming course of events may be vital, but he could not in all honesty claim to have much confidence in him keeping his nerve and remaining calm should things unfortunately go awry. He had made no secret of the fact that he was uneasy about the role which had been assigned to him, but even he must realize that this would be the last chance they would ever have of settling their affairs. He may not be any too enamoured of what was to come himself, but he was practical enough to know that they had no alternative, and had he have informed Ferrers of what he had in mind to deal with the two people who could denounce them irrespective of whether they succeeded or not, then he was as certain as a man could be that he would not even get his accomplice within half a mile of the garrison. If they were unsuccessful in apprehending Richard Ferrers merely because his cousin had failed to do all that was required of him or even perhaps lost his courage at the last minute, then nothing would keep them from standing their trial for treason. Richard Ferrers may not be able to put his hands on those letters at this precise moment in time, but if Lytton was right, and he had every reason to suppose he was, then with Major Neville and General Tuville at his back, it would not be long before that incriminating evidence came to light. It was therefore imperative that he speak to Major Neville tonight, and although he did not expect him to tell him the truth, if there was the slightest chance of gleaning something, however insignificant, which would give him some indication as to the current state of affairs, he had to take it. Not only that, but he had to begin setting their plans in motion for tomorrow night, and if he was to ensure Major Neville was not in a position to thwart their efforts, then he had to see him in order to either invite or command him to his quarters for that fateful drink. It was now almost half past eight and he was feeling tired and just a little anxious, but could neither rest nor relax until he had seen him. Had it have been at all possible he would have spoken to Major Neville last night upon his return from 'The White Hart' but, upon reflection, it was perhaps better that the lateness of the hour had rendered it out of the question, because he doubted whether he could have prevented his temper from getting the better of him and charging him with vindictive mendacity and whatever else Robert had pointed him in the way of.

If Major Denham was surprised at being asked to find Major Neville as well as wondering what it was that required his presence at this hour, he hid it admirably, merely relating the order to a young subaltern.

Not having expected to see Colonel Henderson until the morning Gideon was rather surprised to receive an order to report to him immediately. The young subaltern, flushed and out of breath, could not enlighten him, but it only took Gideon a few minutes to see the reason behind this peremptory summons. At some point after he had left Ferrers Court, William Ferrers must have met with Colonel Henderson to not only consult him regarding the situation in general but also to report what he had witnessed this afternoon between himself and Elizabeth Ferrers.

Gideon had never deluded himself into thinking that he could mislead Colonel Henderson indefinitely, but he had hoped to stretch the deceit for awhile longer in order to grant him precious time in which to put his hands on the evidence which would clear Richard Ferrers' name. As he had no idea that His Grace was in Sussex and had not only met with Colonel Henderson but had sown the seed in his mind about the probable dissimulation he was perpetrating as well as putting forward a plan to bring Richard Ferrers out into the open, he made his way across the courtyard to his quarters in complete ignorance that his fabrication of the facts to date was known or, at least, suspected.

By the time he presented himself to his senior officer, it wanted only fifteen minutes to nine o'clock and as he had arranged to see Lieutenant Beaton at nine he was growing more doubtful as to whether their meeting would be able to take place after all. In view of his dinner engagement with Colonel Henderson being cancelled the previous evening, he could not see him making short work of tonight's meeting as he would be bound to want to know his progress since they last spoke. As Lieutenant Beaton was orderly officer he could not expect this young man to shelve his responsibilities as well as running the risk of being disciplined by Major Denham simply because he expected him to wait and therefore being late for duty. But his main concern was that the longer he left speaking to him the longer it would take to retrieve those letters, and since Richard Ferrers was not the kind of man to sit and wait for ever, it was therefore with a feeling of frustration that he made his way to Colonel Henderson's tower domain.

At the sight of Gideon all Colonel Henderson's exasperation and anger resurfaced, but bearing in mind Robert's strictures, strove to bring both under control. From the moment Gideon entered his room it was clear that something was amiss, and wondered what had occurred to bring about that deep red tinge to his face and the glowering stare to those protuberant pale blue eyes. If he was right and a meeting had taken place between him and William Ferrers, it could be that it had not been any too successful or, perhaps, they had been brought to see that their difficulties were very far from over. As he was in ignorance of His Grace's visit into Sussex and what had been discussed between them yesterday evening, he was left with only speculation.

The dissimulation and duplicity practised by Major Neville had had such a profound impact upon Colonel Henderson that he was unable to trust his voice to speak for several moments. Gideon, standing to attention in front of him, saw the effort he was making to control his temper and knew something quite untoward must have happened. But even had he known that Colonel Henderson had discovered the truth or even suspected it, he would have had no compunction in owning it and certainly he experienced no regrets about his actions, indeed, he considered himself perfectly justified in doing all he could to protect an innocent man from being hung for his crimes. Should he be accused of perpetrating deceit he could not see Colonel Henderson's position improving in any way as he also would be faced with charges he could not possibly answer, and, more to the point, dare not.

"Major Neville," he nodded at length, clearing his throat, "please, do sit down."

"Thank you, Sir."

"I must apologize for the lateness of the hour, Major" he told him, not very graciously, "but I have been unavoidably detained."

"I quite understand, Sir" Gideon acknowledged.

"I had hoped to speak to you earlier," he managed, eyeing him closely, "but as I say, I have been otherwise engaged."

If he was expecting Gideon to show signs of experiencing any kind of embarrassment or discomfiture over the deceit he was executing then he was doomed to disappointment. To his annoyance he bore all the appearance of one who not only had a clear conscience but was also totally unconcerned about being caught out in telling unashamed lies, and this fact alone made his temper rise. Once again he found himself struggling to fight the temptation to throw the accusation at him, but he only had to consider his own position as well as Robert's warning to make him realize the imprudence of doing any such thing.

"I regret our dinner engagement was cancelled yesterday evening," he told him, deploring the fact that he was having to placate this man who had been working behind his back, "but I was unexpectedly called away."

"It's quite all right, Sir" Gideon smiled, infuriating his senior officer, "I shall look forward to dining with you some other time."

To say this was regarded as inflammatory by Colonel Henderson was a gross understatement, almost choking on the retort he could not utter. It was several minutes before he could control himself sufficiently to speak, and when he did so it was obvious to Gideon that the composure in his voice was costing him a tremendous effort. "So, Major, about Miss Ferrers. What progress are you making?"

If, as he suspected, Colonel Henderson had seen William Ferrers since this afternoon, it was logical to assume that he had informed him of what had taken place between him and Elizabeth Ferrers. If there had been no meeting between them then he was not really jeopardizing the situation as far as Richard Ferrers was concerned, and therefore elected to tell him what William Ferrers had witnessed, but from the look on Colonel Henderson's face as he listened to his account of the current position it was difficult to say what conclusions he had arrived at. Feeling something more was needed Gideon expanded gently on this theme. "I was, I need hardly say, disappointed to learn that she was not yet ready to reveal her brother's whereabouts, especially having led me to believe that she was about to come to the point. Although," he conceded, deeming it wise to add extra credence for the delay in concluding this matter, "I suppose when one considers it, it is not surprising that she should experience certain qualms about informing against her own brother."

"*Qualms!*" he barked out before he could stop himself. "As a law abiding citizen she should have none when it comes to informing against scoundrels and rogues like Ferrers!"

The venom in his voice was not lost on Gideon, but it certainly made Colonel Henderson feel better. He may not be able to rake Gideon down as he would have liked, so venting his spleen against the woman he believed was partly responsible for his difficulties, went some way to relieving his feelings.

"I realize, of course," Gideon said with spurious sympathy, "that it makes our task a little more difficult, but I believe that given time she will come round."

"Time!" Henderson bit out. "How much more time does she need?" He glared ferociously at Gideon pointing an accusing finger. "*You!*" he spluttered, "*you* told me that she was on the point of telling us where her brother was to be found!"

"Yes Sir, I did" Gideon confirmed, taking the wind out of Colonel Henderson's sails at this calmly delivered confession, "but it now appears that after further consideration it is not the easy matter she had at first thought."

"You have been far too lenient with her," he was told forcefully. "I warned you with whom you were dealing."

"Yes Sir, you did" Gideon confirmed again still in that calm voice, "but I still believe that arriving at Ferrers Court with armed men at my back or adopting strong-arm tactics will not serve our purpose."

"Then what will?" he demanded, rising agitatedly to his feet, his eyes protruding to their fullest extent. "This matter has gone on far too long," he commented. "It is time to settle it once and for all."

Gideon eyed his senior officer dispassionately. He was definitely feeling the strain of knowing that at any moment he could be called to account for his unsuccessful attempts at committing treason, but he had neither sympathy nor consideration for a man who had attempted to achieve his personal ambitions via this route only to try and hang the crime onto an innocent man when it threatened to rebound on him. Unwittingly echoing His Grace's observations, he was amazed that he and William Ferrers had come this far without detection as neither of them it seemed were capable of exercising restraint or rational thought. None of what he felt for this man was allowed to show however, but whilst he had no liking for appeasing him, he had to do all he could to gain time in order to help Richard Ferrers, and if this meant humouring him then he was quite prepared to do it. "If I may be permitted to suggest, Sir" he offered, "I think another visit to Miss Ferrers tomorrow might be advisable."

Colonel Henderson swung round to face him. "You do, do you?"

"Yes, Sir."

"For what purpose?" he demanded.

"The purpose being, Sir" he said manipulatively, "to remind her that whilst she has so far escaped arrest, that possibility is still open to us."

Those bulbous eyes stared at the man he was growing to heartily despise with every fibre of his being. He could not prove it, of course, but if Robert's supposition was correct, and he had no reason to doubt it was, then all that stood between him and salvation was this man calmly sitting opposite him who appeared to be doing his utmost to foil his efforts to shield himself from disgrace and scandal. "What good will that do?" he demanded, "she has known for some time that she has escaped arrest only by a hairs-breadth!"

"I am aware of that, Sir" Gideon acknowledged, "but perhaps if she knows that she will not be the only one to grace our cells, her aunt perhaps, it may bring her round to our way of thinking."

Dislike Major Neville he may, but this was an idea of some merit, and although he knew it would never come to fruition in view of the plans being laid to deal with Miss Ferrers and her brother once and for all, he felt it behoved him to approve it. "Yes," he nodded, "you could be right Major. If she knows that aunt of hers would also be arrested it could well turn the tide in our favour!"

Gideon heaved a sigh of relief. He had managed to buy another valuable twenty four hours grace. "In that case, Sir" he inclined his head, "I shall speak to her tomorrow and remind her in no uncertain terms of the penalties attached in withholding vital information."

"Yes, you do that Major" Colonel Henderson nodded. "Enough time has been wasted on this matter, and I for one do not intend to waste any more. Impress upon her that we shall no longer wait upon her convenience!"

Gideon rose to his feet. "I shall do my utmost Sir to make clear to Miss Ferrers the imprudence of her failure to cooperate."

"Major Neville," Colonel Henderson forestalled, as Gideon made his way to the door, "you do realize, of course, how imperative it is to apprehend Richard Ferrers?"

"Yes Sir," he nodded, returning the hard stare without a blink, "I have always realized it."

"And Captain Waring?" he asked, the significance of Gideon's words going over his head, "you are keeping in touch with him?"

"I intend to visit him again tomorrow, Sir" he told him calmly, "before I speak to Miss Ferrers."

"Good," he nodded, "good. I expect every effort to be made in capturing Ferrers."

Gideon nodded. "Yes, Sir."

"I fully expect good news from you when I see you tomorrow," he told him significantly. "Shall we say about half past five, Major?"

"Yes, Sir," Gideon inclined his head.

"You may go, Major" he dismissed.

Having to put a curb on his impulses by refraining from informing Gideon in no uncertain terms that he knew of the deceit he had been perpetrating all this time, had rendered the interview a severe trial. At no time did he like being made a fool of, and certainly not now when so much was at stake, but Major Neville's calm self-control, in stark contrast to his own insecurity and agitation, had only served to increase his antagonism towards him. To be obliged to accept those smooth tongued falsehoods as if he believed every word as well as feigning ignorance as to the true state of affairs between him and Elizabeth Ferrers had cost him a tremendous effort, but he promised himself that before many hours were out he would have his revenge. It was several minutes after Gideon had left before he eventually resumed his seat, staring at the closed door with a look of intense concentration on his face, wondering precisely how much Major Neville knew about his participation in treason, a vital necessity, yet something he dare not ask. There were times when he could have sworn he knew nothing at all then, at others, he was absolutely convinced he knew everything and was only waiting for the right moment to denounce him. The thought made him swallow uncomfortably, the visions these thoughts conjured up too horrendous to contemplate, but somehow he managed to pull himself together and slowly pulled several sheets of notepaper towards him with hands that, to his dismay, were far from steady. For close on five minutes he sat looking abstractedly at the sheets of vellum in front of him, the ink drying on the end of his pen, striving to find the right words which would induce Elizabeth Ferrers to leave her home with a complete stranger. William Ferrers may not be the most reliable of accomplices, but he had nevertheless raised a most valid point about the content of the letter which would set in motion a calculated string of events specifically designed to solve their difficulties once and for all. He may have scoffed at his concern, but the truth was that in this one aspect lay the success of such a daring and audacious plan. So much depended on the supposed communiqué from Major Neville being worded with meticulous care; one wrong word or form of address, could end at a stroke his last ditch attempt to save himself and William Ferrers from the scaffold. Not unexpectedly it was a far more difficult letter to compose than he had anticipated, but after numerous failed attempts he finally sat back in his seat, scanning the completed composition with something close to a smile on his face, not unsatisfied with his efforts.

Having bid Major Neville a civil goodnight following his interview with Colonel Henderson, Major Denham, still far from reconciled to his being here, began to wonder more particularly what it was that had required his attendance at such an hour. For reasons he could not explain he was becoming more and more convinced that something out of the ordinary was going forward, what this could be precisely he had no idea, but he would lay his life that it was in some way connected with Richard Ferrers. Although his commanding officer was making no effort whatsoever to enlighten him much less take him into his confidence, he would have had to be blind not to notice that he had been somewhat preoccupied of late, but when, some time later, he was summoned upstairs to Colonel Henderson's room, not only was he quite unprepared for the order he was given, but the very fact that he was seeking out Private Smith surely confirmed his suspicions that something was in the offing.

Private Smith, a man who, having joined the army to escape his criminal past, had come in very useful on more than one occasion and, unless Colonel Henderson had grossly erred, he would do so again. He had not needed to see the look of misgiving which had crossed Major Denham's face upon mentioning his name; he knew perfectly well that apart from the fact that he neither liked nor trusted him, he firmly believed that he was allowed far too much licence and, left to him, he would be instantly discharged from the army to face his accusers in civilian life; either that, or put up for a disciplinary hearing to answer charges of breaching army regulations. It was true that Private Smith's past career would not take too much scrutiny, but nevertheless he had proved his worth more than once when he had required a task to be carried out that he could not entrust to anyone else, but since this matter of saving himself and his accomplice from disgrace or, worse, the scaffold, was of some moment, he was easily able to turn his back on any scruples he may have had. As there was nothing he could do now but await the arrival of this rather suspect individual he took a moment or two to not only steady his nerves with a glass of Judson's best cognac, but also to review the measures taken to ensure that nothing had been overlooked which could possibly foil their plans.

CHAPTER FIFTEEN

It was almost quarter to ten when Gideon eventually arrived back at his quarters fully expecting Lieutenant Beaton to have left, but as he entered the small sitting room he was surprised to find him sitting in a chair idly glancing through a journal thoughtfully provided by Sergeant Taylor.

"My apologies Lieutenant, but as you no doubt know I was summoned to see Colonel Henderson. I thought I would have missed you," he smiled, walking towards him with his hand outstretched. "It is very good of you to wait. I realize you are duty orderly."

"That's quite all right, Sir" he smiled, rising to his feet and taking the hand held out. "Sergeant Taylor told me you had been unexpectedly called out." Refusing the offer of another glass of wine he looked closely at Gideon, his face slightly troubled. "I trust your interview with Colonel Henderson went well."

"It could have been worse," Gideon smiled wryly.

"I may not be able to afford you all the time you need, Major" he told him, "but whilst you may rely on me to do everything in my power, I still don't see how I can possibly help you."

"Thank you," Gideon smiled. "I am afraid however," he apologized, "that there is insufficient time now to fully acquaint you with the details in the short time available before you go on duty."

A slight frown creased his young friend's forehead. "I wonder, Sir" he said thoughtfully, "if you should not dislike it, there is nothing to prevent you from accompanying me. It is most unlikely that Colonel Henderson or Major Denham will leave their quarters at this hour."

Gideon eyed him with respect and admiration, having no difficulty in understanding why Richard Ferrers had placed so much faith in him. "I was hoping you would say that," he smiled. "Providing, of course, you are sure."

"Quite sure, Sir."

Waiting only long enough for Gideon to have a brief word with Sergeant Taylor, they then made their way quietly down the stairs leaving the gatehouse quarters by the back door, emerging into the almost deserted courtyard.

"I never asked you what it was that had brought you here," Lieutenant Beaton commented once they were outside, "but I had no idea it was to do with Richard until Major Denham told me."

"I am afraid I owe you an apology, Lieutenant" Gideon acknowledged.

"Well, I can't imagine what you have to apologize for, Sir" he shook his head, "after all, there was no reason why I should know."

"It is true I am here to find Richard Ferrers," he confirmed, "but *not*," he stressed, "to see him hang for a crime he did not commit."

"I have told no one here about my friendship with Richard," Michael explained, "not because I am ashamed to own him as such," he assured him, "but because almost everyone here hopes to be the one responsible for his arrest." He looked up at Gideon, his eyes troubled. "Even the friends I have made here, all good fellows I promise you," he hastened to add, "would dearly love to be the one who apprehends him. Understandable, of course," he conceded, "after all, no one likes to think of traitors being allowed to escape but, regrettably," he confessed sadly, "none of them would even think to discover the truth, they would regard that as totally irrelevant, for which I believe Colonel Henderson and Major Denham are responsible. The thing is," he pointed out, "I cannot tell them that Richard is not the type of man to turn traitor because they would know at once we were friends, which would ruin any chance I may have of helping him. Having often stayed at Ferrers Court," he explained, "I came to know his family, and I can say without any hesitation that they hold no Jacobite sympathies. I was only posted to this garrison about two months ago," he informed Gideon, "but it was not long before I learned of the searches which had been carried out there, still were in fact until about just over a week ago, and the reason for them; needless to say," he sighed his relief, "I was glad I was not assigned to that duty!" he paused momentarily, his eyes clouding. "I had, of course, learned of my friend's supposed defection before I came here, indeed," he shrugged, "it would have been difficult not to; the name of Ferrers was being bandied about pretty freely, but knowing him and his family as I do I have never believed it. As for his smuggling activities," he smiled, "a circumstance which has aided Colonel Henderson and Major Denham in their efforts to instil into the men the urgent necessity to capture him, well... let us just say, that that is the kind of thing he would do, more to alleviate boredom than anything else."

"What steps have you taken to try and help him?" Gideon asked.

"You seem to be forgetting, Major," he reminded him, "I wear a scarlet coat and in case you had not realized it scarlet coats are looked upon with caution in these parts, even distrust, thanks mostly to Colonel Henderson. With the best will in the world," he remarked, "to attempt even the smallest enquiry about Richard is guaranteed to be met with suspicion, even hostility."

"Yes, I have already gathered as much," Gideon grimaced.

"Even those who do not take part in the trade," he explained, "know those who do, but they will never inform against them. Richard is very well known and respected here, in fact," he nodded, "most of this land forms part of the Ferrers estate, and from all I have managed to discover they would die rather than give him up. With regard to his supposed Jacobite tendencies," he pointed out, "they do not believe it, and they would go to any lengths to shield him from the hangman's noose."

"His sister told me very much the same thing; that everyone loves him," Gideon acknowledged. "I now understand what she meant."

"Not every man commands that level of respect and loyalty," he told him, "but Richard is like his father; a good man who looks after his people. It will not be easy to get any one of them to tell you where he may be found."

"Yes," Gideon nodded, "I understand they are very close lipped."

"Colonel Henderson has totally mismanaged this affair," he admitted frankly. "Perhaps I should not be saying this," he acknowledged, "but I have served under some good officers' Major, but he is not one of them. If he ever discovered I was a friend of Richard's I would be transferred immediately."

"What about Major Denham?" Gideon enquired.

Michael shook his head. "You have seen him for yourself. He is a strict disciplinarian. Whilst I have sometimes thought that he has no liking for Colonel Henderson he respects the rank he carries, and if he was ordered to shoot Richard on sight, he would. It would never even occur to him to question the reason why."

It was very much as Gideon thought. If Richard Ferrers was to be extricated from his difficulties then it appeared that only himself and this young man could help him.

"You never knew Lord Easton, did you Major?" he asked unexpectedly.

"No," Gideon shook his head, "regrettably, I had not that pleasure."

"He was a fine man, indeed, next to my own father I would have trusted him with my life!"

"That's quite an encomium!" Gideon exclaimed, not unimpressed.

"It is true nonetheless," he nodded, "and Richard is exactly like him, which is why he is so well loved."

"I have no reason to doubt his popularity!" Gideon stated truthfully.

"Tell me," Michael asked, "when you saw Richard was he able to tell you very much?"

"More than enough!" Gideon replied briefly.

By now they had traversed the garrison's perimeter, and by the time Gideon had come to the end of recounting his two meetings with Richard Ferrers and what he had disclosed, there was no disguising the look of shock and horror on Michael's face.

"*Good God!*" he exclaimed, stopping dead in his tracks. "You can't mean it?"

"I am afraid I do," Gideon nodded.

"But it's incredible!" he cried. "I can't believe it! *Colonel Henderson and his own cousin!*" It was several stunned moments before he could fully absorb what he had been told, his eyes reflecting his complete and utter horror as he stared up at

Gideon. "I don't suppose there is any chance that Richard could be wrong, is there?" he asked, shaking his head bemused.

"None, I'm afraid," Gideon told him. "Those letters are clearly written and signed by Colonel Henderson and their contents clearly implicate William Ferrers."

"I have never met Richard's cousin," he told him, still reeling from the shock, "but whilst I may not like Colonel Henderson," he admitted, "I never would have thought he would become involved in treason!"

"He is not the first in a position of high rank or trust to throw in his lot with Stuart," Gideon reminded him.

"No, I realize that," he acknowledged painfully. "It just requires a little getting used to."

"I know," Gideon agreed, "but I am afraid we do not have time to adjust to it, especially as Richard's life depends on producing those letters."

"No, of course not" he agreed.

"They are all that stand between him and the hangman's noose," Gideon stated matter of factly, "and somehow or other we have to get our hands on them. The question is," he wanted to know, "can you get me inside the cells without arousing suspicion?"

It seemed for a moment that Lieutenant Beaton had not heard what he had said, but after seeming to consider something for a moment or two he eventually looked up at Gideon, his pleasant smile dawning. "Yes, I can, but not tonight."

Gideon nodded. "When?"

"Tomorrow. The thing is Major," he explained, "a certain Private Elliott, who decided to go absent without leave, is now in the cell block waiting to go before Colonel Henderson tomorrow. I shall need to speak to him in the morning before he presents himself to his commanding officer."

"And?" Gideon prompted.

"And if you were to accompany me," he suggested, "there would be nothing in that to arouse suspicion."

A frown creased Gideon's forehead. "Why should I want to accompany you?"

"You know, Major" he smiled, "I always knew that my love of history would come in useful one day. You see," he told him a little shyly, "I am at present engaged in writing a history of Sussex castles, and at the moment I am studying Hampton Regis garrison."

Gideon smiled appreciatively. "Go on."

"Well, as it happens," he informed him, "the prison block here deserves special attention."

"Indeed!"

"Yes," he nodded.

"And?"

"And Major," he grinned, "it so happens that the oldest part of the prison quarters is late eleventh century."

"Is that so?"

"That is so Major, and as such is of particular interest to me. So much so," he smiled, "that I often go there when I am not on duty." He looked suddenly mischievous. "Imagine my surprise therefore, when I learned that you hold similar interests to mine."

"I do?" Gideon smiled, raising a questioning eyebrow.

"Yes," he nodded, "you do. Upon discovering the prison's original Norman foundations, nothing would do for you but to have a look at them before you return to London."

"I think I know where this is leading," Gideon grinned.

"They know I go there regularly so they won't think anything of it," he explained, "besides, they will expect me to see Private Elliott."

"Are you sure about this?" Gideon asked, suddenly serious.

"Yes, of course," he nodded. "It's the perfect opportunity."

"You do realize," Gideon pointed out, "that if we are discovered, it won't do either of us any good?"

Lieutenant Beaton smiled. "That goes without saying, but since those letters are of vital importance in proving Richard's innocence, that is of very little consequence, besides" he pointed out, "if our positions were reversed, Richard would not hold back in coming to my aid."

"No," Gideon agreed, "he would not."

Lieutenant Beaton pulled out his watch and upon seeing that it wanted only ten minutes to half past eleven suggested to Gideon that they meet here at seven o'clock the following morning. "My duty should finish at nine o'clock tomorrow," he explained, "so while I am with Private Elliott hopefully you should have enough time to try and find those letters."

"Well if Richard was right about where he hid them," he told him, "I should have no difficulty. The only thing that concerns me," he told him, "is if anyone on duty there decides to come with me, or even," he shook his head, "that particular cell is occupied."

"If it is," Lieutenant Beaton shrugged, "we shall just have to improvise. As for anyone wanting to go in with you, they won't," he assured him. "Their interest is as non-existent as their curiosity."

"Very well then, tomorrow it is." Gideon shook his hand and after promising to meet him the following morning thanked him again for his help.

"There's no need to thank me, Major" he shook his head, "like you, I could not live with myself knowing that I was partly responsible for seeing a man hang for something he did not do!"

Gideon returned to his quarters feeling more optimistic than he had for sometime. At last things seemed to be moving in the right direction, and if all went according to plan tomorrow, then it would not be long before Richard Ferrers could take up his rightful place in society again. He tried not to think what would happen if he was unable to put his hands on those letters, but of one thing he could be certain and that was not only would Richard Ferrers feel that he had let him down, but would make the attempt to try and retrieve them himself.

After eating the cold supper Sergeant Taylor had left him, he sat for some time pondering the situation facing him. He was perfectly well aware of the awkward position in which he was placing Lieutenant Beaton, but without his help he could not possibly gain legitimate entry into the prison block. Assuming Richard Ferrers had not mistaken the hiding place then recovering those letters should be a relatively straight-forward matter, but as his future brother-in-law did not strike him as a man who panicked in a crisis, as his quick-wittedness proved when he hid them in the first place, he did not allow himself to worry unduly over this. In fact, by the time he retired to bed he could think of nothing that may occur which could not be adequately dealt with by either himself or Lieutenant Beaton. Short of a surprise visit to the prison quarters by either Colonel Henderson or Major Denham at the precise moment he was searching for them, which seemed unlikely, he was fairly confident that he would soon be a position to relay the good news to Elizabeth. However, being in possession of that correspondence would not mean that her brother's difficulties were automatically over, but they would at least be the means of bringing to an end his enforced exile. His last conscious thought before drifting into oblivion was that he hoped Richard Ferrers would not undo all their efforts by being tempted into making one last trip across the Channel, only to be caught red-handed running illicit goods.

By half past six Gideon had not only bathed and shaved but had also enjoyed a hearty breakfast and was now ready for the task ahead of him. By the time he left his quarters about fifteen minutes to seven the sun was out and already rather warm, promising another beautiful day ahead. He met no one other than the sentries on duty and returning their salutes continued on his way to the appointed spot where he was to meet Lieutenant Beaton, coming upon him standing beneath an ancient archway just out of view to the right of Colonel Henderson's tower quarters. He looked tired and a little pale but greeted Gideon cheerfully, who strongly suspected that he was obviously feeling the effects of too little sleep, no doubt due to the patrol which Major Denham had sent him on yesterday morning, together with a more than ordinarily busy night. Upon having this confirmed he asked if he would prefer to postpone their mission until later when he had rested, but found that his young friend would not hear of it. "By no means!" he exclaimed. "Besides," he added practically, "there will be too many people about then."

Crossing the courtyard in a north-easterly direction they passed the bowling green and walked towards the armoury, a grey stone rectangular building that had been erected some few years earlier on the site of the original Norman foundations resting just beneath the curtain wall. Returning the lone sentry's salute they walked on in silence until they came to the prison block, built of the same grey stone as the armoury. Two sentries, one on either side of the door, stood to attention as they approached and Gideon, who had decided to take his lead from Lieutenant Beaton, immediately fell into character by nodding his head in answer to an architectural description of the building as he followed him inside.

He found himself in a high vaulted and dimly lit corridor with doors on either side, correctly identifying these to be the cells. Following Lieutenant Beaton through the first door on the right they entered a medium sized square shaped room with small windows located high up on the outer wall which, apart from allowing only limited daylight to enter, were at the moment tightly closed. Not only did they prevent fresh air from coming in but also afforded no escape from the heat generated by the naked lights in the sconces which had not yet been turned down. In the middle of the room stood a large oblong table littered with papers, its two front legs supported by wedges of wood fixed under the feet to assist its stability on the uneven stone flagged floor. Corporal Haynes, whose whole demeanour was adequate testimony to his apathy as he sat at the table with the ink drying on the end of his pen, looked up disinterestedly as the door opened. Startled into action as he saw who had entered, the pen suddenly dropping from his nerveless fingers and the legs of his chair scraping on the stone floor, immediately stood to attention with a look of acute discomfort on his face. From beneath his sandy coloured lashes he darted a quick look across at Sergeant Allen, who until now had been lounging against the far wall with a tankard of ale in his ham-like fist, smuggled in by one of his cronies. As he had not expected to receive a visit from Lieutenant Beaton this early he almost dropped the tankard in his surprise, but managing to hold on to it straightened himself up, hoping this current transgression would go unnoticed. He knew he was sailing pretty close to the wind regarding the ever growing list of offences he was accumulating, but although this youthful officer seemed a decent enough young man, he could not fool himself into thinking that he would ignore this further breaching of the regulations. As it was perfectly obvious from the look on Lieutenant Beaton's face that he had seen the tankard he knew there was little point in trying to hide it, so placing it down on the table stood rigidly to attention, mentally preparing himself for being placed on report yet again.

Lieutenant Beaton looked from one to the other, his expression giving nothing away. "This is Major Neville," he informed them at length, as if nothing were amiss. "He is visiting the garrison for a short time only and has expressed a wish to see one or two of the cells, which, as you know, has parts dating back to Norman times. Unfortunately," he explained easily, "this is his only opportunity to

308

do so." Then casually picking up one of the sheets from the table he scanned the half dozen or so lines before looking at Corporal Haynes, still standing rigidly to attention. "I see number two cell is unoccupied."

"Yes, Sir," he replied woodenly.

"Perhaps you will find this cell of interest Major," he said conversationally, turning to Gideon, a smile lighting his eyes. Gideon held his breath. "If you look closely you can still see remnants of the original Norman foundations."

"Indeed!" Gideon exclaimed, trying to do justice to his young friend's efforts as well as to the role he had been designated. "I am looking forward to it."

His enthusiasm did not fool Lieutenant Beaton, but he played his part admirably. "It may not be as perfect an example as others you have seen, but I think I can safely say you will not be disappointed."

Gideon replied suitably, and Lieutenant Beaton, feeling he had prepared the ground sufficiently for the search of those letters, turned back to Corporal Haynes. "I see Private Elliott is your only detainee at present, and in number one cell," relieved that two of their concerns at least had been removed.

"Yes, Sir."

"Has he said anything?" he enquired steadily.

"No, Sir. Not a word."

Lieutenant Beaton nodded. "He is due to see Colonel Henderson at nine o'clock, make sure he is ready. I will see him now." Giving the sheet a final cursory glance, he handed it back to Corporal Haynes and moved to walk out of the room, but as if bethinking himself of something turned and looked at Sergeant Allen who braced himself for the inevitable. "By the by, Sergeant," he smiled, "to say you are cognizant with army regulations you seem to be contravening them with alarming regularity. Were I to report you to Major Denham you would doubtless lose a stripe, perhaps all three. You have a poor disciplinary record Sergeant," he commented, "but you are a good soldier. I shall not report you on this occasion, but I promise you that should I find you drinking on duty again, I shall have no compunction in doing so."

Sergeant Allen let out a sigh of relief. "Thank you, Sir."

"Do not thank me," he shook his head, "I am doing you no favours; it is merely that you are much too good a man to lose," he told him. "We need men like you." Inclining his head towards the tankard on the table, he smiled "You may as well finish that, it is far too good an ale to throw away."

For the first time Gideon had an opportunity to see his young friend at work and liked what he saw. Despite his youth and obvious inexperience he dealt with these two unfortunates in a manner that not only commanded his respect but reinforced his opinion that given time he would go far in his career. "Tell me; what reliance do you place on Sergeant Allen keeping out of trouble?" Gideon asked in his ear when he had closed the door behind them.

"Very little I'm afraid," he smiled, his voice hardly above a whisper. "I know I should have put him on report, but it's true what I said; he is a good soldier, apart from which," he offered, "if he was demoted he could never survive on a private's pay." Then for the benefit of whoever may be listening he flung open the door to the second cell pointing out some interesting facts. "I shall return as soon as I can Major," he said loud enough for anyone to hear, "but now I must see Private Elliott."

Left alone in the small stark cell, Gideon took brief stock of his surroundings, not envying those who enjoyed its meagre cold comforts. Apart from a narrow bed against the far wall and a three legged stool-cum-table in the corner, on top of which stood a water jug and bowl, the cell was completely bare. Fortunately there was sufficient light coming in through the square barred window to allow him to search for that loosened brick without having to resort to a candle or tinder box and without wasting any time bent down to feel the wall that Richard had told him held the letters. Every now and then he paused to listen for anyone approaching but apart from Lieutenant Beaton in the next cell preparing the hapless Elliott for his interview with Colonel Henderson, no noise broke the silence. Working quickly his strong fingers felt the bricks one by one leading inwards from the edge of the door to the corner of the adjoining wall, but despite their deftness they could detect no loose brick. Rising hurriedly to his feet he ran his eye over the full length of the wall before quickly scanning the other walls, rapidly turning over in his mind the conversation he had had with Richard. He had clearly indicated this as being the cell into which he had been briefly incarcerated but upon recalling it in more detail he seemed to recollect him only mentioning the bottom of the wall and not one wall in particular, and unless the bed had been moved since his arrest then there were only two possible ones available. Bending down again he ran the flat of his hand over the whole of the adjoining wall upwards from the floor to a height of three feet, carefully feeling each brick, but just as he was about to think that Richard must have mistaken the cell his fingers found what they had been searching for. Almost at the bottom of the wall near the corner where the two walls met his forefinger caught a brick which moved when touched. Bending down further he saw that to the naked eye it looked to be perfectly in place but by gently levering it back and forth was gradually able to prise it out of position. Considering the cell would have been illuminated by nothing more than a candle at night he could not help but envy Richard's eyesight to have spotted such a cunning hiding place. Heaving a sigh of relief when the brick came easily out of place and with only the slightest sound of a scrape he placed it carefully on the floor before reaching his hand into the darkened space. Immediately his fingers closed round the small oilskin packet but made no attempt to remove it, remaining perfectly still as he paused to listen for any sound, his head turned cautiously towards the door. From the sound of it Lieutenant

Beaton's interview with Private Elliott seemed to be coming to an end but apart from their voices he could detect no other which would suggest someone was approaching. Withdrawing the packet without even stopping to check its contents he slid it into the inside pocket of his coat before hurriedly replacing the brick as silently as he had removed it. By the time Lieutenant Beaton entered the cell Gideon was standing looking down at the floor with something resembling a rapt expression on his face. "Lieutenant!" he exclaimed in what he thought was a praiseworthy attempt at effecting awe. "This is more than I had looked for!"

Lieutenant Beaton, by no means fooled into thinking that his newly found friend had for one moment noticed, much less appreciated, the original Norman flooring towards the rear of the cell, interpreted this to mean he had been successful, whereupon he immediately fell into character. "I knew you would appreciate it, Major. It is something quite out of the ordinary." Then throwing him a significant glance guided him out of the cell and further down the passageway to where an iron grid covered a hole in the floor. "Take a look at this," he suggested.

Doing as he was bid, Gideon lit the tinder box he was handed and looked down to where his companion was pointing. Several feet down he could see the remains of the Norman foundations, and whilst he himself was no historian he was quite impressed with what he saw. Lieutenant Beaton, feeling something more was required, especially as someone had entered the building carrying the prisoner's meagre breakfast, bringing Corporal Haynes into the passageway to take it from him, immediately began to give Gideon a lecture on the history of the garrison and the prison block in particular. Despite Gideon's earnest desire to be gone as quickly as possible, he was nevertheless very much aware of the necessity to give credence to his visit, and although he was perfectly prepared to do all he could to substantiate the reason for him being here he doubted his ability to emulate his companion whose animated flow of historical information, commanded his admiration. In an effort to do justice to his role of keen historian he put forward several questions which drew a pained expression from Lieutenant Beaton. Immediately he knew he had erred, but as he shrewdly suspected that neither Corporal Haynes nor Sergeant Allen would have the least idea of what they were talking about, continued to play his part until his exasperated guide deemed it wise to make their exit.

Having given Private Elliott his breakfast, Corporal Haynes left the cell and after locking the door behind him looked disgustedly down the passageway at the two officers who appeared more engrossed in the past than the present. Returning to his desk he looked across at Sergeant Allen nodding his head disparagingly. "Norman remains!" he scoffed. "Yer'd think they'd 'ave somethin' betta ter do!"

Sergeant Allen was too used to seeing Lieutenant Beaton indulging his passion for ancient relics to take any notice of it and was therefore able to shrug off his subordinate's comment. "Leave the lad alone," he told him. "'E ain't doin' no 'arm."

Corporal Haynes smiled and looked knowingly across at his sergeant. "Yer wouldn't be sayin' that if 'e'd put yer on a charge."

"Mebbe not," he nodded, "but 'e's a good lad. Not many 'ud 'ave turned a blind eye." Sergeant Allen liked Lieutenant Beaton, but it was true what Haynes had said and counted himself fortunate to be let off from his current misdemeanour.

Having emerged from the prison block Lieutenant Beaton waited only until they were out of earshot of the sentries before letting out his pent up breath. "Phew!"

Gideon laughed. "I know," he agreed with heartfelt sympathy.

"It's all very well for you to laugh," he was told, "but you may have asked some more appropriate questions!"

"I'm sorry," Gideon apologized, "but I felt I ought to make some input. I thought you would be pleased."

"Pleased!" he echoed. "Don't you know that William II came *before* Henry II and not *after*?"

Gideon's eyes were alight. "I never was any good at history," he confessed guiltily.

"I can see that!" Lieutenant Beaton exclaimed. "Yes, and that's another thing," he said with feeling, "when next you see Richard you may tell him from me that the next time he finds himself in a fix, not to look to me to help him out of it!"

Gideon burst out laughing. "Confess," he challenged, "you enjoyed it."

Lieutenant Beaton looked up at him and finding himself quite unable to resist Gideon's laugh as well as the absurdity of the situation in which they found themselves, laughed too. "Well, yes" he acknowledged, "I did. I don't mind admitting though," he told him, "there were one or two moments when I thought we may be rumbled."

"So did I," Gideon nodded.

"You have them safe?" he asked, suddenly serious.

"Yes, they're in my pocket," Gideon nodded, "thanks to you."

"That's a relief because I ..."

Gideon glanced down at him as he broke off, then looking straight ahead saw the reason for it. Striding towards them from the opposite side of the courtyard was Major Denham, and from the looks of it he was in no good humour. "Lieutenant," he called, "a moment, if you please."

"I wonder what he wants?" Gideon remarked.

"As long as it's nothing to do with Richard," he commented, "I don't care."

"Lieutenant, I assume you know Private Elliott is up before Colonel Henderson this morning," he stated pungently when he came up to them, his eyes narrowing at the sight of Gideon, not at all pleased to find this young officer in his company.

"Yes Sir, I have just left him."

"And *you* Major Neville," he said somewhat sarcastically, looking up into Gideon's impassive face, "have you too seen Private Elliott?"

"No Major, not Private Elliott," he shook his head, "Norman remains!"

"I see," he nodded, affronted by such levity, gaining the very strong impression that Gideon was laughing at him. "Well," he dismissed, "having seen them, I will not detain you any longer by asking what you thought of them. I am sure you have things to do," not at all pleased that he could not take him to task. "Lieutenant," he said sharply turning away from Gideon, "I shall expect to receive your report in half an hour."

"Yes Sir," he nodded.

"Well, Major?" he asked, raising an eyebrow as Gideon had made no effort to move away. "Is there something else?"

"No, nothing whatever," Gideon replied calmly.

"In that case, Major" he dismissed, "I shall not keep you from your duties."

Gideon had no choice but to leave and could only hope that his young friend would not be subjected to too stern an interview with Major Denham, a man whom he believed was just as bad an officer as Colonel Henderson.

As he walked towards his own quarters he could not help but silently congratulate them both on the acquisition of those letters which symbolized the beginning of the end of Richard Ferrers' enforced exile. He knew that most of the credit for the successful outcome of their enterprise was due to Lieutenant Beaton and fully realized the awkward position in which he had placed him, but took some comfort from knowing that Richard's imminent freedom would far outweigh the risks he had taken. Unfortunately, there had been no opportunity to thank him properly before he left the garrison, but promised himself a word of thanks to that young man upon his return, without whom he would not now be in possession of those letters.

He knew he could not pacify Colonel Henderson indefinitely, but he must try and draw the deceit out for as long as he possibly could. He may have those letters safe, but there was still some way to go before Richard Ferrers could take up his place in society again. He had not needed Colonel Henderson to remind him about paying another visit to Captain Waring, he had already considered this as a necessity and had decided to call on him prior to his visit to Ferrers Court. Even though he was in possession of the evidence needed to prove Richard innocent of treason, there still remained the charges of smuggling hanging over his head. He was filled with some hope of achieving his acquittal of these accusations in view of the fact that no one, not even Captain Waring, had actually caught him in the act of running goods, and if only this adventurous young man would take heed and refrain from any further involvement in this illicit trade, he may yet come out of it unscathed.

As far as Colonel Henderson was concerned, Gideon could only guess at his reasons for throwing in his lot with Stuart. He very much doubted that loyalty or belief in his cause had played any part in his actions, but from what he had so far been privileged to see of him he thought that it was most probably personal ambition which had been the deciding factor. Richard Ferrers may well be right when he said that Colonel Henderson had no prospects of promotion and that he had been living far above his means for some considerable time, but the contents of that correspondence were enough to seal his fate irrespective of his motives.

A brief reading of those all important letters in the privacy of his room, was enough to inform Gideon that it appeared Colonel Henderson was the one who had taken the leading role and William Ferrers had been nothing more than a pawn, but even though only three of those six letters mentioned his name as well as his willingness to participate in what was to follow, it was sufficient to condemn him along with his accomplice. If either of them had had even the smallest belief in The Pretender and his cause he could have found it in him to have some sympathy for them, but to embark on a path of treason for no other purpose than personal gain then trying to incriminate an innocent man to protect themselves when it all went horribly wrong, he found quite unforgivable.

Unaware of the plan being put together to make an end of Richard Ferrers once and for all by using his sister as bait as well as to ensure his own inability to come to their assistance, he set out for Seaford and Ferrers Court in a more optimistic frame of mind. Whilst Richard Ferrers was not out of the wood yet, he had every hope that before too long he would be reinstated to his title and dignities; providing, of course, that that mercurial young man would continue to remain out of trouble.

CHAPTER SIXTEEN

By the time Elizabeth had said goodbye to Gideon she had recovered sufficiently from the initial shock of what he had disclosed to her, but it was some considerable time before she could fully comprehend all she had learned. The discovery that Colonel Henderson and William had taken part in treason only to place the blame onto her brother when their endeavour had failed, still made her furiously angry. She knew Gideon was right in that William must not know or even suspect that they knew the truth, but having to maintain friendly relations with him instead of taxing him about his betrayal was going to take all her resolve. She only had to think of her father and his untimely death brought about by those distressing searches resulting from their treachery, and she felt consumed with renewed anger. Nothing would have given her greater pleasure than to be able to throw their perfidy at them, and the knowledge that she could not only exacerbated her temper. She knew she had to hold her tongue for Richard's sake, but how she was going to manage this in view of what she had been told she had no idea.

If she thought that by spending time alone would help to assemble the wreckage of her chaotic thoughts she was mistaken. A cauldron of emotions ran riot inside her and by the time Salmon entered the sitting room over an hour later she was no nearer coming to terms with them than she had before. The only thing that lightened the gloom of an otherwise disastrous day was the knowledge that Gideon loved her. Not even the joint disloyalty of two people whom she heartily disliked but never suspected of such infamous conduct, could suppress the memory of the way he had made her feel when he had held and kissed her. Recollections of those moments in his arms were her only solace, and had it not been for Richard's dilemma and her cousin's intrigues she would have been the happiest of women.

Salmon, putting his head round the door with something akin to stealth, took one look at her face and knew precisely what was going through her mind. Nothing would have pleased him more than to be able to send William Ferrers and his henchman Whitney packing, but bearing in mind the Major's words of caution he had to strenuously fight down this overwhelming inclination. Elizabeth, upon hearing the door quietly open, turned to see who had entered. For one moment she thought it was her cousin, but upon seeing Salmon let out a sigh of relief. "Oh, it's you, Salmon!" she cried. "I thought perhaps it was William."

"No, Mistress" he shook his head, closing the door behind him and walking further into the room. "As a matter of fact," he told her, his eyes brightening, "that's what I've come to tell you."

"Tell me what?" she asked, not at all sure she could cope with any more surprises today.

"He's gone out, about half an hour after Major Neville had left," he explained. "He told me to tell you that he would be out for some considerable time and you were not to await dinner."

"*Very* considerate of him!" she scorned, her eyes sparkling afresh. "I suppose it is too much to hope that he won't return!"

"As to that Mistress," he shook his head, "I should think it most unlikely; his man's still here as well as all his gear. I can't see your cousin leaving either behind."

"More's the pity!" she exclaimed. "Where is Whitney now?"

"In the kitchen," he told her disgustedly, jerking his head in that direction.

She nodded, eyeing Salmon thoughtfully. "Major Neville told me he had spoken to you about my cousin and Colonel Henderson."

"Yes," he told her, "he did, and quite a shock it was too."

"I still can't believe it," she shook her head. "To think that all this time he has been working against Richard! It's infamous!"

"I never suspicioned it," he shook his head, "not once."

She wrung her hands. "If only Major Neville can get his hands on those letters!"

"He will, never fear" he assured her. "He don't strike me as a man who is easily balked."

"No, I know," she nodded, "but anything could happen to prevent him from doing so."

"Now that's enough of that," he chided. "Nothing's going to happen."

"I hope not," she said devoutly, "because the longer those letters remain out of our reach the more I worry over Richard."

"There's no need to fret yourself over him," he told her.

She frowned. "Perhaps not, but I know how heedless he can be."

"You leave Master Richard to me and the Major," he advised. "We'll see him safe."

"Oh Salmon!" she cried between despair and laughter. "What would we do without you?"

"Never mind that!" he affectionately scolded. "It's your aunt you've got to think of now."

"Yes," she sighed, "I know. Somehow or other I have got to break the news to her about William."

"Well, she don't like him," Salmon put in helpfully, "so perhaps it won't turn out as bad as you think."

"She may not like him," she conceded, "but it's still going to be a terrible shock to her!"

She knew she had to be told, and that it would come better from her than anyone, but even so as she climbed the stairs she was conscious of a sickening thud in the pit of her stomach. There was never going to be a right time to tell her something of this magnitude and she supposed that now was as good a moment as any. Whatever her aunt may think of William he was still her nephew, and she would not like to think that a member of her family had not only turned his hand to treason but had attempted to shelve the blame onto his cousin.

Taking a deep breath she tapped on her aunt's door and putting her head round it was surprised to find that that redoubtable lady, instead of being laid down upon her bed as she expected, was sitting in the winged chair by the fire with a shawl draped round her shoulders and a blanket over her knees. At the sound of the door opening her aunt looked up and upon seeing who it was told her to come in. "There's no need to tiptoe like that!" she admonished in her forthright way.

"I thought you might be asleep," she smiled, kissing her cheek.

"Well I ain't," she told her belligerently. "How anyone could sleep with all this going on, I don't know!"

Elizabeth knelt down beside her taking one bony hand in her two warm ones. "Dearest Aunt," she soothed, looking up into the face which appeared to be suddenly so much older. "You're having a terrible time of it, aren't you?"

"And you can keep that silly talk for the Major!" she told her briskly, the look in her eyes at variance with the primness of her lips.

"Does that mean you like him?" she asked, already knowing the answer.

"I like him well enough," she was told, "but not as well as you it seems!" When her niece made no reply to this she looked sharply down at her. "I take it you *do* like him?"

"Yes, very much" she nodded.

"Now don't be missish girl!" she was told sternly. "I saw the pair of you downstairs this afternoon, and unless you're playing some deep game or other, I'd say you more than liked him!" She twitched her shawl with her free hand. "As for *him*" she pointed out, "I've never seen a man so betwattled before!"

Elizabeth burst out laughing. "Oh Aunt!" she cried. "You're wonderful!"

"That's as may be," she nodded, "but the two of you can't go around smelling of April and May and expect people to believe you ain't in love!"

"*Do* we go around smelling of April and May?" she asked, her face slightly flushed.

Her aunt pinched her cheek. "You minx!" she admonished. "You know you do."

"I am so glad you like him," she confessed.

"I daresay, but you already knew that," she told her shrewdly. Elizabeth darted a quick look up at her. "I may be an old woman," she pointed out, "but I am not yet in my dotage! Why do I get the feeling you want to tell me something and you're going the long way round to do it?"

"I'm sorry," she apologized, "it's just that …"

"Just what?" she cut in sharply. "You think I might go off in an apoplexy, is that it?"

"No, of course it is not," she asserted, "but it *is* true that I have to tell you something; it's just that I know it's going to be a shock to you."

The old eyes suddenly took on a sharp expression. "It's not Richard!" she demanded, her long fingers clenching in Elizabeth's.

"No," she hastily assured her, "at least, not directly."

"Out with it girl!" she told her. "Don't keep me hanging on in suspense!"

Taking a deep breath Elizabeth told her the truth, haltingly at first then more resolutely until the tale was told. For several minutes her aunt sat in silence, only the twitching of her fingers and the solemn expression in her eyes giving any indication as to the extent of her bewilderment and shock. For one awful moment it seemed to her niece that she was indeed in danger of succumbing to an apoplexy as her face became ashen, taking on a haggard appearance which seriously alarmed her. Calling for her aunt's attendant who came hurrying into the bedchamber from the adjacent dressing room in the full expectation of finding her mistress extinct, took one knowledgeable look at her and knew that she was very much alive, although in need of a strong stimulant. Disappearing into the dressing room she returned seconds later carrying a glass of hartshorn and water which was immediately waved away. However, the joint persuasions of her niece and Miss Calne were enough to cause her to give way, sipping the liquid with evident distaste. "I'm all right!" she bit out testily when her two overseers tried to make her finish the restorative and coax her into lying down.   "I don't need mollycoddling any more than I need this repulsive stuff!"

"Indeed, Ma'am," Miss Calne told her concernedly, "you should drink it all, then go to bed."

A few well chosen words were enough to send her faithful companion back into the dressing room, prophesying disaster if she refused to do what was best for her as she did so.

"Miss Calne is right," Elizabeth told her, "you really should lie down. You've received a terrible shock."

Those piercing eyes glared at her niece and waiting only until Miss Calne was no longer within earshot did she demand to know whether all she had been told were indeed true.

Elizabeth nodded. "Yes, it's true." To her immense relief that haggard expression was gradually disappearing and the colour was beginning to creep back into her aunt's cheeks, but it was clear that the news of her nephew's activities had

had a profound affect on her. "I wish I could have spared you," she told her sincerely, rubbing the cold arthritic hands, "but you had to know."

Her aunt nodded absently, staring blindly into the fire. "You say Major Neville saw Richard last night?"

"Yes."

"Is he well?" she asked urgently, turning to face her niece.

"Yes," she assured her. "Major Neville gave me his word he was."

"That is something I suppose," she sighed. "Even so, to think that he, a Ferrers, is on the run is insupportable!"

"I know," she acknowledged, "but once Major Neville puts his hands on those letters it should not be long before Richard can come home."

"You pay a lot of store by this Major Neville," she commented, glancing up at her niece, "but do you think he will be able to put his hands on them?"

"Yes," she told her firmly, "I do. He told me he is going to try and find them tonight, but if he does not he will try again."

Her aunt nodded, lapsing into silence for several minutes. "These letters," she questioned at length, "you say Colonel Henderson wrote them and that they clearly implicate William?"

"Yes," she confirmed gently, "there is no doubt he was deeply involved with Colonel Henderson."

"I always knew William was a fool," she bit out, her voice becoming noticeably stronger, "but not *that* big a fool!"

"A fool or not," Elizabeth pointed out, "he and Colonel Henderson have rendered Richard's position untenable."

"I am perfectly aware of Richard's position!" she snapped, agitatedly tapping her fingers on the arm of the chair. "What I am not aware of are William's reasons."

"According to Major Neville," she told her, "Richard seems to think that William's motive was money, and then there was the title."

"Ha!" she scoffed, "that don't surprise me; he always did covet *that*. Heaven help us if that day ever dawns! As for money," she commented scathingly, "he never did know how to keep his purse!"

"As far as Colonel Henderson is concerned," Elizabeth shrugged, "Richard believes that ..."

"I ain't interested in *him*" she cut in dismissively, "he can go to the devil, but William is my nevvy after all said."

Elizabeth looked closely at her, a frown suddenly creasing her forehead. "What are you saying, Aunt?"

"I thought I had made myself plain enough," she said briskly, those eagle eyes looking straight at her.

"Well, no" Elizabeth said a little bewildered, "I'm afraid you have not."

319

The fingers tapped faster. "You don't want for sense girl," she said irritably.

"Perhaps not," she shook her head, "but I am afraid I don't know what you mean."

"Don't be obtuse girl!" she told her sharply. "William, for all his faults, *is* a Ferrers!"

Elizabeth stared dazedly at her aunt, hardly daring to believe that she had understood her correctly. "I don't understand," she shook her head. "Are you saying that …?"

"I'm saying girl," she broke in firmly, "that I want William's name kept out of this."

"Kept out …!" Bereft of speech Elizabeth rose hurriedly to her feet, her face rather flushed and her eyes sparkling. As much as she loved her aunt and knew without question that she wanted her favourite nephew restored to his rights and dignities, this firmly delivered announcement took her quite by surprise. It was several moments before she could trust her voice to speak, and her aunt, apparently unmoved by her shock and obvious annoyance, sat calmly back in her chair looking up at her niece with a determined look on her face. "But Aunt, you can't mean it!" she exclaimed, horrified.

"Well I *do* mean it!" she bit out, agitatedly bringing her hand down onto the arm of the chair. "This family's seen enough scandal without adding any more to it."

"You don't know what you are asking!" Elizabeth cried.

"Well I do," she nodded mutinously.

"But you know that the only way Richard's innocence can be proven is by producing those letters."

"I know perfectly well the importance of them," she told her irritably, "but if William's name is in them then some other means must be found to clear Richard's name."

"There *are* no other means," she said vehemently, "if there were Richard would not now be hiding out somewhere but here, where he belongs. Without them he is lost."

As none of her arguments were being attended to she strode over to the window to stare blindly out at the park beyond. She could not understand what had got into her aunt; that she loved Richard was unquestionable, but why this sudden need to protect William when he had done his utmost to discredit her brother was beyond her. She felt the tears sting her eyes and impatiently brushed them away. After all they had been through and endured she would have sworn that her aunt would have welcomed this one and only opportunity to save Richard, instead of which she was doing all she could to save William!

"Come here child," her aunt called in a much milder tone.

Choking back her tears and anguish she took a deep breath and did as she was bid, standing rigidly upright in front of her aunt's chair, her flushed face and stormy eyes telling that formidable old lady more than any words could have.

"Take that look off your face," she was told, but the voice was much kinder, more like the aunt she knew. Raising her hands she took both her niece's into them, necessitating Elizabeth to kneel down in front of her, her eyes mistily defiant. "Do you really believe that I care a button for that wastrel I call my nephew or that I don't care for Richard?" she asked earnestly, leaning forward as her fingers gripped Elizabeth's. "Well, do you?" she asked when she received no reply. "I love Richard as though he were my own son and you my own daughter," she declared fervently. "I would give my life if it meant his innocence could be proven so that he could come home."

"Then why ...?" Elizabeth shook her head, her dark blue eyes swimming, unable to say more.

"Because child," she told her gently, her old eyes softening, "whilst I married a Winsetton I'm a Ferrers." She cupped her niece's soft cheeks in her long fingers. "I don't care the snap of my fingers for William, but I *do* care about my family and protecting its honour. I cannot sit by and let another Ferrers be besmirched by scandal."

"But Aunt," Elizabeth sniffed, covering one of the hands on her cheek with her own, her temper gradually receding, "it's impossible to save them both. We *cannot* rescue Richard without those letters!"

Patting the soft cheek her aunt then leaned back in her chair, exhausted from her emotional exertions. "Then a way must be found," she said tiredly.

Elizabeth rose to her feet, looking thoughtfully down at her aunt. "There *is* no other way, and supposing we *can* protect William," she pointed out reasonably, "what of Richard? Do you think he will like it when he learns that one of the men responsible for his difficulties is allowed to go free? And William," she wanted to know, "do you really expect him to be grateful?"

"Of course Richard won't like it," she admitted, "and as for William," she shrugged, "I expect nothing from him but ingratitude and even more folly! This Major Neville of yours," she nodded, "he seems a capable young man; I am sure the task will not be beyond him."

"It's a Herculean task!" she exclaimed.

"Nevertheless," she said unequivocally, "the attempt must be made."

"But it's impossible!" Elizabeth cried. "Without those letters Richard stands no chance at all of clearing his name; and however capable Major Neville may be, not even he can conjure up evidence out of mid air!"

"I'm not asking him to conjure up evidence," her aunt snapped, "merely to find some other way of helping Richard."

"There is no other way!" Elizabeth replied frustratedly. "Richard's every

321

dependence rests on those letters! Were it otherwise" she stated firmly, "we would not have been subjected to such indignities that have been heaped upon us by Colonel Henderson. He knows, if you do not," she nodded, "their significance and the harm they could do him and William."

"I am perfectly aware of what they signify!" her aunt bit out, bringing her hand to rest on the arm of her chair with considerable force.

"I don't think you do," Elizabeth shook her head, "but depend upon it, William does!" Withstanding the glare darted at her, she continued inexorably, "If we suppress those letters you know perfectly well what will happen; Richard will be caught and hung and William will have achieved his ambition - sixth Viscount Easton! Is that what you want?" she asked.

"Of course it's not!" her aunt snapped. "The very thought of having him holding the reins makes me sick to the stomach, and as for Richard being caught and hung, I doubt the Major will allow that to happen."

"I fail to see how he could prevent it when there is no evidence to the contrary," Elizabeth said irritably. "However, since I see your mind is quite made up, I shall approach the Major with your proposal, but how on earth you expect him to save Richard without those letters I don't know!"

"I don't care how he manages it," her aunt ground out stubbornly, "but I will not see another nevvy of mine be tainted with treason!"

Seeing that her aunt would not be moved from this standpoint she knew it was futile to argue the point with her any further, reiterating that she would speak to Major Neville when next she saw him, to which that formidable old lady nodded and closed her eyes.

Uncertain which aspect of the whole thing upset her most Elizabeth went to her bedchamber and shut herself away to think matters through. If she did not know better she would say she was living in a dream; so unreal was it. At no point did she even think that her aunt would make such a stipulation especially when she considered that those letters were Richard's only chance to clear his name. When she had told her aunt that it would be a Herculean task to help Richard without those letters, she had meant it. No matter how she tried she could think of no other way of helping him to prove his innocence, and however much she may trust Gideon and have the utmost faith in him, she doubted even he could save her brother without them.

When she thought of the risks he would be taking in order to help Richard she went cold with fear, but whether he managed to get his hands on them tonight or tomorrow night made no difference, it was all going to be to no avail, and the worst of it was she could not get word to him to advise him of this new and startling development.

She knew implicitly that her aunt would do anything to save Richard, but that she could even think for one moment that William must be saved from his own folly was too incredible. William may be a Ferrers but it meant little to him, were it otherwise he would not have embarked on a venture which he must have known was doomed to failure. She was no traitor, but even so she could admit to feeling some sympathy for those whose convictions had led them down this path, but even had her cousin possessed such firmly held persuasions, the fact that he had incriminated her brother in order to save himself would have killed at a stroke any sympathy she may have felt. Whilst she acknowledged that their conversations had never encompassed politics which naturally rendered her ignorant of any beliefs he may hold, knowing him as well as she did she found it hard to believe that he possessed any at all.

It came as no surprise to her when Miss Calne later informed her that her mistress was not well enough to join her downstairs for dinner, but would instead take a little something in her room. As her own appetite had deserted her she sent a message to inform Salmon that not only her aunt but she too would not be coming downstairs for dinner. Apart from the fact that the mere thought of food made her feel sick, her stomach churning over, there was no telling when William would return and as her aunt's announcement was still a source of considerable aggravation, she was in no mood to see him when he did.

Upon hearing that both ladies would not be partaking of dinner, Salmon drew his own conclusions, nevertheless he would have been astounded to learn that these fell very wide of the mark. At no point would he have believed it to be possible that Clara Winsetton would be prepared to throw away the only opportunity which would save her nephew from the hangman's noose merely in order to protect a man who had attempted to further his own ends through embarking on treason and then doing his best to discredit his cousin.

However, since he was in ignorance of what had taken place between them he began to wonder how Major Neville would fare tonight in attempting to get his hands on those letters. It was true that prior to his first visit to Ferrers Court he had had neither faith nor trust in the military, indeed, they had given him no cause to feel either, but having met this young man he had at once seen that he was a very different kettle of fish to those others they had had in the house. He only had to think of Colonel Henderson and his band of cutthroats and what they had put his late lordship and his daughter through to engender in him a deep dislike of red-coats, but it had been obvious from the beginning that Major Neville was not of their calibre.

Irrespective of Major Neville's feelings for his mistress he knew he genuinely had her brother's interests at heart and was prepared to do all he could to help him. He could only guess at how he would go about retrieving the evidence which would save his high spirited young master, but he had seen enough of him to feel sufficiently confident in that should he fail tonight then he would make the attempt again. In many ways he reminded him of Richard in that once he had set his mind to something he was not one who gave up easily and certainly not because of a set-back but, in one respect, it had to be said there was a world of difference and that was Richard lacked the steadiness which was an integral part of Major Neville's character. At no point did it even cross his mind that the Major would fail in his mission, but he realized the longer it took him to get those letters the more restless Richard would become. Long association with him was enough to instil in him a real fear that he would take it into his head to play a hand in the game himself, thereby placing him in even more jeopardy and increasing his chances of being caught. He shook his head over the business but as his own hands were tied and there was nothing he could practically do other than whatever was needed to try and temper his master's impulsive behaviour as well as looking after the ladies, he went along to the kitchen for his supper in a mood of considerable disquiet.

Elizabeth ventured downstairs the following morning earlier than usual in the hope of running Salmon to earth to pour her aunt's staggering decision into his ears before William left his bedchamber. There may not be anything Salmon could do to persuade that formidable lady into changing her mind, but so used to confiding all her troubles to him was she that now was no exception.

Not surprisingly he was astounded at such a disclosure, scratching his head in perplexity. He had the greatest respect for Clara Winsetton, not that he would ever tell her so, but this desire to protect William from exposure and punishment at the expense of Richard's life, was the very last thing he had expected. He could not find fault with her motives, like him she had the interests of the Ferrers family at heart, but that she should want to shield an ingrate and wastrel like William Ferrers, a man he had never really looked upon as one of the family, was beyond him. He looked his stupefaction and it was several moments before he could speak, eventually giving vent to his feelings so vehemently that Elizabeth, who had never yet known him be so voluble, stared in surprise. She fully understood his feelings but whilst she could offer no satisfactory explanation to account for her aunt's unexpected wish which would either appease or satisfy him, she did eventually manage to instil in him the continued necessity to say or do nothing to make William suspicious. It was clear from the look on his wrinkled face that holding his tongue in the face of such provocation would be a severe trial, but even though she could not say that she had completely won him over, by the time she left him she felt quite confident that he would keep his promise.

As she always had a slice of bread and butter in her room which always seemed to sustain her until luncheon, she had no fear of running into her cousin or her aunt over the breakfast table, but since she was still in no frame of mind to face her cousin as though nothing had happened and she was at a loss to know what to say to her aunt, she was really rather thankful that they were still in their bedchambers. To make matters worse she was not entirely sure whether Gideon would come to see her today or not, irrespective of what he had said in front of William yesterday, but such was the turmoil she was in she admitted to herself that just to see his tall figure and hear his voice making light of her concerns, would have afforded her a great deal of comfort.

Unaware of Elizabeth's dilemma over her aunt's unexpected wish to save William from the results of his own treacherous behaviour, Gideon was looking forward to seeing her again, and in happy expectation of this left the garrison, making his way first towards Seaford. He had not intended making a long stay there but Captain Waring, bearing all the hallmarks of having endured a sleepless night, was determined to pour his difficulties into Gideon's ears. He sympathized with the problems facing him and understood the irritation and despair of one who had suffered yet another setback in his efforts to try and stem the trade. Captain Waring was clearly frustrated but in spite of the many attempts to thwart his exertions he remained resolute in seeing this illicit trafficking curtailed once and for all, and since he was an honest man who could not be bought or bribed in return for turning a blind eye, Gideon foresaw his future as being even more frustrating than it was at present.

Upon enquiring if he had anything further to tell him about Richard Ferrers he shook his head, saying disappointingly that he had had neither sighting nor word of him, but held out every hope that sooner or later this nefarious individual would be caught and hung, especially as he was on the point of being 'gazetted'. "You mark my words, Major" he nodded confidently, "it won't be long before he's dangling from the end of a rope! These so-called friends of his won't be so eager to hide him once they know they can earn themselves five hundred pounds in return for handing him over to the authorities!"

However pleased Gideon was to learn that Richard Ferrers had apparently gone to ground, in view of his imminent 'gazetting' and Captain Waring's hopes because of it, whatever relief he felt was short-lived. He could not delude himself into thinking that this extremely zealous Excise Officer was wrong in his assumptions about Richard's associates. Richard Ferrers may uphold them, indeed, he had been vehement in his defence of their loyalty, but he could not deny that Captain Waring had spoken no less than the truth. From the moment he had learned of His Grace's intention of 'gazetting' him, he had doubted the continued allegiance of those whose very reason for embarking on this illicit trade in the first place was for financial gain. Five hundred pounds was surely more than enough motive to make some men break ranks and inform on their friends, being fully prepared to risk everything, even their lives should they be discovered by their accomplices, in the hope of acquiring such a sum. Richard Ferrers, adamantly refusing to believe that one of his accomplices would be guilty of committing such a heinous crime, was certainly walking a very fine line indeed, and whilst, for the present at least, or so it seemed, he was keeping his word by not taking part in any more nocturnal activities, his position was anything but enviable and very far from secure.

Gideon could only hope that Lieutenant Beaton was right when he had said that his friend was held in high regard by everyone who knew him, because as far as he could see over the next few days Richard Ferrers was going to need all the good-will he could get. Powerful forces were ranged against him and as their desperation grew so would their attempts to ensnare him, and if this meant betrayal from within by someone he trusted due to monetary inducement, then his immediate future looked rather bleak to say the least.

He had told Elizabeth that once those letters were in his possession then her brother would be safe, but he had deliberately refrained from telling her that acquiring them was only the first step on the path to reinstating Richard. He knew perfectly well that he could not approach Colonel Henderson with the evidence that would see him face his trial, not only because it was running an unnecessary risk, but out of courtesy to his rank any charges put forward would have to be done by an officer of equal rank or above, as would his eventual arrest. It was therefore imperative that he return to London to consult with General Turville at the earliest opportunity, his only worry being that Richard Ferrers would not remain inactive for very long.

Keeping these concerns to himself he made his way to Ferrers Court, arriving just as the stable clock struck midday. Leaving his horse in the care of a groom he strode round to the front of the house unaware of the fresh problems besetting the inhabitants. However, it was apparent from the moment Salmon opened the door to him that something was wrong, but before he could enquire if anything were amiss Elizabeth, looking over the banister to see who had arrived, fled down the stairs, her relief at seeing him plainly evident on her face. Taking hold of her outstretched hands and holding them in a strong warm clasp, he looked from one to the other asking calmly what had occurred. Salmon, whose faith in Gideon was now implicit, was just as pleased to see him as his mistress because if anyone could help them out of this latest fix he could, but just as he was about to tell him Elizabeth forestalled him.

"Oh Gideon, thank goodness you've come!" she cried, looking up at him. "Something quite untoward has occurred!"

"That's true enough, Major" Salmon nodded darkly.

"It's not Richard?" he asked urgently.

"No," she shook her head, "it's not Richard, it's - oh, we can't talk here," she told him, "William may return at any moment. Come in here." Pulling him into the small sitting room where only two days before she had had that unforgettable conversation with William, she left Salmon in the hall to keep a watchful eye for her cousin. It was not until she had closed the door behind her and turned to face him that she realized it was one thing to rehearse what she would say to him in the privacy of her bedchamber but quite another when he was standing right in front of her, especially when she considered all his efforts on her brother's behalf.

After several failed attempts to tell him of her aunt's resolve to protect William, Gideon took a step nearer and taking hold of her cold hands looked down at her, his eyes warm and encouraging. "Is it so bad that you cannot tell me?" he asked gently. "I thought you trusted me."

"You know I do," she told him earnestly. "It's just that …"

"Just what?" he urged, raising her hands to his lips. "Has William been plaguing you?"

She shook her head. "No, not that precisely."

Whatever it was that had happened since he was here yesterday it was clearly something she found difficult to impart, so in order to give her time to collect herself he smiled down at her. "Then while you think of the right words to tell me the worst," he said in mock horror, "let me tell *you* something," kissing her forehead. "Early this morning, Lieutenant Beaton and I managed to get hold of those letters," her eyes widened at this, and nodding his head in confirmation went on to tell her how they had achieved it.

"Oh Gideon, that's wonderful news!" she cried. "But how clever of you both!"

"I knew you would be pleased," he smiled disarmingly down at her. "Speaking for myself I …" He broke off as she suddenly burst into tears, covering her face with both hands. "My darling," he urged, taking hold of her hands. "What has happened? You *must* tell me."

"Oh Gideon," she sniffed, "when I think of the danger you were exposed to in retrieving those letters."

"My darling, I was in no danger," he told her softly, wrapping his arms around her. "Is that what has been worrying you?"

"Yes," she nodded, "*that*, and my aunt."

He eased himself a little away from her, his eyes searching her face. "Your aunt? Are you saying that she too has taken up smuggling?" he asked amusedly.

She laughed as he had intended her to. "No," she sniffed, fumbling for her handkerchief, "although I think that would be preferable."

"To what?" he asked gently.

She looked up at him, her eyes mirroring her distress, but gradually by dint of coaxing and making her laugh he managed to get her to tell him what was troubling her. "I'm sorry," she hiccuped when she had come to the end of her disjointed confession, "but I cannot persuade her into changing her mind. She is adamant that William must be protected."

Whatever it was he had expected it was definitely not this, but he supposed he should have when he considered the kind of woman Clara Winsetton was. She may have no time for her nephew but he could see why she wanted the Ferrers name to have no more scandal than necessary attached to it. Nevertheless, her determination to save William had certainly posed a problem, because even though only three of those letters mentioned him by name, he could not see Colonel Henderson taking sole responsibility in order to accommodate the feelings of an old lady he had long since taken in dislike.

"I have been striving how best to tell you ever since," she told him haltingly, "but now that I have I would not blame you if you washed your hands of us!"

"No," he shook his head, "I won't wash my hands of you," he promised, his voice a caress.

"You *will* speak to my aunt before you leave, won't you?" she asked, looking up at him.

He nodded, then taking her in his arms held her close as she gave vent to a fresh flood of tears. She was no coward, on the contrary, he knew her to be a woman of courage and spirit, but she had endured more than enough recently and with the exception of her aunt and Salmon there had been no one to whom she could turn for solace or advice. This latest obstacle, coming on top of everything else she had suffered, had clearly been too much for her, and as she clung to him for much needed comfort and support he vowed that no matter what the outcome of Richard's difficulties, he was determined to keep her safe from any further harm or misfortune.

By the time he left her outside her aunt's bedchamber door she was more calm and in control of herself, her only concern being how he was going to persuade her aunt into changing her mind. When he had kissed her and told her that everything would come out all right, she may have wondered how he could possibly solve this ever worsening tangle, but at no point did she ever doubt he would.

Having been informed by Miss Calne that the Major had arrived, catching sight of him through the window, Clara Winsetton waited for him to come and see her in a mood which her niece would have had no hesitation in describing as querulous. She knew perfectly well that her ultimatum had not found favour with Elizabeth and unless she missed her guess she knew it would not with Salmon either, and although she realized her nephew was as worthless as he was undeserving, she was determined to see the Ferrers name upheld.

"Come in, Major" she called in answer to his tap on the door. "Thank you for coming to see me," she nodded when he had closed it behind him.

"It is a pleasure, Ma'am," he smiled, crossing the floor to where she sat in the winged chair by the fire, raising her cold bony hand to his lips. "I trust I find you well?"

"I could be better," she told him forthrightly, "but that's another story!

Please, do sit down, Major."

"Thank you, Ma'am" he inclined his head, lifting the tails of his coat and easing himself into the chair opposite her.

"I take it my niece has told you?" she asked, clenching and unclenching her right hand on the arm of the chair, eyeing him closely.

"Yes Ma'am," he nodded, "she has."

"I sense you do not like it overmuch," she remarked candidly.

"Not that precisely," he shook his head, "but I must confess to some surprise especially when I consider the affection in which you hold Richard, and yet you wish to protect one of the men who is largely responsible for his present predicament."

Her eagle eyes looked searchingly at him. "In case you had forgotten Major, one of those men happens to be my nephew."

"No," he replied calmly, "I had not forgotten."

"Are you saying that the task is beyond you?" she demanded, her fingers twitching her shawl.

"By no means," he assured her.

"What then?"

"Are you not forgetting his accomplice?" he reminded her.

"If you mean Colonel Henderson," she scorned, "I do not intend to waste any time in considering *him*! He's not my concern."

"Then he should be," Gideon told her with equal frankness. "In not considering him you are making a grave mistake."

"What do you mean?" she demanded, leaning slightly forward in her chair.

"Whilst I accept my acquaintance with Colonel Henderson is not of long duration," he acknowledged, "I have seen enough of him to be able to say that if you think for one moment he will do the gentlemanly thing and shoulder the blame himself, you are quite mistaken. He is far too much the coward for that."

She digested this for a moment or two, asking at length "These letters; have you managed to get hold of them?"

"Yes," he confirmed, "I have them safe."

She nodded considering, her fingers tapping on the arm of the chair as was usual when she was agitated. "How many are there?" she asked urgently.

"There are six in all, Ma'am" he informed her.

"I see," she nodded again "and do they all mention my nephew?"

In view of Richard's situation he was tempted to withhold the truth from her but only a moment's thought was enough to tell him that it would not answer; for one thing there was always the possibility that something could go wrong and, for another, to offer her a lie would be to hold her in contempt which was really quite repugnant to him. "Only three of them name your nephew and his willingness to participate," he told her truthfully.

"So the others could still be used against Colonel Henderson?" she questioned.

"Yes, they could," he confirmed, "but in view of your intention to keep William's name out of it, I cannot see how that will answer."

"Major Neville," she admonished, "are you deliberately trying to thwart me?"

"By no means," he assured her, not unsympathetic to her desire to protect her family, "but you cannot have fully considered."

"There is nothing to consider!" she bit out.

"I beg pardon, Ma'am," he contradicted, "but there is everything to consider. If, as I believe you to mean, I suppress those letters which mention William and only produce the other three, not only could I be facing charges of withholding evidence, but there is every likelihood that Colonel Henderson will openly accuse William of complicity therefore rendering it necessary for him to stand trial in his own defence. You have seen Colonel Henderson for yourself," he reminded her, "therefore you must know the kind of man he is; he *will* name names. Even if William could deflect the accusations made against him the scandal such an action would create will defeat your desire to protect him as well as the Ferrers name," he smiled disarmingly in response to the look she threw at him. "Believe me, Ma'am" he shook his head, "it will not serve."

"Then what will?" she demanded, trying to ignore that smile which she was by no means impervious to, "or don't you know?"

He eyed her steadily for a moment. "No Ma'am, I don't," he admitted frankly. "The need to protect William from the consequences of his own folly had not entered into my calculations, and whilst I am not saying the task is impossible, at this precise moment in time I fail to see how I can save them both."

She considered this in frustrating silence, but although it was not what she wanted to hear she preferred it to false promises. "I suppose there's no need for me to tell you that Elizabeth has no liking for it," she bit out, "nor, I'll be bound, does Salmon!"

Like Salmon he could not fault her motives, but it was clear she had not considered the ramifications of such a request. "Did you really expect them to?" he asked gently.

She looked at him, her eyes sharp and keen, fully prepared to see contempt in those brown depths but there was none. "No," she confessed at length, "I did not."

"And what of Richard?" he prompted. "How do you think he will take it when he learns of your wish to protect his cousin?"

"Badly," she nodded. "There's never been any love lost between 'em," she twitched her shawl, "no use pretending there has."

"In that case, Ma'am" he suggested tentatively, "do you not think it would

330

be better to let William overcome his own difficulties?"

"No I don't!" she barked out. "Leaving him to untangle his affairs would only lead to even more trouble, creating a far bigger scandal which would be beyond anyone's doing anything about! May as well expect him to fly to the moon!"

As it was clear her mind was made up and that nothing he could say would divert her, he reluctantly accepted the charge laid upon him, but nevertheless felt it behoved him to warn her that his efforts may not bring forth the result she wanted. She seemed to accept this well enough, but as he bowed over her hand he told her truthfully, "I cannot pretend to having a liking for your scheme, Ma'am and, whilst I am momentarily at a loss as to how I am to achieve it, I give you my word that I will do all I can to accomplish the task."

She gripped his fingers. "Thank you, Major. I know you don't like it, nor do I if it comes to that," she admitted, "the fool deserves all he gets, but I cannot stand by and see the Ferrers name dragged any deeper into the dirt!"

"I do not doubt either your motives or intentions, Ma'am," he assured her, "only the gratitude of their recipient."

She looked knowingly up at him. "There's no need to say it, Major" she nodded, "my niece has already done so, most eloquently in fact." He smiled down at her. "No doubt you're thinking I'm nothing but a foolish old woman?" she said provocatively.

"No," he shook his head, "nothing so discourteous has entered my head I promise you."

Her fingers gripped his tighter still. "I can see why Elizabeth has taken such a liking to you, Major" she told him, "but if you can bring both my nephews' about, you will not only have the love of my niece but the undying gratitude of an old woman!"

He raised her hand to his lips. "Whilst it is a very great pleasure to serve you both, Ma'am" he smiled, "I fear that should I fail your niece in bringing her brother off safe then I shall need all your gratitude to reinstate me with her."

"Nonsense!" she cried. "Elizabeth places great store in you, as *I* do."

"You're most kind, Ma'am," he inclined his head, "but I do most sincerely hope that I shall not fail either of you," he told her earnestly.

He bowed over hand again and turned to leave, but just as he had reached the door she forestalled him. "And if it should come to a choice, Major?" she questioned.

It was a moment or two before he spoke, but he held her penetrating stare without a blink. "Whilst I have no wish to disoblige you, Ma'am" he told her kindly, "my first duty must be to Richard."

She nodded, then sinking back in her chair watched him close the door quietly behind him.

Although he had given his word to do everything possible to save William Ferrers, honesty compelled him to admit that he failed to see what he could possibly do to protect him from the consequences of his own treasonable actions. Whilst producing even only three of those letters would prevent Richard from climbing the scaffold they would not serve where his cousin was concerned. He had spoken no less than the truth when he had said Colonel Henderson would not shoulder the blame himself, but would name William as his accomplice, in fact he would not be in the least surprised to discover that, with a man like His Grace at his back, he may not even face his trial at all. Nevertheless, whatever his own thoughts regarding William Ferrers he had given his word that he would do everything possible to keep his name out of it, but as he descended the stairs he was very far from knowing how he was going to set about it.

Elizabeth, anxiously awaiting him in the hall, knew immediately she set eyes on him as he rounded the bend in the stairs that he had not been able to dissuade her aunt. Had it not been for William pointing the finger at Richard ensuring he took the blame, she would not have been so unsympathetic to her aunt's feelings, as it was she was by no means reconciled to the scheme.

"My darling," he said gently, after recounting his interview with her aunt, "I realize how difficult this is for you to accept, but I have had a duty laid upon me which I am honour bound to try and discharge. This does not mean that I have relegated Richard to second place," he told her when he saw the slight frown which had descended onto her forehead. "My first duty is, and always has been, to Richard. You must believe that."

"You know I do," she told him earnestly, her eyes reflecting all she felt. "It's just that if anything were to happen to Richard, I couldn't bear it!"

"Nothing is going to happen to Richard," he assured her, taking hold of her agitated hands in his. "Haven't I already given you my word on that?"

"Yes," she nodded.

"Never doubt it," he told her sincerely. "Whilst I acknowledge that your aunt's decision was something I had not looked for, I could not have ignored her plea, but although I have promised her to do all I can for William, I have no intention of putting his safety before Richard's." He raised her hands to his lips. "Do not be thinking she is doing this for William," he told her, "she's not."

"I know she's not," she acknowledged. "She's inordinately proud of being a Ferrers, which is why all of this has been so very painful for her," she smiled up at him. "You must know I do not blame you for giving your word to her; she has placed you in a most awkward position but, Gideon," she shook her head, "how *can* you possibly save them both? Surely those letters will not serve where William is concerned?"

"No, they won't," he agreed. "Whilst they will be more than enough to ensure Richard's safety, they hold no value for William for reasons I have already given. Indeed," he shook his head, "far from protecting him, they will condemn him!"

"So how will you contrive to keep his name out of it?" she asked, her eyes searching his face.

He shrugged helplessly. "I wish to God I knew! At this moment in time," he confessed, "I am totally at a loss to see how it can be done."

"What are you going to do now?" she asked.

"Now," he sighed, "I am afraid I must leave you to prepare for a journey to London tomorrow." He saw the look which crossed her face and experienced such a feeling of pain mingled with joy that he held her close. "My darling," he urged, "I must. Although I have submitted a report to General Turville matters have now reached a point where I need to consult him before anything else can be done. And who knows?" he grimaced, with more hope than conviction, "perhaps he can offer a solution where your cousin is concerned."

She clung to him. "Will you be gone for very long?"

"Only a few days," he promised, kissing the top of her head. "General Turville will return with me in order for him to charge and arrest Colonel Henderson for treason."

"Can't *you* do that?" she asked, moving a little away from him.

"No," he shook his head. "Believe me," he assured her, "nothing would give me greater satisfaction, but his rank, if not the man, demands courtesy."

He then went on to tell her about his forthcoming meeting with Colonel Henderson later that afternoon, but upon her asking what reason he would give for his departure for London tomorrow he raised a questioning eyebrow, offering doubtfully, "Family affairs?"

She smiled, but asked sceptically, "Do you think he will be believe you?"

"Probably not," he shook his head. "But no matter what reason I give I can't see him believing it, and to tell him the truth is out of the question. The chances are I would get no further than the garrison gatehouse."

"He's *despicable!*" she exclaimed.

"Yes, he is," Gideon agreed, "but having to placate him is far more important than gratifying our own desires. What is it?" he asked as he saw her bite her bottom lip.

"I was just thinking, what will you tell him about your visit here today? Isn't he expecting my capitulation?"

"Yes," Gideon nodded, a smile lurking at the back of his eyes, "but unfortunately," he grinned, "upon my arrival at Ferrers Court I was informed that you were indisposed and not receiving visitors."

She laughed. "I really can't see him believing that!"

"Nor can I," he agreed, "but at all costs I need time to see General Tuville."

"But what if he comes here while you are away?" she demanded urgently.

"What shall I say to him?"

As this eventuality had already occurred to him, he had his answer ready. "You are far too ill to see him." Her brows rose at this. "My darling," he smiled, "Colonel Henderson may be desperate to see an end to this matter, but I hardly think that even he will break down your bedchamber door in order to speak to you!"

She considered this, but just as she was about to say something she saw Salmon approaching from the rear of the hall.

Having been on the watch for William with still no sign of him, Salmon decided to desert his post. Upon learning what had transpired between Clara Winsetton and the Major he gave forceful vent to his feelings, telling Gideon in no uncertain terms that he for one would not lift a finger to help a man who had not only brought disgrace on the name he bore, but had virtually pushed his uncle into the grave. He then went on to further inform him that should William escape the full penalty of the law then it would be a gross miscarriage of justice, for which he hoped Clara Winsetton would be satisfied when it was seen that she had had a hand in allowing a guilty man, and a traitor to boot, to go free while an innocent man hung for his crimes.

"You have no need to fear on that score, Salmon" Gideon assured him. "Richard will not mount the scaffold, I shall see to that. As far as William is concerned I am no more enamoured of the idea than you are, but I have had a duty laid upon me and I shall endeavour to carry it out to the best of my ability."

"A worthless rasher of wind!" Salmon exclaimed disgustedly.

"Very probably," Gideon nodded, "nevertheless, I shall make the attempt."

He was fully conscious of the justification for every embittered word Salmon had uttered and were it not for the fact that he had given his word to Clara Winsetton he would gladly leave William Ferrers to his own devices. Upon hearing this Salmon grunted something unintelligible to which it seemed only Elizabeth was able to interpret, hastily begging him to hush as it was not helping. His face told its own story and it therefore took the combined efforts of Gideon and Elizabeth to impress upon him that Richard was not to be told of this latest development. It took every ounce of persuasion Gideon possessed to extract Salmon's promise to say nothing of this to Richard but, however reluctantly he gave it, Gideon believed he meant to keep it.

When Salmon learned of Gideon's departure for London the next day he felt it incumbent upon him to reiterate that his young master would not remain docile for long and although he may have given his word that he would do nothing to jeopardize his position any further, he could not see it lasting. Upon being told that Richard would not have to wait much longer to see his affairs settled, he replied tartly that that was all very well, but keeping him quiet in the meantime was going to be no easy matter.

"I am aware of that," Gideon sympathized, "but you must try Salmon, as well as impressing upon him the need for patience."

Salmon looked his frustration, but after a moment's thought nodded his head signifying that he would do what he could.

"If only he won't say anything to Richard!" Elizabeth said fervently, as she watched Salmon make his way to the stables to order Gideon's horse to be made ready.

"He won't," Gideon assured her. "He knows Richard better than anyone and what he is capable of and, although he has no liking for this idea of your aunt's, he won't say or do anything which could incite him into doing something reckless."

Upon reflection she was brought to agree with this, but just as she was about to raise another point with him, he took her back into his arms, forestalling her by saying, "My darling, we have discussed your brother, your aunt's ultimatum, whether or not we can help William and, even," he pulled a face, "what tale I shall offer Colonel Henderson, and whilst I am not questioning the importance of any of these things, all I want to hear right now is how much you will miss me while I am away."

The look in his eyes made her heart jump, and when his arms tightened around her crushing her to him and his lips fastened onto hers it was impossible for her to say anything at all, but her response to his kisses was answer enough.

CHAPTER SEVENTEEN

When Gideon eventually left Ferrers Court it was almost half past two. In view of his meeting with Colonel Henderson at half past five and his pending return to town tomorrow, he had not intended staying as long as he had, but in view of what had greeted him on his arrival, he could not have ignored or dismissed it.

Clara Winsetton's ultimatum had come as a complete surprise, but he supposed he should have been prepared for something like this. He was honest enough to admit that had he have been able to dissuade her from her fell intention he would have done so, but it had been clear from the outset of his interview with her that her mind was made up. He fully appreciated her feelings and the reasons behind her wish to keep William's name out of it, but whether he was deserving of it was another matter.

The end of Richard's difficulties was in sight, and if only he would refrain from showing himself or embarking on another crazy exploit, then it should be a relatively straightforward matter to extricate him from the charge of smuggling. Thankfully, no one had ever actually caught him in the act of running illicit cargoes and once those letters were produced and Colonel Henderson had been discredited, then he envisaged no difficulty in exonerating him of the charge of treason.

William, on the other hand, was another matter entirely. Those letters were quite useless as far as he was concerned if for no other reason than Colonel Henderson would not go down without a fight; he would certainly name him as his partner in sedition. He was not the type of man who, having embarked on such a dangerous path, only to find it crumble beneath him, would either stand up and face the consequences of his actions or to shoulder the responsibility himself. From what Gideon had been privileged to see of William Ferrers he had no doubt at all that he had allowed himself to be persuaded into the role of traitor simply because of his envy of Richard and his ambition to take possession of the title, making him easy prey to the likes of Colonel Henderson. Even so, how to disentangle him from his unenviable predicament and without any adverse repercussions rebounding on the Ferrers family, had him in a quandary. No matter how hard he tried he could find no way out for William Ferrers, especially as no reliance whatsoever could be placed upon Colonel Henderson either admitting that his accomplice had played a minor role only in events or that he was working alone. As far as His Grace was concerned it was still very far from clear whether he knew the truth or not about Colonel Henderson's venture into treason. If he did then his reasons for assisting him were inexplicable particularly when one considered his views and his close connection with the King. If, on the other hand, he believed his friend's tale about Richard Ferrers then one did not have to look far to see his reasons. If this was indeed the case, then it immediately raised the question as to why the search for Richard Ferrers, and in such a surreptitious manner, had not been instigated until he had escaped from custody? The more Gideon considered it the more convinced he became that having learned from Richard about those letters being in his possession, Colonel Henderson had been faced with little choice but to approach His Grace for aid. But however plausible this was, it still left the question as to why Lytton had aided him in the first place as he would doubtless have demanded to know why Henderson could not have dealt with this matter himself. Knowing His Grace it would not have taken him long to get the truth out of Henderson, and therefore he would have learned about those letters and their damning contents. He did not think that Colonel Henderson would have been able to have withstood His Grace's relentless questioning for very long before confessing the truth to him, and in view of this failed to see what possible reason Lytton could have for involving himself in something of this nature. No matter how he tried Gideon could find no suitable explanation for Lytton's involvement, but whatever his reason he had clearly indicated, if not by word then by deed, that he fully intended to support his friend. Although his motives for offering assistance were as yet unknown, he had proved beyond doubt how far he was prepared to go the moment he had announced his intention of 'gazetting' Richard Ferrers. Whether this would prove successful remained to be seen, but in the event that it was not then it was logical to assume that other means would have to be found. Under normal circumstances he doubted very much whether His Grace would even give the time of day to a man like William Ferrers, much less know that he even existed, and therefore totally indifferent as to whether he was hung or not but, unfortunately, William Ferrers was inextricably linked with Colonel Henderson, and saving him would necessarily mean saving them both. If this meant throwing Richard Ferrers to the lions, then he would have no hesitation in doing so.

Whatever it was that had persuaded Lytton to show his hand in this, it was fairly certain he could be relied upon to do everything possible to save his old friend, even at the expense of his accomplice. He would have no compunction in leaving William Ferrers to his own devices should the need arise, and more than capable of discrediting anything that that unfortunate young man could put forward in his own defence. Faced with the combined forces of two men, one of whom at least would never dared be questioned, William Ferrers would stand no chance at all. In his own way he was walking just as fine a line as Richard, but where he could be reasonably certain of coming out of this in one piece, his cousin could not. Those letters therefore were the one saving grace as far as Richard was concerned; irrefutable proof that he was no traitor and which no court of law could either ignore or disregard. His Grace was no fool, on the contrary, he was most astute and, unless Gideon had miscalculated where he was concerned, he felt sure that he must know the truth about Colonel Henderson. He may not be able to explain his reasons for acting in this matter, but Lytton would know the danger those letters posed and that they were by far the most incriminating piece of evidence against his old friend.

He had spoken no less than the truth when he had told Clara Winsetton that he could not save both her nephews' on those letters alone and, by the time he arrived back at the garrison, he was forced to admit that that stilled held true. He was no nearer finding a solution to the problem than he was when it was first put to him, and whilst he was not admitting that the task was beyond him, he was honest enough to own that he failed to see how it could be achieved. He could only hope therefore that General Turville may have a suggestion or two to put forward because, try as he did, he could see no happy ending for William Ferrers. He may have no liking for it but he was determined to make the attempt if, for no other reason, than he had given his word and therefore believed it incumbent upon him to honour it.

Having handed his horse into the care of a groom, he made his way back across the courtyard to his quarters with a look of deep concentration on his face. He could have done without this meeting with Colonel Henderson but since there was no way of avoiding it, the best he could hope for was that he would accept not only his reasons for what he would regard as a most unexpected and inconvenient return to town, but also his failure to ascertain Richard's whereabouts from his sister. He would not put it beyond Colonel Henderson to visit Ferrers Court in his absence, so desperate was he to solve matters that this would be precisely the kind of thing he would do. Even so, he believed he had prepared the ground sufficiently with Elizabeth should he take it into his head to do just that. He may have shown no regard for the feelings of the Ferrers family to date, but Gideon doubted even he would have the audacity to invade a lady's bedchamber specifically in order to discover whether she was indeed unwell or not.

As it was by now widely known around the garrison that Major Neville had been sent here to try and track down Richard Ferrers, Sergeant Taylor was somewhat surprised at being asked to pack his bag ready for a brief return to London tomorrow. Having known no other life than the army he had served under both good and bad officers, but he was a good judge of character, and unless he was very much mistaken, which he doubted, Major Neville was definitely one of the former, apart from which he struck him as being not only a decent man but an extremely fair one. Naturally, the Major had not confided in him, but he had gained the very strong impression that he was by no means convinced of Richard

Ferrers' guilt; unlike Colonel Henderson who had hunted him remorselessly for months. He did not hold with traitors, but whether this young man was guilty or not, if he stood any chance of a fair hearing, then it seemed to him that Major Neville was the only man to ensure it. Considering the enormity of the situation therefore, Major Neville's unexpected return to London was incomprehensible, but as he was offering him no reason to account for it, he merely did as he was bid.

Gideon had a pretty shrewd idea what was going through his mind, but whilst he looked upon Sergeant Taylor as being a good soldier and a man who could be relied upon, especially in a crisis, he saw no reason to either enlighten him or take him into his confidence. It was one thing to entrust a sealed letter to him, but the less people who knew the truth the better for Richard Ferrers, particularly now as matters were reaching a critical stage.

Having finished the note he had written to Lieutenant Beaton, purely as a precautionary measure, he briefly raised his eyes from the sheet of paper to look thoughtfully across at Sergeant Taylor as he gathered his belongings together. This old soldier may be dependable, but he nevertheless felt somewhat relieved to know that he had hidden those letters safe with no chance of them being found accidentally. There would be time enough to remove them from their hiding place before he left in the morning; on no account could he carry them with him to his meeting with Colonel Henderson. Sealing the letter he then handed it to Sergeant Taylor who promised to deliver it to Lieutenant Beaton personally as soon as he had finished attending to his packing, whereupon Gideon left his quarters.

By the time he crossed the courtyard it was almost half past five and dusk was setting in and the rain, which had begun some little while ago, was by now coming down heavily.   Apart from the fact that years of soldiering had rendered him immune to the weather, so intent was he on the matter in hand that he gave very little notice either to the heavy downpour or to the carriage which was just passing through the archway entrance at a breakneck speed, eventually coming to a clamouring halt just to the right of the tower building.

Fully expecting to be met by Major Denham who seldom, if ever, seemed to leave his room, he was a little surprised to see he was nowhere in sight and that Colonel Henderson was occupying his domain, sitting comfortably back in the Major's chair waiting for him.

"Ah, Major Neville!" he cried, rising to his feet when he saw who had entered, prepared to put his grievances over this young man's dissimulation to the back of his mind for the time being, taking much solace from knowing that very soon this menace to his peace of mind would not be around to cause him any further concerns. Even so, he could not deny that Gideon was a handsome young man, and his manners, whilst irritating in the extreme to one in his disturbingly anxious state, whose desire for a speedy conclusion to his affairs were paramount, were impeccable; having no difficulty in understanding why Miss Ferrers clearly found him so attractive.

"Good evening, Sir" Gideon saluted.

Regardless of his feelings for this man standing to attention before him and his urgent desire to rake him down for the deceiving villain he was, Colonel Henderson felt an explanation to account for his aide's sudden absence was more important. It may stick in his throat to have to adhere to Lytton's strictures on his dealings with Major Neville, but considering the enormity of what was to come he decided that giving in to his natural impulses could, on this occasion, only hamper the successful outcome he was hoping for, so after nervously clearing his throat he embarked on his lengthy tale, which, even in his own ears, lacked conviction. As he prudently skirted around the fact that Major Denham had by no means liked the idea of being sent to keep vigil with Captain Waring for a spurious pending run, he could only hope that Major Neville accepted it more readily than had Major Denham.

To say that Major Denham had by no means liked the idea was a gross understatement. In his opinion he was convinced that it would turn out to be nothing more than another wild goose chase, and would therefore much prefer to leave it to Captain Waring, who seemed more than capable of dealing with it himself. As Major Denham had continued to strenuously argue the futility of such an action, Colonel Henderson had been rather nonplussed as to how to get rid of him as his absence was vital if tonight's plan was going to work, finally resorting to pulling rank by turning a request into an order.

As Captain Waring had not mentioned anything to Gideon this morning about having received word of a pending run tonight or that he was expecting Major Denham to keep him company during what would doubtless be a long and fruitless wait, Gideon wondered if there was another reason to account for his absence which Colonel Henderson did not want him to know about. He could only hope that it had nothing to do with Richard, but querying it could well lead to questions being asked he would rather not answer, merely nodding, "I see, Sir."

"Shall we go to my room, Major?" he asked, already beginning to lead the way.

"As you wish, Sir" Gideon inclined his head, much preferring to remain where he was.

"Please, do sit down Major," he invited when they had reached his upstairs room, indicating the chair on the opposite side of his desk.

"Thank you, Sir."

"So," he smiled as he made himself comfortable, "what news do you bring me?" he asked, raising a questioning eyebrow.

Although Gideon received several nods of approval as he related his meeting with Captain Waring, it was clear that his senior officer was on edge and doing his best to hide it. This was no less than the truth. Considering the enormity of what he had planned for tonight and his hopes resulting from it, not the least being to rid himself of this man sitting opposite him who seemed to be making it his sole aim to thwart him, he was extremely nervous and his attempts to brazen the interview out without him discovering the truth, was placing him under considerable strain.

"Good man, Waring" he commented. "Although," he pointed out, "his task is a hard one. I do not envy him. Of course," he nodded, taking a pinch of snuff, "I daresay that tonight's run will turn out to be nothing but a hoax as Major Denham seems to think, but every effort has to be made to stem this damnable trade!"

"Yes, Sir."

"Yes," he nodded. "These thieving rogues lead him a merry dance! But sooner or later they will be brought to see that their nefarious behaviour will not be tolerated, and once Richard Ferrers is caught and hung," he nodded vigorously, "they will not be so eager to embark on any more runs!"

"I realize his position is a difficult one," Gideon acknowledged, trying to hide his abhorrence, "but do you really believe that eliminating one man will make any difference?"

Colonel Henderson stared at him in disbelief. "Can you deny that Richard Ferrers encourages them?" he argued.

"As I have never met Richard Ferrers," he shrugged, easily able to condone this blatant lie with the knowledge that he was trying to save an innocent man from the gallows, "and Captain Waring admits that he has never been caught running cargoes at all, I really couldn't say, Sir."

Colonel Henderson's face became suffused with angry colour, and his previous mood of amiable patience was fast evaporating, but realizing that losing his temper, although relieving his feelings, would not serve him in the least. Thanks to Lytton putting him in the way of the true state of affairs, he was firmly convinced that Major Neville, if not hand in glove with the rogues himself, was certainly sympathetic, since it appeared that he was on closer terms with Miss Ferrers than he had ever suspected. As it was not in his interests to alert Major Neville either to what was going forward this evening or to the fact that he was aware of the underhanded game he had been playing all along, he bit down the angry words rising inside him. It took a few moments for him to regain control over his emotions, but eventually he mastered his overwhelming desire to throw the truth at him. "Now, about Miss Ferrers? What news there?" he demanded eagerly, leaning forward on his elbows, his bulbous blue eyes regarding Gideon expectantly.

"I very much regret, Sir" Gideon told him calmly, looking dispassionately at his senior officer, "I was unable to speak with her."

Those protruding eyes almost started out of their sockets at this. "*Unable!*

What do you mean, *unable*?" he demanded, clasping and unclasping his hands.

"I am afraid Miss Ferrers was indisposed and not receiving visitors," Gideon replied smoothly, fully aware that this was not the answer Colonel Henderson was hoping for.

"*Indisposed*!" he exclaimed, sitting bolt upright. "What do you mean, *indisposed*?"

"I understand Miss Ferrers was feeling unwell, Sir."

"Unwell! What was wrong with her?" he asked, clapping his hands on the arms of his chair and looking long and hard at Gideon.

"I really couldn't say, Sir" Gideon shook his head.

By no means pleased with this, Colonel Henderson eyed Gideon narrowly, his face taking on a dull red tinge. "You did not think to question it?" he thundered.

"I saw no reason to, Sir" Gideon replied unperturbedly, crossing one long leg negligently over the other.

"No reason!" he barked out. "What do you mean, *no reason*?"

"No, Sir" Gideon shook his head. "My knowledge of Miss Ferrers has never led me to believe that she would succumb to deceit merely in order to shelve her responsibilities."

As this was precisely what Colonel Henderson believed she had been doing all along, he stared across at Gideon with his mouth wide open. If he had needed proof to substantiate Robert's theory then surely this was it! Irrespective of the plan he was putting forward to solve his difficulties this calmly uttered statement merely added to his growing dislike for this man, who seemed to be quite unperturbed at the dissimulation he was perpetrating. He tried to tell himself that no matter what actually took place today at Ferrers Court it was quite beside the point, being totally irrelevant considering that after tonight it would not matter in the least, even so the very thought that he had been duped all this time angered him beyond bearing. Nevertheless, he had to somehow keep his tongue, but no matter how difficult this proved to be, he promised himself that before the evening was out he would repay Major Neville handsomely for daring to take him for a fool. It cost him a tremendous effort to ignore the angry words which rose to his lips, but eventually he managed to overcome his impulses.

The expression on Colonel Henderson's face, giving him the appearance of having been stuffed, was enough to tell Gideon that he was struggling to keep his temper, but short of calling him a liar there was very little he could do but accept what he had been told. "I regret that I was unable to speak with her regarding her brother," he remarked, "but other than invading the privacy of a lady's bedchamber to see for myself that she was indeed laid down upon her bed, there really was nothing else I could do but accept what I had been told."

In his dilemma, Colonel Henderson failed to appreciate such scruples. In his opinion Miss Ferrers deserved no such consideration, but was able to take some comfort from knowing that his plans to deal with her and her brother would go some way to recompensing him for all the trouble and humiliation he had suffered at their hands. Unfortunately, it was at this precise moment that a disturbing spectre raised its head. If what he had been told was true and Miss Ferrers was indeed laid down upon her bed, then no guarantee could be placed upon her accompanying Private Smith in response to the supposed letter from Major Neville, but even more disturbing was the recollection of what he had actually written. When he had put pen to paper he had automatically assumed that Major Neville and Miss Ferrers, whatever the true nature of their relationship, would, if nothing else, at least converse, but now he could not be certain as to what in fact did take place today at Ferrers Court, and knowing this resourceful young lady from experience, he had no doubt that she would immediately read the letter for what it actually was. Of course, there was every possibility that it was nothing but a ruse in order to gain precious time for their own devious ends, although what these may be he had no very clear idea. Nevertheless he still felt reasonably confident that, ill or not, Miss Ferrers would not fail to respond to what she believed was the Major's plea to go to him in order to discuss her brother's affairs. Commonsense told him that nothing would prevent her from going with Private Smith especially when he considered what was in all probability the true state of affairs existing between her and Major Neville. But despite this reasoning he could not quite rid his mind of doubt in that his plans could well be ruined, and this fact alone made him sweat, causing him to wipe his forehead with his handkerchief.

"I realize, of course," he acknowledged, clearing his throat, "that you were placed in a most awkward position but, really Major" he shook his head, "I cannot help but think that Miss Ferrers is merely playing for time."

Not having expected to come off so lightly from such a confession, Gideon looked narrowly across at his senior officer unable to believe that he was accepting his excuse quite so readily particularly when he considered the seriousness of his position, and therefore felt it behoved him to tread carefully. He knew he could trust Elizabeth and Salmon to play their part should Colonel Henderson take it into his head to descend upon them while he was visiting General Turville, but he must do all he could to try and prevent this from happening, and in an attempt to do this said warily, "You could be right Sir in thinking that Miss Ferrers is playing for time, but do you not think," he recommended cleverly, "that in allowing her to believe she has succeeded, it may well serve our purpose?"

"What do you mean?" he asked cautiously, those protruding eyes staring at Gideon from their fullest extent, suspecting some trick.

"In permitting Miss Ferrers to believe that we are showing her consideration," he explained, "it may well be that in a few days time, providing, of course, we do not press her in the meantime," he suggested meaningfully, "it could well be that by then she will have come to realize we are not the ogres she had at first thought but, on the contrary, prepared to understand her predicament."

In spite of his ever growing hatred for this man, Colonel Henderson could not but applaud his efforts, even so he felt it expedient to continue to show some sign of disapproval, which was not difficult considering the lengths they were prepared to go to in order to deceive him. His denunciation of the inhabitants of Ferrers Court, Elizabeth Ferrers in particular, whilst pithy and scathingly to the point, was nevertheless genuinely heartfelt, expressing his deep and intense dislike of them.

However much Gideon wanted to take up the cudgels in their defence he knew he could not. So close was Richard Ferrers to gaining his freedom that he could not allow anything to stand in the way of that. He may have neither liking nor respect for this man, but mollifying him for a while longer was essential, even if it meant embarking on yet more mendacity. Since he was unaware that His Grace was in Sussex and had already put his views forward together with the outline of a plan calculated to bring about the downfall of Richard Ferrers, he had no reason to suppose that Colonel Henderson had any idea that he was being deliberately mislead. Upon being asked when next he intended visiting such a den of liars and traitors, Gideon, interpreting this venomous description to mean Ferrers Court, explained that it would not be for a few more days as he had to return to London tomorrow on urgent family affairs.

"*Family affairs!*" he echoed, when he had recovered from the shock of this calmly uttered announcement. "What affairs?" he choked, spilling snuff down his coat.

"Private matters which require my immediate attention, Sir" Gideon explained without a blink.

"But this is very sudden, Major!" he exclaimed, rising hurriedly to his feet. "You never mentioned anything about the possibility of a return to town when you arrived."

Gideon had fully expected something like this and was quite prepared for it. "No, Sir" he shook his head. "Regrettably," he offered untruthfully, "I had hoped that my affairs would await the conclusion of this matter but, unfortunately, I had miscalculated how long it would take to deal with it." He saw that Colonel Henderson was on the point of spluttering something in answer to this, but quickly forestalled him. "I realize now that I was quite wrong in thinking that I could make an end of this business within a few days, but as we are going to allow Miss Ferrers several days grace," he reminded him smoothly, "my absence from the garrison will not really interfere with that."

There was really no argument to this reasoning but Colonel Henderson, eyeing Gideon closely, felt exasperated beyond endurance. Were it not for the fact that after tonight Major Neville would not be around to either meddle in his affairs or to frustrate his plans, he felt consumed with anger to know that he had deliberately manipulated him into a position which he could have done absolutely nothing about. Reluctant though he was to admit it, he had to acknowledge that Major Neville had played an extremely good hand, had done so in fact ever since he first came here just over six days ago. It was becoming increasingly clear to him that Major Neville, either out of loyalty to General Turville or for reasons of his own, believed in Richard Ferrers' innocence. Nothing else could explain away his deceit all this time, but if this was in fact the truth of it, and he failed to see how it could be otherwise, especially in view of what Robert had told him, it left him wondering if he knew that it was he and William Ferrers who were the real traitors and not Richard Ferrers. Then, of course, there was the question of those letters! If Major Neville knew that Richard Ferrers was innocent, then did he know about that incriminating correspondence? If so, did he know where those letters were hidden or, God forbid, did he already have them safe in his possession? But more than this was the terrifying thought that Major Neville's sudden and unexpected visit to town had nothing whatever to do with family affairs, but was specifically to lay the truth before General Turville. This could well be the case, particularly when he considered that to date he had done nothing but lie and cover up to protect the Ferrers family! If all this were not bad enough it cast doubts on Miss Ferrers' compliance with that letter. Did she know of the Major's return to town tomorrow or not? If she did then that letter would surely make her question why Major Neville was requesting her presence later this evening instead of preparing for a journey to London the next morning. Despite the plans set in motion, these nerve-racking thoughts sent a shiver down his spine and once again he had to wipe his forehead with his handkerchief. He was standing on the brink of disaster for which this man was partly responsible, but even though he told himself that now was not the time to lose his head, it took several minutes before he could pull himself together sufficiently to say, "I see your point, Major."

Gideon, witnessing these barely concealed signs of torment, had a fair idea of what was going through his mind, merely nodded in response to this. This man had known no compunction in blaming an innocent man for his own crimes; deliberately pointing the finger at Richard Ferrers with the help of his cousin. He had no more liking for saving William Ferrers than either Elizabeth or Salmon, and were it not for the fact that he had given his word to a lady, whose pride in her family went far beyond what William Ferrers deserved, he would willingly have left him to his fate. But Colonel Henderson was a different matter entirely. He experienced no remorse about the deceit he was perpetrating any more than he did over the fact that he was deliberately manoeuvring him towards his trial for treason. He very much doubted whether his forebears loyalty to the Stuarts had rubbed off onto him, had this been the case he could have felt some sympathy for his declaring for The Pretender. As it was, he had, with cold-blooded detachment, sought to have an honourable name besmirched as well as being the prime instigator in Viscount Easton's early death. Unaware of what was scheduled for this evening, Gideon watched his senior officer mentally grappling with his dilemma with complete disinterest, totally unmoved by the fear he must no doubt be experiencing.

"I see your thinking is not entirely without its merits," Colonel Henderson managed, regaining some control over himself, returning his handkerchief to his pocket with fingers that were far from steady. "However," he nodded, taking another pinch of snuff, "whilst I shall grant Miss Ferrers a few days grace, be under no illusion," he warned, "upon your return from London, I shall personally accompany you to Ferrers Court. Should Miss Ferrers still show signs of procrastination she shall immediately be placed under arrest. If this does not get her talking, then it will certainly bring her brother out into the open, whereupon he will be arrested." He looked at Gideon to see what affect this had had upon him but nothing could be gleaned from the impassive face looking calmly back at him. "Of course," he shrugged, "we must not forget that he is not only a traitor but a vicious criminal, and however unfortunate," he offered with spurious regret, "one must take into account that there is every likelihood of him trying to evade capture or, having been arrested, he will most probably make the attempt to escape. Should either of these possibilities occur," he shrugged, "there will be no alternative open to us but to shoot him on sight!"

So filled with disgust was he at this man's barely concealed pleasure at the thought of either eventuality coming to pass, that it was several minutes before Gideon could trust himself to speak. He had known for a long time that Colonel Henderson would do everything possible to ensure that Richard Ferrers never came to trial, indeed, it was the one thing he must avoid at all costs if he were to escape condemnation and arrest himself but, to have to sit and listen as well as offering his approval and support for such an action, was something he had no stomach for. As Colonel Henderson clearly expected a favourable response from him, he merely nodded. "Yes Sir," feeling the words stick in his throat.

"Now, Major" he said bracingly, "I think this calls for a celebratory drink."

"A drink, Sir?" Gideon asked, his eyes widening in surprise. "May I ask what cause we have to celebrate?"

"Why, the success of your excellent strategy, of course!" he smiled.

"Thank you, Sir" Gideon replied doubtfully, not at all honoured by this tribute. "But do you not think we are being somewhat premature?"

"You're far too modest, Major" Henderson told him, heading for the table behind his desk where a staggering array of decanters and glasses stood. "Now, tell me, which do you prefer; port or cognac?"

"If you don't mind, Sir" Gideon apologized, rising to his feet, the thought of celebrating something so iniquitous filling him with sickening disgust, "I ..."

"I *insist*, Major" he was told firmly.

"Very well, Sir" Gideon nodded reluctantly, "if you insist. I will take a glass of cognac."

Turning his back on Gideon, Colonel Henderson, in an effort to steady his nerves, began to entertain him with pieces of idle gossip and snippets of information to which his guest was taking very little notice. On the whole this meeting had gone far better than he had hoped, resulting in a precious stay of execution for the Ferrers family, and whilst he had no liking for what Colonel Henderson had proposed he had not envisaged sharing a glass of cognac with him to celebrate the fact. The urgency to save Richard Ferrers from this man's machinations occupied his thoughts to the exclusion of everything else, so much so that he entirely failed to notice the deft movement of Colonel Henderson's left hand as he retrieved a small glass phial hiding behind the array of decanters on the table, quickly and dexterously removing the top and emptying its contents into one of the glasses. Despite the ease with which he did this his hand visibly shook, and even if there were no plans in motion, he had never felt more like a stimulant than he did at this moment. Even in his own ears his voice sounded a little too forced and his conversation rather inconsequential, while at the same time he could not help wondering if William Ferrers had arrived or what he would do should his accomplice's nerves fail him.

Taking hold of the glass he had been handed Gideon stared down at the rich amber liquid that glowed in the light from the chandelier with barely concealed distaste. He was not averse to a glass of brandy, yet right now he felt it would choke him, but as he had been given no opportunity to refuse, he half raised the glass in answer to the toast Colonel Henderson was about to propose.

"To a successful conclusion!" he announced, taking a generous mouthful. "Come along, Major" he urged when Gideon made no effort to raise the glass to his lips, "it is much too good a cognac to waste."

He waited anxiously while Gideon made no move to take a drink, wondering what on earth he would do if he refused it. He could, of course, hit him over the head, but something told him that that would probably be easier said than done. Then to his relief he saw Gideon raise the glass to his lips and swallow some of the cognac which he himself was all too fond of. Taking advantage by encouraging him, with a heartiness he was far from feeling, to drink up. "You will take another, Major?"

"No, thank you Sir," Gideon shook his head, eager to be gone. "Thank you for your hospitality, Sir" he smiled, "but with your permission I will take my leave of you. There are certain things I must attend to before my departure tomorrow morning."

"Of course," he nodded, "I quite understand."

As Colonel Henderson needed a few more minutes for the drug to take effect, after all it would not do for him to collapse in the courtyard, he deliberately detained him by regaling him with an amusing anecdote, his eyes covertly watching his every move. "I hope your affairs are speedily concluded, Major," he nodded at length, "and look forward to seeing you back with us within a few days."

"Thank you, Sir" Gideon inclined his head.

"Your contribution to this business has been invaluable," he told him. "Indeed," he continued, "it is due to your efforts that we have progressed thus far."

"Thank you, Sir" Gideon said again growing uncomfortably aware that for some inexplicable reason he felt as though his legs no longer belonged to him and that his head was beginning to swim. Placing his half empty glass on the desk he raised an unsteady hand to his temple, shaking his head, his other hand quickly grasping the back of the chair as he felt himself sway.

"Is something wrong, Major?" Henderson enquired, his eyes watchful.

Colonel Henderson's voice seemed to be coming from a long way off, and his face getting further away, but even so Gideon retained sufficient alertness to notice the quick, almost furtive, glance Colonel Henderson threw at his glass, and although his vision was becoming more and more blurred and the room seemed to be moving around him, there came the awful realization that something had been put into his drink.

Colonel Henderson, who was now standing right in front of him, saw the recognition in those brown eyes, but just as Gideon was about to say something his legs gave way under him, collapsing into a lifeless heap on the floor.

For several minutes Colonel Henderson did not move, staring almost dazedly at Gideon's inanimate body as it lay on the floor in front of him. He had no need to be told the enormity of taking such drastic action, but necessity was a hard master and self-preservation even more so. There was no way if he could help it that he was going to be charged with treason all because a slip of a girl stubbornly refused to give her brother up. Had she have done so then none of this would have been necessary, on top of which, Major Neville was not only in league with her and her brother but doing his utmost to bring about his downfall; apart from which he was still smarting from knowing that Major Neville had been playing him for a fool all this time. He may not know the whole truth but it was evident he knew enough to be dangerous if left unchecked. From the moment the idea came to him, so blindingly audacious, he knew that not to take the opportunity Providence was offering him would be foolhardy. It may not be in Robert's plans to do away with the Major any more than it was Elizabeth Ferrers, but it was certainly expedient as far as he was concerned.

Absently moving Gideon's glass away from the edge of the table he then looked down at his lifeless body with satisfaction, his loose mouth parting into a smile. Two birds with one stone and all thanks to Miss Ferrers! This was the only way his safety could be assured, and with no hint of blame rebounding on him or William Ferrers; it was the perfect solution to all their difficulties. After swallowing the remains in his glass he bent down to ascertain that Gideon was indeed unconscious, but apart from a faint pulse no sign of life could be evinced. Rising to his feet he hurried over to the door and pulling it open with nervous fingers shouted to William Ferrers who had been waiting in Major Denham's room trying not to think of what he was aligned to, not to mention the repercussions should this night's work come to nothing.

After running up the stairs two at a time he joined his accomplice considerably flushed and out of breath, but one look at the unconscious body lying on the floor caused him to turn quite pale. Not until he had seen Major Neville enter the tower quarters did he feel it safe to jump down from the box of the carriage to creep stealthily inside, heartily relieved to know that Major Denham would not be there to fire questions at him. Too nervous to sit down he had paced the floor clenching and unclenching his hands as he wondered what was going on in the room above. Although he could hear their voices he could not make out what was being said, and therefore had no idea how the meeting was progressing. He was by no means reconciled to the idea of drugging Major Neville, foreseeing all manner of problems arising from it, but as Colonel Henderson had dictated the course of this evening's events, apparently with His Grace's blessing, he had no choice but to fall in with whatever was suggested. He could only hope that Henderson would have no difficulty in rendering the Major unconscious, because from what he had seen of him he had not struck him as being either slow on the uptake or stupid. But more than this was his concern about abducting his cousin. Admittedly, she had proved extremely recalcitrant when it came to revealing her brother's whereabouts, but if only she had been a little more conciliatory or prepared to see the problem from another point of view other than Richard's, then this desperate action could have been avoided. It was not simply because Elizabeth was not fool enough to be coaxed out of her home without a good reason for doing so that worried him so much as Richard getting to hear of it. The intention, of course, was that he should, but whilst it was all very well for Henderson to assure him that he would make certain he did, Richard was no fool and would be bound to realize it was a trap and therefore no guarantee could be placed on him falling into it. Henderson was relying heavily on him coming to his sister's rescue, and when one remembered the close relationship between brother and sister, there was no reason to suppose otherwise, but he was honest enough to admit to himself that the thought of coming face to face with his cousin was something he was not looking forward to. The thought of meeting Richard after all that had happened, not to mention the abduction of his sister, was enough to make him inwardly cringe, and if there was any way he could have avoided it he would. He may not have enjoyed the most comfortable of relationships with Richard, but by dint of placatory measures and careful manoeuvring, especially on his part, they had somehow managed to exist together without any show of open hostility. Nevertheless, he would have to be a fool not to realize that Richard had nothing but contempt for him, and this being so he would be in no frame of mind to consider their relationship when he learned about what had happened to his sister. Deep in his heart he knew that Richard would not give a moment's consideration to the fact that a trap had been laid for him any more than he would to them being cousins', and the mere thought of what he would do to him made him feel sick. The best he could hope for therefore, was that the first and, in his opinion, the most favoured part of their two pronged plan, would succeed, obviating the need for him to come to Elizabeth's aid and thereby preventing them from coming face to face with one another. But no matter which way it developed, there was one overriding aspect that caused him more concern than anything else Should this evening's events prove successful, although at this moment in time he was not at all sure they would, what would they do with Elizabeth? It seemed to him that it would be the height of folly to allow her to go free because no reliance whatever could be placed on her holding her tongue and keeping what had happened to herself. By the same token they could not keep her prisoner for ever, which left only one possible option; the very idea of which rendered him almost paralysed with dread.

By the time he was eventually called upstairs he had already built himself up into a highly nervous state and the sight of the lifeless body in front of him was all that was needed to put the finishing touches to his agitation. He swallowed convulsively, his eyes dilating as he shot a scared look from Major Neville's insensible form to Colonel Henderson, who was himself by now quite on edge with apprehension. Both men were extremely tense, but it was Colonel Henderson who pulled himself together first, sharply recommending his accomplice to stop standing like a stock and hurry. At these tersely delivered words William Ferrers was jolted back to the matter in hand, but although he had been assured that the Major was fully unconscious and would remain so for several hours, nothing would convince him that he would not come round before they had him safely bestowed in the cellar of Hamstoke House.

William Ferrers was himself only a slightly built man and therefore his attempts to raise Gideon into an upright position was not as easy as either of them had predicted. Colonel Henderson, muttering something under his breath, eventually came to his assistance, and between them they somehow managed to carry or drag Gideon's dead weight body down the steps to Major Denham's room, propping him up against the wall while William Ferrers pulled open the heavy oak door to peer apprehensively all around in the gathering darkness to make sure that no one was about. The thought of having to drag Gideon's inert body down even more steps was more than William Ferrers could bear, but as there was no avoiding it, he stepped back inside and putting his arm around his waist managed to drag him down those outside steps, his sword clanking abnormally loud on each one while the toes of his boots scraped on the stone, heartily relieved when he was finally able to bundle him headfirst into the carriage. It was a moment or two before he was able to recover his breath sufficiently to climb onto the box, during which time he was not only getting soaking wet but had to endure listening to his accomplice's instructions yet again. He was already well aware of what he had to do, considering any further recapitulation as unnecessary, not only that but it was far too dangerous to linger as anyone could come along and see something was amiss. Already he could see a number of soldiers frequenting the courtyard and the last thing he wanted or needed was to be accosted by one of them as to what was going on. Eventually though he made his escape from Colonel Henderson, pulling away at such a speed that more than one curious stare was aimed in his direction.

CHAPTER EIGHTEEN

Following Gideon's departure, Elizabeth spent the next hour or so with her aunt, at the end of which time they had resumed their happy and comfortable relationship. She knew perfectly well the reasons behind her decision to protect William, and whilst she would never really be brought to accept it, it was thanks in part to Gideon's persuasions and her aunt's palpable distress over what was happening to her family, that she finally resigned herself to the inevitable.

That her cousin was totally undeserving of the efforts being made on his behalf was certain, but whether he would appreciate them was not. She had never once known William consider anyone other than himself, and on the few occasions he had, there had always been an element of personal benefit attached. She dreaded to think what Richard would say, much less do, when he learned of this, because she could see no way of keeping it from him, but as there were other and more pressing problems facing them and protecting William from the repercussions of his own actions was really anything but a foregone conclusion, she decided to put it to the back of her mind. There would be time enough later for explanations; providing, of course, all Gideon's attempts on Richard's behalf to save him from the unthinkable proved successful!

For a woman of her spirit and independence she was surprised to discover how much she had come to depend on Gideon, but the truth was that after months of intense anxiety as well as striving to find a way of alleviating the difficulties which beset Richard without success, she had been only too relieved to lay her worries onto the capable shoulders of a man who not only believed in his innocence but was in a far better position to assist him than she would ever be. It had not taken Salmon's assurances that he was a gentleman and the very antithesis of Colonel Henderson or the fact that General Turville had been a friend of her father's, that had persuaded her to trust him; her own judgement had told her she could. From the moment she had first laid eyes on him she had been irresistibly drawn to him, and inexperienced though she was she would have had to be blind not to notice that he had felt the same compelling attraction, and whatever misgivings had assailed her upon discovering the purpose of his visit, these were very soon put to flight.

Despite the fact that her parent's marriage had been a love match and they had remained devoted to one another throughout their life together, her aunt had nevertheless felt it prudent to warn her that that happy circumstance was the exception rather than the rule, and therefore she was not to look for love in marriage.   As long as her husband was good to her she advised, giving her no cause for complaint or sorrow, then she could count herself most fortunate. She had certainly seen more than enough evidence to substantiate this statement during her time in London for the season, but somehow she refused to believe that there was nothing more to marriage than either convenience or financial expediency, and knew beyond doubt that she could not marry solely for these reasons and no other.   Those offers for her hand therefore, much to her aunt's disapproval, had been politely declined without the least regret, much preferring to remain single for the rest of her days than to be married to a man for whom she felt not the slightest spark of love.   Her father, upon discovering such ingratitude from his indignant sister, stating that she washed her hands of her niece, had merely smiled and embraced his daughter, telling her that he for one had no desire to push her into a marriage which would be distasteful to her. Those aspirants to her hand, whether genuinely in love with her or not, may have been charming as well as persuasive in their efforts to win her, knowing to a nicety how to evoke a response from the object of their gallantry, but none of them had kept her awake at night much less made her heart jump or her pulses race.

Having had her fill of the military, she would never have thought it possible that she could have fallen in love with a red-coat, and certainly not at first sight.   It seemed incredible therefore, that she could have tumbled headlong into love with a man without knowing the first thing about him, especially one who wore the King's uniform.   She had always believed that love would take time to grow and develop and not hit one like a thunderbolt when one least expected it, but from the moment of first making his acquaintance she had been very conscious of him as well as the alien sensations he had evoked inside her.   She would have had to be blind or totally insensate not to recognize the affect she had had on Gideon as well as his awareness of her, but whilst she had no explanation to account for this phenomenon, she did know that her feelings had nothing whatever to do with Salmon's assurances as to his integrity or the fact that he was prepared to help Richard.   It was a startling revelation to discover that a man who had been totally unknown to her only a week previously, would come to mean as much to her as her own brother, or that she could miss him so much that even before he had disappeared from sight down the avenue, she longed to be with him again. She would always love Richard, indeed, he meant everything to her, but her feelings for Gideon were quite different.   She could lay no claim to having experience in these matters, but the woman inside her knew she had not mistaken her heart and that Gideon was the only man she would ever love or make her feel as though her heart would burst from sheer joy when he kissed her. If anything were to happen to Richard she would find it impossible to fill the gap his loss would leave in her life, but the mere thought of losing the only man she could not live without was far too painful to contemplate.   That she could feel this way over someone who had

353

unexpectedly entered her life only a few short days ago, was so remarkable that she had to pinch herself several times to ensure she had not dreamt the whole; but, if nothing else, it certainly justified her refusal of those most obliging offers!

She knew that Gideon had no alternative but to visit General Turville if Richard's affairs were to be settled as speedily as possible, but even so she hoped he would return soon, as not only did she feel quite bereft without him, but the sooner Richard was back where he belonged the better.

When she thought of the dangers Gideon had been exposed to in trying to retrieve those letters on Richard's behalf she went cold with fear. No one knew better than she what Colonel Henderson and her cousin were capable of, and therefore tried to banish the images from her mind as to what could have happened if by some mischance he had been discovered in the cell block during his attempt to gain the evidence necessary to clear Richard of any wrong doing. She realized only too well that it would be in Colonel Henderson's and her cousin's interests to ensure that any proof of their complicity in treason must never see the light of day, and this being so they would stop at nothing to suppress the disclosure of any evidence against them. Gideon may have succeeded in misleading Colonel Henderson thus far, but he was no fool and sooner or later he was bound to discover the mendacity which had been perpetrated against him, and once he did, then the chances were that he would keep a closer eye on Gideon rendering it difficult for him to make any kind of manoeuvre to assist Richard. She could only hope and pray therefore that Colonel Henderson would not discover the truth surrounding the recovery of those letters before Gideon could reach London and put them before General Turville.

Salmon, no nearer to liking the scheme proposed to shield William than he ever was, maintained a dignified silence; only his occasional sniffs giving any indication as to his feelings. Elizabeth however, knew precisely what these were, but since there was nothing she could personally do to change matters, decided the least said to him about it the better.

Since her aunt had announced she was far too exhausted to join her niece for dinner that evening, Elizabeth debated whether she too would shun the dinner table, but since her cousin had left the house some time previously stating, for the second evening in a row, that he would not be back to dine with her, she decided she would venture down to the dining room after all. As there was some time yet before she need change her gown she sat by the fire in the sitting room pondering the situation facing them with her chin propped in her hand, gazing through the window at the sodden landscape outside. The rain, which had been threatening all day, by half past four had begun in earnest, beating relentlessly against the window panes, bringing to mind how, as children, she and Richard would both choose a rivulet to see which one reached the bottom of the window first. As a ride was out of the question in such weather there was nothing she could do to work off her growing frustration and had to content herself with tapping her foot on the floor. Richard's difficulties may be well on the way to being solved, but he was by no means out of the wood yet. They had always been very close and his relationship with Jane had not changed that, and prior to the advent of Gideon in her life, next to her father she loved him most of all, and would do anything to help protect the brother she adored from the forces bearing down upon him.

As a child she had followed him almost everywhere, and now, as she looked back, she could only marvel at his patience when he had been off on some adventure with his friends only to turn round to find his sister in tow. As she could not be shaken off like Jane, she had been allowed to accompany them, taking part in their boisterous activities including climbing trees which had necessarily meant torn dresses as well as cuts and bruises. He in turn indulged and protected her, shielding her from the consequences of her conduct, which, had said her mother, was very far from ladylike, blaming Richard for encouraging her. A smile played at the corner of her mouth as she recalled these reminiscences, and even though she had outgrown such hoydenish behaviour, she would not trade those happy carefree days or her memories of them for anything. If she were in trouble, then Richard would not hesitate in coming to her rescue and if there was anything she could do to hasten his reinstatement, then it would not be lacking.

So lost in thought was she that she barely heard the clanging of the bell in the distance and Salmon, entering the sitting room some minutes later, found it necessary to attract her attention twice before she became aware she was no longer alone. Looking from the letter he held in his hand and then at her, said with foreboding, "From the Major."

"Gideon?" she questioned, rising hurriedly to her feet, taking the letter held out to her. As she broke the seal he went on to tell her that the man who delivered it, a Private Smith, was waiting for her in the hall. She looked from the letter to Salmon, a worried expression entering her eyes. "I don't understand," she shook her head, reading it for the second time.

"My Dear Miss Ferrers,

I have no wish to alarm you, but since we spoke this afternoon a circumstance has arisen concerning Richard, about which I must speak with you. As it is not possible for me to come to you, if you would accompany the bearer of this letter, he will bring you safely to me.

Private Smith is entirely trustworthy and has my fullest confidence. You may therefore repose your trust in him.

Yours, Major Neville

"What could he have possibly discovered since leaving here?" Handing the letter to Salmon for him to read. "Does this mean he will not be returning to

355

London tomorrow after all?"

"You mustn't go!" Salmon urged, looking up from the letter into her troubled face. "It's a trap."

"A trap!" she exclaimed. "It can't be," she shook her head. "It's from Gideon."

"That's what it *says*," he said sceptically, "but *I've* never heard the Major speak of this Private Smith!"

"No, nor have I," she acknowledged. Torn between concern for Richard and Salmon's caution, she debated the issue, chewing her bottom lip.

"I have to go Salmon," she told him at length. "Something must have happened to Richard."

"You don't know that, Mistress" he shook his head, following in her wake as she left the sitting room. "If only you'd wait and think a minute!"

"If Gideon did not write this letter, then who did?" she demanded seeing the concern etched all over his craggy face. Whilst she was grateful for his care of them she knew that she had little choice but to go. "Salmon," she pleaded, coming to an abrupt halt resting a hand on his arm, "I have to go, you must see that he would not have written to me if it were not important."

"Supposing he *did* write it," he put in doubtfully.

"But who else could have written it if not …?"

"Precisely!" he nodded as she looked at him in horror.

"No," she shook her head after giving it some thought. "I don't credit it. Colonel Henderson cannot have done!"

Salmon went on to warn her that not only was Colonel Henderson dangerous, but so desperate did he regard his situation that he would not put anything beyond him.

"I realize that," she conceded, "but I cannot ignore it! If something has happened, then I must go."

"You don't know anything *has* happened," he told her. "Besides," he pointed out, believing he was throwing down a clincher, "just look at the way it's worded."

"What do you mean?" she asked sharply, unfolding the single sheet and scanning it again.

"Well," he nodded, "to say the Major's been haunting the house for days and the pair of you get along wondrous great, it's as though he barely knows you!"

He was quite right of course, but then this could easily be due to the fact that it had obviously been written in haste. Upon hearing this Salmon shook his head, saying frustratedly, "I *wish* you wouldn't go."

"Salmon," she cried, "it could be a trap as you say, I don't know, although why you should think it is is more than I can tell, but whether it is or not I must go."

Not all his warnings were having the slightest impact on her, and as he walked beside her along the length of the great hall he continued to advise caution, but although she nodded her head in acknowledgement it was clear she was taking no notice.

Private Smith, who had been patiently awaiting her in the hall, had spent his time looking about him with interest. He may have taken the King's shilling in order to escape the consequences of his illegal activities, but he had not totally abandoned his past career, over the course of which he had turned his hand to most things. From what he could see of it if the rest of the house was anything like the hall, a veritable storehouse of treasures, then it was certainly worth a closer look, but although attempting to remove one or two little items he had already spied with a knowledgeable eye would be simple enough, passing them on would not be so easy.

It had not taken Colonel Henderson long to learn about his nefarious past and put it to good use, and Private Smith, not averse to a little underhand dealing, had no objection in coming to the aid of his commanding officer as favours could always be turned to good account, especially when he saw that he was a man more concerned with appearances than ethics. His timely assistance had therefore resulted in him being excused duty on more than one occasion, and whilst this had raised eyebrows in certain quarters, no one had dared question it, not even Major Denham. He may not know of Colonel Henderson's dalliance with treason, but in view of what he had managed to discover he would lay any odds that tonight's scheme was in some way connected with Richard Ferrers. He knew enough to realize that this elusive individual was posing problems which Colonel Henderson was clearly having difficulty in solving, were it otherwise then why else would this officer from London be here? If the Major had been making any headway at all in apprehending Richard Ferrers then he would wager any odds that he would not be here now on the point of committing what was no less than abduction! He may have no qualms about doing whatever was asked of him, but removing Miss Ferrers from her home was very different to what he had previously set his hand to and certainly could not be ranked alongside that of smuggling letters in and out for Colonel Henderson or to sneaking in the port and cognac he was so very partial to. But even though he had accepted the task given him without question he nevertheless had the distinct feeling that should anything go wrong or, worse, something happen to Miss Ferrers, then it would be he who would have to pay the piper and not his commanding officer. Not only this, but if all he had heard about Richard Ferrers were true, then it would go ill with whoever harmed his sister and, no matter how much the sweetener he had been given, it would not do him a mite of good.

None of these thoughts however were allowed to show, and when Elizabeth finally joined him in the hall she saw nothing in this fresh complexioned young man to cause her to feel either anxiety or concern, indeed, he was extremely polite and courteous, removing his hat on her entrance and executing a tolerable bow, enquiring if he had the honour of addressing Miss Ferrers.

"Yes," she nodded, "I am Miss Ferrers."

"Major Neville sends his compliments, Ma'am" he told her.

"I understand I am to accompany you," she said, indicating the letter in her hand. "Where is it you are taking me?"

"You would not know the place," he replied, avoiding Salmon's eye, "but Major Neville required me to tell you that he offers you his apologies for removing you from your home at such an hour, but he will personally escort you back later." This may not have been word for word what Colonel Henderson had been drumming into his head ever since last night, but it was near enough.

Elizabeth nodded, but Salmon, still dubious about the whole affair, opened his mouth to ply this young man with one or two pertinent questions, but to his vexation was immediately forestalled by Elizabeth who unceremoniously took hold of his arm and pulled him to one side. Private Smith, who had no doubt that he could deal with this old man adequately enough should the need arise, much preferred to keep things as pleasant as possible without arousing suspicion and thereby creating the devil of a stir. If Richard Ferrers was as handy with his pistols as he had been led to believe, then he wanted to give him no more encouragement than was necessary to seek him out for causing harm to either his sister or family retainer, and was therefore extremely relieved when he saw her run up the stairs to return not long after with a cloak draped around her shoulders. He had not been able to make out what had been said between them, but from the looks of it her overseer was by no means mollified, and certainly not enough to prevent him from throwing several sharp looks in his direction. Colonel Henderson, confident that this young woman would fall in with his plan to abduct her without question, had given him no instructions about what to do should she refuse to accompany him. As he had never before been called upon to remove a young lady from the protection of her home against her will, he had no very clear idea of what he would do should she prove obstructive, and was therefore glad to know that he would not have to make any kind of attempt to forcibly eject her.

A few more words with Salmon and she was ready to leave following Private Smith outside, where he strode ahead to quickly open the carriage door for her. The last thing he wanted was for this family stalwart to finally persuade her into not going at the last minute, and in order to prevent any such eventuality he took hold of her arm and assisted her to step inside. Immediately the door was closed upon her he jumped nimbly up onto the box, whipping up the horses without any loss of time.

Pulling her cloak closer around her she looked back to catch a glimpse of Salmon standing where she had left him, making no attempt to go inside but watching the coach as it disappeared down the avenue. Too nervous to sit back against the squabs she sat stiffly upright with her hands clasped tightly on her lap. Having emerged through the main gates, leaving the grounds of Ferrers Court behind, they turned left, making their way towards Little Turton, but when the carriage eventually rumbled on straight through the village she very soon lost track of their direction. She leaned forward in her seat to peer outside but the rapidly fading light made it difficult to catch sight of any familiar landmarks. It may have been a well sprung vehicle but this did not prevent her from being jolted at regular intervals as it sped over roads which were either uneven or in a bad state of repair rendering parts into quagmires. In an effort to take her mind off whether or not she had made the right decision in embarking on such a journey as well as her concerns over Richard and the authenticity of that letter, she attempted again to look out of the window to see if she could make out some recognizable sight, but due to the falling darkness as well as the worsening state of the glass in the windows and doors, which were becoming liberally splashed with mud, it was becoming increasingly more difficult to identify her surroundings. Occasionally she caught a glimpse of a light in the distance but as it was impossible to say where they were coming from, she realized it was futile to continually try and discover where she was, sinking back against the squabs not daring to think where she would finally find herself. Every now and then Salmon's warnings came forcibly to mind, but somehow she managed to ignore them, telling herself that he was being unduly cautious. If only Gideon had given some indication as to her destination she would have felt a little better, but after giving it some thought realized that she must have been right in the first place when she had told Salmon he had most probably written the letter in haste and either overlooked it or decided it was unimportant. After what seemed like an eternity it was noticeable that they were reducing their speed, and as she leaned forward to look out she could see they were entering a village. She had no idea which one it was, but once they reached the other end of what appeared to be the main street, their speed picked up again, only to slacken a short time later as it veered off the main road. From the sound of the crunching noise made by the carriage wheels she gained the impression that they were travelling down a driveway, and when she eventually managed to see lights emanating from what appeared to be a private dwelling she was convinced of it. Somehow this seemed to settle her nerves, and when they finally stopped and Private Smith jumped down to open the door and to hand her down, she felt a little more cheered.

She found herself standing outside what appeared to be a grey stone three-storey house with neat flower beds beneath the sash windows on either side of the front door, but before she could look around her more particularly she was straightaway assisted up the three shallow steps whereupon the door was opened to her by a man in a light blue liveried uniform. Having bowed her in, Private

Smith wished her goodnight, the heavy oak door closing with a thud behind her as she stepped further into the square and lofty hall. She heard the carriage being driven away, and just as she was beginning to wonder where Gideon was and whose house he had had her conveyed to, the man in the liveried uniform, in a voice as impartial as his expression, asked her to follow him. He led her across the stone flagged floor to a mahogany door which faced the main front door, bowing as he opened it for her to enter. At first she did not think anyone was in the room, but when she heard the door close with a snap behind her, she swung round to stare in horror at the very last person she wanted to see.

"*You!*" she cried, her eyes reflecting her shock and dismay.

"Good evening, Miss Ferrers" Colonel Henderson bowed mockingly, unable to prevent the satisfied smile which came to his lips over his successful strategy.

He was certainly relieved that this particular part of his plan had worked, because whilst he knew that nothing would have kept her away from Major Neville under normal circumstances, he had dreaded to think what he would have done had she really been unwell and unable to comply with the letter's request, or even took it for what it actually was!

"Where is Major Neville?" she asked urgently, her eyes darting round the room.

"Major Neville?" he repeated, raising a questioning eyebrow. "I am very much afraid that it will be some considerable time before you can see him," he informed her, his eyes glinting. "He is at the moment," he told her gratifyingly, "what one might call 'indisposed'."

"What have you done with him?" she demanded, her eyes blazing.

"Nothing to alarm you," he assured her, determined to keep his temper on a tight rein. "I have merely rendered it impossible for him to intervene in my plans; something he has been in the habit of doing thus far "

"What do you mean?" she demanded, her heart beating so fast she could hardly breathe.

He took time to answer this, slowly raising a pinch of snuff to his nostril, a tiny residue falling onto his scarlet coat which he flicked off with a thick forefinger. "It would seem that you and Major Neville have been extremely busy of late. Oh yes," he nodded when he saw her expression, "I know how the two of you have been working against me and doing your utmost to protect your brother, but *you* must know that I cannot allow such a thing to continue."

"*You* sent that letter!" she accused, her brain reeling in shock and anger over her own stupidity in not listening to Salmon and her own instincts. "It was nothing but a trick to get me here!" she cried, her face very much flushed.

"I regret the necessity for such deceit but, you see," he apologized mockingly, "I knew you would not come here by my invitation."

"Where am I? Why am I here?" she asked sharply.

"You would not know the place were I to tell you," he informed her. "As for the reason you are here," he shrugged, "I should have thought that would be obvious."

"What it is you want?" she demanded, her eyes darting towards the door.

"Why, what I have always wanted, Miss Ferrers," he told her softly. "Your brother."

"So, you're at that again!" she scorned, wondering if there was some way she could reach the door before he could stop her.

"I never left it, Miss Ferrers" he told her readily, realizing what was going through her mind.

"I have told you I don't know how many times that I have no idea where my brother is," she said heatedly, frantically trying to think of a way out of this predicament.

"And *I* have told *you* I don't know how many times that I do not believe you," he smiled, frustrating any attempt on her part to escape by positioning himself between her and the door.

"Do you really believe that by bringing me here you will frighten me into revealing his whereabouts?" she asked scathingly. "I would die rather!" she flung at him.

"That *could* turn out to be quite a prophetic statement, Miss Ferrers" he warned menacingly, experiencing no twinge of conscious at the thought of ridding himself of this obdurate young woman who had caused him far too many problems.

"You wouldn't *dare* lay a hand on me!" she cried, her eyes flashing.

"You underrate me, Miss Ferrers" he told her. "This matter is now of some moment."

"For you, certainly!" she flung at him, taking some small satisfaction from the deep red tinge that flooded his face.

"So, you know that much!" he remarked at length, not at all certain whether to be glad or not that she had discovered the truth but, if nothing else, it reinforced his belief that not only were brother and sister working together as he had always suspected but also that Major Neville had joined with them against him. This did not necessarily mean that his position was entirely hopeless; without those letters they could do nothing to further Ferrers' cause, and he could only hope that by laying Major Neville by the heels he had managed to thwart any attempt on his part to retrieve them. Of course, if he had them in his possession already then it placed a very different light on the matter, but considering the Major's present and rather hopeless position he did not allow himself to worry unduly over it, because should this indeed turn out to be the case after all, then all was still not lost. In fact, he had no doubt that he would be able to prise the whereabouts of those letters out of him, especially once he knew that he held Elizabeth Ferrers captive.

"Yes, I know!" she nodded, her eyes sparkling. "I know too that you and my cousin will surely hang for what you have done!"

"We shall see your brother hang instead," he told her, biting down on his anger.

"You must be optimistic indeed to think so," she said contemptuously, "especially when one considers how he has so far managed to elude you!"

"His elusiveness," he informed her with satisfaction, "is about to come to an end."

She threw him a scornful look. "You really believe that by holding me here against my will I shall be brought into giving Richard up?"

"No," he shook his head. "You see, that is not why you are here."

She looked straight at him and knew instantly the significance of this evening's events. "This is nothing but a trap!" she cried. "You have brought me here in order to draw my brother out into the open!" Oh why hadn't she listened to Salmon?

"Do not look so shocked," he told her, "your presence here is entirely your own fault. Had you given your brother up to me when I first asked you to, you would not be here now."

She cast him such a look that momentarily it quite startled him. He knew perfectly well what she thought of him, but the contempt and disgust in those wide blue eyes made him swallow uncomfortably. "You really are quite despicable!" she threw at him.

"I am anything you please," he bit out, his face flushing, "but I *will* have your brother!"

She looked scathingly across at him. "You really think that Richard is stupid enough to fall into such a trap?" she scorned. "You will have to do better, I think!" she exclaimed.

He fully realized what she was trying to do and at any other time he would not have been unappreciative of her efforts, but not only was he in no mood for delaying tactics but so convinced was he that his strategy would work, especially now that he had scaled the one hurdle which could make or break his plans, that he was not going to allow her to either undermine him or to try and persuade him that he had misread her brother's character. His experience of Richard Ferrers was such that he found it impossible to believe that he would not come to her aid, in fact so certain was he that he would not only rise to the bait but could be relied upon to totally disregard the fact that a trap had been cunningly laid for him. He may question the rumours which filtered through to him about the abduction of his sister, but he believed he had by now come to a pretty fair estimate of that young man's character, and unless he had grossly underestimated him, he had no doubt at all that he would be more than prepared to risk his own safety in order to come to her rescue.

When Robert had outlined the rudiments of a plan to draw Richard Ferrers into a trap the finer elements of it had been left to him, and so carefully had he set about the matter that he failed to see a chink in its armour, much less how it could go wrong, particularly when he considered how close brother and sister were. Richard Ferrers had proved more than once just how astute he really was but, when faced with the knowledge that his sister was in difficulties, he was fairly sure that he knew him sufficiently well to be able to say that he would not hesitate in coming to her assistance, irrespective of the consequences to himself. Ordinarily he would have to agree with her when she said that her brother was not stupid enough to be taken in by his scheming but, on this occasion, she had grossly erred, although she did not know it. He had left no room for error or miscalculation; his plans having been too cleverly laid for anything to go awry, and once this young man was in his custody he had no doubt at all that he would soon be brought to tell him where those letters were hidden, or if Major Neville had indeed already located them on his behalf, especially when he knew that his sister would suffer for his silence. Robert had more than once condemned him for his inefficiency but this time he would prove him wrong.

Something in his face told Elizabeth that she had failed in her attempt to dent his confidence, but by no means deterred tried another tack. "You can't seriously believe that Richard will calmly walk in through the front door and exchange himself for me?" she asked astounded.

He considered for a moment, looking at her flushed and angry face, her expression a nice mix of contempt and disbelief. Taking a moment or two to answer her he helped himself to another pinch of snuff, and not until he had returned the small silver box to his pocket did he say, "No, I don't expect any such thing."

She tilted her head in enquiry, her eyes questioning, but nothing quite prepared her for his disclosure.

"You know, Miss Ferrers" he sighed, "between you, you and your brother have put me to no small inconvenience and, now, it appears Major Neville has joined your ranks against me. But, now" he enlightened her with malicious relish, "it is *I* who have the upper hand. I see you doubt that!" he remarked as he saw the look of scepticism which crossed her face. "I promise you it is so," he nodded. "You see," he told her pleasurably, "I suspected that Major Neville was more closely allied to you and your brother than he led me to believe," he lied glibly, having no wish to appear dull-witted or slow on the uptake, "but once I had those suspicions confirmed" he confessed, "it was no small matter to put two and two together and read between the lines of what he had told me about the current state of affairs. So, you see," he shrugged, "even if I had believed him when he told me

363

that you were indisposed and laid down upon your bed, I knew that nothing would keep you from him and that you would respond to the plea to accompany Private Smith." He watched in contented silence the various emotions which flitted across her face, and after congratulating himself on succeeding in forcing her into submission at last said, with a confidence she could not mistake, "Upon hearing the rumours I have caused to be spread, your brother will automatically assume that I have you safe at the garrison and will, unless I have grossly misjudged him," he shook his head doubtfully, "immediately make his way there to effect a rescue, only to discover that every soldier has been placed on alert with orders to arrest him but, should he prove uncooperative by attempting to escape, they are to shoot him on sight." Ignoring her shocked gasp, he continued "*If*, by some miracle, he does escape detection and manages to make his way to my quarters after all, far from finding his sister somewhat dramatically tied to a chair," he grimaced, "he will find a letter instead informing him that I have you here. Should he again be fortunate enough to leave the garrison without being seen he will, or so I would have thought, come straight here to secure your release, where I shall deal with him once and for all, and *this* time," he told her firmly, "there will be no Major Neville to come to his assistance."

She knew he was desperate to escape the penalties of his treachery but that he would resort to such devious tactics as this shocked her. "My God!" she exclaimed, when she had eventually found her voice. "You must be mad!"

"No," he shook his head, "I am quite sane, I assure you." As if to prove this point he told her unsympathetically, "Having done your possible to thwart my efforts to seek out your brother you have rendered it necessary for me to apprehend him by any means at my disposal, and however much you may deprecate the methods I have been forced to adopt, you must agree that they are foolproof. So you see, Miss Ferrers" he smiled unpleasantly, "you *will* lead me to him one way or the other."

She shook her head, bewildered. "I can't believe you would go to such lengths!"

"Desperation, Miss Ferrers" he inclined his head, "knows no bounds."

"You really would see an innocent man shot in order to hide your crimes!" she exclaimed, choked. "You don't seriously expect to get away with it?"

"Oh, but I do," he told her. "And as for the Major," he pointed out in answer to her unspoken question, "I am afraid that all his strenuous efforts on your behalf have been for nothing. You must see," he shook his head, "that with or without those letters he has clearly gleaned enough information to not only damage my reputation but could do me irreparable harm. It would therefore be an act of gross stupidity on my part to ignore this and allow him to take his findings to Sir John Turville." He raised a sceptical eyebrow. "Surely you did not really believe that I would be taken in by such a tale as returning to town on 'family affairs'?" he asked, easily overlooking his earlier panic and alarm when he had heard this.

She did not need to have this statement interpreted its significance was plain enough. She turned deathly pale at the thought of what he was intending and her eyes were huge with fear as she stared at him, her small hands gripping the back of a chair to support her. The look in his eyes were such that she knew he was not lying or merely trying to frighten her, and for one horrifying moment she thought she was going to faint from the enormity of it. It was with a tremendous effort that she remained on her feet, and her voice was hardly above a whisper as she demanded, "What are you going to do to him?"

"You do not want for sense, Miss Ferrers" he replied meaningfully, pleased to know that at long last he had finally managed to emerge the victor from an encounter with her.

Disgust, fear and an overwhelming sense of nausea swept over her as she saw the satisfied look which descended onto his face as he witnessed her reaction, but pride and sheer determination prevented her from swooning at his feet. But just when she thought she had succeeded in not letting him see her panic the awful suspicion crossed her mind that if he was prepared to rid himself of two people who could denounce him and her cousin then the same could be said of her, and therefore he could not afford to allow her to leave here alive. For the first time since leaving home she felt really afraid but, despite her efforts to prevent him from seeing her fears, they were clearly reflected on her face.

"I am glad to see your position has not escaped you," he pointed out, his pale blue eyes glinting.

Frightened she may be but again that pride came to her aid, her eyes flashing as she told him scornfully, "I was right, you *are* despicable, but if I am to die then I can think of no better reason than that it should be in my brother's cause, which is right and just!" The only answer she received to this was an ironical raising of his eyebrows, but the hold on his temper was beginning to weaken at her continued stubborn defiance and determination to obstruct him. "At least I shall die knowing that I did not give my brother up to the likes of you!" she flung at him.

"Very fine talking," he sneered, "but I wonder if you will still be of the same mind when the time draws near?" Having lived with the threat of the hangman's noose all this time he believed he could speak with some authority on the subject, but as this menace was fast receding due to what he considered to be his unassailable position, his ever growing confidence was clearly mirrored in his face, leaving her with no doubt that she would not leave here alive.

Without stopping to think of what she was doing she made an effort to reach the door, but before she even got half way he grabbed her by the shoulders and thrust her back into the room.

"That really was quite foolish, Miss Ferrers" he sighed, shaking his head.

"You can't keep me here," she flung at him. "Salmon knows where I am."

He raised an eyebrow. "You mean he was in the carriage with you?" he asked in mock surprise.

"Of course he wasn't," she said irritably, "but he knows ..."

"Precisely," he nodded. "He knows no more than you where you are, so you see" he offered, "you cannot expect help from that or any other quarter."

"You are *contemptible!*" she scorned.

Ignoring this, he reminded her, "Had you not been so stubborn in refusing to divulge your brother's whereabouts in the first place, you would not be here now and certainly not awaiting a most ignominious and unnecessary end."

"Give my brother up to the likes of you!" she scorned. "A traitor! Never!" her eyes flashed.

He flushed, but bit down his annoyance. "You realize," he pointed out with more calmness than he felt, "that you have just proved how necessary it is that you do not repeat what you know."

"Do with me what you will," she threw at him, "but you will surely pay for your crimes!"

It would have given him tremendous satisfaction to have shaken this intractable and obstinate woman, whose fierce loyalty to her brother had caused him all manner of problems, but as this would serve no purpose he merely swallowed, saying as calmly as he could, "An empty wish, I assure you."

She was just on the point of responding to this when the door opened and her cousin walked in, looking rather pale and not just a little scared, which was hardly surprising. He had been through enough recently to last him a lifetime and if all that were not bad enough he had since learned what Colonel Henderson had in store for Major Neville and Elizabeth. He had argued strenuously against such drastic measures but, again, he had been overborn, allowing himself to be persuaded that it was the only sensible thing they could do bearing in mind the danger they both posed to their safety. This may be so, but the very idea of committing what was nothing short of cold-blooded murder made him shiver convulsively, and when he finally managed to pluck up the courage to ask the question he dreaded hearing the answer to, he had found it necessary to not only sit down but take a generous mouthful of cognac. He may have told himself that doing away with Richard was a necessary evil if they were going to come out of this imbroglio unscathed, but he had since discovered that talking about something was a far cry from actually doing it, and even though Richard's death would pave the way to everything he had always coveted, as well as being easily explained away, especially as no one would really question the shooting of a known fugitive, he nevertheless felt sick at the thought. But it could not be said that he looked upon Major Neville's death or Elizabeth's for that matter, in the same way. Getting rid of a man who wore the King's uniform would not be as straightforward a matter and certainly not as easy to explain, particularly as he was engaged on official duties. He hoped and prayed that making an end of either of them would not fall into his lap because he was honest enough to admit that he had neither the nerve nor the stomach for it. He had no more desire to have his neck stretched than the next man, but he realized that if this was to be prevented then he had no choice but to go through with this scheme to the bitter end, even if it meant disposing of two more people to ensure it. Nevertheless, the very thought of making an end of Elizabeth was something he could not contemplate without revulsion. It was true that she had proved herself to be Richard's most stalwart partisan, defending him every step of the way and causing them no end of difficulties in so doing, but no matter how infuriating he may find her indomitable defence of her brother he could not pretend to having a liking for it. No matter what exigencies had decreed her death as necessary he could not lightly ignore the blood ties which bound them together, any more than he could the enormity of putting a period to her existence.   He was therefore not entirely certain whether to feel relief or not when he was told that both deeds would be carried out by someone who knew their business well enough to make sure that no suspicions would be aroused when their bodies were found.

It seemed to him that Henderson knew some pretty suspect individuals, none of whom he had the least desire to know anything about, in fact, the more he kept his distance from them the better. The inclusion of Private Smith into their plans had by no means pleased him, firmly of the opinion that to bring in a third party was far too risky, but to discover that yet another confederate was to join their number seemed to him to border on insanity. The more people who were involved in this business could only increase their chances of discovery as no reliance could be placed upon them keeping their mouths shut but, upon pointing this fact out to Henderson, he was sharply told that if he wanted the task of dealing with Major Neville as well as his cousin then he was welcome to it. Resigned but by no means reconciled he prepared himself for the inevitable, pouring himself another glass of brandy that went some way to restoring his dwindling confidence which, not unexpectedly, disappeared as soon as he laid eyes on his cousin.

Even now, he was still feeling the effects of his exertions from having to carry the Major's body down several narrow flights of steps and into the waiting carriage. It had been a nerve-racking moment when he had seen Major Neville lying unconscious on the floor and even more so when he had tried to get him down the stairs and into the carriage without being seen. Major Neville was far heavier than he had anticipated and, even now, he was not certain which had been the most difficult, getting him out of Henderson's tower quarters and into the carriage or getting him out of the carriage and into the house, then down the narrow stairway to the cellar. He had no idea how long it would be before Major Neville would regain consciousness, but he had lived in dread of the drug wearing off before he had him safely bestowed in the cellar. It seemed to him that they would never escape from this mire they had made for themselves as no sooner had they overcome one hurdle than they found themselves faced with another. His nerves had certainly been required to bear more than they could adequately cope with and should anything else arise which needed to be dealt with then he did not think that he would be in any fit state to avert any more disasters. But as it was by far too late for regrets and he was in too deep to withdraw now, he had no option but to see this through no matter what the consequences.

That second glass of brandy had given him a much needed boost, but the look of disgust and contempt on his cousin's face when he entered the room was sufficient to strip away the last vestige of confidence and resolution he had, particularly when he considered what her fate was to be.

"Elizabeth ..." he began, taking a hasty step towards her.

"*You!*" she scorned, her face angrily flushed and her eyes sparkling dangerously. "I might have known you would be a party to this night's treachery!"

"Elizabeth," he pleaded, "you *must* listen to ..." He got no further as she rounded on him, causing him to take a step backward.

"What a *coward* you are!" she cried. "Daring to lay the blame for your crimes onto Richard! I see now why my father and brother never liked you. You really are beneath contempt!" Her eyes flashed. "*You* step into my father's shoes," she disparaged, "you are not worthy!"

He turned scarlet at this denunciation made worse by the amusement on Colonel Henderson's face. "You're being unfair."

Before he realized what was happening she took a step towards him, surprising not only himself but Colonel Henderson as well, by giving him a resounding slap across the face. "You disgust me" she bit out. "Go away. Get out of my sight; both of you!" she throbbed. "I can't bear to look upon you!" Upon which she strode over to the fireplace and turned her back on them, her whole body trembling with anger and shock.

Across the space which separated them Colonel Henderson and William Ferrers, who was tenderly rubbing his stinging cheek, eyed one another questioningly, wondering what on earth they were going to do with this stubborn and recalcitrant young woman.

"Very well, Miss Ferrers" Colonel Henderson nodded, "we will leave you for the moment." When she made no effort to move or speak he told her, "We will await the outcome of tonight's affair. I am quite sure that by now your brother will have heard of your dilemma."

She swung round at that, her hands clenched into small tight fists. "I hope he does come," she told them angrily. "He will make you both sorry you ever embarked on this night's work."

Ignoring this, Colonel Henderson warned, "Do not be so foolish as to attempt to escape. I think you will find it quite a fruitless task. The windows are securely locked, and this door," he indicated with a nod of his head, "will be locked from the outside."

William Ferrers, looking from Colonel Henderson's exasperated face to his cousin's flushed and tempestuous one, was not at all sure whether to hope that his cousin would indeed be arrested or, failing this, shot on sight as he attempted to gain access into the garrison, or if he may escape and turn up here in defence of his sister. In theory Colonel Henderson's two pronged plan appeared perfect and to all intents and purposes his cousin should not leave the garrison alive, but knowing Richard as well as he did he felt the chances of him escaping and making his way here safe and sound to be a pretty safe bet. The very thought of his cousin overcoming such tremendous odds and turning up at Hamstoke House filled him with trepidation and although his face still stung from that slap, honesty compelled him to admit that that would be nothing compared to what Richard would mete out to him.

Elizabeth eyed both men with such loathing that momentarily they were taken aback. In his own way Colonel Henderson was not looking forward with any real pleasure at coming face to face with Richard Ferrers either. Despite his outward show of confidence and bravado, he secretly hoped that, having made it to the garrison, he would either be arrested or, better still, shot while attempting to evade arrest. He swallowed anxiously at the thought of what tonight's scheming would bring, but should it transpire that Richard Ferrers did make it to Hamstoke House against all the odds after all, then providing William Ferrers not only played his part but kept his nerve, he felt sufficiently hopeful that between the two of them they could deal adequately enough with his cousin.

Unable to find words suitable to express her impotency and frustration, Elizabeth picked up a china ornament sitting on a nearby side table and threw it at her captors, and whilst it did neither of them any harm it considerably relieved her feelings, especially when she considered that through her stupidity Richard was on the point of being arrested - perhaps worse!

CHAPTER NINETEEN

Elizabeth's attempt to plant a seed of doubt in Colonel Henderson's mind may have fallen somewhat wide of the mark, but the rumours he had caused to be spread and which eventually filtered through to her brother's ears, resulted in just such a response as he could have wished for.

Having undergone all manner of agonies and doubts about the success or failure of the forthcoming course of action to lay Richard Ferrers by the heels once and for all over the last twenty four hours, his nerves had been stretched to breaking point, rendering him even more tetchy and irritable. Added to this was the unaccustomed exertion of all the preparation involved needed to achieve his goal which he could not delegate to another, including a discreet call upon an individual whose employer, a man he regularly dined and played cards with and whom he knew to be currently away from home, followed by a visit into Lewes.

He had known for a long time that Judson was in the habit of receiving smuggled goods, indeed, he had often sampled some himself, and although he was quite willing to turn a blind eye in return for Judson's discretion regarding his visits to the lady whose husband would by no means appreciate his attentions to his wife, he was not slow to make use of his disreputable reputation. Despite its outward appearance of respectability 'The Peal of Bells' was a regular haunt for quite a number of those who participated in running contraband, as not only did they know of the landlord's sympathetic views towards illicit trading but also his willingness to relieve them of some of their merchandise. As far as Colonel Henderson was concerned it made no difference whether they were cronies of Richard Ferrers or not, as far as he was concerned they were birds of the same feather with no scruples between them, and therefore he had no doubt that they would do all they could to help and protect one of their own by passing the word on about his sister.

His instructions to Judson had been concise as well as abundantly clear, but they had nevertheless placed that unfortunate individual in a most awkward position. On the one hand he was in no hurry to lose such a lucrative customer as Colonel Henderson but, on the other, he was by no means eager to have too much attention paid to his cellar. Colonel Henderson was in an excellent position to put a stop to his profitable little sideline if he so wished, and the only thing which prevented him from doing so was his desire to keep his affair with Mrs. Jaynes a secret. It made no odds to him what folk did providing they left him alone to tend to his own affairs without interference and therefore the Colonel's regular visits to this kind-hearted woman was nothing to do with him. He had never yet snitched, and resented the fact that Colonel Henderson thought him capable of such a thing. Were he to do so however the worst that would happen as far as he could see was that the lady's husband may have something to say on the subject, but since this gentleman was seldom to be found at home then the chances were he would continue to remain in ignorance of it. Of course, there was always the possibility that Colonel Henderson would be the focus of some ribald amusement for a spell, but if his understanding of human nature was correct then he had no doubt that the affair would most probably be viewed with indulgence and soon forgotten, whereas his somewhat suspect dealings would not.

Colonel Henderson may be one of his best customers, but he had never struck him as a man being overly inclined to carry out his military duties, much preferring the comfort of his private parlour to concerning himself with what was going on at the garrison. The only interest or enthusiasm he had ever known him show where his soldierly responsibilities were concerned was when Richard Ferrers' name was mentioned; his embittered remarks leaving him in no doubt that he regarded this individual as his arch enemy. Apart from having the unpleasant title of traitor hanging over his head, whether true or not he neither knew nor cared, he could only guess at what this young man had done other than participate in the trade to engender such a dislike in him, but whatever it was Colonel Henderson seemed determined to entrap him one way or the other. He had of course heard of Richard Ferrers, but as this enterprising young man had never come in his way, he could make no judgement about him one way or the other, even so he had no liking for what he had been asked to do. He had a pretty good idea what would result from his refusal to cooperate, and reluctantly deemed it prudent to do as he was bid. He did not approve of underhanded trickery and dirty dealings because in his own way he was fairly honest and above board, but Colonel Henderson's resolve to apprehend this thorn in his flesh meant that he was prepared to do anything to achieve it even if that meant using himself as a collaborator, and therefore knew he had no choice but to do as he asked if he did not want to come to the notice of the local Magistrate. It was therefore with the greatest reluctance that he agreed to do it, but there was no denying that when he casually dropped a careless reference across the counter of his tap room at '*The Peal of Bells*' to a number of his regular and somewhat nefarious customers to the effect that he had heard Elizabeth Ferrers had been removed from her home by Colonel Henderson, the news had spread like wildfire.

Lieutenant Beaton had not exaggerated when he had told Gideon that scarlet coats were looked upon with suspicion and distrust, so when it became known that Richard Ferrers' sister had been taken by Colonel Henderson the feelings of outrage this engendered more than reinforced his statement. There was not a soul for miles around who did not know of the malicious rumours which had been set abroad about Richard Ferrers' political intrigues, not that they believed them for a moment, or of the respect in which he was held.   As far as his smuggling activities were concerned they neither held it against him nor sought a reason for it, but it did not take much for them to realize that this particular red-coat was setting a neatly laid trap to draw him out into the open and was not above using his sister to do it. Colonel Henderson and Captain Waring may describe them as thieving rogues, but whilst they were ready to admit to depriving His Majesty's Government of its rightful tax, which they considered to be entirely the members own fault, they did not hold with such sneaky and devious tactics as these two men were clearly resorting to, taking it for granted that Captain Waring, far from having no idea as to what was being planned, was heavily involved in laying the trap. Not only as members of the fraternity but as ordinary decent folk they therefore considered it to be their duty to get word to Richard Ferrers as quickly as possible.

It could not be said that Colonel Henderson was a man who possessed the keenest intelligence, a fact to which Major Denham could have testified, but when it came to his own self-preservation he was capable of great mental agility, and it had therefore been with carefully calculated deliberation that he had arranged this evening's events. Elizabeth may have been appalled to learn that a trap had been laid for her brother, but the architect of the devious strategy employed to accomplish his ambush experienced no qualms or feelings of remorse over what he regarded as a masterstroke of genius. With Machiavellian intent he had purposely withheld the location of where Elizabeth Ferrers had been taken in order to make her brother believe she was being held at the garrison, maliciously guiding him there to effect her rescue. By guile and dexterous management he had let it be known he had received word that Richard Ferrers was proposing to gain access to the garrison, for what purpose he deliberately did not specify, but the whole barracks was to be placed on alert and every man, irrespective of his rank, was to remain on duty until they were stood down by him. His orders were unequivocal; under no circumstances was Richard Ferrers to be allowed to escape, he was to be arrested and detained for questioning, but should he decide to evade capture by making a run for it he was to be shot on sight. Unfortunately, he knew from bitter experience just how capable Richard Ferrers was in extricating himself from insuperable odds, and therefore had decided to adopt a precautionary measure in case he did somehow manage to sneak in without being seen. Should this be the case he knew he could rely on him to make his way to the tower quarters where he would no doubt expect to find his sister. He would find that letter instead which, unless he grossly erred, would ultimately bring him to Hamstoke House. Whatever the outcome, he was guaranteed Richard Ferrers dead or alive!

It was not to be expected that a man of Richard Ferrers' temperament would remain kicking his heels indefinitely. When he had given his word to Major

Neville that he would refrain from taking any further part in his nocturnal activities he had meant it, but after only a few days of inactivity frustration was beginning to set in. Since he could not apply himself to the administration and welfare of his estates, any more than he could walk abroad without being arrested, smuggling run goods under the noses of the Excisemen had provided an outlet for his restless energy. He may not have been bred to the life but it had offered him much needed protection from his pursuers, as well as presenting him with the opportunity of staving off boredom.

His father may not have objected to accepting the odd keg of brandy, even going so far as to look indulgently upon a trade which was outside of the law, but he would certainly not have approved of his son and heir joining their number. His son and heir would certainly not have done so had circumstances not rendered it expedient.

His confederates had asked no questions or demanded explanations, willing to protect and help him prove his innocence without the need for either. Having known Richard Ferrers and his family all their lives, holding each and every one of them in high regard, as far as they were concerned it was not a matter of shielding a traitor or a fugitive from justice, but protecting one of their own. If Richard Ferrers said he was innocent then that was enough for them, neither doubting his word nor that he would eventually be reinstated. They were behind him to a man. Colonel Henderson and Captain Waring may describe them as iniquitous rogues and vagabonds, but he knew them to be decent men. In return he not only gave them loyalty but also his share of the profits from their runs, fully realizing, like his father, that they had turned to smuggling out of necessity and not because they were the vicious cutthroats some deemed them to be. That would not prevent the direst punishment being handed out to them if they were caught however. For those like Jim Caites, skipper of *'The Queen of the Sea'*, who knew more about tides and currents than anyone as well as how to handle a craft in all kinds of weather, they could expect to receive anything from three to seven years service in the Royal Navy, where conditions were far from favourable. For the rest, they would be heavily fined and imprisoned for a considerable length of time or, which was more often the case, they would be hung and their dead bodies displayed in chains at crossroads. It was a brutal end to contemplate, but perhaps it was better than abject poverty if they did not supplement their meagre income by running contraband.

He had meant what he said to Major Neville in that he had no regrets about embarking on such a dangerous mission, and were it not for the devastating consequences resulting from his actions, he could have faced his own uncertain future with equanimity. But the death of his father, his estrangement from Jane and the constant harassment of his sister, had engendered in him a firm resolve to repay his cousin and Colonel Henderson for such brutality ensuing from their tyrannical devices to ensnare him and retrieve those letters. As far as their participation in the late rebellion was concerned, he was determined they would face their trial for treason, receiving the full penalty of the law.

He did not condone what Stuart attempted, but he did have some sympathy for those who had believed in his cause and rallied to his banner. He knew without doubt that neither his cousin nor Colonel Henderson held the least degree of allegiance to The Pretender, their support stemming from purely personal motives and aspiring ambitions, and therefore they were the worst kind of traitors. He had never once known William show loyalty to anyone other than himself, and his attempt to throw the blame onto him, resulting in his present predicament, was nothing more than the actions of a coward.

He had told Major Neville no less than the truth when he had said that he knew precisely what was going on at his home, indeed, it would have been impossible for him not to have done so. Nevertheless, the frustration he had experienced over being unable to do anything to prevent its constant invasion, had only increased his dislike of Colonel Henderson, and his cousin especially. With the exception of Salmon and his aunt, his sister had had no support or protection, fending off the attacks to her home and privacy as best she could. She had suffered all manner of abuse on his behalf, standing loyal and firm against overwhelming odds, as well as suffering the loss of their father without him being their to support her, for which he would never forgive them.

Until the arrival of Major Neville it had seemed his cause, if not lost, was looking more and more bleak with no hope of him being reinstated. Without those letters he could say or do nothing in his own defence, and whilst he was by nature optimistic there had been times when he felt quite despondent as to his future. He had no reason to trust the military but, like Salmon he had soon been brought to see that this particular red-coat was by no means of the same cut as those others he had come into contact with and therefore instinctively knew that he was the only one who could free him from his unenviable position.

He knew without question that Major Neville would make every effort to put his hands on those letters as quickly as possible and that Michael, once assured of the Major's sincerity, would also come to his aid. He refused to believe that Michael was now more a soldier than a friend, and despite Salmon's reservation on this point, he adamantly maintained his faith in him.

He himself had no reason to question either Major Neville's sincerity or integrity, much less his word. He did not strike him as a man given over to making false promises any more than he thought he was laying a trap for him or working hand in glove with Colonel Henderson. Had there been the slightest reason to doubt his honesty then Salmon would have spotted it. Not much got past this canny Sussex man who had not only watched over them both from childhood, but who had the family's interests at heart and in whom they all had complete faith and confidence. The Major was certainly cautious, and although this was a trait his father had always approved of, he nevertheless hoped that he would not take too long in obtaining the evidence needed to clear his name, because honesty compelled him to admit that much more of this hiding out could well prove to be more than he could tolerate.

But thanks to the cunningly contrived plot by Colonel Henderson, his days of hiding out were almost at an end. It was not to be expected that the rumours which had been deliberately circulated would not come to his ears or that his reaction would be anything other than what was intended. He may be unaware of the finer points attached to the scheme but he was neither stupid nor lacking in intelligence and saw the abduction of his sister for precisely what it was; a carefully laid plan to entrap him. The only thing he was not sure of was how involved his cousin was in this latest despicable venture. William and Colonel Henderson had already proved how far they were prepared to go to ensure that no wind of blame fell on them, but in daring to callously use his sister in order to serve this purpose, they had gone their length!

Sitting with his cronies in 'The Moonshadow', all of whom were recommending caution and offering advice as to how best to set about combating this latest manoeuvre, to which he was taking absolutely no notice, they looked worriedly from one to the other, wondering how this night's work would end. They watched helplessly as he leaned back in his chair, his long white fingers proficiently priming a pair of pistols with silver sights that glinted wickedly in the light from the candles on the table, his formidable expression bringing to an end any further warnings. They did not expect him to let his sister's abduction go unanswered, but they did wish he would stop and think a little before going headlong into something which could well end up the worse for him. They knew Colonel Henderson was not a man to be trusted, and that his cousin seemed to bend with whatever favourable wind happened to be blowing, but although Richard Ferrers might have right on his side, they could not rid their minds of the thought that this could well end badly for him.

They had never before known Richard Ferrers act rashly, but from the look on his face it was clear he was in no frame of mind to stop and consider the consequences of his actions any more than he was prepared to listen to their entreaties for caution. His marksmanship with a pistol was renowned, indeed, prior to his difficulties he had been known to shoot the pips out of a playing card from some considerable distance therefore, should he take aim, there would be no possibility of him missing his target, but other than firing a warning shot overhead, Richard Ferrers had never purposely aimed at a man before, much less attempted to kill one. Nevertheless, from what his friends could see of it nothing short of a miracle would prevent him from using those vicious looking weapons on the two men he held responsible for not only his father's death but the brutal treatment of his sister.

Their earnest and vociferous insistence to let them accompany him on his mission were promptly cast aside, telling them that this was a matter for him alone, so it was therefore with heartfelt relief that they saw Salmon entering the tap room. Since their efforts to dissuade him from doing something he could well come to regret had fallen on deaf ears, they could only hope that Salmon would succeed where they had failed, he being the only one who could possibly persuade him to think things through before going off half cocked.

It had not taken Salmon long to make up his mind about informing his young master of this latest development, and although he knew he would not receive the news with open arms, he had to be told. Nothing would disabuse his mind that Major Neville had not written that letter, in fact, he would stake his life on it. The more he thought about it the more convinced he became that it was nothing but a cleverly devised plot to ensnare Richard by using his sister as bait. This naturally brought him to wondering where the Major was now. He knew he was going to London to see Sir John, but that was not until tomorrow, and if Colonel Henderson did write that letter, and he was absolutely positive he had, then it was logical to assume that any plan to get his young mistress out of the house could only be done if the Major was not around to spoil things.

Having made up his mind to seek out Richard and tell him, he then told Clara Winsetton about her niece being lured out of the house by what he considered to be a skilfully contrived ruse and what his intentions were to try and prevent the very worst from happening, but even before he came to the end of his explanations, it was patently obvious that she blamed him entirely for being fool enough to let her go. Salmon was perfectly aware that he should have made more of an effort to discourage her from leaving the house, but he had recognized that stubborn look on her face and knew it was useless to remonstrate with her further. Clara Winsetton sniffed her disapproval, but upon being told that the only chance they had of getting her back was for him to go and see Master Richard, she told him in no uncertain terms that if he had the least spark of feeling or concern he would not have let her go in the first place. As expected she had fault to find with his intention of tracking her nephew down to tell him what had happened, stating argumentatively that knowing Richard from experience he could be depended upon to do something stupid, thereby jeopardizing any chance he had of gaining his freedom. Salmon realized only too well the risk he was running, but he knew too that should anything happen to his sister and he had done nothing to avert it, Richard would never forgive him.

He had no proof that that letter was bogus, but so convinced was he that something did not ring true about it, he could not just sit back and do nothing, and by the time he entered 'The Moonshadow' about an hour later he was in such a highly anxious state that the sight of Richard priming his pistols and clearly in a mood ripe for murder, only made him worry more.

Salmon may be as convinced as a man could be that Colonel Henderson was behind his young mistress's abduction, for he deemed it as nothing less, but he had not the slightest suspicion that word of it had already filtered through to her brother, or that Colonel Henderson had ensured it would. He glanced apprehensively from the pistols Richard was expertly handling to his face, which at the moment was exceptionally grim, and could not help but wonder what had put him in such a mood. At first he thought he had decided to make one last run, and his heart sank, his immediate errand temporarily forgotten as he was swiftly assailed with visions of him being caught and arrested, killing at a stroke all the Major's efforts to clear his name. It was not unusual for him to take his pistols on a nocturnal venture, and although he knew Richard to be a crack shot he knew too that apart from firing into the air as a diversionary measure to aid their escape from the Preventive Officers, he had never deliberately aimed at any one, but there was something about Richard tonight which gave him cause for grave concern. He may not know what had brought that forbidding look to his face, but he recognized it all too well and that remonstrance of any kind, though politely attended to, would go unheeded. Familiarity with his impulsive young master was more than sufficient to tell him that although he had not been bred to a life of illegally transporting goods there was no denying that he gained a certain degree of excitement from running contraband under the very noses of the Excisemen as well as viewing such escapades with an enthusiasm which at the moment was clearly lacking. In view of the absence of any obvious zeal to suggest a run was imminent therefore, he concluded that his initial conjecture of a trip across the Channel had been quite wrong, and something else was the cause of his anger. As he had not yet been told that those letters were now safe, for one horrifying moment he wondered if he had heard of something happening to the Major and decided to go to his aid or just merely took it into his head to try and retrieve them himself. This would not surprise him, especially when he remembered the times he had only just managed to dissuade him from attempting so foolish an undertaking, because such was the expression on his face that he could not at all discount the idea. Not unnaturally, the reason for seeking Richard out in the first place was momentarily relegated to the back of his mind, his eyes transfixed on that resolute face and the deft slim fingers priming those vicious looking weapons.

So intent was Richard on the task in hand that it was several moments before he caught sight of Salmon from out the corner of his eye, his unyielding expression not softening at the sight of him. In Salmon's agitated state of mind it seemed to take Richard the devil of a time to finish what he was doing, having to wait with what patience he could muster until he had raised first one pistol and then the other to his eye, looking down the length of both barrels before finally turning to his henchman, his eyes glistening as he heard Salmon tentatively enquire if he was going out tonight. Upon being told that he was not Salmon let out a sigh of relief but, unfortunately, his peace of mind was only short-lived when he was firmly told, "I have other fish to fry!"

From the looks on the faces of Richard's cronies as they shook their heads at Salmon, indicating that not one of their warnings had been heeded, it was obvious that something untoward was going forward, and knew it must have something to do with those letters. Glancing from the downcast group sitting gloomily around the table to Richard's harsh face exhibiting an unwavering determination to see through to the bitter end whatever it was that had brought on this fit of wrath, Salmon suddenly realized that it must have something to do with his sister, and somehow or other he had got wind of what had happened; nothing else could possibly account for the mood he was in. As it was patently obvious to the meanest intelligence that he was clearly in no frame of mind to either listen to reason or endure having questions thrown at him, Salmon was by no means eager to exacerbate his darkening humour, thereby increasing the chances of him doing something which would put an end to any chance he had of gaining his freedom, but he had not come all this way for nothing, and whether Richard liked it or not he was going to say what he had come for. If his sister's abduction was not the source of his present mood then he failed to see what it could possibly be, but since he could think of nothing which could adequately explain his present fury other than knowing his sister had been enticed out of her home by stealth and cunning, then he would not be any too pleased to learn that he had not acquainted him to this fact. Clearing his throat, Salmon looked down at the young man he had watched over and cared for from childhood, indeed, he valued Richard just as if he were his own son, but tonight's unprecedented events overrode his caution in attempting to reason with him when in this frame of mind. "Sir," he said firmly, "unless this other business you say you have to attend to is connected with your sister, then I am very much afraid it will have to wait."

"It is," Richard bit out, springing agilely to his feet, his eyes searching Salmon's face. "So, that's what you're doing here, is it?"

"Yes Sir, it is," Salmon nodded. "I am extremely concerned for her safety." Before Richard could say anything further Salmon began to recount the evening's proceedings as well as his fear that that letter had not been written by the Major and that his young mistress had been seized. "I therefore felt it to be my duty to come and tell you."

"I know she has!" Richard bit out. "And I know precisely whom I have to thank for it!"

"So that's the reason for those pistols!" he exclaimed. "But how is it that you know, Sir?" he asked, bewildered.

Salmon, rather concerned to see that murderous glint in his eyes, listened in astonished silence as Richard explained how he had come to hear of it by several people he knew and who conducted their business at '*The Peal of Bells*'. "T'would seem Henderson's been extremely busy!" he nodded darkly. "But I'll see him damned for this night's work!" he ground out.

Salmon eyed him aghast. "That's the dandy!" he exclaimed when he had found his voice. "Walk straight into a trap. You're in enough trouble without adding to it!"

"So, what are you saying?" he demanded, thrusting a pistol into each capacious pocket of his long oilskin overcoat, "that I just leave my sister to that pair of cutthroats while I save my own skin!"

"Of course I'm not," he replied irritably, "but this has to be thought out. For one thing," he pointed out reasonably, "you don't know where they have got her held."

"I know, but I'd lay my life they have her held at the garrison; that's why I'm going there to see Michael," he told him unequivocally.

Salmon stared incredulously up at him. "Brandishing those things!" he cried, indicating the weapons he had just thrust into his pockets. "'Sides, you'll never get through the gate," he told him. "Why, they'll arrest you on sight!"

"I'll just have to take that chance," he told him, picking up his tricorne and placing it on his head. "Anyway," he dismissed, "I don't intend going in through the gate."

"Salmon's right, Sir" one of his cronies put in. "They'll arrest you sure as check!"

"You can't just walk into the place and ask to see him!" Salmon exclaimed frustratedly.

"I don't intend to," he said firmly, putting Salmon to one side, the glint in those blue eyes proving just how determined he was. "He must have quarters there; I'll just have to try and find them!"

Salmon's remonstrating as to the insanity of such a strategy, which was by no means guaranteed to work, fell on deaf ears, so turned instead to the question of Major Neville. "But what about the Major?" he demanded, going on to explain his visit earlier in the day and the fact that he had managed to put his hands on those letters. "His intention was to return to London tomorrow to see Sir John. What could they have done to him?"

"You say he has them?" he asked sharply, gripping Salmon's arm, immense relief flooding through him upon learning of the safe acquisition of those letters.

"Yes, Sir" Salmon nodded. "But what do you think they could have done to him?"

Almost immediately the light faded from his eyes as he considered the Major's probable plight. "If you are right," Richard said grimly, "and I believe you are, he knows nothing about that letter to entice my sister out of her home, and it's my guess they won't risk him going anywhere tomorrow. For all we know Henderson may be aware, or, at least, have some idea, as to the reason for his visit to town. In either case they daren't risk having him around to spoil their game; they'll have to make sure he's out of the way. God knows what they've done to him or where they have him held!" he exclaimed. "I only hope those letters are still safe!"

Salmon, who had been hoping this too, tried again to make him see reason, but as Richard was taking no notice and there seemed to be nothing else anyone could do or say which would prevent him from his fell intention, he sat down at the table and thrust his head into his hands.

"You go home and wait there," Richard told him, gripping his shoulder. "I'll come to you as soon as I can."

Taking a much needed pull of ale which had been set in front of him, Salmon shook his head wonderingly as he watched Richard stride purposefully out of '*The Moonshadow*', feeling entirely helpless to stop him from going headlong into trouble, hoping against hope that by this time tomorrow his young master would not be dangling from the end of a rope or lying dead in a ditch somewhere!

Mounting his black stallion which had been brought round to the front of the inn some minutes earlier, Richard trotted away from '*The Moonshadow*' with a look of grim determination on his face. Not until he was clear of the village did he give his mount full rein; as impervious to the weather as he was to the danger which awaited him. He knew this country like the back of his hand; every road and dirt track was known to him, and even though there was no moon he had no difficulty in finding his way, the ground being eaten up beneath his horse's hooves. Anger spurred him on, only slowing down to a trot when he rode through a village or skirted a few isolated cottages, the thought of his sister being held captive driving all other considerations, even the fact that he was being led into a trap, from his mind. About a mile outside the village of Durston he turned left down a narrow lane, rendered treacherous by the deep ruts and pot-holes which overflowed with water and mud from the earlier torrential downpour, but with careful manoeuvring he managed to negotiate this without much trouble, eventually coming upon a cultivated field where, on the other side, he would reach the main road which led directly to Hampton Regis.

Nothing impeded his passage across the field and being no stranger to this route, he reached the far side without mishap until he came to the narrow gap in the hedge which gave access to the road. Pausing only long enough to fasten his black ankle length riding coat up to the neck and to pull his tricorne further down over his eyes, he nudged his horse a little further out of the opening so he could peer up and down, relieved but not surprised to find that no other traveller but himself was about on such a dirty night. Spurring his horse on he headed towards the town at a brisk trot looking cautiously all about him as he did so, hoping that nothing would hinder his passage through Hampton Regis. Being a garrison as well as a market town there were usually plenty of people about at this time of an evening, especially red-coats either on their way to *'The White Hart'* or returning from there to the garrison, but due to the sudden change in the weather, even a short distance would ensure a thorough soaking, he saw no one apart from the odd passer-by. Easing to a walking pace he entered the town's main street which inclined upwards veering to the right, progressing through the town and passing *'The White Hart'* on his right until some little way further along he came to the main gatehouse entrance of the garrison on his left. Without looking to either right or left he caught sight of the four guards on duty from out the corner of his eye; two on either side of the ancient gateway with their muskets slung over their shoulders. As there were generally only two guards on duty at any one time at the main entrance this addition to the customary number was all he needed to prove that tonight's venture was nothing but a deviously contrived attempt to draw him into a trap. If Colonel Henderson was indeed holding his sister here then it was safe to assume that he had warned them to be on the watch for him, but although they looked suspiciously at him as he rode unconcernedly past, no cry went up for him to halt allowing him to continue down the street unmolested. Turning into the gradual left-handed bend of the road he continued along it for some little way following the curtain wall of the garrison which stood high up on a grassy embankment to his left until he came to a section where the wall dipped slightly in height. On the opposite side of the road he saw that the handful of cottages which lay back some little way were evincing no sign of life behind the closed doors and drawn curtains, but as the occupants were not unused to assisting members of the fraternity he had no fears of being given up to the authorities should they suddenly discover his presence. Taking only a moment to look quickly behind him to ensure he was not being followed he pulled up and dismounted, leading his horse into the narrow pathway that separated the last cottage from the field behind a hedge, tethering his horse to a gate at the far end which was partly hidden by a derelict outbuilding and overhanging trees.

Pulling his muffler up over the lower of half of his face he walked back to the road and looked cautiously all around before running across it to climb the steep and grassy mound which formed the basis of the curtain wall. Memories of his escape from the same spot came to mind, but dismissing them he concentrated on the matter in hand, pausing momentarily to take another look around him. Upon seeing that no one was in sight he placed his hands on top of the wall and heaved himself up onto it to look down into the courtyard below. From his vantage point he could see every inch of the inside of the garrison compound and that every corner and building was heavily guarded. For several minutes he made no effort to move, lying flat on top of the two foot wide wall to scan the ground below him. Immediately beneath stood a stone grey two storey block which thankfully had almost a three foot gap between it and the base of the wall which was completely unguarded. Swinging his legs and body round he grabbed hold of the edge of the wall to drop silently down onto the dirt and pebble area several feet below, remaining perfectly still until he was certain that no one had seen or heard him. After quickly dusting himself off he trod quietly to the corner of the building to peer round to see who or what stood in his way, but either because no one had thought that entrance would be gained via this particular spot or that the building shielding him from view posed any threat, he could see no soldier on this side of the courtyard.

He had no idea which block housed Michael's quarters or, indeed, if he was in the garrison, but if he waited here all night he had to see him. He may not be in Colonel Henderson's confidence but he would surely know more of what was going on than he did, and if his sister was being held here, although he could not see them placing her in the prison quarters, then Michael may at least know where she would most likely be kept.

How long he stood there waiting for his chance to move he had no idea but after what seemed an eternity the guards on duty were changed and it was while this formal procedure was taking place, none of them it seemed taking either the time or the trouble to look in his direction, he took the opportunity to leave his hiding place. Bending almost double and keeping well within the shadows between the wall and the buildings, his black clothes a perfect camouflage in the darkness, he gradually inched his way towards the gatehouse archway on his left, coming to a halt within a couple of feet of it in order to stretch his head out to see whether the guards were still positioned on the street side. Relieved to find that they were and that the inner archway was unprotected, too thankful at this obvious dereliction of duty to question it, he moved stealthily forward, keeping an eye on the inner compound to ensure that the guards were still occupied in their manoeuvres, to make his way towards a gap he had seen between two blocks of buildings on the opposite side. Arriving at this shelter without being seen or encountering any mishap, he positioned himself there in the shadows with a perfect view of the whole of the inner courtyard in the hope of catching sight of his friend.

As promised, Sergeant Taylor delivered Gideon's letter to Lieutenant Beaton but this was not until about seven o'clock when he had eventually come in from his duties. Waiting only until he was alone he broke the seal and spread out the single sheet of paper upon which was written a dozen or so lines in a strong upright hand. It was brief and to the point merely advising him of his meeting with Colonel Henderson at half past five and that he was returning to London the following morning to see General Turville. He could not promise finding the time to speak to him until his return from town, but should anything untoward occur he was to take those letters from their hiding place in his room to Sir John immediately.

Having seen Colonel Henderson leave the barracks about fifteen minutes to seven o'clock and with no sign of Major Neville since, he could not help but wonder if he had suspected something may happen or that he expected his plans to go awry through no fault of his own. He could not rid his mind that a carefully laid trap had been laid to ensnare Richard, because he could see no other reason for either that letter or the fact that the garrison had been placed on full alert as well as the absence of Major Denham, not to mention that there had been no sign of Major Neville since he had left his quarters. Folding the letter and putting it in his inside pocket, he frowned down into the empty fireplace, unable to dispel the thought that something was very wrong. Had Major Neville returned to his quarters after his meeting had finished surely Sergeant Taylor would have said so, but he had not. The more he considered it the more ominous it seemed, and he became increasingly convinced that something was dreadfully amiss and could not prevent the unpalatable thought creeping into his mind that Colonel Henderson could well have discovered the truth about the game Major Neville had considered it necessary to play in order to protect Richard. He neither liked nor respected Colonel Henderson, and he certainly did not trust him, but in view of what the Major had confided to him he could well understand his desperation in apprehending his friend before he could tell the truth.

Deciding that he could not sit back and do nothing he left his room and made his way across the courtyard to the gatehouse quarters, only to have it confirmed by Sergeant Taylor that he had not seen Major Neville since he left a few minutes before half past five to see Colonel Henderson. Having spotted Gideon's packed bag on the floor, he plied the practical Yorkshireman with questions, none of which he could answer. As there seemed to be nothing more Sergeant Taylor could tell him, he strode over to the stables to ascertain if Major Neville had left the garrison but was informed by the farrier sergeant on duty that he had not laid eyes on him since he returned several hours ago, and his mare was still in her stall. Disappointed but by no means deterred he then walked the short distance to the tower quarters, knowing full well that Major Denham was away from the garrison and he would therefore not be asked questions he would much rather not answer. He did not think that Major Neville would still be there since Colonel Henderson had left sometime previously, but it was certainly worth a try, and upon entering Major Denham's room to find it empty he ran up the stairs two at a time. There was no sign of life and certainly no sign of Major Neville, in fact apart from the two glasses which had been left on the desk there was nothing to show that he had been here at all, but although everything appeared as it always did, for some inexplicable reason he could not shrug off the feeling that something was not quite right. He could not pin-point what this was precisely but that something had occurred he was certain, but since there was really nothing more he could do here he turned to leave, catching sight of a sealed letter propped up on the desk as he did so. He could not explain why but somehow he felt it to be significant and picking it up was somewhat surprised to find that it was addressed to Richard Ferrers in bold letters on the front. A frown creased his forehead as he stared back and forth from that letter balancing in his hand to those glasses standing innocuously on the desk, one drained of its contents and the other more than half full. On their own they seemed quite harmless but when put together with the letter as well as the garrison's state of alert, not to mention Major Denham's absence, they suddenly took on a whole new significance. Reaching out a hand to pick up the glass which still held some of its contents, instinctively knowing it would not be Colonel Henderson's as he was far too fond of it to leave any, he raised it to his nostrils, but when he could detect no odour which would suggest that something had been added to the brandy he dipped a forefinger into the remains and carefully tasted it with the tip of his tongue, discovering to his horror that a drug of some kind had indeed be slipped into it.

When he had been informed that the garrison was to be put on alert due to word having been received that Richard Ferrers may attempt to gain entry, he was somewhat taken aback; in fact he was incredulous. It was not only because he knew Richard was not that big a fool to take such an enormous risk, but he failed to see what possible reason he could have for undertaking such a dangerous enterprise. As he was unaware that Elizabeth Ferrers had been taken hostage, he was at a loss to understand what he could possibly hope to gain by coming to the garrison. He knew that Major Neville had visited Ferrers Court earlier today and would therefore have informed them that he had those letters safe, so it was a fairly foregone conclusion that they would get word to Richard. This being so he could see no conceivable reason which would necessitate him coming anywhere near the place. The more he pondered it the more certain he became that he had stepped into the middle of a cleverly calculated scheme to entrap Richard, because as far as he could make out nothing else could satisfactorily explain his findings as well as the apparent disappearance of Major Neville. Then there was Major Denham! He may not approve of smuggling goods, indeed, his opinion on the trade was well known, but even so he had never before known him join Captain Waring in keeping a nightly lookout for them, and could only speculate as to whether or not he was party to what was obviously planned or if he had been merely put out of the way in order to prevent him from discovering what was going forward, which, after further thought, seemed likely. Whatever this plan was it was clear that they could not risk either Major Denham or Major Neville doing anything to thwart it and therefore had to get them out of the way, but where Major Neville was now he had no idea. Since there were no clues that he could see which would give him some indication where to look for him, he decided there was nothing more to do here for the moment, so pocketing the letter he made his way back down the stairs, leaving the tower quarters with a look of deep foreboding on his face.

If he was honest he really had no idea what to do next, not because he was incapable of formulating some kind of counter-action, but simply because what he had gleaned so far was not enough on which to build anything constructive. It seemed the only way this evening's events would make sense was for him to read that letter, at least by doing so he may be able to do something to try and prevent Richard from being either arrested or shot and even, if he was fortunate, discover where Major Neville was to be found.

Hurrying back to his quarters, mechanically returning salutes to those whom he passed, he failed to share their enthusiasm for the task ahead, knowing that most of them would have no hesitation in shooting Richard Ferrers on sight. Considering that Colonel Henderson had ordered every soldier to be on duty and positioned strategically around the garrison, he must be in no doubt that Richard Ferrers would risk all in coming here tonight, as well as being extremely confident of holding a pretty good hand. Not even he would raise the alert otherwise! Whatever ruse had been employed to entice him he could only hope that his friend would see it for what it really was and not fall into the trap cunningly set for him. From what he could see of it it would take a miracle for him to not only get in and out of the garrison without being seen, but to come off with his life.

It was just as he was within a few feet of his quarters that he thought he heard something but dismissing it walked on until he was almost at the entrance door to the block which housed his rooms when it came again. Pausing to take a look around him he stepped back to look both right and left, the naked flames of the lights in their flambeaux throwing out long shadows all around, deceiving the eye.

"Pst!"

Peering into the dark shadows that separated the two blocks of quarters, he whispered urgently, "Who's there?" his heart beginning to thud, knowing it could only be one person.

"Michael!" came the imperative reply.

Taking a few more steps in the direction where the voice was coming from, he saw a gloved hand emerge, beckoning him. Turning quickly round to ensure that no sentries were nearby to see or hear anything he darted into the entry coming to a halt in front of the dark figure, his eyes staring up at the partially covered face. "*Good God!*" he exclaimed thunderstruck. "Richard! Are you mad?" he cried, gripping the hand eagerly held out. "What in God's name ...?" he began.

"Never mind that now," he whispered,

"Never mind!" Michael repeated aghast.

"I take it all of this is for me?" he asked, indicating the number of soldiers on duty with a nod of his head.

Michael glanced in the direction he was looking then back again. "All in your honour, Richard," he confirmed.

"I thought so," he nodded, then turning back to face his friend, told him urgently "I need to talk to you."

"And I *you*," he returned, "but not here."

"Where then?" Richard enquired.

"My room," he told him, darting a quick look at the courtyard.

"Is anyone likely to come in?" Richard demanded.

"No," he shook his head, "we won't be disturbed," he assured him. After making sure all of the sentries were not in the immediate vicinity, he signalled the all clear, whereupon Richard slid unobtrusively out of the entry to quickly follow him into the building and up the first flight of stairs two at a time.

Entering his rooms, Lieutenant Beaton hurriedly drew the curtains and lit a candle, then locking the door turned to his friend. "I don't know what it is that has brought you here," he told him frankly, "but you must be mad to make the attempt, especially as I cannot help but think a carefully laid trap has been laid to ensnare you! In case you had not realized it," he pointed out dryly, jerking his head in the direction of the courtyard, "Colonel Henderson has had the whole garrison put on alert due to having received word you were going to try and gain entry tonight, and that if you succeeded you were to be arrested or," he nodded significantly, "to be shot on sight if you proved obstructive. Beats me how the devil you managed to get inside with all these sentries about the place!"

"Yes," Richard nodded, eyeing his friend thoughtfully. "I thought something of the kind was planned and when I saw the extra guards on duty I was sure of it," swallowing a generous mouthful of the wine Michael handed him before telling him how he had scaled the wall.

"Well," Michael sighed, "I can't say I'm not impressed because I am, but I am afraid your way out is not going to be so easy. By now," he pointed out, "the guards will have increased in number. Colonel Henderson," he explained, "did not see fit to give a reason to account for your attempt to secure access any more than he was to identify the person from whom he had received word; personally," he told him, fortifying himself with a much needed drink, "I think it's nothing but a ruse, but you're running the devil of a risk in coming here!"

"Damn it, I know!" Richard dismissed irritably.

"They are not out there for nothing!" Michael told him determinedly. "And if it is a trap," he told him firmly, "which I am convinced it is, then I did not think you of all people would be fool enough to take the bait!"

"I tell you I had to come," Richard replied insistently.

"So you say, but you haven't yet told me why." After eyeing his friend fixedly for a moment or two, he said shrewdly, "If you want to know whether I believe you are guilty of treason, the answer is no, and as for trusting me," he nodded, "you obviously do or we would not be here now."

Richard grinned and gripped his shoulder. "I never doubted you," he shook his head.

"I'm relieved to hear it," Michael replied, adding candidly, "but what the devil you're doing here now with every soldier on the look out for you, I *don't* know!"

An ugly look suddenly descended on Richard's face. "I know damn well it's a trap!" he exclaimed through clenched teeth. "And the bait, as you call it," he ground out, "is my sister. Colonel Henderson has abducted her in an attempt to draw me out into the open."

Not unnaturally this statement took him quite by surprise, but once having recovered from the shock he began to understand the reasons behind that letter he had found and the evening's events so far. "So that's how he did it," he said, almost to himself.

"A neat little trick," Richard acknowledged before demanding abruptly, "What about Major Neville?"

"I don't know," Michael shook his head, "his bag is packed ready for his visit to town tomorrow, but he's not been seen since he left his quarters just before half past five to see Colonel Henderson, who himself left the garrison about quarter to seven or thereabouts." He then went on to tell him all that the Major had confided to him and about how they had retrieved the letters from the prison quarters and his subsequent visit to Ferrers Court.

"Yes," Richard nodded, finishing off the last of his wine, "Salmon told me about that. What beats me though," he shook his head, his eyes narrowing, "is what the devil they have done with him!"

"I wish I knew," Michael replied earnestly, going on to tell him about the letter he had received from Gideon followed by his discovery of the drugged wine and Colonel Henderson's letter, handing both over to him.

"Drugged!" Richard exclaimed, disgustedly.

Michael nodded and waited for him to read both letters, at the end of which his friend looked murderous. "I'll cut his liver out for this!" he exclaimed, giving the letter to Michael to read.

"*My Dear Ferrers*" it began.

"*Should you put your hands on this letter, then it is clear you have managed to perform what I would have thought to be an impossible task by not being either shot or arrested. By the time you read this your sister will have been in my charge for some time. No harm will come to her I assure you, providing you are sensible and present yourself to me at Hamstoke House. I feel sure you must know it, but in case you do not you will find it less than a mile to the north of Glynde. I shall await you there together with your cousin and sister.*

Incidentally, please do not expect Major Neville to come to your assistance as he has done thus far; he is presently in no position to offer you aid nor will be for some considerable time.

"Yours,

Colonel Henderson"

"Very well, my friend" Richard said with menacing softness, briefly scanning Henderson's letter which Michael had just returned to him, "it shall be as you say!"

Michael Beaton knew his friend of old, and that once having set his mind to something he was not easily diverted, but from the look on his face it was clear that nothing short of knocking him out for his own protection would keep him away from Hamstoke House.

"My letters," Richard asked sharply, "I take it you can put your hands on them?"

"If they are where Major Neville says they are in his letter, yes" he nodded.

Richard thought for a moment. "According to Salmon Major Neville told him and my sister he was going to town tomorrow to put his findings before Sir John, there is no way he would have told Henderson that; in fact" he recollected, "he told them he was putting forward the reason for his unexpected absence as family affairs."

"And Colonel Henderson didn't believe it," Michael supplied, "or," he nodded, "he could have planned this evening before being told of the Major's plans to return to town, so if he did suspect something getting him out of the way would serve both purposes."

"Precisely!" Richard nodded. "Apart from the fact that he could not allow the Major to get wind of tonight's scheme and do anything to prevent it, he daren't have let him leave here with such damning information. That's why they drugged him and now have him hidden somewhere, probably at this Hamstoke House place, and it's my guess," he said grimly, "that they fully intend to deal with him permanently once they have me out of the way."

"I can only assume that's why Colonel Henderson has sent Major Denham off for the night to share a vigil with Captain Waring," Michael told him, pulling down the corners of his mouth. "He daren't have anyone here who could possibly prevent his plans from going ahead." Richard nodded, his brain racing. "Do you think Henderson would confide what he has in mind to your cousin?"

"Yes," Richard nodded, a dangerous light entering his eyes. "Henderson could not manage this on his own, and whilst William is not the kind of man I would trust or rely on, they are both of them in so deep that they are totally dependent upon each other."

"And your sister?" Michael enquired tentatively, glancing up at the saturnine face frowning straight ahead of him at nothing in particular.

Richard did not pretend to misunderstand him. The thought that the same fate they had planned for Major Neville awaited his sister was not lost on him. "She's safe enough until they have me," he said in a strangled voice.

"I can't help but feel," Michael pointed out, breaching an awkward gap, "that should we find Major Neville at Hamstoke House, I doubt he will be in any condition to tell us anything for awhile."

Richard nodded. "Wait a minute!" he exclaimed, a thought suddenly occurring to him. "Isn't that where Sir Evelyn Joyce lives?"

"Yes," Michael inclined his head, "now you mention it I believe it is. Good God!" he cried thunderstruck, "don't tell me he's in on this too!"

"No," Ferrers shook his head. "I know m'father never liked him, but he's no traitor."

"Then why lend his home to such as this?" he demanded.

"What makes you think he knows anything about it?" Richard asked, raising a questioning eyebrow, before pulling out an elegant gold timepiece from his inner pocket to see that it wanted only a few minutes to nine o'clock, briskly announcing that he must be going.

"Not without me you're not," Michael told him firmly.

"Now I think it is *you* who are mad!" Richard grinned.

"And if I don't," he asked, "how do you propose getting out of the garrison?"

"I got in, didn't I?"

"Yes," he conceded, "you did, but you may not be so lucky getting out."

"Are you saying I can't?" he asked provocatively.

"No," Michael shook his head, unable to resist that smile, "but if it were at all possible for you to look through the window," inclining his head in that direction, "you would see that since your arrival the number of guards on duty has increased."

Richard considered for a moment, eyeing his friend speculatively. "So what do you suggest?"

"The only chance you have of leaving here in one piece," Michael told him truthfully, "is to allow me to distract them."

Richard nodded. "Yes, I think you're right, but how will you manage it?"

"Let me worry about that," he smiled, going over to the window and taking a brief look outside.

"Michael," Richard said earnestly, "I *have* to get out of here!"

"I know," he nodded, turning back to his friend, "and you will, we both will."

"Are you sure about coming with me?" Richard asked urgently.

Michael Beaton grinned. "I certainly can't let you go alone."

"You *do* know," he told him seriously, "that if this goes against me, you could end up facing a court of honour or whatever they call it."

"It is," he confirmed, "but I don't think so," he shook his head, "anyway, the mood you're in you will probably run them through or shoot on sight."

"Not on sight, no" Richard shook head, an ugly look entering his eyes.

"Richard" Michael said earnestly, "you can't make this a killing matter. Leave it to the law. Those letters will serve you better than the sword or the pistol."

"No doubt," he agreed, "but they won't give me half as much satisfaction."

As it was evident his friend was in no frame of mind to listen to reason, he decided to say nothing further for the present, hoping that when the time came he would be able to curtail his more vengeful, if not unreasonable, desires. However, he did manage to persuade him to leave those letters were they were for the present; convincing him that they would be far safer in Major Neville's quarters rather than on his person.

Descending the stairs without running into anyone, Michael whispered the all clear to Richard who, after pulling his hat down over his eyes and his muffler up over his mouth, ran down the stairs to pin himself against the wall behind the main front door, waiting with what patience he could muster while Michael stepped outside. Surveying the courtyard from every angle he had to wait almost five minutes before two pairs of sentries passed each other then himself before the ideal opportunity presented itself to signal it was safe for him to slip into the space alongside the two blocks of buildings.

As two pairs of sentries were walking up and down on either side of the lawn in the middle of the courtyard, and those nearest to him passing at regular intervals, with four more over at the far wall where the armoury and prison block were situated, it was going to be impossible to get Richard across such a wide space without being seen. Since leaving Colonel Henderson's room he now saw that two guards were on duty at the foot of the steps leading to the round tower quarters with at least a dozen soldiers mustered a little way to the right of the archway which formed part of the old gatehouse entrance. Walking slowly towards the main gate he saw that Colonel Henderson had also taken the extra precaution of placing extra soldiers on duty, two on the outer entrance and two on the inner, and if all this were not bad enough he could see that Richard's point of entry into the garrison as well as his proposed escape route, was now cut off due to being heavily guarded. Looking at the scene all around him with a sinking heart he knew it was going to take a minor miracle to get Richard out of here, not to mention himself. As far as he could see the safest escape route was through the main gate, and although there may not be enough buildings to afford him protection it was the shortest distance from where Richard was hiding.

By the time he had come upon the two soldiers on the inner gate, having recollected their duty by taking up their correct positions, he had made up his mind that this was the best, in fact, the only way to get out of the garrison, and having followed up his salute with an enquiry as to whether they had as yet caught sight of anyone, said firmly "Keep your eyes open, we don't want him to slip through our fingers!" Returning to where Richard was waiting impatiently, Michael stood with his back to him surveying the scene intently before turning his head slightly and whispering, "Be ready in a couple of minutes. Head straight for the main gatehouse, that's our only chance of getting out of here. I'll follow you." Without waiting for Richard's reply he then took two or three steps towards where the edge of the lawn met the gravel path, glancing cautiously all around him. He had not exaggerated about it taking a miracle to get Richard out of here, but as far as he could see it was going to have to be now or never, so taking a deep and resolute breath he pushed his head slightly pushed forward, his eyes peering intently into the distant shadows. "Sergeant!" he called suddenly, waving to one of the men standing by the inner gate, "Come here, hurry man!" he ordered. "Over there, quickly," pointing in the direction of the furthest corner of the curtain wall. Then nudging the bemused sergeant in front of him turned to the rest of the men on the gate, shouting "All of you, hurry! It's Ferrers, he's got in over the wall!" Immediately every soldier, with the exception of the two guards on the street side of the gatehouse entrance, left his post to run in the direction Michael was pointing, his eager cries of hurry receiving precisely the kind of response he could have hoped for. Waiting only until they had all rushed ahead of him did he turn and run towards the entrance, catching sight of Richard as he emerged from the shadows to run the short distance to the arched gateway, their exit into the main street challenged by the guards who were not at all sure which surprised them the most, the sight of Richard Ferrers who had been under their noses all the time or that of an officer aiding his escape. Finally recovering from the initial shock they galvanized themselves into action by hurriedly removing the muskets from their shoulders and crying for them to halt in the name of the King. Upon discovering their order was being ignored they came on purposefully with their muskets raised at the aiming position, but Richard, who had born down upon the one with unexpected swiftness, felt the musket knocked out of his hands and himself sent sprawling with a nicely timed hit to the jawbone. Michael, who was right behind his friend, ran full tilt into the other, delivering a head butt to the stomach which not only winded him sufficiently to enable Michael to land him a flush hit full in the face which sent him reeling against the wall, but his musket clattering to the ground beside him.

"Follow me," Richard told him as loudly as he dared as they left the guards lying where they had fallen and the cries and shouts inside the stronghold behind them, emerging from the garrison to race down the main street until finally bearing left where the row of cottages came into the sight. Following in the direction Richard pointed Michael followed him across the narrow road until they reached the safety of the dirt track adjacent to the last cottage, only then stopping and pausing for breath. In the still night air the noise and confusion coming from the other side of the garrison wall could clearly be heard, and as Michael glanced in that direction Richard commented, "They'll be chasing one another for hours."

"Hopefully," Michael nodded, then turning back to look at his friend saw the amusement on his face, and burst out laughing.

"We'll make a fugitive of you yet!" Richard told him, slapping him on the back. "The way you got us both out of there was masterly!"

"Sheer good luck, I assure you" he dismissed, not at all certain whether he would like the life of a fugitive or not.

"It was more than that," Richard confirmed, leading the way to where he had left his horse, "I couldn't have got out without you."

"What now?" he asked, pushing away several overhanging branches as he followed in Richard's wake.

"Now," he was told firmly, "we make our way to Hamstoke House."

Upon being assured that his horse would easily carry both of them as far as Fairbourne, where someone he knew would happily mount him for the remainder of the night, Michael climbed nimbly up behind Richard to the startling discovery that he was really rather enjoying himself. Not for the world would he tell Richard that he was deliberately closing his mind as to what his father would say if he knew that his only son was assisting a man who was not only hailed as a traitor but also a known smuggler on the point of being 'gazetted'.

CHAPTER TWENTY

Had William Ferrers not been so taken up with his own concerns and the horrifying prospect of what awaited their two captives, intensifying his anguish to the point where he could think of little else, he would have had some suspicion of what was in his cousin's mind, being precisely the kind of thing she would do in the circumstances. Having long since recognized her as a strong minded and determined young woman who was not easily intimidated or diverted from her set intention once her mind was made up, he would have strenuously advised his confederate as to the folly of leaving her alone. As it was he was only too relieved to be free of her company, if only for a short while, being in no hurry to have a repeat performance from someone whom he had no hesitation in describing as a termagant and who should have been brought to bridle long since. He may not be a man given over to self-analysis, but the truth was he was just a little afraid of his cousin, a woman who possessed far more courage and strength of mind than himself, were it otherwise then none of them would be in this predicament now. He owned that she had endured a great deal of late, but however much he may regret his uncle's sudden demise, an unfortunate incident to which he denied any involvement whatsoever, blaming Henderson's forceful and brutal tactics, anyone else would have admitted defeat, but she had proved just how resilient she was to set-backs and adversity. Time and again she had defied them, denying any knowledge of her brother's dealings or whereabouts; her resolve and spirit, far from being broken, had emerged in tact from the aftermath of her anger and grief over the invasion of her privacy and the death of her father, to enable her to persist in thwarting them at every turn, shielding her brother with a fierce loyalty that went beyond his comprehension. His face still smarted from that resounding slap, proving just how stubborn and intractable she was, and it would be long before he would forget the look of disgust and anger in her eyes as she had rounded on him. Had he have been privileged to either read her mind or see her actions at this precise moment, it would have proved beyond doubt just how obstinate and single-minded she was in refusing to give in, even when the odds stacked against her were overwhelming, but it would also have filled him with fear and alarm, because if she did escape and somehow manage to reach her brother, then everything he and Colonel Henderson were striving for would all have been for nothing. But worse than this was the thought of what Richard would do to him, something he could not dismiss from a mind which was already over burdened with care.

Elizabeth may have been shocked and appalled by this evening's unexpected turn of events, especially when she considered what almost certainly lay in store for her, but she was by no means cowed into submission. As she had no idea what they had done to Gideon or where they had him held, rendering it impossible for him to come to her rescue or avert disaster for Richard, she was fully determined to liberate herself as well as him, if at all possible. Still furiously angry over her own stupidity in not seeing through such contemptuous deceit or heeding Salmon's warnings, she knew she had to do all she could to try and get out of here so word could be got to Richard to warn him of the trap which had been cunningly laid for him.

She had no idea whose house she was in but from what she had seen so far it was clearly the home of someone who could easily afford such luxury, but right now she was certainly in no mood to appreciate the fine furniture ranged all around the room any more than she was to see how the gold and blue of the carpet acted as a perfect foil for the delicate blue on the walls, upon which hung antique mirrors and numerous portraits. As her father and Sir Evelyn Joyce had only been on nodding terms, neither it seemed being over fond of the other, and no visits had ever been exchanged between them, she did not know that she was currently enjoying his absent hospitality, but although the establishment as well as its owner were unknown to her, she deemed it to be extremely unlikely that it belonged to Colonel Henderson. But identifying the owner of so grand a house was of far less importance than her escape, and waiting only until her captors had left her, locking the door securely behind them, she bent her mind to this vital task, quickly coming to the conclusion that the window was her best and safest way out, only to discover upon examination that it was securely locked, refusing all her efforts to open it. Disappointed but by no means deterred she surveyed the room, looking about her for something suitable to force its release from where it nestled inside the frame. Keeping an ear open in case her cousin or Colonel Henderson returned unexpectedly she frantically searched the room for a suitable tool, opening and closing the drawers of several tables as well as a huge desk until finally coming upon something she thought would do the trick. No doubt Gideon or Richard would have told her that such a delicate piece as the mother of pearl handled paper-knife would not serve her purpose, but so determined was she to get out of here that she picked it up eagerly, giving no thought to whether or not her cousin and Colonel Henderson had seen fit to set guards in the grounds. Treading softly over to the door she placed her ear against it but when no sound could be heard she sped across to the window to begin plying her ineffectual implement. Placing the tip of the knife at the base of the window where it fitted into the frame she bore down on the handle with all her strength, but despite her efforts it remained secure. Straightening up she impatiently removed her cloak to throw it carelessly onto a nearby chair before beginning a second attempt, but after pressing strenuously down on the handle with her right hand whilst at the same time trying to raise the window with her left one, it was to her horror that she heard the paper-knife snap, falling to the floor at her feet in two broken pieces.

She could have cried with vexation, but overcoming this temporary set-back began another search for something far more practical. Unfortunately, there was nothing she could see which would serve her purpose and heaving a deep sigh sat heavily down on a chair, propping her chin in her hands as she turned over the problem of her escape. If she tried to break the glass there would be no way she could muffle the sound, which would inevitably bring her cousin and Colonel Henderson into the room to discover what was happening. Deciding therefore that the window could not after all be her escape route she then turned her attention to the door, and although she knew it was locked she could not help but think it was worth a try. She had, of course, heard Richard jokingly comment about picking locks, much to her father's displeasure, but surely it had to be worth the attempt. Rising to her feet she walked over to the door and knelt down to press her eye against the keyhole to discover that Colonel Henderson had thankfully removed the key thereby enabling her to see into the hall. Admittedly there were blind spots on either side due to the restricted view, but from what she could make out the hall appeared to be completely deserted. Never having picked a lock in her life before, the opportunity to do so never having come in her way, she was not entirely certain how to set about it, but as this was not the time to allow such a trivial thing as that to deter her, she removed a pin from her hair and began to straighten it. When she was finally satisfied that it was level enough she held it between her thumb and forefinger and inserted it into the lock. She had no way of knowing whether it would work or not but after several attempts of moving it around she was somewhat disappointed to find that her efforts were proving to be of no use whatsoever. Again and again she tried but the door remained firmly locked, her pin doing absolutely nothing but making her thumb and finger sore, and she would have thrown it to the floor in her impatience had it not been for the sound of a door opening and closing across the hall followed by approaching footsteps coming to an abrupt hall on the other side of the door. Quickly grabbing her cloak and resuming her seat she waited in expectant silence for the door to open, but as neither her cousin nor Colonel Henderson entered she let out her breath as she heard whoever it was walk away and retreat back into the room across the hall. Deciding it was wiser to remain where she was for awhile in case one or the other of them did come back to check on her she continued to sit down, pondering her predicament while she waited. After almost ten minutes had past she deemed it safe to attempt her escape again, and rising to her feet turned her attention once more to the window, striding purposefully towards it and thrusting back the curtains to grip the bottom half of it. She tried with all her strength to lift it but it would not budge, but just as she was on the point of stamping her foot in sheer frustration two faces suddenly appeared at the window making her almost jump out of her skin, looking back at them in astonishment.

Having managed to leave Hampton Regis behind them without being followed, Richard and Michael made the four mile journey to Fairbourne without any mishap where, as Richard had rightly promised, his crony was only too happy to mount his friend. Upon setting eyes on the animal Michael cocked a pained eyebrow at Richard, to which his friend burst out laughing and its owner looked affronted. It may not have been the most attractive looking mount he had ever sat astride, but he certainly had stamina and by the time they reached their destination, via a safe but circuitous route, he was feeling a little more magnanimous towards his four-legged friend.

Although it had stopped raining by the time they arrived at Hamstoke House over an hour later, Michael had cause to be grateful to Richard's unidentified acquaintance for the heavy and serviceable coat he had so generously bestowed upon him. It had certainly seen better days and perhaps would have been the better for a clean, which the stale odour distastefully invading his nostrils testified, but not only did it protect him from the constant dripping from the branches of the trees as they rode beneath them, but it staved off the cold and damp chill which had followed in the downpour's wake. Apart from the occasional remark, very little conversation took place between them, but as soon as they came within sight of Hamstoke House Richard, his every instinct on the alert, laid a warning hand on his friend's arm, then after a few whispered instructions they both dismounted, whereupon Richard handed his rein to Michael before treading softly towards the main front gates, surprisingly standing wide open, to disappear from sight to make a quick reconnoitre of the grounds.

No stranger to constructing a plan of campaign, he had realized immediately that Colonel Henderson, in his efforts to ensnare him, had not seen fit to position either guards or dogs to patrol the grounds, wanting him to gain entry to Hamstoke House entirely unmolested, unlike the garrison where every soldier had been placed on full alert. In using his sister as bait Henderson had played a masterstroke, knowing perfectly well that he would do everything in his power to come to her aid, and were he not so angry at employing such a devious method of entrapment he could almost have applauded the two-pronged plan Henderson had put together. Indeed, it was a brilliant calculation; should the first part fail then the second was bound to succeed, and once his sister and the Major had been permanently and surreptitiously dealt with to ensure they were no longer in a position to give an account of the true story, they would be in the clear with no accusing fingers pointed in their direction. His temper may have abated sufficiently for him to keep a clear head, but he was still in no frame of mind to appreciate either the niceties or the realities of such a line of attack. Unless he missed his guess, and he was certain he hadn't, he would lay a heavy wager that

Henderson and his cousin were fully expecting him to break down the door in order to rescue his sister, brandishing pistols and threatening all manner of dire consequences, thereby providing them with a justifiable reason to put a period to his existence without any probing questions being asked. If the truth be told, they would in all probability be exonerated of any wrong-doing in shooting a man labelled as a traitor turned smuggler who had unlawfully entered a private dwelling for nefarious reasons, thereby escaping the consequences of their treasonable actions. But he was more than fly to the time of day; recognizing the objective behind the strategy for what it was and for that reason had no intention of being caught in the web they had weaved to rid themselves of him. His only chance of coming through this unscathed as well as rescuing his sister and the Major was to effect an entrance to the house without them being aware of it, thus gaining the upper hand by taking them completely by surprise.

Several minutes elapsed before he reappeared signalling to Michael that all was clear, then leading their horses through the open gates turned a little to the right following the wall a little way before leaving their mounts tethered to some untamed brambles, sheltered by an abundance of bushes and trees out of sight of the house or visible to any late wayfarer passing by on the road. Apart from the sound of the trees rustling in the slight breeze, shedding a constant stream of raindrops down onto them, no sound broke the night's silence. Striding silently on the grass verge running parallel to the curved drive, they headed towards the front of the house where a light was clearly visible from the window just to the right of the main front door, and although the curtains were drawn it was most likely that someone was presently occupying that room. They doubted it would be where they would hold Elizabeth, most probably Colonel Henderson and William were using it, and therefore walked round to rear of the house, thankfully unimpeded by bushes or a thicket or anything equally as obstructive, in a quick reconnoitre to find a suitable means of entry. Being built on symmetrical lines the house had corresponding rooms back and front, but upon turning the corner of the house it was immediately obvious that access could not be gained via the two end windows, being quite inaccessible due to the locked shutters and covering grille. The middle window, which they calculated to be a study of some kind, appeared to be a room immediately facing the main front door, from which a light was just visible behind the curtains, clearly indicating it was currently being used. After putting his ear to the glass and detecting no sound emanating from within, Richard consulted his friend who had been looking vigilantly all about him, deciding that although they could not be certain who or what they would find inside, this was where they would gain access to the house. It was just as Richard was about to remove a very useful tool from one of his voluminous overcoat pockets that the curtains were pulled wide open to reveal his sister.

Upon recognizing her brother Elizabeth almost squealed her delight, but clapping a hand over her mouth managed to stop herself from crying out, watching excitedly as he extricated the implement from his coat pocket to prise open the window. In the stillness the sound of Richard forcing open the casement seemed abnormally loud, and for one awful moment Elizabeth had the dreadful feeling that the noise would be heard by either her cousin or Colonel Henderson, and in her anguish ran to the door to put her eye to the keyhole to ensure that it had not attracted attention. To her relief no one had entered the hall to investigate, but not until Richard had pulled up the window and climbed inside did she leave her post, rushing towards him to fling herself into his arms, totally heedless of the fact that he was not alone.

"Oh, Richard!" she sobbed when he had released her from a suffocating hug, her slim fingers gripping his shoulders. "Is it really you?"

"Yes," he grinned, holding her at arms length and looking closely down at her, "it's really me," kissing her cheek.

"Oh, I am so glad to see you!" she exclaimed between tears and laughter. "I have been so terribly afraid for you!"

"*Stoopid!*" he gently admonished. "Didn't you know I'm indestructible?" he smiled as he saw the tears welling up in her eyes, giving her another hug before introducing her to Michael.

"A pleasure to make your acquaintance, Miss Ferrers" he bowed, his face slightly tinged with colour.

"How do you do," she smiled.

"He does very well," Richard intervened grinning, knowing his friend was none too handy in making polite pleasantries to the ladies. She looked from one to the other, but suddenly the irrepressible laughter she remembered so well sprung to her brother's eyes. "What's that done to you?" he asked amusedly, indicating the broken pieces of china on the floor.

She followed his glance and smiled, but said unrepentant, "I threw it at Colonel Henderson and William."

"Well that's all right then," he nodded, needing no further explanation. "What were you doing at the window?" he enquired.

"Trying to escape," she sniffed into her handkerchief.

"What! With that thing?" he laughed, indicating the broken paper-knife on the floor.

"I couldn't find anything else," she said defensively. "Besides, I had to try and get out of here to warn you. Oh, Richard!" she exclaimed. "You must not be found here; all of this and my presence here is nothing but a trap to bring you out into the open!"

"I know it is," he replied grimly.

"You know!" she gasped. "But how? I mean ..."

"Salmon came to tell me what had happened," he told her briefly "but I already knew of what was afoot, thanks to a friend of mine."

"Well if you knew that, why risk coming here?" she demanded.

"You didn't think I would leave you in the hands of those two, did you?" he demanded.

"You mean you came here to rescue me?" she asked, her eyes widening and her heart touched.

"Yes," he nodded, "*that,* and to call those two to account."

"You've been to the garrison!" she exclaimed. "You must have been mad to go there!" she told him, gripping his arm. "Colonel Henderson made it very clear to me what he expects from tonight's scheme. He wanted you to go there because he was hoping you would either be arrested or shot trying to escape!" even now the thought made her shudder, clinging to him to ensure herself he was actually here in front of her. "But that's not all!" she sobbed into his shoulder, the relief of knowing he was alive and safe beginning to take its inevitable course, taking comfort from his strong arms as he held her close against him, her pent up emotions finding an outlet in disjointedly telling him everything that had happened from the moment she had received the bogus letter to what lay in store for her and Gideon.

Having endured all manner of abuse and incivility on his behalf over the last twelve months by Colonel Henderson, Richard, who truly loved his sister, regarded her emotional outburst as being perfectly normal, but knew very well that he was the one responsible for all her sufferings. But when he released her and pointed this fact out to her she would not hear of it, saying that in spite of everything, even the pain of losing her father, she would not have wanted, or, indeed, expected him to do anything different, but her concerns for his safety were very real and could not be easily assuaged. Even though he assured her that not only would he ensure that nothing happened to her or the Major but that it would take more than those two to trick him, she was not entirely convinced. It therefore took a little time for him to allay her fears but eventually she nodded acceptance, before listening eagerly to his account of all that had happened since he had learned of her abduction.

Looking at Michael with heartfelt gratitude, she held out her hand to him saying fervently "Oh, thank you for coming to Richard's aid! I knew Gideon was right in that we could depend on you."

"A pleasure," he bowed over her hand, his colour a little high, having by now rid himself of his borrowed coat.

"Is it true," she asked worriedly, looking from one to the other, "that they drugged him?"

"Yes," Michael nodded, before Richard could open his mouth, "I am afraid so."

"Speaking of the Major," Richard commented, ignoring his sister's use of his first name, "is he here, do you know?"

She shook her head. "No, I mean I don't know. I have no idea where they have him held."

Richard frowned. "Well, we have to find him, but it's my guess they have him laid up here somewhere. The cellar perhaps!"

"Here!" she cried.

"Well," he nodded, "it would make sense."

"Richard," she said urgently, her wide blue eyes searching his face and her hand resting on his arm, "Colonel Henderson left me in no doubt what they intended for Gideon. They are going to k-kill him; and they *must* not!" she shook her head, vehemently.

In view of what he had discovered he was not at all surprised. They may not be entirely certain how much the Major knew, but the fact that they had drugged him surely proved that they suspected he knew enough to expose them and therefore could not run the risk of having him inform against them, besides which, they dare not allow him to roam free and spoil their plans for tonight. He knew perfectly well that the only way they could be guaranteed his silence was by putting an end to his existence, but as her face told him more than any words could have that Major Neville clearly meant as much to her as she did to him, he could not find it in his heart to confirm this. "Of course they're not," he assured her, covering her cold hand with his. "They merely needed to get him out of the way tonight as well as to frighten you a little."

"No" she shook her head, "he was very clear about it," she blinked away a tear. "Oh Richard!" she cried, "I couldn't bear it if anything were to happen to him. We *must* do something!"

Glancing across at Michael, who appeared to be deep in thought, he squeezed her hand, promising again that they would ensure no harm came to the Major. Upon hearing this Michael raised his eyes to his friend's face saying that under no circumstances could they leave him to their tender mercies and therefore whatever Richard decided to do he could count on his full support. Elizabeth threw him a grateful look which brought another tinge of colour to his cheeks, but as she had no reason to question his sincerity and her faith in her brother was as absolute as ever, she never doubted for a moment that they would save Gideon from the fate Colonel Henderson and William had in store for him. Having had some of her worries allayed she then turned her mind to something which had been nagging at her for some minutes, and turning to Richard asked him about what had happened to him since she had last seen him. "It's too long a story to go into now," he told her, fully conscious that she deserved to be told, especially after what she had suffered on his behalf. "I promise I will tell you everything later," he smiled, taking hold of her hands, "but right now we have other things to think about." She nodded. "Now," he urged, "how many of them are there?"

"Apart from William and Colonel Henderson," she told him, "I have seen no one other than a footman."

He nodded, a frown descending on his forehead. "What about the man who brought you here?"

"Private Smith?" she shook her head. "I assume he has left. He did not come inside with me."

"We didn't see anyone when we reconnoitred the place," he told her, "so as I see it there's only three of them, and I can't see this footman being much of a problem."

Michael, who had strode over to the door keeping an ear cocked for the past few minutes, looked up at this; recognition on his face.

"You know him?" Richard asked sharply.

Michael nodded. "Yes, although" he pointed out, "I have had very little dealings with him."

"Well, we're going to have dealings with him before much longer!" Richard nodded grimly.

Before Michael could reply to this he heard the sound of a door opening across the hall followed by footsteps approaching and immediately attracted Richard's attention to this. Nodding his comprehension, Richard hurriedly whispered brief instructions to his sister then after indicating the spot where he wanted his friend to stand he quickly positioned himself behind the door, pulling the pistols out of his pockets as he did so while Michael drew his sword in readiness.

Elizabeth may well be of the opinion that Colonel Henderson and her cousin deserved to be punished for their crimes, but as she stared wide eyed from her brother to Michael she hoped that it would not be necessary for them to put these weapons to use. However, knowing there was nothing she could do except wait anxiously to see what would happen she promptly resumed her seat, not daring to think how tonight would end.

Almost immediately she heard the key being inserted into the lock and turned, and despite Richard's instructions she could not prevent herself from casting a quick look in his direction, observing that he had pinned himself flat against the wall, his pistols to the ready, and a grimly determined look on his face. Michael too had positioned himself out of eye line, his sword held firmly in his right hand, the blade, glinting wickedly in the light from the chandeliers, pointing upright against his face as he waited for whoever it was to enter. Elizabeth was by no means afraid of William or Colonel Henderson, only of what they could do to Richard and Gideon, but even so she swallowed nervously as the door slowly opened, her breath suddenly constricted in her lungs as she saw William standing on the threshold steadily regarding her. To her immense relief he looked to neither right nor left as he stepped further into the room, but although she withstood his searching gaze unflinchingly, even defiantly, she could only hope he would not read anything in her flushed face other than anger at being kept imprisoned here. Upon being asked if she required anything she merely shook her head, not daring to trust her voice, but apart from a shrug of his narrow shoulders he made no attempt to say anything else. It was just as he was on the point of leaving that he heard the faint click of the door closing behind him, but before he could turn round to see what was happening Michael came up behind him clapping his left hand over his mouth before pressing the point of his sword delicately under his chin.

"One move; one sound," he told him ominously, "and it will be the last thing you ever do."

If Elizabeth was a little surprised to hear Michael speak in that coldly determined voice, William almost collapsed where he stood, but worse was to come as he stared in horror at the dark and menacing figure emerging from behind the door where he had remained hidden, levelling a vicious pair of pistols to his face with hands that, to his overwrought nerves, were alarmingly steady. Even had Richard's face not been partially covered, he knew precisely who the masked figure was and from the look in those blue eyes he knew he would be shown no mercy. He tried to cry out but the hand over his mouth closed tighter and in his fright threw a desperate and beseeching look at Richard who appeared totally impervious to his plight. For some inscrutable reason there seemed to be something quite hypnotic about those pistols, his startled eyes drawn involuntarily to those long barrels, the silver sights glinting wickedly in the light cast from the chandeliers. His head began to pound and his heart thudded painfully in his chest, and even if his unknown assailant was not covering his mouth with his hand his throat felt so dry and constricted that it would have been impossible for him to have cried out.

"What's the matter, Cousin?" Richard invited softly, pulling the muffler away from his mouth, his white teeth glinting. "You seem surprised to see me, but for the life of me though I cannot conceive why," he mocked. William stared with horrified eyes at his cousin. "No, no," he shook his head, "you are not looking upon a ghost! Thanks to my friend here," indicating Michael with a nod of his head, "I contrived to evade capture or being shot as an escapee!" he grimaced. "Was that not the intention of tonight's charade?" he asked, raising an eyebrow.

William tried to shake his head in denial, but even if that sword point were not dangerously poised it would have been impossible for him to have moved or even attempted to open his mouth.

"I feel I must congratulate you on such a cleverly executed plan," he told him sardonically, "should the first part fail then the second will do equally as well. Do not attempt to deny it," Richard warned, his eyes scathingly contemptuous as they swept over his cousin's pale face, remaining quite unmoved as he saw the fear etched into every inch of it, the beads of perspiration breaking out on his forehead.

William again tried to shake his head, but Richard, ignoring this attempt to acquit himself of any wrong doing smiled, a cold parting of the lips that put fear into his heart. "Yet something tells me you are wishing that the first part of your plan had worked," he remarked menacingly, raising a questioning eyebrow. William tried to splutter something but when the hand over his mouth tightened even more, he tried instead to move his head, but that sword point, delicately pressed further into his chin, made him think better of it. Richard eyed his cousin dispassionately. "By the time I have finished with you," he promised softly, "you will be praying it had." William quaked at the look in his cousin's eyes and knew a moment of sheer terror as he watched those pistols come within an inch of his face. "Was it your idea to use my sister as bait, or Henderson's?" he demanded. "You really are quite despicable," he scorned, "and what you have done is beneath contempt, but when you use my sister in such a way as this, you have gone your length."

Again William tried to move his head but to no avail, his terrified eyes flitting from Richard's unyielding face to those pistols which he knew perfectly well his cousin was most skilful at handling.

"What a lily-livered coward you are!" he snarled. Something like the cry of an animal in pain could be heard deep within William's throat, but Richard, who had always known his cousin to possess neither courage nor moral fibre, merely threw him a disdainful look. "Even now," he scorned "you cannot stand up for what you have done! Do not worry," he assured him, lowering his pistols, "I shall not kill you, unless of course you give me cause," he told him coldly.

Elizabeth, who had found it impossible to remain seated, rose nervously to her feet, looking from her cousin to Richard expectantly. He may have said he would not kill William, but the stifled attempt to deny any involvement in what had taken place acted like a flame to gunpowder on her brother. She wanted nothing more than for this terrible nightmare to end, but she dreaded the outcome of tonight's affair especially when her cousin, even now, could not bring himself to admit his treasonable activities or the part he had played in attempting Richard's downfall.

From childhood she had loved and adored her brother, she knew she always would, but she could not deny that he had changed since she had seen him last. It may be indefinable, indeed, it was so subtle that it could easily have been non-existent, but knowing him as well as she did she recognized it immediately. She knew he would not kill William in cold blood, but she had to acknowledge that her cousin's lack of courage and strength of character were provocative to say the least. Nevertheless, it was with relief that she saw Richard drop his pistols from William's frightened face, whose relief was clearly as heartfelt as her own.

From the moment her aunt had told her what her intentions were about protecting William from the consequences of his own folly she had known that Richard for one would never accept it. She herself was still not entirely convinced of the wisdom of such a resolve, but since her aunt could not be moved she had deemed it wiser to say nothing and to await developments. However, she was not at all certain whether to be glad or not that there had been no time to tell Richard about it, but from the look on his face it was evident that he was clearly in no frame of mind to show magnanimity towards his cousin.

"Do not be thinking however, that our relationship will prevent me from using these," Richard warned, indicating his pistols. "When my friend removes his hand should you try and cry out or make a sound of any kind, it will be the last thing you ever do. Do I make myself clear?"

William managed a nod, heartily relieved to feel the sword removed from under his chin and the hand from over his mouth, but his relief did not extend to gratitude, and now the immediate danger point had passed, said peevishly, "Well, now that you *are* here, what is it you want?"

"What a question!" Richard exclaimed, removing his hat. "And here was I thinking we had so much to say to one another."

William eyed him with loathing, but just one glance at those pistols still held firmly in those beautifully shaped hands, warned him to tread carefully. "I suppose you think that I am to blame for Elizabeth being brought here?"

"*You,*" he nodded, "and your equally devious associate."

"I was not in favour of this," he told him hastily. "Useless I daresay to expect you to believe that!"

"Quite!"

"What are you going to do?" William asked, his voice rising nervously.

"Keep your voice down!" Richard ordered. "I don't want Henderson joining us yet. As for what I mean to do," he smiled wickedly, "what would you do to someone who had sold you to the devil?"

William swallowed. Richard may have smiled but there was nothing either friendly or cousinly in the smile. "You think it was I who …"

"You know," Richard said smoothly, his tone disparaging, "I always knew you were a coward."

William flushed. "If this is the kind of humour you are in Cousin," he expostulated, "then it is pointless saying anything further." He turned to leave but Michael was before him, barring his way. Apart from the fact that he wore a scarlet coat denoting he was a soldier, he had no idea who Richard's accomplice was, but since it was clear that he too was determined to keep him here, he spun round to face Richard.

"Try that again Cousin," Richard warned, "and I *will* kill you."

William swallowed. He may hate his cousin with every fibre of his being but he knew when he was beaten. He should have known that Richard was far too astute to be taken in by a hoax of this nature, and even though it was true when he said he had had no liking for any of this, he had allowed himself to be persuaded into going along with it, because not to have done so would have meant the hangman's noose. From the looks of it though, it appeared it still did, as Richard clearly had every intention of handing him and Henderson over to the authorities. Nevertheless, he had to try to do all he could to save himself and if that meant placating his cousin he was quite prepared to do so. But from the look on Richard's face it was obvious he was in no mood to be placated.

"Do not try my patience too far," Richard advised softly, taking a step nearer to him. "You already have a deal to answer for."

"You cannot prove anything!" William shot at him.

"You think not?" Richard asked, holding on to his temper with an effort. "I may not be able to prove that you and Henderson were responsible for hastening my father's death, but we both know that your hounding of him as well as my home and sister brought on that heart attack." William swallowed, licking his extremely dry lips. "As for your part in the late rebellion," he went on, "and your determined efforts to point the finger in my direction, you seem to be forgetting those letters. Oh yes," he nodded, when he saw the look on his cousin's face. "I have them safe."

William went rather white about the mouth. There seemed to be no doubt that his cousin was speaking the truth and that he did indeed have that incriminating evidence in his possession. Once those letters were produced nothing could prevent him from climbing the scaffold, and since he was unaware of Gideon's promise to his aunt, he was now more convinced than ever that he had to appease Richard at all costs, no matter how unpalatable the thought. "You mean you really *would* produce them?" he asked, not quite able to keep the note of panic out of his voice. "I *am* your cousin, after all" he reminded him.

Richard's eyebrows rose. "A connection you have been oddly reluctant to recognize before!" he derided.

William flushed, knowing perfectly well what he meant by this scathing response, but biting down the angry words which rose to his lips, decided to try a more conciliatory tack. "I realize how things must appear to you," he offered, "but I had no hand in 'gazetting' you, nor did I ask you to take up smuggling, besides which" he smiled nervously, not liking the ugly look which had descended onto Richard's face, "you seem to be forgetting that, like it or not, we *do* bear the same name, and should I go to the scaffold then every Ferrers will always bear the shame of it!" As soon as the words had left his lips he knew he had erred; just one look at Richard's face was enough to tell him they would have been best left unsaid.

"Very fine talking!" Richard scorned, his lips thinning. "You *dare* to speak of shame! Had you the least semblance of honour or pride in the name you bear, you would never have embarked on such a course as treason in the first place." William swallowed. "Had your so-called allegiance to Stuart stemmed from belief in his cause instead of your own and then attempting to disinherit me by implication, I could have found it in me to have some sympathy for you but as it is," he told him disdainfully, "I find you rouse nothing in me but contempt. As for our name" he inclined his head, his eyes glinting, "I believe it is well enough established to withstand your trial for treason and subsequent hanging."

William blenched at the thought, his eyes staring panic-stricken at his cousin. "You wouldn't …!"

"You underrate me," Richard told him coldly.

"But Richard …" he began.

"By handing you both over to the law you will have the opportunity to speak in your own defence. An opportunity," he reminded him, "you were fully prepared to deny me."

"I promise you I would …" he began desperately.

"Save your eloquence," Richard advised. "It will not serve you. Now" he demanded, "you are going to answer some questions. Apart from you and Henderson and that footman, who else is here?"

William debated whether to tell him, but just one look at those pistols made him realize the futility of such a refusal. He shook his head. "No one."

"And Major Neville? What have you done with him?"

"He is not dead if that is what you are thinking!" he cried, trying desperately to think of some way out of this predicament.

"It is to be hoped for your sake he is not," Richard warned ominously. "Where do you have him held?" he demanded. "Well," he pressed when William made no attempt to answer.

"He's in the cellar, damn you!" he bit out irritably.

"And the key?"

"I have it here."

Richard held out his hand. "I will take that."

Again William hesitated, but since his cousin was more than capable of forcibly wresting it from him, reluctantly dug a hand into his coat pocket and handed it to him.

"Now, about this Private Smith," he urged. "Apart from bringing my sister here, what else has he been asked to do?"

It was several moments before William answered, debating whether to do so or not, but one look at his cousin's grimly taut face as well as those weapons were enough to decide him against making a heroic stand. "He was to return to the garrison."

"And?"

Ferrers swallowed. "He - he was to discover what had happened to you and report back here."

Richard nodded. By his calculations it would be close on an hour's ride to Hampton Regis, if not more in this weather, and the same back, and therefore it was reasonable to suppose that they could not expect to see him for some little time. Should he return sooner than anticipated then he was more than confident that between him and Michael they could adequately deal with Private Smith.

"Now I want you to get Henderson in here," he told him curtly.

William stared, but asked warily "Why?"

"I should have thought that was obvious," Richard bit out. "And do not be thinking of alerting him," he warned.

Between those pistols and that sword, both of which were still pointing menacingly in his direction, he decided that refusal would be futile, so opening the door he called out to his accomplice in a voice which even in his own ears seemed not to belong to him.

Having settled himself down to a glass of port while William Ferrers checked on his cousin, Colonel Henderson believed he had more than earned this well deserved drink. When he had laid his plans for this evening he had hoped they would pay dividends, but never had he dared to hope that they would run as smoothly as they had. So benign was his mood, especially as Richard Ferrers had not shown himself at Hamtoke House, because surely he would have arrived by now if he were going to, it was safe to assume that he was either in custody at the garrison or had been shot trying to evade capture; besides which, Major Neville was safely tucked away where he could do no harm, and Miss Ferrers was securely held just across the hall. All he had to do now was to wait for Private Smith to bring the news to him that Richard Ferrers had indeed been dealt with, one way or the other.

But despite his feelings of satisfaction over a job well done, he could not delude himself into thinking that he was out of the wood yet, on the contrary, his problems were by no means over. Although it would relieve his mind to know that Richard Ferrers was securely locked in a prison cell instead of roaming free, until he had those letters in his possession then he could neither relax nor take it for granted that he had seen the last of his difficulties. More than anyone did Richard Ferrers know the significance of those letters, but no amount of optimism could lead him into believing that he would tell him their whereabouts any more than he would refrain from citing them in his own defence should he ever come to trial. That damning evidence was Richard Ferrers' ace in the hole, a circumstance which that young man was perfectly well aware of, but somehow or other he had to find those letters, if he did not then everything he was striving for would be for nothing and both he and William Ferrers would be taking a walk to the scaffold.

But even supposing matters could be settled satisfactorily where Richard Ferrers was concerned, there still remained the question of his sister and Major Neville. He could not deceive himself into thinking that either of them would keep silent, in fact he took it as a foregone conclusion that at the earliest opportunity they would take steps to bring him to account, not only for his treasonable activities but for his part in the downfall of Richard Ferrers. In view of this therefore he had no option but to take certain steps to ensure they never informed against them, and although William Ferrers had not been any too enamoured of the solution for dealing with Major Neville, he had positively reeled when he learned of the same fate for his cousin, but unless a miracle occurred to obviate this he failed to see what other measures could be adopted in the circumstances.

Upon hearing William Ferrers call to him he sighed his impatience; it seemed that not only was he expected to devise ways of extricating them both from their difficulties, but also to oversee his accomplice who apparently could not even deal adequately with his own cousin!

Taking a moment to drain his glass before placing it down on a side table he rose to his feet, his face mirroring his irritation as he crossed the room to open the door, muttering something under his breath as he did so. He could see William Ferrers standing by the open door of the rear saloon waiting for him to join him, his face pale and drawn and looking for all the world like someone who had suffered a severe shock. He knew Ferrers' nerves were on the point of collapse, but he fervently hoped that he would hold himself together for awhile longer because whether he liked the tasks ahead of them or not his assistance was going to be needed if they were going to clear themselves of all the loose ends which could possibly denounce them. It never so much as crossed his mind that his quarry was the source of his confederate's present nervousness and that he was at this very moment standing beside his cousin with a pair of vicious looking pistols aimed at him.

"Well?" he demanded peevishly as he approached. "What is it?"

"M-my c-cousin," William stammered, "she w-wishes to speak to you."

"What about?" he asked, coming to an abrupt halt only inches away from him, his eyes instantly suspicious; fully expecting Miss Ferrers to be playing some off some trick.

"She will only t-talk to you," he faltered, uncomfortably aware of what would happen to him if he failed to get Henderson into the room.

"Devil take her!" he exclaimed frustratedly, brushing past him into the room. "Well," he shot at her, "what is it you have to say to me that cannot be said to your cousin?" he demanded, looking fiercely down at her as she sat with her hands folded on her lap.

Before she could speak he heard the door click shut behind him, but thinking it was William Ferrers took little or no notice of it, but irritably demanded again what it was she wished to say. To his annoyance she made no effort to speak and just as he was on the point of remonstrating with her about the unwisdom of trying to make a fool of him or pushing him too far, to his horror he caught sight of a dark clad figure emerging from behind the door, holding a pistol in each slender white hand.

"*Ferrers!*" he cried aghast, his eyes starting from their sockets.

"At your service," Richard bowed mockingly, his eyes glinting as wickedly as the silver sights on those long barrels.

The sight of his adversary bearing down upon him with all the air and confidence of a man in complete control, not only of himself but the present situation, made him feel sick. There was no denying that Ferrers' stealthy entrance was an unlooked for eventuality which had not entered into his calculations, but the knowledge that he had cleverly turned his plans on their end and could, even now despite all his efforts, expose him as a traitor, made him feel as if were standing on the edge of a precipice. Shock, incredulity and a tardy recognition that he should have considered Ferrers was capable of attempting something of this nature, if not as a potential probability, then at the very least a remote possibility, rendered him acutely conscious to the fact that he had grossly underestimated this young man who, in his ever growing despair, seemed to have taken on the mantle of his Nemesis; as difficult to shake off as he was to dispose of!

CHAPTER TWENTY ONE

Gideon opened his eyes to the painful discovery that not only did his head feel as if it was being rhythmically pounded but that his ineffectual attempts to raise himself made the room swim around him, causing him to sink thankfully back onto the cold stone floor where he had been left. In the dim light cast by the candle burning in its holder he could see he was enjoying the sparse comforts of a cellar, but in whose house it was or how long he had been here he had no idea, and since trying to retrieve his watch from his inside coat pocket required too much exertion, he was only too glad to close his eyes again and remain where he was.

He had no way of knowing how long he lay there but after what seemed an eternity he could feel a tingling sensation begin to spring to life in his legs and body and with it the diminishing of that overwhelming sense of nausea whenever he tried to move, as well as the pounding in his head. His mouth felt extremely dry and he was very thirsty, but although he was able to make out a water jug sitting on a table against the far wall he was for the moment quite unable to reach it. He knew there was nothing he could do but remain helpless and inert on the floor until such time that his legs regained sufficient strength to take his weight, but while his body was temporarily incapable of functioning properly his brain was not. He was easily able to recollect the fact that Colonel Henderson had drugged his wine; the reasons why he should have done so however were unclear, but for the moment at least he felt quite incapable of applying his mind to finding any suitable explanation to account for it.

To his annoyance he realized he must have succumbed to the residual effects of the drug without being aware of it, because when he opened his heavy lids sometime later it was to discover that the candle had almost burned down in its holder, but at least that throbbing in his head had now ceased and from his tentative attempts to move his legs it seemed they had regained their strength sufficiently for him to try and get to his feet. Cautiously attempting to try and raise himself he slowly managed to heave himself up off the floor, but so giddy did it make him that he was grateful to drop onto an old chair conveniently placed a short distance away from him, leaning forward with his head held in his hands until the dizziness had passed. After a couple of minutes he again tried to stand up, but even though the room still seemed to be moving around him he managed, albeit unsteadily, to walk over to where the water jug and bowl rested on the table, thankfully pouring at least half of the jug's contents over his head, giving no more than a brief thought to the fact that at some point during the evening's most unusual events he had lost his wig. Raking his trembling fingers through his hair, he shook off the residue of water then after swallowing a generous mouthful, leaned heavily on his splayed hands resting on the table, trying to assimilate what had happened.

He supposed he should have known, or at least suspected, that something was not quite right when he discovered the absence of Major Denham as well as Colonel Henderson's insistence that he share a drink with him. He could not believe he had been stupid enough to be taken in by such a trick and could only assume the reason for such a ploy was that matters must have reached crisis point for Colonel Henderson and William Ferrers. If they had found it necessary to resort to such a strategy as drugging his wine as well as getting rid of Major Denham, then something must either have occurred which they wanted no one to know about or they were putting together some kind of plan which made it essential that neither of them were around to thwart it. It could even be that his own mendacity had been discovered and his being here was nothing more than an attempt to prevent him from laying the truth before General Turville, but however plausible this sounded he could not rid his mind that something far more devious was behind it. If they had deemed it necessary to adopt such drastic measures, then he believed that more than his silence was the cause of tonight's events, and it was more than probable that something must be going forward for which they would want neither witnesses nor interference. The more he considered it the more certain he became that the only thing which would require such extreme tactics as far as he could see was if they were orchestrating a scheme of some kind to try and ensnare Richard Ferrers. He knew this was nothing but conjecture but in view of what had happened so far it was the only possible reason that made any sense, and by ensuring the absence of two people, one of whom would do everything possible to try and prevent it, he was sure of it.

If he was right and something was scheduled for tonight to ambush Richard Ferrers, then at all costs he had to get out of this cellar, but although he was gradually beginning to get his strength back the room still had a tendency to sway around him. He knew he should be grateful that his hands and feet had not been tied, but he supposed neither of his captors had deemed this necessary in view of him being unconscious.

If his calculations were correct, then whatever it was that had motivated them into taking such desperate measures, Richard Ferrers was in more danger now than he had ever been. His acquaintance with the future sixth Viscount may be of short duration, but he believed he had assessed that young man's character accurately enough. If a trap had indeed been laid for him as he suspected then Richard was certainly astute enough to read it for precisely what it was, and could certainly be depended upon to accept the challenge, because that is how he would see it, without a thought for his own safety. He may not be able to work out the

411

rudiments of such a plan, but nevertheless he was convinced that something had been arranged to bring about either the arrest or, which they would regard as preferable, the demise of Richard Ferrers. He could of course be quite wrong and his being here could after all be due to Colonel Henderson having got wind of the dissimulation he had been perpetrating and was simply ensuring that he did not return to London to put the facts before General Turville, but somehow he did not think so. As he was unaware of Lytton's arrival in Hampton Regis and his subsequent meeting with Colonel Henderson at 'The White Hart', he failed to see how either he or William Ferrers could possibly have discovered the truth, or at least come to suspect he was withholding it from them, and therefore he was left with only one conclusion.

Although that dousing of cold water had gone a long way to clearing his head he still felt somewhat sluggish, but after straightening himself up and flexing his shoulders and stretching his legs and body, he turned his attention to the door which he instinctively knew would be locked even without turning the handle. It was just as he was about to cross the floor that he heard the sound of footsteps hurriedly descending the stairs outside and quickly positioned himself behind the door, pulling out his sword as he did so, surprised that this had not been taken from him, waiting for whoever it was to enter.

Almost immediately he heard the key being turned in the lock followed by the scraping of the door as it slowly opened over the uneven flagstones. Having fully prepared himself to see either Colonel Henderson or William Ferrers it was therefore something of a shock to find himself coming face to face with Lieutenant Beaton instead, and for one brief moment wondered if he was suffering some kind of delusion as a result of whatever had been slipped into his drink.

Despite Richard's assurances that he would not shoot either of the two men he held personally responsible for his father's death, Michael had nevertheless been somewhat hesitant to leave him alone with them even though it was extremely unlikely he would in fact harm them, and certainly not in front of his sister. Nevertheless, he could not rule out the possibility that he could well be goaded into doing something grave enough to seriously hamper his chances of clearing his name, and as for Colonel Henderson it was difficult to say which shocked him the most; coming face to face with his quarry or discovering that one of his junior officers had ranged himself against him.

Colonel Henderson, his initial shock receding, could not help but think he had stepped into a nightmare, because although he had achieved his objective in getting Richard Ferrers here, it was certainly not in the way he had anticipated nor could he say it was the success he had hoped for. Staring incredulously from Lieutenant Beaton, whose sword was still suggestively unsheathed, to those fearsome barrels with their silver sights glinting wickedly in the light from the chandelier, he was forced to face up to the fact that he could not now lay claim to disposing of Richard Ferrers in the manner he had hoped; certainly not with a witness to denounce him as a liar. Looking transfixed from one pistol to the other, his mouth wide open and his eyes protruding to their fullest extent as he sought in vain to find words suitable to express his feelings, made several attempts to say something, but so bereft of speech was he that he could do no more than swallow, his heart beginning to beat uncomfortably fast in his breast. He saw the glint in Richard Ferrers' eyes and knew instinctively that even though his plan had accomplished its aim he really had attained no more than a hollow victory. However much it went against the grain to admit it he knew, if William Ferrers did not, that his quarry had the upper hand and unless he was very much mistaken it would take all his ingenuity to turn the tables in their favour thereby extricating them from this unenviable state of affairs. From the looks of it though Richard Ferrers was in no mood to be appeased and certainly far too intelligent to be caught out by any more tricks. With those pistols levelled unerringly at him and Lieutenant Beaton's sword pointing provocatively in William Ferrers' direction, he realized it would take nothing short of divine intervention for them to leave here in one piece. Clearly, no dependence could be placed on his accomplice attempting anything in the way of redeeming the situation, indeed, he was looking extremely nervous and unless he grossly mistook the case, he bore all the signs of one who was on the point of physical and mental collapse.

It was no less than the truth. Beneath that briefly exhibited bravado a moment or two ago William Ferrers was extremely frightened. With the exception of Elizabeth no one knew his cousin better than he, and that being so he could not see Richard letting them off lightly. It was not only because he blamed them for what had happened to his father and their venture into treason, bringing with it all the ills which had befallen his cousin, but also the indignities suffered by his sister culminating in her abduction in order to bring him out into the open. He knew Richard had every intention of seeing them both face their trial for treason resulting in an inevitable walk to the scaffold, but knowing his cousin he felt it reasonably safe to assume that he would extort his own retribution first.

Michael Beaton may have no regrets about his participation in tonight's events, after all he had no stomach to see an innocent man hang whilst the guilty went free, but there was no mistaking the glitter in those blue eyes and the satisfied smile which touched those well shaped lips as he faced his antagonists. Like Elizabeth Ferrers he sensed the subtle change in Richard but, again like her, could not quite pinpoint what it was. He did not think that since they were at Eton together his friend had changed to such a degree that he would disregard his upbringing, and certainly not to the extent whereby he would shoot two men, who, despite the swords they carried, were virtually unarmed as they would be dead before they even unsheathed them, no matter what crimes they had committed. He perfectly understood the provocation his friend had suffered at their hands, but whilst he had readily turned his hand to smuggling, he did not think that Richard's recent experiences had turned him into a cold blooded killer.

Removing Colonel Henderson's sword from its scabbard and holding onto it in his left hand, he glanced from his commanding officer's face, suffused with angry colour, to Richard's coldly determined one, and saw at a glance that a silent battle of wills was taking place between them.

Since setting his plans in motion Colonel Henderson had allowed himself to picture the scene when he eventually came face to face with Richard Ferrers and had taken great pleasure from it, but at no time did he think it would be he on the defensive and not his quarry. One look at that resolute face however was enough to inform him that he had been outwitted by a man who was far more sagacious than he had realized, and that he had read far more into this evening's schemes than he had thought. He knew perfectly well that Richard Ferrers not only blamed him and his cousin for all the ills which had descended on him and his family and was determined they should answer for them, but also to bring them to account for their part in the late rebellion. From the looks of it though he gained the strong impression that he was in no hurry to hand either of them over to the law, but resolved to extract his pound of flesh first in order to repay them in some measure for all that had happened. Shocked and bewildered at the way things had transpired it was therefore several minutes before he could find his voice to speak, words temporarily escaping him as he stared in turn from that single-minded face to the barrels of those pistols.

"We meet again, Henderson!" Richard mocked softly, his eyes glinting dangerously. "Though not in the way you had hoped, I'll wager!"

"Why you ... !" he spluttered, instinctively going for his sword only to realize too late that it had been taken from him.

"Always so impulsive, are you not?" Richard smiled, but there was nothing friendly in that thin parting of the lips.

"I'll see you hang for this!" he exclaimed furiously, his bulbous blue eyes glaring ferociously at this inflammatory remark. "As for you," he declared, spinning round to face Lieutenant Beaton, "I personally shall see to it that you face disciplinary action!"

A deep throated laugh left Richard's lips. "A pleasant daydream, but you seem to have forgotten one important point, Henderson" he reminded him, "I am very much afraid you will be in no position to discipline anyone, and the only ones you will see hung are yourselves," Richard informed him inexorably, glancing significantly across at his cousin.

Elizabeth, who knew her brother better than anyone, saw he was holding onto his temper with a tremendous effort, and wondered if he would be so restrained if she were not here. In her agitation she rose to her feet, her small hands gripping the edges of her cloak, her eyes wide with anguish as she looked from one to the other, wishing Gideon were here as he would perhaps be the only one who could prevent the very worst from happening. She did not think her brother would shoot either Colonel Henderson or William in cold blood, but she had to acknowledge that they had certainly given him cause, even so she hoped and prayed that he would continue to keep his anger in check until such time as both of them could be handed over to the authorities or, in the interim, Gideon put in an appearance to curtail Richard's understandable desire for the settling of scores.

Something very similar was going through Michael Beaton's mind also. He could not deny that his friend had endured much recently and his desire to inflict his own personal brand of justice was perfectly reasonable, but nevertheless he could see no good ensuing from allowing Richard to give vent to his feelings. From the looks of it however, it would take all his persuasions, even his sister's, to instil into Richard the need for caution, and that to take matters into his own hands would merely serve to make his own position infinitely worse. He may not like Colonel Henderson, much less respect him, but he saw at a glance what he was attempting to do, and with Richard in this mood it would not take much provocation for him to lose what control he had.

William Ferrers, looking from one to the other like a scared rabbit, swallowed nervously, especially after hearing his cousin say what was no less than the truth. For perhaps the very first time since embarking on this ill-fated venture he was really frightened and fearful of the consequences of his participation in what had seemed to him a sure fire way of attaining what he had always coveted. If he were honest he had to admit that he had not particularly cared whether Stuart succeeded or not, his sole aim in contributing to his cause was from purely personal reasons and not because he desired to see him or his family reinstated to their former grandeur. It seemed to him that from the very beginning one thing after another had gone wrong necessitating hastily put together contingency plans which invariably had turned out to be flawed. He knew that he had neither the nerve nor the ingenuity to continue with an enterprise that was clearly destined to end in disaster, and whilst he had no wish to climb the scaffold he could think of nothing to say or do which would either placate his cousin or persuade him into letting them go. He inwardly winced at Richard's scorn should the attempt even be made, and therefore decided that his best course of action was to wait and see, because even though his cousin had made it clear what the outcome of their activities was going to be, he held out some hope that their relationship may just tip the scales in his favour.

Since Colonel Henderson's threats of hanging and a court martial had been dismissed by Richard Ferrers with a calm disregard to the fact that his position was still precarious, at least as far as he was concerned, he eyed his quarry with something akin to loathing. His temper as well as his frustration were even more exacerbated upon hearing him ask Lieutenant Beaton to find something with which to tie them both up, his face turning almost purple at the very idea of such an indignity.

"You're crowing mighty loud now, Ferrers," he warned as he was pushed unceremoniously into a chair by his junior officer, "but I'll make you pay for this, see if I don't!"

Richard Ferrers raised an eyebrow at this. "Indeed, and how do you propose to do that, bearing in mind that before too long you will be standing your trial for treason?"

"You little ..." he spluttered attempting a lunge forward only to find himself pushed back into the chair.

"I would advise you to watch your words, Henderson" Richard cautioned ominously, "these pistols of mine have devlish light triggers."

Having ensured himself that Colonel Henderson was securely tied to the chair, Lieutenant Beaton then turned his attention to William Ferrers who, much to the disgust of his accomplice, made a bolt for the door. "You fool!" Henderson exclaimed, believing he would have been better employed in attempting to retrieve either one of their swords which had been taken from them under duress or Lieutenant Beaton's own where he had put them on the floor, instead of trying to escape.

"Most unwise, Cousin" Richard advised with a shake of his head, watching his friend push him into a chair.

"Damn you, Richard!" he cried shrilly, his eyes starting from their sockets. "You can't mean to kill us in cold blood!"

"I must confess," he acknowledged, "that when faced with such a lily-livered coward as you I am sorely tempted, but I will refrain, for now at least," he inclined his head mockingly, "to indulge my desire to rid the world of the likes of you."

"You don't seriously expect to get away with this, do you?" Henderson challenged, the calmness which had enveloped him over the last hour or so completely deserting him and panic beginning to creep in. "Adding murder to your list of crimes will not help you."

"No," he acknowledged, holding his temper, "but those letters will." He saw the look of horror which crossed his face and was well satisfied. "Oh yes," he nodded, his eyes glinting, "I have them safe." Receiving a nod from his friend indicating that their prisoners were securely tied, he then tossed him the keys for the cellar. "See what you can do for the Major." He saw the hesitancy on Michael's face and knew instantly the reason for it. "Have no fear," he promised him, "I will not kill them while your back is turned."

Being assured that Richard meant it Michael let himself out of the room and hurriedly made his way towards a narrow passage leading off the rear of the hall where on the right at the far end a single door stood slightly ajar. Picking up a candle from the table resting against the wall he pushed the door open and quickly ran down the steps, unlocking the cellar door at the bottom with somewhat unsteady fingers. Upon learning that the Major had been drugged he had not known quite what he would discover upon his entry, but to find himself coming face to face with Major Neville clearly in a mood to do battle with his sword unsheathed instead of lying unconscious on the floor, made him take a hasty step backwards.

Having fully prepared himself to be confronted by either Colonel Henderson or William Ferrers it came as something of a surprise to Gideon to find himself looking down into the rather flushed face of Lieutenant Beaton who, if he was not mistaken, had expected to find himself laying eyes on a corpse. Heaving a sigh of relief he immediately sheathed his sword and stepped out from behind the door, exclaiming "You!"

"Are you all right, Sir?" he asked anxiously, his eyes searching Gideon's rather pale face.

"*No*, Lieutenant," he said firmly, "I don't mind saying that I am not all right," raking a hand through his already dishevelled hair.

"You must be feeling like the devil!" he exclaimed.

"Well, that is one way of putting it I suppose," he smiled, "but as you would expect I have felt better."

"I don't doubt it," he nodded comprehendingly. "In fact, Richard asked me to come and render you all possible assistance," he offered.

Gideon eyed him closely. "Richard!" he repeated. "Lieutenant," he sighed, "I realize my wine was drugged and unless I am very much mistaken I think I know why; but although I cannot at the moment, for reasons which are patently obvious," he explained reasonably, "work out the basics of the plan to apprehend Richard, which I assume your presence here signifies has somehow or other gone awry, and my head still feels as if it's being pounded, beyond that I am quite in the dark. Just what the *devil's* going on?"

Michael Beaton looked a little uncomfortable, but deciding that Major Neville would not be fobbed off, said hesitantly "Well Sir, that's rather a long story."

"I had a feeling it might be," he replied resignedly, glad to sit down again.

"Is there anything I can get you, Sir?" he asked, a little alarmed at the Major's somewhat haggard face and tousled appearance.

Gideon shook his head. "No, thank you. Well," he invited, "you may as well tell me the worst."

"Oh, it's not as bad as that, Sir" he assured him.

"If it's anything to do with Richard," he told him tartly, "it's bound to be every *bit* as bad as that!"

417

To say that the story which poured off Michael's tongue came as something of a shock was a gross understatement, and for several moments Gideon could do nothing but stare up at his young friend as one stunned.   However desperate Colonel Henderson was to settle his affairs and without any adverse repercussions rebounding on himself and William Ferrers, he had never considered him capable of abducting Elizabeth in order to entrap her brother. He had known from their very first meeting that Colonel Henderson mistrusted her, indeed, he had made no secret of the fact that he was of the unshakeable conviction that she knew far more than she was saying, and that she had been working hand in glove with Richard from the **very** beginning in order to bring about his downfall.   Apart from the fact that he **had** dared to use one whose very life meant more to him than his own, and in so callous and devious a manner, proved how frantic he actually was in attempting to bring matters to a speedy conclusion before his position developed to the point where it was beyond doing anything about.   Such cunning generated no admiration or endorsement in his breast, but he was compelled to admit, albeit reluctantly, that it was nevertheless a most cleverly devised plan.   A plan which would doubtless have succeeded if it had been designed to entrap someone other than Richard Ferrers, a young man who had struck him from the outset as being more than ordinarily astute, and which had been clearly demonstrated when he had read his sister's abduction for precisely what it was. This last ditch attempt of Colonel Henderson's to rid himself of Richard Ferrers as well as ensuring that that incriminating evidence came into his possession was unquestionably outrageous, it was certainly risky, as any number of things could have arisen to cast it all awry. Not only had he relied heavily on Elizabeth complying with that bogus letter and Richard taking the bait he had so deviously enticed him with, but also on being able to get rid of not only himself by making it impossible for him to decline his hospitality in order to offer him drugged cognac but also Major Denham by sending him off on what was in all probability a wild good chase with Captain Waring. The scurrilous means he had adopted to secure the successful outcome of his schemes may have fallen into place precisely the way he had planned but in view of the way things had apparently turned out they could not be said to have gained him very much.   Even so, to learn that his future brother-in-law was at this moment upstairs acting as not only protector to his sister but also as gaoler to the two men he had vowed to repay in full for their crimes, alarmed him.   Like Lieutenant Beaton he doubted Richard would do anything in front of his sister, but considering the provocation his two prisoners had meted out he placed no reliance on Elizabeth's presence as being sufficient to temper his very natural desire for revenge.

"Good God!" he exclaimed, rising hurriedly to his feet, the legs of the chair scraping violently on the stone flagged floor. "Are you telling me that after all that has happened you have left that young madcap alone with those two brandishing a pair of pistols!"

"It's quite all right, Sir" he assured him, "he won't use them, I promise you."

"I wish I were as confident as you in that belief!" he bit out, making straight for the door, surprising Lieutenant Beaton by mounting the cellar stairs two at a time.

Not daring to think what he would find upon entering the rear saloon, Gideon thrust open the door to find Colonel Henderson and William Ferrers tied securely to their chairs with Richard sitting astride another in front of them, his pistols resting on the back and aimed with deadly accuracy in their direction, while Elizabeth, despite sitting bolt upright in her chair, was looking tired and apprehensive.

Upon his entrance four pairs of eyes stared at him with varying degrees of emotion, but it was Elizabeth who found her voice first, crying out his name with heartfelt relief before jumping out of her seat and speeding across the room to fling herself into his arms. "Oh Gideon!" she cried, clinging to him. "Thank God you are safe! When I think of what they have done to you!"

He held her tight against him. "My darling," he soothed, "I was in no danger, I promise you."

"But they could have …!" she began tearfully.

"But they did not," he assured her gently, looking down into her pale and drawn face, wiping away a stray tear with his forefinger. "As you can see," he smiled, "I am quite safe."

"Major Neville!" Colonel Henderson thundered disregarding this tender scene, "you surely do not mean to allow this madman to kill us!" indicating Richard Ferrers with a nod of his head.

Ignoring this and everyone else, Gideon guided Elizabeth back to her chair and eased her gently down onto it, raising her hand to his lips, responding to her silent plea with a reassuring smile.

"Did you hear what I said, Major?" he demanded, paying no heed to this touching picture, his frustration exacerbated by what he regarded as his undignified position.

Richard's attempts to get information out of either Colonel Henderson or his cousin as to Sir Evelyn's part in tonight's affair as well as when he would be likely to return to his home proving unsuccessful, he had somehow managed to restrain his overwhelming desire to get it out of them by other means. He may have a score to settle with these two men, but he knew very well that by indulging his natural impulses would gain him nothing but a transient gratification and giving vent to his feelings would certainly not serve him in the least, besides which he could not subject his sister to such an ordeal. William, who had been ordered by his accomplice to say nothing, although it would have been quite impossible for him to have done so, so terrified was he, could do nothing but stare as one transfixed at those vicious looking weapons aimed in their direction.

Over the preceding months Richard Ferrers may have been sustained by the knowledge that he would repay them handsomely for their part in recent events, but apart from the fact that he was no cold-blooded killer, more practical matters were now occupying his thoughts. Those letters may prove him innocent of treason but they had yet to be produced to the authorities, and as they were at the moment hidden safely in the Major's quarters back at the garrison, the question of how they were to be retrieved and taken to London to Sir John posed something of a problem. Then there was the matter of taking Colonel Henderson and his cousin to a place of safety until such time as those letters could do their work. The more he thought about it the more risky it seemed to take them to the garrison to be held in the prison block there until other measures could be adopted until they faced their trial for treason as no reliance could be placed on either of them not trying to talk the guards into releasing them. He would stake his life that Sir Evelyn was no traitor, but since neither Colonel Henderson nor his cousin were forthcoming as to whether or not he knew what was taking placing under his own roof during his absence or, indeed, just how far the footman was in their confidence, he considered it not only foolhardy but dangerous to keep them here any longer than was necessary. Then, of course, there was the question of the man whom Henderson had persuaded to remove his sister from her home. According to Elizabeth his name was Private Smith, and although Michael had verified that he was indeed a member of the military stationed at the garrison, his part in tonight's affair and the prospect of his return to Hamstoke House, could not be overlooked, but as both his captives were as uncommunicative about this individual as they were about everything else, he was left with only guesses which were as numerous as they were unhelpful.

Employing his time while he waited for Michael to return with Gideon by trying to work out the problems facing them, he instantly raised his head as the door opened and both men walked in. Gideon's somewhat dishevelled appearance and the rather strained look on his face were enough to tell him that he had had a most uncomfortable time, thanks to this unscrupulous pair of individuals in front of him, but his tousled and damp hair, crumpled and dusty coat and blemished white gaiters, which not all Gideon's efforts could renovate, in no way deterred his sister from going to him. Observing her immediate response at the sight of him with brotherly forbearance, he had to admit that he had never before seen her face glow quite like that. Apart from the fact that he had nothing against the Major and was in no doubt that he would make Elizabeth an excellent husband, it was clear that both parties concerned felt the same about each other, and therefore would know no hesitation in giving their marriage his blessing and approval, providing of course he could extricate himself from his present difficulties!

"Good evening, Major" he inclined his head, thwarting Henderson's indignant response to Gideon's lack of interest to his demand, amusement written all over his face. "I am sorry you have had a rather uncomfortable time of it, but we came to your rescue just as soon as we possibly could."

"So I see," he replied wryly, attempting to smarten himself up, glancing significantly from the prisoners to those pistols.

"You must not be thinking however, that we put their confinement before your release out of choice" he smiled irrepressibly, rising easily to his feet, "but I felt sure you would understand that curtailing their movements took precedence over setting you free."

"A wise precaution," Gideon inclined his head. "I am certainly indebted to you, I would be even more so if you could dispense with those things," indicating the pistols still in his hands.

Richard appeared to give consideration to this request, his good humour disappearing as his eyes raked contemptuously over Colonel Henderson and his cousin, but after what seemed an inner struggle he nodded his head, returning the pistols to his pockets.

"Major Neville!" Colonel Henderson barked out, his face taking on a purple tinge. "I repeat; are you just going to stand there and do *nothing*?" conveniently overlooking his contribution to Gideon's present disorderly appearance. "You cannot, surely, mean to stand by and allow him to kill us!"

Gideon eyed him dispassionately. "Give me one good reason why I should not?" he asked calmly, quite unmoved by their plight.

"Reason!" he echoed, shocked at such a response. "Good God man, you wear the King's uniform; surely *that* is reason enough!"

"Coming from a man who readily abandoned the obligation that comes with the uniform, I find such an observation sits oddly on your shoulders," he pointed out coldly. "If it were left to me," he told him unequivocally, "I should have no compunction in leaving your fate in the hands of others," glancing significantly at Richard.

"Thank you, Major!" Richard inclined his head. "That was well said."

"Do not thank me," Gideon told him. "Whilst I accept you have justification on your side, I cannot and *will* not allow you to shoot them."

"Do you think I might?" he asked provocatively, an irrepressible twinkle in his eye.

"I think it very probable," Gideon nodded, "but I am sure you will agree that by allowing those letters and the law to do their work they will serve us all better. Besides," he smiled, "I do not think my father would appreciate it knowing that his daughter-in-law's brother was hanged for murder!"

Not unexpectedly Richard burst out laughing at this to which Gideon told him he was a young fool, but if he had been expecting some show of relief from their captives, or for some visible signs of embarrassment or remorse by Colonel Henderson over drugging his wine and his brief incarceration, then he was doomed to disappointment.

Colonel Henderson, far from regretting what he considered to be a necessity, stared up at Gideon with something akin to loathing. Having witnessed that display of affection between him and Miss Ferrers and the humorous exchange with her brother, he had no difficulty in understanding his deliberate mendacity throughout this whole affair and if nothing else, it certainly proved just how closely aligned to the Ferrers family he actually was; just as Lytton had claimed. Clearly, he could expect no support from Gideon or, indeed, Lieutenant Beaton, both of whom were fellow officers, and from the looks of it he could expect none from William Ferrers either. Subjecting his present circumstances to a rapid review and coming to the conclusion that there was no escape, he was forced into facing the awful realization that his position was perilous to say the least, and his long-term prospects, if, indeed, he had any, did not look any too good. Should he be fortunate enough to leave here in one piece, then he supposed that as a last ditch attempt he could call on Lytton, but it took only a moment to realize that Robert, not only a great believer in self-preservation but extremely sensitive about letting it be seen that he was involved in something as sordid as treason, would not allow himself to be blackmailed into coming to his rescue yet again. Having made his stance perfectly clear on the last occasion they met, he knew he could count on no further support from Robert, and should he attempt to use his past transgression against him, he knew without being told that a man of his standing would have no difficulty in deflecting any damaging accusations he may put forward.   Panic, exacerbated by fear born from the knowledge that there were no more avenues of escape available to him, began to creep in, and ultimately his temper overrode what little judgement he had left, and the angry tirade which left his lips proved to his listeners just how desperate he really was.

William Ferrers, who had for some little time been of the belief that their enterprise was doomed to failure, was now convinced that their days were numbered, if not by a ball from one of his cousin's pistols, then from the due processes of the law.   For as long as he could remember he had resented and envied Richard more than anyone else, longing for the day when the Ferrers inheritance would be his. It had been his intense jealousy of Richard as well as his overriding desire to be the sixth Viscount Easton which had brought him to where he now stood, and for perhaps the first time since embarking on such an ambitious course he acknowledged the futility of his resentment.   In his more optimistic moods he had convinced himself that he was indeed the man he professed to be to all his acquaintance; purposeful, determined and a man of his word, but in the cold light of day, such as now when his life hung in the balance, he was honest enough to admit that he was none of these things. He was weak and easily led, and for a man like Henderson these flaws in his character had been cleverly and skilfully drawn out; his assurances of a promising future finally persuading him into a course of action which, instead of securing him what he wanted above all else, had brought him to the point where he was only inches away from death. Despite his bravado a short time ago he was a very frightened man, to which his wilting body in the chair was adequate testimony. Colonel Henderson's determination to drag this nightmare out to the bitter end was more than his nerves could stand, and as he waited almost comatose for the axe to fall he knew his only hope lay in Major Neville, a man whom, he was convinced, held him in the utmost contempt.

Gideon may well do, but he was neither cruel nor vindictive and could see little point in tormenting a man who was already on the verge of nervous collapse. He had no more liking now for Clara Winsetton's wish to protect her nephew than he ever had, but to send a man to the gallows whose only real crime was to possess a weak will and envious nature would serve no purpose whatsoever. His role in recent events had been minor, merely doing as he was bid, the real culprit and instigator of all that had happened, and one who deserved to face his trial as well as the scaffold, was Colonel Henderson. His instincts told him that Richard Ferrers was a decent and honest man, and certainly no brutal killer, but it was going to take all his powers of persuasion to convince him that his cousin had learned a valuable lesson and that there seemed little likelihood of him embarking on any more future ventures, and therefore he should allow his cousin to go free.

From his conversation with Michael Beaton in the cellar it was clear that Elizabeth had not told her brother about her aunt's wishes regarding William, had she have done so then he doubted William would have remained unmolested. He was still very far from certain how to set about extricating William without Colonel Henderson implicating him in some way, but before this could be worked out he had the unenviable task of informing Richard of something he was clearly in no mood to hear.

From the look on Gideon's face Elizabeth had a very shrewd idea what he was thinking but knew too that her brother was in no frame of mind to receive such unwelcome news. She realized now that she should have told him herself, but the truth was she had been so relieved to see him that every other consideration, apart from his own and Gideon's immediate safety, had been forgotten. When she had recalled it to mind it had been too late, or rather, she had hoped it still would not be necessary to tell him, but now the time had come when he must be told, and deemed it to be her responsibility. From the moment she had discovered her cousin's perfidy she had been determined to make him pay for his crimes and especially for helping to bring about the death of her father, but seeing him now, terrified and fearful, with his head sunk on his chest and almost paralysed with dread, she could not find it in her heart to see him climb the scaffold. Like Gideon, she realized his role in recent events had been minor in comparison to Colonel Henderson, whom she would have no regrets in handing over to the authorities, but her cousin, through weakness and ambition, had been easily led, merely doing as he had been told. That did not mean she forgave him, not at all, but she could, to some extent at least, perceive the reason for his participation in all that had gone before, and firmly believed that he had been punished enough and therefore saw no reason why he should mount the scaffold.

Since Colonel Henderson could clearly count on no support from Major Neville and William Ferrers was in no condition mentally or physically to even try to retrieve their situation, he had been brought to realize that it was left to him to make a final attempt at salvaging their position. Refusing to accept that matters were hopeless he had frantically searched for a solution to the dilemma facing them, but try as he did he could come up with nothing that would extricate them from this present crisis. Nothing that was until he attempted a lunge forward in response to Gideon's inflammatory remark.

As the silken cords tying the heavy brocade curtains were all that Lieutenant Beaton had been able to find for the purpose of securing them to their chairs, had, during a succession of attempts to break free by Colonel Henderson, gradually begun to loosen. Although they had been pulled as tight as possible that last lunge had been sufficient to make them even more susceptible to the rigorous movement of his hands behind his back, and being a far bigger and heavier man than Lieutenant Beaton he had no difficulty in working them free, until eventually he was able to slide them over his hands, gripping them tight in his fingers until the right moment.

Unaware of the efforts being made by Colonel Henderson to free himself, Gideon turned to Richard, who was at the moment in the process of removing his voluminous overcoat, in order to speak to him about his cousin, when Elizabeth rose to her feet to intervene. She suspected from the look on Gideon's face that he was about to tell him of her aunt's stipulation and knew that she must be the one to break the news to him, but just as she was almost abreast of them, to her surprise as well as everyone else, Colonel Henderson rose suddenly to his feet and with remarkable swiftness for a man of his size grabbed hold of her and pulled her roughly against him, dragging her towards the door with his right arm around her neck and his left one across her body.

"Why you …!" exclaimed Richard taking a hasty step towards them, an ugly look on his face.

"Don't move," Henderson ordered, his over bright eyes bulging and his face a deep shade of purple. "I'll break her neck if you do."

"Henderson," Gideon said with more calmness than he felt, placing a restraining grip on Richard's arm, "let her go."

Having recovered a little from the shock of what was happening, Elizabeth began to wriggle in his arms only to find the grip tightening, her wide blue eyes scared and expectant as they looked from her brother to Gideon.

"You hurt her, Henderson" Richard threatened "and I swear I'll kill you; which is what I should have done before."

"Then it is a pity for you you did not," he bit out. "You two," nodding at Gideon and Michael, "remove your swords, and please do not try anything stupid."

Michael looked his indecision, but after receiving a confirming nod from Gideon unbuckled his sword belt and threw it on the floor next to Gideon's.

"Now kick them over here," he ordered. "Careful Major," he warned. "I have only to move my arm a fraction and I'll break Miss Ferrers' neck."

Gideon knew he would, so doing as he was bid kicked one and then the other in the direction of the door, having to contain his anger as well as his impatience until the appropriate time when he could make a move. For the moment it was far too dangerous to risk anything, the slightest attempt to do so could mean Elizabeth's life; Colonel Henderson, being far beyond the point of all reasoning, would have no hesitation in doing what he said. For a man in his position he would not give a moment's thought to taking her life, knowing he could only be hung once irrespective of how many lives he took.

Glaring at Richard he ordered, "Now, untie him," nodding his head in his accomplice's direction.

"I'm damned if I will!" Richard snarled.

"You know what will happen to your sister if you refuse," he warned. "Do not make the mistake of failing to take me seriously. I am not going to take a walk to the scaffold!"

"You won't get away with this Henderson," Gideon told him, his calm voice at variance to the blazing anger in his eyes and the fierce pounding of his heart when he thought of the danger Elizabeth was in.

"You think not?" he asked, his eyes darting from one to the other. "As long as I have Miss Ferrers I believe I will. Now, unless you want me to hurt your sister, I suggest you do as I ask and untie him."

Having come to the end of his mental as well as his emotional reserves, William Ferrers, having lost all sense of what was going on around him, was only vaguely aware of what was happening but when he raised his eyes to see his cousin bearing down upon him with such a ferocious look on his face he instinctively cowered in his chair. Something between a whimper and a cry of pain escaped his dry throat and for one terrifying moment he thought his end had come, almost fainting with fright as he felt the cords around his wrists being untied, wondering what his cousin was going to do to him.

Fury and impotence were acting on Richard like a flame to gunpowder and in his frustration pulled his cousin roughly out of the chair with one hand and thrust him towards Colonel Henderson. *"Here's* your accomplice, Henderson!" he ground out. "Much good may he do you!"

The force of Richard's thrust caused William to stumble, his hand quickly grabbing hold of Henderson's vacated chair in his efforts to save himself from falling to the floor. Managing to pick himself up he staggered to where Henderson was standing, his trembling fingers attempting to set his wig straight, his face pale and drawn beneath the rouge. He caught sight of his cousin's eyes upon him, cold and merciless and wished, not for the first time, that he was anywhere but here, but worse was to come when he heard Henderson instruct him to retrieve his cousin's pistols from his discarded overcoat, turning startled eyes towards his accomplice as though he had not heard correctly. "The p-pistols?" he stammered.

"Yes, damn it!" he snapped irritably. "Be quick about it."

"Be careful Cousin," Richard mocked softly, the febrile glint in his eyes making William pause, "they might go off."

Staring from his cousin to Henderson with painful indecision he wrung his hands not knowing what to do.

"Hurry up man!" Henderson shot at him. "We haven't got all night!"

Galvanized into action he picked up Richard's coat with hands that visibly shook, extracting the pistols from the pockets as though they were live coals. Holding Elizabeth round the waist with his left arm and removing his right hand from around her neck Colonel Henderson took hold of one of the pistols, ordering William Ferrers to keep his cousin as well as Major Neville and the Lieutenant covered with the other. Placing the nozzle against Elizabeth's temple, he eyed his audience with a mix of excitement and satisfaction. "All of you against that wall," he ordered.

"Don't be a fool Henderson," Gideon bit out, keeping his eyes on those weapons. "Put the pistol down and let Miss Ferrers go. There's nowhere to run to."

"Do as I say!" he barked, indicating the wall with a wave of the pistol.

Taking advantage of the moment Elizabeth struggled with all her strength to break free, but Henderson's hold on her was too strong, and tears of frustration and fear began to well up at the back of her eyes. Casting a frightened look at her brother and Gideon, both of whom could do very little with two pistols aimed at them, especially as William's could well go off accidentally in the highly nervous state he was in, tried again to wriggle out of his arm, but almost immediately the nozzle was once more pressed against her temple. "You know I will shoot her," he warned, his protruding eyes bulging even more. "Back against the wall I say!"

Reluctantly they did as they were told, then after nodding his head satisfyingly he instructed William Ferrers to tie them up one by one and when he had done so he was to bring the carriage round to the front door.

William's lack of moral fibre may have been a contributing factor in bringing him to where he now stood but he retained sufficient commonsense to realize that running away would do them no good at all, not only that but his hands were shaking so much he could barely hold Richard's pistol let alone manage to tie anyone up. Like it or not they had come to the end of the road, and even supposing they did make it to the carriage he doubted they would get very far besides, he was tired of running and whilst he had no desire to have his neck stretched, neither had he any desire to try and make a run for it and possibly end up being shot. Surprising himself as well as his audience he shook his head. "No. No, I won't."

Gideon and Richard, taken somewhat aback at this startling and unexpected defiance, glanced significantly at one another, and Lieutenant Beaton, who had never experienced anything as remotely exciting as this evening's events, stared at both of them with his mouth wide open.

Colonel Henderson, furious at his accomplice's rebelliousness, angrily shouted his order again to which he received a firm shake of the head. "Damn you, Ferrers!" he spluttered. "Do you want to go to the gallows?" From out the corner of his eye he saw Gideon take a tentative step forward, but spinning round cautioned him as to the unwisdom of doing anything foolish.

"It's over, Henderson" Gideon shook his head. "You may as well put the pistol down and let Miss Ferrers go."

William, who had by now dropped the pistol he had been holding as if it were contaminated, not only looked exhausted but utterly defeated, his eyes staring blankly ahead and his whole body shaking with reaction and fear, but Henderson, determined to make good his escape with or without him, ordered him one last time to do as he had been told. When he neither answered nor even looked in his direction, Henderson, frantically aware that he was on his own and the gallows were beckoning, lost what little self-control he had, and before anyone realized what was happening raised his pistol and fired, whereupon William Ferrers dropped to the floor.

Panic, desperation and a feeling of sheer hopelessness engulfed him all at once, and upon seeing his three adversaries bearing down upon him threw the empty pistol down onto the floor. Quickly pushing Elizabeth away from him to try and impede their passage in order to give him precious seconds in which to bend down and pick up the pistol William Ferrers had dropped, he discovered to his horror upon rising to his feet that his back was against the door. With his face purple and blotched, and his eyes protruding to their fullest extent he unsteadily pointed the weapon at them, momentarily making them pause, but the footman's unexpected arrival in the hall and his forceful attempts to open the door caused Henderson to lose his balance slightly, his finger jerking uncontrollably on the trigger. The explosion, coming so soon after the first, brought forth another demand to know what was going on from the footman on the other side of the door, a demand which went unanswered by the room's occupants as they saw Elizabeth collapse unconscious to the floor.

CHAPTER TWENTY TWO

General Turville may have questioned Colonel Henderson's mishandling of this affair, even going so far as to suspect his motives for tracking down Richard Ferrers with such uncompromising vengeance, but at no time had he thought him a party to treason. When he had sent Gideon into Sussex he had had no idea just what his investigations would reveal, but upon learning the full extent of Henderson's involvement together with that of Richard Ferrers' own cousin, not only profoundly shocked him, but greatly disturbed him.

From the moment Lytton had approached him on this he had gained the very strong impression that dirty work was in the offing, but although he could not say why this should be he had nevertheless been quite perturbed over the business. Try as he did he could not rid his mind of the distasteful thought that there was more to the apprehension of Richard Ferrers than he had been told, and for reasons he could not put his finger on had found himself questioning Colonel Henderson's part in the affair. If, as Lytton had led him to believe, Richard Ferrers was indeed a traitor then why should it be necessary to conduct a search for him so furtively instead of out in the open, but more than this why had it taken so long to instigate one? For a man in Colonel Henderson's position, who would surely have had little trouble in tracking down someone virtually on his doorstep, the reason for him to bring in Lytton was inexplicable. He could not help but wonder if Henderson's failure to capture Richard Ferrers had its roots in incompetence, but even this did not fully explain the need to seek him out with such ruthless determination. Since this left him with only one conclusion he wondered if there could well be a far more personal reason to account for the urgency to arrest him and had begun to speculate what his friend's son had done to generate such extreme measures being taken against him, but at no time had he suspected Colonel Henderson of treasonable activities, much less Jasper's own nephew. It therefore came as a reeling blow to discover that a man of Henderson's standing and one, moreover, who wore the King's uniform, had lent himself to the furtherance of Stuart's cause, resulting in him pointing the finger at an innocent man when the insurrection had failed. His reasons for embarking on such a course still remained something of a mystery, but if Richard Ferrers was right when he had told Gideon that he had most probably entered into the business from personal gain and hopes of high office, then he had been doomed to disappointment. One would have thought that a man who had attained high rank within the military would have had enough sense to realize that Stuart would have promised all manner of things if it meant gaining support for his cause, but clearly Henderson had not paused to consider such a necessary act of deception.

Then, of course, there was the disclosure that Richard Ferrers' own cousin had been working hand in glove with Colonel Henderson. He knew very little about William Ferrers but according to Gideon it seemed most likely that his motivation for throwing in his lot with Henderson had stemmed primarily from envy and personal ambition rather than political beliefs. He could well imagine Richard Ferrers' shock upon discovering that his own cousin was one of the men responsible for not only feeding information to Stuart but also ensuring that the finger of blame was cast in his direction.

Clearly, Gideon had gained the trust of Miss Ferrers, which, bearing in mind her animosity towards the military, must have been considerable in view of all she had endured, was no mean feat; it had certainly born fruit. If Gideon was right, and he had no reason to suppose otherwise, then obtaining those letters was paramount if Richard Ferrers was to take up his place in society again. He placed great store not only in Gideon's tact and discretion but also his abilities, and had no doubt that he would find a way of gaining entry into the prison block to retrieve the evidence needed to conclude this matter once and for all, ensuring that the guilty faced their trial for treason and an innocent man went free.

With regard to Richard Ferrers' smuggling activities, he had no reason to question Gideon's confidence in that these could easily be explained away due to the fact that no one had ever actually caught him red-handed in the act of running goods, even though he was in fact an active member of the fraternity. If all Gideon had reported was true, and he had no reason to doubt it was, then he could well understand his old friend's son embarking on this illicit career. Obviously, Colonel Henderson had got wind of Ferrers' nocturnal activities and decided to use the information against him in an attempt to damage his reputation even more. It would certainly add much needed weight to the charge of treason as well as gaining Henderson much needed sympathy and support in apprehending him in a locality which, for the most part, fell within the Ferrers estate.

What could not be so easily explained away was Lytton's involvement. Like Gideon, he was at a loss to understand what could possibly have induced him to come to Henderson's aid. Admittedly they were old friends, but Lytton was nothing if not astute, and it would surely not have taken a man of his perspicacity long to discover Henderson's participation in the late rebellion. His Grace, who could be quite remorseless in his dealings, would have had little trouble in prising the truth out of him and this being so he doubted Henderson would have withstood His Grace's unremitting questioning for very long before confessing the whole. Nevertheless, this did not explain how a man of Lytton's firmly held beliefs and unquestionable loyalty to His Majesty, had allowed himself to be persuaded into offering Henderson assistance once he was in possession of the facts. His willingness to support his old friend therefore continued to remain an enigma, but this did not alter the fact that His Grace was a powerful force to be reckoned with and certainly not one to be disregarded with impunity.

But of one thing he could be certain, and that was Gideon would need all the assistance he could get if this matter was to be resolved, especially if, as he strongly suspected, Colonel Henderson decided to call on His Grace in his attempts to prove obstructive to Gideon's pursuance of the law. He may place the greatest store in his Personal Staff Officer's adroitness and tact, but he possessed neither the authority nor the rank to either arrest Colonel Henderson or to place him in safe custody. It was therefore imperative he go to Gideon's support without any further loss of time, and in view of this considerably startled his orderly by brusquely ordering him to prepare for an immediate journey into Sussex, unaware of the stirring events about to be played out at Hamstoke House.

From the moment Gideon had learned of Colonel Henderson's part in Stuart's attempt at insurrection he had been all too well aware of the difficulties which would arise should he attempt to place him under arrest for treason. He was fully conscious of the fact that he lacked both the rank or the authority to charge a senior officer with any offence, let alone something as serious as sedition, and that such a prerogative would fall within the jurisdiction of General Turville or some other officer of equal rank. Unfortunately, matters had developed in a way that he had neither expected nor looked for, but at this moment in time, as he looked horror-struck at Elizabeth's lifeless body at his feet, he could happily have disregarded the dictates of military etiquette by inflicting the direst punishment on Colonel Henderson.

But gratifying his natural urges would not help Elizabeth, so leaving her brother to deal adequately with him and Lieutenant Beaton to ascertain that William Ferrers was indeed dead, he knelt down beside her to establish the extent of her wound. Her face was ashen and the blood seeped steadily from the hole in her shoulder, but to his immense relief he was able to detect a faint pulse and without wasting any time effortlessly ripped away her sleeve with his strong fingers in order for him to take a closer look. He saw that the ball was not as deeply embedded as he had at first thought, but as there was no time to waste in waiting for a surgeon to be brought, he somehow had to pack that hole and stem the flow of blood until one could tend her. It was therefore with a complete disregard for her maidenly modesty that he raised her skirts in order for him to tear off strips from her petticoat, his strong fingers making easy work of the delicate material, then grabbing hold of a decanter of brandy from a nearby table, he soaked one of the strips with the amber liquid and began to clean the wound, after which he worked with a calm efficiency that had its roots in experience rather than emotional detachment. His fingers were remarkably steady as they packed that gaping hole with one after the other of the fine lawn strips that had made up her petticoats which he tightly rolled into swabs in order to staunch the blood which was steadily oozing from the wound.

Having dealt suitably with Colonel Henderson by knocking him senseless, Richard was at Gideon's side in two strides, kneeling down beside him to look at his sister, his face as white as her own. For several stunned moments he found it impossible to speak, glancing sideways at Gideon's taut face as he concentrated on packing that opening as tight as he could. He was not overly squeamish any more than he was a stranger to the sight of blood, but as he stared down at the torn flesh of his sister's shoulder, he was conscious of a feeling of nausea welling up inside him. Her loyalty and devotion to him had been unwavering and certainly beyond question; suffering all manner of abuse and humiliation in his cause, and this was her reward! From childhood they had been best friends as well as brother and sister; he protective and shielding and she totally trusting as well as looking up to him as a fount of all knowledge, and he knew that should anything happen to her because of him he would never forgive himself.

To their infinite relief they saw her briefly open her eyes to stare dazedly up at them, Richard taking the opportunity to pull a flask from his pocket and gently raise her head to swallow a little, but her consciousness was only short-lived as the pain of Gideon's probing fingers proved too much to bear. Richard heard Gideon's sharp intake of breath, and could only marvel at the way he was holding himself together, working quickly and efficiently in order to save the life of the woman he loved; his fingers deft and sure as they continued to plug that gaping hole.

Michael, having made sure that life was extinct in William Ferrers and that Colonel Henderson would be unconscious for some considerable time, thanks in part to him striking his head on the door handle as he fell to the floor as a result of the force of Richard's fist, managed to move his dead weight body to one side in order to allow him to open the door to the terrified footman. It was clear from the look on his face as he tried to peer over Michael's shoulder that he had not expected such goings on when he had allowed Colonel Henderson to use his master's home during his absence, and was therefore extremely fearful of the consequences in allowing the chance to make extra money get the better of him. Deciding that the less he saw the better, Michael stepped out into the hall closing the door of the rear saloon behind him, trying to calm the shattered nerves of Sir Evelyn's servant whilst at the same time instructing him to bring a bowl of warm water and a towel. It took time and patience to achieve both, but eventually he managed to soothe his alarms sufficiently to enable him to carry out his instructions, returning some minutes later with the required items, then having handed these over he opened the door of the saloon to allow Michael to enter, disappointed when he was firmly excluded but told to keep himself within hearing.

After what seemed the devil of a long time to Richard's over-stretched nerves, it was with relief that he saw Gideon place the last makeshift swab into place, finishing off his handiwork with a covering pad and tying an improvised bandage round the dressing to keep it in place.

"Hopefully that should hold," he said tautly, rising slowly to his feet and immersing his blood stained hands into the bowl of warm water which had been placed on the table, looking anxiously down at Elizabeth's inanimate body. "Tell me," he asked at length, having subjected their situation to a rapid review, discarding the towel "how far is Ferrers Court from here by your reckoning?"

"About seven or eight miles," Richard replied, rising unhurriedly to his feet. "Damn it man!" he exclaimed horrified, suddenly realizing what was in his mind. "She'll never make it!"

"Yes she will," Gideon said firmly. "She *has* to."

"I tell you she won't!" he bit out. "That hole will burst wide open before she's gone a mile over these roads!"

"We have no choice," Gideon told him. "Not only can we not bring a doctor here to treat her," he told him firmly, "but we have to clear this place before we leave tonight."

"Clear the place!" Richard echoed, wondering if the shock had temporarily deranged Gideon. "For God's sake man, there's been cold-blooded murder committed here tonight!"

"I am aware of that," Gideon told him. "Lieutenant," he called over his shoulder, ignoring Richard's growing exasperation.

"Yes, Sir."

"Get that footman in here."

"Yes, Sir," springing to the order instantly.

Paying no heed to Richard's vehement arguments as to the insanity of what he was proposing, Gideon inserted a hand into the inner pocket of his coat to pull out a pocket book from which he tore off a sheet and handed it to Richard, requesting him to write down the name and direction of their physician together with a note that his attendance was needed urgently at Ferrers Court. Although Richard was still of the opinion that it was far too dangerous to risk his sister's life by jolting her over roads that were in such a shocking state of disrepair, he strode over to the desk and dipping the pen in the standish did as he was asked, handing the sheet back to Gideon reiterating his objections, all of which went unanswered as the door opened and the footman walked in.

This unfortunate individual, agog with curiosity as well as fearful of the repercussions which could ensue from such unprecedented events, had placed an eye and then an ear to the keyhole in an attempt to discover what was going on behind the mahogany door, only to stumble in an undignified heap at Michael's feet when it was unexpectedly opened. Having hastily got to his feet, he entered the saloon with a string of apologies and explanations falling off his tongue, but upon setting eyes on Colonel Henderson, whose unconscious bulk had been manoeuvred into a wing chair, William Ferrers' corpse stretched out on the hearth with his cousin's voluminous overcoat thrown over him and Elizabeth Ferrers lying as if dead on the floor, he stared from one to the other with such a look of horror and shock that for several moments he was unable to utter a word.

"What's your name?" Gideon asked abruptly, bringing him back to earth with a jolt.

"C-Cartwright, Sir," he managed, staring at Gideon as one bemused.

"Tell me Cartwright," Gideon asked, "where is Sir Evelyn?"

"In town, Sir," he replied anxiously, looking from one to the other warily.

"How long for?"

"M-Monday w-week, Sir," he stammered nervously.

"I take it Sir Evelyn and Colonel Henderson are acquaintances?"

"Yes, S-Sir" he confirmed, wringing nervous hands together. "They p-play c-cards together Sir, once a w-week."

"Did Colonel Henderson persuade you into allowing him to use your master's home this evening?" Upon receiving a frightened nod, Gideon asked "For what purpose?"

Cartwright looked a little uncomfortable, but explained "The Colonel said he had need of a private room, Sir. He didn't tell me why, he just said that a few acquaintances w-would be joining him and that he would make it worth my while, especially if I said nothing to Sir Evelyn."

Gideon nodded. "Greased you in the fist did he?" Upon receiving an assenting nod, he commented, "I hope it was indeed worth your while! Now tell me, is there someone here who could convey a message to Doctor Jarvey at Little Turton?"

"Little Turton!" he exclaimed. "But that's all of six or seven miles, Sir!" still unsure what was going to happen to him, not to mention all these bodies lying around the room.

"I am aware of the distance. Are you here alone, or are there other servants in the house?" Gideon asked sharply.

"There's only me and Davy, the stable boy Sir," he explained. "Williams the groom and all the house servants having gone to town with Sir Evelyn."

"Take this to the stable boy," Gideon ordered, handing him the note. "Tell him it's urgent and he's to waste no time. I take it there are horses and a carriage of some kind in the stables?"

"Yes, Sir" he nodded. "Well, what I mean, Sir," he corrected himself, "is that the carriage in the stables is one that is not used now; Sir Evelyn having gone to town in the other."

"What happened to the carriages which must have been used to bring me and the lady here?" Gideon demanded.

"I'm afraid they're gone, Sir" he replied penitently, feeling as though this was somehow his fault. "The first one, Sir" he explained, "the one that you were brought here in, was driven away by someone the Colonel had brought with him specially for that purpose. The carriage that the lady arrived in, Sir" he clarified, "was driven away by the man who brought her here."

This came as no surprise but it was disappointing all the same; doubtless both carriages had been used with the same callous disregard for their owners as that of Hamstoke House. "Well, that can't be helped," Gideon sighed. "Is there another vehicle other than the carriage?" he asked briskly.

"There's only the trap her late ladyship used, Sir" he offered.

"We'll need that as well," Gideon said firmly. "Lieutenant, go with Cartwright to the stables and get the carriage and trap ready to bring round to the front door as soon as you can, and make sure that the boy leaves here immediately with that message."

"Yes, Sir" he nodded.

"But, Sir," Cartwright said almost tearfully, "I can't say that the carriage is in any fit state to be used, not having been out since her ladyship passed on, and as for the horses, Sir" he urged, "there's only two carriage horses in the stables and one other, which Davy will need if he's to take this message. The nag that pulls the cart has not been between shafts since I don't know when!"

"That can't be helped," Gideon bit out. "It will have to do."

Cartwright, about to argue the wisdom of using a nag that was good for nothing but eating its head off, unexpectedly found a firm hand under his arm propelling him inexorably out of the room.

Waiting only until they were alone Gideon turned to Richard, explaining "You must take Elizabeth to Ferrers Court in the carriage, where I hope Doctor Jarvey will not be too long in arriving."

"Damn it, Gideon!" Richard exclaimed, making use of his first name as though they had known one another all their lives. "Subjecting her to a seven mile drive over roads that are in no fit condition for someone with a hole in their shoulder, is running the devil of a risk!"

"Do you think I don't know that?" Gideon bit out, glancing down at Elizabeth's inanimate body. "Her life is just as important to me as it is to you, but apart from the fact that I believe my handiwork will hold until she's tended by the doctor, you must see that her presence here will only create the devil of scandal. Once that ball is removed she will be in no fit condition to be moved for some considerable time, and under no circumstances can we allow Sir Evelyn to return here to find your sister recovering from a pistol wound."

"Scandal!" Richard echoed eyeing Gideon a little bemused, wondering what was in his mind. "I fail to see how that can be avoided after what has happened here tonight!"

"*Nothing* has happened here tonight. We have not come within ten miles of the place," Gideon told him quietly, stunning his future brother-in-law. "I am afraid you will also have to take Colonel Henderson with you, we cannot risk taking him to the garrison. I'll bring William to Ferrers Court in the trap."

Richard stared incredulously up at Gideon as though he could not believe what he had heard, much less what he was suggesting.

In view of this evening's unprecedented events Gideon knew that this was really not the right time to inform him of his aunt's wish to protect William, and also that his death at the hands of his accomplice had, however unintentionally, created the means of absolving William of any involvement. He supposed there would never be a right time to tell him something like this, but if they were to prevent an outright scandal resulting from tonight's fiasco, then he was faced with very little choice, especially as he needed Richard's help in order to achieve it.

It was not to be expected that Richard would take such tidings calmly, in fact his reaction was precisely how Gideon had predicted it would be and was therefore prepared for the angry outburst which left his lips once he had overcome his incredulity. Not surprisingly, he determinedly refused to accept such an honourable end to his cousin's deceitful career as that recommended by Gideon and adamantly refused to agree to something he clearly found to be not only quite repugnant to him, but downright untrue. As far as destroying those letters which mentioned William was concerned, so incensed was he that he vigorously rejected the idea, informing Gideon in no uncertain terms that he would have nothing to do with it. Gideon had no doubt that given time he would be able to bring Richard round, but as time was not in their favour he could not waste what little they had by resorting to tact and diplomacy in trying to win him over to the scheme. He was therefore obliged to point out that whilst he had no liking for covering up the truth any more than he did, when faced with the harsh realities of what would follow if they did not do everything in their power to avert more trouble coming their way, there was nothing else they could do.

Richard, still not convinced, paced frustratingly up and down, his face echoing his disgust as he considered everything Gideon had said, suddenly coming to an abrupt halt only feet away from him. "Are you seriously suggesting that I say that William, far from being in league with Henderson, was in fact working with us in order to reveal the truth about him?" In response to Gideon's confirming nod a pugnacious look descended on Richard's face. "No, damme, I won't do it!" he exclaimed. "Why, it's more than flesh an' blood can stand!"

"I realize that," Gideon replied calmly.

"Do you?" Richard bit out. "And do you also realize that there is every possibility that Henderson won't tell the same tale? Why, he'll sing like a bird at the earliest opportunity!"

"Very probably," Gideon agreed, "but there is nothing we can do about that."

"Damn it man!" Richard cried, impatiently removing his hat and slapping it against his thigh. "He'll bring all to ruin!"

"I realize that too," Gideon acknowledged, "but you cannot have considered. His position is most awkward to say the least. He has committed cold-blooded murder here tonight and in front of four witnesses, not to mention his participation in treason, to which those letters testify. The chances are that any claims he puts forward will be looked upon as nothing more than an attempt to exonerate himself and without those three letters naming William as his accomplice his accusations towards him will not be taken seriously." Gideon paused for a moment. "I have no idea if my strategies will work or not," he smiled, "but since this situation has been thrust upon us, we are having to make the best of it."

Richard heaved a sigh, after which he took another frustrated turn up and down as if by doing something energetic it would help clear his mind, eventually coming to a halt in front of Gideon, raking his long fingers through his hair. "Very well," he conceded reluctantly. "I'll take Henderson to The Court until this General of yours shows his face, although how I shall be able to keep my hands off him I don't know!" he exclaimed. "As for William," he shook his head, "I suppose there's nothing else we *can* do," he admitted grudgingly. "But I don't like it!"

Gideon gripped his shoulder, not unsympathetic to his feelings. "Nor do I, but you must see that we cannot leave William's body here," he reasoned, "and as for Henderson," he shrugged, "it is by far too dangerous to leave him where we cannot keep our eyes on him. I dare not run the risk of taking him back to the garrison to await the arrival of General Turville."

Richard considered this, saying at length. "I was thinking about that earlier. I would not at all put it beyond him to talk the guards into letting them go."

"I too have thought of that possibility; which is why he must go with you," Gideon nodded. "We have to anticipate every eventuality which could give rise to a scandal as well as impede our efforts to exonerate you, both of which are at risk if we left him at the garrison. There would be no way he would keep his mouth shut."

"Talking of averting scandals," Richard reminded him, "what are we going to do about this Private Smith? According to my cousin after he left here he was to return to the garrison to discover what had happened to me and then report back here to Henderson. We have to do something about him," he urged.

"I know," Gideon nodded, rapidly turning this problem over in his mind. "However," he smiled at length, "I think there may be a way of dealing with him."

"It's to be hoped so," Richard replied tartly, "because I tell you now that running goods is a damn sight more easier than thinking up ways of getting us out of this mess!" Gideon laughed and was just about to respond to this when Richard clapped a hand to his forehead, a thought suddenly occurring to him, "Good God!" he cried.

"What is it?" Gideon asked sharply, envisaging another hurdle to scale.

"I forgot, Michael and I have left our horses near the entrance!"

Gideon heaved a sigh of relief; compared to everything else this was a small matter. "Don't worry, I'll take care of them. What's more," he grinned, "if those nags of Sir Evelyn's don't come up to scratch, they will come in very useful."

A smile suddenly lit Richard's eyes. "I once called you cautious," he grinned, "but after this I'm not so sure. Do you think all this will work?" he asked, indicating the muddle surrounding them.

"It *has* to," Gideon told him, a slight frown creasing his forehead. He was just about to say something when the door opened and Michael walked in followed by Cartwright. "Is everything ready?"

"Yes, Sir" he nodded. "The carriage and trap are round the front and the stable boy left with the message ten minutes ago."

"Cartwright, don't you go anywhere until I have spoken with you," Gideon ordered, before helping Richard lift Colonel Henderson's dead-weight body out of the chair to carry him through the hall and down the three shallow steps to the driveway. Michael, who had run on ahead, had the carriage door open ready, whereupon they hurled their unconscious captive inside and dropped him unceremoniously onto the floor. Returning to the house, Richard, by no means pleased that his overcoat had been used for covering his cousin, demanded of his friend if he could not have found something else as he pulled the voluminous garment off him, picking his pistols up off the floor and returning them to the pockets. Gideon, leaving them to see to William Ferrers, knelt down beside Elizabeth to gently pick her up in his arms to carry her out to the carriage. He kissed her forehead and she stirred in his arms, her eyes opening to stare dazedly up at him, but only for a moment, but it relieved his mind of a dreadful fear. Once his cousin's body had been placed into the trap with his small dress sword thrown onto the floor beside him and covered with an old horse blanket, Richard climbed up into the coach ready to take his sister's lifeless body from Gideon, who carefully handed his precious charge into her brother's care. As both men understood each other's anxiety over Elizabeth it was quite unnecessary to voice it, and apart from Gideon saying, "I'll join you at Ferrers Court as soon as I've finished here," no words were needed between them. After firmly closing the door and giving Michael his instructions as well as seeking directions to Ferrers Court, he stepped back to watch as Michael jumped up onto the box, gently easing his team down the drive and through the main gate.

Returning to the house Gideon strode across the hall and into the rear sitting room where he had spent the most traumatic hour of his life, his glance automatically taking in the pool of blood on the carpet where Elizabeth had fallen.

He could only hope and pray that she would live, but despite his promptness he had to admit that she had lost a fair amount of blood, and whilst he was no stranger to dealing with wounds any more than he was to seeing fallen comrades in the field, it was the first time he had had to work on someone who meant more to him than life itself.

He had neither sympathy nor understanding for Henderson, and whilst there was no doubting his intention to murder William Ferrers he was easily able to acquit him of attempting to murder Elizabeth. That pistol going off had been nothing but a sheer accident, but even so he did not think he would ever forget the horror he had felt when he saw her slump to the floor at his feet. It had been an instinctive reaction which had guided his hand in attempting to prevent the very worst from happening, but even now he still had no very clear idea of how he had managed to set aside his personal feelings in order for him to tend to that hole in her shoulder. He had been perfectly willing to leave Henderson in Richard's capable hands, and could only marvel that he had not killed him there and then, had he have done so there would have been more than enough justification. Nevertheless, he was relieved to know that his future brother-in-law had done no such thing, but merely knocked him senseless; to have one corpse on their hands was bad enough, but to have two would have taken the devil of a lot of explaining!

"You wanted to speak to me, Sir?" Cartwright asked, entering the sitting room in Gideon's wake, wishing, and not for the first time during the last hour or so, that he had not acceded to Colonel Henderson's request to use Sir Evelyn's home in his absence.

"Yes," he nodded, swinging round to face him. "Tell me, the man who brought the lady here, Private Smith, do you know him?"

"No, Sir. I've never seen him before," not at all sure whether to be glad or not that he could deny all knowledge of him.

"Can you tell me anything at all about him?" Gideon questioned.

"No Sir," he shook his head, "nothing. Colonel Henderson just told me that a Private Smith from the garrison would be arriving in a carriage with a lady and I was to show her in here. The young man never even came into the house, Sir."

"Can you describe him?" he asked.

"Well Sir," he shrugged, "I only caught a glimpse of him, but I think I would know him again if I saw him," attempting to describe Private Smith as best he could, hoping this would go some way to earning himself a reprieve for his part in tonight's fiasco.

Gideon nodded. "No, don't go yet," he ordered as he saw Cartwright about to leave, "I've not finished with you." Sitting down at the writing desk, he pulled a pen and a sheet of paper towards him, taking a few minutes to scribble a note to Private Smith, after which he affixed a wafer and wrote his name on the front. Upon discovering that his senior officer's plans had come to nothing but had in fact been arrested, because there was no way something of this magnitude could be kept quiet indefinitely, there was every possibility that this nefarious individual may well abscond. It was extremely doubtful whether he would respond to the letter deciding instead to either make a run for it or go to ground somewhere until the coast was clear, in which case he would have to rely on Major Denham to effect a search, but having some idea of what he looked like would at least assist him in keeping his eye open for him.

Cartwright, whose expression was a nice mix of curiosity and apprehension, waited in nervous silence until he had finished, making a solemn oath as he did so that never again would he allow himself to get into this kind of a fix if only the Good Lord would spare him on this occasion.

Rising to his feet Gideon handed him the note with strict instructions that he was to hand it to Private Smith personally who he understood was due to return here at some point tonight. "You are to say nothing to him about what has happened here," he ordered firmly. "Is that understood?" Although he received a confirming nod Gideon nevertheless felt it behoved him to reinforce his warning. "Should he ask you where Colonel Henderson and his friend are or enquires about the lady, you are only to say they have left with me but you don't know where we have gone to. Under no circumstances," Gideon cautioned, "are you to mention anything to him about what you have seen."

"It shall be as you say, Sir" Cartwright assured him solemnly, his eyes pleading leniency as they looked at Gideon's stern face. "I - I never dreamed this would happen Sir," he shook his head. "I ..."

"Clearly not," Gideon bit out. "I take it you will be able to clear up this mess so the room appears as normal?" indicating the room with a nod of his head.

"Yes Sir," he assured him, regarding this as a small price to pay for coming out of this as well as he had.

"About the carriage and trap," Gideon said briskly, "they will be returned here before Sir Evelyn arrives back from town?"

Upon receiving another nod in response to this, Gideon picked up Colonel Henderson's sword off the floor before casting a quick glance around the room to ensure nothing had been left behind. Having satisfied himself that he had not overlooked any incriminating evidence he opened the door to leave but paused momentarily looking directly at Cartwright, saying meaningfully, "Cartwright, no one has been here tonight; none of this ever happened."

Cartwright swallowed. "No Sir, of course not, Sir," he replied comprehendingly, unable to believe he was not going to be reported to his master and therefore discharged.

"Should anything leak out about this evening's events," Gideon warned, "which leads to rumour or gossip, I shall know where to look for the mischief maker. I hope I make myself clear?" he asked, watching the relief cross his face.

"Yes Sir; perfectly."

"Let this be a lesson to you Cartwright," Gideon advised. "I doubt Sir Evelyn would be any too pleased to know that you had abused his home as well as his trust in this way." Without waiting for a response he turned on his heel and left.

By now it was well after midnight but although the rain had stopped the air was damp and chill, and pausing only long enough to ensure that William Ferrers' body was well covered and Henderson's sword was thrown down beside his accomplice's small sword, climbed up into the trap and trotted down the drive until he came to the entrance where he pulled up and jumped down. He saw the horses were still where Richard and Michael had left them and after quickly untying their reins walked them the short distance to the trap where he hitched them up behind, before climbing back onto the box and making his way to Ferrers Court.

CHAPTER TWENTY THREE

By the time Salmon arrived back at Ferrers Court after leaving the 'The Moonshadow' so convinced was he that Richard's lifeless body would be brought back home on a stretcher, his nerves were well and truly on the fret. Trying to remonstrate with Richard when he was in this kind of humour was a waste of time but nevertheless he felt he had to try and make him see the futility of going full tilt into something which could well end up the worse for him. He knew Richard was neither a coward nor a fool, seeing his sister's abduction for precisely what it was, a cleverly laid plan to ensnare him, but undeterred by the possible consequences to himself he had gone headlong to her rescue in a mood ripe for murder. He supposed he should have known better than to think that any words of his would have prevented him from doing everything he could to protect her, and whilst he expected no less of a man of his integrity, he would have felt a little easier in his mind had he not taken those pistols with him.

Miss Calne, no stranger to Clara Winsetton's odd humours, had never before known her to be so tetchy and irritable as she was this evening, and believed that this latest spate of vexation had its roots in Miss Elizabeth leaving the house so peremptory, which she shrewdly guessed had something to do with her brother's unfortunate troubles. So out of sorts was her mistress that during the last hour or so she had found herself on the receiving end of her sharp tongue, and was therefore more than a little relieved when that redoubtable old lady abruptly informed her that she was going downstairs. Wrapping a shawl around her bony shoulders and leaning heavily on her cane, resisting her companion's offer to assist her with the acid rejoinder that she was not yet decrepit, she slowly descended the stairs to find Salmon pacing anxiously up and down in the hall.

Having prised the outcome of his meeting with Richard out of him upon his return from the 'The Moonshadow', she had immediately denounced him as a fool, telling him in no uncertain terms that had he been firmer with her niece then none of this would be happening. He had been about to tell her that her niece, as well she knew, could be as stubborn as her brother, and had taken no heed of his warnings, but before he could open his mouth to tell her how it had come about or explain his efforts to dissuade her, she had walked majestically out of the room. Although she was perfectly well aware of Elizabeth's stubborn streak, she still believed he should have made more of an effort to prevent her from leaving the house in the first place. As well as being extremely concerned for her safety she knew that Richard, in an attempt to protect his sister, would be more than likely to neglect his own by throwing caution to the winds and riding hotfoot to her defence. Whilst this was exactly the kind of thing he would do, she considered he was in more than enough trouble as it was without adding to it, and Salmon's contribution, albeit unintentional, had merely served to put Richard in more danger as well as Elizabeth.

But as she descended the stairs to find Salmon pacing up and down, the embodiment of anxiety, she knew she had been too harsh in her judgement and could not help but feel sorry for him, but indulging his mood of wretchedness would serve no purpose. His devotion to the Ferrers family, and to Richard in particular, was as absolute as it was indisputable, and therefore his distress over her nephew's current activities had the effect of softening her expression, her old eyes looking at him with such understanding that for once both of these seasoned sparring partners were as one.

As both of them could only hazard a guess as to what had happened to Major Neville at the hands of Colonel Henderson and William, as far as she was concerned it was useless to place their dependence on him in coming to the rescue of either Elizabeth or Richard. Since her nephew could be relied upon to go headlong into a situation without a thought for the consequences to himself, putting his sister's safety before his own, it was a great pity that the Major was momentarily unable to take a hand, if for no other reason than to curb Richard's more energetic response. Despite her own growing anxiety she knew perfectly well that as there was nothing either of them could do but await the outcome of tonight's events with what patience and courage they could muster, there was very little point in indulging one's fancy by imagining all manner of morbid eventualities.

Salmon, having been on the listen for the past hour or more for the sound of an approaching carriage in the full expectation of it bearing the lifeless body of his young master, was not at all sure whether to be glad or not at her suggestion that he would be better employed doing something useful instead of walking up and down like a cat on hot bricks. Although he would rather die than admit to holding this formidable woman in the highest regard, he knew she was right, but he could neither settle nor feel easy, and the longer time went by without any news, the more unsettled he became.

Deciding it was time that she took matters into her own capable hands, Clara Winsetton bid him assist her down the remaining few steps of the stairs, after which he could make himself useful by bringing some wine to the small sitting room. Realizing that nothing would persuade him to leave his post, this cosy apartment was near enough to the front door to hear a vehicle approach, and although she fully expected him to jump up and down like a jack rabbit at the slightest sound, she was more than capable of stemming his more agitated starts.

Having returned to the sitting room some minutes later carrying the huge silver tray laden with decanters and glasses from the late Lord Easton's library, he handed her a glass of wine, after which she invited him to pour himself one. Upon shaking his head with the heartfelt announcement that he felt it would choke him, she virtually ordered him to join her in a glass, stating that she would much prefer him to be drunk than sober if this was the kind of humour he was in. Deciding that he had enough on his mind without provoking her even more he did as he was told, then reluctantly sat down on the edge of a chair which she impatiently indicated with the tip of her cane. But after several glasses of the future sixth Viscount's best claret both his devotees were beginning to feel the effects of the rich ruby liquid sufficiently enough to unbend towards one another. So much so that after an hour they found themselves reminiscing over the many scrapes in which Richard had found himself as well as being in complete agreement that his many good qualities had seen him turn out to be as equally well liked and respected as ever his father had been. Priding herself on the successful outcome of her tactics in keeping Salmon occupied until they received news of Richard and Elizabeth, she was just on the point of recalling some half forgotten episode when the sound of carriage wheels approaching made her pause. Salmon, darting a quick look at her, rose to his feet on the instant, treading over to the window where he cautiously lifted the edge of the curtain to peer anxiously through it. His eye fell on a travelling carriage coming to an abrupt halt, whose crest on the door panel was indiscernible in the darkness, but there was no mistaking the scarlet coat of the man on the box, and for one hopeful moment wondered if it could possibly be Major Neville. His hope however was short-lived as he watched with disappointment a young man, who was quite unknown to him, jump nimbly to the ground and quickly open the door, whereupon a dark figure stepped out. He did not need either the moon or a lantern to recognize Master Richard, and without waiting to see anything more entered the hall just as the front door was being imperatively kicked with a loud cry to open up. Preparing himself for the worst Salmon flung open the door, considerably taken aback to find himself looking at Richard's grim face as he came in carrying his sister's lifeless body in his arms; but apart from telling Salmon to do all he could to help Michael and that he was to expect the arrival of Dr. Jarvey, he wasted no time in either making conversation or answering his questions, but mounted the stairs two at a time.

Having fully expected to see Richard being brought home either dead or wounded, it was something of a shock to see that it was his sister instead, and upon setting eyes on Lieutenant Beaton entering the house in Richard's wake, knew that this evening had gone every bit as bad as he had predicted. Nevertheless, he was pleased to know that Richard's faith in his friend had not been misplaced.

Clara Winsetton, who had just emerged from the sitting room into the hall, looked from Salmon to Michael, who had only that second entered the house, with a questioning eyebrow. As Richard had had no time to offer an explanation it fell to Michael to step into the breach, so executing an exquisite bow, offered "Lieutenant Beaton, at your service Ma'am." Hiding her alarm by subjecting him to a fierce stare from out of her eagle eyes, she heard him explain, "I am Richard's friend, Michael. I know we have not met before, but you may have heard Richard mention me, Ma'am."

She looked closely at him for a few moments before nodding. "Yes, I do remember him mentioning you. Was that my nephew who came in just now?"

"Yes, Ma'am" he nodded, feeling some clarification was required. "I must apologize for this disturbance, but I feel sure you will understand when I tell you that I am afraid your niece has sustained an injury, a ball in the shoulder to be precise," he explained a little awkwardly as he saw the shock which crossed both their faces. "Richard has brought her home, and whilst there is no time now for him to tell you the circumstances of this evening's events, he will no doubt do so in due course. Doctor Jarvey has been summoned and he will be here directly."

Listening to this polite and concise explanation with a calmness she was far from feeling, she nodded her head. "Thank you, Michael," instantly making use of his first name. "I must go to her at once. Salmon," she said evenly, "you will wait here until Jarvey arrives when you will show him to my niece's room immediately. In the meantime," she told him, "you will provide refreshment for Michael and offer him all the assistance you can." On which parting note she slowly climbed the stairs, experiencing an acute pain which had very little to do with old age and aching limbs, leaving the two men to watch her slow ascent until she turned the bend and was lost from sight.

"It's all my fault!" Salmon cried, turning to face Michael, wringing his hands. "I should never have let her go."

"You must not say so," he shook his head, having seen enough of Elizabeth to feel confident to say that once her mind was made up nothing would change it. "None of you were to know what would happen. It was a very cleverly executed ploy."

"She will be all right, won't she?" Salmon asked ignoring this reasoning, his concern evident in his eyes. "If anything happened to her I'd never forgive myself!"

"I think so," he smiled tentatively, "thanks to Major Neville."

"Major Neville!" he exclaimed, searching the younger man's face. "I thought that …"

"I am afraid," Michael shook his head, "that there is more to this evening than Miss Ferrers being wounded."

Salmon had a feeling there was, but nothing quite prepared him for the full sum of tonight's dealings, staring up at Michael in complete astonishment as the story unfolded. "Mr. William dead!" he shook his head, his voice hardly above a whisper.

"I am afraid there was nothing any one of us could have done to have prevented it; it happened so quickly," Michael explained, wishing Major Neville were here as he felt quite inadequate to the task thrust upon him.

"And Henderson?" he questioned. "You say he's outside in the carriage?"

"Yes," Michael nodded. "When his pistol went off accidentally and Miss Ferrers fell to the floor, Richard became so enraged that he knocked him senseless."

The old eyes gleamed, but only for a moment, the full realization not lost on him. "But where are we to put him, Sir?" he asked.

"Major Neville could not risk taking him to the garrison in case he attempted to bribe the guards into letting him go," he told him. "He thought it safer to bring him here to await the arrival of General Turville."

"And that's another thing!" he cried, running a hand through his grizzled hair. "What are we to do with Mr. William?"

Before Michael could answer these questions the sound of a vehicle approaching had the effect of stemming any further conversation, and Salmon, quickly pulling open the door, watched with relief as Doctor Jarvey alighted from the gig.

Doctor Jarvey, a man of middle height and spare frame with a habitually harassed expression, had been physician to the Ferrers family for more years than he cared to remember, but they were not the most lucrative of patients; all of them it seemed being possessed with remarkable good health. Apart from Richard sustaining a broken leg when he was twelve years old and Miss Elizabeth spraining her ankle when she was only knee high, with the exception of the late Lady Ferrers' tragic illness and Lord Easton's heart attack, there had seldom been need to attend the residents at Ferrers Court, and therefore it had come as something of a shock to receive that hastily scribbled note that his attendance was urgently required.

After bidding Salmon a curt good evening followed by an immediate demand to know why his presence was necessary, and at such an hour, he flung off his heavy coat and subjected Lieutenant Beaton to intense scrutiny, causing that young man to cast an appealing look at Salmon for his assistance. Upon learning the reason for his immediate attendance he looked aghast, words momentarily failing him, but pulling himself together he insisted he be taken to Miss Ferrers without further delay, keeping his reflections to himself as he followed Salmon up the stairs.

Opening his eyes to the sickening sensation that his head was being repeatedly pounded and the feeling that his jaw was broken, Colonel Henderson tried somewhat unsuccessfully to raise himself from his undignified and uncomfortable position on the floor of the carriage. It was several minutes before he was able to piece together the hazy recollections which were flitting in and out of his brain, but gradually they began to slide into place with horrendous clarity.

His plans to deal with Richard Ferrers once and for all having gone horribly awry, being his last ditch attempt to salvage a situation which had gone quite beyond him, there was no denying the fact that he had lost his head and panicked. Shooting William Ferrers may have been the spur-of-the-moment action of a desperate and frightened man, but it did not alter the fact that he had committed cold-blooded murder and in front of witnesses who would be only too willing to testify against him.

It was regrettable that one of those witnesses had been the unfortunate victim of such a tragic accident, but that pistol going off had been the result of a most dreadful circumstance beyond his control and not because he had intended to shoot her. He had not known which had shaken him the most; seeing Miss Ferrers fall unconscious to the floor or her brother bearing down upon him with such a look of murder on his face that he thought he would kill him there and then. His spluttering protestations that it had been an accident had barely left his lips when he felt his jaw come into contact with that surprisingly powerful fist, the force of the blow causing him to reel backwards and strike his head on the heavy handle of the door, a black chasm opening up before him as he crumpled to the floor, knowing no more until he opened his eyes a moment or two ago. He supposed he should be grateful for escaping with his life, but he could not delude himself into thinking that it would be spared for very much longer; nothing now it seemed could prevent him from climbing the scaffold, not only for the murder of William Ferrers but also his participation in treason.

Since the back of his head was extremely tender to the touch and his efforts to raise himself made him feel quite nauseous, he really had no choice but to remain where he had been unceremoniously thrown onto the floor of the carriage. As it was impossible for him to look outside in order to see where he was he could only speculate the location, and it was then that he began to contemplate what was going to happen to him. For one terrifying moment the dreadful suspicion crossed his mind as to whether he was going to be done away with without even the pretence of a trial, but before he had time to consider this further the carriage door was suddenly pulled open and two pairs of hands grabbed hold of his legs.

Overcoming his fear by putting on an extremely brave face, he instantly plied them with questions, to which neither of his captors were taking the slightest bit of notice. "I demand to know ..." he began furiously.

"You're in no position to demand anything," Salmon told him forthrightly, pulling him roughly to his feet.

He knew that voice, and unless he was very much mistaken, which he doubted, he had been brought to Ferrers Court, and although the reason for this momentarily escaped him he could not help but fear the worst. Looking from Lieutenant Beaton's uncommunicative face to Salmon's inflexible one, he knew it would be useless to try and talk them into letting him go, but before he could even put this to the test the sound of wheels approaching made him quickly turn his head, his anger mounting when he saw Major Neville bringing Sir Evelyn's old and well-worn trap to a halt behind the carriage.

Descending a little stiffly down onto the drive Gideon walked towards them, completely ignoring Colonel Henderson by enquiring of Salmon if that was the doctor's gig. Upon being told that it was and he was at this very moment tending to Miss Ferrers Gideon nodded, disregarding Henderson's blustering demands to know what the devil they meant to do with him by instructing them to get him quickly into the house.

Richard, after an affectionate hug quickly followed by a brief inquisition by his aunt, had been summarily banished from his sister's room in order that her maid and Miss Calne could undress her and put her to bed, leaving him with nothing to do but content himself with pacing up and down the landing in growing frustration until the arrival of Dr. Jarvey.

It was not to be expected that Dr. Jarvey was in ignorance of Richard's current difficulties; like everyone else hereabouts he was perfectly well aware of the charges laid against him. However, whilst it was not for him to give an opinion and he could only speculate as to whether Miss Ferrers' injury was in any way connected with her brother's activities, it did not take much to realize that something pretty untoward had been going forward. He did not approve of such goings on as this and upon setting eyes on Richard pacing exasperatedly up and down he cast him such a look of censure that Richard was moved to expostulate that he was here to tend his sister and not give him a lecture. As it was patently obvious that that worthy practitioner was not prepared to waste time in either listening to his explanations or to answering questions as to the probable outcome of his visit to Elizabeth, Richard found himself with nothing to do but descend the stairs and wait with what patience he could muster for him to emerge from his sister's room.

Having taken advantage of his employer's absence to spend a few convivial hours at the inn in Little Turton, Whitney returned to Ferrers Court slightly the worse for wear to find the place a hive of activity, just catching sight of Dr. Jarvey's retreating figure at the top of the stairs. He would not normally have entered the house by the front door, but upon setting startled if bleary eyes on three vehicles outside he could not help but wonder what was happening. At first, he could only stand and stare in blank astonishment at what was going on around him, but it soon began to dawn on him that something quite unexpected had occurred. Holding onto the banister post with his left hand in order to steady himself, the effects of his potations not having yet begun to wear off, he watched almost mesmerized as Salmon and two men in scarlet coats, one of whom looked vaguely familiar, half dragged and half carried Colonel Henderson into the small sitting room.

As no one had as yet noticed his arrival he rather hoped to escape detection by making his way up the stairs to his employer's room in order to see if he was here or, if not, to lay out his night gear without anyone being the wiser. It was just as he was about to attempt the ascent that he heard a firm tread rounding the bend in the stairs and as he half turned his head to see who it was, the movement, slight though it was, was sufficient for him to lose his balance and topple backwards, ending up lying on his back on the first few steps of the stairs, thereby impeding Richard's descent. Gaining his feet with more haste than dignity, he looked up into Richard's dark and forbidding face as he came down the remaining steps in the faint hope that his condition would go unnoticed.

"Whitney!" Richard exclaimed. "What the devil are you doing man?" Having by now regained some of his poise he mumbled an incoherent apology, to which Richard stated unequivocally, "Whitney, you're drunk!"

"Only a very little, Sir" he slurred.

"Well, now that you *are* here," Richard told him, "you can make yourself useful."

"Is there something you wish me to do, Sir?" he managed to ask, only just managing to stop himself from swaying to and fro by grabbing hold of the banister post, the reason for his employer's cousin being here at all momentarily escaping him.

"Yes," Richard nodded, "I am afraid to say there is. Prepare yourself for a shock, Whitney" he warned, "your master's dead."

Opening his eyes to their fullest extent, he stared at Richard dumfounded. "*Dead*, Sir?" he repeated, this unexpected disclosure having the immediate affect of sobering him up.

"That's what I said," Richard nodded. "I'm sorry to have to be the one to break such news to you," he told him, "but I shall need you to assist in carrying him to his room."

"I - I don't understand, Sir!" he exclaimed, shocked.

"I am not entirely sure that *I* do," Richard told him truthfully, "but there is no time now to explain it all to you," much preferring to wait until he had spoken with Gideon before going into any detail.

"But, Sir ..." he began.

"Just stay where you are for the moment," Richard told him. "I shall be with you directly."

Whitney, watching Richard stride into the small sitting room and close the door with a snap behind him, sunk heavily onto the bottom step of the stairs, dropping his aching head into his hands. He had no idea whether he knew of his cousin's venture into treason or not, but if he had William's accomplice here then it stood a very good chance that he did.

As his participation in William Ferrers' treacherous enterprise had amounted to nothing more than adopting the role of go-between, he did not think he could be found guilty of treason by association; surely he could not be held responsible for another man's political persuasions! He swallowed uncomfortably. If only that were true! His late employer, as he well knew, had no more political persuasions than he had himself, and if he had decided to embark on such a dangerous path as furthering or supporting insurrection, then who was he to tell him that he could not? However logical this reasoning, he was nevertheless astute enough to realize that his future was looking anything but the comfortable existence he had thought it would be. If Richard Ferrers had indeed discovered the truth about his cousin's involvement with Stuart then it was reasonable to assume that he also knew of his attempts to discredit him and step into his shoes. Whatever differences had existed between the cousins', surely no one could blame him for what one of them had tried to do! His dealings with Richard Ferrers had been slight, but he had never been given cause to believe that he would seek revenge by deliberately trying to ruin a man who had been nothing more than a paid servant.

William Ferrers may not have been the most dependable of men as well as possessing his fair share of faults, but his death had left him not only without employment but in a most precarious position. He could only speculate at what had gone wrong tonight, but clearly something quite untoward had occurred resulting in the death of a man whose future had been so closely aligned with his own. Had William Ferrers' plans been successful, because from the looks of it they had evidently failed, then he himself could have lived quite comfortably on the back of his good fortune for the unforeseeable future. Now though, his prospects were anything but certain, and if he was not careful he could find himself in a whole load of trouble. The thought made him sweat, especially as he wondered what was going on behind the closed door to the sitting room and the possible fate that awaited him.

Had he have but known it his fate was the last thing on the minds of the room's occupants. They may have Colonel Henderson laid by the heels, but it was not only impractical to keep him here indefinitely but extremely dangerous. Yet try as they did they could find no other solution to the immediate problem of keeping him secure until General Turville placed him in safe custody and those letters were handed into his keeping. Since Richard had submitted to Gideon's proposal about ensuring his cousin's good name, albeit reluctantly, there seemed to be nothing more they could do now other than bring William's body into the house and taken up to his room.

Upon seeing the door to the sitting room open, Whitney rose unsteadily to his feet, preparing himself for the worst, his face pale and drawn as he watched them walk purposefully towards him. He may tell himself that the authorities could not hang a charge of treason around his neck simply because his employer had been unwise enough to embroil himself in Stuart's cause, but he was not so drunk nor lost to all sense of reasoning that he could fool himself into believing that they did not know, or at least suspect, the minor role he had played. Even so, he could not prevent the sigh of relief which escaped his lips when they made no mention about his participation in recent events.

Richard and Gideon may have taken the decision in that the less Whitney knew the better, but they were not naive enough to believe that he was in total ignorance of what had taken place. On the contrary, they realized perfectly well that William must have taken him part way into his confidence at least. They doubted his role would have been anything more important than running errands between his employer and Henderson, but even so it would be foolish to believe that Whitney was either blind or stupid or that he would fail to see that his late employer had met his end by a bullet wound to the chest. It went against all logic to assume that Whitney had been in ignorance of William's activities or that he had had a meeting this evening with Colonel Henderson, and therefore he would be bound to want to know how he had come to be shot, if for no other reason than curiosity. If their understanding of the case was correct, and they had no reason to suppose otherwise, then Whitney would not want his involvement, however small, advertised to the world any more than they did theirs. Indeed, the look on his face told them that he was a very frightened man and not merely from finding himself suddenly unemployed. The hopeful glance he threw at them was enough to tell them that they had not erred in their calculations. Whitney was extremely fearful of the consequences accruing from his marginal participation in his late employer's activities, and was therefore extremely relieved when he learned that the worst was not going to befall him. He perfectly understood the inference attached to their version of recent events and certainly did not need to have it reinforced that William Ferrers, far from being engaged in treason, was in fact assisting his cousin to reveal the truth about Henderson. He had no idea whether the tale would be swallowed by the authorities, but he for one was not about to argue the point; as far as he was concerned all that mattered to him was that as he was not going to take a walk to the gallows after all!

Richard, still far from reconciled with the story they had set in motion, cast a significant glance up at Gideon which left him in no doubt of his feelings. Whilst Gideon had no liking for the lie they were putting abroad any more than he did, he failed to see what else they could do given the unlooked for set of circumstances in which they found themselves.

Salmon, also far from happy with the way things had turned out, gave it as his opinion that they were asking for trouble. Waiting only until Whitney and Michael had turned the bend in the stairs carrying William's covered body to his room, he told them bluntly, "If you think you can trust that squinty eyed ferret your cousin called a valet to keep his mouth shut, then all I can say is you've both lost what sense you had!"

Receiving another meaningful glance from Richard, which Gideon had no difficulty in interpreting to mean 'I told you so', looked from one to the other with such an expression on his face that Richard, goaded beyond endurance, gave it as his opinion that Salmon was right, and if this should blow up in their faces then he for one would not be at all surprised.

"What else can we do?" Gideon asked reasonably, not unsympathetic to their feelings. "Unfortunately, tonight's unlooked for events have forced our hand."

"I daresay," Richard nodded, "but I still don't like to think that William comes out of this smelling of roses! As for Henderson," he said unequivocally, "I'll be damned if I see him escape what's coming to him! I realize we have no choice but to keep him here for the time being," he admitted grudgingly, "but I can't pretend to having a liking for any of it!

"Do you think I do?" Gideon demanded. "Make no mistake about it," he said firmly, "nothing would prevail upon me to see Henderson go free; apart from all he has inflicted on your father and sister, he has taken part in treason, leaking information to Stuart no less, not to mention committing cold-blooded murder and seeking to have an innocent man blamed for his crimes," looking significantly at Richard as he raised his eyes to his face. "As for your cousin," he shrugged, "well, you knew him better than I, but I saw enough of him to know that he was weak and easily led with not an inch of back bone. His jealousy of you and his urgent need of funds were such that they led him into a situation I am quite sure he had come to regret long before tonight's unfortunate events. Henderson's reasons for what he attempted are a little more obscure than William's, and I doubt he will favour us with any, but he took your cousin's measure from the outset and used it for his own ends, even to the point where you became a most useful and convenient scapegoat should anything go wrong, which, of course, it did, when Stuart failed and he became aware that his letters, far from having been disposed of, were in your possession." He paused only long enough to allow this to sink in. "I never agreed with your aunt's wish to keep his name out of it but despite my representations she was determined to shield him. When I learned of what she had in mind, needless to say I was somewhat taken aback, especially when I knew what place you hold in her affections, but I do know that it was not out of consideration for him that she sought my assistance but to uphold the honour and dignity of the Ferrers family. I know you have no cause to love your cousin," he admitted fair-mindedly, "he has done too much against you for that, and whilst I know full well you will not like it, I would be less than honest if I did not tell you that whilst your safety was, and always will be, my first concern, I had every intention of honouring the promise I made her; I still do." He looked unflinchingly at Richard, the inflexible note in his voice not lost on him. "I gave my word, and that is something I don't take lightly, but having done so I will not break it no matter how much you may dislike it. For what it is worth," he offered, "I believe that he has got off extremely lightly considering his offences, but there is no denying that his unexpected death at the hands of his accomplice has rid me of a dilemma I was very far from knowing how to deal with; it has also rid you of what in all probability would have been an embarrassing problem in the future, because although I am convinced that he had learned a late but valuable lesson, there is no gainsaying that William could well have created all manner of difficulties for you."

A thoughtful expression had entered Richard's eyes but he held Gideon's steadily. "I know," he sighed, "all you say is true, but damme he had a deal to answer for!   As for giving your word," he nodded, "I wouldn't expect you to renege on it; in fact, had you have done so," he said candidly, "I would have been greatly disappointed in you."

"So would I," Gideon told him truthfully. "My father told me that a man is only as good as his word; and you know something?" he raised an eyebrow, "he was right."

Richard grinned and gripped his shoulder. "I shall look forward to making your father's acquaintance.   But talking of giving your word; what about Whitney? Do you think he will keep silent?   He may not know what took place tonight at Hamstoke House, but he must have known of the meeting there between William and Henderson."

"I don't think so," Gideon shook his head, still unable to believe that Henderson and William Ferrers had actually had the ingenuity to draw up such an involved plan themselves.   "When one considers the enormity of what they were planning, the fewer people who knew about it the better. Whitney may have been in your cousin's confidence to marked a degree, but I doubt he would have informed him of their intentions for tonight. The more I think about it the more likely it seems that William and Henderson concocted this between them when they met, and although I can't say when this meeting actually took place, it must have been over the last few days.   Considering the little time they had available they managed to put together a quite brilliant plan, but I am convinced your cousin never told Whitney anything about it, but merely gave him leave of absence for tonight."   He saw the frown descend onto Richard's face, and said uncompromisingly,   "I don't like or trust him any more than you, but in this instance I believe we may rely totally upon his continued silence, if for no other reason than he is extremely fearful of what could befall him. He may have had no more loyalty to your cousin than I, but the part he has played, albeit minor, makes him believe that he will be strung up from the nearest gallows should it ever become known. He won't," he shook his head, "but as long as he thinks he will, and he can't possibly know what took place at Hamstoke House unless we tell him,

I see no reason for us to worry ourselves unduly over him. As far as the footman there is concerned," he reasoned, "the same applies. He abused the trust placed in him by his employer for monetary gain and therefore is far too anxious to keep his dealings from coming to Sir Evelyn's attention. The last thing he wants is to be turned off at his age, and although we could not hide the debacle resulting from Henderson's actions he assured me that he could restore the room so no evidence remained of what occurred. Be assured," he told him emphatically, "I left him under no illusion as to what would befall him if he spoke of it to anyone. He is much too fearful to say anything, and therefore your sister's reputation will come to no harm through him." He saw Richard's lips compress in suppressed anger at the mention of his sister, and Gideon, who was himself having to strenuously repress the overwhelming urge to extract retribution from Colonel Henderson, felt it incumbent upon him to point out a most pertinent if painful fact. "You know as well as I that your sister was used as bait to ensnare you, and however despicable the thinking behind the strategy we have to acknowledge, however reluctantly, that it worked; perhaps not in the way it was supposed to, but nevertheless it succeeded in getting you to Hamstoke House. It also succeeded in getting her shot. We are fortunate in that we know the truth of it, but had we left her there for Sir Evelyn to find upon his return home recovering from a ball in her shoulder it would have taken a deal of explaining, in fact," he pointed out frankly, "I fail to see how we *could* have explained it without giving rise to gossip and innuendo. Dissimulation is as abhorrent to me as it is to you," he told him unequivocally, "but regrettably there are times when telling the truth can only do more harm than good." Pressing home his advantage he continued inexorably, "Do want your sister's name to be bandied about as well as being the subject of hearsay and insinuations, which would have been the case had we left her at Hamstoke House? No, of course you do not!" he said confidently. "As for William," he pointed out, "I have no more wish than you to see him hailed a hero instead of the villain he was, and whilst I accept that Henderson may still try to do you damage through him, which, unfortunately, is a risk we shall have to take, even if he can't produce those letters substantiating him as his accomplice, your position is still far too vulnerable for us to be too nice in our dealings!"

After digesting this for a moment or two, Richard finally came to accept that Gideon had spoken no less than the truth, the mulish look gradually beginning to recede from his face. No more than they did Gideon like the idea that William was to be discharged of any wrong doing and his name to remain unsullied, but unfortunately the realities of tonight's events had left them with no other course of action open to them. "Of course," he shrugged, "if you have a better idea of extricating us from the difficulties surrounding us as a result of what has occurred tonight, then I should be happy to hear it."

Having dug his hands into the capacious pockets of his coat, Richard broodingly scrutinized the toe of his right boot, but commonsense told him that Gideon was right. However much he may resent shielding his cousin from condemnation he knew there was no alternative, especially if he wanted to protect his sister from the gossip which would follow, and eventually nodded his head in reluctant acknowledgment. He could not argue against Gideon's line of reasoning any more than he could come up with anything better than the strategy he had worked around the tragedy of recent events, recognizing that it was the only feasible answer to their difficulties.

Salmon, who had been nodding his head in agreement, had been more than a little relieved to learn that the Major had been able to avert disaster befalling the family by his timely intervention in this evening's unusual events, and whilst he had no doubt that Richard could have managed things himself, there was no denying that the Major, unlike his young master, was a man who did not act rashly but clearly thought things through. Having by now come to regard Gideon as quite one of the family Salmon, although fully agreeing with all he had said, was still very wary of placing any trust in Whitney and allowed his scepticism regarding his silence to show, but just as he was on the point of voicing this Richard forestalled him by recommending him to take that look off his face and make himself useful by bringing the drinks tray to the great hall. Deciding against arguing the point further he did as he was bid, but not without muttering something under his breath to the effect that he would not be at all surprised to find that they had not heard the last of him, whereupon Richard turned on his heel and strode across to the great hall, lighting a branch of candles which stood on the table before pulling out a chair and sinking down onto it. Upon seeing Gideon follow him inside he stretched out his right leg and kicked a chair out, inviting him to join him, his hands thrust deep into his pockets.

As it had been decided that Michael and Salmon would take it in turns to watch over Colonel Henderson, and Richard and Gideon would wait for Dr. Jarvey downstairs, it seemed that for the moment nothing more could be done. As both men were taken up with their own thoughts as well as wondering what was happening upstairs, neither attempted to make conversation, but their mood lightened considerably when Salmon, placing the tray down on the long oak table with some force, looked at his young master with something akin to long-suffering, saying docilely "If that's all Sir, I'll return to the sitting room."

Richard, eyeing his life-long devotee narrowly, suddenly burst out laughing. "Lay it on a bit thicker why don't you? No doubt the Major is already thinking I make you eat the scraps off the floor!" pouring him a glass of wine.

Salmon sniffed, taking the glass he was handed. "I'm sure I don't know to what you're referring."

"The devil you don't!" Richard nodded.

Salmon, who was just on the point of responding to this, heard the sound of footsteps coming down the stairs and stepping into the hall saw Michael descend the last the step whereupon he signalled him to join them. Not until the door to the great hall was pushed to behind them did Richard ask his friend about Whitney, and upon being told that having found the whole experience quite distressing and had retired to his room, Salmon, snorting his doubt as well as his disgust, reiterated his opinion that he would make a run for it at the earliest opportunity and shouting his tale as he went.

Since Gideon had already discounted this theory for very practical reasons and Richard had been brought to admit that he was right, they did not share Salmon's view, who, upon discovering that his warnings were going unheeded, emptied the contents in his glass and left them to begin his watch over the prisoner, murmuring something quite unintelligible under his breath as he left. Richard, after watching his henchman's retreat with an amused eye, poured out three glasses of wine handing one each to Gideon and Michael. "Here, you both look as though you need it; you've certainly earned it."

Taking the glass held out to him Gideon eyed the rich ruby liquid before glancing up at his future brother-in-law with a gleam of pure amusement. "Your yield?" he enquired, raising a questioning eyebrow.

"What! Lord no!" Richard exclaimed unabashed. "We don't run anything as good as this. M'father was very particular about his wine. Brandy now" he grinned, "that's another matter! If you'd like some ..." he suggested provocatively, his eyes alight.

"Thank you," Gideon inclined his head, recognizing, and not for the first time, just how irresistible Richard's smile really was, "but I think the wine will suffice." Richard burst out laughing, but just as he was on the point of responding to this, the door opened to admit Dr. Jarvey, his face a nice mix of disapproval and incredulity upon witnessing such frivolity at a time like this. Upon seeing who had entered the laughter instantly died on Richard's lips, his eyes narrowing slightly, by no means certain that he liked the silent condemnation on the doctor's thin and harassed face.

Stepping further into the room, Dr. Jarvey looked from one to the other before bringing his gaze back to rest on Richard. Although his dealings with the Ferrers family had been scant he had been far better acquainted with the father than with the son, and whilst all he had ever heard about him, in spite of his difficulties, certainly seemed favourable, he saw in an instant that he was dealing with a very different man to his late lordship. He could not see the recently departed Lord Easton callously disregarding his daughter's dilemma by indulging in a drinking session with his companions whilst she lay in such a serious condition upstairs, and it was therefore with a look of severe censure that he eyed the discredited sixth Viscount, who, from the expression on his face, was by no means pleased at such disapproval.

Dr. Jarvey, who had his own opinions about what had occurred this evening, even though they were unsubstantiated, found it hard to believe that his patient would have suffered such an injury in the normal course of events. As Clara Winsetton had made no attempt to enlighten him as to the cause of her niece's wound except to say that she had met with an accident, and it seemed most unlikely that Richard Ferrers would admit to the fact that it was his illicit undertakings which had brought it about, he could only hope that the Major, who, from the looks of it, seemed to be man of apparent calm good sense, would see fit to explain it to him.

Richard may not be overly acquainted with Dr. Jarvey, but he was neither stupid nor lacking in intelligence, and knew precisely what was going through his mind. He supposed that given the circumstances it was a natural conclusion to arrive at, but even so it did not make the assumption any more palatable. Having to let the supposition pass unchallenged or, which was infinitely worse, to stand by and let his associates be unjustly maligned, tried his patience to the limits, and it was therefore in a somewhat argumentative tone that he demanded to be told how his sister did.

Interpreting Richard's attitude to mean that he had hit the nail on the head as to the real cause of Miss Ferrers' injury, Dr. Jarvey pursed his lips in silent reproof, but since it was not his place to take this young man to task for either his way of life or his morals, he bit back the censorious words hovering on his lips, regarding it as a blessing his father was not here to witness such behaviour.

Reading the infuriating look which had descended on Richard's face as a result of the doctor's barely concealed feelings, Gideon decided it was time to step into what bore all the hallmarks of an uncomfortable breach, but before he could open his mouth to speak, Richard, who had been striving to bite down the angry denial on his lips with an effort and finding the task impossible, wrathfully demanded of his silent accuser, "Do you honestly believe that I would do anything which could possibly put my sister's life at risk! Just what kind of a man do you think I am?"

Despite the fact that everything he had ever heard about Richard Ferrers belied the official description of him as being a traitorous rogue and vicious cutthroat, he nevertheless felt quite unable to answer this pointed question. Even so, there was a ring of sincerity in his vehemence which he could neither discount nor ignore and although he still believed that something untoward had occurred to bring about his patient's injury, he was forced to reconsider his original opinion in that her brother's illicit activities had had something to do with it. Also coming under rapid review was his initial impression that the Major's presence in company with the Lieutenant had signified that Richard Ferrers had been placed under arrest. Had this indeed been the case then he could not see this young man celebrating the fact by sharing a drink with them, and therefore could only guess as to what had brought them here. But whatever the reason he could not approve of the kind of joviality he had witnessed, especially when he considered the circumstances in which they found themselves, but as he was neither a heartless nor an unfeeling man he was quite prepared to overlook it, even going so far as to put their behaviour down to shock, and in view of this felt it behoved him to offer his apologies.

Not unnaturally this sudden change of attitude took Richard a little aback, especially coming hard on the heels of his unspoken accusation, causing him to eye the doctor circumspectly for a moment or two. His blue eyes, suspicious and wary, searched the impassive face in front of him wondering whether there was some kind of ulterior motive behind the apology, but since he could detect nothing in Jarvey's demeanour to suggest this, his resentment began to recede. "Yes, well" he nodded at length, slightly mollified, "never mind that! What about my sister?"

He had not missed the anxiety in Richard Ferrers' voice, clearly reflecting his concerns for her, but whilst Dr. Jarvey was prepared to acquit him of deliberately placing her in danger he still held to the belief that something pretty unusual had taken place. Nevertheless, it was becoming increasingly obvious that Ferrers was not going to give him an explanation regarding the circumstances surrounding his sister's injury, and since his scarlet-coated acquaintances appeared to be equally as reticent, he had no choice but to accept this unsatisfactory state of affairs no matter how distasteful. He may find this whole episode and the mystery attached to it to be quite repugnant as well as being far removed from his regular impeccably conducted medical dealings, but he could not deny that he was somewhat relieved to see that severe look leave Ferrers' face. Richard may not have openly accused him of any misconduct, but he had seen enough of this young man to realize that he was more than ordinarily astute, and that not only would he have had to be blind not to recognize his own suspicions but quite capable of acting upon the provocation his condemnation had engendered. Upon seeing that no pugilistic retribution was going to be executed, he swallowed, saying steadily, "Yes Sir, I think I can safely say that Miss Ferrers will make an excellent recovery. I've removed the ball from her shoulder, but she has lost a deal of blood." Just as Richard was on the point of offering his thanks, Dr. Jarvey cleared his throat, forestalling him by saying candidly, "I feel it only fair to tell you however, that it is not I who deserves your thanks, but whoever packed that wound."

"Well," Richard shrugged, looking gratefully across at Gideon, "I can't take the praise for that," he told him truthfully. "That honour goes to the Major here."

Turning to Gideon, Dr. Jarvey inclined his head. "My compliments Major on such promptness; you certainly saved Miss Ferrers' life by your actions."

It was a moment or two before Gideon replied to this. He had no need to be told how fortunate they had been in averting a tragedy tonight, and the mere thought of just how close they had come to losing Elizabeth was more than he could contemplate. Not only this, but he had no desire to set this worthy practitioner thinking again and wondering why it had not been her own brother who had come to her immediate aid, especially as he was unaware of the captive across the hall as well as William Ferrers' dead body upstairs. To enlighten him about both at this precise moment in time would be foolish as well as unwise as not only could it possibly impede their efforts to bring a traitor and murderer to justice but would, out of necessity, require a lengthy explanation for which he was in no frame of mind to offer. "You're most kind Doctor," he nodded, "but anyone would have done as much."

"You think so?" Jarvey raised an enquiring eyebrow. "I am afraid I do not share your reliance on that point. In any event," he nodded, "your efforts certainly prevented a tragedy from occurring."

"I am afraid you exaggerate my efforts," Gideon smiled fleetingly.

"You do yourself an injustice, Major" he told him. "Believe me, I know what I am talking about. I have more than once removed a ball from a patient and the loss of blood is usually copious, especially when the shot was fired at such close range." From out the corner of his eye he caught the swift look which passed between Richard and the Lieutenant, and knew instantly that his instincts were not misplaced. "Had you not stemmed the flow," he continued smoothly, still looking at Gideon, "then I should be reporting most adversely on Miss Ferrers' condition." He may have no personal experience of the military but he prided himself on possessing a wealth of knowledge where human nature was concerned, and therefore held it as his opinion that the Major was either the most self-effacing young man he had ever met or he was doing his best to try and draw his attention away from events which he had no hesitation in deeming as pretty irregular.

"Can we see her?" Richard demanded urgently.

"I would rather you didn't, Sir," Jarvey replied apologetically. "I have given her a cordial which will help her rest more easily, and if left undisturbed she should sleep until morning."

"Damn it man, that's my sister lying upstairs!" Richard exclaimed frustrated, taking several hasty steps towards the doctor.

"I know it, Sir," Jarvey acknowledged, "but she has been through quite an ordeal and I would much prefer it if you did not disturb her. I shall call again tomorrow to see how she goes on."

Richard, far from satisfied with this, was just about to argue the point when Gideon, realizing that nothing would move the doctor from this stance, intervened by saying in his quiet way, "Your attendance on Miss Ferrers at such an hour is much appreciated Doctor, but you will, I am sure, understand our very natural concerns."

As Dr. Jarvey had no idea where Gideon and Michael fitted into the sequence of events and no one it seemed was going to enlighten him, he looked closely from one to the other, but as they appeared to be expecting some kind of a response from him, he swallowed, saying cautiously, "I understand, of course, that you are extremely anxious about Miss Ferrers, but I can only repeat that I would prefer it if she were not disturbed tonight. But tell me Major," he asked calmly, casting a glance at Gideon, "what is your connection with Miss Ferrers and the events of this evening?"

Goaded beyond endurance, Richard raked a hand through his hair, eyeing the doctor with something akin to resentment. "Damn it man!" he exclaimed. "The Major here is going to marry my sister!"

Considerably startled by this, Dr. Jarvey looked his astonishment. "Indeed, Sir!" he managed, having pulled himself together. "Then I can only say," he offered, turning to Gideon, "that I am surprised that *you* of all people should have allowed something of this magnitude to happen."

"Is that so!" Richard exclaimed exasperatedly, before Gideon could respond. "Well *you*" he told him forthrightly, "can take that Friday face off. What happened to my sister was an accident and something none of us could either have foreseen or prevented, but if you think for one moment that any one of us allowed it to happen deliberately, then you are a bigger fool than I took you for!"

Had Gideon been asked for his advice he would have strongly recommended Richard to curtail his temper as he could see no good ensuing from setting the doctor's back up, especially given his strongly held suspicions, but to his surprise and, apparently, Richard's as well, Dr. Jarvey took this rebuke extremely well.

"I prefer to regard that comment as never said, Sir" he told Richard magnanimously, inclining his head, "and instead point out that I merely have my patient's best interests at heart, thereby creating an earnest desire to learn what possible contingency could have arisen to occasion such an injury."

If he thought that this politely worded reprimand would bring forth either an explanation or an apology from Richard he was very much mistaken, but he did have the satisfaction of seeing the slight tinge of colour which crept into his rather pale cheeks.

"Damn you, Jarvey!" Richard cried, not without a touch of humour. "It would serve you right if I sent you packing and brought in another man!"

"You could, of course, Sir" he nodded, unperturbed, "but to do so would mean an explanation will be required, not only to account for my dismissal but for that ball in your sister's shoulder."

Again Richard raked a hand through his already disordered hair, knowing that the doctor had spoken no less than the truth. Until this General Turville arrived to take matters in hand, it was out of the question to try and explain recent events, and not only to Dr. Jarvey. Looking from one to the other with an inscrutable expression on his face, Dr. Jarvey, keeping his reflections to himself, made no attempt to prise the truth out of them but instead reiterated his belief that Miss Ferrers would take no permanent hurt from her injury. Nevertheless, he felt it behoved him to repeat that under no circumstances could he permit them to disturb her tonight, but if, after his examination tomorrow, her condition had improved, then he would have no objection to her receiving visitors.

Since nothing would move him from this stance her three well-wishers had to be content with this ruling, but so frustrated was Richard in not to being allowed to see his sister, that upon shaking hands with the doctor he warned him that no matter what her condition tomorrow, nothing would keep him from seeing her. Bowing his unruffled acceptance of this Dr. Jarvey, politely declining a glass of wine, bid them goodnight, failing to see the infinitesimal nod Richard gave to Michael, who, interpreting it to mean that he was to make sure the door to the small sitting room was firmly shut, unobtrusively left the great hall. Dr. Jarvey, pausing only long enough to pick up his bag and saying he could find his own way out, followed in Michael's wake, oblivious to the strenuous efforts behind the closed sitting room door to keep the captive from drawing attention to his presence as well as his plight.

By now it wanted only ten minutes to two o'clock and even though there were still matters they needed to discuss, both men were feeling much too tired to enter into a lengthy dialogue, but there was one aspect about this evening's events which Richard felt he could not leave until the morning. After refilling their glasses and handing Gideon's to him, Richard, taking a generous mouthful, asked, "What do we do about my cousin? What I mean is," he frowned, "shouldn't we report his death to the Magistrate or something?"

"Ordinarily yes," Gideon nodded, draining his glass, "but since these are not ordinary circumstances I feel that trying to explain William's death to a Magistrate would not only be somewhat awkward but virtually impossible. Apart from anything else," he shrugged, "it could well impede General Turville's investigations. The last thing we need," he told him firmly, "is a well meaning but overawed Magistrate or official who finds himself coerced into letting Colonel Henderson go."

"Yes, of course," Richard agreed, "I had not thought of that."

"Even so," Gideon mused, taking a sip of wine, "I feel perhaps we ought to tell Dr. Jarvey, if for no other reason than to pronounce life extinct and to record his death." He smiled at Richard's horrified stare. "I know it's going to be just as awkward to explain it to Jarvey as it would to a Magistrate, but I feel we really have no choice."

"Devil take it, Gideon!" he cried, "he's already suspicious about how my sister received that ball in her shoulder, and to bring him face to face with

William's dead body is only going to make him all the more determined to find out the truth."

"He will have to be told the truth sooner or later," Gideon acknowledged, "but I feel that until General Turville has taken the matter into his own hands, we can't risk telling Jarvey too much; for one thing," he nodded, "it could so easily jeopardize your position."

"You mean you want me to fob him off!" Richard said knowingly.

"I'm afraid so," Gideon nodded. "If you tell him that all will be revealed when you are in a better position to do so, he may well accept that."

"Yes, well" Richard eyed him doubtfully "he may, but don't blame me if he goes blabbing it all over!" he warned, unable to resist Gideon's infectious laughter. "So," he enquired when his paroxysm had abated, "when is it you mean to see Sir John?"

"Tomorrow," Gideon told him, "but first I have to return to the garrison to collect my gear as well as those letters."

"Well," Richard told him emphatically, "you're going nowhere tonight. You're staying here."

"Thank you," Gideon smiled. "I was going to ask if you objected to my racking up here for the night as I am far too tired to attempt the journey back to Hampton Regis at this hour."

"Object!" Richard cried, putting his glass down on the table with some force. "Damn it man! After all you have done! Besides," he grinned irrepressibly, "I count you as one of the family," immediately setting up a shout for Salmon in order that a room could be prepared for him. Gideon, promptly declining this luxury on the grounds that he would be quite comfortable where he was, found himself overruled by being informed that putting someone up on a makeshift bed may be the way things were done in other households, but it was certainly not the way they treated guests at Ferrers Court. Gideon's assertion that he would be perfectly alright where he was and that he much preferred to remain in close proximity to the sitting room across the way, was also dismissed. However, the offer of food was not so easily rejected, realizing with acute awareness that he had eaten nothing since breakfast and therefore Salmon's pronouncement seconds later that only a cold collation could be put together as cook had long since retired, was heartily welcomed.

"And Salmon," Richard forestalled him, "when you and Michael have eaten you had better give Henderson something. Yes, I know; you'd much rather choke him than feed him!" he commented amusingly, upon seeing the look which had descended onto Salmon's face, "But I can do without another corpse on my hands, thank you!"

With their prisoner secure and his two guards more than prepared to keep vigil over him for what was left of the night, Richard and Gideon eventually climbed the stairs to their rooms. After such an eventful day followed by several glasses of wine and what had proved to be a sustaining repast washed down by a number of tankards of ale, both men were ready for their bed, and Richard, climbing the stairs with his hand tucked under Gideon's arm, rounded off what was left of the night by regaling him with some of his adventures. Nevertheless, it was evident to Gideon that the strain of recent events was beginning to show on Richard's face, and by the time they arrived at his bedchamber door he strongly suspected that there was something he wanted to say.

Richard, correctly interpreting Gideon's expression of enquiry, asked concernedly, "My sister; she will be all right, won't she?"

It had taken every ounce of will power Gideon had possessed to prevent himself from disregarding Dr. Jarvey's instructions and forcing his way to her bedside in order to assure himself that she was indeed alright. The very thought that the woman he loved was at this very moment struggling to combat the results of such an attack was more than he could bear, and had several times found it necessary to severely restrain his natural impulses by rushing to her side. Having himself sustained a ball in the shoulder he knew from experience just how painful and weakening it was, and had it been at all possible to have exchanged places with her, he would have been more than prepared to endure the agonies of such an injury again. However, despite his concerns and anxiety, Dr. Jarvey had not struck him as being either incompetent or one given over to offering false hope, and therefore felt confident enough in that worthy's ability and diagnosis to say that he felt sure she would.

Richard nodded, then after struggling to find the right words in which to thank Gideon for all he had done, which were dismissed as unnecessary, gripped his hand and turned to enter his room, but instead of opening the door stood perfectly still for a moment or two with his hand on the handle, before turning to Gideon. "Y'know," he grimaced, "I never thought I'd sleep in my own bed again!"

Since it was clear Richard expected no reply to this and Gideon could not think of one suitable they parted company, both men taken up with their own thoughts, the one to thank his good fortune for sending him a guardian angel just in the nick of time and the other to fervently hope that nothing now would go awry with their plans.

CHAPTER TWENTY FOUR

Major Denham's nightly vigil in company with Captain Waring turned out to be every bit as frustrating and unproductive as he had known it would be, reinforcing his long held belief that one could not trust informants. He was not at all surprised that this evening's watch had come up empty handed, bitterly animadverting to his long-suffering associate that one could never be sure what their motives were for coming forward with information. Since he could speak from first hand experience he had known from the moment Colonel Henderson had broached the matter to him that it would be nothing but a waste of time, but since his senior officer, who had made no effort to enlighten him who the informant was, had turned his request into an order he had found himself with no option but to do as he was told.

Bitterly resentful at being used in such a way, he whiled away the fruitless hours of waiting for the lugger to come into view in agreeable contemplation of what he would say to Colonel Henderson when he returned to the garrison. The handful of men he had taken with him, carefully hidden and ready to pounce once the cargo had been brought ashore, were beginning to get restless, but since neither he nor Captain Waring could give any indication as to how long their wait would be, his irritation had quickly grown into aggrieved antagonism. He could not say whether Richard Ferrers would be on board the incoming vessel or not, but he would stake his life that somewhere along the way he was at the bottom of whatever was going on tonight. He was by no means keen on the idea of a fugitive from justice like Ferrers getting away, but he could not help feeling somewhat mollified to know that this young man's failure to show himself would considerably exasperate Colonel Henderson.

As the minutes slowly and tediously turned into hours it was becoming increasingly clear to all concerned that no cargo was going to be landed tonight, or at least, not at this particular spot. By half past five, frustrated beyond bearing, Major Denham decided to call a halt to the vigil, pithily informing Captain Waring that since it was starting to get light he could not see any smuggler worth his salt attempting a landing now. Reluctantly agreeing to this, Captain Waring rose to his feet, briefly scanning the horizon one final time for a last minute sighting, but as nothing met his searching gaze he slowly and dejectedly walked back to where he had left his horse, closely followed by Major Denham and his men.

Although the rain had long since ceased, Major Denham was not only feeling exceedingly uncomfortable due to his damp clothes which had gradually dried on him during the night but utterly disheartened, turning down his companion's invitation to join him in something warm and invigorating before beginning his return journey to Hampton Regis. Birling Gap, a notorious location for smuggling contraband ashore, had been totally deserted tonight with not the slightest sign of any landing, and as he made his gruelling and protracted way back to the garrison, conscious of the disgruntled comments among the men, he promised himself that someone would pay for his ignominious and unrewarding wait.

By the time he arrived back at the garrison it was almost seven o'clock, and so belligerent was his mood that had he have been fortunate enough to have come upon Colonel Henderson he would have discharged himself of his grievances; as it was he saw no sign of him, having instead to make do with venting his spleen on a hapless private as he passed him on the way to the stables. He was not at all certain whether to be pleased or not that Colonel Henderson was nowhere in sight, his tower domain evincing no sign of him, because although divesting himself of his vexation would have made him feel a whole lot better the chances were that by succumbing to his overwhelming impulse, it could easily result in a disciplinary hearing. He may have neither liking nor regard for Colonel Henderson, much less confidence in his military abilities, but nevertheless he was a senior officer whose rank certainly demanded respect. Not for the first time he found himself questioning his Colonel's dedication and commitment, because as far as he could ascertain he possessed neither of these essential qualities, and could only wonder how on earth he had ever managed to attain his position.

It was not until he had changed into a dry uniform followed by a substantial breakfast that he embarked on a search for his missing Colonel, but not all his enquiries brought forth a favourable response; no one it seemed having any idea where he was. The answers to his probing questions may not have elicited any encouraging replies, but what they did reveal came as a severe shock. He was extremely taken aback upon discovering that in his absence the garrison had been placed on full alert last night in the expectation of a visit from Richard Ferrers, especially as he had been under the impression that it was Ferrers he had been sent out on a watch to apprehend. From what he could gather, given the confusion which seemed to have everyone running aimlessly around the garrison last night with no precise idea of who or what they were chasing, none of them it seemed could be absolutely certain whether this enterprising young man had in fact attempted an entry or not. Under normal circumstances the absence of Colonel Henderson, a not an unheard of occurrence, would not have attracted his attention quite so particularly, but given all the factors of the last twelve hours or so, he somehow felt it imperative that he locate him. Returning to his tower room he sat in contemplation for several minutes, his agile brain turning over recent events as well as wondering who it was that had shared a drink with him the previous evening, those two glasses suddenly taking on a critical significance. He could not remember Colonel Henderson mentioning that he was expecting anyone to join him last night, but whoever it was he felt certain that this unknown visitor had played a pivotal role in his senior officer's disappearance. As Colonel Henderson was not in the habit of inviting fellow officers to either dine or share a drink with him he began to wonder more particularly about last night's unidentified guest. It was just as he was on the point of mentally scanning Colonel Henderson's acquaintances in the vicinity to try and discover which one of them he would be most likely to invite to the garrison or, failing this, would find it necessary to pay him a call unexpectedly, that he suddenly bethought himself of Major Neville.

Although he knew nothing to this young man's detriment he could not honestly lay claim to a liking for him. There was something about him which suggested underhand dealings, and whilst he could only hazard a guess as to what these may be, he could not rid his mind of the feeling that he was largely instrumental in Colonel Henderson's disappearance. Naturally, he was aware of the reason for the Major's visit to Hampton Regis and that he was under Sir John's personal orders, but the feeling that something did not quite ring true persisted to niggle at him, and decided to approach Sergeant Taylor in the hope that he may be able to shed some light onto the matter. But upon being told some minutes later by that wary and somewhat uncommunicative man that he had not seen the Major since he left his quarters yesterday evening to see Colonel Henderson, he became more than ever convinced that Sir John's representative had not only been the one Colonel Henderson had entertained in his quarters, but also that he was responsible for his disappearance. What he could not explain was why Major Neville had not returned to collect his cloak bag which was still packed and waiting where he had left it, but since Sergeant Taylor could offer no satisfactory explanation to account for it any more than he could tell him where the Major was likely to be, he found himself with no choice but to make as dignified an exit as he could. Unfortunately for him, he fared no better with the sergeant whose duties also incorporated attending the junior officers, including Lieutenant Beaton, but upon seeing who had entered this young man's room, became immediately inarticulate and quite unable to offer anything in the way of an explanation to account for his unexpected absence, to which Major Denham's eyes narrowed sharply. He was fully aware of the friendship which had sprung to life between Major Neville and the Lieutenant, and unless he was very much mistaken, he was as convinced as he could be that the two of them were up to something which had necessitated both their absences from the garrison. What this was he had no idea, but he was determined to get to the bottom of what he was fast coming to believe as something rather havey-cavey, and unless he had grossly miscalculated he was convinced that Richard Ferrers formed an integral part of it.

Deciding that very careful thought was required before embarking on the next step, after all it would not do to alert the officers' and men that their Colonel had vanished, he returned to his tower room where, over an hour later, despite intense deliberation, found himself no nearer to solving the dilemma facing him. Of course, the prolonged absence of his senior officer could be nothing more serious than that he had decided to visit his lady friend Mrs. Jaynes in Lewes, which would explain why no one knew his whereabouts, under no circumstances would he want this affair to be broadcast around the garrison, but however probable this was it did not explain the drinking glasses or the combined absence of Major Neville and Lieutenant Beaton, any more than it did Colonel Henderson's insistence that he join Captain Waring last night in what had turned out to be a fruitless vigil. Another cause of concern was the fact that following his own departure to join Captain Waring the whole garrison had been placed on full alert in anticipation of Richard Ferrers attempting an entry. He himself had had no word about the possibility of this young man trying to gain access from any of his usual sources, and since he was in ignorance of the abduction of Elizabeth Ferrers, which in turn set in motion the events which followed, he was quite unable to account for this. It seemed that no sooner had he found a satisfactory explanation to one aspect of the mystery than it was immediately discounted as instead of clarifying the situation it merely made it all the more inexplicable. But when, some time later, he was informed that General Sir John Turville had arrived and was desirous of speaking to Colonel Henderson and Major Neville, such a feeling of foreboding enveloped him that it was several moments before he could steel himself to greet him. Upon informing him that neither of them were at the moment in the garrison, indeed, he had no idea where they could be and his enquiries had led nowhere, followed by a brief account of the previous evening's events, he saw Sir John's bushy eyebrows snap together.

Having quickly summed up Major Denham, he nevertheless recognized a diligent man behind the self-importance, and instinctively knew that whatever his thoughts and feelings towards Colonel Henderson, he could be relied upon to do his duty. It gave him no pleasure or satisfaction to divulge something as detrimental as the accusation of treason against a fellow officer, but however distasteful such a disclosure was, he had to bear in mind that an innocent man's life hung in the balance. Major Denham, totally unprepared for what he heard, was so shocked that he could only stare dazedly across the desk at that harsh and craggy face. It was impossible for him to assess his thoughts because what he had learned was so far removed to what he had believed to be true, that the enormity of it was too much for him to comprehend. He may not like Colonel Henderson, but at no point had he ever so much as suspected that he had been deeply involved in treason, and never to the extent that he had in fact alerted The Pretender to military deployments here. He was not certain which aspect of the case sickened him the most; the fact that Richard Ferrers' own cousin had played a part in the affair or his senior officer was a traitor and had attempted to hang his crimes onto a man who was clearly innocent of such a damning charge.   As far as Richard Ferrers' smuggling activities were concerned he preferred to reserve judgement on that, but one thing he did know and that was Sir John could count on him offering all the assistance at his command to bring to justice a man, albeit his senior officer, who had so far forgot his loyalties by embarking on insurrection.   In the meantime though, he had to try and keep Sir John reasonably occupied as well as trying to provide answers to his imperative and probing questions until such time that Colonel Henderson or Major Neville returned to the garrison.

Having spent most of what remained of the night in a fitful sleep, his mind unremittingly re-living the past few hours with agonizing clarity, Gideon, deciding it was useless to remain in bed tossing and turning any longer, flung back the bedclothes just as the long case clock outside his room chimed half past five. As he was more than capable of looking after himself as well as having no aversion to washing and shaving in cold water, and thanks to the razor and other essential commodities thoughtfully provided by Salmon, he emerged from his room sometime later, his coat and breeches brushed and his boots polished, looking perfectly presentable.   Treading softly along the upstairs passageways, the whole house shrouded in silence, he headed for the stairs with the intention of visiting their captive, not only to relieve his overseers of the burden of watching over him for awhile, but to try and discover the answer to a question for which he did not require an audience, but as he approached Elizabeth's room to his surprise the door unexpectedly opened and Clara Winsetton stepped out. As no one other than her niece and Miss Calne had ever seen her without her finery or her face powdered and rouged, the mere thought of anyone else catching a glimpse of her with her hair disarrayed beneath her nightcap as well as her face being totally devoid of any cosmetic aid, was a great mortification to her.

As neither of them had expected to see the other so early in the morning they were both taken a little aback, but Gideon, who was by no means dismayed at the sight of her so unadorned, bowed. "Good morning, Ma'am."   Correctly interpreting the sharp twitch she gave to the shawl loosely draped around her shoulders as well as her look of horror as being perfectly normal for such a proud and formidable old lady to be caught unawares, he was immediately put in mind of his own grandmother who had never been known to leave her room until she was certain she was fit to be seen.

"Major Neville!" she exclaimed, discomfited.

He had no idea whether she had been sitting up with her niece all night or not, but regardless of her obvious anguish at being discovered in such a disorderly state, it was clear from her pale and drawn face that not only was she extremely worried about Elizabeth but also that last night's events had taken quite a toll.

Her sharp eyes scrutinized him keenly, but when, after several moments, she could detect nothing in his demeanour to suggest that she had given him a disgust of her, she visibly relaxed, asking him what he was doing up so early. Upon being told that he had been unable to sleep, much preferring to be out of bed and doing something useful she nodded understandingly, dismissing his apology for having startled her.

As he was unaware of Sir John's imminent arrival into Sussex, he fully intended leaving Ferrers Court just as soon as he had seen Elizabeth, but since he had no idea what time Dr. Jarvey would arrive, in fact he did not expect to see him much before eleven o'clock, and Richard's affairs had reached the point where they needed to be speedily resolved, especially in view of the guest in the sitting room, he knew he could not delay his departure any longer than was necessary. But whatever the urgency to settle Richard's affairs he also needed to satisfy himself that Elizabeth was indeed recovering as well as Dr. Jarvey had claimed, besides which, he wanted to see her, and could not leave without doing so. He knew perfectly well how it would appear should he be seen entering her bedchamber, and even though he believed his credit with the Ferrers family to be sufficient for them to acquit him of holding any ungentlemanly motives, to take advantage of this would be quite repugnant to him.

"I am pleased to report that she spent a comfortable night," she told him in answer to his enquiry. "I can, of course, only hazard a guess as to what it was Jarvey administered," she grimaced, "such an evil looking concoction if ever I saw one, but she was much calmer after she had drunk it. Although," she pointed out, "I suspect it was your efforts rather than Jarvey's that did the trick. Richard told me what you did last night."

"I am afraid he overstates the case, Ma'am. My efforts ..."

"Saved her life!" she told him unequivocally. "A circumstance which places me very much in your debt. An obligation I am very conscious of, I promise you." "Indeed, Ma'am" he shook his head, "I did nothing."

"You do yourself a gross injustice, Major," she said firmly. "We both know that were it not for you she would not be here. I am under quite an obligation."

"There is no need to feel under any obligation, I assure you," he attested, shaking his head. "But if indeed you do feel that some debt is owed me, then you can discharge it by granting me permission to see her."

She eyed him closely. "What, now?" she asked cautiously.

He nodded. "If you please, Ma'am."

She pursed her lips at this. "It would be most irregular!"

"Yes, I know," he smiled, "and I would not ask it of you, but as I have no idea what time Dr. Jarvey is due to arrive, and Colonel Henderson cannot remain here indefinitely, I cannot delay my departure to town any longer than is necessary."

"Richard did mention something about it now I recall," she mused, "but I was not fully attending. However," she said more briskly, "if your leaving here means that Richard's affairs can be concluded satisfactorily as well as ridding us of that scoundrel downstairs, I am a little more inclined to allow it; not that I hold with this kind of thing!" she said almost as an afterthought.

"I promise not to do anything too reprehensible?" he told her meekly, his eyes gleaming.

She was quite unable to resist his smile. "You are indeed a rogue who was surely born to be hung!" she told him, the tartness in her voice totally belied by the twinkle in her eyes.

"Does that mean I can see her?" he urged, his own smiling irresistibly back at her.

She had no difficulty in understanding why her niece had fallen in love with him; she herself was conscious of his many attractive qualities, and even though she knew that he was neither devious nor calculating, she felt she would be failing in her duty to allow such a visit. Nevertheless, she was a kind hearted woman as well as a sensible one who knew perfectly well that it was not his intention to attempt to ravish her niece and certainly not whilst she was so poorly, or with the presence of Miss Calne in the adjoining dressing room. "Very well," she agreed, "but only for a moment."

"Thank you," he inclined his head.

She hesitated. "You can, *indeed*, save Richard, Major?" her voice urgent.

"Yes Ma'am, I can," he confirmed, meeting her look directly.

She nodded. "I'm glad. It's time he was home where he belongs. About William" she commented, a frown descending onto her forehead and her eyes clouding over, "I want you to know that I do not hold you responsible for what happened to him."

He sighed. "You are most kind Ma'am, but I blame myself; I should have been more prepared."

"Nonsense! According to Richard it was beyond anyone's doing anything about."

"Perhaps," he grimaced.

"There's no 'perhaps' about it!" she declared abruptly. "If anyone is to blame it is that devious reprobate belowstairs." She read the expression on his face with unerring accuracy, and said more gently "You must not take it so much to heart Major. Were it not for you," she reminded him, laying a hand on his arm "heaven only knows what would have become of Richard, and as for Elizabeth - well, you know how much we are all of us beholden to you."

He covered her cold bony hand with his warm one. "You have it quite wrong, Ma'am," he assured her. "I am the one who is beholden: not only to you for your generosity but Richard also, without whom I would never have met his sister." He bowed over her hand and raised to his lips, before smiling up at her.

"For that, I shall be eternally grateful."

She nodded. "That was handsomely said, Major" she acknowledged, "and although I know you mean it, you and I cannot hide from the truth. Had it not been for you Richard would most probably be dead by now. As for William" she conceded, "his death is to be regretted, of course, but had it been otherwise he would be here now in Richard's place! I realize how that sounds," she acknowledged, "and no one is more sadder than I over what has happened to him, but the names of Ferrers and all it stands for would have been ruined within a twelvemonth had he taken possession of the title. I hope I am not an unfeeling woman," she nodded, "but it would not have been right for William to take up my brother's dignities under such circumstances!" Without giving him time to respond to this she walked away in the direction of her own bedchamber, leaving him a prey to his own thoughts as he silently turned the handle of Elizabeth's door before quietly entering the darkened room.

Although the heavy brocade curtains were drawn casting the room into darkness there was more than enough light illumining the scene from the dying embers of the fire, showing him his path to the big four poster set against the far wall adjacent to the window. To his left he could see the door leading to the adjoining dressing room standing ajar from behind which he could easily hear the rhythmic breathing of Miss Calne as she lay asleep. Manoeuvring his way between carefully arranged chairs and a low bow-legged table displaying a vase of flowers, he made his way over to the bed to stand for several moments looking down at the lifeless form of the woman he would give his life to save, his face revealing the various emotions he was experiencing. Her thick dark hair, free of pins and totally unadorned, was spread in a cloud on the pillow surrounding her pale face, slightly turned towards the window, with her right hand under her cheek and her left arm reposing in a sling resting on top of the coverlet. He was conscious of an overwhelming sense of failure as he recalled the promise he had made to himself to protect her and keep her safe from harm and this, coupled with the painful knowledge that he had done neither, let alone shield her from such misfortune as receiving a ball in the shoulder, only served to increase his anguish and impotence causing him to berate himself for his own lack of awareness. It gave him no solace to know that there had been absolutely nothing he could have done to prevent it as Colonel Henderson's actions had been sudden and quite unexpected. He knew perfectly well that he had not meant to shoot her; that pistol going off had been nothing but a sheer accident which none of them could have foreseen, but even so he was conscious of an ever growing desire to inflict the most dire punishment on him, and the knowledge that he could not only contributed to his frustration. No matter what chastisement he felt Colonel Henderson deserved for such a transgression, he was a man who had to be protected at all costs, even against himself, if Richard was to come off safe. Even now, he would never quite know how he had managed to put aside his feelings, much less his horror, in order to try and save the life of the woman without whom he could not envisage his future. He had known for some little time that the day would come when he would have to choose a suitable bride, especially now Aubrey was no longer alive and his marriage would take on the same importance, but whilst his parents had been fortunate enough to enjoy what was commonly called a love match, he himself was not so optimistic in that he looked for the same affection and devotion in his own marriage. Having always been a man who took his military and family responsibilities very seriously, he experienced no regrets about resigning his commission, a decision which had not been as difficult to make as his friends had believed it would be. Nevertheless, prior to this he been quite content to live the life of a carefree bachelor, enjoying not only the company of his many friends but also the pleasures and diversions derived from female connections without commitment by either party. It seemed incredible therefore that little more than a week ago not only had he never heard of Elizabeth Ferrers, but had been relatively satisfied with his life, and certainly there had been no one for whom he had felt in the least degree inclined to offer his name. From the moment he had first set eyes on her he had known instinctively that he had at long last found the woman with whom he wanted to share the rest of his life, rendering his previous affairs as empty and meaningless. He was honest enough to admit that he wanted to make love to her with every fibre of his being, but what he felt for her went far deeper than merely wanting to satisfy his own very human needs and desires. It transcended mere physical attraction, embracing all the trifling as well as important aspects of life from taking enjoyment together out of simple little things, to conveying a confidence one would not share with another living soul and to protecting and caring for her for the rest of his life, and the mere thought of losing her was far too horrendous to contemplate.

Suddenly he became aware of a narrow ray of early morning sunlight picking out the delicate lace edge of the pillow as it found its way through a slight gap in the curtains and which, in a few moments, would be full in her face. Stepping over to the window he gently pulled the curtains together cutting off the sliver of light, only to hear a low voiced murmur behind him. Turning round he saw her move her head slightly before slowly opening her eyes to look dazedly around her, her gaze eventually coming to rest on his tall figure. He kept perfectly still in the hope that she would think she was dreaming, because although he had no intention of doing anything reprehensible as he had light-heartedly told her aunt, it was nonetheless true to say that he was finding it extremely difficult to refrain from taking her in his arms and holding her close against him.

"Gideon?" she cried faintly. "Is that you?"

"Yes," he said softly, coming up to the bed. "I had not meant to disturb you. Forgive me."

"It must be very early," she said weakly, "but I am so glad you have come!" She tried to move her left arm into a more comfortable position only to wince as a shaft of pain shot through her, causing her to bite on her bottom lip, but managed to say with the same irrepressible humour which characterized her brother, "I must confess that having a gentleman steal into my bedchamber at such an hour is a most romantic gesture; I only wish I were in a better position to receive such a visit."

Sitting down on the edge of the bed he gently altered the position of her arm which had the immediate affect of easing the throbbing in her shoulder. "I am full of romantic gestures," he smiled, tenderly kissing her long white fingers before resting them back on the coverlet, "as you will eventually discover, but whilst I would like to be able to say that coming here this morning is one such example from my extensive repertoire," he pulled a face, "I am afraid to say it is no such thing." Her eyes looked an enquiry. "No," he shook his head, his eyes alight. "At the risk of seeming to be a very weak spirited and humdrum fellow, I sought permission."

She smiled, as he had intended, and listened with a mixture of amusement and sadness as he recounted his conversation with her aunt. "I am not surprised she let you see me; she likes you," she told him truthfully.

"And I like her; very much" he admitted frankly. "Which is why I feel my failure to help William so particularly."

Her eyes clouded. "Poor William!" she sighed. "I know he deserved to be punished for what he did, but surely he did not warrant such an end, and by the hand of his own accomplice!"

"His death is regrettable," Gideon nodded, "for your aunt's sake if nothing else, but although I could not quite agree with her decision, I had every intention of doing everything I could for him. However, even now I must confess that had he not met his end by the hand of Colonel Henderson I fail to see how he could have been saved from facing his trial."

"Speaking of Colonel Henderson," she wanted to know, "what will…?"

"He need not worry you any more," he assured her, raising her right hand to his lips before going on to tell her all that had happened after she had fallen unconscious to the floor.

"You mean he has been tied up downstairs all night?" she cried, after listening incredulously to the tale which unfolded.

He nodded. "Since we could not risk taking him to the garrison in case he coerced someone into releasing him," he explained, "yes. You see, there was nowhere else we *could* take him."

She considered for a moment. "Although I can see the sense of that," she nodded, "I only hope Salmon and Richard will be able to refrain from keeping their hands off him!" she exclaimed. "But about Richard," she asked, a slight frown creasing her forehead, "does this mean he is safe now?"

"Once I can put those letters into General Turville's hands and he formally places Colonel Henderson under arrest, yes," he promised her.

She winced suddenly as another dart of pain caught her unawares, the ramifications of last night's events momentarily taking second place as she yet again tried to ease her arm into a less painful position.

"It *will* get better," he assured her softly, gently manoeuvring her arm to make it more comfortable for her. "I promise."

She smiled lovingly up at him. "It feels better already; as I do for seeing you."

"That's far more than I deserve," he told her candidly. "I should have done everything possible to have prevented this from happening. I blame myself for exposing you to such an ordeal. It is unforgivable!"

"You must not think that," she shook her head. "It was not your fault. No one could have foreseen it."

"Perhaps not," he shrugged, his eyes a little grave, "but somehow that does not make me feel any better."

Slipping her right hand out of his she placed her fingers over his lips, silencing any further self-recrimination. "My darling," she begged, "please do not blame yourself. I do not. How could I," she shook her head, "when my aunt told me what you did for me?"

He kissed her fingers then taking hold of her hand in both of his, held it against his chest as if it were the most precious thing in the world. "I love you more than life itself," he told her in a deep voice, "so much so that the thought of losing you is more than I can bear!"

Although she felt extremely weak, indeed, the slightest effort rendered her quite exhausted, she was nevertheless overjoyed to see him and hear these words, and would, were it at all possible, cast herself into his arms. She had no very clear recollections of what had happened after Colonel Henderson had thrust her from him; it had all happened so quickly that she never really felt the ball penetrate her shoulder at all. All she could remember, and that vaguely, was briefly opening her eyes to see Richard and Gideon looking concernedly down at her. After that, she knew no more until waking up to find herself being put to bed by her maid and Miss Calne in readiness for the arrival of Dr. Jarvey, whereupon he had immediately set about the painful task of extricating the ball from her shoulder. Through a haze of pain she dimly remembered him asking her to explain how she had come to be wounded, immediately followed by her aunt's terse recommendations to him to stop plying her with questions she was clearly in no fit state to answer. She must have passed out then because she knew nothing more until a moment ago to find Gideon looking down at her. "Ssh!" she soothed. "You're not going to lose me. I'm a Ferrers, remember? We're not so easily got rid of!"

He smiled perfunctorily at this, but the truth was it could all have turned out so very differently, and the knowledge that he could have lost her was something he would not forget in a hurry. His quick thinking may have saved her life, but had he thought a little quicker then the chances were that he could have prevented her being shot in the first place, thereby saving her from the agonizing pain she was now suffering. If by some means he could have exchanged places with her in order to relieve her of what he knew from experience was a painful ordeal, he would, but as it was not possible he could only look on in frustrating impotence and berate himself for being totally unprepared for what had happened.

"I know," he acknowledged, squeezing her hand, "but I would have given anything to have spared you this!"

"You could not have done more than save my life," she told him lovingly, her eyes warm and tender as they looked up into his troubled face. "How can I ever repay you for that?"

"By loving me," he told her simply, pressing his lips into her palm.

Her heart skipped a beat at these words, the pain in her shoulder momentarily forgotten. "That is such an easy obligation to discharge," she smiled. "If I could love you any more I would."

He looked down into her pale and drawn face, his eyes dark and intense as he read the unspoken message in her eyes, fighting the overwhelming urge to throw restraint to the wind by taking her in his arms and holding her close against him.

She sensed the inner struggle raging inside him and although she wanted him to take her in his arms and kiss her, she was so attuned to him that she knew were he to do so he would feel that he had contravened his own personal code of honour by abusing the trust her aunt had placed in him. As she had no wish to put him under such an intolerable burden by trying to get him to break his word, she asked instead when he intended to go to London in order to settle her brother's affairs, upon which he told her that he was intending to leave Ferrers Court immediately after breakfast.

She nodded. "I know you have to go," she acknowledged, "Richard's affairs must be settled as speedily as possible; he cannot any longer go on in this way, but I shall miss you so dreadfully!"

"If it were not for the fact that you were lying here injured," he told her earnestly, "which should unquestionably give you protection from any advances I may wish to make, as well as giving my word to your aunt not half an hour ago that I would do nothing reprehensible, I would show you just how much I will miss *you*. Indeed, I would know no hesitation in taking you in my arms and kissing you until you begged me to stop," he assured her in a deep voice.

"Do you think I would tell my aunt if you did?" she teased, taking comfort

475

from the warm strength of his fingers as they held her own.

"No," he shook his head, "but even though I want nothing more than to take you in my arms and do just that, to do so would be taking an unforgivable advantage of both of you."

It was no more than she had come to expect from him, but could not refrain from saying, "I think she would forgive you;" adding huskily, "I know *I* would."

"My darling..." he began raggedly.

"Would it be so very bad if you *did* kiss me?" she asked softly, removing her hand out of his and laying it gently on his arm. "I may be incapacitated," she told him lightly, "but I hope I am not so fragile that I would break merely because you have."

He knew her to be quite inexperienced in matters of love and the arts of seduction, but although this avowal was no calculated act of enticement, it was nevertheless far more potent than any intentionally perpetrated skill because of the purity of the motives behind it, and the affect it had on him was such that he knew he was losing the battle to hold onto his self-control.

She may be unsophisticated when it came to using her charms into stimulating a man into making love to her, but she was nevertheless woman enough to understand the meaning of the look in his eyes as a result of her words, and to take pleasure from them.

"My darling," he cried thickly, "you don't know what you are asking!"

"I think I do," she acknowledged. "I know you promised my aunt that you would not do anything reprehensible, indeed," she smiled, "it would be extremely difficult for you to do so given the circumstances," indicating her left arm with a slight turn of her head, "not to mention Miss Calne asleep in the dressing room, which she is very much aware of I assure you, but whilst I have no wish to be the one to cause you to break your word to her," she told him truthfully, all the love she had for him reflected in her eyes, "I am not asking you to make love to me, not here; not like this," she shook her head, "just to kiss me."

He may yearn for the day when he could make love to her, but he was no callow and impatient youth in the throes of a first love affair, but a man who, after a number of extremely agreeable liaisons, had finally found the one woman with whom he wanted to share his life and endow his name as well as to love and cherish for the rest of his life. He had no intention of stealing a few illicit moments with her purely to satisfy his very natural desires, on the contrary, he wanted nothing to taint or mar the love they shared, and nor, apparently, did she, but he was honest enough to admit that he had wanted to kiss her from the moment he had stood looking down at her as she had lain asleep. But honesty compelled him to own that should he do so not only would he be behaving in a way that would bring down the well deserved criticism he would receive should it become known, but he would find it extremely difficult to contain his ever growing need for her, and had therefore fought the temptation to make any move to do so. But this heartfelt declaration together with the look on her face had the effect of tearing him in two with indecision, bringing something resembling an agonized groan from deep within his throat as he tried to ignore her irresistible but innocent tempting and assert his own good sense, but before he could stop and question the wisdom of what he was doing, lowered his head to brush her parted lips with his own. He had not intended it to be a passionate kiss, but her quivering response to the delicate touch of his lips as they gently brushed her sensitive and receptive ones, as well as feeling her right arm slide around his neck drawing him down to her, acted on his senses like a powerful stimulant, killing at a stroke any desire to curb his very natural needs. He had no regrets whatsoever about falling in love with her and certainly none when it came to demonstrating that love, and although somewhere in the far recesses of his consciousness he was vaguely aware of the fact that he really should have known better than to think he could remain unaffected by the taste and touch of her and that such a brief and fleeting contact would be sufficient to assuage the torrent of emotions rioting inside him, as their demands of each other intensified this was naturally relegated to the back of his mind.

When Elizabeth looked back on this moment she was candid enough to admit to herself that the question as to the rights and wrongs of her actions had never so much as entered her head, or if it had, she had not been aware of it. All she had known with any certainty was that she loved Gideon more than life and that she was where she wanted to be; in his arms and receiving his kisses, kisses which rendered her acutely susceptible to not only her own ever growing needs and desires but his also. Had Miss Calne or her aunt chosen that particular moment to enter her room she could have put forward no defence at being discovered in such a compromising situation, useless to tell them that it was so very difficult to keep a hold on reality when one was being subjected to the most exquisite and hypnotic seduction. She was quite sure that Dr. Jarvey would have thoroughly deprecated such behaviour, especially when he had specifically stipulated no visitors and plenty of rest, but somehow being in Gideon's arms and taking pleasure from his drugging kisses were far more beneficial than any medicine he could have prescribed.

After what seemed like an eternity Gideon reluctantly released her mouth from the crushing confinement of his and slowly raised himself into a sitting position, his eyes dark and smouldering as he looked lovingly down into her flushed face, his breathing somewhat uneven and his colour a little high, and it was therefore several moments before he could speak. "I had not meant to kiss you like that," he smiled, his voice raw. "I have no excuses to put forward, none whatsoever;" he shook his head, "except to say it palpably demonstrates what I have known from the moment I first saw you, which is I am not proof against either my love for you or the effect you have on me. But if nothing else," he told her hoarsely, "I hope at least it assures you of how much I shall miss you."

She slid her hand down his arm until it came to rest on his hand, convulsing beneath her touch, her large blue eyes travelling up to his face to see him brace himself in an effort to keep from taking her in his arms once more.   It had been an instinctive and moving reaction to what had just passed between them, and not from any desire to deliberately entice him into kissing her again, although she knew that should he do so she would do nothing whatever to prevent it, both of which he was perfectly well aware.   She heard him rasp out a sigh which seemed to come from deep within him, telling her more than any words could have just how much he loved her and the frustration he was experiencing in that the circumstances were such they precluded him from further demonstrating his feelings.

"You may take it I *am* assured," she told him softly, smiling lovingly up at him, the pain and discomfort of her injured arm momentarily forgotten, "not only as to how much you will miss me but how much you love me." He clasped her hand in both of his and pressed it to his lips. "Of course," she pointed out mischievously, "you do realize that you have now set a precedent, and I shall therefore expect an even greater show of assurance on your return as to how glad you are to see me again!"

"Minx!" he cried hoarsely, his eyes devouring her before bending his head to brush her lips with his one last time, after which he hurriedly left the room to prevent his emotions from completely overpowering him.

Unaware that he had been with Elizabeth for over an hour it was with some surprise that Gideon saw the time was a couple of minutes after half past seven and that the household staff were already busy about their duties. Acknowledging the brief bobs from two maids' as they passed him with a nod of his head he continued down the stairs and made his way directly to the small sitting room to find Salmon and Michael Beaton still at their post. From the looks of it Michael was clearly feeling the strain of his nightly vigil far more than Salmon, who, upon his entrance, looked as though he was more than prepared to continue keeping guard over his prisoner for as long as necessary.   Recommending Michael to get something to eat and them some rest, Gideon turned his attention to Salmon who, after commenting that the Lieutenant was as good a man as any that he had seen and that he had indeed proved a good friend to Richard, advised him in a quiet aside that although Colonel Henderson had made numerous attempts to break free he was nevertheless as safe as houses with no chance of him going anywhere. Casting a brief glance at their prisoner Gideon then turned his attention back to Salmon, not at all surprised to discover that getting rid of this stalwart was not going to be the easy matter it had with Michael.

"I don't trust him," he told him unequivocally, prepared to stand his ground and stay put.

"Nor do I," Gideon nodded, "but I need to speak with him alone."

Salmon looked as belligerent as he did mulish, but seeing the determination on Gideon's face said grudgingly, "Very well Major if that's what you want, but I don't like it. I'll be within calling if you need me." After throwing Colonel Henderson a look of pure aversion he stalked out of the sitting room, closing the door with a snap behind him.

For several moments the two men eyed one another; the one calculatingly and the other with open hostility. Gideon was neither a violent nor an aggressive man, but he had to exert all his self-control to prevent himself from exacting the most dire punishment on the man responsible for Elizabeth's present condition. What he had done to Richard was unforgivable and he was determined to see him receive his just rewards for that, but that he should dare to harm in any way the one person whose life was more precious to him than his own, was unpardonable. He may acquit him of deliberately intending to shoot Elizabeth but the very fact that he had had her abducted and then held her to ransom in order to bring Richard out into the open, was, despite his obvious desperation to conclude his affairs, an act of calculated vindictiveness, for which he could not exonerate him.

He stood looking dispassionately down at the man who commanded neither his respect nor sympathy with a coldness rarely seen in those brown eyes, but it made Colonel Henderson swallow an uncomfortable lump which had suddenly appeared in his throat. "You and I are going to have a little talk," Gideon told him, with admirable restraint. "I must counsel you however, that it would be most inadvisable for you to attempt anything. Do I make myself clear?" Upon receiving an assenting nod, Gideon pulled up an upright chair, sitting astride this exquisite piece of antiquity to lean forward with his arms resting on the back, bearing all the appearance of one who was quite prepared to remain where he was until he got what he came for. His eyes raked dismissively over Colonel Henderson's florid face wondering, and not for the first time, how on earth he could ever have believed that Stuart, should his insurrection have prospered, been stupid enough to offer him a position even remotely carrying the power and authority he desperately craved. When he thought of what he had put the Ferrers family through, Elizabeth in particular, who, not only having to contend with her father's death alone but was now paying the penalty of this man's intrigues by lying upstairs recovering from a ball in her shoulder, his anger rose afresh, but biting down on this he said calmly, "I shall be leaving here soon to return to London, when I shall see General Turville and present those letters to him. Oh yes," he nodded, catching the glance Colonel Henderson threw at him. "I have them safe. He will accompany me back here whereupon he will immediately place you under arrest for treason and the cold-blooded murder of William Ferrers."

"Blast your eyes!" Henderson spat venomously, pulling on the ropes with all the force he could muster. "I'll see you damned for this!"

"Save your eloquence as well as your strength for what lies ahead of you," Gideon cautioned coldly. "They will not serve you here."

"I should have made an end of you when I had the chance!" he snarled.

"Then it was a pity for you you did not," Gideon acknowledged. "But I am not here to bandy words with you any more than I am to hear your excuses. You must know, as I do," he pointed out, "that this is the end of the road for you. There is nothing more you can do to stave off the inevitable and nowhere else you can run to in order to escape your actions."

"Ha!" Henderson scorned, his face a deep purple. "You think you have me laid by the heels do you? Well, let me tell you," he cried, "that I still have a trick or two up my sleeve! By God, I am not done yet!"

"By that I take you to mean His Grace," Gideon nodded. "Well, I am sorry to disappoint you," he shook his head, "but in that you are fair and far off. But speaking of His Grace," he raised an eyebrow, "I *would* be interested to learn how you managed to persuade him into assisting you to bring about the irrevocable downfall of Richard Ferrers."

"I daresay you would," Henderson bit out, making another futile attempt to break free of his bonds. "But I have no intention of telling you."

"Was it his idea to 'gazette' him, or yours?" Gideon asked firmly, ignoring his prisoner's efforts to provoke him.

As sleep had been virtually impossible due not only to his manacled position but also the anger which threatened to consume him, not to mention the panic and fear he seemed powerless to suppress, Colonel Henderson was certainly in no frame of mind to come face to face with his principal gaoler. He had no intention of answering any of his questions either now or at any time, much preferring to rely on General Turville's protection and sympathy as a senior officer who surely would not allow him to be either harassed or verbally besieged by a man of inferior rank, and who would certainly shield him against the threats menacingly put forward by Salmon during the night. From soldierly fellowship if nothing else he felt sure that General Turville would ensure his protection and safe conduct away from this unlawfully convened prison to a secure lodging in London to await his trial, an occurrence which, although the mere thought filled him with dread, short of a miracle, he could see no way of avoiding. No matter what arguments he had tried to console his fevered brain with, he could not delude himself into thinking that those letters were not in Neville's possession or that they would not be produced against him, but if only he could reach London in the safety of Turville's escort, then the chances were relatively good that he could get word to Lytton to come to his defence. Robert may have said that should last night's plans come to nothing then he would not hesitate in washing his hands of the whole affair, but he was fairly sure that when faced with his fait accompli he would soon re-assess his position. After all, what he knew about Robert's past transgression was more than enough to ensure that the disclosure would be extremely damaging to not only his reputation but the future of his house, and that alone would surely spur Lytton into coming to his aid; his failure to do so would mean the consequences of such a refusal would be too horrendous for a man of his arrogance and pride to contemplate.

Something in Henderson's demeanour told Gideon that he was not going to be either provoked or influenced into divulging information, and short of extracting it from him by other and more painful methods of persuasion, he instead tried a more subtle approach in the hope that it would loosen his tongue. He saw little point in attempting anything in the way of exerting physical pressure on him as it would achieve nothing of value and besides which, he did not advocate or approve such brutal and ruthless methods. "I can, of course, understand your reticence in not wanting to talk," he remarked candidly, "after all there is always the possibility that you could in some way incriminate yourself, but as I am no lawyer," he shrugged, "I really could not say with any degree of certainty how you would stand legally on this point. However," he pointed out practically, "whilst I may not be a lawyer, not that that really signifies because you are going to the gallows irrespective of what you say or not to me," he told him confidently, "I somehow cannot see His Grace rendering you the same courtesy by observing a similar obligation." The only response he received to this was a ferocious glare from out of Henderson's protuberant blue eyes and an inarticulate splutter. "Or is it because you think that by keeping faith with him he will reward you by coming to your assistance?" he shrugged. "If you *are* labouring under the conviction that His Grace will come to your aid, then you are destined to disappointment," he warned him. "Do not misunderstand me," he shook his head, "I easily acquit him of treason. How do I know this?" he raised an eyebrow when Henderson opened his mouth to speak, "because his loyalties, unlike yours," he inclined his head mockingly, "are too well known to be questioned, but whatever means you adopted to attach him to your side will not be sufficient to hold him there. He will do all he can to protect himself at no matter what cost, and if that means leaving you to your own devices as well as denying all knowledge of any involvement, he will do so."

Despite his profound dislike of this man sitting calmly opposite him, Colonel Henderson could not deny that he had spoken no less than the truth. During the small hours when he had considered his predicament he may have talked himself into believing that Robert would do anything rather than face the consequences of his past misdemeanour, even going so far as to rescuing him from his trial and execution, and like a man grasping for a much needed lifeline he had convinced himself that he had hit upon the means of his salvation, but Gideon's calm reasoning shattered any hopes he had, plummeting them into the abyss of disillusionment and forcing him to face the unpalatable truth. He knew Lytton would do everything possible to extricate himself from this affair and should he attempt to dangle his past misdeed over his head yet again in order to help liberate him from the hangman's noose, he knew that his threats would yield nothing but disappointment.

Seeing the indecision which had suddenly descended onto his deeply flushed face, Gideon pressed home his advantage. "I can, of course, only speculate how your enterprise began and the reasons behind it, but it needs no ingenuity to know you are relying heavily upon His Grace coming to your aid as he has thus far by successfully bringing about a reprieve, although by what means I know not," he shook head. "Unfortunately, what neither you nor William Ferrers paused to consider when you enlisted his aid, was that whilst he was in a prime position to assist you in tracking down Richard Ferrers, the same reliance could not be placed on his ability or, indeed, his willingness, to shield you from denunciation should all efforts to apprehend him fail, as indeed has proved to be the case. But even if he was prepared to facilitate you by saving you from having to face your trial, it would be quite impossible for him to do so by virtue of his complicity, which has clearly left him exposed to charges of being an accessory to treason after the fact; an indictment even he will find difficult to answer or defend." Colonel Henderson, who had not even considered this, turned quite pale, and so great was his fear and agitation that he could hardly utter a word. Taking advantage of this, Gideon went on smoothly, "Of course, if His Grace were to find himself in the position of having to answer such serious allegations, he could easily claim that he knew nothing of your treasonable activities and that he offered you assistance to apprehend a traitor and fugitive in the firmly held belief that he was doing whatever was necessary in the interests of justice, and with His Majesty at his back," he reminded him, "there would be no difficulty. You see my point, Henderson" Gideon asked, raising an eyebrow. "If His Grace *did* know of your involvement why then come to your aid? What inducement could you possibly have offered to persuade a man of his unquestionable loyalty to help you out of such a fix?" He let this sink in for a moment or two before continuing inexorably, "Should this in fact turn out to be the case, then as I have already pointed out he will be in no position to aid you further as he will be far too occupied looking to himself. However, if he *was* in complete ignorance of your activities, then you can neither look nor, indeed, expect any. In either event, he will leave you dangling in the wind to face your fate alone, but whichever way it was does not really matter in the least," he pointed out, rising to his feet. "As far as *you* are concerned you are on your own and may as well accept the fact that no help is going to be forthcoming." Returning the chair to its original position, he turned and stood for a moment looking down at the beaten figure of Colonel Henderson, before saying "Come what may you are going to have to answer for your crimes; and even if you can evade the gallows for treason, there is no way you can avoid the same over the murder of William Ferrers, a man who, despite his usefulness in providing the perfect scapegoat in his cousin, was hardly the type to recruit as a reliable accomplice. By shooting him, if I may say so," he told him candidly, "was your biggest mistake. Whatever chance you may have had of buying an acquittal for treason, his murder has rendered that possibility no longer viable. *Richard* Ferrers is now a 'gazetted' man," he told him coolly, "an appellation he does not deserve. Was that Lytton's idea?" he asked sharply.

Colonel Henderson, whose head had slumped dejectedly onto his chest, looked up at this, his eyes mirroring not only his fear but the fact that there was nothing else he could do to stave off the inevitable. He had done all he could to save himself but he was honest enough to admit that there was nothing left; those letters and William Ferrers' murder were two inescapable facts that would see him climb the scaffold. He knew Major Neville, a man on whom he had misguidedly pinned his hopes, was right when he said that nothing now would induce Lytton to either aid or support him; and however frightening the thought he was forced to admit that he was a defeated man with no hope of succour from any quarter. He doubted Lytton would be charged with such serious allegations, and if he were they probably would never be taken very seriously by the authorities. A man in Robert's position knew more than one way to survive crises and setbacks, but of one thing he could be sure of and that was there would be no room in Lytton's thoughts for such as himself.

When he made no answer to this question Gideon suggested quietly, "You have nothing whatever to gain from withholding anything, and whilst confessing the whole truth to me will not alter in any way what is going to happen to you, surely knowing you have acknowledged your offences as well as saving an innocent man from the consequences of 'gazetting', will go some way to putting right the terrible wrong you set in motion."

Henderson nodded. Apparently he did, because when Gideon left the sitting room half an hour later he finally had the answer to the question which had for long occupied his mind.

CHAPTER TWENTY FIVE

By the time he left the sitting room it was apparent that Richard's homecoming was already known to every member of the household. It was also apparent that even had he been the traitor and vicious cutthroat he had been advertised to be, it was patently obvious that it would not have mattered one jot to the inhabitants of Ferrers Court. Upon entering the breakfast room in Salmon's wake to find his host already halfway through a substantial meal, it was clear from the heavily laden table that someone had indeed brought out the fatted calf for his delectation.

"I had not looked to see you up this early," Gideon remarked, sitting down on the chair Richard had kicked out for him, eyeing the multi-coloured dressing gown in some astonishment.

"What!" he cried, his mouth full of roast beef, "lie abed the first day I have been home for over a twelvemonth! No, I thank you!"

Gideon eyed his future brother-in-law with a mixture of amusement and apprehension, asking warily "What are your plans?"

Richard cast him a glance of pure mischief, putting him in mind of his sister. They were not alike, the resemblance being more in the way of certain facial expressions that definite features, but that look was unmistakable. "Why, do you think I may do something I oughtn't?"

"The thought had occurred to me," Gideon smiled, spreading a liberal portion of mustard onto a generous slice of beef Salmon had just placed in front of him. "Do not forget," he reminded him, "you are now a 'gazetted' man, and until that is lifted and our friend in the sitting room is formally charged and taken into custody by General Turville, *your* position is still somewhat precarious."

At the mention of the prisoner in the sitting room, Salmon, who had been no more successful in trying to prise information out of Gideon regarding his talk with Colonel Henderson any more than he had in making Richard see the unwisdom of remaining at Ferrers Court whilst they were housing their captive, was goaded beyond endurance as he glared from one to the other. Since neither of them seemed to be at all interested in what he had say, he thrust a tankard of ale down in front of Gideon, grumbling something in the broadest of Sussex, casting a reproachful glance at his young master as he did so. As Gideon was not at all sure which one of them Salmon was addressing, which was perhaps just as well since he found his utterances quite unintelligible,   he cast a look across at Richard who, thankfully, appeared to be having no difficulty in interpreting this outburst.

"Yes, I daresay!" he exclaimed. "But I wish you'd take yourself off and that Friday face of yours with you! Egad, it's enough to give anyone a fit of the dismals!"

Salmon heaved a sigh, then turning to Gideon cried, "I've told him till I'm blue in the face Major that while we have that scoundrel here it's not safe for him to be under the same roof!"

"I agree," Gideon acknowledged calmly, surprising both Salmon and Richard who looked at him as though they could not believe their ears.

"What!" Richard cried. "You too?"

"Salmon is quite right," Gideon nodded, selecting another slice of beef from the serving dish. "As I remarked earlier, your position is still precarious and it would be foolish to run any unnecessary risks at this stage."

"So what are you saying?" Richard demanded. "I go and hide myself away!"

"That would be the sensible thing to do, yes" Gideon nodded, not expecting him to take any notice.

"Well, I won't do it!" he cried, banging his empty tankard down on the table. "Why, it's more than flesh and blood can stand! I won't be driven out of my own home like a criminal!"

"*There!*" Salmon snorted disgustedly. "You see what I mean Major? That's all I can get out of him."

"Are *you* still here?" Richard demanded, eyeing his henchman steadily.

"I'm going," Salmon told him firmly, "but I still say it, you won't be happy until you're knee deep in trouble again!"

"Well, go on," Richard invited when Salmon had left, "say what you have to."

Placing his napkin down on the table with slow deliberation, Gideon looked across at Richard whose face clearly echoed his feelings, and knew that it was going to take great tact and a lot of persuasion to convince him that Salmon had spoken no less than the truth. "You don't want for sense Richard," he told him, "any more than you need me to confirm what you already know. Apart from the fact that you are now a 'gazetted' man with a price on your head you are still wanted for treason, and until I can return here with General Turville for him to formally charge Henderson and place him under arrest and those letters are given in evidence, as well as removing the threat hanging over your head which that label has consequently brought with it, that is not going to change." He saw the frown descend onto Richard's forehead. "You told me that your friends were not the kind of men to turn tail on you, very well," he nodded, "I accept that, but like it or not you have made enemies; Captain Waring for one. You may never have been caught red-handed running goods, but thanks to Colonel Henderson he firmly believes that you are nothing short of a cold-blooded felon who is responsible for masterminding all the illicit activities taking place along this stretch of coast, and he would like nothing more than to apprehend you by whatever means at his disposal, and should he get wind of you being here, then I would not at all put it beyond him to either come here looking for you or informing against you at the garrison. Remember too," he pointed out, "you have no friend in Major Denham. However," he shrugged, "since you are determined to remain here irrespective of the risks you are running, oblige me in one thing at least; stay indoors and do not venture out."

The frown on Richard's forehead deepened as he contemplated what Gideon had said, knowing perfectly well that no matter how unpalatable, every word he had uttered was true. It was also true that he was tired of hiding out and evading the Preventive Officers as well as the soldiers from the garrison, and although this had been a necessary as well as a regular occurrence over the recent past, the time had now come when he wanted to put an end to his energetic activities.

"Believe me," Gideon told him earnestly, "I would not advise such a precaution unless I thought it prudent to do so."

Richard cast him a glance from under his lashes, acknowledging at length, "I know." A semblance of a smile touched his well shaped lips. "I stand very much in your debt Gideon; I assure you I am most conscious of it."

"You owe me nothing," Gideon assured him.

"You may say that if you wish," Richard shrugged, "but we both know it's true. I also know that were it not for you I would not be here now. In fact," he added, leaning forward and pouring himself another tankard of ale, "I dread to think where I *would* be if you had not come along when you did." He swallowed a generous mouthful. "But whilst I accept that what you say is true, you must see that I cannot look to my own safety while my sister is lying upstairs recovering from a ball in her shoulder. It may have been an accident, but what happened to her is entirely my fault, and I cannot desert her now; she deserves better than that, especially when I think of all she has endured on my behalf. I can see you disapprove of that," he remarked as he saw Gideon's lips compress, "but my mind's quite made up. Do not be thinking I am disregarding your advice," he smiled, "I am not, but nothing would induce me to leave here now. However," he promised, "in view of what you have said, I give you my word that I will not venture out."

The determination which had settled on Richard's face told Gideon that he was irrevocably set on this course, but even so he felt it behoved him to make one more attempt try to make him realize that his position was still hanging dangerously in the balance. "Your sentiments do you credit," he told him sincerely, "but although I fully understand your very natural anxiety where she is concerned, indeed, I thought something like this was in your head, I promise you she will make a full recovery with or without your presence here." In response to Richard's raised eyebrow, Gideon explained about his visit to see her earlier, furnishing him with a slightly edited version as to what had passed between them. "She is very conscious of your position," he nodded, defending this falsehood with his conscience by telling himself that although she had not actually come out and said it, he knew it to be true, apart from which, it was imperative Richard was not found at Ferrers Court until his affairs were concluded, "and worrying over you while things have still to be settled could only impede her recovery."

After digesting this for a moment or two, Richard eyed his benefactor with a more than ordinarily close eye. "So," he said slowly, "you've seen Elizabeth."

"Yes," Gideon nodded, not shrinking from the concentrated look focused on him from out of those piercing blue eyes, "I wanted to satisfy myself that she was indeed all right before I left here to see General Turville. Since Dr. Jarvey refused to allow either of us to see her last night and I have no idea what time he is due to arrive today and your affairs will not wait on his convenience, I took the opportunity when it arose. I'm sorry if you do not approve of that," Gideon told him firmly, "but Elizabeth means as much to me as you, I think."

"Damn you, Gideon!" he exclaimed, "I'm not accusing you of anything, but what beats me is why my aunt permitted you to see her and not me!"

Gideon smiled. "I can't answer that."

"No," Richard nodded darkly, "but it seems to me you can twist her round your little finger."

Gideon laughed. "Perhaps, but whatever the reason it does not alter your position in any way." He paused momentarily before asking, with more hope than optimism, "I don't suppose I can persuade you into changing your mind about remaining here?"

Richard shook his head. "Not a chance!"

As it was patently obvious that he would not be moved from this stance, Gideon gave up any further move to try and persuade him. "Of course," he smiled down at him as he rose to his feet, "I would be somewhat reassured if you gave me your word that during my absence you will refrain from inflicting any kind of retribution on our prisoner; quite understandable given the circumstances I know," he acknowledged, "but I do not think you will have any further trouble from him."

Richard cocked an eyebrow. "Salmon told me you had spoken to him earlier. What passed between you exactly?"

"Let us just say," Gideon inclined his head, "that he has finally been brought to accept that the game is up and that he cannot look to His Grace for any further assistance or support."

After tossing off the remainder of his ale Richard rose to his feet and took several steps towards Gideon, his eyes narrowing slightly. "Is that so?" he said slowly.

"That is so," Gideon confirmed.

"And did Henderson happen to mention what had brought His Grace into this business in the first place?" Richard asked, thrusting his hands into the capacious pockets of his dressing gown.

"He did touch upon it, yes" Gideon nodded.

"I get the feeling he more than touched upon it," Richard commented thoughtfully.

"As a matter of fact, he did" Gideon affirmed, his eyes alight.

When Gideon made no effort to expand on this, Richard exclaimed, "Damn it Gideon! After all that has happened I thought you trusted me!"

"I'd trust you with my life," he told him, gripping his shoulder, "but not with this; at least," he corrected himself, "not yet."

"Why not?" Richard demanded, his eyes sparkling.

"Because the mood you are in you are most likely to act upon it, and if all our efforts to prove you innocent are not to be checked at this stage," he told him firmly, "I think it best if you don't know."

"You *do* still want to marry my sister I take it?" Richard enquired, not quite able to hide the smile in his eyes. "Because if you do," he reminded him, "she needs my permission."

Gideon, who had reached the door by now, turned at this and smiled. "Are you saying that you would withhold it?"

"If you don't tell me what Henderson said, yes."

Gideon smiled. "You won't," he told him confidently.

"Oh, why not?" raising a questioning eyebrow.

"Because you love her too much to make her unhappy," Gideon replied easily.

"You have all the answers, don't you?" Richard stated amusedly.

"No," Gideon shook his head, unable to resist that smile, "only some."

Richard burst out laughing at this, then putting a hand through Gideon's arm walked with him out of the breakfast room and up the stairs, accepting his apologies for having to leave him to settle things here while he was away, with a careless shrug. It was just as Gideon was on the point of leaving Ferrers Court that General Turville, due to the urgency attached to his presence at Hampton Regis, having left London at an extremely early hour, permitting only two stops on the way to rest the horses, arrived unannounced at the garrison in company with half a dozen men, taking Major Denham completely by surprise.

He was only too aware of the difficulties besetting Colonel Henderson in his attempts to track down Richard Ferrers, but whilst he may have neither liking nor respect for his commanding officer, he had by no means liked the idea that a traitor turned smuggler was roaming free conducting his illicit activities and had therefore done all he could to assist him in his efforts to apprehend this young man, being too much the soldier to question his orders. In view of what General Turville disclosed to him about Richard Ferrers he had at no point suspected the truth behind those searches at Ferrers Court, and certainly had never found it necessary to question the means his senior officer had adopted to try and seek him out, accepting his strenuous, though severe, attempts as being perfectly understandable given the kind of man they were dealing with. As far as Elizabeth Ferrers was concerned, he had kept an uncharacteristically open mind. She could well be in league with her brother, even going so far as to offer him shelter as Colonel Henderson seemed to think, but as nothing had come to light to prove this, he had regarded her hostility as perfectly natural given the numerous searches of her home and the resultant death of her father. Being an honest as well as a straightforward man he had looked upon the exploits of Richard Ferrers as not only disloyal but nothing short of iniquitous and he by no means liked the idea of knowing that a man who was claimed a traitor then turning his hand to smuggling in order to evade the law was still at large, and had therefore considered it to be his duty to do everything in his power to seek him out, at no point pausing to consider that Richard Ferrers may well be innocent. He had certainly questioned Colonel Henderson's merit to the rank he held as well as to his commitment to the assignment of garrison commander, but even given the ease with which he shelved his duties as well as the regularity of his disappearances, he had never been given cause to doubt either his reasons or his dedication in hunting down Richard Ferrers, and certainly not his loyalty, but Sir John's disclosure came as a reeling blow.

Whether he liked it or not, General Turville had been faced with little choice but to acquaint him with the circumstances surrounding this unexpected visit, and although he was reluctant to impart such damaging news there was no way it could be avoided as not only was Major Denham's assistance necessary but such a scandal could not be kept in check indefinitely and sooner or later he would come to learn of the dishonourable conduct of his commanding officer. It gave him no pleasure or satisfaction to either accuse or arrest a fellow officer, and certainly not for something as serious as treason, but since those letters clearly proved beyond doubt that he was heavily involved with The Pretender, he was faced with no alternative but to embark upon a course of action he would much rather have not. Nevertheless, he was not a man to shrink from his responsibilities however distasteful, besides which he had no stomach to see an innocent man hang for another's crimes, and therefore knew no hesitation in carrying out the task ahead of him.

When he had sent Gideon into Sussex he had had no very clear idea of what he would discover, but although he had questioned Colonel Henderson's part in the affair he had never at any time thought that he would turn out to be the conspirator. It may not explain how Henderson had managed to persuade His Grace into offering his assistance, but if nothing else it explained why he had moved heaven and earth to find Richard Ferrers; with such damning evidence in that young man's possession he could not afford to allow him to roam free. Gideon had certainly repaid the confidence he had in him, but whilst his report had been concise and to the point, there were still a number of questions to which he had no answers, but since it appeared that both Colonel Henderson and Gideon were nowhere to be found and Major Denham could not enlighten him, he spent the time in awaiting the arrival of one or both of them with what patience he could muster.

It had taken Major Denham only a matter of minutes to see that he was dealing with a very different type of man altogether to Colonel Henderson, but although he had no suitable explanation to account for the disappearance of his comamnding officer or Major Neville, he was at least able to substantiate his efforts to locate the two men who appeared to hold the key to last night's bewildering events by sending for Sergeant Taylor. Withstanding Sir John's ferocious stare with unruffled calm, he could unfortunately add nothing to what he had already told Major Denham; he had not seen Major Neville since he had left his quarters last night about half past five to see Colonel Henderson and that his bag was still packed where he had left it in readiness for his return to London today.

"This Lieutenant Beaton," Sir John barked when Sergeant Taylor had left, "you say he too has disappeared?"

"Yes, Sir" Major Denham confirmed, beginning to feel a little uncomfortable.

Sir John took several frustrating paces up and down before coming to an abrupt halt on the other side of the desk. "What has he to do with this?"

"I really couldn't say, Sir" he shook his head. "I know he and Major Neville struck up quite an acquaintance, but I would not have thought that he has anything to do with this business."

"So, you just allow your officers to come and go as they please, do you?" he thundered, his eyes scowling beneath his bushy eyebrows.

"Not at all, Sir" Major Denham shook his head, hating to feel at either a disadvantage or worse, inept. "You may rest assured, Sir" he promised, "that he *will* be dealt with."

"So I should hope," Sir John bit out. "It seems to me that things are pretty lax around here!"

Had Major Denham not been so taken up in allowing himself to infer that this scathing observation was meant as a personal attack, he would have known that such a caustic outburst had been merely a manifestation of Sir John's frustration and not a condemnation on his abilities to maintain discipline. As it was he felt extremely aggrieved that circumstances beyond his control had resulted in such an indictment being laid at his door, but since General Turville appeared to be engrossed in his own thoughts and far from receptive to explanations, he had no choice but to let the opportunity to defend himself pass. Needless to say the next hour or so proved to be a severe trial for both men. Sir John, desirous of settling this unpalatable affair as soon as may be possible, had no way of knowing where either Gideon or Colonel Henderson were, much less what had happened to them, saw no point in wasting time by searching for them all over which would doubtless prove to be as exhausting as it would fruitless. Unfortunately, he was never at his best when having to wait upon developments, much preferring to be up and doing, but because there was nothing he could possibly do other than await the arrival of one or the other of them, his temper as well as his frustration began to escalate.

As far as Major Denham was concerned not only was he finding it difficult to comprehend the full extent of his commanding officer's perfidy, but failed to see what else he could personally do to render his guest's wait more agreeable, much less offer some kind of practical suggestion which would at least give some indication as to where either man was likely to be found. There was always the possibility that one or both of them were at Ferrers Court, but as he was unaware of precisely what had taken place last night, and he was in complete ignorance of the true state of affairs between Major Neville and Elizabeth Ferrers, he was momentarily at a loss to put forward a satisfactory reason to account for this.

Gideon, having finally managed to leave Ferrers Court about half an hour later than anticipated, eventually arrived at the garrison just as the gatehouse clock struck fifteen minutes past eleven. As he had no intention of remaining any longer than it would take him to collect his bag and retrieve those letters, fully expecting to be in London by early evening, providing, of course, nothing untoward occurred to delay his progress, he was somewhat surprised to learn from Sergeant Taylor, having hurried up to his quarters the moment he had seen him guide his horse through the archway, of General Turville's unexpected arrival well over an hour previously. Clearly, Sir John had decided to act upon his report by coming into Sussex, a circumstance which, although it took him a little by surprise, relieved him of the necessity of returning to London, thereby saving precious time and reducing the risk of Richard taking matters into his own hands. Dismissing Sergeant Taylor with instructions to take his horse to the stables he waited only long enough to cast a glance through the window to ensure that there was no possibility of him returning. Having satisfied himself that he was indeed heading in that direction he quickly strode across to the fireplace and bending down rested his left hand on the front brickwork and inserted his right one up the chimney breast until he felt the small ledge at the back of the projecting wall. Although the grate still housed the dying embers of the previous evening's fire there was insufficient heat to prevent him from running his fingers along the ledge until they found the bundle of letters he had placed there the night before, and after taking hold of them rose quickly to his feet and tore off the oilskin covering to swiftly sift out the three which named William Ferrers as accomplice. Richard may well be right when he had said that there was nothing to stop Colonel Henderson from naming William at his trial, possibly in an effort to make it appear that he had been the one to engineer the whole thing or even, perhaps, out of a malicious desire to deal the Ferrers family one final wounding blow, but without those letters to substantiate his claim such accusations could not be acted upon, indeed the chances were they would not be taken seriously but merely looked upon as a last ditch attempt to save himself. Whatever Colonel Henderson may or may not say at his trial was beyond his doing anything about, but he was determined those letters were not going to be produced; not out of sympathy for William Ferrers nor because he felt he had already received punishment for his part in what had occurred, but simply because he had given his word to a lady who had already seen her family suffer enough. Releasing the buckle on the strap of his bag he flung it open and pulled out a shirt into which he folded those three remaining letters, before concealing them in the middle of his other belongings, then putting the other letters in the inside pocket of his tunic he fastened the bag before leaving his rooms to make his way across the courtyard to the tower quarters.

General Turville, who had spent most of his time in looking at maps of the area and going through Colonel Henderson's papers in company with Major Denham in case somewhere amongst them there may be some indication as to what had occurred or where he may be likely to go, was certainly relieved at the arrival of his Personal Staff Officer. Upon seeing him walk in he dropped the papers he held in his hand, returning his salute almost as if it were an afterthought, totally disregarding the fact that he was not wearing his white wig, a circumstance that had not escaped Major Denham, who looked at Gideon with strong disapproval.

"I am glad to see you, Sir" Gideon told him with heartfelt sincerity, his outstretched hand being wrung in an iron grip, having neither the time nor the inclination to apologize for not being properly dressed. "Your arrival at this moment is most opportune Sir, particularly as I had intended to leave for London to day to put the whole matter before you. I have returned here directly from Ferrers Court merely in order to collect my gear," Gideon explained. "You must have left London very early and ridden non-stop Sir," Gideon smiled, "to get here in so short a time."

"Well before daybreak" Turville nodded, adding reminiscently, "reminded me of when I was campaigning as a young subaltern."

"Well, your arrival is certainly most timely, Sir" Gideon told him.

"Considering the circumstances," he pointed out gruffly, "there was no time to waste."

"I hope, Major" Major Denham said markedly, cutting unceremoniously into this exchange, "that you are in a position to tell us where Colonel Henderson is. He is nowhere to be found, and considering the most unusual events which appear to have taken place last night as well as the disappearance of yourself and Lieutenant Beaton, we are quite at a loss."

Gideon eyed him meditatively for a moment or two before saying steadily, "My disappearance, and that of Lieutenant Beaton, was rather forced upon us."

"I hope you can explain that, Major!" he nodded, his eyes narrowing.

Before Gideon could reply to this General Turville, who by no means liked the idea that Major Denham was on the point of taking Gideon to task, snapped "I have no reason to doubt that he can." Then turning to Gideon said, "The content of your report, though not at all what I expected, was sufficient to tell me that my presence here was needed as soon as possible if this regrettable affair is to be concluded, and it appears I was right. But tell me," he asked, "do you indeed know where Colonel Henderson is?"

"Yes Sir, I do," he nodded. "At this precise moment he is under guard at Ferrers Court."

Not unnaturally this announcement held is auditors speechless but it was Major Denham who found his voice first. "Under guard!" he exclaimed. "What the devil do you mean?"

"Precisely that," Gideon replied, returning his look quite unperturbed. "Last night's unusual events, as you so describe them," he inclined his head, "precipitated a course of action which, however unfortunate, was nevertheless very necessary." Turning to Sir John, whose face clearly echoed his concern, said evenly "You may believe me when I tell you Sir, that had it been at all possible to have brought Colonel Henderson here I would have done so, but since it would have created as much embarrassment as it would speculation, I considered it wiser to adopt the course I did."

Major Denham, still reeling from the shock of discovering that his commanding officer had embroiled himself in something as serious as treason, may have been forced into owning that he had misjudged Gideon, but this did not mean he liked him any better. His feelings towards him were not likely to improve when he realized that something of this magnitude had been going on under his very nose and he had known nothing about it. It did little for either his pride or self-esteem to know that he had failed to pick up on the signs which, in hindsight, were blatantly obvious and that it had taken an outsider to unveil the truth. Although he would rather die than admit it, even to himself, he would have much preferred to be the one who had discovered what was going on and not someone brought in from London, and his feelings of resentment were such that he could not resist asking, "And just what was it that prompted this course of action, Major? Whatever Colonel Henderson has done his rank demands fair treatment. Do not forget," he reminded him, "we are talking of a senior officer!"

"I do not forget it," Gideon assured him. "But considering he was prepared to deny Richard Ferrers' rank the same courtesy when he set out to hound him and his family, he has been treated with as much respect as possible."

General Turville may have spent only a short time in Major Denham's company, but he was shrewd enough to draw some pretty accurate conclusions; correctly deducing the bitterness he must be feeling towards Gideon, but when he saw his barely concealed resentment prudently deemed it time to intervene. Authoritatively reminding Major Denham that whatever he may think, Major Neville had been acting under his direct orders and, furthermore, he had never been given cause to question either his diligence or integrity, and if he had considered his actions last night to be necessary then he for one had no doubt there was a perfectly good reason.

"I'm sorry, Sir" Major Denham apologized, hating to be put on the defensive, "I meant no offence."

Ignoring this, General Turville looked directly at Gideon. "What *did* happen last night?"

"Well, Sir" Gideon shook his head, "to understand that one has to know all that has gone before." He then went on to recount all that had happened since he had come into Sussex culminating with the stirring events of the previous evening, his auditors listening to every word in incredulous silence. To say that the story which unfolded both shocked and astounded them was a gross understatement but it was General Turville who found his voice first. "Good God!" he cried, rising hurriedly to his feet, "It's worse than I thought!"

"Not very pleasant, I know," Gideon acknowledged, "but once panic had set in I am afraid that any commonsense he had left him, especially when he saw that William Ferrers was not prepared to go any further with the venture."

After taking several frustrated turns around the room he came to an abrupt halt in front of Gideon, demanding, "And Miss Ferrers?"

"Fortunately, she's going to make a full recovery, Sir."

"Thank God!" he cried.

"Are you saying that Sir Evelyn was a party to all this?" Major Denham asked shocked, his face rather pale.

"By no means," Gideon shook his head. "According to his man, Sir Evelyn is spending some time in town and knows nothing about it. I believe Sir Evelyn and Colonel Henderson are acquaintances, and therefore he was able to persuade Cartwright into allowing him the use of Hamstoke House for the evening."

"But what makes you think he will keep his word and say nothing to him?" he demanded.

"Because he is much too afraid of losing his position," Gideon said simply. "Should Sir Evelyn ever discover that his home had been used without his knowledge and for such illicit purposes, he would have to be a most magnanimous employer indeed to let it pass."

"So that's why he drugged your wine and sent me off on a wild goose chase!" he said broodingly.

"Yes," Gideon nodded. "If his plan was to work, and I say *his* plan," not wanting to alert Major Denham to his doubts as to the architect of the scheme, "because William Ferrers was in no condition to formulate any plan for their recovery, then he had to rid himself of the only two people who could possibly have thwarted his plot."

"It was a damned risky one!" Sir John commented, thrusting his hands deep into his pockets. "Devious too. A two pronged attack!"

"Yes, it was," Gideon acknowledged. "Any number of things could have gone wrong, but the key to its success or failure was in Miss Ferrers' abduction. Having made sure that word had been put abroad, knowing perfectly well that it would reach Richard's ears, Colonel Henderson knew that he would move heaven and earth to go to his sister's aid, which is why the letter he wrote to her had to be very carefully composed."

"Yes, I see that," Major Denham nodded, "but why write a letter supposedly from you, why not from another?"

"Because at some point Colonel Henderson had discovered the true state of affairs which exists between us," Gideon told him unashamedly, aware of the glance General Turville cast at him from under his lashes, "and knew that she would not hesitate to leave her home alone if she knew she were coming to see me."

Major Denham, deciding it wiser to keep his thoughts on this to himself, said instead, "But she was not alone; you mentioned that she accompanied Private Smith to Hamstoke House."

"Yes, that's true," Gideon acknowledged, "but she believed he was acting as my advocate and therefore would have trusted him. Colonel Henderson would have known this, but more to the point he himself must have trusted Private Smith sufficiently to recruit him for such a task. I take it you know this man?"

"Yes," Major Denham nodded, "I do. I can tell you that I have reason to believe Colonel Henderson made use of Private Smith on more than one occasion," he told them regretfully, "for which he was rewarded with, shall I say, certain inducements. I also feel it to be my duty to have to tell you that before he joined the army I am reliably informed that his past career was - well," he shrugged, "let us just say, not as honest as one would wish."

Gideon, who was not overly surprised at this, nodded. "Well, whatever his past career, he must be found. I doubt very much whether he was in Colonel Henderson's confidence to the point where he knew of his treasonable activities, but he must, at the very least, have known that what he had been asked to do was unlawful; abduction is a serious offence." Looking from Sir John to Major Denham, he said resignedly, "Even giving him the benefit of the doubt by saying there really has not been either sufficient time or the opportunity for him to approach me in response to the note I left Cartwright to hand to him upon his return to Hamstoke House, the truth is that I cannot see him responding to it. I believe it to be a pretty accurate assumption to say that he will make good his escape as soon as he possibly can. I was rather hoping you could perhaps help there," Gideon said optimistically.

"Yes, of course. I shall be happy to do whatever lies in my power to apprehend him," Major Denham assured him. "I promise he will not be allowed to get away with this."

"Thank you, Major" Sir John nodded. "And now," he sighed, looking at Gideon, his bushy eyebrows snapping together, "about William Ferrers. Are you indeed telling us that Richard Ferrers is in agreement with setting abroad the tale that far from being Henderson's accomplice he was in fact working with his cousin in order to bring him out into the open?"

A twisted smile touched Gideon's lips as he recalled Richard's initial reaction to the suggestion, but deciding to keep this to himself said quite composedly, "Yes Sir. We are both of the opinion that no good could possibly result from dragging his name through the dirt. Whatever he did he has received just punishment for, apart from which," he stressed, "I gave my word to Clara Winsetton that I would do all I could to keep his name out of it."

"That's all very well," Major Denham pointed out, the look on his face adequate testimony to what he felt about allowing a law-breaker to go free, "but surely you cannot have considered the consequences of such a decision."

"I assure you I am very much alive to them," Gideon told him firmly. "I do not like the idea of shielding William Ferrers any more than you do," he said unequivocally, "nor, if it comes to that, does Richard Ferrers or his sister, but given what can only be described as exceptional circumstances, not only do I fail to see what good would come from disclosing his involvement, which," he reiterated, "was minor, but I will not go back on my word."

"You say you are alive to the consequences," Major Denham observed, "I beg to differ. For one thing," he pointed out, "you cannot have considered; there is absolutely nothing whatever to prevent Colonel Henderson from naming him at his trial."

"He does have a point, Gideon" Sir John pointed out fairly. "A man with his back against the wall is capable of anything in order to save himself."

"I realize that Sir," Gideon acknowledged "but as I have already said, without those letters naming William there is very little chance of anyone believing him."

"That's as may be," Major Denham nodded, "but I believe I have the advantage of you where Colonel Henderson is concerned," he said firmly. "You may believe me when I tell you that he will do everything in his power to avoid the very worst from happening."

"Perhaps," Gideon inclined his head, "but something tells me there will be no startling declaration from Colonel Henderson either at his trial or any other time."

General Turville, who had been sitting on the edge of the desk regarding the toe of his boot, raised his head at this to cast a quick look up at Gideon who, unless he was very much mistaken, knew more than he was saying. He gained the very strong impression that there was something he wished to convey to him but much preferred to do so out of Major Denham's hearing, and if it was in anyway connected with His Grace, which he firmly suspected it was, then he could well understand why. "Major Denham," he said quietly, twisting himself round in order to face him, "would you be good enough to please give us a moment?"

It seemed at first as though he was going to argue the point, but realizing that this could easily be turned into an order and he did not want to appear at a disadvantage in front of Major Neville, he said in a rather strained voice, "Yes, of course, Sir. I'll begin making some enquiries about Private Smith."

Waiting only until the door had closed behind him, General Turville rose to his feet, his sharp eyes scanning Gideon's face intently. "All right Gideon," he nodded, "let me have the whole tale. I take it this claim of yours in that Colonel Henderson won't make any last minute declaration is in some way connected with His Grace?"

"Yes Sir, it is," he said firmly.

"I thought so," he sighed. "Well," he nodded, "it's perhaps better not to discuss it in front of Major Denham, because although he knows the truth about Colonel Henderson, the less he knows about Lytton the better." Taking a revivifying pinch of snuff he eyed Gideon closely, "I must tell you however, that according to Major Denham, Henderson had a meeting with His Grace the other night at *'The White Hart'*, or, at least," he sighed, "so he believes. According to him a letter was delivered to Colonel Henderson by a waiter from 'The *White Hart'* and although he was not told who the letter was from, the crest on the wafer was enough to enlighten him as to the writer. Apparently," he shrugged, "Colonel Henderson left the garrison not long after, and although he cannot say for certain that that is where he went, I think we can safely say it was."

"The other night!" Gideon exclaimed surprised. "I had no idea he had come into Sussex. So," he mused, "that's why Colonel Henderson cancelled our engagement!"

"The Lord only knows what passed between them," he scorned, "but I'd lay my life last night's events had their roots in Lytton's mind and not Henderson's."

"Yes Sir" Gideon agreed, "I am convinced of it. Even before you told me of His Grace's visit into Sussex I knew that neither Colonel Henderson nor William

Ferrers had the ability to formulate something so ingenious, and whilst I had no idea that His Grace had seen Colonel Henderson it did occur to me that it was precisely the kind of intricate idea which would appeal to him. I cannot help but think that it was more a case of Lytton outlining the scheme and leaving its implementation to them."

"Yes," he nodded, "I agree. So, what do you know that I do not?" indicating he take a seat.

"Well, Sir" Gideon sighed, easing himself onto the chair, "unlikely though it may seem, as far as Colonel Henderson is concerned I envisage no further difficulties or unforeseen eventualities; in fact," he nodded, "he seems quite reconciled to his fate."

"Really!" Sir John raised sceptical eyebrow. "I must say considering the position in which he finds himself, I would have thought that he would be fighting tooth and nail to find a way to extricate himself from his predicament." But after hearing Gideon's account of his interview with Colonel Henderson earlier that morning his expression, which had been extremely grim, lightened perceptibly. "Yes," he inclined his head, "I tend to agree with you. Without Lytton's support Henderson's position is most disagreeable, and as you rightly say His Grace is perfectly placed to deflect any claims or accusations made against him, and even if this does not turn out to be the case he will not risk openly defending Henderson now; to do so would only raise questions about what he himself knew of this affair as well as whether or not he knew of Henderson's involvement," he took another pinch of snuff, "in which case there would be nothing to prevent Henderson from divulging the truth," he shook his head, "His Grace is not fool enough to jeopardize his reputation by risking such an eventuality for a man like Henderson! By the way," he asked, "I take it you have those letters safe?"

"Yes, Sir" Gideon confirmed, "I have them in my pocket."

"Then I shall relieve you of them," he told him, holding out his hand.

"With pleasure, Sir" Gideon grinned, removing them from his inside pocket and handing them to him. "I feel as though I have been carrying hot coals around!"

"I don't wonder!" Sir John cried, putting them into his own pocket without even scanning them. "And those that mention William Ferrers?"

Gideon smiled. "I have those safe too, Sir."

"But?" he queried, raising a bushy eyebrow.

"I had rather hoped you had forgotten those, Sir!" he smiled.

"I daresay, but you must acknowledge that they could well turn out to be as hot a coal as these!" patting his pocket.

"Yes, I know," he agreed, "but the thing is Sir, I was going to place them into Richard's care; after all, William was his cousin."

Sir John considered this for a moment or two. "Well," he conceded, "I suppose he has more right than anyone else to them, but I can't claim a liking for it!"

"Without those letters, Sir" Gideon reminded him, "any accusation Colonel Henderson may put forward cannot be taken further, and whilst I believe there is little chance of him doing so in view of the reasons I have already given, if William Ferrers' name is to be kept out of it, or, at least," he amended "if whatever is hurled at him cannot stick without evidence, disposing of those letters is essential."

Sir John pursed his lips. "Do not misunderstand me, Gideon," he shook his head, "I admire you for honouring your word, but, upon reflection, do you think you were wise in giving such a promise to Clara Winsetton?"

Gideon sighed. "To be quite honest, Sir," he said truthfully, "wisdom did not enter into it. Despite my representations that she allow William to settle his own affairs, her mind was quite made up. Although," he admitted, "I knew that it was not William she wanted to protect so much as the family, having already suffered at the hands of her nephew and his accomplice. Even though she knew that I was faced with the devil of a dilemma in attempting to save them both and that those letters were no good where William was concerned, I was not proof against such a plea!"

General Turville nodded. "Well, there's no denying that Ferrers' death, however regrettable, has certainly relieved you of a burden."

"That's as may be, Sir" he agreed, "yet somehow it does not make me feel any better."

Rising to his feet he gripped Gideon's shoulder, conveying his understanding more than any words could have, but since he had suddenly bethought himself of something which could possibly generate more problems than William Ferrers' participation ever could, asked "When you spoke to Henderson this morning, I don't suppose he gave any indication as to how he managed to persuade Lytton to assist him, did he?"

"As a matter of fact he did," Gideon replied gravely, vacating his chair.

General Turrville eyed him closely, "And?"

It was a moment or two before Gideon replied to this, and when he did his voice clearly reflected his distaste for such tactics. "It would appear he suborned His Grace by the simple expedient of blackmail."

At this General Turville almost dropped his snuff box and those bushy eyebrows snapped together, a deep frown creasing his forehead. "*What?*" he thundered. "You don't mean it?"

"I am very much afraid that I do, Sir."

"But what in the name of all that's wonderful could Henderson have over him?" he cried.

"A confession, Sir!" Gideon replied flatly.

"A confession!" he repeated, bewildered.

Gideon nodded. "According to Colonel Henderson," he explained, "one evening, when they were both in their cups, oh many years ago now," he shrugged, "His Grace made the colossal error of confiding something quite monumental to him; so monumental in fact that should it ever become known, his name as well as his reputation would be ruined for ever." Before Sir John could find words to respond to this he continued, "I have no idea whether His Grace recollected the disclosure or not once he had sobered up, but Colonel Henderson clearly remembered it and had no compunction in using it against him when his efforts to apprehend Richard proved futile."

Still trying to comprehend all he had heard, he managed to ask "Did Henderson happen to mention what the confession was?"

It was a moment or two before Gideon responded to this. "When I asked him how he had managed to bring His Grace into this in the first place I had not expected him to enter into any great detail, I merely thought that telling me how he had coerced him by holding a confession over his head would be the end of it; I had not expected him to tell me what it was His Grace had actually confided," he paused momentarily, "but that was precisely what he did do. I must admit," he shook his head, "had I have been able to have stemmed Henderson's flow I would, but once he began talking nothing could stop him. I don't mind saying, Sir," he grimaced, "that in view of what he told me I cannot help but feel that I have exchanged one hot coal for another!"

"As bad as that!" he exclaimed, pursing his lips.

"It is certainly not a very flattering tale, but judge for yourself, Sir" Gideon invited, perching himself on the edge of the desk. "I know nothing of Lytton's past," he shrugged, "but from what Henderson told me it seems that during his travels on the Continent, when he was quite a young man, he came upon a woman for whom he formed quite a passion. When Lytton eventually returned to England she came with him, whereupon he found her a discreet little house in a quiet part of town and maintained her in some style. It was at this moment in Lytton's life when the marriage his father had long since arranged for him to The Honourable Anne Fortescue, took place. Although it was not a love match I understand that it was a reasonably happy marriage, but it did not prevent His Grace from continuing his affair. With no brothers or other male relatives Lytton was the last of his name and his marriage to Anne Fortescue would ensure the line was secure, but by some quirk of fate," he grimaced, "it would seem that both ladies gave birth to a boy the same night, within an hour of each other. The lady who had been delivered of his illegitimate son died within minutes of giving birth, whilst his legitimate son died within an hour of his. Her Grace it seems had rather a difficult time and fell unconscious the moment the child was born, so did not see her son until several hours later. It fell to the physician to inform His Grace that due to complications his wife would not be able to bear any more children, at the same time word was delivered to Lytton about his illegitimate son and the death of his mother, and at some point throughout these proceedings Lytton took the decision to exchange babies." Gideon swallowed, saying with difficulty, "When Her Grace regained consciousness and was given the child to hold, she had no idea that it was not the baby she had given birth to but was, in fact, her husband's illegitimate son. *Her son*," he managed, "was buried with Lytton's mistress."

Having listened to this with his eyes bulging from their sockets in shocked disbelief, General Turville was quite unable to speak for several moments, capable of nothing more than staring at Gideon as though he had never seen him before. "My God!" he exclaimed at last. "That's the most diabolical thing I have ever heard in my life!"

"I know," Gideon sighed. "One does not credit even a man like Lytton with such a devious concept."

"And Her Grace," Sir John queried, "she never knew the deception which had been perpetrated?"

"Apparently not. Henderson told me that up until the day she died three years ago, she was in complete ignorance of it; as is the son. Although," he acknowledged, "when one considers the strong resemblance between father and son, who *would* question it?"

"It's incredible!" Sir John cried, clapping a huge paw to his brow.

"Yes, it is," Gideon agreed, feeling quite sick at the thought. "I can't say how he managed it, but he could not have done it alone, which means that whoever aided him must have been greased handsomely in the fist to keep silent, including the physicians who attended both ladies."

"It's a miracle it never leaked out!" Sir John cried. "When one considers it, Lytton was running the devil of a risk, because no matter how much he paid them he was leaving himself wide open for blackmail. His abettors would know that he would rather die than have something like this spread abroad!"

"When one bears in mind His Grace's position and the power he holds," Gideon pointed out "they were probably too afraid to. Should it ever do so however, his reputation would be ruined and his name not worth the paper it is written on; not to mention his son being disinherited on the grounds of illegitimacy."

"Why, in God's name, did he ever entrust something of this magnitude to Henderson?" Sir John demanded, looking up at Gideon. "I mean, would *you* confide a secret of this enormity to a man like that?"

"No, Sir," Gideon shook his head, "I would not but, in fairness to His Grace, he *was* drunk at the time."

"Paralytic I would have thought!" Sir John stated unequivocally. He paused for a moment, before saying distastefully, "But Henderson had not forgotten it and was more than prepared to use it against him in order to enlist his aid."

"Yes, Sir" Gideon nodded. "How bitterly His Grace must have regretted that momentary lapse!"

"Who else knows of all this?" Sir John demanded.

"No one, Sir."

"Good! Let's keep it that way."

Gideon looked down at him considering for a moment or two, a frown creasing his forehead. "The thing is, Sir," he said carefully, "I was going to tell Richard, not the whole but the bare bones of it," he hastened to add when he saw the look on his senior officer's face, "enough to help him understand why Lytton was brought into this business and how he came to be 'gazetted'. I think, Sir," he suggested, "he is owed that much, especially when one considers what the family have suffered."

"Very well," he conceded at length, "but only the bare bones mind you!"

"Thank you Sir," Gideon nodded. "By the way, Sir" he asked, "what is happening about this 'gazetting'?"

"I almost forgot about that," Sir John grinned ashamedly. "I have arranged for a letter to be published in the London Gazette exonerating Richard Ferrers of any illegal activities or wrong doing. With luck" he nodded, "that should see the end of any problems arising there."

"That will be a tremendous relief to him, Sir" Gideon told him.

Sir John nodded a little absently, suddenly attacked by a none too pleasant thought, and upon being asked by Gideon if anything were amiss, said irritably, "His Grace! I shall, of course, have to report our findings to him and the fact that I have lifted that infamous 'gazetting'. I had hoped that he was still at 'The White Hart' but according to the orderly Major Denham sent hot foot there this morning it appears he left yesterday and is most probably back in town by now." Gideon did not need any further explanation, but Sir John, still recovering from the shock of what had been disclosed to him, raised helpless hands in a gesture of frustration. "Considering how he has aided and abetted Henderson and William Ferrers all this time, albeit through coercion, it's going to be difficult enough to tell him the truth as it is without letting him suspect we know the role he has played, but how the devil I am to face him knowing what I do, God knows! I suppose," he conceded, rising to his feet, "it is perhaps as well that he is no longer in Sussex, at least it will give me time to come to terms with his infamy. On no account must he even suspect that we know what happened all those years ago!"

"No, Sir" Gideon agreed wholeheartedly. "Having been handed a live coal once, I am in no hurry to receive another!"

Sir John laughed, then gripping Gideon's shoulder said, "Live coal or not, you don't need me to tell you what an excellent job of work you have done and that you have more than justified my faith and trust in you, but you do realize that should Lytton even so much as suspect we know the truth, it won't do either of us any good!"

"That thought has occurred to me, Sir" Gideon smiled.

"I see," Sir John nodded. "And has it also occurred to you that if he does learn of it, not to mention if our plans should go awry where Henderson and William Ferrers are concerned, they will most probably hang us both from the same rope!"

Gideon laughed. "I don't think it will come to that, Sir."

"No!" he exclaimed. "Well, let us hope you are right! Now though," he said firmly, "it's time we went to Ferrers Court; the sooner my task with Henderson is done the better!"

CHAPTER TWENTY SIX

Not long after Gideon had left Ferrers Court, Richard, discarding his flamboyant dressing gown for his more habitual attire, descended the stairs to check on his unwelcome guest before visiting his aunt.

He could find no fault with Gideon's thinking, much less his actions, especially where his sister was concerned, but he was still far from reconciled to giving house room to a man whom he had no hesitation in deeming his enemy, even for only a short time. He realized, of course, that the circumstances had been somewhat awkward, preventing them from taking him to the garrison, and therefore failed to see where else they could have taken him, but the sooner he was removed from under his roof the better pleased he would be. He could only hope therefore that Gideon would make all speed in returning to Ferrers Court, because he was human enough to admit that the temptation to mete out his own brand of justice was almost impossible to resist. He was deeply in Gideon's debt, not only for arriving just in the nick of time to save him from utter despair but retrieving those letters which would prove his innocence, indeed, he was very conscious of his obligation to him, but he could not quite dispel the frustration he felt at being told only half the story about his meeting with Henderson. He would give a monkey to know what had passed between them earlier to give rise to his future brother-in-law's assurances that their prisoner had finally resolved himself to his lot, because although he was not doubting Gideon's assertion that they would see no more attempts to escape or hear any further venomous utterances pass his lips, his behaviour so far had not led him to suppose that he would suddenly change either his attitude or his resolution. In his opinion a man in Henderson's precarious position would stop at nothing to either effect an escape or to try and induce his captors into letting him go, attempting to instil into their minds the gross error of keeping him incarcerated; bearing in mind that he was not without influential friends. But when Richard entered the small sitting room it was to the surprising discovery that Henderson, no longer bound hand and foot, was stretched out fast asleep on a sofa with his henchman reclining rather uncomfortably on a chair, barely able to keep his eyes open and not a sign of Michael.

Salmon, upon hearing the door open, was jerked instantly awake, all semblance of sleep deserting him as he saw the astonishment on Richard's face as he scanned the scene in front of him. Rising hurriedly to his feet he briefly explained that Major Neville had suggested Henderson be untied as he did not envisage him attempting any more heroics and that Michael should take the opportunity to snatch a bite to eat and a couple of hours sleep. It was on the tip of Richard's tongue to enquire if he too had been given leave to sleep while their prisoner virtually did as he wished, but only a moment's reflection was sufficient to remind him that Salmon was by far too old to be keeping nightly vigils. Guiltily aware that he had expected much from his aged friend, he looked down into the wizened features of the man who had not only been a part of his life for as long as he could remember but had given loyal and devoted service to the family without a thought for himself. Although Salmon would strenuously deny that the last twenty four hours had taken quite a toll, in fact he had argued vigorously when the Major and Michael had suggested he take a break instead, it was nevertheless obvious that trying to remain wide awake during what had been an eventful night had been rather a strain. Acknowledging that he had used Salmon abominably, Richard merely nodded and smiled recommending that he too get something to eat as well as several hours sleep and that he himself would remain with Henderson until Michael returned. Salmon was just about to dispute the point when Michael entered the sitting room looking refreshed and more like himself. It had been unfortunate that a succession of nightly duties followed by that patrol which Major Denham had ordered he go out on had resulted in him having very little sleep over the last few days, and although he had been perfectly willing to give way to Salmon, Richard's stalwart would not hear of leaving his post. However, upon setting eyes on their prisoner lying fast asleep as though he had not a care in the world, he eyed his friend wonderingly.

"Ay, you may stare!" Richard exclaimed. "It seems the Major holds out no fear that he will create any more difficulties!"

Brooking no further argument from Salmon, who clearly had no intention of vacating his vigil, Richard manoeuvred him unceremoniously out of the sitting room with a firmness that belied the affection he had for him, telling him in no uncertain terms that he was no good to him half asleep, then remaining only long enough to issue explicit instructions to Michael he took himself off upstairs with the sole intention of visiting his aunt. Having reached the first landing he stopped momentarily, a deep frown suddenly furrowing his forehead as he bethought himself of William and that arrangements would have to be made about his interment. Whatever his crimes William was a Ferrers, and every Ferrers before him had been buried in the crypt in the family church in the grounds of Ferrers Court, and whilst he may question the rights and wrongs of a traitor being laid to rest among his illustrious ancestors, he knew he had little choice but to grant his cousin that same final mark of distinction.

Without thinking what he was doing he slowly made his way to William's room and quietly opened the door, treading softly across to where his cousin was laid out on top of the big four-poster, his slim person covered by a white sheet. He stood beside the bed for a moment or two considering, then drawing the sheet from off the pasty white face he looked down at the man who had done his utmost to not only bring the name of Ferrers into disrepute, but also his downfall. He was conscious of no misgivings in his dealings in uncovering the identity of a traitor and bringing him to account for his actions, but he could not deny the discovery that his cousin had played a role in Colonel Henderson's treasonable schemes, irrespective of the extent, had come as a tremendous shock. There may not have been much love lost between them but, even so, he did not like to think that his cousin had been involved in something as abhorrent as treason, and whilst there could be any number of reasons for him doing so, he was as convinced as a man could be that their origins stemmed more from monetary gain rather than conviction. Knowing something of his expensive and ruinous lifestyle, he could see how attractive the promise of money would be, especially to a man who continually found himself in urgent need of funds; this exigency requiring him to unsuccessfully try and recoup his losses via the tables or the turf. Handing over *iou's* was all very well when the punter had funds to honour them or, at least, some future prospects to induce the recipient to accept them, but William's had by no means been certain, indeed, they had been anything but a foregone conclusion.

Coveting the title was a far cry from actually standing next in line, a circumstance William seemed to have either forgotten or overlooked when he had pledged his credit all over town, clearly placing all his hopes on his cousin being legally disposed of by either being shot as an escapee from custody or hung as a traitor. He could well imagine William's growing anxiety over his continued avoidance of whichever fate awaited him, not only because the longer it took to apprehend him the worse William's financial circumstances would become, but also because his constant evasion of arrest not only served to prolong William's wait to become the next Viscount Easton, but he would never know a moment's peace of mind whilst he was at liberty. William's boastful bravado may have served in hiding the truth from his friends and acquaintances, but he had been no more able to hide the truth from himself any more than he could his uncle or cousin and this, coupled with his intense jealousy of him, had no doubt all contributed to his involvement in treason. Being a naturally weak man who not only bowed to a stronger will than his own but one who would do anything to avoid altercation or being brought to account for his actions, he could well understand William's ever growing fears as he learned of his own continued evasion of the law.

The Pretender, young and handsome and fighting for a cause against overwhelming odds, personified a romantic and chivalrous figure, and coupled with his promise of rewards for services rendered to those who supported him would prove irresistible to a man like his cousin. He had no doubt that Colonel Henderson was not only the instigator in bringing about their treasonable partnership, but also the architect behind their activities, he certainly had the ideal man in William; as suggestible as he was easily led.   He had neither time nor sympathy for men like Henderson and his cousin, possessing no thoughts or beliefs other than what would benefit themselves but, on the contrary, further their own ambitions or line their own pockets, condemning those men who, albeit traitors, were truly loyal to their convictions. Unfortunately, what Colonel Henderson and his cousin had failed to take into consideration was the possibility that Stuart's attempt at insurrection could quite easily go awry and that should this indeed prove to be the case, then he would not only look to his own safety but would give no thought whatever to his adherents.

It must have been a devastating blow to learn that Stuart's efforts had failed, turning their dreams into ashes, and worse, the realization that at any moment they could be denounced as traitors, leaving them fearful and anxious. He could well understand their desperate efforts to avoid accusing fingers being pointed in their direction by seeking to implicate others, but although his cousin had made an unexpected stand by refusing to follow Colonel Henderson's orders at the last minute, realizing that there was nothing else they could do to stave off disaster, he was still of the opinion that William had got off lightly by meeting his end at the hands of his accomplice rather than through the due process of law.   He may believe that William had got off far too lightly from his recent venture into treason, but he was not by nature a vengeful or vindictive man and by the time he left his cousin's room he had been brought to acknowledge, albeit reluctantly, that unless he wanted the name of Ferrers to be dragged into even more scandal, he had no choice but to accept the tale Gideon proposed to put forward in that William, far from being a traitor, had in fact assisted in their efforts to expose one. He could only hope and pray therefore that Colonel Henderson would not decide to undo all they were striving for by making a last minute declaration at his trial to the contrary.

Having given instructions that a message was to be sent to Reverend Parton to come and see him as well as to Whitney informing him to make himself available later that day as he wished to have a word with him regarding his late employer and his position as valet, he then spent the next two hours with his aunt, during the course of which he learned precisely how the household had fared during his absence.   Clara Winsetton, perfectly aware of her nephew's sentiments, did her best to explain the reasons behind her request to Gideon to protect William from the consequences of his actions, but even though Richard knew that this desire stemmed from the purest of motives, he could not help but feel that his cousin had not been worthy of such loyalty.

Dr. Jarvey, arriving at Ferrers Court half way through the morning, was somewhat surprised to find his passage to Miss Ferrers' room impeded by her brother's insistence that he speak to him on another matter before he saw his sister.

He could read nothing amiss in Richard's expression, but these words filled him with foreboding, and unless he grossly mistook the case he would lay his life that it had something to do with last night's unprecedented events. But upon hearing the calmly delivered announcement that his cousin was lying dead on his bed as a direct result of being shot the previous evening and he wished him to officially pronounce life extinct and to record the death, shocked him to the very core of his being, and not until he had followed Richard into his cousin's room and pulled off the sheet exposing the stiffening remains of William's body, did he find his voice. "Good God, Sir!" he exclaimed, horrified. "Why did you not mention this to me last night when there was every chance I could have ...?"

"I am afraid he was beyond any aid you could have administered, Jarvey" Richard told him firmly. "He was dead as soon as he hit the floor! Besides," he pointed out practically, "it was far more important for you to tend my sister than to waste time on a man who was past doing anything with!"

Appalled by such reasoning as well as his apparent callous disregard, for he saw it as nothing less, he cast a glance up at Richard from under his lashes, and was shocked to see that there were no traces of regret or sorrow on his face. He was not a man given over to listening to tale-bearing or spiteful rumours, but if only half of what he had heard about the ill feeling which existed between the cousins' were true, then he could to some degree understand why Richard Ferrers was not entirely heartbroken at William's unfortunate death. Nevertheless, when he considered the dubious events of last night and the unsatisfactory answers he had received to his questions about Miss Ferrers' wound, his growing suspicions upon his departure from Ferrers Court that something quite untoward had occurred, were now rekindled with a vengeance. From the looks of it though Richard Ferrers was in no frame of mind to either assuage his curiosity or to explain the precise nature of the proceedings which had brought about that injury to his sister or the death of his cousin, nevertheless the mysterious circumstances surrounding such goings-on made him feel rather uneasy, and therefore felt it incumbent upon him to ask some pretty pertinent questions; none of which Richard was in a position to answer.

From the troubled expression on Dr. Jarvey's face Richard knew that nothing less than the truth would satisfy him, but to do so could well mean running the risk of jeopardizing their efforts to bring Colonel Henderson to justice. He realized the methods they were adopting to bring this about were somewhat unorthodox, but even so he felt fairly confident that the good doctor would take a pretty dim view of taking the law into one's own hands, regarding it as being totally unjustifiable, irrespective of the provocation involved. As an honest and diligent man he would most probably see it as his duty to demand to see the prisoner in the sitting room and perhaps even make the attempt to release him or, which was more than likely, report such goings on to the nearest Magistrate.

Under no circumstances could he allow this to happen, but how to avoid it as well as satisfy Jarvey's very natural curiosity momentarily eluded him. For a man used to command and making spur-of-the-moment decisions, Richard experienced a rare moment of vacillation bringing forth an exasperated sigh, which was immediately interpreted by that industrious practitioner to mean that he was extremely reluctant to enter into an explanation.

Strongly suspecting Richard Ferrers of deliberately erecting a wall of silence in order to prevent him from discovering the truth regarding last night's irregular proceedings, pushed him to the limits of his endurance. Were it not for the fact that he knew he was sincerely attached to his sister and would never intentionally place her in jeopardy as well as being most anxious over her present condition, he would say that he looked upon the whole affair, not as an amusing interlude precisely, but certainly with a detachment he wholeheartedly deprecated.

"I realize an explanation is due to you, Jarvey" Richard told him coolly, not at all pleased to find himself being closely scrutinized, "but I am afraid at this present moment I am quite unable to give you one."

"*Sir*," Jarvey said awfully, "your sister is at this very moment recovering from a ball in her shoulder and your cousin," pointing an imperious finger down at William's lifeless body, "lies dead upon his bed as a result of being shot, and you say you cannot give me an explanation to account for either!" he exclaimed incredulously.

"That is precisely what I am saying," Richard nodded. "And you can take that look off your face!" he told him irritably as he saw the frown descend on the harassed face looking perturbedly up at him. "Whatever you may think, I did not pull the trigger!"

"*Sir*," he ejaculated, aghast, "I assure you that ...!"

"Oh, didn't you!" Richard scoffed, just as exasperated as Jarvey. "Seems mighty like it to me!"

As no such thought had entered his head he regarded this rebuke as a personal affront, indeed, he took great exception to it, but as he found himself torn between Richard's vehemence and his own sense of right and wrong, Dr. Jarvey looked every inch his frustration, clearly undecided what he should do about this unsatisfactory state of affairs. Whilst he admitted that it was not his place to tell Richard how to conduct his affairs, he was nevertheless most reluctant to officially record a death when the circumstances leading up to it were shrouded in mystery, but since this young man seemed to have little or no understanding of official procedures, felt it behoved him to try and explain them to him. Richard, who had been plagued by official procedures for the past year and more, needed no reminding about the bureaucracy which abounded nor any instruction into its intricacies, but when he stringently pointed this fact out to the fraught doctor, immediately found himself being eyed quite severely, which did nothing to alleviate his temper.   His temper was even further exacerbated when he was told, somewhat forthrightly, that he would never have thought so from his unresponsive demeanour and his uncooperative attitude, Jarvey going on to reiterate his misgivings about the whole affair, which considerably relieved his lacerated feelings. He could not deny that he would feel far happier if this uncommunicative young man would open up a little and set his mind at rest on one or two points at least, but from the looks of it he was no nearer doing so now than he was before. It was just on the tip of his tongue to remonstrate with him as to the seriousness of his position when he saw the rather taut expression which had suddenly descended onto Richard's face and the sombre look creep into his eyes, and whilst he was relieved to see that some kind of recognition as to the gravity of the circumstances facing him had at last penetrated, it nevertheless made him pause from chastising him further.   He was as sure as a man could be that what had occurred had its roots in Richard Ferrers' troubles, and although he had never believed him capable of treason, it could not be argued that his sister's injury and his cousin's death, irrespective of whether he was innocent or not, could have come about through other causes. Clearing his throat a little uncomfortably, he said, in a much milder tone than he otherwise would have, "I do realize the awkwardness of your position Sir, but..."

"That doesn't cover the half of it, Jarvey!" Richard exclaimed, raking a hand through his hair. "But you are right," he conceded, "an explanation *is* due to you, but the devil's in it that I cannot; at least," he amended, "not yet."

Having pulled the sheet back over William's body, Dr. Jarvey straightened himself up, sighing, "I am not accusing you of either harming your sister or murdering your cousin," he assured him, "I hope I have more sense than that," he pointed out matter-of-factly, "but you must own, Sir," he urged, "that something most untoward occurred last night which must be answered."

"Untoward!" Richard cried. "Egad, I should rather think it was!"

"Well, Sir?" Jarvey encouraged, raising an eyebrow.

Despite his frustration Richard was not unmindful of the justification of Dr. Jarvey's observations and knew that whether he liked it or not some kind of explanation would have to be offered to account for the momentous events of last night, and after several moments of intense consideration gave him a somewhat edited version of events.

Not unnaturally, Richard's disclosure came as a severe shock to the law-abiding doctor, who, despite several attempts to open his mouth, seemed momentarily incapable of saying anything in response to this. Richard, correctly interpreting the myriad of emotions which crossed his face, nodded his verification of what he had divulged.

"Good God!" he exclaimed at length, horror-struck, not quite certain which aspect of the case shocked him the most; the fact that William had been deliberately murdered in an attempt to thwart his efforts in the apprehension of a traitor or that Miss Ferrers had been the most unfortunate victim of an accident for the same reason, both apparently at the hands of the man Richard Ferrers had evidence to see hang for treason and which would ultimately clear his name. "I can hardly believe my ears, Sir!" he shook his head, his eyes staring blindly up at Richard.

"Pretty, ain't it!" Richard replied derisively.

As Dr. Jarvey had by this time arrived at a fairly accurate assessment of Richard's sense of humour, he received this remark with a somewhat deprecating look, and although he had come to realize that this outward façade of indifference merely served to cloak his very real concerns, he nevertheless wished that he would begin to take his position a little more seriously. He was not surprised that Richard had refrained from revealing the name of the man responsible for his present predicament as to do so could quite well jeopardize his only chance of being exonerated, and therefore did not attempt to persuade him. Instead, he accepted his promise that all would be divulged once the perpetrator had been formally arrested and he himself was reinstated to his title and dignities, but whilst he regarded this as quite understandable given the circumstances, had he have known that at this very moment the architect of Richard's difficulties was enjoying house room at Ferrers Court, he would not have been so acquiescent. Thankfully for his peace of mind however, he was totally unaware of this, and was therefore able to assure Richard, in blissful ignorance of the prisoner below stairs, that he would do all that was officially required of him, before making his way to his sister's bedchamber.

It was almost half an hour later when Dr. Jarvey emerged from Elizabeth's room to find Richard pacing the floor outside her door, pleased to convey the satisfying news that his sister was progressing just as she ought. The deeply furrowed frown on Richard's forehead lifted at this, but descended again almost at once when he was told that he would much prefer her to remain undisturbed until tomorrow as she was still rather weak, the inevitable result of losing so much blood, and therefore too much excitement was to be avoided at all costs. It was on the tip of Richard's tongue to argue this point but Dr. Jarvey, apart from catching sight of the martial light which had entered those blue eyes, was not unsympathetic to his concerns, forestalled any argument by granting permission for him to see her, but only providing he did not to stay too long.

Frustrated beyond bearing to know that not only had William escaped facing his trial for treason but was in fact to figure as a champion in the cause of truth and justice, as well as Colonel Henderson being under his very own roof and he could do nothing to him, not to mention his own part in bringing about his sister's injury, Dr. Jarvey's stipulation coming as it did, acted on him like a flame to gunpowder. He had every reason to thank Gideon for the quickness in which he dealt with his sister's wound last night and certainly had no objection whatever to his earlier visit to her room, but so exasperated did he feel over his own impotence to settle matters as he saw fit, that he was goaded into pointing out to his aunt when Dr. Jarvey had left that it looked well when her own brother had been barred her room at such a time and a man who had been unknown to them until a week ago, had been allowed to see her. Clara Winsetton, who believed that a visit from Major Neville had done her far more good than any prescribed potion or rest could have, merely raised an eyebrow, to which he replied by shutting the door with a snap behind him.

The sight of Elizabeth lying ashen faced with her left arm reposing in a sling resting limply on top of the coverlet, renewed his feelings of resentment towards the co-conspirators as well as exacerbating his own vexation, but her calm acceptance of what had happened the night before in addition to her assurances that it was perhaps for the best that their cousin's name was kept out of it, went some way to soothing his ruffled feathers. But it was not only his feelings towards his cousin and Colonel Henderson that rankled, it was also the fact that he was the one responsible for her present predicament, and not even her word of honour that she did not blame him in the least, made him feel any better. Like Gideon, he believed he should have prevented this from happening, but even when she told him that there had been nothing anyone could have done as it had all happened so quickly, did very little to appease him. In spite of her assurances, the overwhelming sense of failure to protect his sister weighed heavily on his conscience, and when he could not even give her a favourable answer as to how long it would be before Gideon was likely to return merely served to increase his wretchedness. Although his own eagerness for Gideon's speedy return to Ferrers Court in company with General Turville stemmed from very different reasons, primarily in order for his affairs to be settled, he had no difficulty in understanding his sister urgent desire to see him again; after all, wasn't he eager to see Jane? Nevertheless, he was realistic enough to know that it would be at least two days before they could expect to see them, and the hopeful look on her face as she gazed up at him turned to one of disappointment when he told her that he did not look to see Gideon for at least a couple of days.

She knew perfectly well that finalizing her brother's affairs were far more important than her own longing to see Gideon again, but even so she was not quite able to hide her regret upon hearing this.

"*Stoopid!*" he murmured with brotherly affection, his cares momentarily forgotten. "It's almost a day's march to London! Can't expect him to get there and back in so short a time!"

She summoned up a smile. "No, of course not. It's just that …"

"You miss him," he supplied gently. She nodded, whereupon he squeezed her free hand, his eyes scrutinizing her face. "You like him very much, don't you!" he commented at length.

"Yes," she nodded, "very much. Don't you?"

"Yes," he confirmed, without a second's thought, "I do," adding humorously, "for all he's a red-coat!"

She smiled. "I'm glad," she told him seriously, "because if you did not, then I would be forced to choose between you; and I really could not bear that!"

He looked at her as though he were seeing her for the first time. "You love him very much?" he asked softly.

"With all my heart," she replied sincerely, her eyes corroborating the truth of this. "Indeed, I could not live without him!"

He nodded. "I thought so. In fact," he told her, patting her hand, "Gideon told me much the same thing about you. In fact," he told her amusedly, "he was quite emphatic. He told me to my face that he would marry you with or without my permission."

Her heart may have soared at this, but it did not prevent her from biting anxiously on her bottom lip, asking warily "Do you object to our marriage?"

"And if I did?" he questioned, raising an eyebrow.

"It would upset me very much," she told him truthfully, her eyes clouding.

"That's what I thought," he nodded. "So it's just as well I'm not going to withhold either my consent or my blessing, isn't it?" he told her, a smile lighting his eyes.

Her own searched his face, her fingers suddenly gripping his hand. "You mean it?" she cried huskily.

"*Idiot!*" he laughed, bending down to kiss her forehead. "Do you really think I want to see my sister made unhappy?"

"Oh Richard!" she cried between tears and laughter. "I can't tell you how happy that makes me!"

"There's no need. I can see it does. Indeed," he grinned, "I foresee a very happy future for you both, even though I've no doubt you will manage to twist him round your little finger!"

This naturally brought a mischievous laugh from her which, predictably, led to several minutes of sibling amusement with both parties recalling past incidents to either reinforce or repudiate such a claim. Having won and lost ground in the encounter she finally withdrew in good order, agreeing to a truce only on condition that he tell her all that happened to him since he had left home.

He was sorely tempted to give her an abridged account of events, but only a moment's thought was enough to tell him that she deserved no less than the truth, especially after all she had endured on his behalf. However, by the time he came to the end of his narrative, so horrified was she that he willingly answered all of her questions in the hope that it would dispel any fears she had as to his safety throughout his exploits. She remained unconvinced that he had come through with no hurt, and after reiterating that he had emerged without a scratch deemed it time to take his leave in order that she could rest.

However tired she was she could not let him leave without reluctantly reminding him that although matters were in a fair way to being finalized he must do nothing to jeopardize the successful outcome of his reinstatement. He did not pretend to misunderstand her, and the smile which had won him many friends dawned as he promised her that he had no intention of taking part in one last run and that if it was Colonel Henderson's presence in the house that was worrying her, then she could be assured he would not lay a hand on him - even though the temptation was irresistible. With this she had to be content, but just as he was about to leave her she forestalled him, and turning his head looked a little ruefully as he said, "I know what it is you want to say, but I promise you there's not the least need to be anxious. I shall not make any attempt to see Jane clandestinely. I shall not see her until my affairs are settled, even though I want to more than anything else in life."

"But surely now ..."

"I would be indulging optimism too far if I allowed myself to think that Sir Arthur would not only receive me but grant his permission for me to even speak with Jane, let alone give his blessing to reinstating our betrothal," he grimaced, his eyes clouding.

"What if I sent a message," she offered, "requesting Jane to visit me as I am unwell? Surely Sir Arthur would have no objection, especially as he has no idea that you are home."

He walked back to her bedside and kissed her cheek. "You are without doubt the best of sisters'," he said affectionately, "far better than I deserve after what I allowed to happen to you." She opened her mouth to refute this, but placing a finger on her parted lips, shook his head. "I know you and Jane have exchanged letters via her father's groom and Salmon, and that you have secretly met, but when I see Jane," he told her firmly, "I want it to be out in the open and not a case of stealing a few illicit moments with her behind her father's back. Do you understand?" he asked gently.

"Yes, of course I do," she said fervently, reaching up her right hand to lay it gently against his face. "It's just that she longs to see you."

"I'm surprised he hasn't packed her off to London again to that aunt of hers!" he exclaimed, his eyes hardening.

"Sir Arthur did threaten to," she told him, "but after making her promise that she make no contact with us here thereby lessening the chances of seeing you, he has not done so."

"Obliging of him!" he scorned, unable to bear the thought of Jane being subjected to his high-handed dictates.

"You won't ..."

He patted the hand still resting against his cheek before laying it back down on top of the coverlet. "No," he assured her. "I promise I won't do anything stupid by forcing an issue with him."

But as he quietly closed the door behind him she knew that should Gideon be delayed in returning to Ferrers Court, then she could only hope and pray that Richard's resolve to refrain from taking part in any nocturnal trips across the Channel and keeping his distance from Sir Arthur would hold out.

He was perfectly aware of his sister's anxiety about his probable actions should there be a delay in settling his affairs satisfactorily, despite his earnest assurances to the contrary. He had set her mind at rest as best he could but although he had no intention of doing anything to mar his chances of extricating himself from his difficulties at this delicate stage, he too hoped that nothing would arise to cause him to put this resolve to the test. Inactivity and idleness were anathema to him, and even though running goods had provided an outlet for his boredom, he was loath to think that the rest of his life would be spent in dodging the Preventives. Once his affairs were settled then he had every intention of setting his mind as well as his energies into the management of his vast estates, but until then he had to find a way of occupying himself, which, considering his promise to Gideon about not venturing beyond the front door until such time as matters were resolved, somewhat limited his scope of useful employment.

His interview with Whitney after luncheon did much to render him more optimistic. It was obvious from the expression on Whitney's face that there was not the least need to put the fear of God into him about the repercussions which would ensue should he decide to tell all he knew. That astute individual, by no means eager to mention his late employer's dealings with any one, had no need to have the wisdom of keeping his mouth shut impressed upon him. His participation in recent events had been minor; his role merely that of go-between, but not a soul would believe him, and since he had no desire to have his neck stretched he deemed it to be far safer in keeping his tongue well and truly between his teeth. Fear of the dire consequences attaching to his role of valet-cum-jack-of-all-trades for William Ferrers, which could so easily be misconstrued or, worse, embellished, was very much at the forefront of his mind, making him nervous and fearful. In view of the way things had turned out, as far as he was concerned the less people who knew about his connection with William Ferrers the better, in fact, the more distance he could put between himself and what had happened, the happier he would be.

Richard, who shared Salmon's dislike as well as his distrust of Whitney, recognized instantly the apprehension which emanated from him as he stood nervously upright, his whole demeanour one of agitation as he tried to shut out the terrifying prospect of climbing the scaffold for his lesser part in events. He knew the role Richard Ferrers had played in uncovering the identity of Jacobite collaborators, and hoped his assurances of his continued silence would be sufficient to prevent him from taking matters to the bitter end.

Richard had no taste for impeding the course of justice any more than he had for allowing traitors to go free, but like his father before him he was a fair and just man, and one, moreover, who had no difficulty in understanding either the awkward position Whitney's former employment had placed him in and his fear of what could ensue because of it. He saw little point in handing this man over to the authorities, indeed, he saw nothing to be gained from it especially when he considered the decision to keep his cousin's name out of it. Appeasing his own sense of right and right and wrong by seeing this man face his trial for complicity in treason may help dispel the nasty taste in his mouth engendered by the knowledge that his cousin was about to figure as a hero, but it would also kill at a stroke the aim in view.

Knowing something of the appalling state of his cousin's financial affairs he would lay a considerable sum on the chance that Whitney had not been paid since he did not know when, and upon having this confirmed tossed a small purse of coins at him which he had pulled out of his pocket. His cousin may not have been the most reliable of men, but he would hazard a pretty good guess that he had relied heavily on Whitney, not only for keeping creditors at bay, but also as a messenger between himself and Colonel Henderson, and although he had neither liking nor trust for this man, he supposed he deserved something for his trouble. He had no doubt that Salmon would look upon it as hush money, which in a way it was, but Richard, as shrewd a man as his father ever was, instinctively knew that with or without payment, Whitney was far too terrified to say or do anything which would bring about any adverse repercussions on himself or obstruct their ambition to end this matter, if not satisfactorily, then without creating the devil of a hue and cry. Besides, he very much doubted if he had sufficient funds on him to buy himself a ticket on the stage to whichever destination he had in mind, and if providing him with the means to put as much distance between himself and Ferrers Court as possible, then he considered it well worth it.

Whitney, not expecting to get off so lightly, much less receive a handsome purse, was so surprised at not being handed over to the nearest Magistrate that he could do no more than stare at his late employer's cousin as though one struck dumb. Indescribable relief held him speechless for several moments and when he did eventually find his voice he could do no more than stammer his disjointed thanks, not needing Richard's warning that he hoped this would be a lesson to him. He had no need to be cautioned about becoming involved in similar enterprises in the future, one venture into rebellion was more than enough for him, and after offering his assurances on this point so eager to be gone was he in case Richard Ferrers experienced a change of heart that his somewhat undignified and hasty exit from the book room coincided with Salmon's emergence from the sitting room as he went to open the door in answer to Reverend Parton's tug at the bell pull.

Reverend Parton had enjoyed the living of Little Turton and surrounding area for a good many years and not only knew the Ferrers family well but all his parishioners by name. Like Dr. Jarvey he was aware of Richard's troubles but unlike that worthy practitioner, thanks to his cosy chats with Salmon, cronies of long-standing, over a drop or two of something warm and invigorating, he was fully cognizant with the true circumstances surrounding his hasty departure and his subsequent efforts to bring the culprits to justice and thereby reinstate himself.

Being known as sympathetic to the trade, Reverend Parton was by no means shocked to learn of Richard's venture into illicit trafficking and certainly thought no less of him because of it. He himself was known to take possession of a keg or two of brandy, indeed, he even went so far as to allow church property to be used for hiding run goods until a more safe haven could be found. He may be a man of the cloth, but he could readily sympathize with those who were forced by Government measures to supplement their meagre income by illicit cargo trafficking. Of course, two wrongs did not make a right as he well knew, but even though he was honest enough to admit that by assisting the Gentleman he was condoning illegal activities, he also knew that in some small way he was helping to alleviate the sufferings of his parishioners. Just as the good Lord with the loaves and the fishes provided much needed sustenance for the poor, so too was he by offering a temporary asylum for run goods, and until the authorities came to their senses and decreased the heavy burden of taxation, then he would continue to assist his flock in any way he could.

Richard, all too familiar with the Reverend's sentiments, greeted him warmly; his slim hand vigorously shaken between two massive paws which held it in a strong firm clasp. "It's good to see you again, Parton" he smiled, having to look a long way up into the gaunt face beaming down at him. "Thank you for coming."

"It's good to see you too, My Lord; back home, where you belong!" he cried enthusiastically, easing himself into the wing chair Richard indicated by the fireplace.

"I am afraid you are a little premature, Parton" Richard smiled ruefully, "I am not reinstated yet."

Reverend Parton leaned forward in his seat, staring aghast at Richard. "But if you are not reinstated, how comes it about you are here?" he demanded. "I confess that when I received a message to attend you here I had hoped to learn that that infamous 'gazetting' had been lifted."

Richard, who knew he received his intelligence from Salmon, sighed "Not yet," unaware of General Turville's letter rescinding this. "But whilst my affairs are in a way to being settled, I am afraid I am not quite out of the wood yet," he told him ruefully.

"Drat those red-coats!" he exclaimed vehemently, taking the glass of wine offered. "Are they so blind that they cannot see the truth?"

"It would appear so," Richard nodded, sitting down opposite the ferocious cleric.

"But are you not running a terrible risk?" he enquired, bemused.

"I am afraid necessity outweighs the risk, Parton" Richard told him.

"The devil fly away with the military!" he scorned, raking a hand through his iron grey hair. "By God!" he thundered. "They have a lot to answer for!"

"Very probably," Richard shrugged, "but it is due to the unwavering diligence of one red-coat in particular that I am here," he told him firmly, "and not dangling from the end of a rope!"

Reverend Parton was just about to take a revivifying drink of his wine when his hand stilled at this, an arrested expression entering his dark grey eyes. "You don't say!" he exclaimed.

"I do say," Richard confirmed. "Were it not for Major Neville, I dread to think what case I would be in at this moment!"

"And who," he demanded, "is Major Neville?"

"The man to whom I am eternally indebted," Richard told him unequivocally.

As Reverend Parton's opinion of the military as well as the Preventives were no higher than anyone else's he looked sceptical, but by the time Richard came to the end of his version of recent events, the scepticism had been replaced with one of incredulity, indeed, so shocked was he by all he had heard that it was several moments before he could find his voice. He was not sure which aspect of the matter appalled him the most; Miss Ferrers' injury, William's complicity or Colonel Henderson's iniquities, resulting in his present incarceration at Ferrers Court. "Good God!" he ejaculated at last. "It's worse than I thought!"

Had Dr. Jarvey been privileged to have witnessed this conversation he would have been extremely affronted at the way Richard easily confided in the Reverend, exhibiting none of the reticence he had shown with him. But Richard, on far more intimate terms with Parton than Jarvey, had no such qualms about confiding in him. "Not very gratifying to discover one's own cousin is involved in something as sordid as treason, I know" Richard acknowledged, "but nevertheless, I aim to keep his name out of it as well as seeing him properly buried." He took a sip of his wine, his eyes steadily regarding the astonished parson. "Which is why I asked you to come and see me, Parton" he nodded. "Will you oblige me by overseeing William's interment?"

Apart from the fact that Reverend Parton had no liking for allowing traitors to go free, he had never liked William Ferrers over much; too shifty by half he thought him. Admittedly, he had not been so well acquainted with him as he was with Richard, but he had seen enough of him to take him in dislike; easily reading the avarice and envy he was not quite able to hide behind the forced smile. Nevertheless, he had not thought him capable of treason and Colonel Henderson even less so, and was therefore deeply shocked to think that between them they had not only hounded Miss Ferrers to the point of harassment but had driven her father to an early grave, and if all that were not bad enough they had tried to place the blame onto a man who was totally innocent of any wrong-doing in order to escape their crimes. Then, to crown all, they had rounded off their iniquities by inflicting a most grievous wound on a lady who had done nothing to deserve such treatment. If anyone were to ask him what he thought, he would say that as far as he could see the only good thing to emerge from last night's events was the fact that one of them at least, had received some form of punishment for his activities. Even so, to think that he was being asked to preside over the interment of a man who had shown neither loyalty nor respect to the name he bore, even treating it with contempt, was expecting an awful lot, but since Richard, despite his courteous request, was determined to do full honour to his cousin, he found himself torn between his repugnance to participate in such a ceremony and his Christian duty. It was one thing to turn a blind eye to smuggling, even going so far as to hide run goods, but treasonable activities was something quite different, and he for one did not hold with it, and it therefore took him several minutes of intense soul searching before he agreed to do it.   However, upon receiving Richard's gratitude, he felt it behoved him to point out that were it not for the affection and respect in which he had held his late father as well as himself, no power on earth would have induced him to lay to rest a man who had so far forgotten his duty to not only his king and country but to his family also.

"I am fully conscious of what I am asking of you, Parton" Richard assured him, "but, indeed, I can do no other than give my cousin a Christian burial." Upon seeing that his guest was still far from convinced, said, with a smile few could resist, "You have no liking for it I know, but if it comforts you at all, neither have I, but you must see that to do otherwise would not only be dishonouring the name I bear but would bring it into disrepute."

"Ay," Parton nodded, "I know, and your sentiments are just what I have come to expect from you, but if you think for one moment that your cousin would have afforded the same courtesy to you, then you are fair and far off. Why," he cried emphatically, "he was prepared to see you hang without the slightest misgiving!"

"That's as may be," Richard shrugged, knowing this to be no less than the truth. "But we are not talking about *my* death, Parton."

"No," he said forcefully, "but we would have been if this Major had not come along when he did to put a spoke in their wheel!" Waiting only until he had finished the last of the wine in his glass did he say, "Ay, I can see you don't like being held up in comparison to your cousin, but the truth is, My Lord," he pointed out inexorably, totally disregarding the fact that he was not yet reinstated to the Viscountcy, "that your cousin was not fit to be mentioned in the same breath as you and your late father, and whilst I am prepared to accommodate your wishes regarding his interment, I will have you know that it is for your sake and not his that I do so!"

"And I shall always be indebted to you," Richard told him with a most disarming smile, rising to his feet. "But, indeed, Parton" he acknowledged, "you must allow it to be the only thing we can do."

Having risen to his feet to stand towering above his host with a most forbidding expression on his face, his high cheek bones slightly tinged with heated colour, he conceded at length, "The only thing I *will* allow My Lord, begging your pardon," he offered, "is that you are truly the gentleman your father raised you to be, were it otherwise," he opined, "I would not have acceded to your request."

Deeply touched by this gruffly delivered compliment, Richard, grasping the outstretched hand eagerly held out, placed his own into it, expressing his heartfelt thanks. He knew quite well what he had asked of him, because despite Parton's sympathetic leanings towards the trade as well as his freely given assistance, he was by nature an honest and religious man, whose sense of right and wrong had been sorely tested by his request. He knew too that he had spoken no less than the truth when he had reminded him of how quick his cousin had been to ensure he climb the scaffold in order to save himself from exposure as well as to enable him to step into his shoes, thereby severing any ties or feelings of loyalty one for the other. He could not argue against this reasoning, but even though he would never really become reconciled to the fact that William was going to figure as an upholder of truth and justice by featuring as an active participant in uncovering the identity of a traitor when the very opposite was true, much less forgive him for his contribution to his father's death, he knew no other course was open to him. The truth was he was still of the same mind as he had been last night in that his cousin had got off extremely light for his crimes, especially when he thought of his sister lying upstairs recovering from a ball in her shoulder, albeit by the hand of William's accomplice. Honesty compelled him to admit however, that in the heat of last night's wrath he could easily have dispensed his own kind of justice and to the devil with the consequences, but now, in the cold light of day, he had to acknowledge that to have done so would have been an act of pure revenge. However reprehensible his cousin's transgressions, there had been that belated attempt at atonement at the end, and that innate sense of chivalry which guided his hand in all he did had dictated he accord him that final mark of respect as well as laying him to rest in the family vault. Not to have done so would have been an act of unspeakable dishonour; a circumstance he could not contemplate without revulsion or have reconciled with his conscience.

It had not taken Michael or Gideon very long to deduce that the majority of the local population were extremely partisan, and none more so than the Reverend Parton whose loyalty to the Ferrers family, especially to the future sixth viscount, was unwavering. Richard, deeply touched by such devotion, knew this as well as anyone, and was therefore not surprised when the exasperated cleric demanded to see the prisoner in the sitting room. Having a very good idea of what would ensue as a result of such a meeting, for it was not to be supposed that Parton intended to offer him spiritual comfort, Richard laughed, amusedly accusing him of taking advantage of his calling, a charge which he made no attempt to deny. That ferocious stare, rather daunting to the uninitiated, was enough to inform Richard that it would go ill with Henderson if he decided to put into execution his very excellent pugilistic skills, which, from the looks of it, was what he intended.

"I agree Henderson stands in need of a good hiding," Richard confessed, "but, really Parton," he smiled, shepherding him out of the book room with a firm hand on his shoulder, "it would not do, truly it would not."

"Hm!" he snorted disgustedly. "It's to be hoped the authorities are not so lenient as you appear to be!"

Richard laughed. "You have it quite wrong, Parton" he shook his head. "Nothing would give me greater pleasure than to be able to bring him to book in the manner you describe, but if I am to come off unscathed, then both you and I must restrain our very natural impulses."

This very sound reasoning caused Reverend Parton to stop dead in his tracks, realizing that, however much it went against the grain, Colonel Henderson must remain unmolested. "Ay," he nodded at length, looking down at Richard, "you're in the right of it My Lord. I suppose it would not do for him to stand his trial looking as though he'd already received his punishment!"

Richard burst out laughing at that, patting Parton's shoulder. "No," he shook his head, "it would not do at all."

Eventually managing to assure his devotee that his willingly offered services to act as self-imposed judge and juror as well as gaoler were not in the least necessary, he escorted him to the stables where he had left his gig, a mutual agreement having been arrived at regarding William's interment.

By the time Richard lost sight of Parton's retreating figure, it was almost half past four, the stable clock chiming the half hour as he passed the lily pond with the innocent looking cupid staring angelically at him, before running up the few shallow steps into the rear of the house.

Guiltily aware that he had not checked on the prisoner since his visit earlier that morning, he strode through the hall to the small sitting room, fully prepared for hostility from their captive and a scolding from Salmon. But upon crossing the threshold he discovered that Henderson's overseers, instead of exhibiting signs of tedium or expressing some complaint which he had fully expected, were in the middle of a game of cards, and apart from an acknowledging nod of the head from his henchman and a friendly smile from Michael, there was nothing to suggest that they had had enough of their assignment. As for Colonel Henderson, apart from a belligerent stare cast in his direction, far from displaying resentment he was exceedingly docile, flicking through the pages of a periodical as though he had not a care in the world, and upon being told in a quiet aside by Salmon, who had momentarily discarded his game to stand beside him, that there had been none of the antics of last night, Richard was beginning to think that Gideon had spoken no less than the truth when he had said he anticipated no further trouble from their captive. He did not need either Salmon or Michael to tell him that he was very much subdued; indeed, his whole demeanour demonstrated complete capitulation as he sat in the chair, his food hardly touched on the plate beside him. Having fully expected to find him securely bound in order to prevent any further attempts to free himself as well as hearing more vituperative remarks leave his lips, he was somewhat taken aback to find him so meek. He had managed to refrain from pressing Gideon with questions as to what had actually passed between himself and Henderson to bring about this unlooked for change in their prisoner's attitude, but although he intended to hold Gideon to his promise to reveal their conversation upon his return to Ferrers Court, the truth was he was far too relieved to find him so submissive. Nevertheless, the suspicion crossed his mind that there was every possibility that Henderson was playing off some trick, merely waiting to take them off their guard before making an attempt to escape, especially as he was no longer bound to the chair, but after a closer scrutiny of the unruffled figure in front of him, he was forced to concede that Gideon had been right after all; and could not help but wonder yet again just what had taken place between the two men earlier that morning. In fact, so startling was the change in him that he could quite well be looking at a very different man to the one he knew and was, unless he was grossly mistaken, like one fully resigned to his fate. If he did not know better he would say that either Salmon or Michael had slipped something into his drink to deaden his senses, but before he could explore this fanciful theory further the sound of horses hooves approaching the house met his ears.

Salmon and Michael, who had by now become firm friends, glanced at one another expectantly, while Richard strode over to the window to see who could possibly be descending on them. Peering over his shoulder, Salmon was just as taken aback as Richard to see Gideon in company with half a dozen men, and one other, whom he had no difficulty in recognizing as General Turville. Not having expected to see Gideon until the day after tomorrow at the earliest, his arrival took them all by surprise, but Richard, whose need to settle his affairs as well as ridding the house of their unwelcome guest, had become paramount, was extremely relieved.

Salmon, his old eyes lighting up with relief, made his way into the hall to open the heavy front door, leaving Richard to follow leisurely behind.

CHAPTER TWENTY SEVEN

"I know you said you would not linger long on the road," Richard remarked amused as he strolled into the hall, "but unless you grew wings since you left here this morning and flew there and back, I'd be mighty interested to learn how you managed it so quickly."

"However much I would like to take credit for performing such an impressive feat," Gideon smiled, gripping his outstretched hand, "I regret to confess I cannot. General Turville is the one who demands both your awe and admiration; he was awaiting my return at the garrison which negated the need to journey to town." Richard looked from Gideon to Sir John, a faint sign of recognition in his blue eyes. "Richard, allow me to introduce General Turville to you."

"There's no need to introduce us," General Turville told him before turning back to Richard. "I'd know you for Jasper's son anywhere. You have the look of him!"

"Thank you, Sir" Richard nodded, finding his hand lost in Sir John's huge paw. "I can claim to having a vague recollection of you only," he confessed apologetically, "but I am sure you will allow that that is due to our paths having seldom crossed rather than from incivility." He smiled ruefully. "I only wish your visit here could have been under happier circumstances, and not due to such an extremity as this."

Sir John nodded, his bushy eyebrows snapping together. "It is to be regretted, of course," he acknowledged, "but never did I think the next time I put a foot inside Ferrers Court it would be for such a reason as this," he shook his head. "A man of Henderson's standing!" he exclaimed shocked, still trying to come to terms with his perfidy. "Your cousin, too!"

"Yes, indeed Sir" Richard concurred quietly.

"Monstrous betrayal!" Sir John exclaimed strongly. "Damnable business. Damnable!"

"As you say, Sir" Richard endorsed, "damnable!"

"I knew something damned ugly was in the wind the moment Lytton first broached the matter to me," he said forcefully, "but never did I suspect the truth of it."

"Nor did I, Sir" Richard shook his head, a twisted smile touching his lips. "A salutary lesson, indeed."

Sir John nodded, then pulling himself together said heartily, a manner he adopted when his emotions threatened to overcome him, "Well, m'boy, you don't need me to tell you that your father and I were good friends long before you were breeched," clearing his throat. "And I don't mind telling you that I was deeply shocked over his death!"

"Thank you, Sir. It is certainly a circumstance that none of us shall hurriedly forget," Richard said regretfully.

"Ay," he nodded, "and who can blame you." Catching sight of Salmon he turned his head, exclaiming, "Many's the time I've spent under this roof with your father! Eh, Salmon!"

"Yes, Sir," Salmon inclined his head, this remembrance conjuring up long forgotten memories of happier times.

"You don't need me to tell you in what esteem I held your father," he told Richard, "which is why I am here now to do all I can to help his son."

"Thank you, Sir" Richard nodded, glancing from Sir John to Gideon a little ruefully. "I must confess to not having looked for you so soon, but your arrival, I need hardly say, is most opportune. However," he acknowledged, "I cannot help but feel you must be very much shocked over what has happened. I realize how distasteful all of this must be to you."

Sir John disclaimed any such thing with an impatient wave of his hand. "You did precisely what I would have expected Jasper's son to do!"

"Thank you, sir. Even so," Richard conceded, "I would be less than honest if I did not tell you that when Gideon informed me how you refused to believe me guilty of treason, I was, needless to say, extremely relieved, especially as my father and Sir Matthew are no longer alive to substantiate my story. I don't mind admitting," he grimaced, "that my affairs had reached the point where I could do very little while those letters remained out of my reach. Indeed," he admitted frankly, "without them, I'm all to pieces; they are all that stand between me and the gallows. In fact," he declared with a touch of wry humour, "if I can't do anything about this damned 'gazetting' that's most probably where I shall end up!"

"Let me set your mind at rest on that at least," General Turville told him earnestly. "I have arranged for it that that malicious notice is to be withdrawn with immediate effect and another to take its place exonerating you of any transgression. Major Denham has been put in full possession of all the facts and he will ensure that all military personnel at the garrison are made aware that you are no longer a wanted man; including Captain Waring," he nodded significantly.

The effect this news had on Richard was such that he could do no more than stare blindly from Gideon to Sir John, speech momentarily deserting him as relief flooded through him. Not unnaturally it took a few moments to take in all that he had been told, but slowly the realization that he was no longer going to have to dodge the Preventive Officers as well as the soldiers for the rest of his life began to seep into his bemused brain, and raised a somewhat unsteady hand to his brow.

"I know its insertion was only a couple of days ago," Sir John continued, "but since no one it seems has yet taken advantage of the 'gazetting' I do not anticipate any further difficulties there!"

Since Richard had never doubted his associates loyalty, and none of them, perhaps with the exception of Reverend Parton, read The London Gazette, he was far too relieved to learn that the notice had been rescinded to make any comment, and therefore let this pass. "I...I don't quite know what to say, Sir" Richard managed, shaking his head, a tremulous smile touching his well shaped lips.

"There's no need to say anything," Sir John assured him.

"Indeed there is, Sir" Richard said firmly. "I am fully alive to everything both of you have done on my behalf," looking at each one in turn.

Sir John, forestalling Richard's further attempts to render his thanks, categorically denied that any were in the least necessary, but, on the contrary, owed to him for uncovering the identity of the real traitors. "Knowing your father as well as I did," he told him, "I found it inconceivable that his son had turned traitor and therefore had no difficulty in believing you innocent. Thanks to Gideon's detailed report I set out for Sussex immediately to not only relieve you of your guest, but to tell you that you won't have to wait much longer to be reinstated." Gripping Richard's shoulder with a firm hand, he smiled, "Your father was inordinately proud of you m'boy, but then you must know that. Well," he sighed, "there's no denying you have set us all in a bustle of late with your antics, but I think you need lose no more sleep!"

"Thank you, Sir" was all that Richard was able to say.

"Now," Sir John nodded determinedly, "I'll see Henderson." Then as if bethinking himself of something, turned back to Richard. "Do you think food and drink could be provided for my men?"

"Yes of course, Sir" Richard smiled, "the horses too will be attended to."

A huge grin crossed Sir John's face at this. "I take it that you have no objection to entertaining red-coats at Ferrers Court on *this* occasion?"

Richard laughed. "None at all Sir; they are for once most welcome."

Sir John laughed, then disappearing into the small sitting room closed the door quietly behind him.

Following a handshake and a few brief words with Gideon, Michael, shrewdly suspecting that he wanted time alone with Richard to discuss matters, accompanied Salmon outside to tend the soldiers who had accompanied Sir John, both men vehemently denying that the previous night's events had taken quite a toll, sternly rejecting Richard's claim that they were worn out and must get some rest.

Not until Richard had shut the door of the book room behind them and poured out two glasses of wine, did he say "Tell me; did I hear aright, or was that a flight of my imagination just now?" inclining his head in the direction of the hall.

"No flight of imagination, Richard" Gideon assured him, a smile lighting his eyes. "Short of Henderson being found guilty at his trial followed by a public declaration, you are now virtually a free man. My felicitations!" he smiled, raising the glass he was handed in salute.

"Well, I don't mind saying it makes good hearing, but it's going to take the devil of a time getting used to!" he grinned, taking a seat opposite him and returning the gesture.

"I can understand that," Gideon nodded.

"The thing is," Richard confessed, "I've been dodging the Preventives and Henderson's horde for so long that to suddenly find I no longer have to, makes me feel something's devlish wrong!"

Gideon laughed. "What! Are you saying you want Sir John to overturn his findings?"

"Devil a bit!" he grinned. "I may do idiotic things now and then, but I don't fly in the face of good fortune! Egad!" he cried, "I don't think Salmon could stand it!"

"If it comes to that," Gideon told him, between amusement and frankness, "neither could I."

Richard laughed, then after raising his glass and inclining his head to Gideon, said, "My freedom apart, I don't mind saying that I'm glad to see you! I thought I'd be housing that scoundrel for several more days!"

"Has there been any trouble with him since I left earlier?" Gideon enquired. "No," Richard shook his head, "he's been pretty docile. But it's not him I was thinking of; it's Salmon and Michael. They've been watching over him for twelve hours and more, adamantly refusing to allow me to take a turn in watching him, although" he acknowledged fair-mindedly, "that's most probably due to the fact that they think I would lay hands on him," he grimaced "and although they assured me, still do in fact, that they are more than capable of keeping vigil for another twelve hours if need be, they need some rest. Salmon especially," he acknowledged, not quite able to hide the affection he had for him. "But will he admit to being worn out?" he demanded. "No, of course he won't; devil take him! Why the deuce he needs to put me before anything else God knows!"

"What else did you expect?" Gideon smiled. "The man's devoted to you."

"I know," Richard conceded. "The thing is, Gideon" he confessed, "he's been here for ever; watching over all of us without a thought for himself. Ever since I can remember he's been a part of our lives." A cloud descended onto his forehead. "Over the last twelve months or so he's been more of a rock than ever; God knows what I would have done without him; keeping an eye out for me as well as watching over my sister and shielding her from all manner of abuse and incivilities. And what do I do to thank him for all this?" he shot out, tossing off the remainder of his wine, "expect him to watch over the very man who caused all the bother in the first place!"

"Do you think he minds that?" Gideon asked. "I would say not," he shook his head. "From what I have been privileged to see of him, whatever service he renders stems from affection and not duty."

"I know," Richard sighed, raking a hand through his hair.

"You know, Richard," Gideon offered, "it has been my experience that men like Salmon do not want expressions of gratitude, even though we feel they are owed them. My father has just such a one, Penny. He has been at Burroughs Croft ever since he was a boy, and I am sure that should my father ever offer thanks of any kind he would be so offended he would pack up his bags on the instant."

"Oh, devil take it!" Richard exclaimed, slapping his hand to his cheek. "I'm blue devilled, Gideon, and that's the truth of it!"

"It's no wonder," Gideon replied, "you've been through much. But your days of being blue devilled are almost at an end. Very soon now you will be exonerated and reinstated."

Richard eyed him squarely. "Yes, and we both know I have you to thank."

"I seem to recall," Gideon reminded him, "expressing the observation that no thanks are in the least necessary."

"Well, they are" Richard said with finality. "Good God, Gideon!" he cried, sitting bolt upright. "Do you think I am not aware of the risks you have run on my behalf in bringing me to this point? Not to mention what you did for Elizabeth! Nothing I could ever do would suffice to pay the debt I owe you!"

"There is no debt," Gideon said firmly, looking straight across at Richard. "And you will oblige me by not mentioning it further."

Richard did not mistake the inflexible note which had crept into his voice, but after eyeing him closely for a moment or two, nodded his head. "Very well; but at least you will allow me to thank you, just once."

Gideon was quite happy for him to do so, but it was clear to him that nothing would disabuse Richard's mind that he was under an obligation to him, but whilst he had come to expect no less from a man of his integrity, he nevertheless looked upon his own actions as merely doing his duty in ensuring an innocent man did not go to the gallows.

"And now, if you have had your fill of showering me with gratitude," Gideon said amusedly, "perhaps you will tell me something of more moment. Did Jarvey see Elizabeth this morning? How is she progressing?"

Richard was pleased to be able to report that Jarvey was very well pleased with his sister's progress, but could not advocate her determined efforts to be allowed to leave her bed quite yet. Perhaps in a day or two he would permit it, but it was much too soon after enduring such a painful procedure of having a ball removed from her shoulder; *that,* he insisted, was quite out of the question.

"Clearly, he does not know my sister if he thinks she will lie abed indefinitely! Be warned Gideon," he smiled, pointing his glass at him, "once Elizabeth has taken something into her head, she is not easily diverted!"

"I know," Gideon smiled fondly, one very recent recollection springing to mind, adequately proving that his love had a mind of her own, "but nor am I. Which is why I shall tell her she must not disregard Jarvey so readily. She must not be allowed to have her own way in this."

Richard, who was just in the process of handing him another glass of wine, paused, eyeing Gideon amusedly, "A piece of advice Gideon," relinquishing the glass into his hand, "if you want Elizabeth to do something, then tell her she must do the opposite!"

"Yes," Gideon grinned, "I have already discovered that, but being one who can speak from painful experience, she would be well advised to mind Jarvey."

Richard, eyeing his future brother-in-law closely, was fast coming to the conclusion that whilst his sister would no doubt twist him round her little finger nine times out of ten, Gideon would nevertheless know to a nicety how to handle her. Having resumed his seat he then went on to recount all that had passed between himself and the doctor, immediately following this up by relating his meetings with Whitney and Reverend Parton.

Gideon heard him out in silence, nodding his head here and there, asking only when he had finished, "Is William's body still in his room?"

Richard shook his head. "No. I've had it removed to the ice house until Turner, the estate carpenter, has finished preparing his casket, when he can be placed in the church ready for his interment."

"And Whitney? You say he has left?"

"Yes," Richard nodded, "with sufficient funds to compensate him for any wages he did not receive. You were right about him," he conceded, "I saw enough to convince me that I do not anticipate any trouble there. In fact," he told him, "he was far too relieved to be leaving here with a whole skin. If I know Whitney, by this time he will have put as many miles between himself and Ferrers Court as possible. Unfortunately," he pointed out, "his absence means someone will have to visit my cousin's lodgings to sort out his belongings, and I've no doubt," he nodded, "that there will be a large number of debts to settle. I dread to think what state his affairs are in, but I'll put Pritchard onto that."

Gideon nodded thoughtfully, saying at length "I am sure we're right about Whitney. I am convinced his role involved nothing more than that of a messenger of some kind, indeed, I saw the relief on his face last night when he realized we were going to take no action against him. I doubt very much whether he will be treading down such an adventurous path again. As for Jarvey," he commented, "he did not strike me as being a man who could be fobbed off indefinitely, but you were quite right in telling him what you did. To have told him anything else, especially at this stage, could easily lead to your position being jeopardized."

"Yes," Richard agreed with feeling, "don't I know it! I've had my fill of jeopardy, thank you!"

"Exactly so," Gideon smiled, "which is why I think you had better have these to obviate any further such risks." Placing his glass down onto a small side table, he dug his hand into the inner pocket of his coat to pull out three sheets of well-worn vellum which he held out to Richard.

Richard's heart suddenly began to beat rather fast as he leaned slowly forward in his chair, reaching out a somewhat unsteady hand to take them from Gideon, his intense blue eyes glancing from those smiling brown ones back to the letters. "My letters!" he cried in a strangled voice.

"Three of them, yes," Gideon nodded. "As you know, they clearly implicate William. The others," he informed him, "are with General Turville." He watched in silence as Richard's trembling fingers slowly spread open each folded sheet in turn, taking time to read every single seditious word written in Colonel Henderson's large, sloping hand. He already knew the contents, but to see again, after all that had occurred, his cousin's willingness to participate in The Pretender's attempt at insurrection, only served to increase his disgust and his feelings of impotence.

"You will, of course, do with them as seems best to you," Gideon said calmly when Richard looked up from the pages in his hand, "but considering the harm they could do to the Ferrers name, my advice is to destroy them."

A sombre look entered Richard's eyes as they steadily held Gideon's, knowing he had spoken no less than the truth.

Gideon was not unmindful of the pain and distress William Ferrers' actions had wreaked, and that Richard was by no means in favour of the plan adopted to keep his cousin's name free from the taint of treason. Clara Winsetton's ultimatum had been as unexpected as it was fraught with difficulties, not the least being winning Richard over to the idea, creating a situation that, even now, had William not met his end in the way he had, Gideon failed to see how he could have possibly accomplished such a daunting task. He was himself far from happy with the outcome of events, but if they were to keep the proceedings of last night at Hamstoke House to themselves, thereby ensuring no questions were raised about Elizabeth as well as upholding the Ferrers name with its honour intact, then for the life of him he could not see what else they could possibly do.

Richard, perfectly well aware that should he decide to go ahead regardless and produce those letters incriminating William, whilst it would go a long way to satisfying his own code of justice, it would also mean bringing shame on the name he bore; a name of which his father had been inordinately proud, and one he was determined to maintain with integrity. Not only that, but he could not expose his sister to gossip and speculation merely in order to gratify his own need to see justice done, to do so would be an act of unspeakable dishonour; as repugnant to him as it was unjust to her. "Yes," he said in a muted voice, "after all, what else can be done with them?" Rising to his feet he prodded the logs with an elegantly booted foot until the unburned tops were facing down allowing the flames to curl around them, then throwing the sheets of vellum onto the fire rested his right hand on the mantelpiece and watched as they crackled and shrivelled in the blaze. "Such a wanton act of destruction," he remarked plaintively, straightening up, "seems almost iniquitous when one considers the difficulties you must have encountered in retrieving them. By the way," he asked, raising a questioning eyebrow at Gideon, "how *did* you manage it? In all the commotion last night I forgot to enquire."

"I thought you would never ask," Gideon told him amusedly, attempting to strike a lighter note in order to try and dispel the sombre look which had entered Richard's eyes. "And here I've been all this time eager to puff off my efforts on your behalf!"

"Yes, of course," he grinned. "I saw at the outset you were a boaster! Was it difficult?" he asked soberly.

"Nothing to signify," Gideon shook his head.

"You make light of what must have been a quite hazardous task!" Richard commented, not fooled by this disclaimer. "Remember," he nodded, resuming his seat, "I have been striving to discover a way of placing my hands on them for some appreciable time. No one knows better than I how daunting a prospect it was."

"A daunting prospect, yes" Gideon acknowledged, "but not an insuperable one; thanks to Michael. The predicament was not in placing my hands on them, but gaining entrance to the prison block."

"Yes," Richard replied with feeling. "Don't I know it!"

"It was due wholly to Michael's daring," Gideon smiled, "that my entrance was effected with no difficulties, in fact," he nodded, "he carried it off with great aplomb."

Richard's eyes suddenly brimmed with laughter. "Did he, by God! I'd have given a monkey to have seen it! Not one for words is Michael," he emphasized, "except when it comes to riding that damned hobby horse of his. Egad!" he grinned. "I wish I'd been there!"

Gideon smiled. "You would have been quite impressed. I know I was."

Glad that he had kept faith with Michael, Richard listened to Gideon's recital with keen interest, nodding his head here and there with approval, ending by bursting out laughing when told of Michael's horror over Gideon's lack of historical knowledge. "You know," he pointed out fair-mindedly, "you have to hand it to him! Pluck to the backbone! I mean," he offered judiciously, "just look at the way he got the two of us out of the garrison last night; splendid work! Shouldn't be at all surprised if he made general one day!"

"Without a doubt," Gideon agreed. "Although he made light of his part in last night's proceedings when he imparted them to me in the cellar, I have to say that I have seen enough of his capabilities to be quite convinced that that prophecy will come true as well as commanding my utmost respect."

The French ormolu clock on the mantelpiece chiming the hour, brought to Richard's mind the length of time General Turville had been with Colonel Henderson, instantly stating that he would very much like to know what was going forward between the two men in the small sitting room. This in turn made him recollect Gideon's promise that morning to tell him what he had said to make Henderson so docile and compliant. "Because short of drugging him," he said frankly, not without a touch of humour, "I can't for the life of me begin to imagine how you managed it."

"It really wasn't that difficult," Gideon shrugged. "Oh, I admit at first he was somewhat belligerent, even defiant, but once he had been made to realize that he could no longer look to Lytton for support, he knew his case was lost. In fact," he nodded, "I suspect he knew that the moment he shot William."

A crease descended onto Richard's forehead. "That's all very, but if Lytton has been assisting him all this time, why should he fail to do so now?"

"For the simple reason that his position will not suffer any such further displays of support," Gideon replied smoothly.

Richard's eyes narrowed. "What position?" he asked warily.

Pausing only to drain the remains in his glass, Gideon explained, "You know Richard, from the very beginning the one thing that has always puzzled me has been Lytton's involvement. No matter how I tried I could find no reason to account for it and no argument I offered myself satisfactorily explained why he was concerning himself so particularly in ensuring your arrest. Even when taking into account his well known views as well as his friendship with Henderson, they did not make his motives any clearer. *Never*, until your advent on the scene, has Lytton ever taken such a personal interest in the arrest of a Jacobite as he has with you. His determination to make an end of you as quickly as possible and without anyone being the wiser," he stated candidly, "does, you must agree, give rise to a number of questions."

Richard, who had been listening to this with intent concentration nodded comprehendingly. "Yes, it does. In fact," he told him, "I too have wondered why he was so eager to ally himself with Henderson."

"Eager never entered into it," Gideon shook his head. "A man like His Grace," he said firmly, "would surely want to know why Henderson had failed repeatedly to apprehend you and then, having done so, allowed you to escape, especially with armed men at his back. He would no doubt demand to know why he had been called upon to lend weight to the search, and Lytton is far too astute to be taken in by lies or prevarication, and I very much doubt," he nodded, "that Henderson would have been able to withstand his persistent and relentless questioning for very long. In fact," he said confidently, "it's my guess that had it not been for you informing him that you had not only set eyes on those letters but had them safe, he would not have found it necessary to apply to Lytton. Henderson knew the damning significance of that correspondence and in sheer desperation, when all those searches here had failed, he requested assistance from his old friend, and Lytton, don't forget," he reminded him, "is in a position to offer every assistance."

"So what are you saying?" Richard demanded. "That Lytton got the truth out of him and went along regardless to cover up his treason!"

Gideon shook his head. "No, although I must confess that that is what originally occurred to me, but it only took a very little thought to make me see that I was quite wrong. At the same time however," he shrugged, "I failed to see how Lytton could be unaware of the truth, and it made no sense to me to believe that he had taken Henderson's word on trust. Distrustful of Lytton I may be," he pointed out, "but he is far too loyal to betray the very things he believes in." He smiled across at Richard, whose face clearly echoed his confusion. "Therein you see, lay my dilemma!"

"*Your* dilemma; well I like that!" Richard grinned. "In case you had forgotten, I was the one on the receiving end of their collaboration!"

Gideon laughed. "No, I have not forgotten, but don't you see Richard, I had to discover the truth surrounding Lytton's involvement as well as the need to 'gazette' you ."

"So what are you saying" he insisted, "that Henderson did in fact tell you the truth about how he persuaded Lytton to join ranks with him?"

"That is precisely what I am telling you," Gideon confirmed.

"Is it though!" he mused at length, eyeing Gideon narrowly. "Well, I suppose you'd better tell me the worst!"

But the story which unfolded was far worse than Richard had ever suspected, and so shocked and appalled was he that it was several minutes after Gideon had finished telling him what had passed between himself and Henderson before he could find his voice sufficiently to utter, hardly above a whisper, "My God! You can't mean it?"

"I'm afraid I do," Gideon nodded gravely. "Not very edifying I know."

"Why, it's the most iniquitous and despicable thing I ever heard in my life!" Richard cried.

"Yes it is," Gideon sighed. "One hesitates to think that even His Grace is capable of such contemptible infamy."

"Contemptible is right," Richard ground out disgustedly, taking a moment to refill their glasses. "It's the most diabolical thing ever I heard! And you say Lady Lytton never knew of the deception?" handing Gideon his glass.

"No," Gideon shook his head, "no more than does his son."

"My God!" Richard exclaimed, almost choking on his wine, "I was forgetting his son. Should this ever leak out he'll be declared illegitimate and disinherited. Marquis of Blane today; plain Eugene Beresford tomorrow!"

"Yes. I am afraid he is as much a victim of his father's machinations as you are," Gideon pointed out fair-mindedly.

"More so, I'd say" Richard said emphatically. "What beats me though, is how he managed it; what I mean is, he must have greased the doctors' and attendants handsomely in the fist to buy their silence!"

"Either that," Gideon nodded, "or they knew him too well not to take his warnings seriously as to what would befall them should they talk. Whichever way it was he was running the devil of a risk as any one of them could let something slip at any time either because they had a grievance to settle or perhaps imbibed too much, which," he inclined his head, "was in fact what he himself did in his cups one night."

A frown creased Richard's forehead as he considered something. "Y'know, it's hard to believe that a man like Lytton was intoxicated to the point where he actually confided something of such magnitude to anyone, but to Henderson of all people! I mean," he pointed his glass at Gideon, "would *you* entrust something of that nature to a man like that, and worse," he nodded, "completely forget the incident? Which I'm sure he must have. I certainly would not!"

"No, nor would I," Gideon agreed. "And there's another thing of which I am certain, and that is apart from the fact that Lytton would have been extremely shocked by Henderson's recollection, especially as he most probably had no memory of what took place between them that night, and the use to which Henderson was prepared to put his confidence, but also that he would no doubt be thinking of repaying his old friend for such an insult, for Lytton would regard it as nothing less. Which is why," Gideon said pointedly, "this disclosure must not go beyond ourselves."

"Lord no!" Richard exclaimed. "The last thing I want is to have Lytton on my tail. I've done enough looking over my shoulder!"

"Precisely!" Gideon confirmed. "Which is why General Turville and I do not intend pursuing it further. We are convinced that no good could possibly ensue from exposing such an abhorrent deceit; for his son it would be catastrophic and whilst I feel that His Grace deserves to be brought to account for such infamy, his son most certainly does not warrant the condemnation and ostracism such an exposure would inevitably bring in its wake. What's the matter" Gideon asked as he saw a cloud suddenly descend onto Richard's face, "I thought you agreed we would take no action. Are you now saying you don't approve?

"I may agree that it's best for all concerned to leave well alone, but as for approving, no, damme, I don't!" he thundered. "Why, it's more than flesh an' blood can stand! Here's my cousin immersed in treason and shot by his own accomplice, and yet far from being recognized as such he's destined to figure as the embodiment of devotion and loyalty, conjoining with me in hot pursuit of a traitor; and now Lytton also escapes from the consequences of his iniquities!" briskly tossing off his wine. "And they dared to call me a vicious cutthroat!"

"Yes, I know," Gideon acknowledged, not unsympathetic. "It's grossly unfair, but given all the factors I fail to see what else we can do."

"Oh, I see that," he admitted, "but it don't mean I have to like it."

"Do you think I do," Gideon asked steadily, "or Sir John for that matter?"

Richard raked a ruthless hand through his hair, his eyes smouldering as he was forced to acknowledge that he had no choice but to accept the unpalatable fact that whether they liked it or not, they were completely hemmed in. "No, of course I don't, he replied irritably, "it's just that ...."

Gideon had a very shrewd idea of what Richard had been about to say, but as Sir John entered the room immediately following his tap on the door, it was left unsaid. From the looks on Sir John's face, it was evident that he had not relished the task he had been faced with; his expression a nice mix of revulsion and resignation. For a man of his strongly held beliefs and rigid principals it was beyond his comprehension how a man could so easily set these aside for personal ambition and profit, and since the prisoner in the small sitting room had done precisely that, he had found the interview a severe trial to not only his patience but also his sense of justice. No more than Gideon and Richard did he like the idea that criminals and traitors were allowed to be either set free or shielded; as far as he was concerned William Ferrers had got off lightly and as for His Grace there really was very little they could do to see him face the penalties for his deceit, but he would see himself damned before he allowed Colonel Henderson to escape the full penalty of the law and was therefore determined to see him face his trial for treason and the cold-blooded murder of his accomplice.

Apart from Sir John informing them that he envisaged no further attempts from Henderson to either obstruct or impede the forthcoming course of events, whatever had passed between the two men Gideon and Richard were destined never to know. It had been a painful affair from start to finish, and Sir John for one would be extremely relieved to see the end of the matter once and for all. Sickened and appalled by all he had discovered, his only gratification was knowing that his old friend's son would soon be exonerated and able take up his rightful place in society again where he belonged with his rights and dignities intact.

After consulting his watch and checking it with the clock on the mantelpiece, Sir John eyed the weather with misgiving, as the rain, which had begun as a light drizzle ten minutes before, was now coming down in earnest, and the daylight was already giving way to early dusk. It had been his intention to escort his prisoner direct to London breaking the journey at the garrison at Drayton Weir, a few miles from the Surrey border for the night, and not to the garrison at Hampton Regis in order to prevent as much embarrassment and awkwardness as possible for all parties concerned, as well as not wishing to delay the painful necessity of convening his trial any longer than was necessary in order that an innocent man could be speedily vindicated, but the sudden change in the weather made him reassess his plans. He may have no fear of Colonel Henderson attempting any heroics in the way of trying to escape, but he nevertheless considered it far too risky to set out on the journey at this juncture, because although there was sufficient daylight at the moment and it was only a few minutes after six o'clock, it would not be long before total darkness set in.

Gideon, seeing the sense of this argument, fully concurred with his senior officer as to the wisdom of remaining at Ferrers Court tonight and postponing their departure until the morning.

Richard, looking from one to the other with a wary look in his eye, rose to his feet, demanding one of them to repeat what he thought he had heard. "What!" he cried incredulously, when Sir John reaffirmed his intention. "Do you mean you want me to house that scoundrel for one more night?" He caught the gleam of pure amusement in Gideon's eyes. "No!" he shook his head. "Devil take it, I won't do it!" he told him, not quite able to suppress the smile hovering at the corner of his mouth as Gideon gripped his shoulder. "Yes," he nodded darkly, "it's all very well for you to laugh, but I've had my fill of playing host to that rogue."

"It's monstrous to ask it of you," Gideon said, his shoulders shaking at Richard's horrified expression, "but, indeed, you know it is for the best."

"I don't know any such thing," Richard replied, unable to resist Gideon's smile, "but since I am clearly outnumbered, I suppose I shall have to say yes."

General Turville, patting him on the shoulder, acknowledged the justification of his reluctance. "Your feelings are perfectly understandable, I assure you" he nodded, "it's the devil of a thing to ask of you. But you need have no worries" he assured him, "my own men will take turns in guarding him, providing, of course," he smiled, "you have no objection to them entering the house."

Accepting the inevitable, Richard assured him he had none, whereupon he immediately gave orders that rooms were to be prepared for their guests and the soldiers Sir John had brought with him to be taken care of. Salmon, upon being informed of the plan, merely sniffed, informing his young master with dark humour that much more of this and they would have to start charging Colonel Henderson for house room.

Having learned of the small invasion of Ferrers Court from her aunt, Elizabeth waited expectantly for Gideon to come and see her, but it was not until he had left his room sometime later, shaved and reasonably presentable with clean clothes extracted from his cloak bag, to go downstairs to dinner, did he visit her.

He would have liked to have seen her immediately upon his return, but as this had not been possible, he had had to contain his impatience as best he could. Richard, who experienced no qualms or reservations about leaving Gideon alone with his sister, accompanied him up the stairs quite prepared to permit the visit there and then, but just as they reached Elizabeth's bedchamber door his aunt, who was just emerging, announced that Elizabeth was by no means in a fit condition to receive visitors. Conveniently overlooking the one she had permitted first thing that morning, she told her nephew, incorporating the Major in her quelling statement, that Elizabeth needed to rest and if either of them thought that she was going to allow such a thing, then they were very much mistaken. Clara Winsetton, not proof against her nephew's charm and cajoling, eventually capitulated, but not without warning Gideon that if he thought for one moment that he could invade a lady's bedchamber as and when it suited him, then he was fair and far off. Raising her hand to his lips, he smiled up at her, breaking down every last defence she had, but rallying her forces gently rapped his knuckles with her bony fingers, admonishing him for the rogue she had always known him to be. Conscious of an ever-growing affection for this redoubtable old lady, Gideon had no intention of abusing the trust she placed in him, but as he entered Elizabeth's room sometime later, to find her sitting up in bed supported by a mound of pillows with her hair unconfined and falling over her shoulders, he found it necessary to sternly suppress his very natural impulses at the sight of her. She was still rather pale and her deep blue eyes reflected the effects of the constant throbbing in her left arm, which lay in its sling on top of the coverlet, but upon seeing Gideon enter the room, all the pain and discomfort she had been enduring was momentarily forgotten, her eyes lighting up at his entrance.

Her aunt, who was finding herself becoming more irresistibly drawn to the Major, was by no means averse to assisting in their romance, within limits, of course. Although she had deemed it incumbent upon her to at least make a show of frowning upon Gideon when he requested to see her niece whilst she was abed, she not only knew that he would behave impeccably towards her, but also considered it necessary to present her niece looking reasonably well turned-out to the man who was clearly besotted with her. Miss Calne, by no means reconciled to a single gentleman visiting the bedchamber of a single lady, no matter what the circumstances, kept her tongue with difficulty, as she followed her mistress's instructions regarding her niece's appearance, but could not deny that Miss Elizabeth made a very beautiful invalid.

Treading softly across the room to the big four-poster, Gideon sat gently down beside her, taking her right hand in his and planting a kiss on its soft palm. "Missed me?" he asked softly, his eyes smiling warmly down at her.

She returned the smile, but a roguish impulse made her say, "After seeing you only this morning! No," she shook her head, her voice a caress, "not at all."

His eyes lit up at this, sending a quiver spiralling through her, surprising and exciting her when he kissed her wrist, raising his eyes to her delicately tinged face. "Missed me?" he asked again.

She shook her head, saying a little breathlessly, "No."

Leaning forward a little and lowering his head, he then caressed the inner curve of her elbow with a feather light brush of his lips before again raising his eyes to hers. "Missed me?" he asked again, more intently, his voice a little unsteady.

She shook her head, biting down on her bottom lip as her skin burned from the touch of his lips and the gentle but urgent grip of his fingers on her arm. "Not at all" she managed, the breath almost stilling in her lungs, the rights and wrongs of what she was doing momentarily pushed to the back of her mind.

She heard his sharp intake of breath as he looked up into her flushed face, his eyes burning with a need which precisely matched her own, a smile touching his lips before kissing her invitingly parted ones with a slow thoroughness which rendered her incapable of saying or doing anything other than responding to it. Eventually raising his head, he looked deep into her eyes, demanding urgently "Missed me?"

"Yes," she told him breathlessly, "you must know I have, so very much."

Had Miss Calne been privileged to have witnessed this amorous display instead of being briskly shepherded out of the room by her strong minded mistress, she would have felt herself to be perfectly justified in not only demanding the Major make an immediate exit, but ensuring no more such visits were allowed. Having long ago concluded that men cared for nothing but their own bestial pleasures, she had happily turned her back on the male sex without a moment's regret. Indeed, the very idea of permitting one to touch her so intimately was so repugnant to her that the very thought made her shudder with revulsion. To have seen Miss Elizabeth positively encouraging the Major's advances, for she would have described her behaviour as nothing less, would have deeply offended her sensibilities. It was therefore as well for her peace of mind as well as her sense of propriety that she remained in ignorance of what she would have had no hesitation in deeming a disgraceful episode.

Miss Elizabeth meanwhile, far from being imbued with feelings of shock and revulsion, was conscious only of an overwhelming sense of exhilaration and well-being. She had no need for Miss Calne to tell her that for a single lady to entertain a gentleman in her bedchamber, even though he was her future husband and she virtually an invalid, was not at all the thing. She knew it perfectly well. The only defence she could have put forward were she ever challenged was that she was deeply love. When she had playfully denied missing him she had not intended to either tease or incite him into such a stimulating display of lovemaking, and as she had never before been subjected to anything more than a polite kiss of her finger tips from hopeful suitors for her hand, she had not expected him to tantalizingly prise the answer out of her in such a devastatingly provocative way. Her response to such an irresistible onslaught had its roots in love and not from having personal knowledge of the skilful arts of seduction, guaranteed to inflame a man's natural desires. During the whole of her life she had never experienced anything remotely like the emotions Gideon aroused inside her, but she was neither ashamed nor embarrassed in that he had expressed his love for her in such an ardent way before his ring was even on her finger. She could no more have resisted his kisses than she could prevent the sun from shining, but as she lay contentedly back against the pillows with her hand held in Gideon's strong and comforting clasp and his eyes lovingly looking down at her, she knew no desire to either resist or repulse his lovemaking.

Elizabeth's mischievous response had been adorably irresistible, evoking all Gideon's very human needs and desires, and as he was not made of stone but flesh and blood, had found it impossible to resist her. He had promised himself that he would not allow his feelings for her to get the better of him, but he could no more have withstood her response than he could deny his feelings for her. His love rendered him acutely susceptible to her every spontaneous and unaffected gesture, and he was honest enough to admit that it was becoming increasingly more difficult for him to withstand the affect she had on him. He knew her aunt and Richard trusted him implicitly and whilst he retained enough self-control to give them no cause to censure his conduct, it was nevertheless true that the more he saw of Elizabeth the more he loved and wanted her; longing for the day when he could make her his own and show her how much he loved her without any feelings of guilt or sense of betrayal to those who had placed their trust in him. Until then he somehow had to exert every restraint over his emotions, but as he looked down at her he knew it was going to take every ounce of self-discipline he possessed to carry out this noble, if somewhat fragile, resolve.

So attuned to him was she that Elizabeth instinctively knew what was going through his mind, and for the second time that day sought to help him in his efforts, but such was her love for him that she knew it was going to be as arduous for her as it was for him. But it was so very difficult to maintain good intentions to do something you knew to be right when the man you loved with every fibre of your being was looking at you in just such a way, and the warmth of his hand holding yours made you feel as though your heart would burst with love and need. If only those dark brown eyes would not smile quite so lovingly down at her or his very nearness fill her with longing, it would be so much easier to sustain her determination. As it was, she was finding it extremely difficult to retain any semblance of rational thinking, especially as his thumb had begun to rhythmically caress the palm of her hand, slowly demolishing her fixed purpose.

She was therefore not at all certain whether to be glad or not when the opiate Dr. Jarvey had insisted she take earlier began to wear off and the pain in her left arm, which had begun to throb rather painfully some minutes before but had not until now intruded on her consciousness, was gradually becoming quite acute and could no longer be ignored. In an effort to relieve it she gently moved her left arm which had been lying on top of the coverlet, but the movement brought on a sudden shaft of pain which darted its whole length making her close her eyes on a agonized gasp and her hand to clench into a tight fist.

Immediately Gideon released the hand he had been holding and strode round to the other side of the bed, his own experience of suffering the same misfortune not only making it possible for him to empathize with her but also knowing how to place her arm in a more comfortable position. She winced at his touch, her face losing its colour as she experienced a momentary sensation of nausea, thankful to lean against his shoulder, but other than pulling a face made no demur as he put the glass of Dr. Jarvey's prepared sedative to her lips.

"Perhaps now," he said tenderly, drawing her closer against him, "you will not disregard Jarvey so readily. You are in no fit condition to leave your bed. Yes," he nodded as she looked a question, "Richard told me how you tried to persuade him into allowing you to get up, but I am afraid I must insist that you do precisely what he says."

"Yes, but ..." she began faintly.

"No 'buts', my darling" he shook his head. "You will oblige me by following his instructions."

She sighed, accepting this without comment, contented to remain safe in his arms and doing nothing more strenuous than snuggling her head against his shoulder, listening to him telling her about what had transpired downstairs and Richard's horror at the thought of playing host to Colonel Henderson for one more night. As the sedative was by this time beginning to take effect and her eyelids refused to remain open, she could only offer the ghost of a smile, and Gideon, looking closely down at her gently laid her back against the pillows. She did not stir when he kissed the top of her head or pulled the coverlet over her and made her comfortable, nor did she hear him leave the room and close the door softly behind him.

By no means reconciled to the house being invaded by a parcel of red-coats, rendering it more like a barracks than a gentleman's home, any more than she was to having that reprobate under their roof for one more night, Clara Winsetton nevertheless believed that Sir John, a once regular visitor to The Court, should be dined in style, in company with the Major and Lieutenant Beaton. As it had been some appreciable time since they had entertained she was therefore determined to do full justice to the occasion by not only overriding Richard's instructions that they would dine in the great hall due to it being conveniently within earshot of the small sitting room, but would open up the dining room instead, as well as decking herself out in all her finery.

Always an imposing figure, she never looked more formidable than when heavily painted and rouged and wearing a wig which stood almost twelve inches from the top of her head, elaborately decorated with feathers and a diamond chip that perfectly matched the diamonds around her throat and dangling from her ears. Her dress, a stiff creation in dove coloured satin with massive hoops exposing a white underdress of silk edged with Brussels lace, rustled with every step she took, and Gideon, just emerging from Elizabeth's room in time to see her leave her own and walk towards him, admirably concealed a smile of pure appreciation at the sight of so awe-inspiring a lady. Not for the first time since making her acquaintance she forcibly put him in mind of his own grandmother whom he and Aubrey had adored, just such a redoubtable old lady whose forthright facade hid a heart as generous as it was kind.

As she had by now come to look upon him, if not in quite the same way as she did Richard, then certainly with indulgence for one whom she had a decided partiality, and therefore knew no qualms in taking him to task. Upon hearing the long-case clock further down the passageway chime the hour, she eyed Gideon closely, saying meaningfully, "You have been with my niece an unconscionable time, Major."

"Yes, Ma'am," he smiled, bowing over her hand, "but I promise you I comported myself with all the decorum you could have wished for."

Her eyes narrowed as she looked up into his perfectly grave face, only his eyes revealing the laughter welling up inside him. "Hm!" she sniffed. "I don't doubt your idea of decorum differs greatly to my own."

"Perhaps, Ma'am" Gideon agreed amusedly, "but since she has set up no cry to be rescued from any advances I may have made, I think there is every likelihood they could well correspond."

"Vastly diverting!" she replied dampingly, not quite able to prevent the responsive twitch at the corner of her mouth. "And I daresay you would have me believe that you made none!"

"And would you have me believe that you thought I would not?" he asked, the smile in his eyes more pronounced.

A rich chuckle left her lips at this. "Well, that's what I call giving me my own again! But tell me," she asked, indicating her niece's bedchamber door with a nod of her head, "how did you leave her?"

"Having persuaded her to drink the sedative Dr. Jarvey left her," he told her, "she is now asleep and should remain so until the morning."

She sighed her relief before saying, with a tartness completely belied by the smile in her eyes, "Clearly your powers of persuasion into getting her to swallow that foul stuff are far greater than mine; useless I suppose to ask how you managed it."

"If you wish to spare my blushes Ma'am," he smiled, "yes."

After rapping him over the arm with her furled fan and apostrophizing him for a rascal, said seriously, "You know, were it not for my brother's death and Richard's affairs, she would even now be enjoying another season. Although," she nodded, "I have every reason to suppose she would be married by now, especially as her first season was a great success. Did she tell you?"

"No, Ma'am," he shook his head, "she did not."

"Well, that don't surprise me," she nodded. "She is not conceited, nor is she one for puffing off her own successes. Three offers of marriage she received and all from most eligible young men."

"I am not surprised" he told her. "She is very beautiful."

"Yes, she is. Her mother was just such a one. I daresay," she said astutely, eying him shrewdly "you must be quite a judge; clearly you've known many beautiful women."

He laughed at that. "Yes Ma'am, I have," he told her truthfully, "but not as many as you apparently seem to think. Whilst I am not without experience," he confessed, "I am no philanderer."

"I never supposed it, Major" she replied candidly. "You ain't no libertine, *nor* did I suppose you were merely indulging in a flirtation to while away the hours until Richard's affairs were settled and you returned to town. Had that have been the case," she told him firmly, "I would never have permitted you to visit my niece in the privacy of her bedchamber, and certainly not without the presence of myself or Miss Calne." She hunched a shoulder, saying in her blunt way, "I don't hold with men getting married too young, it's asking for trouble. Seen too many of 'em go wrong. A man should look about him first; acquire some experience. How old are you?"

"Nine and twenty, Ma'am," he replied unsteadily.

"A good age," she nodded. "Tell me," she asked abruptly, "is it because my niece is beautiful that you love her?"

"No," he shook his head, quite unperturbed by this direct question, "but I would not be entirely honest if I did not say that upon first setting eyes on her she quite bowled me over, but I had not been long in her company before I saw there was more to your niece than a beautiful face."

"Yes, there is" she agreed. "And what precisely did *you* see?"

"I could give you any number of things, but the only one of any importance is that I saw a woman without whom the rest of my life would be totally meaningless," he told her with perfect sincerity.

She nodded, apparently satisfied with this answer. "Three offers of marriage!" she repeated, not without a touch of pride. "In her *first* season too. And then," she said frustrated, "after having me traipsing around with her to all manner of routs, balls and the like, what do you think?"

"I cannot imagine, Ma'am," he said without a tremor.

"Refused 'em; everyone! When I asked her why, do you know what she replied?" He shook his head. "Said she wasn't in love with any one of 'em! I could have boxed the chit's ears!"

"I would say that that's a very good reason for refusing," he said reasonably, "although," he smiled, "I must confess to having every sympathy for her rejected suitors."

"However," she acknowledged, ignoring this, "I'm bound to say that it's worked out better than I could ever have hoped for; because there's no denying when a young girl turns down three offers of marriage word gets about, and the tattle mongers or, rather," she corrected herself, "the mammas' of daughters' who are in despair over their failure to attach a man's interest, being as they can't hold a candle to Elizabeth, are bound to talk!"

"*Absente reo*" he remarked.

She looked warily at him. "That sounds very clever Major."

"It is Latin, Ma'am" he smiled. "Roughly translated it means 'behind someone's back'."

"Ha!" she scoffed. "You have it in a nutshell, Major!"

"Regrettably," he shrugged, "it is all too often the case."

"Yes," she sighed. "I am afraid to say you are right."

"To pay heed to it," he smiled, "is to condone it; far better not and therefore rise above it."

She was very much impressed with this, but felt impelled to say, "Very likely, but there are those to whom I would very dearly love to impart a few home truths!"

"I have no doubt you would do it admirably," he nodded, his eyes alight, "but Elizabeth needs no justification."

"No," she agreed firmly, "she does not. You know," she told him, "I told my niece not to look for love in marriage; not that I was not very happy with Sir Thomas," she assured him, "but not everyone was as fortunate as my brother in enjoying a happy marriage."

"I know," he nodded, "which is why I was not so optimistic in finding the same affection in my own marriage as that enjoyed by my parent's."

"Ha!" she cried. "How any man could not love your mother I don't know; such a captivating and adorable little piece. Had all the men in a tizzy as I recall" she told him, chuckling. "Then along comes your father, and before the cat could lick her ear they made a match of it!" She looked kindly down on him, saying fondly "My niece could look as high as she chooses for a husband; which is why I was out of all patience with her when she turned down the hand of two of her hopeful suitors at least, the one being an heir to an earldom and the other to a Marquis but, upon reflection," she admitted, "I'm glad to say she did. I've never seen Elizabeth happier, for which I have you to thank. She loves you very much, Major!"

"I know," he nodded, "and I can't tell you how happy that makes me, because if she did not," he said disconsolately, looking directly at her, "I would be utterly desolate." Upon which he proffered his arm and escorted her down the stairs.

Richard, seeing nothing to marvel at in his aunt's attire, kept her tolerably well entertained during dinner, but Michael, looking somewhat warily at her, especially as she had taken on a somewhat formidable appearance in her paint and powder compared to when he saw her yesterday evening, was immediately put in mind of a maiden aunt who had terrified every member of his family with her caustic comments. However, since she appeared to be in a most receptive mood and showed no inclination to either reduce him to schoolboy status or treat him as an intrusive red-coat, was, to his enormous relief, genuinely amused by some interesting anecdotes he had dared to impart. Sir John, all too familiar with Clara Winsetton, knew to a nicety how to deal with her, and since she had long ago taken a liking to this military friend of her brother's, thoroughly enjoyed reminiscing with him over happier days. A number of times throughout dinner Gideon caught her darting a swift glance across the table at him, but since their relationship, short though it was, was progressing quite amicably with a good understanding growing up between them, apart from the occasional remark one to the other, neither felt compelled to make polite conversation. By the time dinner came to an end, in no way the lengthy affair Clara Winsetton was used to sitting down to, it was clear to her nephew and guests that she was looking rather tired, and although she would never admit such a thing, excused herself instead on the grounds that they no doubt had important matters to discuss, and would therefore leave them with the decanter of port. Richard, escorting her out of the dining room got no further than the foot of the stairs, whereupon he was summarily told that she was no decrepit who needed to be taken to her bedchamber. He laughed, kissed her affectionately on the cheek and told her that she was nothing but a cantankerous old woman, an epithet to which she took no exception, but, on the contrary, liked very well, laid her hand against his cheek, saying that it did her heart good to see him back home where he belonged. Unfortunately choosing that moment to leave the sitting room having taken Colonel Henderson something to eat, Salmon was immediately charged with the task of helping her up the stairs, blatantly disregarding her claim that she was no decrepit, admirably hiding her fondness for him by announcing in quelling accents that he would be far more useful by assisting her to her room instead of feeding the very man who would have willingly seen her nephew hang from the nearest gallows. Over her head two pairs of eyes met, speaking volumes one to the other, but both clearly reflecting the love and pride they had in this redoubtable woman without whom they would not be without.

Following her departure from the dining room, the port and cognac passed freely up and down the table, its occupants discussing the quick succession of recent events and their possible consequences. Having been taken fully into Richard's confidence, though not to the extent that he was told the precise nature of Lytton's perfidy, Michael was firmly of the opinion that whatever heinous crime His Grace had committed all those years ago, should remain in the past, as he for one was none to eager to come to Lytton's attention.

Sir John, who had been mulling over the incident with an ever darkening brow, was by no means happy to allow such a transgression to go unpunished, and would, with the greatest alacrity, see him denounced were it not for the repercussions which would befall the innocent from such a disclosure. Although this view of the matter was the general consensus of opinion, Gideon had not failed to notice that Richard had been looking pensively down into his glass at the candlelight playing on the rich ruby liquid for some few minutes and shrewdly guessed his thoughts. Should they ultimately decide that Lytton's criminal deception all those years ago be made public after all, whilst it may go a long way to satisfying their own ideas of right and wrong it would do untold damage to too many people to justify reversing their decision. Richard knew this was true, but it would be long before he would be able to accept it, if ever, and since he had spoken no less than the truth to Gideon when he said that he had had enough of looking over his shoulder, he was realistic enough to know that there was nothing whatever they could do in order to bring him to his just deserts.

But it was not only His Grace's iniquities which brought that brooding frown to his brow or the sombre look in his eyes; another, and far more personal reason was occupying his mind, indeed, it had been encroaching on his consciousness all day, and waiting only until he was alone with Gideon, did he broach the matter to him. Michael, having already retired, and Sir John, deeming it prudent to take a look at their prisoner before following suit, Richard strolled unhurriedly out of the dining room with his arm tucked under Gideon's, laughing at some humorous anecdote whilst at the same time striving for the right words to mention the matter which was very close to his heart. As he already felt himself to be under an immeasurable obligation to Gideon it seemed to him the height of impertinence to request one more service from him, and although he knew he would not fail him he nevertheless felt a little embarrassed to solicit one final favour.

Saluting the soldier standing guard outside the small sitting room, Gideon then leisurely climbed the stairs side by side with Richard, paying polite attention to his idle observations on a number of inconsequential subjects with unfailing patience and good humour, but by the time they reached the first landing it was evident that Richard's mental pursuit for topics to discuss was floundering, and Gideon, deciding it was time to bring his agony of inner deliberation to an end, said amusedly, "You know Richard, all of this is most interesting, not to say quite entertaining, but don't you think it's time to tell me what is really on your mind?"

Richard stopped and looked at Gideon, a sheepish grin twisting his lips. "I suppose I should have known better than to think I could hoodwink you."

"Yes," Gideon smiled, "you should. What is it?" When Richard made no immediate answer he asked, "Is it Henderson's trial that is troubling you?"

"No," he shook his head. "Nothing like that."

Whatever it was that was perturbing Richard, it was undoubtedly something he found a little awkward to discuss, yet clearly it was creating a problem that he obviously could not deal with himself. Rapidly going over recent events in his mind he recalled the conversation he had had with Elizabeth the morning he had come upon her unexpectedly at Cuckmere Valley, and by dint of elimination eventually arrived at what he considered to be the crux of the matter. Looking down at Richard's bent head he said thoughtfully, "Would I be right in thinking that you are dwelling on Miss Trench and that she is the cause of your melancholy?" Richard's head shot up at that, a tinge of colour creeping into his face. "I thought so," Gideon nodded understandingly. "Would it help at all" he said encouragingly, gripping his shoulder, "if I told you that I am seldom, if ever, shocked or embarrassed. I presume your present dejection has something to do with the fact that you have not seen her for some considerable time and are eager to do so."

Richard sighed, a rueful smile playing at the corner of his lips. "That's about the size of it. The thing is," he shrugged, "if I go to see Sir Arthur myself I would not be at all surprised if he set the dogs onto me, let alone granting me an interview."

"Stiff rumped, is he?" Gideon observed shrewdly .

"Let us just say," he said dryly, "that he's mighty prone to standing on his dignity when he's a mind; certainly as far as I am concerned I am *persona non grata,* in fact" he explained, suddenly grim, "he has forbidden any contact between the two households; so much so," he said wretchedly, "that he refused to attend my father's funeral due to my dealings, for which I can only assume he was afraid the taint of traitor would fall onto him through association." A derisive smile touched his lips at the thought, but it was gone in a moment. "It's only thanks to letters being smuggled in by her father's groom and Salmon, bosom cronies," he explained, smiling up at Gideon, "that Jane and Elizabeth have been able to meet, were it not for that," he told him, "I would never have known that Sir Arthur had every intention of packing Jane off back to London to stay with her aunt because he feared that the two of us would meet clandestinely. It was only on Jane's sworn assurance that she would have no contact with anyone here and running the risk of seeing me, that he relented and permitted her to remain at The Manor." After briefly scrutinizing the shine on his boots, he said, not a little defiantly, "So desperate was I to see Jane that I did contemplate something of that nature, but the truth is I couldn't do it," he shook his head. "To place her in a situation where she would have to lie to her parents, even such a blinkered man like Sir Arthur, would have been unpardonable."

"Yes, it would" Gideon agreed, "even so," he smiled, "I can quite well understand why you felt the need."

"The thing is," Richard told him gloomily, "even if he did agree to let me speak to him, I cannot see him being persuaded by anything I might say."

Observing Richard's downhearted demeanour he said intuitively, "In view of this then, I take it you would like me to be your advocate and plead your cause to Sir Arthur? No doubt," he pointed out amusedly, "that coming from a man who wears the King's uniform my entreaty will carry far more weight."

Richard looked a little sheepish. "Frankly, yes." Then upon seeing the twinkle in Gideon's eyes, grinned. "It's the devil of a thing to ask of you, especially after all you have done already. I've no right; none at all!"

"My understanding," Gideon reminded him, brooking no argument, "is that I was sent here to try and do what I could to settle your affairs, now unless I am grossly at fault," he told him affably, "your affairs are not yet settled and nor are they likely to be until this final impediment is scaled."

Richard heaved a sigh. "I knew you would understand."

"I do," Gideon nodded, "I just hope that Sir Arthur does too."

Richard nodded, then raking a hand through his hair, a gesture Gideon had come to recognize as his expression of frustration, said "The thing is Gideon, I've not laid eyes on Jane this age; over twelve months in fact, and if I don't see her soon I think I'll go stark mad!"

"Well," Gideon sighed, his eyes alight, "seeing as how my father would take as much exception to my future wife's brother being out of his senses as much as he would to him being a murderer, assuming that is I had allowed you to vent your spleen on Colonel Henderson and William last night, I suppose it behoves me to put forward all the tact and diplomacy at my command."

Something between a groan and a deep hearted sigh left Richard's lips, grasping Gideon's hand saying "Thank you. It seems I shall never be out of your debt!"

"Surely you did not think I would refuse?" Gideon smiled, raising an eyebrow in mock horror.

"No," Richard shook his head, "the devil's in it that I knew you would not; which is why I was reluctant to ask such a thing of you after everything else you have done."

546

Gideon pulled a face. "You know, much more of this and I shall become quite puffed up in my own conceit!"

"No, you won't," Richard laughed. "I only wish there was something I could do for you."

Gideon's eyes lit up. "As a matter of fact," he nodded, "now you mention it, there is something."

"If it's in my power to do it, you have but to name it." Richard invited.

"It is," Gideon nodded. "Grant me permission to ask for your sister's hand."

"What!" Richard cried, "I thought I had."

"Not in so many words," Gideon shook his head.

"Well if that don't beat the Dutch!" he laughed. "Of course you have it," he told him, gripping the hand held out to him. "Not that I envisage her saying no!"

"If she does," Gideon told him, a smile lighting his eyes, "then I shall be applying to you to plead *my* cause!"

CHAPTER TWENTY EIGHT

Like his recently deceased accomplice, Colonel Henderson was not a man given over to self-analysis or wasting even so much as a moment's thought on those who had suffered from whatever action he had taken.   He had done whatever he had considered necessary in order to protect himself and William Ferrers from the consequences of their involvement in treason, and if that had meant pointing the finger at an innocent man, then so be it.   So desperate had he been to shield them both from exposure and denunciation as traitors that he had been prepared to do anything or sacrifice anyone in an attempt to achieve it.   Over the last twelve months or more, he had carried out an untiring campaign on the Ferrers family with complete and utter disregard for either their dignity or feelings, and his relentless persecution, far from finding either Richard Ferrers hiding out at his home or those damning letters, had accomplished nothing except being instrumental in the untimely death of Jasper Ferrers.   The longer it had taken to apprehend his quarry as well as placing his hands on that correspondence, the more desperate he had become and it had therefore been as a last ditch attempt to prevent a complete debacle from occurring that he had coerced Robert into assisting him by daring to hold his past misdemeanour over his head.   But even with such a powerful and influential friend at his back, Richard Ferrers had continued to remain elusive. His last hope therefore had been what he had firmly believed to be a foolproof plan, but although its execution could not be faulted it had never so much as crossed his mind that it would be turned against him with such devastating effect by the very man it had been designed to ensnare; a man who was neither a coward nor a fool.

Having considered it expedient to not only make an end of Major Neville but Elizabeth Ferrers as well in order to prevent them from divulging all they knew, he had regarded it as imperative that their demise should be engineered in such a way that no wind of blame could be attached to either himself or William Ferrers.   All the actions he had taken the other night to finally settle their affairs having unfortunately   gone horrendously awry, he had employed unplanned measures which had been forced upon him by the combined effects of surprise and panic, resulting in the deliberate and cold-blooded murder of his accomplice and the accidental shooting of Elizabeth Ferrers, an act which immediately added fuel to Richard Ferrers' fire.   No one had been more taken aback than he upon seeing her slump unconscious to the floor, but before he could even make his escape or ascertain the extent of her injury, he had seen her brother bear down upon him with such a murderous look on his face, that he had genuinely believed he would strangle him with his bare hands.

Upon first discovering that he had been brought to Ferrers Court, trussed up and thrust ignominiously onto the floor of a carriage, he had feared the worst especially when he considered all that had gone before, but apart from numerous menacing looks cast in his direction by his reluctant host as well as his henchman, not to mention Lieutenant Beaton, a man whose role in the sequence of events he still found difficult to fathom or understand, he had to admit that on the whole he had been treated reasonably well. The truth was that it would not have surprised him if Richard Ferrers had dispensed his own brand of retribution for what he had done, not only to his sister but also being instrumental in the death of his father, without even waiting for a trial and sentence to be passed.

But as the minutes turned into hours with no physical harm being threatened or carried out to his person, he had begun to feel more hopeful as to still being able to come out of this fiasco with a whole skin. During the night time hours the panic he had experienced earlier in the evening had gradually evaporated to be replaced by an illusory calm frame of mind which enabled him to talk himself into believing that Lytton, despite his refusal to offer further assistance, would come to his aid yet again. Confident he still had the power to command his on-going support due to the damning information he possessed, his optimism steadily grew until he had convinced himself that his current predicament was nothing but a transitory phase and that even before Sir John could set plans in motion to get his trial underway, he would be released and exonerated of any wrong-doing.

It presented a pleasing picture, and one which entered his dreams during what was left of the night, awaking in a mood of considerable well-being some hours later, sufficiently restored to sanguinity. But thanks to Major Neville, a man whom he had long since wished at the devil, he was soon disabused of any hope he had cherished of receiving help from His Grace. Despise him he may, but he had been forced to admit that he had spoken no less than the truth when he had said he could no longer count on support from Lytton. Robert would undoubtedly look to himself, because there was no way he would allow either his name or reputation to be sullied, and certainly not by association with a man like himself who was currently under arrest for not only taking part in insurrection but for cold-blooded murder. Even discounting his treasonable activities, he had callously taken the life of a man, who, no matter what his crimes, had been given no chance to defend himself, put to death in front of witnesses, two of whom wore the King's uniform, and as a result could expect no reprieve or last minute stay of execution through His Grace's intercession. But that last flickering flame of optimism still lingered; his hold over Robert! That, surely, was more than enough to rally his old friend to his cause once more! No man, especially one so full of pride as he, would allow such a deceit as the one he had committed all those years ago, to be made public knowledge. But unfortunately, even this final vestige of hope was shattered by Major Neville's quiet reminder that His Grace, a man of dexterous ability and outstanding adroitness, and one, moreover, who could claim the most powerful ally in the land, would have no difficulty in extricating himself from such an embarrassing and humiliating accusation.

Beaten into submission at last by this soberly delivered but unpleasant fact, he was finally brought to accept his inescapable and unenviable fate. It was small consolation to know that he had escaped detection for so long due to his own inexhaustible efforts, and had almost succeeded, but now that every remnant of hope had gone, and there was nothing further he could do to stave off the inevitable, every last ounce of fight he had had left him, leaving him depleted of all mental and physical reserves; his whole body, slumping heavily forward in his seat, symbolizing his defeat as well as his resignation to the unpreventable.

It had been this inertia and passivity which had led Richard to laughingly question Gideon as to whether he had slipped something into his drink to render him more manageable, but upon learning the truth of what had passed between the two men, he had found no difficulty in understanding such a capitulation. But for his temporary prisoner, humiliation and shame were to be added to his already over burdened state of mind, when Sir John promptly reminded him of not only his betrayal of trust to his King and country, but also to the name he bore; a name which had been synonymous with the Stuarts. His declaration of support to Charles Edward Stuart therefore, was all the more contemptuous given as it was without the smallest degree of conviction in the cause that this representative of a fated dynasty had strived to bring to a successful conclusion. What had made his deeds even more dishonourable was that, unlike his father and grandfather, who had stood shoulder to shoulder with the Stuarts throughout all their adversities, had done so openly and for all men to see, with pride and nobility, not covertly or for personal ambition and profit, and certainly without any thought of pointing the finger at an innocent man when Stuart hopes disintegrated, resulting in that iniquitous 'gazetting'. Not content with this, he had added the murder of his accomplice to his already treacherous crimes, an act of sheer cold-bloodedness which, should he have somehow managed to have bought an acquittal for his treason, would be enough to see him hang. Struggling to eat his last meal at Ferrers Court, every mouthful sticking in his throat, he could not rid his mind of the thought that before the day was out he would be enjoying incarceration in far less luxuriant and comfortable surroundings than those in which he currently found himself. The prospect was certainly daunting, especially when he considered that he would not be imprisoned for long, having to face his trial almost immediately upon his arrival in town. He could not even enliven his spirits with the thought of laying the blame at William Ferrers' door, because as Major Neville had made perfectly clear to him, even if he could produce those letters advertising his willingness to participate, there still remained the other three clearly indicating his own readiness; but more than this, there were four people at least who would be ready to swear that William Ferrers, far from being a traitor, had conjoined with his cousin to seek him out. Only now, when it was far too late, did the enormity of what he had embarked on come home to him, and the very thought of the evidence contained in those letters being presented at his hearing, convicting him without the need for any explanation, was something he found hard to contemplate. But worse than this, was the shock and incredulity which would follow his denouncement, bringing with it the inevitable taint and ignominy of treason which would unquestionably attach to his name; staining the reputations of his proud and noble forebears for all time, a dishonourable indictment which was undeserving to men who had never betrayed either their beliefs or loyalties.

Honesty compelled him to admit that he could not suffer to see such a public demonstration of abhorrence any more than he could approach his trial and ultimate execution with either equanimity or courage, and therefore concluded that the only way to obviate the risk of exhibiting the slightest hint of cowardice or dishonour was by ensuring that his end was not brought about by a public executioner.

Unaware of what was going through their prisoner's mind a brief consultation was held over breakfast, as a result of which it was agreed that Michael would return to Hampton Regis and Gideon, following his meeting with Sir Arthur, would then join up with Sir John somewhere on the road to London.

Since no heroics or last minute attempt to escape were envisaged and Colonel Henderson would be encircled by the six armed men who had accompanied Sir John, it was considered safe enough to allow him to ride to town rather than in the coach generously offered by Richard.

This gesture immediately put Gideon in mind of Sir Evelyn's coach and trap, to which Richard assured him that two of the stable lads had returned them yesterday, and all that remained was for Michael to discover from Major Denham the situation regarding Private Smith. Having left Ferrers Court some ten minutes earlier on a borrowed and far better bred horse than the one which had been loaned him the other night, Michael had bidden farewell to Sir John and Gideon, promising his friend that he would visit again soon when, hopefully, his affairs would be settled.

Having leisurely consumed a hearty breakfast, Richard, still wearing his startlingly flamboyant dressing gown over his shirt and breeches, sauntered into the hall some minutes later, amusedly watching the hectic preparations for departure. Upon seeing Gideon come down the stairs carrying his hat and gloves, the clock in the hall just striking half past eight, he stepped up to him and nodding his head in the direction of the sitting room, grinned "And I thought the army was organized!"

"Quiet, bantling!" Gideon ordered cheerfully. "Unless you want us to leave here without him."

"And relinquish him to my tender mercies!" Richard smiled.

"When you put it like that," Gideon nodded, "perhaps not."

"I thought not!" Richard smiled, then casting a mischievous glance up at him said irrepressibly that now he was respectable again life would seem deadly flat.

Gideon's eyes twinkled in response to this. "Yes," he marvelled, shaking his head bemused, "I can't begin to imagine how you will contrive to stave off boredom!"

Richard burst out laughing at this, but just as he was on the point of responding the door to the small sitting room opened and General Turville walked out immediately followed by Colonel Henderson with two soldiers on either side of him firmly gripping his arms. Suddenly he appeared so much older; his face pale and drawn and the bulbous blue eyes, looking to neither right nor left, stared dazedly ahead of him as he was led outside to where the other four soldiers were waiting. Pausing only to have a brief word with Gideon and Richard, General Turville then donned his hat and gloves and strode purposefully out of the front door which was being held open by Salmon, issuing brisk orders as he did so.

Richard was neither vindictive nor callous, but he would have been less than honest if he did not acknowledge to feeling immense relief in knowing that a man guilty of treason and cold-blooded murder was about to face his trial for both calumnies. He and his family had suffered too much at the hands of Colonel Henderson for him to feel any regret about the end which awaited him, believing he was only receiving his just deserts for all the wrongdoing he had engineered. Even so, he was not so heartless and unsympathetic that he could not understand the affect such a discovery and ultimate arrest of a fellow officer would have on Gideon and Sir John. To men of their integrity it had been an extremely distasteful affair, but to allow Colonel Henderson's crimes to go unpunished, or even to turn a blind eye and allow an innocent man to take the blame in order to shield his reputation, would have been quite repugnant to them. From out the corner of his eye Richard saw Gideon walk towards the door, absently pulling his gloves through his hand as he stepped outside to watch the cavalcade as it made its way down the avenue, and crossing the hall to join him, followed Gideon's glance, making no effort to speak until they were lost from sight. "Try not to take it too much to heart, Gideon" he advised considerately, seeing the sombre expression which had entered his eyes, bringing a hand to rest on his shoulder. "Henderson dealt his own cards and played his hand how he saw fit."

"Yes, I know" Gideon sighed, "but I wasn't thinking of Colonel Henderson so much as knowing that when this becomes known, as it very soon will," he nodded, "every man who wears a scarlet coat is going to be judged by what he has done."

"Perhaps," he replied, thoughtfully. "But people have short memories, besides which, once they see what you and Sir John have done any loss of faith they may have had in the military will soon be re-established. Aren't I proof of that?" he smiled.

"You forget," Gideon reminded him, "not everyone know us as well as you."

"Exactly so," he grinned, "which is why you should regard me as a shining example for the multitude!"

Gideon laughed. "I suppose that's meant to comfort me?"

"But of course!" Richard replied genially, his eyes alight. "What else?"

"I shudder to think," Gideon replied, a responding twinkle in his eye.

Richard broke into laughter. "Oh ye of little faith! Haven't I promised to behave myself! What else is it you wish me to do?"

"Only a small thing," Gideon smiled.

"Well?" he said warily.

"Convey a message to Elizabeth for me."

"Is that all?" he said relieved. "I thought for a moment that you wanted me to keep to the house again! Because if you did" he told him unabashed, "it would make things deuced awkward!" Gideon cocked an eyebrow and Richard continued easily, "The thing is, I have to return that nag to Jo- er - the friend of mine who loaned it to Michael the other night. He wouldn't like it if one of the lads took it over instead. He's devlish shy, y'know!"

Gideon smiled. "I see. I take it this friend is a member of the fraternity?"

"No," Richard grinned, "just sympathetic."

"*That*, of course," Gideon smiled, "makes all the difference. I quite see how that renders his suspicions as perfectly understandable. In that case" he sighed resignedly, "I suppose you had better return it, after all," he said ironically, "we don't want him thinking you've stolen it. To have you charged with theft would, I think, tax even my powers!"

Richard patted him on the shoulder. "Never!" he cried. "I have every faith in you! What is it you want me to tell Elizabeth?" grinning irrepressibly as he requested him to spare his blushes.

"Having seen from the outset that you are a man of exquisite sensibility," Gideon pointed out, his eyes gleaming, "and not wishing to embarrass you by expecting you to pass on any *tendre le mot de l'amor* on my behalf, I considered it diplomatic to write them down. If you would be so kind," he smiled, handing Richard the sealed letter he had pulled out of his pocket.

As this proved too much for Richard's self-control, he fell into a paroxysm of laughter, which, after only a very few seconds, infected Gideon with the same affliction. "Egad!" Richard cried, putting the letter into his pocket, "I don't know what you deserve for that!"

"Only that you will engage to deliver my note," Gideon replied on a tremor.

"You must know I will. Come," he offered unsteadily, "I'll walk with you to the stables."

"What!" Gideon exclaimed, indicating his exotic dressing gown with a nod of his head. "In that abomination!"

Accepting this criticism with the good-humoured retort that if he wanted him to convey his *billet-doux* to Elizabeth, he would thank him to show more respect for his attire, then tucking a hand through Gideon's arm strolled round to the rear of the house in companionable conversation. By the time they reached the stables Gideon's grey mare was being led out with his cloak bag securely attached, and after casting a knowledgeable eye over its various points and commenting favourably, Richard looked up, saying "Gideon, about Sir Arthur; I can't vouch for his reception of you."

"Of course not. But if he's as high starched as you say," he nodded, running a hand down his mare's silken neck, "I daresay I can expect a rather cool welcome."

"I realize what I'm asking is a great imposition," Richard acknowledged, "but should you manage to persuade him as to the truth of things, my debt to you will be increased a hundred-fold, and that, you must know," he smiled, "I could never repay or offer sufficient thanks."

Hoisting himself up into the saddle, Gideon looked down into the apprehensive face staring up at him and his attractive smile dawned. "I've told you," he reminded him good-naturedly, "this debt you seem to think you owe me is quite imaginary, and as for thanks" he shook his head, "I don't need them, but if you think I do, then offer them to Miss Trench with my compliments. I feel sure," he remarked amusedly, reaching down to grasp Richard's hand, "that you will know precisely how to bestow them upon her." He was just about to give his horse the office to move off when he said, "I shall return as soon as I can, but I expect it will not be for several days." Whereupon he turned his horse and trotted out of the stable yard in the direction of the avenue, raising a hand in farewell without a backward glance before he was lost from Richard's sight.

For a man of Major Denham's unbending disposition being brought to acknowledge that he was wrong was something he could not face with equanimity, but however much it irked him, he had to admit that he had grossly misjudged Major Neville. He had been bitterly resentful upon first discovering that Colonel Henderson had seen fit to bring in a man from outside and had failed to see the reason for it, as it not only cast aspersions on the proficiency and abilities of the soldiers under his command, but could, if not carefully handled, lead to all manner of discontent among them leading to questions being asked as to the competency of their commanding officer. Equally as galling was the knowledge that Colonel Henderson had sought the support of His Grace the Duke of Lytton without so much as a word to him, a man who certainly carried enough weight to influence Sir John into assisting him with this matter, the result being that Major Neville had come into Sussex under the direct orders of General Turville to undertake the task of apprehending Richard Ferrers. As neither Colonel Henderson nor Major Neville had seen fit to confide in him, he had been left with nothing but speculation, and even though he had not taken to the Major he had been quite convinced that despite his military punctilio as well as his tact and discretion, he had no liking for the man who was after all a senior officer. Indeed, so much had been kept from him, even the fact that Lieutenant Beaton was a friend of Richard Ferrers and had come to his aid as well as being in the thick of events the other night while he had been kept kicking his heels with Captain Waring waiting on a bogus run. His trustworthiness as well as his pride had taken quite a beating, but these were minor ills in comparison to the shock he had received upon learning the truth from General Turville and Major Neville. Colonel Henderson may not have commanded his respect, but even so he had never so much as suspected that his commanding officer had embroiled himself in insurrection together with Richard Ferrers' cousin and had pointed a traitorous finger at that innocent young man in order to protect themselves. The plan they had devised to ensnare Richard Ferrers was, however devious, really quite brilliant, but even though he could appreciate this from a purely tactical point of view, a sickening disgust enveloped him as he considered what could have ensued had it have proved successful.

As a no nonsense type of man who believed that rules were not made to be broken, much less bent, he had found life in the army suited him very well, and since he had neither the time nor the inclination to marry, his military career and resultant duties had become his whole life, indeed, he had needed nothing else. In his opinion it was unthinkable for a soldier to question his orders, in fact it would have been a gross breach of discipline to have done so. He could not deny that Richard Ferrers had led them all a merry dance, but although he now shuddered in self-reproach at the thought of being at the forefront of participating in effecting his arrest and organizing all those searches and inquisitions on Colonel Henderson's behalf, he took small comfort from telling himself that he had been merely carrying out his orders. Admittedly, he had not known the truth or the existence of those letters and had therefore believed Colonel Henderson when he had issued orders regarding the apprehension of Richard Ferrers, a traitor turned smuggler, by any means available, and although he had no liking much less respect for his commanding officer he had carried out his orders diligently and with precision, unaware that he had been assisting him in his private war against the Ferrers family in order to ensure his own self-protection. Unfortunately, instead of making him feel better, it merely served to emphasize how unwilling he had been to delve into this affair more closely, but more than this it showed how indoctrinated into the observance of protocol he was to even question a senior officer's orders. A disciplinarian he may be, but he was a stickler for the truth as well as being able to distinguish right from wrong, and therefore set out to atone for this dereliction of duty, for he saw his actions as nothing less, by setting about tracking down Private Smith with a determination that was as grim as it was rigorous.

His hapless quarry, having restored the borrowed carriage to its gullible owner and appropriated a horse from the garrison stables, returned to Hamstoke House in the expectation of finding Colonel Henderson and his accomplice still there together with Miss Ferrers, suffered a severe shock upon discovering them gone. The sight of Cartwright attempting to clear the remains of the earlier scene of mayhem, almost incoherent with dread as he bemoaned the evening's events, caused him to fear the worst, and the content of Gideon's letter, far from assuaging his alarm, merely served to exacerbate it as well as his rising tide of panic. Without Colonel Henderson's protection and backing he was well and truly lost; and knew that returning to the garrison would be foolhardy as by now the cry would have gone out, or at least, it very soon would.

He had no well-wisher in Major Denham and knew that he would like nothing better than to put him on a charge, after all there would be no difficulty about this considering his ever growing list of offences, and only Colonel Henderson's protection had prevented him from doing so. But now that Colonel Henderson's illegal activities were known and he was virtually under house arrest as well as his accomplice dead, his own future suddenly looked extremely bleak. Although Major Neville's note had not stipulated what Colonel Henderson's crimes were, it nevertheless left him in no doubt as to their seriousness and that he himself was heavily implicated by virtue of abducting Miss Ferrers. If he complied with Major Neville's request by either handing himself over to Major Denham or, indeed, even to himself, with assurances of protection until such time as he could be placed into General Turville's safe custody, then he could be certain of facing his trial, and he was quite sure that his past career would very soon become known and used against him, which would do very little if anything to assist him. Should he in fact fail to surrender himself then he could see nothing but an uncertain future on the run as a fugitive from justice, and although at the moment this seemed to be by far the better option, there were no guarantees as to how long he could evade capture and arrest. He had made himself indispensable to Colonel Henderson, who, in return for services rendered, had ensured him being excused certain duties and effectively permitting him to do very much as he pleased, but now that he was no longer around to shield him from Major Denham he decided that he would much prefer to take his chances and hope that he could make it across the Channel to France before he was sighted and apprehended. Unfortunately for him however, every penny he had was safely tucked away at the garrison, and as no captain would allow him to board his vessel without payment up front, then he had no choice but to return there to collect his belongings as well as his ill-gotten gains. According to his calculations there had not been sufficient time for Major Neville to report his findings to Major Denham, and therefore felt it safe to make his way back to Hampton Regis while it was still dark, thereby cutting down the risk of being seen.

Having made the decision to trust to luck in reaching the coast to board a packet to France, where he had no doubt he could put his many talents to profitable use, his spirits began to rise, especially when he considered that it would only be for an indefinite period. He had no intention of remaining there for the rest of his days, and once the hue and cry had died down here then he had every expectation of returning, by which time he doubted they would still be on the look out for him. Unfortunately however, his calculations had failed to take into account the most mundane of eventualities such as discovering his horse had cast a shoe, a circumstance that could not have been more mistimed. Ordinarily this would not have posed a problem, but with no blacksmith within a three mile radius of Hamstoke House and every horse and vehicle in the stables having been taken by Major Neville, this unlooked for incident began to assume gigantic proportions. Having more than enough on his mind and even more to do, Cartwright could offer no suggestion to solve his difficulty other than that of leaving the nag here and walking back to Hampton Regis, especially as remaining at Hamstoke House until the morning when he could arrange to have his horse shod was out of the question. There really seemed to be nothing else he could do but walk every inch of the way back, a prospect he was not looking forward to with any obvious degree of pleasure, because not only had it come on to rain again but it would mean he would not reach the garrison before it began to get light.

As it was no business of his what Colonel Henderson got up to providing he kept to his part of the bargain by shielding him from any disciplinary action Major Denham may wish to impose as well as greasing him in the fist, he had asked no questions, believing that ignorance would serve him better, but he had certainly not expected to find himself in such a fix as this. Since he had no idea where Major Neville had taken Colonel Henderson he could waste no time in trying to find him, and even if he did he failed to see what he could do considering that his own position would likely be such as to render him quite useless. It was therefore in a mood of considerable bitterness and resentment that he set out on the long trek back to Hampton Regis, having to continually avoid the pot holes made treacherous by the heavy rain, as well as leaving the road altogether to skirt hamlets and villages in case the word had already gone out, giving not a moment's thought to the horse he had left behind at Hamstoke House or how Cartwright would either return it or explain its presence to Sir Evelyn. After almost three hours of trudging in the pouring rain with hardly a stitch on him that was not soaked through, he arrived at the garrison, his temper all the more exacerbated by the fact that it was now quite light and his entrance, far from being the unobtrusive access he had planned, was witnessed by the guards on the gatehouse. But from their reception it was obvious that no order had been given to either apprehend or arrest him which could only mean that news of recent events had not yet been carried to Major Denham. Used to his antics, the guards, apart from knowing looks and ribald teasing, allowed him to pass into the courtyard unmolested, unaware of the sigh of relief which left his lips as he made his way to the privates' quarters.

By the time Major Denham had recovered sufficiently from learning of his commanding officer's iniquitous activities from Sir John and Major Neville to begin a search of the garrison for Private Smith, it was just turned quarter past twelve. Unfortunately, as several hours had passed this nefarious individual, on another purloined horse from the stable while the farrier sergeant was out of the way, having emerged from the garrison within half an hour of his arrival without any mishap, was halfway to the coast, blissfully unaware that he was about to be pursued and apprehended.

Michael, presenting himself to Major Denham over an hour after leaving Ferrers Court, was apprehensive of his reception, because even though he had been placed under General Turville's orders, albeit temporarily, he knew his senior officer well enough to feel confident that he would most probably be subjected to a sharp reprimand. It was therefore much to his astonishment that no such reproof was forthcoming, indeed, so benign was Major Denham that for a moment he wondered if he were imagining it, never for one second thinking that it was his own shame over his dogmatic belief in discipline that almost caused an innocent man to hang, but when he was invited to take a seat and tell him precisely what had occurred over the last thirty six hours or so, he felt quite unable to do so. Major Denham, realizing that there was more to this young officer than he had been led to suppose and that perhaps his strict discipline in the past was responsible for his present uncertainty, began to issue words of encouragement in a voice as near to buoyancy as he could manage, requesting him to enlighten him as to the recent sequence of events. Swallowing an uncomfortable lump which had suddenly formed in his throat, Michael, casting an anxious glance at the unusually softened features of his senior officer, but detecting nothing to suggest he was being led into condemning himself to a charge of dereliction of duty or something equally as detrimental to his career, relaxed sufficiently to be able to relate the course of events and the part he had played in them. Much to his relief Major Denham nodded his head approvingly, saying that although it was to be deeply regretted that Colonel Henderson had taken such a despicable course, he would have expected no less from an officer in the King's service to expose such a felony no matter how distasteful.

Considerably heartened by this, Michael then enquired about Private Smith and was told that a thorough search was in hand covering a wide radius, including the coastal ports in case he decided to try and cross the Channel to France. A perfunctory smile left Major Denham's lips as he offered congratulations on a job well done, and without waiting for a response he quickly followed this up by saying that in view of the hectic time he had had of late, he was excused duty until tomorrow, advising that he catch up on his sleep. Unable to believe he had heard him correctly, Michael looked warily across the desk at the face which was steadily regarding him, his doubt clearly visible. "That is an order, Lieutenant" he said firmly. "You are no good to me half asleep!"

Somehow Michael found his voice to thank him, then after saluting he hurriedly made his exit, dazed and a little confused by the unexpected change in Major Denham's attitude. By far too relieved to look into the reasons to account for this, he fervently hoped that this augured well for their future dealings and also that Gideon's interview with Sir Arthur had progressed equally as well.

Having risen from the breakfast table a bare half hour before Gideon arrived at The Manor, Sir Arthur, who had not long sat down in his book room to peruse a copy of the London Gazette or some other periodical, a daily ritual which every member of the household was perfectly well aware of and fully respected, or, to be more precise, dared not disturb him, was not best pleased when informed that he had a visitor, and a Major to boot. Since he had no idea what a representative of the military could possibly want with him, his initial reaction was to adamantly refuse to see him, but being by nature a man who liked to know what was going forward, curiosity won the day and therefore instructed Marsh, his equally interested butler, to show him in. His stiff greeting was certainly not an auspicious beginning to the meeting, but Gideon's unruffled and dexterous handling gradually began to demolish the aloof barrier he had erected as well as having a most beneficial affect on the man who held Richard's happiness in the palm of his hand. Richard may have gone headlong into a situation which had brought near disastrous results down on his head, but he was not so careless or ramshackle as to recklessly disregard the dictates governing society. He may feel like scaling the ramparts and carrying Miss Trench off across his saddle bow, something which would hold instant appeal to that adventurous young man, but as this would surely condemn them both in the eyes of polite society, he was left instead to wait for Sir Arthur to relent with what patience he could muster.

Gideon was perfectly happy to promote Richard's cause, but it had taken time and patience to persuade his host that he was speaking the truth and not practising some cruel cajolery merely to aid and abet the star crossed lovers. Initially, Sir Arthur, every inch the man Richard had described him to be, was very much on his dignity and very far from relenting, listening to the edited version of the tale Gideon saw fit to unfold with patent distrust, clearly suspecting a trick of some kind, but when he eventually realized that it was indeed no ruse but the unvarnished truth, with baffled incredulity. Gideon, fast gaining the impression that it was not Richard's innocence which Sir Arthur had difficulty in coming to terms with, so much as knowing that he had all this time judged him on gossip alone, as well as severing all ties with his father and Ferrers Court, had allowed him time to take in all he had been told. This ostracism, based purely on the rumours he had heard which had been maliciously put abroad by Colonel Henderson and William Ferrers, had now placed him in the disagreeable position of having to face the unpalatable thought of offering an apology. Like Major Denham, he could not bear to think that he was in the wrong, but an innate sense of justice made it possible for him to accept that on this occasion he had been too easily swayed by gossip. His dread of scandal or anything which could taint his name even by association, had ultimately dictated he take his prejudice to the unpardonable length of cutting all ties with the Ferrers family, even going so far as to boycott Jasper's obsequies. His wife and daughter had certainly acquiesced with this decree, but he had seen the reproof which they had not been quite able to hide in their eyes, and whilst this had had very little affect on him, for some reason the steady look in Major Neville's made him feel rather ashamed. Gideon neither accused nor demanded, on the contrary, his tact and diplomacy were sufficient to render it impossible for Sir Arthur to forbid his daughter visiting Ferrers Court in order to see Richard and his sister, and since Jane had made it abundantly clear, if not by deed such as meeting him clandestinely, then by word, that she would marry Richard or no one, he was brought to finally accept the inevitable. Prior to ostracizing himself and his wife and daughter from the Ferrers family, he had not been averse to a marriage between Jane and Richard, indeed, he could think of no better alliance, and since she had turned down very eligible offers for her hand, he had been quite happy to relinquish her into Richard's care. Naturally, this view had undergone something of a change over the recent past, and the very thought of tying his daughter up in matrimony to a man hailed as a traitor turned smuggler, was so repugnant to him that he had seriously toyed with the idea of packing her off back to London to Aunt Matty without any further ado. Only her strenuous assurances that she would make no contact with Elizabeth or, indeed, anyone at Ferrers Court, or, more particularly, attempt to see Richard secretly, that he relented and permitted her to remain at The Manor. In happy ignorance of the secret correspondence between herself and Elizabeth as well as their arranged meetings when out riding, together with his acknowledgement that he had made a gross error of judgement, he eventually rang the bell pull for Marsh, requesting his daughter's presence in a voice of contrite acceptance.

Although there would only ever be one woman for him, as soon as Gideon set eyes on Jane Trench, quietly entering her father's inner sanctum in answer to his summons, he had no difficulty in understanding why Richard had fallen head over heels in love with her. Despite the fact that she was dressed in the very height of fashion, her hair was simply arranged and adorned only by a narrow band of ribbon threaded through the rich brown curls. Beneath her air of gentle calm, which was in marked contrast to Richard's more energetic nature, and her evident sincere filial respect, nothing could quite hide either her intelligence or independent spirit, components of her character which had enabled her to not only withstand her father's directives but endure her separation from Richard. Having quietly closed the door behind her she glanced enquiringly from one to the other, holding out her slender white hand as her father introduced Gideon to her, her large brown eyes conveying her puzzlement as to what the Major could possibly be doing here. Upon being told that he had come on Richard's behalf, the horrifying thought flashed into her mind that he had been injured or, worse, killed, making her heart skip a beat and all the colour leave her face. "Richard!" she exclaimed unsteadily, a trembling hand stealing to her throat, her eyes dilating in fear as she looked from her father to Gideon.

"No, no" her father assured her in a far more gentle tone than she was used to, taking several steps towards her and clasping her hands. "He is quite safe, I promise you." If he had needed further proof of his daughter's unalterable feelings for Richard Ferrers, then this spontaneous demonstration of alarm and dread at the thought of something happening to him, was surely it.

Having achieved his objective, Gideon deemed it time to depart, believing that Sir Arthur and his daughter did not need a spectator intruding in their conversation, so after reinforcing her father's assurances as to Richard's safety and relating the good news that he would soon be reinstated, politely took his leave. Had it not been for Sir Arthur's head groom, a life-long crony of Salmon, detaining him to enquire if he was the Major who had been helping Master Richard as he handed him the bridle, he would have left The Manor long before Jane came running up to him in the stable yard. After having his hand vigorously wrung by a huge and calloused paw, Gideon listened good humouredly to his acerbic opinions about the way Richard and his family had been treated, adding that he daresn't think what would have happened had he not come along when he did. Making no attempt to stem the pent-up flow of bitter reproach which left his lips about certain members of the military as well as those closer to home, indicating the house with a nod of his head, Gideon stood patiently waiting for him to come to the end of his catalogue of grievances. Keeping his own counsel, he nodded and smiled where appropriate before deftly extricating himself from one who clearly regarded him as not only a very good sort of a man, but Richard's saviour, finally ending by offering his sincere gratitude for all he had done for his late lordship's son. It had not taken this indignant monologue to inform him of the partisanship which abounded for Richard hereabouts, it merely confirmed what he had always known; that Richard and his family were held in very high regard. It was just as he was about to climb into the saddle when he heard a voice calling him, and turning round saw Jane Trench running towards him.

"Oh, Major Neville!" she cried breathlessly, "I am so glad to have caught you before you left."

"Miss Trench," Gideon bowed. "Is there something I can do for you?"

"No, no" she assured him. "It is merely that I wanted to thank you."

"Thank me?" he raised an eyebrow. "For what, pray?" he smiled.

"For all you have done," she said eagerly. "There are no words to express my gratitude."

"Indeed," he shook his head, "I have done nothing, I assure you."

"Yes," she said urgently, "you have, more than you know. You see," she smiled nervously, "I never believed Richard to be guilty, but my father, well…let us just say he can be a little proud at times, and…well, he is not a bad man, Major. Indeed," she told him sincerely, "he is the best of fathers'. It is merely …"

"You need say no more, Miss Trench" Gideon smiled kindly. "I understand perfectly."

"Yes, I think you do" she nodded, gratefully. "But you see, Major" she explained, "I know how difficult it is to turn my father away from something he has decided upon; he is not easily diverted." She hesitated for a moment. "My father told me a little of what passed between you, not everything, of course, but I realize what a task you must have had." She smiled tremulously up at him. "Would it be impertinent if I asked how you managed it?"

"Not at all. I merely told him the truth, Miss Trench" he said simply, "that Richard Ferrers is innocent of treason and that the real perpetrator is, as we speak, being escorted to London in order to face his trial. I told him too that Richard is most desirous of seeing you," he smiled down at her, emphasizing, *"as soon as possible."*

Her eyes lit up at this and the colour flooded her cheeks. "Is…is that true. Does Richard indeed wish to see me?" she asked excitedly. "I mean, after all my father has said and done!"

"With as much impatience as you wish to see him" Gideon replied sincerely.

"Yes, I am impatient to see him," she replied truthfully, her colour deepening. "Tell me, how…how is Richard?" she asked apprehensively, her eyes searching his face. "It has been so long since I have seen him."

"I promise you he is well, in fact," he told her truthfully, "when I left him this morning he was in excellent spirits;" he hesitated, not wishing to embarrass her, then said with quiet sincerity, "but he is missing you very much."

She let out a sigh of relief. "How can I ever thank you?" she asked earnestly, resting a light hand on his arm.

"There is nothing to thank me for, I assure you," he shook his head. "Upon my honour there is not."

"You may say that, Major" she smiled, "but it is due to your representations that my father is permitting me to visit Ferrers Court after luncheon. In fact," she smiled shyly, unable to prevent the warm glow from entering her eyes, "he told me that he is even willing to see Richard tomorrow morning."

After taking her hand and raising it to his lips, he said with real pleasure, "I am glad of that." He smiled down at her. "And knowing that that happy circumstance makes you as delighted as I know it will Richard, renders any obligation you felt owed me is now discharged." Then after bowing over her hand climbed into the saddle.

"Major," she forestalled him, "you say the obligation is discharged and there is nothing to thank you for, but, indeed, there is; you have given me what I thought to be lost for ever, and you must allow me to do so now as it is most unlikely that we shall meet again."

"On the contrary, Miss Trench" he smiled amusingly down at her, "since I am soon to become Richard's brother-in-law that makes us in some sort related, and therefore we shall most certainly meet again."

Her eyes widened at this. "You mean you are going to marry Elizabeth?"

"That is precisely what I mean," he grinned. "Although," he pointed out ruefully, "I have not yet got round to formally asking her."

She smiled. "You must know Major, that Elizabeth is my oldest and dearest friend."

"I *do* know," he nodded.

"It is because of our friendship," she told him, "that I feel her present indisposition so particularly, and also that I can safely say she will not decline your most obliging offer."

"I trust your conviction entirely, Miss Trench" he smiled, leaning down to take her hand and raise it to his lips.

"Major Neville," she insisted, gripping his fingers, "I know you say I owe you nothing, but I am fully conscious of the debt I owe you for bringing my father round. You *must* at least allow me to acknowledge it."

"Very well, Miss Trench," he nodded, "I will allow you to acknowledge it." Then looking down into her upturned face, a twinkle lurking at the back of his eyes, said humorously "However, if, indeed, you believe you do stand in my debt and wish to remunerate it, you may do so by attempting to keep Richard out of trouble, at least," he smiled, "until my return in a few days time."

She laughed. "You may be sure of it, Major."

He brushed her hand with his lips. "It has been a very great pleasure to

563

meet *and* serve you Miss Trench, and look forward to seeing you again soon." Upon which he straightened up then turned his horse and trotted out through the gate towards the main entrance, pleased to know that he was not too far behind General Turville.

Following Gideon's departure, Richard waited only long enough to issue instructions to a groom before striding up the rear steps into the house and setting up a cry for Salmon. Half an hour later, having discarded his vivid dressing gown for his more habitual black coat, he tapped softly on Elizabeth's door, a little surprised to find it opened almost immediately by Miss Calne. Adamantly refusing him admittance to his sister's room on the grounds that she had only a moment ago woken up and was not yet fit to be seen, softened her refusal by adding that she would be ready to receive visitors later, providing, of course, Dr. Jarvey considered her well enough, but in the meantime if he would care to hand over the Major's letter she would make sure she received it. Richard, instantly taking exception to this, stated impatiently that he was not a visitor but her brother and if she thought she could prevent him from seeing Elizabeth then she was very much mistaken. Miss Calne, her abhorrence of men apart, not only believed that even a brother should not enter his sister's room until she was decently presentable, but was sufficiently well acquainted with his impetuosity to enable her to withstand his fierce demand to allow him to see her with tolerable equanimity. Nothing, she told him determinedly, seeing the pugnacious expression descend on his face, would move her from this stance, and therefore had the doubtful pleasure of watching him stride away towards the stairs in a mood of considerable irritation.

All too familiar with Miss Calne's notions of propriety, Elizabeth was not at all surprised to learn that she had barred her brother her bedchamber, but easily forgave her for depriving her of his company the instant she was handed Gideon's note. Had Miss Calne the least idea that it contained such affectionate, not to say amorous, words and phrases such as *'my very own darling'* and *'I can't bear to leave you even for a few days'*, she would have been deeply shocked, feeling it to be her duty to snatch it out of her fingers, but since her charge had no intention of relating such spine-tingling expressions of love, she remained in blissful ignorance. Looking at her overseer from under her lashes Elizabeth smiled, then after reading the note a second time kissed the sheet of vellum before folding it back into its creases to place it under her pillow, just as Susan entered the room carrying her cup of chocolate.

Having savoured the contents of Gideon's note again an hour later, its every word evoking the same delicious response, Dr. Jarvey, arriving a bare two minutes after she had returned it to its hideaway under her pillow, took one look at her flushed face and told her firmly she was running a fever, just as he had suspected and therefore it would be necessary to cup her, something he should have done yesterday when he attended her. Since she could hardly tell him that the reason for her inflamed cheeks had nothing whatsoever to do with her wound, but, on the contrary, a far more pleasurable one, it took all her powers of persuasion to dissuade him from carrying out this unpleasant course of action. He pursed his lips and shook his head, warning her vigorously about the folly of dispensing with such a simple remedy which, were she not so stubborn, must know that it would render her more comfortable as well as reduce her high temperature, but as his patient was determined that not one drop of her blood was going to be extracted, he set to work on removing the dressing, protesting and condemning such an imprudent decision while he did so. She may have been able to hide the truth surrounding the cause of her flushed cheeks, but she could not hide the sharp intake of breath or her momentary feeling of giddiness as his fingers deftly uncovered the hole in her shoulder. Inspecting the wound with close scrutiny he then nodded his head approvingly at the way it was healing, but Miss Calne, standing rigidly upright on the opposite of the bed, saw Elizabeth's colour recede as he gently began to pat it with a pad of muslin, onto which he had emptied the contents of a vial which he had retrieved from his bag. It seemed he would never stop dabbing it, but after what seemed an interminable length of time he eventually finished this necessary but painful task, and after applying Basilcum Powder bound a fresh dressing round it and told her that it was coming along just as it should, adding, not without a touch of reproach, that she would be better if she allowed him to bleed her. She shook her head, glad to rest back against the pillows, watching him through half closed lids as he returned his evil looking instruments and paraphernalia to his bag, his face bearing the expression of one who was suffering from exasperation over her recalcitrance in allowing him to cup her and frustration at her brother's adamant refusal to take him fully into his confidence. Of course, he quite appreciated Richard's predicament and his earnest desire to say or do nothing which could possibly impede the enquiry which was currently taking place, but whilst he had agreed to Richard's promise to tell him the whole tale when he was in a better position to do so, it nevertheless rendered carrying out his duties, such as recording his cousin's death and all the officialdom that accompanied it, extremely difficult. Against his better judgement he had allowed himself to be overborne on all counts, but when he heard her weakly mention about leaving her bed he was determined to have his way and categorically refused to sanction such a thing, stating purposefully that she had already seen fit to disregard his advice about being bled, and unless she wished to be confined to bed indefinitely she would do as she was bid, whereupon he wished both ladies good morning.

Having returned Michael's borrowed horse to its owner and spent a good half hour talking to his crony, Richard had then enjoyed a good gallop over the downs before returning home, his frustration at being refused admittance to his sister's room as though he were a schoolboy bent on plaguing the life out of her, having by now disappeared. Being informed by his groom that the doctor had arrived about half an ago, he strode round to the front of the house just as this worthy was about to climb up into his gig, but upon setting eyes on his patient's brother, waited until he came up to him, his frown informing Richard that he was in no very good humour. Upon asking how he had found his sister, the frown deepened, telling him in no uncertain terms that Miss Elizabeth was, without doubt, his most obstinate patient, and if she ended in a high fever then he for one would not be at all surprised considering how she continually ignored his advice. In response to Richard's raised eyebrows he poured forth his grievances, whether actual or imaginary his listener was not at all sure, but if nothing else he gathered from the impassioned outpourings that whilst Elizabeth was progressing just as she ought, he had nevertheless detected signs of a high temperature, but not only had she refused to let him bleed her but had begun to talk of leaving her bed. *"And if, Sir"* he said awfully, climbing onto the box, "you could persuade her as to the folly of disregarding my instructions, which will only hamper her recovery, I would own myself obliged. I shall call again tomorrow, when," he nodded, "I shall expect to find Miss Ferrers more biddable. Good day, Sir!"

Entering the house Richard lingered only long enough to drop his gloves and riding whip onto a table before taking the stairs two at a time, arriving at Elizabeth's bedchamber within half a dozen strides. Without waiting for a response to his tap on the door, he unceremoniously thrust it open, only to be pulled up short by the sight of his sister walking unsteadily towards a chaise longue against the far wall. "What the deuce!" he cried, advancing purposefully towards her.

Having taken advantage of Miss Calne's leaving the room to attend her aunt, she had managed to throw off the covers and sit on the edge of the bed to pull on her dressing gown which lay draped across a chair just to the right of the four poster. Although it had been an agonizing few minutes to try and ease first her left arm into the sleeve and then the other without assistance, she could not help but feel quite proud of her achievement. Refusing to admit that Dr. Jarvey was right when he had said it was much too soon to be thinking of getting out of bed, she considered that the short distance from the four poster to the chaise longue was well within her capabilities. Of all things she detested it was lying in bed doing nothing, after all, it was not as though she were ill, and was therefore convinced her recovery would be greatly assisted if she were not cosseted and treated like an invalid, having everything done for her. No sooner had she put her feet to the floor than she realized her theory was very different to actually putting it into practice, having failed to take into account that her legs, when her full weight was on them, were far too unstable to carry her very far, and that the movement set off the throbbing ache in her arm. "Oh, Richard! Is that you?" she heaved a sigh of relief upon hearing his voice.

"Well, of course it's me!" he replied irritably. "Who the devil do you think it is? And just what, may I ask," he enquired impatiently, "do you think you're doing." Without giving her time to reply to this he picked her effortlessly up in his arms and carried her straight back to bed, to which she took instant exception by telling him roundly that she was not a child. "Then stop acting like one," he told her, his tone a nice mix of severity and anxiety, as he pulled the covers over her. "I've just seen Jarvey," he nodded darkly, "and he's far from pleased with you, let me tell you."

"I daresay ..." she began.

"And if you think," he warned her, "that I am going to be subjected to another homily from him simply because you won't do as you are told, then you are fair and far off!"

She giggled. "Oh no! Did he really?"

"Yes, *really*," he retorted, rather concerned over how pale she looked. "And *you*," he said firmly, brooking no argument, "are going to remain just where you are until he says otherwise." She watched him pick up the glass Dr. Jarvey had left containing the soporific draught which she unequivocally told him was horrid, but ignoring her protests sat down and gently raised her with his right arm, holding the glass menacingly in his other hand. Shaking her head and tightly closing her lips, he said evocatively, "You drank it last night." She shot a look up at him. "Oh, yes" he nodded, "my aunt told me how Gideon got you to swallow it. I can only guess his methods of persuasion," he told her, unable to prevent the twinkle in his eye, "but I am not he. Now drink." She sighed, but dutifully doing what she was told took several sips. "All of it," he ordered, ignoring her screwed up face and putting the glass to her lips. "If Gideon takes my advice," he commented, placing the empty glass down, "he'll beat you." She pulled a face at him. "I doubt he will though!" Then after admonishing her to behave herself and go to sleep, he smiled, asking conspiratorially, "Did Miss Calne give you his letter?" She nodded and smiled up at him, her eyes revealing more than she knew. "Don't worry, he'll be back soon," he promised.

"What about Sir Arthur?" she asked.

"I don't know," he shrugged. "It may have taken Gideon longer to persuade him than I thought. Don't worry your head over it." Then bending down he kissed her forehead and left her to sleep.

He could not pretend to be anything other than worried over his sister. No one knew better than he just how stubborn and determined she could be once she set her mind to something, but could only hope that now she had discovered for herself that attempting anything in the way of getting up was out of the question for the time being, there would be no more such attempts. Taking a look in on his aunt before going downstairs and finding her in a good humour, he kissed her affectionately on the cheek, grinning that she was looking as fine as fivepence. "I can't think why!" she snapped, not quite able to hide the affection she had for him; her eagle eyes softening as they looked up into his face, apostrophizing him as a flatterer. Upon being asked if he had seen Elizabeth yet he told her that he had, and pulling up a chair gave her a brief description of what had happened, at the end of which she gave it as her opinion that the sooner the chit was married the better, because it seemed to her that the only one she would listen to was the Major. He agreed to it, but felt it behoved him to remind her that since Gideon still had a fair bit to do to before they could see the end of their difficulties, not to mention his own affairs such as resigning his commission and visiting his home, it would be awhile yet before he would be walking his sister down the aisle. She accepted this readily enough and Richard, seeing that she was already making wedding plans for which she did not need his input, left her soon after in agreeable contemplation.

Encountering Salmon in the hall as he descended the stairs he told him that there were some letters he needed to write which would require taking to the receiving office, and after being assured that this would be done, he strode into the book room at the rear of the house, closing the door firmly behind him. Ten minutes later, just as he was addressing the first of his letters, an unexpected visit from Captain Waring took him completely by surprise, raising his eyes from the letter to stare incredulously at the very last man he expected to see. But Richard had a sense of humour, and coupled with his generous nature, bore him no grudge for his relentless pursuit of him and therefore was perfectly ready and willing to receive him, walking round the desk with his hand outstretched. At first it seemed as though that diligent young man was going to refuse to take it, but the glint of pure amusement in Richard's blue eyes as they looked at him broke down the stiff reserve he had erected, and unbent sufficiently to shake it. His visit lasted three-quarters of an hour, during the course of which he refused to partake of any refreshment offered, whether this was due to the fact that he could not be certain if the wine had been illegally imported or not Richard was not certain, but accepted his rejection of a liquid stimulant gracefully. Having placed his trust as well as his confidence in Colonel Henderson, Captain Waring had been deeply shocked to learn the truth about a man whom he had regarded as not only above reproach but assiduous in the extreme. To discover these beliefs were totally misplaced had caused him to seriously doubt his own judgement, and although he had never for one moment had reason to doubt him about Richard Ferrers' activities, to now find himself face to face with the man he had hounded without any evidence to prove his involvement in illicit trading, rendered him acutely uncomfortable. Major Denham had been quite explicit in his explanation when accounting for Richard Ferrers' lengthy association with a group of individuals whom he had spent months in tracking down, and that far from participating in the trade had simply adopted them as a means of much needed sanctuary until he had retrieved the evidence to clear his name. He by no means liked the idea of an innocent man taking a walk to the gallows and even less to knowing that he had helped him on his way; his only solace therefore was knowing that he had been merely doing his duty and carrying out his orders, and since his host appeared to be neither vindictive nor hostile by the time he took his leave he had come to the conclusion that Richard Ferrers was in fact a decent and honest man who had been unjustly maligned. Accepting his reason for his actions as well as his apology with good-natured amiability, Richard walked with him to the front door, grasping the hand held out to him while smiling down into the serious grey eyes with such a look of devilment lurking in his blue ones that for one awful moment Captain Waring's soul was seized with doubt; so much so, that as he rode away he was not at all certain whether Richard Ferrers had in fact smuggled contraband or not.

By the time he said goodbye to Captain Waring, quite aware of the uncertainty he had raised in his breast, and returned to the book room to begin writing his second letter, it was almost two o'clock. He was trying not to think of how Gideon had fared at The Manor, but if anyone could persuade Sir Arthur into accepting the truth as well as influencing him to change his decision about himself and Jane, then it was he, but as the minutes ticked by he began to think that he had not been successful. Gideon had left here early this morning, and as it was only a short step to The Manor, he felt sure that whatever the outcome he would have known it by now, not from Gideon himself as the plan was he would immediately set out after Sir John, but he had fully expected a note delivered by the hand of a groom from Sir Arthur either informing him of the meeting's failure and that his decision remained firm or requesting his presence in order to discuss matters. Biting down his frustration he resumed his second letter to Pritchard, the nib of his pen scraping across the vellum as he advised him of the current position and his subsequent instructions in a strong upright hand. Having cast off his gloom for long enough to deal with his correspondence, he was just shaking sand over the three sheets when he heard a tap on the door. Believing it was Salmon he called to him to come in and without looking up, said "Ah, Salmon you're just ..."

"I am afraid I have dismissed Salmon," he was told in a gentle voice that was as familiar to him as his own. "I hope you do not mind."

Looking up at the face he thought he would never see again, he dropped the shaker onto the desk from suddenly nerveless fingers. *"Jane!"* he cried in a strangled voice, the chair scraping on the floorboards as he got up and strode round the desk. "Jane!"

"Hello, Richard," she smiled shyly.

Taking hold of her hands he stood looking down at her slightly bemused. "Is it really you?" he asked unsteadily.

"Yes," she nodded. "It's really me," her large brown eyes lovingly searching his face.

He shook his head, but when he could see that she was no figment of his imagination but very real, a burning need entered his eyes as they hungrily devoured every inch of her "So, Gideon did manage it, after all," he said almost inaudibly.

"If you mean the Major" she smiled, her heart beating so fast she was amazed she could speak at all, "yes. I don't know what he said to papa precisely, but ..."

"It's of no consequence," he shook his head. "You are here and that is all that matters. Just tell me one thing," he asked urgently, "do you still love me?" She could only manage a nod of her head as her throat felt suddenly dry, rendering speech impossible. He smiled, a crooked little smile she remembered so well, then as if he could contain himself no longer he pulled her roughly into his arms and thoroughly kissed her, leaving her breathless and quite convinced that her lips were bruised and several ribs cracked. When she was at last able to speak, and then hardly above a whisper, she pointed out these two very minor inconveniences, to which he laughed, not very steadily, before kissing her again with even more urgency. No cry of protest left her lips or any attempts to escape his strong arms as they crushed her to him, just a joyous capitulation to the man she loved; a capitulation Richard eagerly accepted.

"I thought I would never see you again," he told her in a ragged voice, when he finally released her lips.

"I know," she sighed. "Oh, Richard, how I have prayed for this moment," she cried into his shoulder. "And now it is here, I can hardly believe it!"

"Believe it," Richard said firmly, cupping her face in his trembling fingers.

She smiled mistily up at him. "It is like a miracle!"

"I know," he nodded. "I have so much to thank Gideon for; not the least being my life, but this particular debt I can never repay!" he shook his head.

"You like the Major, don't you?" she said softly.

"Yes; if I didn't," he told her, "I would never permit him to marry my sister. Do you?"

"Oh yes, very much," she said readily. "I know I only met him briefly, but he is a man one can place one's whole trust in."

"*I* certainly have. Without him," he sighed, holding her close, "God only knows where I'd be now!"

"I think he is just the right man for Elizabeth," she smiled, when he had released her from a suffocating hold. "I am so happy for her."

"I daresay she'll have him eating out of her hand nine times out of ten," he remarked amusedly.

"Of course she will," she laughed, "but you need have no fears for her. I know they will be very happy."

Some time later, seated side by side on a small sofa, her head resting comfortably on his shoulder and his arm around her waist, the time seemed to fly by as they had so much to say to one another, and not until a chance look at the clock on the mantelshelf did they realize that two hours had past without them being aware of it. She was in no hurry to leave the warm protection of his arms, but since she had promised her father she would not stay too long, reluctantly raised her head from his shoulder, smiling up at him in a way that rendered it necessary for him to exercise every ounce of restraint. He did not try to detain her, not only because his feelings were such that he could so easily throw caution to the winds and make love to her there and then, but also because he had no wish to alienate Sir Arthur by taking advantage of this visit and thereby run the risk of him reneging on his change of heart.

She was sorry not to see Elizabeth, but she had no wish to disturb her rest, and therefore Richard promised to give Elizabeth her love as well as the posy she had brought with her and left on the table in the hall. In no hurry to part company with her he accompanied her to the stables, and with her arm tucked comfortably in his they slowly made their way round to the rear of the house. A deep chuckle suddenly left her throat, causing him to stop and look down at her, her eyes looking provocatively up him, saying huskily, "I see you are not taking me the to the stables via the shrubbery as I recall you doing on a previous occasion!"

He smiled warmly down at her. "I'll take you anywhere you wish to go," he said hoarsely.

"Oh, Richard!" she cried, laying a hand against his cheek. "Don't you know, I am already where I wish to be."

As a groom had emerged with her horse and was looking in their direction, Richard had to content himself with kissing the palm of her hand, his eyes blazing with an intensity that took her breath away. Disregarding the mounting block which had been brought out for her use, Richard cupped his hands and hoisted her into the saddle himself, then taking her gloved hand kissed it. "Until tomorrow," he said warmly. "Tell your papa I shall see him as he asked at eleven o'clock."

She nodded, then turning her horse rode out of the stable yard, but not until she had gone from sight did he return to the house, a feeling of euphoria tinged with disbelief running through him.

CHAPTER TWENTY NINE

Having made good time, Sir John and his entourage were two miles the other side of Uckfield when Gideon eventually came up with them, and after enquiring how he had fared with Sir Arthur, Sir John then told him that he hoped to make East Grinstead within the next two hours, and if their luck continued and the rain held off, hopefully they would reach London before nightfall. In response to Gideon's enquiry about Colonel Henderson he was told that all things considered he appeared remarkably reconciled to his lot, then twisting round in the saddle to cast an eye over him said, "Not that I'm complaining mind you, but the sooner we reach our destination, the happier I'll be."

Considering the state of the roads their progress was surprisingly swift, reaching East Grinstead by about half past two and so far it seemed that luck was indeed with them, because the rain, despite it being overcast, had held off. Bringing the men to a halt just as they approached the outskirts of the busy market town, Sir John briefly consulted his watch then looking at Gideon riding alongside him at the head of the escort, asked him what he thought about holding up here for a spell in order to rest the horses and have something to eat and drink themselves or continue their journey. As there were as yet still about thirty miles to go and it would take several hours to cover them, Gideon, after taking a look at the men as well as casting an eye over their mounts, decided that they were fit for a few more miles, explaining that the garrison at Drayton Weir was in some sort a half way house and it was only fifteen miles further on, and that far again to London. If they were fortunate in that the light and weather held by the time they had changed horses there and refreshed themselves they could resume their journey and arrive at the barracks before it got dark, but should both these natural elements fail then they could hold up for the night at the garrison. Sir John, after considering this for a moment or two, nodded his head in agreement and in response to his signal the entire party rode forward, clattering along the main street under the interested and fascinated stares of the town's inhabitants.

As nothing untoward occurred to mar or impede their progress they finally arrived at Drayton Weir just as it came onto rain. It seemed at first as though it was only going to be a short light drizzle, but by the time the official preliminaries had been concluded with General Turville and the Colonel in charge of the garrison, all the signs pointed to it lasting well into the night. The decision having been taken to remain until the morning, it was regarded by all concerned that Colonel Henderson, irrespective of his crimes, was an officer and therefore installing him in a cell in the prison block would most likely create awkwardness for the guards and embarrassment for him, and was therefore housed in Colonel Currie's quarters. After ensuring the horses had been stabled and rubbed down and the men fed and quartered, Gideon then joined Sir John and Colonel Currie, together with his staff officer, for dinner, a long drawn out affair that lasted well after lights out.

But despite the lateness of the hour when the evening finally broke up in Colonel Currie's quarters, Sir John and Gideon, together with the escort company, left Drayton Weir betimes, relieved that the previous evening's downpour had given way to a bright sunny morning, auguring a warm day. The last fifteen miles were accomplished without any mishap or hindrance, the party arriving at the barracks just before eleven o'clock, Sir John commenting favourably that they had made good time, then in a quiet aside to Gideon remarked that he was not sorry to get their prisoner here in one piece, because no matter how docile he had proved himself to be, no reliance could be placed on a man in his position continuing to behave rationally.

Having come to accept the inevitable with a calm complacency that was totally out of character, Colonel Henderson was certainly docile, but behind that outward appearance of submission his brain was busily occupied with evaluating the various ways and means of depriving the public as well as its executioner of a trial and execution. He was of the same mind now as he had been when first arriving at such a momentous decision, and whilst it was something he was not looking forward to with any degree of relish, he considered it a far better prospect that witnessing his own public condemnation. He could expect neither understanding nor sympathy, let alone leniency, from the judiciary, and therefore he was more than resigned to the course he was preparing to embark on.

From the moment they had left Ferrers Court until now he could have made a run for it at any time; especially as how they had not deemed it necessary to manacle his hands. Had he have been fortunate enough to have apprehended Richard Ferrers only to discover he had effected an escape he would have known no hesitation in ordering his men to shoot on sight, but General Turville would not have issued such an order to his men, they would merely have ridden after him and apprehended him, keeping him under even closer surveillance. Should he have made such an attempt it would have served no purpose other than to put them on their guard, never leaving him alone for a second, and considering what he intended, such close scrutiny would not serve his purpose in the least. Having gone from the hunter to the hunted may be considered by some to be nothing short of poetic justice, but he could not fail to detect a touch of irony in his unexpected change of fortune.

He was not a particularly brave man, nor did he possess any of the attributes accorded to the heroes of legend. Not for him the rescuing of a lady in distress or rising nobly to the occasion in order to save the day, and certainly not if these deeds posed the least degree of risk to himself. Being a man entirely governed by his own interests and one, moreover, who would always look to himself, had, upon the humiliating discovery that his future prospects in the military were not looking any too propitious, known no hesitation about advancing himself in the cause of a man, who, if successful, could bring him untold rewards. His efforts to promote as well as defend himself had been carried out with a fierce determination that knew no bounds, and were it not for that damning correspondence, not even Major Neville's assiduousness would have been sufficient to denounce him.

Both Sir John and Gideon, relieved to have him safely installed in the barracks, soon began to put in motion the necessary procedures for his trial. The prosecution of a fellow officer for treason as well as cold-blooded murder and abduction could not help but be a most painful affair; but the thought that an innocent man could have gone to the gallows purely on his endorsement, rendered the ordeal less harrowing. It could not be said that Gideon was looking forward to the forthcoming trial with any degree of satisfaction, but he was realistic enough to know that it was not only unavoidable but essential; even justifiable, given the nature of the charges. Had Colonel Henderson embarked on such a course out of conviction, then his reasons for doing so may have met with some sympathy from one or two members of the court especially considering his forebears loyalties, although the sentence could not be anything other than what had been meted out to others, but there would still be the other indictments to answer which could not be looked upon in the same light, and certainly more than enough to see him climb the scaffold. Not even His Grace would support a man on trial for murder and abduction.

Apart from snatching a few minutes here and there to write some personal letters; one to each of his parent's and one to Billings, his father's man of business, and the other to Richard, enclosing one to Elizabeth, his normal duties as well as preparing Colonel Henderson's pending trial in company with civilian officials, whose ideas ran contrary to those of the military, kept Gideon pretty much occupied over the next few days. Far too busy in fact to put his mind to the question of putting his papers in, deciding this would have to wait until after the hearing, but Sir John, who had been pondering this unhappy prospect with more than ordinarily deep thought for some days, rather hoped that he could dissuade him, and broached the matter with him at the earliest opportunity.

"I realize, of course," he said gruffly, "that you have your reasons, but if some way could be found to easing your father's predicament, would you take it?" He saw the crease which descended onto Gideon's forehead, and without giving him time to respond to this, pointed out, "You don't need me to tell you in what good opinion I hold you, or how pleased I am that you have once again justified my faith in you with all you have accomplished of late."

An acknowledging nod of the head was all the answer Gideon vouchsafed to this. He knew full well in what light he was regarded by Sir John, and was sincerely touched by it, but the fact remained his father's heart condition, whilst stable if he refrained from exertion, was precarious, and even though Billings was perfectly capable of holding the reins until he himself took them from him, he could not in all conscience shelve his responsibilities to his father. "I'm sorry, Sir" he offered apologetically, "I cannot. Indeed, Sir," he smiled ruefully, "you must not ask it of me. I *cannot* leave my father with an estate he is in no fit case to administer."

Sir John nodded, reluctantly accepting the inevitable. "I thought that is what you would say," he sighed. "You must not be thinking that I do not honour you for your decision," he told him truthfully, "I do, but the damnable thing is that good officers' are hard to find, and I have been most fortunate in having the very best in you!"

Gideon thanked him warmly for this tribute, to which Sir John impatiently waved a hand. Feeling something more was required, Gideon briefly explained that during the course of his eight years of army service, apart from the months on sick leave, he had not been able to visit his home as often as he would have liked, and when he had it was only fleetingly. It was with unashamed affection that he spoke of his parent's and Burroughs Croft as well as his desire to return there with all possible speed to not only offer his father all the support at his command, but also to endow a home on his wife, stating unequivocally that he had no desire for her to follow the drum.

"It's Elizabeth Ferrers, of course?" Sir John raised an enquiring eyebrow.

"Yes, Sir" Gideon smiled.

"I thought so," he nodded. "Well, I wish you happy m'boy. Couldn't marry into a finer family!"

"No, Sir" Gideon agreed, "I know," going on to explain that although he had thoroughly enjoyed his time in the military he had no reservations about the step he was about to take.

Sir John nodded. "Very well, m'boy," he conceded, seeing that he could not be diverted, "put your papers in when you're ready."

Gideon was just on the point of thanking him when the door was unceremoniously flung open and a young and out of breath subaltern burst in, totally disregarding the practice of knocking on his commanding officer's door. His stricken face was alarmingly pale, bearing all the appearance of one who had undergone a tremendous shock, and his eyes, horrified and dilated, looked fearfully from one to the other as if seeking direction, his mouth opening and closing as he strove to speak. Upon discovering that Major Neville was not at his desk he had experienced a moment of unalloyed dread as he realized with a sickening thud that it would unfortunately fall to him to impart the bad news to General Turville, and without pausing to think, had consequently ran down the corridor to his room, relieved to find the Major there. General Turville, after bending a ferocious stare upon him, demanded to be told what the devil he meant by bursting into his room in such a fashion, but Gideon, after taking one look at the dazed face staring blindly at him, rose to his feet, knowing perfectly well that he would not have entered his commanding officer's room in this way without good cause, suggested he get his breath back and calm down.   This he did, or at least, sufficiently enough to say, "It's the p-prisoner, S-Sir. C-Colonel Henderson; he's dead Sir!"

Sir John rose to his feet, the chair legs scraping on the wooden floorboards. "Dead! What do you mean, dead?"

"H-he's hung himself, Sir!" he managed, covering his face with hands that visibly shook.

Gideon, whose face had suddenly become taut, looked across at Sir John who, staring in disbelief from his Personal Staff Officer to the young Second Lieutenant, bore all the appearance of having been stuffed.   It was Gideon who found his voice first, asking the young officer to tell them, as calmly as he could, what had happened.

It was several moments before Lieutenant Pulman could pull himself together sufficiently to recount what had occurred, but after swallowing and taking several deep breaths, managed, "Well, Sir," looking at Gideon, "as you know I was duty orderly," again he paused in order to compose himself.   "I had gone to the prison block ... because I had to take a report from the sergeant..."

"It's all right, Lieutenant" Gideon said quietly. "Take your time."

He swallowed.   "I had just entered the prison block Sir, about fifteen minutes ago, when I saw Private Bamford taking the prisoner something to eat, there's only one defaulter in the cells at the moment, so I knew it was for the Colonel, Sir." He stole a look at General Turville's stern and reddened face and swallowed, but turning back to face Gideon, continued unsteadily, "I had only been with Sergeant Miller a few seconds when we heard a clatter Sir, then we heard Private Bamford let out a cry before running back down the corridor to the Sergeant's room...I ..."

"Go on, Lieutenant," Gideon said steadily.

"Well, Sir" he nodded, wiping his brow, "he...he told us that he had unlocked the door to his cell and saw the Colonel hanging from a beam; he...he'd hung himself with his sword belt, Sir."

"His sword belt!" exclaimed Sir John, leaning heavily on his splayed hands.

"Yes, Sir" he nodded.   "We...we weren't quite certain what to do Sir," he gulped, not liking the look on General Turville's face, "so we cut him down and laid him on the bed, Sir. He was quite dead, Sir!"

"How the devil did he get his sword belt?" Sir John demanded, standing up to his full height, throwing an accusing stare at the Lieutenant. "I saw Major Neville remove it myself!"

"Who gave him his belt back, Lieutenant?" Gideon asked evenly when he made no answer.

Lieutenant Pulman swallowed almost convulsively and his frightened eyes stared from one senior officer to the other, but since they were waiting for an answer and would not rest until they got one, he said hesitantly, "I ...I'm not quite sure, Sir."

"I know you don't wish to get anyone into trouble," Gideon told him calmly, "but you must tell us. You don't need me to tell you how serious this is."

Lieutenant Pulman, who had no wish to be disciplined for withholding information, nodded, saying carefully "I believe it was Private Bamford, Sir. I understand that the Colonel asked him earlier this morning if he could have it because he said that he felt quite undressed without it, Sir."

"And he believed that!" thundered Sir John, banging the top of his desk with his clenched fist. "Of all the blithering idiots!"

Gideon sighed and rubbed his forehead with his fingers, his eyes clouding as they looked down into the Lieutenant's pale face. "You've told no one about this?"

"No, Sir."

"Good. Let us keep it that way for the time being. This will spread through the barracks like wildfire fast enough as it is, but for now you say nothing; is that understood?"

"Yes, Sir."

"I want you to return to the prison block," he ordered. "Tell Sergeant Miller he is to let no one in, and he and Private Bamford are to remain there. Inform Major Carlisle his presence is required in the prison quarters, but you tell him nothing. General Turville and I will join you directly."

"Yes, Sir" leaving the room on the words.

"How the devil could something like this happen?" General Turville exploded when Lieutenant Pulman had left. "Of all the mutton headed idiots!" he roared. "How could he have been stupid enough to believe such a tale about feeling undressed without his belt?"

Such an act was to be regretted, indeed, it should never have happened, but Gideon could well understand how Private Bamford would have felt overawed by a senior officer, even though that senior officer was in the prison quarters awaiting trial. Taking Colonel Henderson to Ferrers Court from Hamstoke House rather than to the garrison at Hampton Regis had been for this very reason; to prevent a junior officer or ranked man being coerced or persuaded by a senior officer. At the moment though, General Turville was in no frame of mind to listen to extenuating circumstances, and whilst Gideon accepted that Private Bamford would have to be disciplined for an act of such gross carelessness, in fact it was nothing short of dereliction of duty, considering Sir John's mood, he would much prefer to speak with him himself prior to the unavoidable enquiry he would have to face, in the meantime however, his commanding officer was seeking answers that he presently could not give him.

To the uninitiated General Turville's occasional flashes of anger could be quite daunting, but Gideon was not uninitiated and nor did he take them personally any more than he failed to see that there was every justification for them. He was himself extremely vexed over such a thing happening, as not only would it create the inevitable gossip which surrounded such a momentous occurrence, bearing little or no resemblance to the truth, but would also prolong finalizing Richard's affairs. He could only suppose that Colonel Henderson had had this in mind from the moment he realized there was nothing left for him to do to stave off the inescapable; clearly preferring to end his own life rather than face the ignominy of a trial followed by his execution, especially knowing that he could no longer count on His Grace for support. Whether or not he had taken the honourable way out was for others to judge, Gideon's task right now was to try and sort out the chaos created by Private Bamford's gullibility in allowing himself to be manoeuvred into doing something he would not have expected from a raw recruit.

The Surgeon-Major, having matter of factly pronounced life extinct, stared dispassionately down at the deceased for a moment or two before covering it with the coarse woollen blanket, pulling out his snuff box with a detachment that betokened a complete imperviousness to death or injury. A lifetime of army service had rendered him immune to ripped and torn limbs as well as the mangled carcasses of men who had fallen on battlefields such as Preston, Sheriffmuir, Dettingen, Falkirk and, of course, Culloden; such bloody demonstrations of the mortality of man leaving him quite unaffected by the sight of a corpse whose death had been brought about by his own hand.

As Gideon had never adopted the habit of taking snuff, Major Carlisle, a habitual user, proffered his small French enamel box to Sir John, shrugging an indifferent shoulder when it was immediately waved away with an impatient hand. No more than Major Carlisle was Sir John a stranger to the ruptured and mutilated bodies of men who had fallen in battle, but, unlike his Surgeon-Major, he had never been quite able to stand aloof from what was really an inevitable part of the life of a soldier with such unemotional detachment as he was now displaying. He had no fear of death, accepting it to be as much a part of life as anything else, but such unconcealed indifference was as objectionable to him as knowing that a man under his command had acted with such gross stupidity. He may not be able to claim any more of a liking for Colonel Henderson now that he was dead any more than he had when he was alive, but the plain fact was that he had been under his protection whilst awaiting his trial for treason, and apart from casting aspersions on his competence as commanding officer it also meant that Richard Ferrers' affairs would have to be set aside until this regrettable incident could be investigated.

Having relegated his own affairs to the back of his mind due to more important issues, Gideon was more concerned over the difficult and unmerited position in which Sir John found himself as well as the delay in finalizing Richard's affairs. He had no need for Sir John to remind him that rank carries responsibility and therefore he alone was culpable for what had happened, because although he had not personally handed Colonel Henderson his sword belt, he may as well have done, and even though Private Bamford would also have to be disciplined, ultimate liability lay with the commanding officer. He was perfectly well aware in what light Sir John would be regarded in some quarters for allowing something of this gravity to occur, but he was optimistic in that a military Court of Honour as well as a civil Coroner's Panel, both of which were unfortunately inescapable, would exonerate him of not only dereliction of duty but of any wrong-doing. As he could put his papers in at any time with immediate effect, it had been his intention to do precisely that once Colonel Henderson's trial was out of the way, but the unfortunate tragedy which now faced them rendered that completely out of the question. He knew that Sir John would accept his papers of resignation right now if he placed them before him, but to walk away at this time with matters so delicately balanced would be an act of unspeakable dishonour. Such conduct would be unforgivable, and certainly something he could not contemplate without revulsion, any more than he could face his parent's or Elizabeth and her brother with such a discreditable transgression hanging heavy on his conscience. However much he longed to see his home and parent's again as well as Elizabeth, his innate sense of duty would not allow him to do this. What was of far greater importance right now was for him to support and assist his commanding officer in all that was to come, as well as ensuring all the official administration which accompanied these matters, both military and civilian, was carefully arranged.

Of no less importance was the finalizing of Richard's affairs. The longer it took to exonerate and reinstate him the more restless he would become, and whilst he pinned his hopes on Miss Trench to divert his thoughts into less energetic channels, he could not fool himself into believing that he would remain still for very long. Richard had not only placed his life and trust into his hands, but his whole future, and he was therefore determined to honour the confidence placed him no matter what. A less generous man than himself could be forgiven for thinking that by taking his own life, Colonel Henderson had not only opted for the easy way out, but had also determined to render life exceedingly difficult for Richard Ferrers for as long as possible by taking his feud with that young man to his grave.   Gideon did not entirely subscribe to this view, if for no other reason than Colonel Henderson knew that he had those letters in his possession and that they would be produced in evidence and the verdict found in Richard's favour, and therefore any idea he may have had of taking his hatred to the bitter end could, at the very least, have been only a transient thought. He had decided his own fate purely on the grounds of self-interest; to save himself from witnessing his own public demise and humiliation rather than as a last minute attempt to irrevocably rout his adversary.

Gideon's commonsense enabled him to handle the men under his command with a nice mix of fairness and discipline, gaining him the reputation of being well liked and respected by all who served with him; a man who neither lost his head nor punished out of hand. Not only was he a good officer in the field but one who possessed a talent for organization and administration; traits that were to come in useful over the next week or so and which Sir John would sorely miss. Apart from hurrying off a brief note to Richard, he was kept far too busy to give much consideration to his own affairs, but even so it was impossible for him to banish Elizabeth from his thoughts, longing to be with her again and wondering how she was progressing.   Collecting statements, preparing a mound of paperwork, liaising with military and civilian personnel and questioning the men on duty in the prison quarters at the time of Colonel Henderson's death as well as trying to locate any family he may had had, meant that he was on duty for long hours at a stretch, barely grabbing more than a few hours sleep each night.

Private Bamford, having undergone a lengthy period of questioning by Gideon prior to his disciplinary hearing, had merely substantiated what he had believed to be the truth. He may have acted in a manner Gideon would not have expected even from a raw recruit, but it strengthened his belief in that far from being incompetent or inefficient, he had merely been overawed by a high ranking officer who had used his seniority to manipulate and coerce the young man into doing something which had brought about such catastrophic results, an outcome that he could not possibly have foreseen.   In view of what he knew about Colonel Henderson and his probable pre-conceived idea of putting a period to his existence by his own hand, he did not believe that this young man should receive the full penalty of military law or a sentence of any great severity, and upon seeing the fear in that young and freckled face as he was on the point of being escorted out of his room back to the prison quarters, said, not unkindly, "Private Bamford, you have behaved, at the very least, irresponsibly, indeed, you should have known better than to allow yourself to be persuaded by a detainee, irrespective of his rank. Whilst I appreciate that you were not to know the use to which the Colonel would put his sword belt, you should know that you ought to have sought advice before handing it to him if you were uncertain, but the fact remains that you are fully cognizant with army regulations, and regrettably you did not do so.   However," he nodded, a smile touching his lips, "in your defence, I can understand how difficult you must have found it to withstand such persuasion, especially from a man who held a particularly high rank. Nevertheless," he concluded, "I must tell you that whilst your sentencing will be entirely out of my hands, I promise to do all I can to ensure you receive a suitable but fair sentence. That is all Private."

It was thanks, in the main, to Gideon's testimony which included his dealings with Colonel Henderson and the acquisition of those letters as well as the determination of the prisoner to end his own life rather than face public condemnation, that Private Bamford was spared the more gruesome punishments meted out by the military. Instead of the flogging or the wooden horse with those horrendous weights attached to each foot or even riding the gauntlet, where an offender was tied to a horse and lashed as he rode up and down between two lines of men, as he had expected, he was sentenced to six months incarceration with hard labour. It was the best Gideon could have hoped for, because despite his awe and respect for such a high ranking officer, he was nevertheless an experienced soldier of five years service who had contravened the most basic of regulations.

As far as General Tuville's enquiry board was concerned, Gideon had every faith in his fellow officers to distinguish the fact from the fiction without bias or favour, ultimately exonerating his commanding officer of dereliction of duty or negligence in bringing about Colonel Henderson's death whilst in his custody and under his protection. The day following Private Bamford's disciplinary hearing, the senior ranked members of the Military Board of Enquiry, needing no other witness or evidence other than Gideon's testimony and those letters, stated that Gideon's request to Major Carlisle and others to hold themselves available for attendance, was now no longer necessary. Taking less than five minutes they unequivocally concluded that Colonel Henderson, in an attempt to escape his trial and sentence for treason, had, in sane mind, dishonourably taken his own life, and that General Turville, far from being negligent or shelving his responsibilities to not only the men under his command but to the detainee in particular, had done everything within his power to ensure his safety as well as follow the due process of military regulations. In conclusion, and with unreserved apologies, the Board stated its regrets that such a hearing had had to be convened in the first place, and hoped that Sir John would not regard it as either a slur on his integrity or as a personal affront.

Sir John may have been relieved at the outcome, but Gideon knew that in spite of this for a man of his impeccable service and untainted reputation, it would be impossible for him to accept such a humiliating experience; and certainly something he was not likely to forget in a hurry. For himself, he was extremely vexed that a damned good officer and an even better man, had had to be subjected to such an enquiry, and after shaking the huge paw held out to him, dismissing his gratitude for all he had done with a shake of his head, surprised Sir John by the sudden and unexpected expression of resentment which descended onto his face, who demanded to know the reason for it. With more anger than his commanding officer, or, indeed, anyone had ever yet heard from Gideon, he responded, "I had every confidence in the Enquiry finding in your favour, but that you should be subjected to such an ordeal is monstrous! It surely cannot be right Sir, when a man like Henderson, who has committed heinous crimes such as treason, murder and abduction, not to mention the persecution of an innocent man and his family, is, by his own hand, freed from the necessity of facing his trial and sentence."

Sir John, very much touched by this, agreed, but when, later that evening, Lady Turville, who had invited Gideon to join them for dinner, endorsed his bitter observations with several of her own pungent ones, eyed her husband with a defiant nod of her head, as if daring him to contradict her. He had no intention of doing so, but although he could not argue against their annotations there was no denying that the whole affair had left a somewhat nasty taste in his mouth.

Three days later, in the house of the local Magistrate, the four men who made up the civilian Coroner's Investigation Panel, having heard all the testimony and read the written evidence, namely those incriminating letters, judged that the deceased, one Colonel George Samuel Henderson, late of the South East Counties Infantry, had, by his own hand and in full possession of his sanity, taken his own life in order to evade his trial and sentencing for the aforementioned offences. It further stipulated that General Sir John Turville, Commanding Officer of the London and South Eastern Fusiliers, was absolved of any blame surrounding the death of the deceased and was therefore free to resume his duties. Finally, The Honourable Richard Ferrers, only son of Jasper Algernon Fortescue Ferrers, fifth Viscount Easton of Ferrers Court in the county of Sussex, was thereby found not guilty of the charges of treason and smuggling by virtue of irrefutable proof given in evidence. It ended by declaring that all persons, officials and commissioners of His Majesty's Government departments would be so advised and a recommendation put forward that the said The Honourable Richard Ferrers is to receive a notice of exoneration and reinstatement to his title and dignities forthwith. "And *that*, gentleman," stated the Coroner, "concludes the findings and verdict of this Coroner's Panel!"

Gideon would have very much liked to have taken the news to Ferrers Court himself but, unfortunately, affairs still kept him in London, and had to content himself with sending a despatch to Richard enclosing a copy of the Coroner's Panel findings and verdict, and hoped that this would console him until official notification reached him. Also included in the packet was a sealed letter to Elizabeth, imparting his innermost feelings and urgent desire to see her again, hoping that before too long he would be with her once more, when he would find her very much recovered, wishing he could have been there to see her face when she read his letter; taking some solace from knowing that very soon he would be able to show her how much he was missing her.

Despite extensive enquiries it appeared that Colonel Henderson's only living relative was a cousin living many miles distant in Northumberland, whose unequivocal reply to Gideon's letter left him in no doubt that the relationship had been very far from cousinly, and therefore the military could do whatever they wished with George's body.

"'Pon my soul!" ejaculated General Turville, handing the letter back to Gideon, his eyes widening to their fullest extent. "He seems to have made himself obnoxious even to his only relative!"

"So it would appear," Gideon grimaced.

"Well," Sir John sighed, "I suppose we shall have to make some arrangements about his interment. Unfortunately, his suicide renders an orthodox church service a little awkward, so it seems we shall have to have some kind of a burial rite in the barrack chapel; as for his remains," he shrugged, "I daresay they can be interred in the garden at the back of the chapel."

"I'll speak to Reverend Dutton, Sir" Gideon nodded, holding out very little hope that this middle-aged cleric would accommodate their request.

As the barracks came within the parish of this diligent and serious minded parson, and with no resident army chaplain, Reverend Dutton often conducted services in the barracks chapel, but considering the nature of Colonel Henderson's death, neither Gideon nor Sir John looked for a favourable response to their request. Their doubts were not misplaced. As by this time the news had spread about the traitor Colonel and his suicide, Reverend Dutton knew precisely what had brought Gideon to the parsonage, but despite his reluctance to engage in conversation about what he instinctively knew to be the reason for this visit, he nevertheless invited him into the small parlour, determined not to relent one jot in his determination to refuse. It took all the tact and diplomacy at Gideon's command to persuade this uncompromising man of the cloth to conduct a service of interment, but no argument or reason he put forward would make him surrender either his opinion or resolution. In desperation to settle this matter once and for all, Gideon, against his better judgement, was forced into more direct tactics, reasonably informing the outraged cleric that whilst he appreciated how the taking of one's life went against the teachings of the church, and how such a religious man as himself would find it totally unacceptable, the fact remained that he needed a proper burial. Eyeing Gideon considering for several moments, he then began to pace up and down, his brow creased and his lips pursed in thought, before eventually coming to a halt in front of the man who stood towering above him. Resigned but by no means reconciled, he nodded his head, saying with a reluctance which proved just how very far from happy he was, that he would accede to his request, agreeing to conduct a service over the deceased tomorrow morning.

The service, respectable if not lengthy, was attended by Sir John and Gideon and all other senior officers who were not on duty. It could not be said that it was the most inspiring of sermons, but, as Sir John fair-mindedly pointed out as he emerged from the chapel alongside Gideon, that he supposed, given the circumstances, it had been the best the poor Reverend could manage. Gideon agreed to this, but just as he was on the point of saying something, the sight of His Grace's coach entering through the gateway made him pause, exchanging a significant glance with General Turville.   By the time His Grace left 'The White Hart' the morning following his meeting with Colonel Henderson, he had already disassociated himself with the matter that had taken full possession of his friend's mind. He instinctively knew that the plan he had outlined to solve their difficulties once and for all would fail, not through any defect in his initiative, but simply because it was being carried out by two of the most incompetent idiots it had ever been his misfortune to meet. He may not so far have had the privilege of meeting Richard Ferrers, but from all he had gleaned about this enterprising young man, it was clear that he possessed more drive and resourcefulness in his little finger than his cousin did in his whole body. Again and again Richard Ferrers had run rings around his cousin and Henderson, necessitating all manner of dire means having to be implemented in which to try and curtail his antics and secure his arrest, and it was therefore with the utmost confidence that he intuitively knew that this latest scheme to lay him by the heels would be as futile as anything which had gone before. He had already expended considerable time and effort in an attempt to resolve their dilemma, but he had made no idle boast to Henderson when he had unequivocally informed him that this latest contribution on his part to bring matters to a satisfactory conclusion was the end of his participation in what had become, not only a source of considerable grievance, but also one of acute sensitivity. He had become embroiled in this distasteful affair by means of blackmail, and although he knew he had only himself to blame for this, having irresponsibly imparted such damaging news to him all those years ago when in his cups, the fact remained that Henderson had dared to suborn his assistance because of it.   His reputation was so far unsullied, and he was determined it should remain so, but he was nevertheless irrevocably resolved in rewarding Henderson handsomely for daring to treat him with such disdain.   He was in no doubt at all that he would be applied to yet again by one or other of the conspirators pleading for his support once more, the same cry leaving their lips in order to account for yet another failure to entrap Richard Ferrers. But not only would his patience tolerate no more inefficiency or lame excuses to defend their flagrant stupidity and ineptitude, but his profound belief in self-preservation had deemed it time to call a halt to any further support. Of course, there was always the possibility that Henderson would dangle his secret over his head in an effort to rally him to their cause once more, and whilst this was something he could not disregard lightly, he was quite convinced that for a man of his ingenuity and infinite resource, this threat could be more than adequately dealt with.

Having taken the sudden decision to visit his estates in Gloucestershire, for no other reason than a perverse whim, prior to returning to town, he pleasurably turned his mind, while whiling away the tedium of the journey, by evolving a fitting revenge on the man who had dared to treat him with contemptuous disdain. Since all the servants in his many establishments were trained to expect His Grace without notice or prior warning, his unexpected descent upon his principal seat caused them neither alarm nor concern, accepting his unannounced arrival with calm placidity. No one who had the dubious honour of being employed in His Grace's service ever made the error of thinking that carrying out his orders could be delayed to suit their own convenience; so when his under groom, Stope, was instructed by Benson, his very superior valet, only minutes before departing 'The White Hart' , to make all speed to London with various instructions and messages, the order was instantly carried out. Consequently, upon his arrival in Gloucestershire, taking over a week on the road, breaking his leisurely journey at the most select and renowned posting houses, his orders had been strictly discharged with an efficiency he not only expected as his right but without even a word of thanks. His correspondence, brought down from London in a small satinwood box, was placed on a long oak table which took up almost the entire length of the massive entrance hall, and with an infinitesimal nod of his head to a footman, this exquisite example of the craftsman's art was carried into his book room at the rear of the house in readiness for him to go through. Amongst the many letters, some fragranced and tied up with ribbon, were numerous cards of invitation for the pleasure of his company at this ball or card party or some sporting event with friends, but one sealed communication in particular caught his eye, rendering the rest of little importance. Sipping his wine, he eyed the letter in his hand from out of half closed lids, knowing precisely from whom it came. With slow deliberation he put his glass down on the desk and broke the seal, conscious of something stir within him, but having cast a cursory glance over the several sheets and detecting nothing to suggest that his secret had been made known to Sir John, it was therefore with relief that he perused the contents, concise and to the point, more closely.

It came as no surprise to him to discover that the plan to ensnare Richard Ferrers had come to nothing, he had known all along it would, and that Colonel Henderson was now in custody awaiting his trial, and those letters, which had been a source of infinite anxiety to him, were now safe and ready to be produced in evidence which would exonerate Richard Ferrers. What did shock him was the intelligence that William Ferrers had been shot dead by Henderson, an act of cold-blooded murder which had resulted from panic and fear, and the accidental shooting of Miss Ferrers. He had always known George was a fool, but not to the extent where he would lose what little commonsense he had by killing his own accomplice. He supposed he should be thankful to know that as far as he was concerned this matter was now over, especially as Sir John had not suggested that his presence may be required at the trial or even indicated that George had let something slip, but for a man who liked to be prepared for all eventualities, especially ensuring that nothing unfavourable rebounded on himself, then until his friend was actually dangling from the end of a rope, he really could not enjoy complete peace of mind. It was, of course, some degree of comfort to know that he would no longer be required to extricate either Henderson or William Ferrers from their self-imposed difficulties, but he could not help resenting the fact that he had been deprived of the satisfaction of repaying his so-called friend for his audacity in daring to threaten him in the first place.

Threaten! His Grace's heavy lids lowered as he pondered this. Once again he was faced with the unpleasant thought of that disastrous confession he had made, hovering over his head like an avenging Nemesis. Henderson knew perfectly well that he would do everything in his power to prevent such a secret from being made public, and even though his friend was himself on the brink of disaster he may still harbour the thought that such intelligence may yet assist him. Could it be that Henderson believed he still had an ace in the hole left to play? It could. Yes, it very well could. An eleventh hour declaration! But how like George! Dramatic and foolish to the end. Of course, such a public statement would not prevent him from climbing the scaffold, but it could do himself irreparable harm; after all, he had his reputation as well as his son to consider. It would be foolish to take for granted that Henderson would go quietly; no, he would not. He had no doubt that he could deflect any adverse repercussions such an announcement would bring in its wake, even triumph over them, especially from a man who was known to be a traitor; but, even so, mud did have a habit of sticking! But what if he could obviate that risk? Yes, of course, that was a far better prospect! A return to town then was what was required, but even as he rang the bell to issue curt instructions to a footman to prepare for the journey tomorrow, events in London had taken a dramatic turn.

Unlike his journey from Sussex into Gloucestershire, the one to town was not so much leisurely as impeded, due, in the main, to the terrible condition of the roads, made worse by days of heavy rain, taking six frustrating days. It was not to be expected that Colonel Henderson's suicide and the resultant hearings and enquiries would be long in coming to his attention, or the fact that Richard Ferrers had been found to be innocent of all charges laid against him and that the 'gazetting' had been lifted. Within minutes of entering his town house, this startling news, staring boldly up at him from the London Gazette which Parker had placed ready for him on the spindle-legged table along with numerous items of correspondence, had the affect of holding him speechless, and it was some little while before he was able to assimilate all he had read and to ponder how this could possibly harm him or damage his reputation.

However confident he was in his ability to deflect any adverse criticism or damaging accusations, he nevertheless heaved a tremendous sigh of relief when no mention had been made about either his support of Colonel Henderson and the role he had played in attempting to bring about the downfall of an innocent man, or the reason for it.   Had his participation been divulged then it would have clearly led to questions being asked, questions he would much rather not have to answer, but more than this for a man of his eminence to be summoned to an enquiry or Coroner's Panel to either give evidence or offer explanations, would have been as degrading as it would insulting.   It would appear therefore that officially this lamentable affair was over without any testimony or statement required from him but, even so, one nagging doubt still lingered in his mind, because although Sir John had made no mention of it in his letter and there was nothing in the Gazette to either imply he had assisted Henderson or anything to suggest that he had done so merely in order to hide the fact that he had played a cruel cajolery by foisting an illegitimate son onto society, no one knew his old friend better than he. It would be quite in character for him to have either hinted at the truth or stated it categorically to Sir John, in which case a man of his integrity would have felt himself in honour bound to investigate it further, but since there was nothing to substantiate this theory in the news journals he had so far perused, and something of this magnitude would certainly have been reported, he was at a loss to account for Sir John's reticence.   He was not fooled by Sir John's polite and courteous reception of him, he knew perfectly well that he disliked him, and therefore found it hard to believe that he would not have acted upon such damaging information.   Of course, it could well be that Henderson had not said anything at all, in which case he was worrying unduly, but an innate sense of self-preservation told him that it behoved him to discover the truth, and it was this that took him to the barracks the next morning, just as Sir John and Gideon were leaving the chapel following the burial service.

At no time did General Turville welcome a visit from His Grace, and now was no exception, but short of refusing to see him thereby risking the consequences of such an affront, for he would see it as nothing less, he really had no choice but to accept the inevitable. His Grace, always impeccably attired, had certainly done justice to the occasion by wearing a satin coat of peacock blue with sleeves that boasted cuffs at least twelve inches deep, edged with gold brocade and breeches of the same colour. Inserted into the cascade of intricately worked lace at his throat was a diamond pin which glittered in the morning sun, and the ruby ring he always wore on the little finger of his left hand was just visible beneath the same delicate lace which fell over his long white fingers.   The spiral curls of his wig, a really elegant creation in a most delicate shade of blue, stirred gently in the light breeze as he alighted from his coach, making exaggerated if unnecessary use of his long cane. His slim legs, encased in shell-pink stockings, aroused no admiration in Sir John, and upon seeing him tip-toe towards them in extremely high heeled shoes which looked as uncomfortable as they did impractical, was barely able to hide his snort of irritation at such a vision. Gideon may not like His Grace any more than his commanding officer, but his ready sense of the ridiculous brought an appreciative smile to his eyes, looking at Sir John with such unalloyed amusement that despite himself he could not resist the twitch at the corner of his mouth, but by the time they came up to their unwelcome visitor their expressions were such as to arouse no suspicion in his mind. Greeting Sir John and Gideon by executing a most exquisite bow, he immediately offered his profuse and sincere apologies for descending upon them without prior warning or invitation. Since he habitually disregarded these observances to courtesy Sir John received his apology indifferently, merely introducing Gideon to him. A slight inclination of the head from both men was the only recognition exchanged between them, but Sir John, who had shrewdly concluded that His Grace had only one aim in paying them this visit, felt it behoved him to usher his obnoxious guest up to his room.

"So," His Grace mused, after reposing himself gracefully onto the chair he was offered, eyeing Gideon through his eye glass, having to look a long way up into his unsmiling face, "*you* are this Major Neville I have heard so much about!"

Had it been at all possible Gideon would have had no compunction in retiring to his own room to finalize some unfinished work, having neither the time nor the inclination to exchange insincere pleasantries with His Grace, but in view of a significant glance cast at him from General Turville, he had reluctantly accompanied the two men into his commanding officer's room. "Yes, Your Grace," he inclined his head.

"You know, Major," he purred silkily, the thin painted lips parting into the semblance of a smile, "your exploits have left me quite breathless with awe, I assure you. You therefore must permit me to felicitate you on your expeditious, not to say," he inclined his head, "delicate handling of a most painful and regrettable affair."

Having been raised by a father who was most truly a gentleman as well as being a man of the highest principles and integrity, he found Lytton's smooth-tongued utterances dishonest and offensive but, like Sir John, knew that to voice one's repugnance would be extremely dangerous. Resisting the temptation to hurl his words back into his painted face, he merely bowed his head. "Your Grace is most kind, but, indeed, I did nothing."

The painted eyebrows rose at this. "You do yourself a disservice, Major," he rebuked gently. "Indeed," he pointed out, theatrically shrugging his shoulders, "it is due to your unremitting exertions that Richard Ferrers has been spared the gallows!"

"Richard Ferrers *was* an innocent man, Your Grace!" Gideon reminded him unambiguously, not flinching beneath that suddenly cold grey stare.

"So it was eventually proven," he pointed out, the slight edge to his voice not lost on his auditors, causing Sir John to cast an anxious look up at Gideon who, from the looks of it, appeared to be in no frame of mind to either humour His Grace or adopt a conciliatory attitude. "Which is why," Lytton smiled thinly, deciding it behoved him to use a much milder tone considering the delicate nature of his visit, "you must permit me to congratulate you on what was undoubtedly a considerable feat on your part in providing the evidence to clear his name."

This was not only an olive branch from His Grace but a complete volte-face, as unexpected as it was disquieting. Lytton was not only a man one neither took liberties with nor opposed, but one who never forgave a slight or an offence against his person, yet for some reason it seemed to Sir John that he felt it wise to adopt more conciliatory measures. He could not help but wonder whether his initial conclusion had been right after all, in that His Grace was seeking to know whether Henderson had indeed implicated him in some way, and therefore felt it incumbent upon him to adopt a more tolerant approach in the hope that it would reap rewards where his habitual arrogance would not. He knew Gideon was not only an even tempered man but a fair and just one, and one, moreover, who did not lose his head in a crisis. His manners were not only impeccable but an integral part of his character, and his loyalty and integrity were unquestionable, rendering dissimulation or falsity abhorrent to him. He knew that Gideon would not deliberately alienate or offend His Grace, but having to endure such hollow compliments from a man who had done his utmost to put a rope around the neck of an innocent man, would be a severe trial to him.

He was quite right. Gideon had told Richard and Miss Trench that their thanks were not in the least necessary, and that still held true. But their expressions of gratitude had been genuine and sincere, offered from the heart, unlike this man, whose dulcet tongue and honeyed words of praise were as hollow as they were nauseating. Coming from a man who had stopped at nothing to ensure that Richard ended up on the end of a rope or even shot as an escapee, knowing full well that he was completely innocent of any treasonable activity, rendered it extremely difficult for him to offer even the barest of civilities. He could neither charge His Grace with infamous and despicable conduct either towards Richard and his family or the cruel deceit he had played on his wife and son, and the disgust he felt was such that it was several moments before he could respond suitably to His Grace. "Your Grace is most kind," Gideon inclined his head, perfectly aware of Sir John's relief at his deference, knowing how difficult it was for him to pander to this man, "but I can only repeat, I have done nothing other than my duty."

Again those painted eyebrows rose. "Come, come, Major" he chided gently, "whilst this modesty is most becoming in you, you must acknowledge that I cannot allow such self-effacement!"

Sir John, who inwardly winced at this, would have derived immense satisfaction from throwing his painted and powdered visitor down the stairs, but he knew he could not; such an action, however gratifying, could lead to disastrous consequences.

"I assure you, it is no such thing, Your Grace" Gideon shook his head, barely able to conceal his vexation at the thought of having to indulge a man who had ruined more than one life. "My efforts, as you call them, on Richard Ferrers' behalf, were no more than I would accord any man unfortunate enough to be in his position."

"Are you saying, Major," he asked softly, swinging his eyes glass to and fro, "that you believed in his innocence prior to your visit to Hampton Regis?"

"I am saying, Your Grace," Gideon told him truthfully, "that I prefer to keep an open mind until the evidence proves guilt or innocence."

"An admirable philosophy!" he nodded, the smile not quite reaching his eyes. "And from whom did you acquire such wisdom, Major?"

"From my father, Your Grace," Gideon replied simply.

"A most estimable man, clearly!" he remarked, raising a painted eyebrow.

"A *most* estimable man, indeed, Your Grace," Gideon inclined his head.

"Your loyalty is commendable," Lytton applauded, "but did you, I wonder," he asked curiously, his voice silky smooth, "apply that same excellent philosophy to Colonel Henderson?"

"I accorded him all the civility and respect which was his due, both of which he had continually denied to Miss Ferrers and her father, Your Grace," Gideon responded without hesitation.

"I daresay," His Grace nodded, "but that is not *quite* what I asked, is it?" he smiled thinly.

"My orders, Your Grace" Gideon informed him firmly, "pertained to Richard Ferrers and not Colonel Henderson. Since he had not come under suspicion there was no reason for me to adopt *any* philosophy. Colonel Henderson's participation in treason was exposed through his own hand, and not merely the writing of those letters," he explained, "but by his actions to ensnare Richard Ferrers by any means available. He knew that Richard Ferrers had seen those letters and was only waiting to put his hands on them and that once he did they would be enough to see him hang."

"I see," his Grace nodded again, crossing one leg gracefully over the other. "And did Colonel Henderson give you his reasons for engaging in treasonable activities, Major?"

"No, Your Grace, he did not," Gideon shook his head.

"You asked him, of course?" Lytton enquired, again raising a pencilled eyebrow.

"Naturally, Your Grace" Gideon replied stiffly.

"And you made no assumption?" he insisted politely.

"Yes," Gideon nodded, "I made several in fact; but since he refused to corroborate any one of them I saw little point in wasting time in trying to prise the reason out of him."

"It appears therefore, does it not, Major" he said smoothly, taking a delicate pinch of snuff, "that Henderson was just a little reticent in explaining his reasons for such a vile crime?"

"Most reticent, Your Grace," Gideon concurred.

"And yet," he raised a doubtful eyebrow, "he was in your company to a marked degree, and you still say he offered no explanation?"

"None whatsoever, Your Grace," Gideon replied categorically.

"You know, Major," he said thoughtfully, looking up at Gideon through half closed lids, "I must confess to experiencing a little difficulty in believing that. Oh, please do not misunderstand me, Major," he cried contritely upon seeing the tautness which appeared around Gideon's mouth, "but you see, you must, you *really* must," he emphasized, his discoloured teeth accentuating his malevolence, "allow me to have superior knowledge of Henderson. My acquaintanceship with him was, dare I confess it" he shrugged ingenuously, "of long duration, and my familiarity with him permits me to say, without fear of contradiction," he smiled thinly, "that he was not the type of man who could keep his head in a crisis; his tongue," he sighed eloquently, "sadly, all too often allowed him into indiscretion, and now, upon discovering he said nothing to indicate his reasons for such a reckless venture could almost lead me to believe we are discussing a different man entirely. So much so, that I cannot help but wonder," lowering his eyes to scrutinize his painted fingernails "if in fact he *did* impart something to you, for example, an indication as to why he approached me to assist him in the apprehension of an innocent man?"

Not by the flicker of an eye lid did Gideon let it be seen that his suspicions were now confirmed in that His Grace, far from coming here to offer insincere congratulations, was merely trying to ascertain if Henderson had divulged his secret. "No, Your Grace, he imparted nothing."

His Grace nodded, then smiling up at Gideon, said apologetically, "You must forgive my - er, what shall I call it?" he pondered, "ah yes, my inquisition, but you see, Major," he said mournfully, "it is a great mortification to me to learn that one of my oldest friends embarked on something as sordid as treason and then enlisted my aid to apprehend a man who was entirely blameless. I have been most abominably used;" he sighed, "my generosity, my good nature and - dare I say it?" he raised a painted eyebrow, "my privileged position. Such deceit as that," he sighed, "is extremely painful to one of my sensibilities." Sir John snorted at this, quickly turning it into a rather unconvincing cough when Lytton turned his head in his direction. "Ah yes," he nodded "you fully appreciate my suffering, Turville, do you not? Indeed," he shook his head, his curls dancing, "such a betrayal is something one may never recover from. I know I shall not, especially when I recall how a man, with my *unwitting* assistance Turville," he moaned, "could so easily have had his life ended prematurely. It must be a lesson to us all, I fear!" He turned and looked up at Gideon, his lips parting in a smile that sent a shiver down his spine. "I refuse to spare your blushes Major," he shook his head, "because whilst I know how you seek no reward for what you consider to be your duty, you must allow me to offer my thanks, my gratitude and, dare I say it, my unending regard in preventing a most tragic miscarriage of justice."

Over the top of Lytton's head, Sir John and Gideon exchanged exasperated glances, both men pushed to the limits of their patience, but since His Grace fully expected something favourable in response to such a sorrowful but self-exculpatory oration, Gideon thanked him as politely as he could.

"Not at all, Major" Lytton sighed. "It is of great comfort to me to know that you prevented a most regrettable tragedy; had you not have done so, I would have been prostrate with remorse."

"Major," Sir John coughed, seeing the effort it was costing Gideon to maintain any semblance of calm or politeness, "I know you have work awaiting you on your desk. I am sure His Grace will spare you in order for you to attend to it."

His Grace waved a languid hand. "By all means, Major" he nodded. "You must forgive me for detaining you and keeping you away from your duties."

"Thank you, Your Grace. Sir," he saluted, and closed the door behind him.

"I see the Major is a man of infinite tact and discretion," he remarked when Gideon had left.

"Yes, Your Grace," Turville nodded, wishing this obnoxious little man would take himself off, but since he believed he had not yet achieved what he had come for, he envisaged entertaining him for awhile longer.

"You are, indeed, most fortunate to have such a man under your command," he commented, taking out his snuff box with painstaking care.

"I am aware, Your Grace" Turville agreed, "but not for very much longer, I fear."

"Oh!" he raised an eyebrow. "But how is this?"

"Major Neville is on the point of selling out, Your Grace."

"Selling out!" he cried in exaggerated horror. "May I be permitted to ask the reason for this?"

"I understand it is domestic matters," Turville replied uncommunicatively.

"Domestic matters?" he raised an enquiring eyebrow.

"His father, Your Grace" he told him reluctantly, "has not been enjoying the best of health of late."

"I see," Lytton nodded, taking a pinch of snuff. "Regrettable, of course, but how fortunate for us all that he was still in regimentals during this most regrettable affair!"

Turville eyed him guardedly, having a very good idea that he was about to be asked the same question, and in the same roundabout manner, as had been put to Gideon. "Yes, Your Grace" he nodded, "most fortunate."

"Yes, indeed," he nodded, returning the little gold box to his pocket. "It is also most fortunate that the Major is blessed with many fine qualities, two of which, I am sure you will agree," he smiled thinly, inclining his head, "are indispensable for a man in his position." General Turville did not need to have this explained, the subtly veiled inference was enough. "You must not think that I do not admire the Major, Turville, I assure you I do, and, of course, I value and appreciate his very natural desire to spare me pain by refusing to recount any of Henderson's desperate claims to malign me, which, my dear Turville, I feel certain must be the case," he commented painfully, shaking his head. "But the Major's delicacy and consideration," he sighed, "are to be honoured, and so seldom to be found in these modern times. You and I, my dear Turville," he shrugged, "know only too well how the vulgar can misinterpret something, but, alas," he sighed, "once a thing has been uttered, it cannot be retracted, and, of course," he moaned, looking innocently across at his host, "it is so very difficult to dispute."

"Major Neville is a man of the highest integrity, Your Grace!" Turville said earnestly, not appreciating the subtle warning.

"But of course!" he cried, raising an astonished eyebrow. "You misjudge me, Turville. Upon my honour I have nothing but veneration for the Major. His diligence and unfailing industry in this matter have left me quite lost in admiration, I assure you it is so, but this matter has been a most painful affair for all concerned, and I," he inclined his head, "have felt it most acutely. No one knew Henderson better than I, my dear Turville," he said softly, "but I confess, yes," he nodded, "even I can err, Turville, he played me false," shaking his head sorrowfully. "It is of great affliction to me to know that he behaved in such a manner, so much so that, even now, I have not come to terms with his perfidy. When I recall his representations to me to assist him, urgently requesting support, I knew no hesitation, none whatsoever, and yet, to think that he used me in such a manner - it is unpardonable!" He covered his face with a white hand, shaking his head mournfully. "But you and I, my very dear Tuville," he shrugged, "are men of honour, and for that reason I am sure you will enter into my feelings when I say that I shudder to think of what he said to my detriment in an attempt to hide his crimes, the very thought of which," he shuddered eloquently, "causes me acute pain."

Apart from the fact that he found all this flowing eloquence too much for his patience, it was on the tip of Sir John's tongue to tell him to cut line and that his dirty little secret would remain such, but to do so could easily rebound adversely as Lytton was more than capable, as had been proven more than once, of rewarding one for such impertinence and therefore bit down the blistering retort.

"You do understand, do you not, Turville?" Lytton asked, the unruffled calm of his voice softening the threat beneath the surface.

"Perfectly, Your Grace," Sir John nodded, not flinching from that cold warning stare. "But as only the pertinent facts attaching to Henderson's treason were reported at the enquiries convened to investigate this matter, and I am not aware of any implications being put forward about anyone of a detrimental nature, I believe we have finally seen this end of this distressing affair."

Like Gideon, he found the cruel deceit Lytton had perpetrated all those years ago to be equally as abhorrent as William Ferrers' and Henderson's treason, and that he should receive due punishment for this, but the thought of his son, totally ignorant of his father's crime, had influenced their decision to take it no further, in the firm belief that the victim of his offence did not deserve to suffer because of it. He was not fooled by Lytton's smoothly delivered eloquence but as both men held the other's look, understanding one another perfectly, it was as though a silent agreement had been sealed between them. But Sir John, far from happy that this man had committed two unforgivable crimes; the iniquitous deception perpetrated all those years ago and the relentless pursuit of an innocent man in order to protect such a Machiavellian pretence, felt sickened with disgust, but managing to conceal this said, with an innocence that did not fool his guest but considerably relieved his mind, "Both Major Neville and I, Your Grace, believe that this whole episode is best forgotten."

Having read the meaning of this with unerring accuracy, Lytton, after inclining his head in acknowledgment, said softly, "T'would seem the Major has intelligence as well as wisdom, as do you, my dear Tuville. I am, I need hardly say, in full accord with your sentiments about such a painful episode being forgotten, indeed," he raised an eyebrow, "to resurrect something which could only result in distress for all concerned, is not only foolhardy but extremely hazardous," whereupon he rose stately to his feet, smiling down at his troubled host whose face clearly echoed his feelings.

"Your Grace I ..."

"No, no, Tuville" he shook his head, "there is not the least need for you to say more. I assure you," he smiled, "your expression is eloquence itself," upon which he walked towards the door in a rustle of satin, his high heeled shoes tapping on the floorboards like a death knell. He paused for a moment as if considering something, then turning his head a little towards Sir John, his hand holding the edge of the half open door, said, with a cold-blooded detachment that made Sir John shiver, "You know, Tuville," he remarked "whatever repugnance you may feel, there is one thing at least you *must* acknowledge; and that is, it was *positively* inspired!"

CHAPTER THIRTY

It would be long before Gideon and Sir John would forget their interview with Lytton; his clinical unconcern over events which would fill most men with shame, leaving them under no illusion that should his deception and the use to which it was put ever become known, then he would be merciless in his retribution. The uneasy truce which had been mutely drawn up between them therefore, had to be endured for the sake of those whose lives would be irrevocably ruined were it to be contravened, and however distasteful this may prove to be to men whose very lives were grounded in truth and integrity, the acceptance of such a despicable agreement, whilst an extremely bitter pill to swallow, had guaranteed protection for those who were far more worthy than His Grace.

Finally at liberty to attend to his own affairs Gideon put his papers in for resigning his commission two days after his interview with Lytton, a circumstance which very much grieved General Turville, because although there was a long list of men waiting to purchase and his replacement would be with him almost immediately, the thought that he was losing a very capable officer in Gideon did not make this fact any more agreeable to him. He knew Gideon was in the fortunate position whereby he did not have to wait for someone to purchase his commission before he could go home, and consequently expected him to leave almost straightaway, and it was therefore not without deep regret that he was soon to say goodbye to him. He understood his reasons perfectly well, in fact he would not have expected anything else from a man of his integrity, but he could not deny that not only was he losing a damned good officer, but a man of the highest principals and one, moreover, whom he was proud to call friend. He had come to rely heavily on Gideon and never once had he found his faith and trust misplaced, but this business with Richard Ferrers could well have turned out to be a disaster for that young man were it not for him, a man who was about to walk away from the life he had not only enjoyed but took great pride in for the last eight years. He had no doubt that he would make a success of administering his father's estates just as he had his army career, and could only feel that his loss was Sir Matthew's gain, a man who clearly had as much faith in his son as he had himself.

Not surprisingly, Gideon's fellow officers and friends were not about to let him go quietly, and by a carefully contrived ruse managed to entice him to the officers' dining quarters the evening before his departure, his entrance hailed by the sound of trumpets and hurrahs as he was enthusiastically lifted and carried by half a dozen friends the whole length of the room. The wine and claret flowed freely throughout the night; songs were sung, if not always in tune then certainly with gusto; past charmers they had known were brought to mind quickly followed by slurred warnings to Gideon about becoming leg-shackled. Reminiscences were exchanged, some happier than others, while old comrades were remembered, and by the time the dawn began to break over the barracks, Gideon, arm in arm with his friends, walked or staggered backed to their quarters, but none of them were so drunk that they did not know that they would miss him very much.

His goodbye to Sir John next day, although much later than he had intended, was rather more subdued, but it was nonetheless sincere for all that. He had served under General Turville for most of his service and had been proud to do so, and although he had no regrets about resigning his commission, he could not help but feel some sadness. However, this was tempered by a despatch he had received late yesterday, sent post-haste by Lady Neville in reply to both his letters, expressing her delight in having him home again very soon, and that his father, though not restored to full health, was nevertheless much better, and that Doctor Mawe was very well pleased with his progress. She then went on to say how happy they were to hear the news of his forthcoming proposal of marriage to Miss Ferrers, stating that even though neither she nor his father had ever laid eyes on her, and despite the fact he had not long made her acquaintance, they had no reservations as they were certain their son knew his own mind and heart sufficiently to make such a momentous decision. She ended by saying that they looked forward to meeting Miss Ferrers, and hoped that Gideon would bring her to Burroughs Croft with him, for she felt sure he would visit her before coming home, for an indefinite stay, providing, of course, she was well enough to travel, because whilst he had not gone into too much detail about her brother's difficulties, the poor child must be feeling dreadfully pulled from her injury. His father sent him his compliments and looked forward to having him home before the end of next week. In the meantime she remained his most loving and affectionate Mamma.

He could well imagine Penny waiting uncomplainingly for his mother to write a letter so he could hand it to a groom who, he had no doubt, had been pacing up and down outside in readiness to take it for half an hour or more. He smiled fondly as he pictured her emerging from her sitting room, well over the time she said it would take her to scribble a few lines, with her irresistible smile and warm word of thanks for keeping them waiting as she at long last handed the letter over, full of genuine contrition for taking so long. Penny may be his father's man, but he was more than happy to perform any service for her, and would, upon her hurried emergence from her sitting room, merely incline his head and say it was no matter. Clara Winsetton had spoken no less than the truth about his mother, whom he adored, when she had said that his father, who was still very much in love with her, having taken one look at her all those years ago, had found his heart to be irrevocably lost to the young woman who truly was as captivating and as adorable as she had said.

He had witnessed the love which his mother and father shared as well as the little displays of affection which passed between them, and whilst this had made for a very happy and secure childhood for himself and Aubrey, he had never really believed that he would meet a woman for whom he could feel what his father did for his mother or that he would be fortunate enough to have a woman love him in the same way that his mother loved his father. Their marriage was indeed an exception, as had apparently been that of Lord and Lady Ferrers, but he had seen too many marriages simply subsist; their foundations based solely upon the need for an heir to ensure a line or financial expediency and, as was so often the case, the distinction of acquiring a title or adding to existing ones, with no love or feelings of tenderness on either side, both parties, once the succession had been secured by several children, living completely separate but discreet lives, only coming together when occasion demanded.

He had not wanted that sham of a life for himself. To have asked a woman to be his wife purely on the grounds of time-honoured convention, to have offered her his name and all worldly goods as well as to love and honour when none of the essential ingredients were there nor were ever likely to be, would have been quite distasteful to him. If he could not enjoy the wedded bliss shared by his parent's then he would much rather remain a bachelor for the rest of his days, taking his pleasures where he will, at least there was more honesty in that than keeping up the pretence of a marriage where neither party was in love with the other; to turn a blind eye to the extra-marital connection of one's wife diplomatically hovering in the background, or his own mistress established in a neat and discreet little house somewhere. But Aubrey's tragic and unexpected death had meant that he could no longer hold to this belief. The Neville family could trace their lineage back for centuries past in almost an unbroken line from father to son, and although his father would not even consider either coercing or persuading him into marriage because of this, the fact remained that he owed it to his name to marry an eligible female to provide the necessary heir. He had come to accept his marriage as his duty rather than something he felt inclined to do, because although he had met any number of eligible young ladies, all of whom it seemed were not averse to receiving an offer from him, it was unfortunate that not one of them had sparked off a chord inside his heart, leaving him with the painful knowledge that his offer would be made from expediency after all, rather than love.

Having come to accept this regrettable circumstance, if not with enthusiasm then certainly with resignation, he had, quite out of the blue and when he had least expected it, met Elizabeth Ferrers, the woman he had instinctively known to be the one whom he had been searching for for the whole of his adult life. When he had been sent into Sussex it had not been with the intention of looking for a bride, but to try and discover the truth about a young man who stood perilously close to the hangman's noose, little knowing that his sister would turn his life completely upside down within the space of a few short minutes. He could neither explain nor rationalize his feelings, all he knew was that he loved and needed her more than life itself, and could not bear to contemplate even for so much as a second spending the rest of his life without her in it. What made it all the more wonderful was that she fully reciprocated his feelings, because when he had told Clara Winsetton that should she not love him he would be utterly desolate, he had spoken no less than the truth. She may not be the daughter of a Duke or an Earl, but even so her antecedents were impeccable, had they not been, the very thought of having to give her up for an eligible woman of his own order, would be equivalent to tearing the heart from his body.   But, mercifully, this contingency would not be necessary, and the thought of this as well as seeing her and holding her in his arms again after more than two long agonizing weeks caused him to urge his mare on a little quicker, acutely aware that he could not wait for the tall twisted chimneys of Ferrers Court to come into view.

Had Miss Calne or, indeed, her aunt, been privileged to have seen Elizabeth's face upon reading Gideon's letter, handed to her by Richard with a teasing comment that he had no objection to being called upon to act as intermediary between them, they would have needed no further proof of just how much she loved and missed him.   Such as phrases as '*I have only been parted from you for two days, and already I miss you more than I can say*' and '*I long to be with you again, to take you in my arms and show you just how much I love you*' sent such a thrill shooting through her that were it at all possible she would have gone to him on the instant.   Richard, dropping in on her to see how she did an hour or so later, took one look at the letter lying on the coverlet and knew immediately the cause of the colour in her cheeks and the glow in her eyes, and although he only made a light-hearted reference to it he could hazard a pretty good guess as to its contents, and hoped for her sake that Gideon would be back with them soon, because although she was showing a very brave front, he knew she was missing him like the devil. He knew only too well what that was like, being separated from the one you loved more than life itself, longing only for the day when you could be together, and were it not for Gideon he would not now be the happiest man alive, and therefore wished he had the power to hasten his return.   Within a couple of days of receiving Gideon's letter Elizabeth had finally been allowed out of bed by Doctor Jarvey having been plagued by his patient that it was nonsense her remaining in bed when she felt so much better. "You may well," he admonished, "but I am far from happy to allow it. It is far too soon; the least exertion could open up that wound!"

"But I am not going to be doing anything so very taxing," she pointed out.

"I'm sorry, but I cannot …" But he was not proof against her persistent teasing, a nice mix of pleading and coaxing, but although it went very much against his better judgement he eventually gave in, realizing that it would be just like her to contradict his orders and get up when his back was turned. Although she would not admit it, even to herself, the fact remained that her legs were very far from steady when she tried to stand up, glad to be able to sit back down onto the bed or drop onto the nearest chair. Miss Calne, categorically refusing to assist her to get dressed, told her in no uncertain terms that she had yet to meet, with the exception of her aunt, a more stubborn woman, and that she for one would not lift a finger to assist her in what she had no hesitation in describing as madness. Upon this she stalked out of Elizabeth's bedchamber, grumbling something to the effect that she washed her hands of the whole affair, and if Miss Elizabeth ended up ill again or that wound opened, it would be no more than she deserved. But with the help of Susan, Elizabeth eventually managed to get dressed and have her hair brushed and arranged into its usual becoming style, but there was no denying that she still looked rather pale and drawn as she unsteadily left her bedchamber to try and walk along the corridor towards the stairs. Kindly refusing the proffered arm of Susan, who had been her personal attendant since she had been seventeen and who was hovering anxiously in the background, she was determined to make the effort herself, but although she managed to reach the top of the stairs without mishap, honesty compelled her to admit that she seriously doubted whether she would be able to descend the stairs without help. But with the same determination that had driven Colonel Henderson and her cousin to desperation, she turned sideways to rest both her hands on the banister, wincing at the pain in her left arm from the pressure of her weight as she leaned heavily on the polished oak. Taking one step at a time, her legs trembling from the exertion, she had just paused for breath before taking the next step down when Richard came striding into the hall from the rear of the house, looking up thunderstruck to see his sister attempting to come down.

"What the devil?" he exclaimed, taking the steps two at a time.

"Oh, Richard," she smiled, her breathing a little laboured. "I am so glad to see you."

"Just what do you think you're doing?" he demanded.

"Trying to get down the stairs, of course," she told him, her eyes smiling at his thunderous expression. "Doctor Jarvey told me I may get up."

"I daresay he did," he bit out, "but I don't think he meant coming downstairs."

"I am *not* staying in bed another minute!" she declared. "Nor in my room; I am *not* an invalid!"

Seeing the mulish look suddenly descend onto her face, Richard, goaded into saying something under his breath, unceremoniously picked her up in his arms and carried her down the stairs, but upon being told that she could manage for herself now, he said frustrated, "I ought to beat you. Stop wriggling," and without listening to a word she said strode through the great hall and into the sitting room, laying her down on a comfortable settee.

"Thank you," she said meekly, when he straightened himself up.

"Y'know," he told her, seeing the roguish look in her eyes, "if these are the antics you intend kicking up when you're married, then all I can say is that Gideon ought to beat you, regularly!"

She laughed. "He won't."

"Don't be too sure of that!" he nodded.

"I am sure of it," she smiled. "You see, he loves me."

At this Richard burst out laughing. "The fellow has all my sympathies!"

She pulled a face, to which he told her that the sooner Gideon took her off his hands the better, bending down to kiss her cheek, knowing perfectly well that he would miss her when she finally left The Court.

Richard, who had shrewdly guessed that his sister must know the content of Gideon's letters by heart, had not erred in his supposition. Every loving word and phrase were imprinted on her memory for all time, sending tingles spiralling up and down her spine at the thought of them. She longed to see him again, but knew he must be rather busy in settling matters in town, and would come to see her just as soon as he could, and therefore took pleasure in reading both his letters again and again, taking comfort from them until he returned to her. Jane's regular visits were welcome, enjoying their long talks together and discussing her marriage plans to Richard, who, after a lengthy and profitable interview with Sir Arthur, had been pleased to report that he had no objection to their betrothal being reinstated. She did not need Jane or Richard to tell her how very much in love they were, she could see it for herself; the way their eyes lit up when they saw one another and the little, almost infinitesimal, glances they cast in each other's direction or the smiles they exchanged which conveyed so much more than words. She was genuinely pleased for both of them, and knew they would be very happy, but seeing them together only increased her longing for the man who haunted her dreams and for which not even Gideon's letters could compensate her in his absence.

Having persuaded Richard that she was well enough to attend William's funeral, two days later she made the short drive from the house to the Church in the trap sitting beside her aunt, her feelings somewhat mixed as she took her seat next to her and her brother in the front family pew. William, a man who had neither the resolution nor the backbone to think and act for himself, had finally allowed his ambitions and jealousy of Richard to get the better of him, embarking on a venture which anyone with a modicum of commonsense would have known would end in disaster. Since his death she had learned more of his ruinous way of life from Richard and the huge sums of money he owed to his creditors or lost at play, with no hope of defraying the half of them, but that he could actually have believed for one moment that by supporting Stuart, whose attempts at insurrection had been by no means a foregone conclusion, would ensure him the title as well as a position of power in the new Government, surely proved how unrealistic and foolish he was. She may not have liked or trusted him, but she could not help but think that his tragic end could so easily have been avoided had he not allowed himself to be governed by his overriding envy and hopeful if impossible aspirations. His life, which could have been put to far better use than feeding his unreasonable aims and covetous desires, had ended ignominiously and well before it should.

Clara Winsetton, sitting bolt upright beside her niece, whose face looked as if it had been carved in stone, was giving no indication as to her feelings. The truth was she had never liked William, indeed, he was too much like his father; wastrel and caring for nothing or nobody but himself. Added to this, he had embarked on insurrection for no better reason than advancing himself into a position that was as nonsensical as it was criminal, and then, when it threatened to overtake him had dared to point the finger in Richard's direction. Through him and his equally devious accomplice her brother had succumbed to a heart attack brought about due to their scurrilous dealings, and her niece, who had done her best to fend off their despicable behaviour, had ended up being shot. But now, seeing his coffin standing in front of the alter, draped in the richly embroidered Ferrers coat of arms, she was not sure whether to hail his death as a blessing for the Ferrers family or as a woeful waste of a life that could have been prevented, and, perhaps, capable of quite a lot of good.

Richard's thoughts were far from elevating, indeed, he was not at all certain whether to feel relief or grief at his cousin's death. That it had been brought about by his own hand and devious actions could not be denied, nor could the fact that he and William had never really been friends. He had been aware of William's jealousy towards him for a long time, and even though his cousin had done his best to hide this fact, it was nevertheless a potent force in his life. It would be so easy to blame Colonel Henderson for leading his cousin astray with dreams and hopes of a glorious future, but William, through his envy and unrealistic hopes of becoming sixth Viscount Easton, together with his ever growing and desperate need for money, had not taken much persuading to embark on a course that was as dangerous as it was doomed to failure. William may have made a last stand to uphold some semblance of honour in refusing to carry out Colonel Henderson's order, but he still believed that his cousin had got off extremely lightly for his crimes, and totally undeserving of the efforts Gideon had strove to formulate in bringing him off safe. It seemed a little ironic that his efforts had only been possible due to William's death, saving him from disgrace and the scaffold by being posthumously hailed as an advocate of truth and justice. He was not a vengeful nor a vindictive man, but whilst he could find it in him, if not to forgive, then to overlook, William's part in attempting to bring about his downfall, no power on earth could engender one spark of forgiveness in his breast over his contribution in bringing about his father's early death. William had chartered his own course knowing perfectly well what could result from it, but he had gone ahead regardless, and although he was honest enough to admit that his cousin's lack of resolution and weakness of character had been at the root of his difficulties as well as his involvement, his own sense of right and wrong should have told him that his venture into treason with a man who, as Gideon had rightly said, had taken full advantage of him, should have been enough to hold him back from such a fatal path.

It had been out of deference to Richard and the Ferrers family that Reverend Parton had agreed to conduct William's obsequies and not from any liking or respect for the deceased, and therefore the sermon, read out in his deep and powerful voice, had been brief and to the point. He considered himself to be a fair and reasonable man, but there had been nothing venerable he could say about the late departed William Ferrers which would have sat easily on his conscience. He only had to think of his late lordship, driven to an early grave, and his hackles rose in indignation at the very thought of conducting a Christian burial on one of the men responsible, and therefore had to sternly remind himself of his calling in order to carry out the last rites with some semblance of willingness.

Having seen Elizabeth and his aunt safely into the trap, Richard, waiting only long enough to see them drive away, re-entered the church where Reverend Parton awaited him so that the coffin could be placed into the tomb where the caskets of his Uncle Lawrence and Aunt Sophia were, having been recently opened in order that the body of their son could be placed alongside them. Ever since the title had been granted to Edward Ferrers in 1455 by Henry V1, during one of his intermittent periods of rational thought, although most probably initiated by his strong-minded wife Margaret of Anjou, for services rendered at the battle of St. Albans and the Lancastrian cause, every Ferrers had been buried here in the mediaeval church, having miraculously escaped the fire which had gutted the manor house in 1545. The tide may have turned for the son whose father had had a resounding victory at Agincourt, resulting in his imprisonment and brutal death in the Tower of London, but no Ferrers had ever laid a hand in anger on their King or plotted his demise or overthrow by treason, and to think that his cousin had entered into insurrection for no other cause than personal gain, rendered William's dignified entombment a great trial to Richard. His Uncle Lawrence may have thrown good money after bad night after night at the card table, but he had never heard it said that he harboured treasonable intentions or nursed feelings of resentment about anyone, but as Richard looked sombrely at the sepulchre of his father and mother adjacent to that of his aunt and uncle, his thoughts were far from enlivening, doing nothing to lighten his heavy heart. The stonemason from Little

Turton, standing a little way back with his head bowed and hands folded, waited while Reverend Parton said a few words over the entombing, then after Richard had removed the coat of arms and folded it and left the church in company with Parton to walk back to the house, re-sealed the tomb.

William may not have been the most popular member of the Ferrers family, or, indeed, to the rest of the inhabitants at Ferrers Court, but his relatives could not help feeling some sorrow at the death of one of its members, even more so when it was remembered that his end had been brought about through his own scheming. Salmon, more forthright on the subject, had no intention of attending the obsequies of a man who had been instrumental in bringing about the early death of his late lordship, telling Richard that he could not pretend to feeling a sadness merely for appearances sake, and to enter a church to say goodbye to a man he heartily disliked would be tantamount to sacrilege. He fully agreed that Richard had no choice but to attend, as did his aunt and Miss Elizabeth, in fact, it would have created a very odd appearance if they had not, but since Mr. William was not his own kin nor, he added pugnaciously, a Ferrers, at least, not what he would call a Ferrers, then he had not felt himself obliged to pay his last respects.

Richard could not blame him for this, but since he could find no suitable reply and Salmon did not expect one, he turned his mind to the daily routine of running his estates and his thoughts to what lay ahead. Providing nothing untoward occurred he hoped to see Gideon any day now and looked forward to seeing him; not only did he like his future brother-in-law but there were still a few matters he wanted to discuss with him, and, of course, his arrival would no doubt help Elizabeth's recovery, because there was no denying that without him she really was quite forlorn. His surreptitious entries via that subterranean passage apart, if he were honest he had to admit that he had come to believe he would never step foot inside his home again, let alone administer what was his. He had lived in hourly expectation of hearing that William, by some means or other, had managed to establish the illegality of that document he had signed, and were it not for all that had gone before he would feel that, with his cousin's death and Colonel Henderson's trial and sentencing, justice had at last been done. He had no regrets about uncovering the identity of those who had leaked vital information to Stuart, even though one of them turned out to be his own cousin, but he could not deny that the last fifteen months or so had not entirely been a bed of roses. He had told Gideon that he would never forgive himself for his father's death and that still held true, because although he had had his father's blessing and approval for embarking on such a mission, had he not offered his services so readily he would still be alive today. It was a painful thought to take to bed at night, weighing heavily on his conscience, his only solace being that his father, whilst not living to see him proclaimed innocent, had gone to his grave knowing the truth. Then there was Elizabeth. Not only had she defended and supported him but had believed in him implicitly, only to find her reward for all this being a ball in the shoulder, and whilst no one could have foreseen this had it not been for him it would never have happened, although she had never once blamed him. He knew his sister too well to suspect her of lying, in fact, if he knew anything of it she was more than likely to thank him for bringing Gideon into her life, and although he was pleased to know that she had met a man worthy of her, he knew how fortunate they all were to come out of this as well as they had. Gideon may say he was owed no thanks of any kind, but he had not only saved him from taking a walk to the scaffold but had been instrumental in giving Jane back to him, without whom he could not envisage his future, and nothing he could say or do would be sufficient reward for a man whom he had no hesitation in deeming his liberator.

But Gideon's letter, informing him of Colonel Henderson's suicide which arrived at Ferrers Court the day after William's funeral, came as a reeling blow, not at all what he had expected, and so shocked was he that it was close on five minutes before he could fully take in what he had read. He could only hazard a guess as to whether Colonel Henderson had had this mind from the moment he knew there was nothing else he could do to stave off disaster and that he could no longer count on His Grace for support, but whilst those letters would still see him safe, he was far from happy to know that yet another conspirator had escaped the full penalty of the law for his crimes. It seemed that Colonel Henderson had been as dishonourable in death as he had in life, and rather than face his accusers had taken the coward's way out, surely proving that his venture into insurrection had stemmed purely from personal ambitions rather than belief and loyalty. Easily discounting William in having any say simply because he was a follower rather than a leader, he had, nevertheless, in company with Colonel Henderson and His Grace, done his utmost to apprehend him by any means at available, relying heavily on his friends informing against him by having him 'gazetted'. Well, his friends may be illegal traders depriving His Majesty's Government of its rightful duty, but they were far more honest and upright in their dealings than the three of them had ever been in the whole of their lives.

Clara Winsetton, who, upon hearing the news, gave it as her opinion that she had always known Henderson to be a bullying rogue, was not at all surprised to learn he had taken such a coward's way out rather than face his accusers, adding, as Richard was about to leave her to her afternoon's rest, "I know it's not what we wanted, but at least he can do you no more harm."

"I know," he nodded, "but it seems damned unfair all the same!"

"Yes, it does" she agreed, "but then," she pointed out practically, ringing her bell for Miss Calne, "if life were fair you wouldn't have been dodging the soldiers or that fellow Waring, and your father would still be alive!" She saw the sombre look enter those blue eyes, and said gently, "Richard, I know you feel your father's death to be your fault, but truly it was no such thing."

"Perhaps," he shrugged at length, "but somehow that does not make me feel any better." Upon leaving his aunt's room he went in search of Salmon and found him in the sitting room talking to Elizabeth, both of whom looked up as he entered.

Not unnaturally they were extremely shocked at the news, and Salmon, snorting his disgust, surprisingly became quite voluble on the subject, ending by commenting that they should have dealt with him while they had him here.

"An idea not without its merits," Richard smiled perfunctorily, "but whilst that solution had crossed my mind, I can't help thinking it would have created the devil of a stir!"

"And they dared to call you a felon and vicious cutthroat!" Salmon snorted disgustedly.

Richard nodded. "Yes, somewhat ironic, wouldn't you say?"

"I don't know about that Sir," Salmon said truthfully, "all I know," he nodded, "is that two of the nastiest pieces of work I've ever clapped eyes have escaped the law for their crimes!"

"I am aware of that," Richard told him grimly.

"Downright criminal, it is!" he exclaimed, making for the door. "I don't know what the world's coming to, and that's the truth!" closing it with a snap behind him.

"But Richard," Elizabeth asked, laying a hand on his, "does this mean that your affairs are to remain unsettled?"

"No," he shook his head, smiling reassuringly down at her, "according to Gideon," indicating the letter in his hand, "those letters will be produced at this Coroner's Panel he writes about, when hopefully matters will be settled once and for all. Before that however," he nodded, "there's to be another two inquiries, one for this Private who had unwittingly assisted Henderson and the other to question General Tuville."

"To question him!" she exclaimed, surprised. "What on earth for?"

"Well," he admitted, "I'm not that familiar with military procedure and the like, but according to Gideon," he explained, "although he did not personally hand Henderson his sword belt, the fact remains that he was in Turville's custody at the time it happened, and as he is the commanding officer, responsibility rests with him."

"But that is so unfair!" she cried.

"I know," he sighed, "but I have every faith in Gideon doing all he can on his behalf."

"But he could not have known what Colonel Henderson had in his mind," she shook her head. "He must have thought of it well beforehand."

Raking a hand through his hair, Richard looked down at the letter he still held in his hand, saying frustrated, "I'd lay my life he did!"

"But to blame Sir John is monstrous!" she cried, her eyes sparkling. "What a coward Henderson was!"

"Yes," he agreed, "he was."

He sat down beside her, and taking hold of her right hand, said considerately "I am afraid this means we shall not be seeing Gideon for a several days yet. This business is going to keep him pretty busy."

"Yes," she nodded, "I know. It's just that …"

"You miss him," he supplied gently. She looked sideways at him, nodding her head. "I do understand," he smiled sympathetically, "and I wish I could produce him for you right now, but I can't," he patted her hand. "But if nothing else, it will at least give you time to regain your strength; you're still looking a little pulled, y'know."

"I feel much better," she smiled, "truly I do."

He looked sceptical, but over the next few days, having finally discarded the sling, much against Doctor Jarvey's advice, giving her partial use at least of her left arm, he had thankfully come to believe that she was at last in a fair way to being her usual self. After several days of heavy rain, which had kept everyone to the house, the sun eventually broke through allowing her to take steady walks around the gardens in the warm sunshine, considerably relieving her brother's mind when he saw the colour gradually return to her cheeks. He held himself fully responsible for what had happened to her, and even though she did not blame him in the least, he could not rid himself of the guilt which enveloped him, especially when he thought how much more serious it could have been.

Taking advantage of the change in the weather, having decided to walk the short distance from The Manor to Ferrers Court, Jane, entering the house via the back door encountered Salmon in the hall, who, upon laying eyes on her, gave her the nod that the one package from the bundle of letters he had taken from the groom, who had only just returned from the receiving office in Little Turton, was from the Major, prayed it was good news. She knew that Richard's exoneration and reinstatement had still to be officially approved, and after removing her hat and gloves waited a good ten minutes before going to the book room to enquire if all were well. Quietly opening the door to see Richard staring in dazed astonishment at Gideon's third letter, arriving five days after the second, enclosing that all important copy of the Coroner's report with its vital section of exoneration, walked softly over to the desk, kneeling down beside him and looking lovingly up into his face, resting a gentle hand on his arm. Not until he felt the touch of her hand did he make any attempt to move, then turning his head slightly, stared blankly down into her upturned face, saying, with something very close to a sob in his voice, "I'm a free man!"

She nodded, her eyes misty with love and understanding, saying gently, "Yes, my darling."

He gave her a crooked little smile, the letter falling from his suddenly nerveless fingers as he lowered his head to cover his face with hands that visibly shook. For several moments she neither moved nor spoke, her only response to such good news and his reaction to it being the gentle pressure of her fingers on his arm, warm and reassuring and conveying all the love and faith she had always had in him. Then, with the compassion that was an intrinsic part of her nature, realized he most probably wanted to be alone for awhile, to take in the enormity of knowing that at long last he was finally exonerated and reinstated, she rose noiselessly to her feet and was just about to walk away when his right hand shot out and took hold of her left one.

"*No!*" he cried vehemently. "Don't go. Please Jane, I need you!" In one swift movement he was on his feet, the chair legs scraping on the polished floorboards, pulling her roughly into his arms and holding her so close she could hardly breathe. "Jane!" her name seemed to be ripped from his throat as he buried his face in the soft silken mane of her hair, his whole body trembling in mingled relief and the joy of having her near him. "I have been proved innocent! My darling," he cried, "I am now reinstated!" He held her tighter still. "Oh God!" he cried hoarsely, pressing his lips into the softness of her neck, "I can't believe it!"

She moved a little away from him to enable her to look up into his pale and drawn face, her eyes warm and tender, saying, from the bottom of her heart, "I never doubted you would be."

His eyes devoured her as he cupped her face in his unsteady hands, saying in a voice that was raw with emotion, "Now, at last, I can in all honour claim the right to marry you!"

"You've always had honour, Richard" she managed huskily, "I needed no letter to tell me that nor the fact that you were innocent; I've always known these things! As for the rest," she smiled lovingly, "I have always been yours; ready and eager to be claimed by you."

An agonized groan left his lips at this, but since no words of his could properly convey his feelings, he pulled her roughly back into his arms and kissed her with such fierce intensity that she had neither the time nor the inclination to say anything further, letting her response to this ruthless onslaught speak for itself. She knew, had known in fact ever since his troubles began, that had he have been forced to remain on the run for the rest of his life, she would still love and need him, and, like his sister, would never even have considered for one moment turning her back on him.

Emerging from the book room some considerable time later arm in arm with Jane, Richard, upon discovering his aunt and Salmon were in the sitting room, unceremoniously interrupted their lively exchange of views on some topic or other by telling them the good news. Salmon's old eyes immediately filled with tears of relief and Aunt Clara, who had to strenuously blow her nose several times, managed to say, in a voice which brooked no argument, that she had known all along it could not have been any other way. Richard laughed, and after hugging her and kissing her soundly on the cheek said that of course she did, to which she fondly chided him for having no respect for an old woman. Salmon, who, after several congratulatory words with Richard and shaking him vigorously by the hand, had found it necessary to dive into his waistcoat pocket for his handkerchief. Clara Winsetton, herself in danger of succumbing to the natural emotion following months of anxiety and constant worry, hid her feelings by briskly admonishing Salmon to stop behaving like a fool and bring in the decanter tray, because she for one, she nodded defiantly, was in need of a stimulant, besides which, she shrugged, it was only right that they celebrated her nephew's exoneration and reinstatement. Richard was in full agreement with this suggestion, but not, he said, until he had told his sister, who, he was informed, had left the house over an hour ago to take a walk in the gardens and therefore had no idea of the arrival of Gideon's letters. Jane, like Aunt Clara and Salmon, was aware of Elizabeth's unshakable devotion and belief in Richard as well as all the abuse she had suffered on his behalf and of the close bond which had always existed between brother and sister, and therefore made no demur when he said he wanted to be alone with Elizabeth to tell her the good news. The grounds of Ferrers Court were vast, but he had a pretty shrewd idea where she would be and unerringly tracked her down to the rose garden where she had gone to inspect some new blooms, which, Phillips the head gardener had told her two days before, would be out before the end of the week. Upon hearing the sound of firm footsteps approach her along the winding path, she thought it was Phillips coming to talk to her and raised her head in the full expectation of seeing him, but upon setting eyes on her brother, those dark blue depths lit up, saying contritely that she had not meant to stay outside so long, but it was such a beautiful day.

"I thought I would find you here," he told her quietly.

Something in his voice and the look on his face made her pause, cold fingers suddenly clutching at her heart, saying in a strangled voice, "Oh Richard! It's not Gideon? He's not...?"

"No, no" he assured her, squeezing her hand. "He is well, upon my honour he is."

She let out a sigh of relief, her eyes flying to his face as he smiled crookedly down at her, then watched as he slid his hand into his pocket to retrieve two sheets of vellum and one sealed communication, holding her breath expectantly.

"I've received these from Gideon," he told her. "This one's for you," indicating the sealed billet, "but first, I want you to read these." Her fingers shook perceptibly as she took them from him, hardly daring to look at the words written in that strong upright hand, but by the time she had come to the end of Gideon's communication tears of immense relief were falling unheeded down her cheeks and something like a convulsive sob escaped her parted lips. "Oh Richard!" she cried, staring up at her brother, whose blue eyes reflected his own immeasurable relief as well as the unashamed deep and genuine love he had for her as they looked back at her, a tremulous smile hovering on his lips. "Oh Richard!" she cried again between tears and laughter, shrugging helpless shoulders in mingled joy and wonder before falling into the arms he held out to her. The slight discomfort which she still experienced in her arm was completely forgotten as he held her close to him, uncontrollable sobs of indescribable relief racking her body as she clung to him, giving him as much comfort as he was giving her. She could feel the relief emanating from him with every breath he took, but although he was able to prevent his emotions from over spilling he was nevertheless incapable of arresting the deep agonizing sigh which left him like a powerful force.

After what seemed an aeon of time she gently eased herself a little away from him, her eyes warm and tender as they looked searchingly up into his face, hardly daring to believe that the day they had long awaited had finally arrived. "I can't believe it!" she said dazedly, shaking her head. "To know that you are no longer a wanted a man!"

"I know," he grimaced, a slight tremor in his voice, kissing the top of her head, "it's going to take the devil of a lot of getting used to!"

"I have prayed for this day," she told him earnestly, "and whilst I knew you were innocent and nothing anyone could say or do would make me believe otherwise, it is so good to have you home and safe and to know that I shall no longer have to worry over whether you are alive or dead or dreadfully hurt!" He held her tight against him as she gave in to emotions which he knew would take some time to leave her completely. "Promise me something Richard," she said firmly, when she was able.

"*Anything*," he smiled.

"Promise me that never again will you do something like this. I know why you did it, and I am truly proud of you, but I couldn't bear anything to happen to you!"

"I promise," he assured her, "but haven't I told you I am indestructible?"

"Yes," she sniffed, "you have, but you may not be so fortunate next time."

He nodded, saying truthfully, "I know, and next time there will be no Gideon to come to my aid. What a lot I have to thank him for!"

"Yes," she nodded, "but he does not want thanks."

"I know," he sighed, "and the devil's in it, he means it!" He raked a hand through his hair. "But I shall always be indebted to him. I am very conscious of the fact that he gave me back my life and dignities, not to mention Jane and ..." he compressed his lips, "I shall never be able to repay him!"

Taking hold of his hand she said simply, "You like Gideon very much, don't you?"

He nodded. "Yes. Oh, I know I have not known him very long," he admitted, "but the truth is I've come to love him like a brother, in fact," he grimaced, "he's done more for me than any brother would!" He smiled tenderly down at her, squeezing her hand, saying softly, "But not a sister. Thank you."

"For what," she asked, resting her free hand against his cheek.

"For believing in me and loving me the way you do; for enduring the despicable treatment meted out to you, for having to undergo the pain and grief of losing our father alone, but most of all" he said earnestly, "for being my sister!" kissing the palm of her hand. "I told you not long ago that you were the best of sisters'," she nodded, "it's true. I don't need a brother when I have you."

"Oh Richard!" she sniffed, reaching up and kissing his cheek. "I love you very much, and I never believed that tale father and Salmon told me, but even if I had," she told him truthfully, "it would not have made any difference to how I feel about you, nor," she added firmly, "would it have convinced me that you were a traitor, and even if I had known where you were hiding out, nothing anyone could have said or done would have prised it out me."

"I know," he said softly, "which is why I feel so damnably about this," gently touching her arm. "I shall never forgive myself for allowing something like this to happen to you."

"I've told you," she shook her head, "it was not your fault; no one could have foreseen it. *Now*," she said as firmly as she could, a twinkle in her eye, "I want to hear no more about it, because if I do I shall be extremely cross!"

He laughed, pinched her cheek and said very well he wouldn't mention it again. "Shall we return to the house," he asked, "or do you want to remain here to read Gideon's letter, *which*" he said in mock brotherly disapproval, "I've no doubt contains some pretty effusive stuff!"

She laughed and coloured slightly, but said mischievously as she patted her pocket, "Oh, I do hope so, which is why I shall read it later!"

"Hussy!" he laughed, pulling her right hand through his arm to walk slowly back to the house in contented sibling empathy.

Although Gideon's letter began harmlessly enough by explaining the reason for the delay in him returning to Ferrers Court, it nevertheless contained confidences and ardent passages expressing his urgent need to be with her again which were every bit as effusive as Richard had teasingly surmised. Having read it repeatedly over the course of the next two days, her heart beating excitedly each time she re-read every blissful word, she lovingly placed it with the others she had received from him, her fingers not quite steady as she re-tied the bow of the ribbon securely binding them together before carefully depositing her precious bundle into the French enamel box which she kept in the drawer of a Queen Anne cabinet beside her bed. Richard knew perfectly well that the content of Gideon's letter was the reason for his sister's glowing face and sparkling eyes, but knew too that unforeseen events had kept him in town for far longer than he had envisaged, and although his return to Ferrers Court was imminent, he would, were it at all possible, have ridden to London himself to bring Gideon to her.

He was himself eager to see Gideon on his own behalf, because although he continually maintained that no thanks were due to him, he knew perfectly well that he was under a huge obligation which he could never fully discharge, and if it took him for ever, he was determined to offer him his gratitude if nothing else. As it turned out however, he was able to do so within two days of receiving his last letters, Gideon arriving just as the time-piece in the hall struck two o'clock.

At long last the tall twisted chimneys of Ferrers Court came into view, and Gideon, who had taken a real liking to his future brother-in-law, was looking forward to seeing him again, but it was his eagerness to see Elizabeth after more than two long weeks, which caused him to spur his horse on.   Having ridden down the avenue he made his way directly to the stables, where his grey mare was taken by a groom, and not wishing to enter through the rear door, strode quickly round to the front of the house, tugging almost impatiently on the bell pull. Salmon, who had been talking to Richard in his book room, no sooner heard the chimes from the clapper, than he immediately excused himself and hurried to open the door, staring up at Gideon with welcome relief. *"Major Neville, Sir!"* he cried, shaking the hand held out to him.

"Hello, Salmon. How are you?" he smiled, dropping his cloak bag onto the floor.

"None so bad, Major," he nodded, taking the cloak bag from him then relieving him of his long drab riding coat. "I ..."

"He's not the Major any longer, Salmon," came a familiar voice from the rear of the hall.   "So," Richard mused, strolling leisurely forward, his eyes alight as he extended his hand, taking note of Gideon's riding breeches and top boots as well as the superbly tailored mulberry coloured coat, "you've finally gone and done it! You're no longer a red-coat!"

Gripping Richard's hand, he laughed, "As you see, I've finally gone and done it; I'm no longer a red-coat! How are you Richard?"

"Need you ask?" he grinned. "Never better! By the way," he nodded, "I don't know what your immediate plans are, but don't get to thinking you're leaving here just yet. I know you want to get home," he acknowledged, "but you must stay for a couple of days at least."

"I shall be pleased to," Gideon smiled. "I told my parent's to expect me later this week. I am afraid I only have my cloak bag with me; the rest of my gear has been sent home by carrier."

"That's settled then," he said firmly, turning to Salmon to ensure Gideon's room was made ready and his clothes pressed.

Receiving an assenting nod to this, Salmon looked at Gideon, his old eyes lighting up, "It will be a pleasure to have you, Major."

"How much longer are you going to call him the Major?" Richard demanded.

"Begging your pardon, Sir," he told Gideon, "but you'll always be the Major to me."

Richard laughed. "I've a deal to say to you," he told him when Salmon had left.

"Yes," Gideon nodded, "and I to you."

"First though," Richard grinned, patting him on the shoulder, "there's someone whose been waiting with what patience she can muster to see you. They're all in the garden. I'll take you there."

"How is she?" Gideon asked earnestly.

"According to Doctor Jarvey," Richard told him as they walked towards the rear of the hall, not without a touch of pride, "she's the most stubborn patient he has ever had." He then went on to tell him about how he had found her attempting to get out of bed, then several days later, having badgered poor Jarvey to death, made the attempt to get down the stairs. "If you take my advice Gideon," he warned, the light in his eyes giving the lie to his recommendation, "you will beat that chit, at least twice a day!"

Gideon laughed. "I see. And would *you* beat her, at least twice a day?"

Richard smiled, opening the door which led to the gardens at the rear of the house, "No, of course I wouldn't."

"I thought not," Gideon grinned.

"And nor will you by the looks of it!" he laughed.

"No," he shook his head, "I won't."

Upon approaching the oak tree, where, only a few short weeks before, Gideon had sat with Elizabeth, it came as no surprise to Richard to find she was not there sitting in the shade with his aunt and Jane, both of whom were delighted to see him. Clara Winsetton, who knew quality when she saw it, took one look at Gideon and knew instantly that only the finest tailor in town had fashioned his impeccably cut coat, and the delicate lace at his wrists and throat, from which a small diamond pin glinted, was of the finest, all meeting with her unequivocal approval. After eying him up and down considering said, in her forthright manner, that it was about time he put his regimentals to one side.

"Thank you, Ma'am," he said without a tremor, bowing gracefully over her hand, his eyes smiling down into hers. "I trust I find you well?"

She dismissed this with an impatient hand, saying "Never mind that! Well, Major, it seems we have a deal to thank you for."

"Not at all, Ma'am" he shook his head.

She eyed him severely, saying firmly, "Major ..."

"Forgive me, Ma'am" he interrupted gently, "but you appear to be labouring under a misapprehension."

"*Major ...*" she began awfully, her bony fingers gripping the arms of her chair.

"You know," he interrupted again with a most disarming smile, "I do wish you would call me Gideon." She compressed her lips at this, not at all certain whether to take him to task for interrupting her, or for attempting to change the subject. "You see, Ma'am," he said gravely, growing more and more fond of this formidable old lady, "apart from the fact that I am no longer in regimentals, it does happen to be my name."

She twitched her shawl at this, unable to resist his coaxing smile. "I daresay," she snapped, the twinkle in her eye not lost on him or Richard. "And I suppose next you are going to ask if you can call me Aunt!"

"If you should not dislike it Ma'am yes; especially as I am...or rather, I should say," he corrected himself, "have every hope of becoming your nephew, it would be a little less formal, besides," he smiled down at her, "not only would I deem it an honour, but I would like it very much." She snorted, but it was obvious to Richard that she by no means disliked this light-hearted exchange, nor for that matter, Gideon. She pursed her lips, eyeing him closely, nodding "Yes, you have the look of your father, but you have your mother's way with you!"

"Thank you, Ma'am," he inclined his head.

"Very well," she conceded, having made the pretence of giving it some thought, "I suppose I shall have to call you Gideon, because I've no doubt," she said tartly, glancing across at Richard, "that I shall be hounded to distraction if I don't, *but,*" she emphasized, leaning forward to take hold of his hand, her eyes smiling up at him as she squeezed his fingers affectionately, "I shall expect you to behave yourself!"

"Thank you, Ma'am" he smiled, raising her hand to his lips, "I promise I shall not do anything to cause you embarrassment."

"Ha! You can keep that silly talk for my niece," she nodded. "Where is the chit by the way?"

Since no one could enlighten her she pursed her lips, before stating roundly that no one would think she had been lying abed injured for days on end the way she refused to keep still.

Richard laughed, then placing a hand on Gideon's shoulder, said "Gideon, you know Jane I believe?"

"Yes, I have had the pleasure of making Miss Trench's acquaintance," he smiled taking her hand. "How do you do Miss Trench; or may I call you Jane?"

"Oh yes," she smiled, "please do; if I may be permitted to call you Gideon. You did say," she reminded him laughingly, "that we were going to be in some sort related."

"That, at least, is the hope," he smiled.

"I don't know where Elizabeth is, but if you should not dislike it, will you allow me to accompany you to find her?"

"I shall be honoured," he smiled, proffering his arm.

"Well, if that don't beat the Dutch!" Richard laughed. "On the point of offering for my sister and then walks off with my betrothed as calm as you please!"

"These army types," Gideon shook his head sadly, "so very rag-mannered!"

Richard laughed, slapping him on the shoulder. "I shall repay you handsomely, see if I don't!"

"Thank you for allowing me to accompany you," Jane said in her quiet way, slipping her hand comfortably through his arm. "I assure you," she smiled, "I have no intention of playing gooseberry between you and Elizabeth, but I did want the opportunity of a few moments alone with you."

"Is there something you wish to say to me, Jane?" he asked, smiling encouragingly down at her.

"Well, actually there is," she confessed. "You see Gideon, I know you said you require no expressions of gratitude, but, indeed, you must allow me to do so."

"Must I?" he asked, raising a comical eyebrow.

"Yes," she nodded firmly, "you must." She walked alongside him in silence for some little way, then looking up at him said, not a little shyly, "You cannot be unaware of how very happy you have made me. Because of your efforts on Richard's behalf as well as your representations to my papa, you have given me something which I thought was lost to me, indeed," she nodded, coming to a standstill without realizing it, "I am most conscious of the debt I, in fact," she smiled, "all of us, owe you. Richard particularly is very much aware of the obligation he is under."

"Ah," he recollected amusingly, nodding his head comprehendingly, "he did say he had a deal to say to me!" Removing her hand from the crook of his arm he raised it to lips, his eyes conveying so much understanding that she knew precisely what had made her future sister-in-law fall in love him. "You know, Jane," he told her, the sincerity in voice not undermined by the gentle way he spoke, keeping a firm hold of her hand in both of his, "when I say I need no thanks, that is precisely what I mean. My efforts on Richard's behalf as you call them, were not to promote myself in anyone's favour nor because I wished to receive congratulations or expressions of gratitude. I do not advocate hounding an innocent man to the gallows, and that is precisely what Richard was, an innocent man. My actions would have been the same for any man who found himself in Richard's unfortunate position. I simply did my duty, and what I believed to be right," he nodded. "I came into Sussex to do all I could to help a young man whose difficulties were threatening to overpower him and not to perform an act of charity merely because Richard's father and my commanding officer were old friends. I did not expect any reward for whatever service I performed on his behalf," he told her earnestly "and I still do not, and I certainly do not look upon Elizabeth as such. I did not come here in the expectation of falling in love with Richard's sister, that happy circumstance was something I had not anticipated, but my feelings for her have nothing whatever to do with what you may believe I consider is owed me. *Nothing* is owed me," he assured her. "I love Elizabeth more than life and consider myself the luckiest and happiest man alive because of it."

She nodded comprehendingly, "Thank you, Gideon." Then without thinking said, innocently, "But Richard too, claims he is the happiest man alive!"

"And with good cause," he smiled warmly, kissing her fingers before releasing her hand.

The colour flooded her cheeks at what she had said, realizing too late how it appeared, her embarrassment so acute that she hurriedly lowered her eyes, faltering "I'm sorry ... I"

"There is not the least need to be sorry," he assured her, gently raising her chin with his forefinger, forcing her to look up at him. "Nor do I think you a very pushing young female." The laughter in his voice easing her awkwardness. "You have spoken no less than truth, indeed, he is extremely fortunate to have you; and I wish you both very happy."

"Thank you," she smiled shyly. She was just about to say something when suddenly she caught sight of a rose pink vision in the distance before it was lost from sight behind some well kept hedges, his eyes following her glance. "I think you will find Elizabeth is making her way towards the shrubbery," she told him, more composed now, adding considerately, "I know you wish to be alone with her, so I shall leave you now." He brought his gaze back to her face, her eyes smiling up into his. "You know, Gideon," she said softly, resting a reassuring hand on his arm, "I do not think you will be disappointed with her answer to your question." Then without waiting for him to respond to this, she walked back towards the house.

Following in the direction where they had caught a glimpse of Elizabeth, Gideon emerged from the path banked by high hedges on the right into a wide open space, where, in the far distance, could be seen red bricked walls sheltering two rows of glass houses. Laid down immediately in front of them he could see rows of what appeared to be a variety of vegetables growing, and directly at the forefront of these were Tudor knot gardens cleverly interspersed with orderly and symmetrical bordered ones displaying a variety of different flowers, their boxed hedges well clipped and tended. Having come to the end of the path he paused and looked to the right, where, in the distance, he could see the stable clock, then, just as he wondered which path or avenue she could have gone down, he caught a glimpse of deep rose pink walking away from him in company with one of the gardeners, in enthusiastic and animated conversation with a basket over her right arm. A warm glow entered his eyes and a smile touched his well shaped lips as he contentedly watched her, as much at ease talking to an estate worker as she was to anyone else, and not for the first time felt his insides somersault at the sight of her. His strides may have been leisurely as he followed in her wake but he soon caught up with her, not sorry when he saw her companion nod his head in acknowledgement to something she had said and walk away to the far end of the garden.   Her back was turned to him as he approached her, bending down to examine a bloom, and without turning round or looking up at the sound of footsteps behind her, believing it to be Richard, said excitedly, "Oh Richard, what do you think? You know I told you that Phillips is cultivating a new rose in a deep shade of pink, well, he has asked me if I minded if he can call it '*Elizabeth Ferrers*' . Isn't that so kind of him?"

"I think it very kind of him," came the quiet reply; "especially as pink is your colour."

Upon hearing that deep familiar voice she spun round, her basket falling off her arm and tumbling to the ground, spilling some of its contents of cut flowers onto the path as it toppled over onto its side, staring in wide eyed surprise at the man she had been missing with agonizing longing for two weeks past, the colour flooding her cheeks.

"Of course," he pointed out, taking a step nearer to her, his eyes smiling down into hers in a way that made her heart feel as if it were going to burst, "I am not at all sure I approve of a strange man wanting to name a flower after you; a rose especially!"

Seeing him again after what seemed like an eternity, and not in regimentals as she had become used to, was so unexpected that for one awful moment she felt just a little shy and tongue-tied, and something very like a stifled sob caught in her throat, managing croakily,   "He… he's not a strange man," she faltered, "it's …it's Phillips; our head gardener."

"Ah!" he nodded, his eyes alight with amusement and something else which made her draw in her breath, "that, of course, makes all the difference."

How she had desperately missed that gentle teasing and the way he had of looking at her in just such a way as he was now that made her heart stand still! Tears of overwhelming joy began to well up in the back of her eyes and when she saw him hold out his hand to her, sobbed huskily, "Oh Gideon! Is… is it really you at long last?"

"Yes, my darling" he said lovingly, "it's really me," firmly clasping her fingers as she placed them into his. It was just as he was about to draw her into his arms that a small contingent of gardeners emerging from a hidden section of the grounds came into his eye line, carrying various tools and implements which told him they were about to set to work, unless he was very much mistaken, on a section of the gardens quite close to them. Looking round to see what had drawn his attention the sight of this tiny army bearing down upon them struck her as so absurd at such a moment that upon turning to look at Gideon with such a look of comical dismay on his face,   a spontaneous bubble of laughter escaped her. Succumbing to his ready sense of the ridiculous at this diminutive invasion just when he was on the point of kissing her, glanced from the industrious group advancing steadily towards them then back to Elizabeth, whose head was pressed against his shoulder shaking with mirth. "I suppose they *do* have to be here in this very spot right at this moment?" he sighed. "Of course," he commented, in the manner of one who had not given up all hope, "one would think in grounds as vast as this, there would be at least one tiny corner which might, I say *might*," he emphasized, "because one should never build up one's hopes, after all," he shook his head sadly, "which would escape attack from zealous gardeners, unless, of course," he sighed mournfully, "this man Phillips, you know," he reminded her helpfully, "the one with the rose, is conspiring against me and means to thwart my efforts to be alone with you by ensuring that every arbour and secreted bower is regularly patrolled by his legion of supporters! Now please, do not spare me, I beg of you," he urged, the ardent look in his eyes demolishing what little composure she had, "if you prefer Phillips with all the roses at his command to my poor pretensions, then so be it. I'm not saying I understand such a preference," he shrugged bewildered, "but I shall abide by your heart's decision and retire forthwith from the lists with what dignity I can muster!"

This droll absurdity, as stimulating as any fervent protestations of love, evoked an uncontrollable quiver of pleasure which ran the whole length of her body, and looking lovingly up into his face, laid the palm of her hand against his cheek. "Oh, how much I have missed you!" she told him huskily.

Taking hold of her hand and pressing his lips against its soft palm, his eyes burning as they searched her glowing face, told her, in a none too steady voice, "Since it is not possible at this precise moment for me to show you just how much I have missed *you*," referring to the unwelcome invaders busily setting to work just a few yards away from them, "can I take that to mean you *do* know of a secluded corner?"

She nodded, then taking hold of his hand, her basket forgotten, led him out of this part of the garden towards the shrubbery, but hurriedly bypassing this delightful sun trap walked a little way further on until veering a little to the right where she guided him down a path of rose covered archways which ran the full length of this secluded little avenue, where, just half way down, was a discreet little recess, its conveniently placed seat making it a pretty and sweet-scented arbour for two people who wanted to be alone.   Having taken her seat she drew him down beside her, her face a little flushed and her eyes glowing with happiness at seeing him again, telling him that this was one of the places where she and Jane used to play as children because no one ever came here, well, hardly ever.   He found this confession irresistible,   but he had no doubt that in their childlike minds no thoughts of the use for which this secluded little spot had originally been intended, or which it was now being put, had ever occurred to them.

"I see," he said slowly, raising her hand to his lips and kissing its palm, "and what manner of mischief did you get up to?" he asked softly.

"None at all!" she replied a little breathlessly as his lips began to brush her wrist with provocative deliberation.

"None?" he raised a questioning eyebrow, his eyes warm and dark as they looked deep into her own.

"We were very well behaved, I assure you," she managed, holding her breath as he leaned forward a little, his fingers provocatively lifting the lace at her elbow to expose her soft skin, closing her eyes on a barely concealed gasp as he kissed its silken inside, deliciously wonderful memories flooding her mind at the last time he had done this.

"Are you sure about that?" he asked a little thickly, his left hand gently travelling up her right arm to her shoulder, the warmth of his fingers penetrating through the material of her sleeve, feeling herself being irresistibly drawn a little nearer to him, her heart pounding in her breast as he tilted his head a little in order to caress the soft creamy skin of her throat with provocative sensitivity.

"Yes, quite sure," she managed on a sharp intake of breath, her fingers suddenly clutching his arm on a convulsive shudder as his lips seductively paved a trail up the smoothness of her neck with deliberately lingering caresses that forced her head back against his supporting arm, his free hand cupping the side of her face to allow his thumb to rhythmically stroke and tease her parted lips, closing her eyes on a pleasurable gasp as he slowly and tantalizingly tormented his way to her mouth.   But when she could no longer bear the exquisite agony of his delicately stimulating tugs on her bottom lip, already sensitized by his evocative thumb, she cried out his name on a throbbing gasp, her pliant body putting up no resistance when his arms tightened around her, drawing her yieldingly into his strong hard body until she thought her ribs would crack, but this conviction was soon lost sight of when she heard his deep throated cry of need and felt his mouth on hers, arousing and exciting her with slow drugging kisses until she could think of nothing but the sheer pleasure he was giving her and the joy of being held in his arms.

Apart from a slight breeze rustling the heavily scented blossoms all around them and the sun's rays flickering through the foliage, no sound or disturbance broke the spell of this idyllic and sheltered arbour, and not even the stable clock chiming the half hour permeated into the consciousness of the two people who were enjoying its seclusion for a short time.   When Gideon had kissed her before the woman inside her had instinctively known that he had been keeping a tight hold on his emotions, but now, as she rested back against the seat with her soft malleable body partly covered by his powerfully strong torso and his arms crushingly confining her to him, rejoicing in the unrestrained and hungry demands he was making of her mouth, she was left in no doubt.   The diminishing but lingering discomfort of her shoulder was forgotten as she eagerly welcomed and returned his passionate demands, their uncontrolled cries at the pleasure they were giving and receiving only serving to enhance their need of each other, until, after what could have been an aeon of time, he released her mouth and buried his face into the thick softness of her hair.   She could feel the thudding of his heart next to her own and the trembling of his body as he remained pressed against her, his chest heaving for several minutes until gradually he got his breathing sufficiently under control for him to groan hoarsely into the soft dusky curls, "I love you!   I love you more than life itself!" As if to prove this point, his none too steady fingers brushed several ringlets away from her neck, his lips caressing her exposed receptive skin with delicate feather light touches, making her shudder in his arms, feeling rather bereft when, some minutes later, he eased himself a little away from her to enable him to look down into her flushed face, her eyes darkened with desire as they gazed up at him from where she lay with her head back resting in the crook of his arm. "I have missed you so much!" he told her hoarsely.   "These last two weeks without you have been torment. I have ached for you, my darling. I can't bear being parted from you." Without giving her time to respond he lowered his head and kissed her, a slow unhurried kiss that seemed to drain her of all power of movement or thought, delighting in the intimacy they were sharing, justifying her refusal of those most obliging offers for her hand!   After a while his mouth left hers and opening her eyes to look up at him, trembled at the burning need she could see in those dark depths as they hungrily devoured every inch of her flushed face. "Oh, Gideon!" she cried breathlessly, resting a hand on his cheek, "I love you so much.   I have been so miserable without you these last weeks."   He kissed the palm of her hand. "Your letters," she told him huskily, "I have read them over and over because they make me feel as though you are with me."

An agonized groan ripped from his throat at these words before thoroughly kissing her. "I meant every word of them," he pressed against her hair as he held her tight against him.

"They're beautiful words!" she cried.

"My darling," he told her thickly, "you have made me the happiest man alive," then easing himself away from her so he could see her face, said "will you make my happiness complete by consenting to become my wife?"

A stray tear fell from the corner of her eye at this. "Yes, my darling," she said fervently, "oh, yes!"

A deep sigh racked his body, then pulling her roughly to him, comprehensively kissed her. "There is however, one stipulation," he told her urgently when he released her.

"There is?" she enquired breathlessly.

"Mm" he nodded.

"And what is this stipulation?" she asked against his lips.

"That we do not have an overly long betrothal," he managed hoarsely.

"I see. I take it you have a reason for this?" she managed, between kisses.

"I do," he confirmed at length, unable to tear himself completely away from her, "a vitally important one. In fact," he told her, pausing to brush her lips with his, "it is a matter of life and death."

"I see," she mumbled indistinctly against his lips, "as serious as that!"

"Not only serious, but crucial," he informed her thickly, "in fact, if my ring is not upon your finger very soon I shall be driven to the brink of insanity with wanting to make love to you, and that, you know," he shook his head, "will never do."

"No," she agreed huskily, "that will never do," her glowing face and smouldering eyes telling him more than any words could have that she not only perfectly understood but felt precisely the same.

"I knew you would understand," he groaned, deciding that no further words were in the least necessary. "You know," he said ashamedly some minutes later, cradling her against him, "in all the excitement I forgot to ask you about your arm. Forgive me, my darling" he smiled, tenderly rubbing the afflicted area.

"Of course I'll forgive you," she sighed contentedly. "But truly, it is much better. I only have a little discomfort now," she shook her head. "Doctor Jarvey says it is healing just as it ought."

"Mm," she heard the doubtful note in his voice and cast a quick glance up at him from under her lashes, "I must confess to some surprise at that," he admitted, looking down at her, his eyes alight with amusement and something else.

She looked a question, knowing instinctively what he was going to say, the responsive glow in her eyes almost proving too much for his self-control. "Oh, I see," she nodded. "You mean Richard's been telling you about how I tried to get out of bed?"

"About your attempts to get out of bed" he confirmed, "*and* your single-handed foray downstairs, yes," he nodded. "You know," he told her tenderly, pushing a strand of hair away from her flushed face, "I ought to be very cross with you."

"But you're not!" she said caressingly.

"No," he shook his head, "I'm not," he confirmed in a deep voice.

"I am so glad," she smiled up at him. Then, as if a thought had just occurred to her, asked provocatively, "What would you do if you were?"

"Were I to take Richard's advice," he informed her, his voice a caress, "I would beat you, at least twice a day."

She laughed quietly into his shoulder, before raising her eyes to his, asking teasingly, "And will you beat me, at least twice a day?"

The look in his eyes and the deep warmth of his voice made her quiver. "No," he said throatily, holding her tighter, "only once."

She laughed, then gave herself up to a pleasurable few minutes in his arms before it would be time to reluctantly leave their sanctuary.

"You know," he told her gently, when they eventually left their fragrant arbour, her hand tucked in his arm, "I think it may be advisable if we were to take the long way back to the house."

"Oh, why?" she asked, looking up at him.

"Because, my darling," he told her caressingly, looking warmly down at her as he tenderly brushed her flushed face with his forefinger, "just one look at you will suffice to apprise Richard and your aunt as to precisely how we have spent the last hour or so."

"How do I look?" she enquired a little breathlessly.

"Like a woman who has been well and truly kissed," he replied lovingly, "and one, moreover, who has enjoyed it just as much as I." She smiled shyly up at him, rendering it necessary for him to exert every ounce of restraint, but having eventually managed to clamp down on his urgent desire to take her back in his arms, said teasingly, "Although, I doubt they will need evidence of how we have past the time, they are bound to know we have not been exchanging polite pleasantries!"

She blushed and laughed and shook her head, but when she finally came upon her aunt and Richard sitting under the oak tree with Jane, she felt the colour deepen in her cheeks, and was not quite able to meet her brother's indulgent eye or her aunt's penetrating stare, and when she asked if they had enjoyed their stroll around the grounds was quite unable to give her an answer. Richard, who knew precisely how they had been spending the last hour or more, was neither shocked nor filled with the need to question Gideon's behaviour towards his sister, knowing perfectly well that however much he loved her, he could trust him to keep the line until his ring was on her finger. He cast an eye brimming with laughter at Gideon, who had fully expected her to remark on the length of their absence and was therefore not in the least embarrassed or fooled by this seemingly innocent enquiry, returned Richard's look with one of equal amusement. Releasing Elizabeth's arm from the protection of his, he leisurely walked towards her, his eyes laughing down into hers as he bowed over her hand, saying, without a tremor, "Having been absent for over two weeks, I am afraid to confess that we did not stroll very far, my attention, I am sure you will appreciate, being naturally diverted from such a delightful scene by the pleasurable company of your niece, who," he smiled down at her, "has done me the honour of consenting to become my wife."

Glancing across at her brother and receiving an assenting nod of the head and a huge grin, Elizabeth, in answer to Gideon's turn of the head in her direction and his outstretched hand, walked over to where he was standing in front of her aunt. Raising her hand to his lips, she looked up at him, her feelings mirroring his, leaving that redoubtable old lady in no doubt that this was one most obliging offer her niece had no intention of turning down, and one she herself most definitely approved of.

CHAPTER THIRTY ONE

Any hopes either Gideon or Elizabeth may have cherished about spending a little time alone together following their betrothal announcement were dashed almost as soon as they returned to the house, as the arrival of Michael, bringing them news of Private Smith, naturally included Gideon as well as Richard. Aunt Clara, having paused only long enough to have a word with Michael, accepted her niece's proffered arm to assist her up the stairs but not without shrewdly commenting that she had no doubt she would much prefer to talk of love and bride clothes with Jane than accompany her to her bedchamber, to which Elizabeth laughingly replied yes, of course she would, a response which brought forth a cackle of mirth from her aunt. Jane, after being introduced to Michael and thanking him for all his efforts, exchanged a few words with Richard before making her way to the sitting room, leaving him to speak to Salmon while Michael happily renewed his acquaintance with Gideon. Upon becoming aware that his visit had coincided with Gideon's betrothal to Elizabeth Ferrers, he was rendered acutely embarrassed and immediately announced his intention of returning another day. Gideon's whole being may ache with the need to take Elizabeth back into his arms and kiss her, but he too had once been young and inexperienced, not only as a soldier but as a man, and remembered only too well how, at the same age, he had tried to do the right thing without embarrassing either himself or others. Even though he was no longer in regimentals he knew that one word from him would be sufficient to persuade him into taking his leave, but apart from the fact that he would not even consider asking someone to leave another's man's home in which he himself was a guest, it was not in his nature to hurt anyone much less humiliate them. Besides, he liked Michael, but he knew too that without his help Richard would most probably have been arrested or shot at Hampton Regis garrison as a result of Colonel Henderson's despicable scheming, and it was therefore with the smile which had won him many friends that he assured him he was by no means intruding and that he would be most interested to learn of Private Smith's activities and the results of Major Denham's enquiries. Richard, having left Salmon to rejoin them, overheard this, and slapping his friend on the shoulder, laughingly told him not to be absurd, propelling him irresistibly towards the book room. As Elizabeth was by now descending the stairs, Gideon waited for her to come up to him before following Richard and Michael into the book room, but even standing on the first step she still had some way to look up into his face, only just reaching his shoulder, placing her hand in his as he smiled ruefully down at her.

"I'm sorry, my darling" he shook his head, "but I must see Michael."

"I know," she said tenderly, smiling up at him.

"I shall come to you just as soon as I can," he told her softly, kissing her fingers.

"And I shall be here waiting for you," she smiled, reaching up in order for her to briefly touch his lips with her own.

His eyes burned into hers. "I love you," he told her in a deep voice, then after kissing the palm of her hand, made his way to the book room.

Upon his entrance, Michael, who had just sat down, immediately rose to his feet and stood to attention, and Gideon, catching the light of pure amusement in Richard's eyes, said kindly, "It's all right Michael," gently easing him back into his chair, "you no longer have to stand to attention or call me Sir or Major; Gideon will do very nicely."

He blushed and stammered, apologizing that he had meant no offence, but due to Gideon's delicate and tactful handling, he soon found himself slipping back into the easy terms which had existed between them prior to Gideon's return to town, and eventually began to relax, enabling him to relate the events surrounding Private Smith's arrest.

It appeared that this unscrupulous individual had indeed made it as far as Newhaven, and had even managed to book a passage on the next available packet to Dieppe, but thanks to a storm in the Channel which lasted for two whole days followed by several more of unfavourable winds, he had been forced to linger about the town for far longer than he would have liked. The landlord of *The Ship Ashore*, whose hostelry had been bursting at the seams for days due to the inclement weather, had paid no undue attention to the customer occupying his small back bedchamber, and doubted that he would ever have done so had it not been for Molly, the flirty little piece who helped his good lady in the kitchen. As Wednesday was market day and everyone for miles around came to either sell or buy produce of every description, and it was Molly's task to purchase fresh vegetables and whatever else was needed by Mrs. Peat, she generally made the most of her time away from the inn by ogling all the personable young men who came within her orbit. Not surprisingly, the sight of so many soldiers unexpectedly frequenting the town and market place caused her eyes to light up, and taking full advantage of her ample charms began to attract their attention by walking with studied nonchalance past them and swinging her half full basket in her hand, and when one in particular spotted her glances in his direction from under fluttering eyelashes, lowered her eyes and raised a hand to her breast as he walked up to her. Not at all sure whether to feel insulted over the way he paid scant attention to her obvious lures or excitement at being asked if she had seen a man fitting this description whom he had reason to believe may be in Newhaven, rushed back to the inn with her shopping half done, her eyes sparkling and cheeks glowing, bursting into the kitchen and announcing to Mrs. Peat in breathless exuberance, "Oo, you'll neva guess; there's soljers in the town and ..."

The description of the wanted man which escaped her pouting lips may have been interpolated with comments such as "Oo, I wunda wot's 'e's done?" and "It meks me all affeared wen I think on it!" was enough to make Mr. Peat put his thinking cap on, and by the time he had pondered and cogitated he was convinced that the tall, sandy haired and fresh complexioned young man the red-coats were after was the one presently occupying his small back bedchamber. He was not snitch, he hoped that went without saying, but he ran an honest inn and just one whiff that he harboured law-breakers and the like, however unwittingly, would do his profitable little business no good at all. As he told his good lady, "'E ain't dun me a mite of 'arm, an' fer all I no's 'e ain't this ere desprit criminal their a lookin' for, but I ain't teckin' no chancis. Now," he nodded to Mrs. Peat, "up them sters wi' ya' and see if 'e's in." Placing his battered tricorne on his head, he watched her shuffle up the stairs, a little surprised to see her stop and turn round when she was only half way up, and cocking his head demanded to be told what was the matter.

Her ample proportions were not made for such steep and narrow stairs as these, but after catching her breath, asked wheezingly, "Wot do I says ter 'im if 'e's in?"

He sighed. "'Ow shud I no's; yer'll 'ave ter think o' somethin'." Her lips pursed at this. "Jus' meck shua 'e don't go nowere till I gets back wi' the soljers. 'Sides," he nodded firmly as he opened the door, "'e ain't paid 'is shot yet!"

As this clinched the matter, Mrs. Peat continued up the stairs, but her bulk, causing the floorboards to creek alarmingly under her weight, rendered it necessary for her to tip-toe the rest of the way across the first floor landing, arriving at the back bedchamber door in a manner perilously close to stealth. Pressing her ear to the door in an attempt to hear if their guest was indeed in his room, strained every nerve and sinew in an effort to detect any noise from within, but just as she was on the point of thinking the room was empty she heard movement on the other side of the door, and it was just as she was about to knock it that she realized how difficult it would be to hold him in conversation for an indefinite period. Since she was not as verbally inventive as her spouse, she took the sudden decision to lock him in, hoping that he would not notice, or, if he did, that his banging on the door to be let out would not come to the notice of the other guests.

Twenty minutes later, Mr. Peat, with half a dozen armed soldiers following closely behind, returned to his hostelry to be proudly informed by his good lady that the gent in the back bedchamber was in right enough, but just to be on the safe side had taken the precaution of locking him in. Receiving an approving nod of the head from her husband, he escorted the soldiers up the stairs to the first landing, whereupon he unlocked the door before hurriedly stepping aside to allow the red-coats to do their work.

By the time Michael had come to the end of this descriptive recital of Private Smith's apprehension, Gideon's shoulders were shaking and Richard had fallen into a paroxysm of uncontrollable laughter, wiping his streaming eyes with a handkerchief in one hand and slapping the arm of his chair with the other. It was Gideon who managed to find his voice first, asking on a quiver, "Tell me, was his shot eventually paid to Mr. Peat?" to which Richard almost collapsed in his seat, gasping for breath.

"Well," Michael replied unsteadily, "I believe there was something of an altercation between them about this, but from what I can gather from the sergeant who arrested him, he flung his purse at Mr. Peat followed by an item of clothing he had not got round to packing, telling him to help himself, and, while he was at it, why didn't he take the shirt off his back!" This was too much for Richard, and Michael, glancing across at his friend then back to Gideon, whose eyes were brimming with laughter, added, "Then as he was being escorted out of his room I understand he said something to Mr. Peat about Judas and thirty pieces of silver, but by this time the goings on had attracted no small attention from the other guests, and during his struggle to break free, he shouted at the interested on-lookers that if they were not careful they could well find themselves being locked into their bedchambers as well!"

This proved too much for Richard, and Gideon, who had somehow managed to control the laughter building up inside him, gave in to the paroxysm which he could no longer suppress. Michael, who had not intended his rendering of events to be amusing, suddenly saw the absurdity of it all, and burst out laughing.

"Egad!" Richard gasped when he eventually found his breath, "I'd have given a monkey to have seen all this!" wiping his eyes. "Damme!" he cried, "the best stage farce in town is nothing to it! Talk about Bartholomew Fair! Heaven bless Molly and the Peats'!"

Gideon, who had strenuously tried to avoid Richard's eye, finally gave in to his better self and cast an irresistible glance in his direction, whose enjoyment of such a ridiculous charade was quite infectious. "Remind me, Michael," he nodded, his eyes brimful of laughter, "to avoid 'The Ship Ashore' should I ever take it into my head to visit Newhaven!"

"Yes, by God!" Richard exclaimed, his eyes brimming. "Between getting locked into your room and Molly, there's no telling what may happen to a man there!"

Gideon laughed. "Nonsense, Richard! I daresay one would enjoy a most pleasurable stay in such an establishment!"

Having by now recovered sufficiently from his paroxysm Richard strode over to a small side table upon which rested a silver tray bearing a couple of decanters and several glasses, and began to pour out some wine, but turned at this, pointing the stopper at him, "Well, all I can say," he nodded, the laughter even now in his eyes, "is that you must have stayed at some deuced peculiar places!"

"I have," he smiled. "You should have seen the quarters we were sometimes billeted!"

"Really! As bad as that?" he shook his head melancholically. "T'would seem then," he pointed out, the gravity in his voice completely belied by the mirth in his eyes, "that *'The Ship Ashore'* is not as hazardous as I thought!"

A burst of laughter followed this, and over their wine the three men enjoyed a pleasurable fifteen minutes or so in exchanging good-humoured anecdotes and friendly banter, but when Gideon, in response to Richard's outstretched hand gave him his glass to be re-filled, looked across at Michael, asking conversationally, "So tell me, did they have any trouble in getting Private Smith back to Hampton Regis?"

"No, none at all," he shook his head, declining more wine. "It seems that after his outburst at *'The Ship Ashore'* he put up no resistance whatsoever."

"That must have been a relief?" Gideon nodded, knowing from experience the difficulties attached to escorting a prisoner. "Such an escort as that," he commented, "is not without its worries."

"So, where is this Private Smith now?" Richard asked, handing Gideon his wine before resuming his seat.

"At the garrison," Michael nodded.

"I take it he is he due to answer the charges against him quite soon?" Gideon remarked.

"Well," he said slowly, looking at the remnants in his glass then raising his eyes to look from Gideon to Richard, "that's just it," he sighed.

"What's just it?" Richard asked, sipping his wine, his eyes narrowing slightly.

Michael put his empty glass down with slow deliberation, a slight frown creasing his forehead, but met Richard's eye unflinchingly. "The thing is, Richard" he said at length, "whether Private Smith has a military disciplinary hearing or a civilian trial, either could well cause something of a problem."

"Problem?" Richard repeated, leaning forward a little in his chair. "What kind of a problem?"

After casting a brief glance at Gideon, who had a sneaking suspicion of what coming, Michael swallowed, saying reticently "Well, you see Richard, if Private Smith's offence of abduction is heard in either court then it is inevitable that the victim will be named; there will be no way of withholding it or the reason for her seizure. Major Denham is very much aware of this."

"Is he though!" Richard said slowly, a glint in his eye.

"Yes," Michael nodded, feeling a little uncomfortable, wishing he had not been the one delegated to have to break such unwelcome news. "Richard," he said earnestly, "I know Major Denham is no friend of yours but, indeed, he has given this matter a deal of thought. He knows full well that Private Smith had no hand in your sister's injury any more than he did in treason, and since Sir Evelyn still has no idea of the use to which his home was put during his absence that night, he sees no point in alerting him to the truth now, as well as being anxious to keep your sister's name out of it."

"Go on," Richard urged, not very encouragingly.

"The thing is, Richard," he explained, "Private Smith has a list of offences dating back to well before he joined the army, all of which he confessed to Major Denham, as well as his abduction of your sister, not to mention the breaching of army regulations whilst in military service. Both military and civilian offences will bring heavy prison sentences; so, you see Richard," he nodded, "if Private Smith *is* charged with abducting your sister, along with all the rest, then there will be no way the events at Hamstoke House can be kept out of it, but not only that," he emphasized, "your cousin's part in recent events will be made known."

"And?" Richard urged again.

Michael eyed his friend cautiously, saying warily "Major Denham is most desirous of protecting your sister's reputation and ..."

"My sister's what?" he said ominously, sitting bold upright. "Did you say *'my sister's reputation'?*"

"Yes," Michael confirmed unenthusiastically. "Not that she needs ..."

"Devil take it, she doesn't!" he exclaimed, angrily. "Damn it all, Michael!" he said furiously, "you know as well as I that she was lured out of this house; she did not leave it with a stranger of her own free will!"

Gideon, interpreting the look in Richard's eye with unerring accuracy, decided it was time to intervene, and putting his glass down leaned forward a little in seat, asking, "Michael, what is it Major Denham wants precisely?"

Michael, who had every sympathy with his friend, especially as two of the conspirators had already escaped justice and now it seemed that Private Smith was about to do so as well, added to which, he was fiercely protective of his sister, and was therefore just a little relieved at Gideon's intervention. "Major Denham is perfectly happy to charge Private Smith with abduction along with his other offences," he explained uneasily, "but he believes it may be for the best just charging him with the offences prior to his military service together with those breaches of army regulations, but if the charges do include abduction then Miss Ferrers' name will be mentioned as the victim of such a crime. If Private Smith answers charges for his other offences only, then they should be sufficient to carry a hefty sentence, and although he will serve this sentence, not for your sister's abduction," he advised Richard, looking at the incensed face opposite him, "but for all the rest, he will still be imprisoned, and surely," he shrugged helplessly, "that has to be better than nothing. Major Denham is quite prepared to go along with whatever you decide. He is hoping that I will return with your answer."

"I'll wager he is!" Richard scorned, rising hurriedly to his feet. "Well, you may take him my answer, and that is I'll be damned if I see this Private Smith evade what's coming to him!" After finishing off his wine and putting his glass down with some force, he turned to Michael, his face reflecting his anger. "He may not have committed treason or pulled the trigger which wounded my sister, but he must have known something deuced ugly was in the wind when he was asked to seize her! For God's sake, Michael," he demanded, "what kind of a man commits abduction and thinks no harm will come of it?" turning exasperated on his heel and striding over to the window to stare broodingly out of it, a dark frown creasing his forehead and his lips compressed into an angry line causing Michael to cast an appealing glance at Gideon.

It did not go unanswered. "Michael," he said calmly, "would you mind giving us a moment, please?"

"Yes, of course," he nodded, glancing briefly across at Richard, hoping that Gideon would be able to bring his friend round.

As soon as the door had clicked shut behind Michael, Richard spun round, saying wrathfully, "And before you say anything, Gideon; I won't do it! Damme, it's more than flesh an' blood can stand!"

"I know it is," Gideon agreed calmly.

"Do you?" he shot at him, striding over to the tray and pouring himself another glass of wine. "First my cousin comes out of this untarnished, then Henderson decides to escape his just deserts by taking his own life and saving the hangman the trouble, not to mention His Grace's iniquity going unanswered; and now, if Denham has his way, Private Smith too will escape his just deserts; well, I won't have it!" he said firmly.

"Richard," Gideon said quietly, taking a step towards him, "the decision is, of course, yours to make, but listen to what I have to say before you do."

"It makes no difference what you say," Richard said determinedly, "my mind's made up. It was bad enough Henderson and my cousin embroiling themselves in treason in the first place then foisting the blame onto me to save their necks when it all fell apart, but if you think I am going to allow something like abducting my sister to go unanswered then you are quite wrong!"

"Do not misunderstand me, Richard" Gideon said unequivocally, "I do not advocate abduction going unanswered; I am no more enamoured of this than you are, the thought of yet another party to recent events being about to escape the penalties of the law for their crimes renders me as frustrated as you, but I hope I am realistic enough to realize that, given all the factors, it is perhaps for the best." Richard threw him a smouldering look, but undaunted Gideon continued, "Having striven to shield Elizabeth from the gossip and speculation which would inevitably result were it ever to become known of the events at Hamstoke House, because it is futile to think that people will not draw their own conclusions, to have it revealed in open court would only be to undo all our efforts. Believe me," he told him emphatically, "were it not for Elizabeth I would willingly testify at the trial myself as to the full extent of Private Smith's iniquities, but as this is not possible I can only hope that his offences prior to him joining the army as well as during his service will be weighty enough for him to receive a heavy sentence." Richard cast a glance at him, but it was clear that that blazing anger was petering out. "However much either of us may dislike it," Gideon pointed out reasonably, "I have to confess that I am not overly surprised at this, but whilst I have no more liking for it than you, I think we should be grateful to Major Denham, indeed," he nodded, "I had not looked for such consideration in him."

"Consideration!" Richard cried.

"You know, Richard," Gideon told him earnestly, "you don't need me to tell you how I feel about your sister; there are no lengths to which I would not go to shield and protect her, but in this instance I have very little choice but to accept Major Denham's proposal, and nor, for that matter," he nodded, "do you. Elizabeth's reputation needs no defending, we both know that, but whilst I honour you for wanting to bring to justice one who has caused her harm, it would in all probability turn out to be quite detrimental. Do not be thinking however, that I am either happy or reconciled in allowing something like this to pass unchallenged, I am not, indeed," he admitted truthfully, "I am myself conscious of wanting to inflict the direst punishment on Private Smith, but whatever gratification such an act would give me, it would serve no purpose other than that."

Richard, who had been listening to this in brooding silence, suddenly began to pace up and down the room raking a ruthless hand through his hair, finally coming to an abrupt halt in front of Gideon, pointing a finger in some aimless direction. "He may not have pulled the trigger," he declared frustrated, "but he has a deal to answer for! Damme Gideon!" he exclaimed, "my sister could have died!"

A sombre light entered Gideon's eyes at this, his face suddenly taut, saying grimly, "I am hardly likely to forget that. The sight of her lying unconscious at my feet will, I think, haunt me for the rest of my life!" Richard looked up at the dark face in front of him, vividly remembering his quick actions that night in order to save the life of his sister; the life of a woman he knew Gideon loved more than life itself. "Which is why," Gideon nodded, "I think she has suffered enough without the possibility of having to give evidence at a trial."

Having digested this, Richard slowly nodded his head, then looking up at Gideon gave him a crooked little smile. "Damn you, Gideon!" he grinned. "Why are you always right?"

"Not always I'm not," he shook his head, his expression lightening, "but on this occasion I believe I am, and when you have cooled down, you young hothead," he smiled, gripping his shoulder, "you will know it too."

"Damme, I know you're right Gideon!" he exclaimed. "It's just that ...well, devil take it, it sticks in my throat!"

"Do you think it doesn't in mine?" Gideon said earnestly. "Well it does; when I think of all that has gone before and yet not one has faced their trial, it makes me extremely angry, but then I remind myself of what *is* important, which is you are now exonerated and reinstated; no scandal is attached to your name because of William and Elizabeth will not have to endure any spiteful or cruel gossip."

"I know," Richard conceded at length. "All you say is true, and I must seem like the veriest wretch!"

"On the contrary," Gideon shook his head. "I esteem you for wanting to protect your sister; indeed, I would have thought the less of you if you had not wanted to do anything in her defence. But if it is of any consolation at all," he told him unhappily, "I too feel just as impotent as you as well as feeling as though I have failed her, not only in not having considered the eventuality of her being shot but also in knowing that not one of the men responsible for what happened to her have answered for their crimes, or are going to."

Richard sighed. "I know. It's just that when I think ..."

"Don't think, Richard," Gideon advised kindly, "it will serve no purpose other than to drive you to the brink of madness, and as I have already made perfectly clear," he smiled, striving for a lighter note, "my father will most certainly not like that!"

Richard grinned and gripped his shoulder. "Damn you, Gideon I ...! My God!" he cried, slapping a hand to his forehead. "Michael! I was forgetting Michael! What a wretch I am! Not only have I made him feel like the devil's advocate, but I've left him outside! Yes," he warned pointing a finger at Gideon, "it's all very well for you to laugh!" Whereupon he opened the door and called, "Damn you Michael! What the deuce you standing out here for?"

Michael's apologies for bringing him such unwelcome news was brushed aside with the unequivocal announcement that he was the one who should be apologizing. Michael had known very well how Richard would receive such tidings, and whilst he himself had no taste for law-breakers escaping the penalty of the law, especially when he considered the harm they had done, he felt a little like a traitor himself. But honesty compelled him to admit that under the circumstances he failed to see what else could be done and therefore heaved a sigh of relief when Richard accepted Major Denham's proposal for dealing with Private Smith without bringing a charge of abduction against him. He had no liking for this any more than Richard and even though he knew his friend had every justification in being angry, he was extremely relieved that Gideon had somehow or other brought him round to agreeing to Major Denham's proposal. Declining the invitation to stay to dine on the grounds that he already had an engagement with Major Denham, a twinkle crept into Richard's eye, slapping his friend on the shoulder and laughing, "Oh, like that is it? Thought you couldn't abide the man!"

Michael coloured and stammered, stating that since this business with Colonel Henderson and Sir John's letter informing him of his resultant suicide, Major Denham had appeared to have undergone some form of transformation, and whilst he could not lay claim to liking the fellow over much, the fact remained that he was his senior officer, and much preferred relations between them to be as amicable as possible.

"*Stoopid*!" Richard laughed. "Did you think I'd give you the go-by once I knew this?"

They parted on the best of terms, with Michael promising to visit again just as soon as his duties permitted, then after shaking hands with Gideon was escorted to the stables by Richard where he waited with him until his horse had been brought out, glad that their friendship was still undamaged.

"You know, Richard" Gideon told him upon his return to the book room, handing him the glass of wine he had just poured, "I like that young man."

"Yes," Richard nodded, taking his glass and sinking into a chair, "so do I." He took a sip of wine, then resting his head back against the chair closed his eyes, a deep sigh racking his body. "Do I detect a rebuke coming on?" he grinned, opening his eyes and looking across at Gideon.

"No," Gideon shook his head, "not at all. Why, do you think you deserve one?" he smiled.

"Possibly," Richard acknowledged, "I didn't exactly hide my spleen when I heard Michael say what he did." He heaved a deep sigh. "I don't mind admitting that I was damned annoyed, but my anger was not aimed at Michael."

"I know it wasn't," Gideon nodded, "he knows that too. You and your family have been through much, and do not deserve to see the perpetrators of such despicable crimes evade their just deserts; it's hard to accept. But you know Richard," he told him kind-heartedly, "it's very difficult to assist a friend when you are under orders."

"Yes, I know," he sighed, "but Michael assures me I have not given him a disgust of me, which is a relief, because I know damned well what I owe him. Were it not for him God only knows what would have happened to me at the garrison that night, most probably I would have been arrested, tried and strung up, or," he grimaced, "simply shot on sight! I'd hate to lose a damned good friend, but he assures me I have not. So," he nodded, "about Henderson. I must confess I never expected that."

"No," Gideon shook his head, "neither did I but, upon reflection," he admitted, "I really should have considered such an eventuality."

"Perhaps," Richard conceded, "but he must have had this in head for some little time. I suppose we shall never know why he did it, unless, of course, he much preferred what he thought to be the easy way out rather than face his accusers."

"Probably," Gideon sighed. "He may not have entered into insurrection through loyalty or belief in Stuart's cause, as his forebears had, but I think it could well have crossed his mind that he had not only dishonoured them by his actions, but himself as well."

"So, what did happen precisely?" Richard asked.

After taking a revivifying drink of his wine Gideon sat back in his chair, crossing one long leg negligently over the other, before embarking on the unprecedented sequence of events culminating in his meeting with Lytton.

"Well," Richard shrugged, "I don't pretend to having an understanding of military procedure, but it seems damned unfair that Sir John had to endure the ignominy of an inquiry."

"Yes," Gideon agreed, "damned unfair. I suppose if I am honest" he smiled ruefully across at Richard, "I have to confess that I was as angry as you were a moment ago to think that three people have escaped justice. Whilst I accept that culpability for Henderson's suicide lay with the commanding officer, I believed, still do in fact, that it surely cannot be right when the perpetrators of such crimes evade the consequences of their actions whilst the diligent, like Sir John, are questioned as to their dealings, and the innocent, like *you*," he nodded "would have been strung up from the nearest gallows without a moment's hesitation."

"Don't I know it!" Richard cried. "But I suppose the truth is," he sighed, "it will take awhile for me to resign myself to it; were it not for what happened to my father and Elizabeth I might have found it easier to do so, as it is," he shrugged, "I'm far from reconciled."

As only time would ease the pain around Richard's heart concerning his father's death, and nothing he could say or do would either help lessen it or hasten his acceptance, Gideon asked instead about William's funeral.

"It seems this parson of yours was as reluctant to perform the obsequies for Henderson just as much as Parton was for William!" Richard pointed out, after acquainting him with the details. "You should have heard him on the subject; quite eloquent in fact."

"Well," Gideon nodded, "if this Reverend Parton of yours is anything like Reverend Dutton, I can well imagine what he had to say. Trying to persuade a man of the cloth whose beliefs are as unwavering as his principles are inflexible to perform such an office, takes a deal of achieving." He caught the gleam of pure amusement in Richard's eyes, and Gideon, quite unable to resist it, shook his head, "No, don't tell me," he smiled, "this Reverend of yours, is he by chance a member of the fraternity too?"

"No," Richard grinned, "just sympathetic."

"Ah," Gideon nodded knowledgably, "like this sympathetic friend who loaned Michael the horse!"

"Quite so," Richard smiled, "but you mustn't think too badly of him though, even if he does allow church property to be used to store run goods." Upon Gideon raising an eyebrow at this, he laughed, saying "He has some pretty strong views on smuggling, let me tell you."

"Evidently!" Gideon replied, unable to hide the twitch at the corner of his mouth.

"He's had the living here at Little Turton for as long as I can remember," Richard explained, "and knows all his flock by name, but the truth is he has never liked William, even less so when he knew what he had planned to do, but his agreeing to carry out William's obsequies was from loyalty to my father and myself rather than from his Christian duty!"

This was not said to puff off his own consequence or in a conceited manner, but as a simple statement of fact, and Gideon, who had not needed this to prove to him just how popular and well-liked Richard was, had no difficulty in believing it. "It seems I should have sent you to speak to Reverend Dutton," Gideon smiled. "I don't mind saying it took a deal of work to persuade him."

"I know you've had a busy time of late," Richard nodded, "in fact, it has not been easy for any of us, but I don't mind saying I do not envy you your meeting with Lytton."

"I am in no hurry to repeat it, I assure you," Gideon told him unequivocally. "But, you know Richard," he pointed out, "I may find Lytton as offensive as I do objectionable, but I'll say one thing for him; he can carry off something that would make most men recoil with such smooth aplomb that I am not at all certain whether to applaud or revile him."

"The latter, of course," he nodded. "Were it otherwise, Sir John would not have deemed it necessary to release you from what you clearly found to be quite an ordeal."

"An ordeal is precisely what it was. But you're right," Gideon nodded, finishing his wine and rising to his feet. "Should I ever arrive at the point where I admire a man like Lytton, then I shall surely deserve my father's condemnation, as I would my own." He put down his empty glass just as the clock on the mantelpiece struck the half hour, and Richard, raising lazy eyes up at this timepiece, smiled.

"Half past six, and we dine at eight," rising leisurely to his feet. "I take it," he grinned irrepressibly, "you can be ready and presentable by then?"

"I will have you know," Gideon laughed, "that I was getting into my uniform by no other light than a shaft of the moon through a broken window within less than five minutes before you were out of short-coats!"

"I was right," Richard shook his head sadly, "you *are* a boaster!"

"I'm a sad case, indeed!" Gideon laughed, gripping his hand.

"Just one thing," Richard forestalled as they made their way to the door. "About Jane."

"Jane?" he raised an enquiring eyebrow, a smile lurking in his eyes. "She is very beautiful," he acknowledged simply, "and, if I may say so," he offered gravely, "you are extremely fortunate."

"Damn you, Gideon!" he laughed, exasperated. "I know all that. I just wanted to say thank you for ... well, damme you know what I mean!"

"I do," Gideon acknowledged. "I know precisely how you feel to have the woman you love back in your life; a woman you thought was lost to you, but I have told you before there is not the least need to offer me thanks." Richard was about to argue the point, but Gideon, raising a hand, said frankly, "I need neither gratitude nor reward. You have given me your sister for which I shall be eternally in your debt," he smiled, "and, unless I very much mistake the case, that makes us even." Richard, detecting the note of finality in that pleasant voice, nodded. "Very well, if that's how you want it."

"It is," Gideon said firmly. "But speaking of Elizabeth," he said purposefully, "I have already written to my parent's telling them about her, and they are most desirous of meeting her. My mother has suggested I take her home with me for a visit when I leave here providing, of course, she feels well enough to travel. I have not mentioned this to her yet" he nodded, "because I wanted to know if you approved."

Richard, who had been standing listening to Gideon's plea leaning back against the desk with his arms folded across his chest and his eyes fixed firmly on his face, raised an amusing eyebrow at his request for permission. "After all you have done, do you think you need my approval?" his crooked smile twisting his lips.

"What I have done," Gideon shook his head, a little smile playing at the corner of his mouth, "has nothing whatever to do with it. Since your father's death, Elizabeth has been in your guardianship, and will remain so until she either comes of age or marries. However eager I may be to introduce her to my home and parent's, it would not be right nor proper for me to take advantage of what has gone before, or our friendship. To have approached Elizabeth before having spoken to you would have been quite wrong; and really most repugnant to me." He smiled. "I thought you would have known that."

"I do know it," Richard nodded, returning the smile. "Do you think I would have allowed you to offer for my sister had I not? I may do crazy things now and then," he grinned, straightening himself up, "but I know a man of integrity when I see one. If I can place my life into your hands as well as my sister's future," he nodded, "then I think I can entrust her to your care for a week or two."

Returning Gideon's grip on his hand and his shoulder, he laughed, "Don't tell me you thought I would refuse?"

"Well," Gideon sighed, inclining his head, "the thought had crossed my mind; I know how much Elizabeth means to you."

"Yes, she always has, and, needless to say, she always will, but I know how much she means to you" he nodded, "and you to her, and I couldn't bear to see her made unhappy."

"You needn't worry," Gideon assured him, "I shall take the greatest care of her."

"I know you will," Richard nodded, then slipping his hand through his arm left the book room together, his visit from Captain Waring suddenly springing to mind, regaling him with what took place between them. Gideon's sense of the ridiculous as he pictured that diligent young man refusing to partake of refreshment, brought forth a deep throated laugh, agreeing with Richard that he most probably thought it to be run cargo. Coming upon Salmon in the hall Richard enquired if the ladies were still in the sitting room, to which he was told that Miss Jane had already retired to Miss Elizabeth's bedchamber with her in order to change for dinner several minutes ago, further informing him that Sir Arthur's groom had not long brought round a message to say that the carriage would be at the door by ten o'clock to take Miss Jane home, to which he nodded. It was just as he was about to put a foot on the first stair that he turned to Salmon, requesting him to come to his room in ten minutes, then turned and climbed the stairs alongside Gideon.

Disliking the current mode of painting his face or applying patches with equal fervour as he did of adopting an elaborate style of dress or wearing a ridiculously high and farcically arranged or coloured wig, Gideon arrived downstairs three-quarters of an hour later just as Clara Winsetton was leaving the small sitting room, eyeing him closely before bestowing her full approval on his appearance. His knee length coat of royal blue satin edged with a narrow band of silver thread down the front edges and on the turned back cuffs, fitted perfectly across his shoulders. His breeches, clipped just below the knee with small silver buttons instead of the more fashionably huge clocks, were of watered silk in a pale shade of grey which perfectly matched his long fronted waistcoat, from which a small silver fob hung from one pocket. Apart from the diamond pin which nestled in the folds of the heavy fall of lace at his throat the only other adornment was a diamond encrusted clipped bow, a coming of age gift from his mother, neatly tying his dark hair in the nape of his neck. Clara Winsetton, who was by no means averse to a man applying a little something to his face, had to admit that Gideon's needed no embellishment and was very much impressed with what she saw, telling him in her forthright manner that whilst he had presented a very handsome figure in his scarlet regimentals, he most certainly did out of them, to which he thanked her meekly for such favourable comments, the twinkle in his eye bringing forth a deep throated chuckle of laughter from her.

Drawing her bony arm through his, he happily indulged her humour as he escorted her through the great hall and into the sitting room, daring to suggest that she too presented quite a figure, in response to which she playfully rapped him over the knuckles with her fan, the bold patch at the corner of her mouth twitching appreciatively as she told him with as much severity as she could that she was far too old for such silly talk and he would be best advised to keep it for Elizabeth.

"I shall certainly do so," he told her gravely, "especially as I now have your approval."

"Hm!" she snorted. "It seems to me," she told him firmly, "that you wouldn't care whether you had my approval or not!"

"In truth, Ma'am," he smiled, "no, I would not."

"I thought so," she nodded. "Well, I've no doubt you'll know just the right things to say to her," the patch quivering at the corner of her mouth, "lovey-dovey stuff that's enough to turn one bilious, but let me tell you," she tapped the back of his hand with her unfurled fan, "the moment you start saying 'em over the dinner table, I shall retire to my room and so I warn you!"

"And who could blame you, Ma'am?" he said without a tremor, his shoulders shaking. "To utter such sentiments as those which you have in mind whilst the recipient is eating, would, I am sure you will agree, not only show a lamentable want of delicacy on my part, but hardly likely to meet with the response for which they were intended."

A rich throated chuckle left her lips at this, and by the time she entered the sitting room on Gideon's arm, was in such a good humour that she surprised Salmon, having brought in the silver tray with the decanters and glasses, by asking him, not in the brisk way he was accustomed to but quite benignly, how he was feeling. Cocking a questioning eyebrow at Gideon over her head, he saw those brown eyes looking at him with a lurking smile, and interpreting this to mean that he knew precisely how to deal with this cantankerous old lady, who really was quite exceptional, nodded his head comprehendingly, and proceeded to reply to her enquiry.

It had not escaped that sharp-eyed lady's notice that although Gideon bestowed his full attention upon her in ensuring her comfort as well as engaging her in conversation until the others joined them, he also kept one eye on the sitting room door. She was neither stupid nor blind, and she certainly did not need her niece to tell her how the two of them had spent their time this afternoon, it had been clearly writ on both their faces, but never before had she seen Elizabeth look so radiant as she did upon entering the sitting room with Jane to find Gideon there waiting for her; her whole face lighting up at the sight of him. Walking across to where she stood in a few strides, he raised her hand to his lips, his eyes looking down into hers with so much meaning that the colour crept into her cheeks and the responding look which entered those dark blue depths rendered it necessary for him to sternly suppress the overwhelming desire to take her in his arms there and then, but somehow managing this agonizing fete he turned to Jane and smiled down at her, bowing gracefully over her hand. It was just as she was in the middle of saying that Richard would be with them directly, when the door to the sitting room quietly opened and he walked leisurely in, but the man Gideon was used to seeing had undergone a transformation, causing him to stare in surprise.

Having discarded his habitual black coat, riding breeches and knee high boots for a set of clothes which would not have looked out of place at Devonshire House, his aunt, who could not help but approve of his appearance, was nevertheless just a little taken aback at the sight of her nephew decked out in a style he only adopted on rare occasions, as ordinarily when he dined at home he was dressed in a style that was as elegant as it was simple. His coat, fashioned in oyster coloured satin, was slightly nipped in at the waist with fine whalebone strips to stiffen the skirt and edged with gold thread, the turn back cuffs, at least a foot deep, exposing the soft fall of lace which gracefully covered his hands.   A waistcoat of watered silk in the same colour, intricately patterned to form interwoven flowers in a delicate shade of blue and peach with mother of pearl buttons hugged his lithe body, and his satin breeches, in the same delicate peach that formed part of his waistcoat, were fastened just below the knee with gold tassels, and his shapely legs, encased in silk stockings of a pale shade of blue with matching shoes which boasted a heel of at least three inches in height.   Like Gideon, he wore no wig, but his hair had been curled and brushed and tied in the nape of his neck with a black velvet bow to taper into a spiral.   Apart from the heavy gold signet ring on the little finger of his left hand a ruby glittered on the index finger of his right, and in the folds of the heavy fall of lace at his throat nestled a diamond and ruby pin, and Salmon, who had demanded to know what the devil he was playing at when he had helped to create this ensemble, had to admit that he had never looked more like a lord than he did at this moment, putting him in mind of his late lordship.   Flourishing a lace handkerchief in his right hand he executed a most exquisite bow, his eyes glinting wickedly up at Gideon, daring him to comment on the patch he had cunningly placed at the corner of his mouth and the light dusting of powder to his face. Gideon, unable to resist the provocative twitch of Richard's lips burst out laughing, gripping his shoulder. "And you were wondering whether *I* would be dressed in time!"

"I thought you'd like it?" Richard grinned, straightening himself up and returning the handkerchief to his pocket with a deft movement of his hand.

"I take it you don't rig yourself out like this ordinarily?" Gideon laughed when Richard pulled out a small fan and unfurled it.

"Oh, Lord no!" he grinned, making provocative use of the fan. "I used to though, when m'father was alive. Whenever we had guests here to dine or I dined with my father in town and he was entertaining or we were attending an engagement or other, I did; it was something he would insist upon."

"Quite right too!" stated his aunt, looking proudly at her nephew, his eyes laughing as he minced across to her, raising her hand to his lips with such exquisite grace that she said, not quite steadily, "How *very* like your father you are! Not that he minced, of course!" she nodded firmly.

"Oh, Gideon!" Elizabeth smiled up at him, her hand touching his arm. "Doesn't he look quite magnificent?" she said proudly.

He looked down at her hand on his arm then at her, her eyes glowing up into his. "Yes," he nodded, "I have to say he does." Then claiming her hand in his held it in a warm clasp, looking down at her with such love and desire that she caught her breath, saying in a soft caress, "But so do you."

It had not occurred to her that she could have worn a sack tied with string and Gideon would have found her beautiful, and had therefore taken extra pains over her appearance. Having ruthlessly ran an eye over every gown she possessed she finally elected to wear the one her father had liked her in the best, and therefore had no hesitation in pulling out the rustling creation in a crushed strawberry pink satin, resting on narrow hoops to expose a white under dress of cream silk richly embroidered in various shades of blue, gold and yellow, it's deep square neckline a perfect foil for the double row of pearls with a diamond drop centre, which her father had bestowed on her for her presentation at court. Like Richard, she neither liked wearing a wig nor powdering her hair, only doing so when in town for the season, and therefore her dark hair had been curled and dressed with a fine string of pearls threaded through it, entwining the two long spirals which fell over her left shoulder; her only other adornments being a pair of diamond drop earrings and a small patch at the corner of her left eye. Her aunt, having taken a look in on her before going downstairs, had nodded her head in approval at her niece's appearance, declaring that a touch of powder and rouge would not come amiss, but although she dusted a light film of powder over her face nothing would induce her to use the rouge pot, and although she herself was perfectly satisfied with the results of her labours it was not until she saw the unadulterated look of love and adulation in Gideon's eyes that she felt as magnificent as he had said.

Having poured out the wine and offering each one a glass from the ornate silver tray, Salmon then left the sitting room to return ten minutes later to announce that dinner was ready, to which Richard nodded his head before leading the way to the dining room escorting his aunt and Jane. Pulling her arm through his Gideon escorted Elizabeth into dinner several paces behind, then tightening his grip on her fingers with his left one, lowered his head and whispered into her ear, "You know, if I did not know better I would swear that I detect the hand of Phillips at work; deliberately thwarting my attempts to be alone with you!"

She looked up at him at this, something between a choke and a laugh escaping her lips, causing her aunt to briefly turn round, and in the light from the myriad of candles illumining the great hall, she could see the burning intensity in his eyes, her fingers convulsing in his. As the long dining table had been concertinaed to accommodate such a small group, she was not at all certain whether to be glad or not that she was sitting directly opposite Gideon instead of being seated beside him. Although his manners were impeccable, engaging Richard and his aunt seated at both ends of the table, and Jane, immediately next to him, in conversation, his eyes continually focused on her, and although she was able to contribute to whatever was being discussed, she was so very conscious of the man she loved looking at her in such a way that she could only marvel at being able to speak at all. It seemed that Richard too was afflicted with the same condition, allowing his eyes to regularly come to rest on Jane, who too was looking particularly beautiful this evening in a gown of amber satin, her huge pansy brown eyes periodically glancing at Richard in a way which left no one in any doubt as to her feelings for him.

During Richard's absence, the two footmen, both of whom had been in service at Ferrers Court for many years, had been allotted to other duties, which they much preferred to being dismissed, but now he was back home and reinstated as the sixth Viscount Easton, they had donned their uniforms again and resumed their roles with enthusiasm, both taking it upon themselves to inform Richard that it was a pleasure to see him back where he belonged. Salmon, standing stiffly behind Richard's chair, coughed, but Richard, deeply touched by this, turned and whispered something in his ear which made him purse his lips and Richard smile. As Sir Arthur's carriage would soon be arriving to take Jane home Richard and Gideon elected to decline the usual practice of remaining behind in the dining room to partake of a glass of port or brandy following the ladies departure, so after the health of both happy couples had been toasted, they all made themselves comfortable in the great hall, the kindling in the huge fireplace having been lit and the heavy brocade curtains drawn. Elizabeth and Jane sitting with their heads together some little way from the fire, were happily engaged in discussing matters very close to their hearts; and Aunt Clara, after engaging Gideon in a game of piquet, with Richard acting as an interested spectator uninvitingly offering a word or two of advice to his aunt in her ear as to her discards, and losing heavily, very soon afterwards announced her intention to retire, stating that she was far too old to be enduring late nights, to which her irrepressible nephew laughed, saying that had she been winning she would have stayed up all tonight. She scolded him soundly as to his aspersions, affectionately kissed his cheek and told him that she would allow him to escort her up to her bedchamber, then turning to Gideon told him that she would not have lost their game had she not been so tired, his eyes smiling down into hers as he good-humouredly agreed, then pleased her immensely when he bestowed a kiss on her powdered and rouged cheek. Upon their exit from the great hall, he strolled over to where Elizabeth and Jane were sitting, and drawing up a chair engaged Jane in conversation, his eyes meeting Elizabeth's over her head, saying more than any words possibly could. Unfortunately for Jane, her father's carriage arrived at the front door within fifteen minutes of Richard's return, not quite able to hide her disappointment at having to leave, telling Gideon that she may not see him before he leaves Ferrers Court as her mamma wished her attendance at home the next day. He offered his regrets upon hearing this, but told her he hoped to see her again very soon, whereupon he bowed over her hand before she took Richard's arm as he escorted her to the carriage. The door to the great hall having been closed behind them, he turned to Elizabeth without taking a step towards her, his eyes looking down at her with such warmth that her heart turned over. "This is where I place all my faith in Richard's tact and discretion in not returning too soon," he said pointedly.

She looked innocently up at him, the look in her eyes giving the lie to this. "Oh! And why is that?"

"You know *'why is that'*," he told her in a deep voice. "How much longer do you think I am going to wait to have you to myself, even if only for a few minutes?" Holding out his hand to her, he said softly, "Come here."

She dutifully did as he asked, going to him in a rustle of satin with her hands placed piously together in front of her, her lips primly set and her eyes downcast, but the roguish patch at the corner quite ruined the affect of maidenly modesty. "Well, Sir. What is it you want?" she asked demurely, keeping her eyes lowered.

"You know very well what I want," he told her, between amusement and ardour, raising her chin with an unsteady forefinger, her eyes glowing as they looked up into his smouldering brown ones.

"Oh," she nodded comprehendingly, "you mean you want to kiss me?" His eyes burned into hers. "Then why didn't you say so?" she asked, but even before she had folded her arms around his neck two powerfully strong ones had wrapped themselves around her, crushing her to him, his mouth hungrily devouring her responsive one in a kiss that was neither gentle nor coaxing, but one which she welcomed with equal fervour, melting eagerly into him with a need that matched his own. As there was no timepiece in the great hall, not that it would have mattered if there had been as neither of them gave a moment's thought to such a mundane thing as time, they had no idea how long they remained locked in each other's arms, but it seemed that all too soon the pressure of his mouth relaxed until slowly he reluctantly deprived her of it, rendering her quite bereft. For several minutes they clung to one another, her breathing as laboured as his own, and his heartbeat keeping rapid time with what had always been, until he came into her life and turned it upside down, a most reliable organ. Unwillingly he slowly eased himself away from her, looking down into her flushed face, his own colour a little high, with such naked desire that she shuddered, and although it was a difficult enough fete at the best of times, her response was such that he found it necessary to exert every ounce of self-control he had to prevent him from kissing her again.   Cupping her face with his unsteady hands, his eyes lovingly taking in every inch of her face, he told her in a voice which he knew must be his own, first as to how much he loved her, and then about his parent's invitation. "I have spoken to Richard about it," he said hoarsely. "He has no objection.   My darling" he pleaded, "please say you will come!"

She smiled mistily up at him, her voice a soft caress. "Of course I will come." He heaved a deep sigh, but before he could act in response to her acceptance and the unspoken invitation of her parted lips telling him most eloquently that she wanted him to kiss her, the door to the great hall opened, and Richard strolled in.

Having taken his own time in saying goodnight to Jane by slipping into the small sitting room with her, had, upon reluctantly seeing her into the carriage and waiting until it was lost from sight, deliberately delayed his return to the great hall, by no means perturbed to see Gideon unhurriedly remove his arms from around his sister, after all, he had himself been extremely reluctant to release Jane from the confines of his.   "Has Jane gone?" Elizabeth asked, keeping her hand on Gideon's arm as he walked towards them.

"Yes," he nodded. "So," he smiled at her, "I take it Gideon has told you about this visit to his home?" She nodded, her eyes glowing. "And, of course," he kissed her cheek, "you said yes." She nodded again. "I thought so. Gideon," he said firmly, "I shall leave it to you to take this chit in hand, but I still think you should beat her!"   At which she pulled a face at him, causing him to burst out laughing and giving her a hug. "Let me tell you my girl that if this is the way you mean to conduct yourself in front of Gideon's parent's I wouldn't be in the least surprised if they urged him not to marry you!"   He smiled down at her. "And then!" he nodded, "I shall have you back on my hands!"

"I shall be on my best behaviour the whole time," she assured him, taking hold of his hand. "I promise you," she smiled mischievously up at him, a look which Gideon had long since found to be quite irresistible, "you will be very proud of me."

"Stoopid!" he said softly. "I already am."

She kissed his cheek, then glancing from him to Gideon, whose eyes had never left her and were saying the most wonderful things, said she would go to bed and leave them to their claret or whatever it was men drank when the ladies were no longer present, whereupon she laid a hand on Gideon's proffered arm as he escorted her out of the great hall. Upon reaching the foot of the stairs she laid her free hand on his chest, looking up at him with so much love that he drew in his breath. "You know," she told him softly, "I told you that I thought Richard looked quite magnificent," he nodded, his eyes smiling down into hers, "well, I think you do too."

"Thank you," he inclined his head. "I was beginning to wonder whether I met with your approval out of regimentals; I have your aunt's."

"You must know you do," she smiled. "This," she nodded, brushing her fingers over his coat, "is most becoming."

He caught hold of her fingers, his eyes burning down into hers. "If I were to tell you, or rather," he corrected himself unsteadily, "show you of what I think of you," he rasped, "we would be here all night."

The only response she could manage was to place her hand on the back of his head and draw it down to her own, but even standing on the first step she had to raise herself on tip-toe, but willingly accommodating her, he lowered his head, shuddering as he felt her lips on his. The soft, feather light caresses, seductively brushing his sensitized lips brought a groan from deep with his throat, and when he could no longer contain his need of her pulled her roughly against him to kiss her with such demanding intensity, that were it not for his arms around her she was convinced that she would not have been able to stand up on her own. "Oh, Gideon!" she sobbed huskily into his shoulder when she had got her breath back. "I do love you so very much." She eased herself a little away from him, her eyes, still dark with desire, clouded a little as she looked up at him. "I ...Oh Gideon...do ...do you think you're parent's will like me?" she asked anxiously.

"Like you!" he cried, hoarsely. "Oh, my darling," he uttered thickly, "how could they not, when their son adores you!" Deciding no words were necessary to endorse either of these statements, his arms tightened around her and drew her closer into his body, thoroughly kissing her, releasing her only when the timepiece, striking eleven o'clock, intruded into their consciousness. Gideon, resting his forehead against hers, sighed, "I think this is where we must say goodnight."

She looked up at him, nodding her head, her eyes telling him that she did not want to say goodnight any more than he did, but after a brief kiss on her lips and telling her he would see her in the morning, she turned and ascended the stairs without a backward glance, and only waiting until she was lost from sight did he rejoin Richard. By now most of the candles had been extinguished, and in the light from the few remaining and the flames from the fire, the great hall seemed to have dwarfed in size, turning a most impressive space into much more comfortable surroundings. Two huge chairs had been positioned either side of the fireplace with a small table set between them, on top of which rested a tray and numerous decanters and glasses. Richard, lounging in one of the chairs with one ankle crossed over the other and his waistcoat opened, looked up at Gideon from out of half closed lids, the ruby and diamond pin in the lace at his throat and on his little finger glinting in the flames from the fire, told him to help himself and come and join him.   A pack of cards had been set on the table but as Gideon, although an extremely good player, was no gamester, and Richard felt disinclined to play, they reclined at their ease, and because they were each of them comfortable with the other's company conversation flowed naturally between them.   It was not long before they were telling one another about their homes and families which automatically led to discussing recent events before going on to exchange accounts and anecdotes of their exciting careers, ending with Richard revealing the existence of the secret passageway which had been his lifeline, and promising to show it to him tomorrow.   Not until the candles were guttering low in their holders and the last flickering embers of the fire had petered out did they make any attempt to leave; leisurely climbing the stairs to their bedchambers just as the timepiece in the hall struck half past two.

CHAPTER THIRTY TWO

With the exception of Salmon, no one looking at Richard and Gideon the following morning would ever have guessed that they had consumed a substantial amount of claret the night before and did not get to bed until after three o'clock. Running a knowledgeable but indulgent eye over the two men as they descended the stairs into the cellar beneath the kitchens where he was in the process of checking the bottles, he eyed his young master cautiously, having a pretty shrewd idea what they were doing here at seven o'clock in the morning. Upon his commenting that he thought they would still be abed considering how they had made a night of it, Richard, indignantly demanding to know if he thought they could not carry their wine, was cantankerously told that no such thought had entered his head, adding somewhat severely that it was time the passageway was sealed up, besides which, he pointed out tetchily, it was far too early in the morning for him to be up to any tricks. "Devil a bit!" Richard grinned, laying an encouraging hand on his shoulder. "Come on Salmon," he rallied. "I promised to show it Gideon."

Eyeing Gideon as one would a child bent on mischief, for he fully considered him to be one of the family and therefore stood on no ceremony with him, said knowingly, "*I* see, Sir. This time of the morning?"

"Well of course this time of the morning!" Richard cried. "How the deuce can we come down here later when everyone will be about?" Taking Salmon's acquiescence for granted, he moved the chest covering the door to the steps leading down into the passageway, peering into the dark well before him, then taking hold of the candle Salmon had lit, called over his shoulder to Gideon to come and join him. Staying only long enough to tell Salmon to cover the entrance because they would emerge from the other exit and walk back to the house, he descended the steps, cautioning Gideon to have a care.

Gideon, looking all about him in amazement, was most impressed with what he saw, and Richard, who had never really had the time to inspect it very closely, looked all around him as if it were his first time in this subterranean passage. Beneath their feet the ground was soft and slippery, and the atmosphere, despite a natural draught, was dank and musty. Holding their candles aloft, it could be seen that since Richard's last nocturnal exit the cobwebs, gently swaying to and fro in the current of air, had settled and become quite dense, having to continually brush them away. The red bricked walls, crumbling in places under the pressure from the tree roots, was damp to the touch, the trickle of water seeping down them glistening in the glow from the candles. Gideon listened with keen interest as Richard informed him of its history and the reason it was built in the first place, and could not help wondering how many more of these houses had similar means of escape. "So," he remarked amusingly, "this is how you escaped detection, is it?"

"Lord yes!" Richard grinned over his shoulder, easing away a tree root. "I've no idea if Henderson ever did hide men in the grounds keeping watch for me, but I knew I was safe to come and go while this passage was open."

"Does Elizabeth know about this?" Gideon asked with a laugh in his voice, knowing perfectly well that she would like it immensely.

"Lord no!" Richard exclaimed. "M'father forbid me to tell her, because if she knew this was here it would have been just like her to have come down it. In fact," he nodded, "it still would. Yes," he said emphatically, "and that's another thing; it would be best if you did not mention to her how we have spent part of our morning, because I tell you Gideon," he nodded firmly "if you want her to leave here with you tomorrow before the sun sets, it's best you don't. Once she sees this I've a deuced uncomfortable feeling that we won't get her out of it!"

Gideon laughed at this, stating wholeheartedly that he totally agreed.

Having walked the quarter of a mile to the other end, it was with relief that Gideon saw Richard climb the few steps and open the flat wooden door, because although he was neither claustrophobic nor of a nervous disposition, in fact, he would not have missed seeing it for anything, the passageway was bitterly cold, and his hands and feet were becoming quite numb. Snuffing his candle and placing it beside Richard's on the makeshift shelf he ascended the steps and emerged into the bright sunshine, relieved to be in the fresh air, rubbing his hands together as he waited for Richard to replace the wooden door and cover it over with the brambles and branches from the thicket. It was amazing to Gideon to think that the passageway had been there for centuries and was still virtually intact, but more than this was that it was only known to Salmon and Richard. Suddenly a deep throated laugh escaped his lips, impeding his climb out of the ditch and onto the lane, and Richard, who had been dusting his boots, looked up at this, grinning. "You know, Richard" he laughed, "of all the people who have lived in this house over the years, with the exception of those members of your family who used it to escape persecution, it would have to be you who knows about it, and use it too!"

Richard burst out laughing at this. "You sound like Salmon! He says that only I could remember being told something as a child, then not only remembering it but using it too!"

"Well," Gideon nodded, "it's a good thing you did."

"Don't I know it!" he cried. "At least it kept me in touch with my home and Salmon. M'father always intended to have it sealed up," Richard informed him as they began to make their way back to the house, "but for one reason or another it never was."

"I take it that this must be the shortest distance from the house to any point beyond the wall?" Gideon observed, as they began to follow the lane.

"Yes, although" he confessed, "it's most probably as far as they could dig, not only because of the work involved, which" he nodded, "you must agree is prodigious, but also because they probably did not have time to develop one in another direction."

"Yes," Gideon concurred, "I think you're right." He looked at Richard, a thought just occurring to him. "Tell me," he smiled, "did you ever use that passageway to store run goods?"

Richard's blue eyes lit up at that and an irrepressible smile touched his lips. "Well, yes" he admitted, "I must confess it did cross my mind, but when I mentioned it to Salmon he was firmly set against it, and, upon reflection" he acknowledged, "I have to say he was right. So it was never used for that."

"You know, Richard" Gideon said without a tremor, "my life is going to seem dreadfully flat now that you are an upright citizen again!"

"No, is it?" he enquired innocently, raising an eyebrow, to which both men burst out laughing.

Having spent half of the night staring up at the ceiling blissfully reliving her reunion with Gideon with spine tingling clarity and reflecting on the prospect of meeting his parent's, and what was left of it in a deliciously wonderful dream, Elizabeth awoke the following morning to a feeling of intense exhilaration. Resting back against the pillows with her arms tucked under her head she closed her eyes as she lived again those moments in his arms and the unfamiliar sensations he had aroused in her, conscious of wanting to feel them again; her heart beating rather fast at the expectation of seeing him very soon, the thought of which suddenly galvanized her into action.

Susan, a single female of indeterminate age and thin, unprepossessing features, had been personal attendant to Miss Elizabeth since she was seventeen, and nothing, in her opinion, could have suited her better. Having attended the late Lady Ferrers until her sudden and unexpected illness which had sadly resulted in her death, it had been a most fortunate circumstance for her when Miss Elizabeth had requested she look after her instead of retiring to live with her widowed sister, because not only was she extremely fond of her late ladyship's daughter, but it was a real pleasure to dress and take care of a young lady who, like her mother, was as kind as she was beautiful. Like everyone else at Ferrers Court she was aware of the romance which had sprung to life between Miss Elizabeth and the Major, and although it was not her place to discuss her young mistress with the other servants, she had to admit, even if only to herself, that she fully deserved this happiness, especially considering what she had endured over the last twelve months or more.

Unlike Miss Calne, she had no aversion to men, on the contrary she liked them very well, providing, of course, they were kept in their place, but the sad truth was she did not take, unlike her sister, and following the one and only dalliance into courtship when aged just eighteen with the lad who looked after the squire's horses, which lasted a mere few weeks and ended the moment she caught him in the arms of another, she had entered the service of Lady Ferrers, deciding that it was perhaps her lot in life to remain single. This did not mean that she did not interest herself in the affairs of the heart of others, quite the opposite, indeed, she was very much interested to hear of their joys as well as the trials and tribulations which beset their romances, and had, on one occasion, even assisted the young girl who helped cook to bring her young man up to scratch, resulting in a walk down the aisle. And now, having turned down those most obliging offers, something which still made her dab at her eyes and shake her head, it was Miss Elizabeth's turn at last! Of course, it was a pity that it had been Master Richard's difficulties which had brought this young officer into her life, but since he had somehow or other managed to extricate him from the troubles which had beset him, it seemed only fair to her that he be allowed to carry off his sister, just like the knights in days of old. It was during this pleasurable flight into fantasy that she was jolted back to reality by the insistent tugging of the pull requesting her presence. As it was only eight o'clock and not yet time to take Miss Elizabeth her morning cup of chocolate, she wondered if she had suffered a relapse and was feeling poorly due to her recent wound, so hurrying next door in the full expectation of seeing her laid down upon her bed, was considerably taken aback to see that, far from being prostrate, her young charge was casting various gowns from her wardrobe and items of clothing from various cupboard drawers onto her bed. "Oh, Susan!" she cried, "I am so sorry to have startled you but, you see, we are going into Wiltshire tomorrow and I must sort out my things! And then I must go downstairs for breakfast!" Since the young lady she had taken charge of had always partaken of a little something in her room, the mention of breakfasting downstairs caused her to raise an astonished eyebrow, but one look at her young mistress's flushed face and glowing eyes as well as recalling the announcement of her betrothal yesterday, were enough to apprise her of the reason for going downstairs as well as the visit into Wiltshire. Perfectly willing to aid her charge in the course of true love, she instantly sniffed, dabbed at her eyes with the handkerchief she had quickly retrieved from her pocket, then after vigorously blowing her nose she pulled herself together, nodding her head briskly, informing her that, whilst deciding which of her many gowns to take was, of course, most important, first of all she would help her dress and arrange her hair in order for her to go downstairs and partake of breakfast, while she, in the meantime, would summon the footmen to bring her trunks up from the cellar; after which, she smiled happily, they could go through her wardrobe together.

This plan of action being decided upon, Elizabeth, having taken more time than usual in choosing what gown to wear, finally sat down at her mirror to wait with what patience she could muster while Susan brushed and dressed her hair, fidgeting in her seat until those deft fingers finished their work. Unlike Miss Calne, who would have known no hesitation in telling her to keep still unless she wanted to look as though she had been dragged through a bush, Susan merely sighed indulgently, cleverly threading the narrow band of yellow ribbon through the thick dark curls which perfectly matched her gown, eventually standing back to admire her efforts in the mirror with a sigh of satisfaction. In her haste to go downstairs, it seemed to Elizabeth to take Susan an inordinately long time to tend her, but when she finally stood up to look at herself in the long mirror, she could not deny that no one, not even Miss Calne, could dress her hair better than Susan. Thanking this disciple of romance with a kiss on the cheek followed by a breathless "How do I look?" she at long last walked composedly into the dining room in a soft sigh of damask, in marked contrast to having raced along the corridor and down the stairs, having to pause and catch her breath before opening the door, just as Gideon and Richard had almost finished their substantial breakfast.

Richard, having risen to his feet at her entrance, took one look at her and knew precisely how his sister, despite her attempts to appear calm and unruffled, had ran all the way from her bedchamber to the dining room. His eyes laughed down into hers, then bending down to kiss her cheek, whispered in her ear, "*Stoopid!* Did you think he would disappear?"

She smiled and blushed as she returned his hug before turning to face Gideon, who had also risen at her entrance, and was now standing by his chair looking down at her in such a way that her heart seemed to somersault. Somehow she managed an unsteady "Good morning, Gideon," as he took both her hands in his, but instead of raising them to his lips lowered his head and lightly kissed her cheek, his deep voiced "Good morning, Elizabeth" doing absolutely nothing to steady her ever increasing pulse rate.

Richard, who knew that his sister always had a light breakfast which consisted of just a slice of bread and butter in her room, which always seemed to sustain her until luncheon, forbore to tease her about this sudden change in her habits, knowing perfectly well that it was Gideon's presence which had brought about this alteration to her routine. Clearly, Salmon knew this too, because upon him entering the dining room carrying a jug of ale, looked so surprised to see her seated at the table that he stared opened mouthed at her, in response to which she cast him such a look of wide eyed innocence that any comment he was about to make died at birth. Gideon, who had learned from Richard earlier that the love of his life never came down to breakfast and was now struggling to uphold the fact that she did, had to sternly suppress the smile hovering at the corner of his mouth as well as the burning desire to take this adorable creature in his arms and kiss her.

Instead, he had to content himself in watching her as she tried to compose herself before informing Salmon, without directly looking at him, that she would have her usual cup of chocolate and those delicious hot scones that only cook knew how to make!   Salmon, eyeing her closely, saw the pleading look she darted at him from under her lashes, and although he knew precisely what had brought her downstairs this morning, he could not resist that desperate appeal, and said he would go and see if they were ready.

Richard, casting an amusing glance at his sister, whose sole attention seemed to be fixed on the napkin she was unfolding, fully understood the reason for her unexpected actions this morning, but as he had no intention of either teasing or embarrassing her, told her conversationally that he and Gideon had already been out, taking a walk around the grounds.

She looked up at that, her colour still a little high, so very conscious of Gideon looking at her, but managed with reasonable calm, "Have you?"

He nodded, helping himself to some more ale, before asking her if she had any plans for this morning because he had promised Gideon to show him around some of the estate.   She looked across at Gideon, who, having finished his breakfast, was sitting perfectly relaxed in his seat, unlike the lady who was striving to behave as though her presence at the breakfast table was an every day occurrence, but succeeding only in floundering adorably.   In the middle of her jumbled reply, which incorporated everything from having to consult with Susan about what to pack, seeing Aunt Clara, writing a note to Jane and having a word with Phillips about his rose, not daring to look at Gideon when she said this, Salmon returned with a tray carrying her cup of chocolate and a dish of scones. Not by a word or gesture did he betray his feelings, but after removing the cover and setting these delicacies out in front of her, glanced down at her bent head with such a knowing look on his face that Gideon found it all he could do to keep from going to her and taking her in his arms. Looking down at the array in front of her, she swallowed, then casting a swift glance up at Salmon, whose expression was as eloquent as his demeanour was forbearing, offered a faint thank you.   No one made scones better than cook, indeed, she had been known to eat several and thoroughly enjoyed them, but right now, as she stared down at these mouth-watering delights, whatever appetite she may have had deserted her.   Richard, having by now finished his breakfast, glanced from Gideon to his sister, a picture of innocence as she sipped her chocolate, responding to a remark Gideon had just made with such a look on her face that he deemed it time to leave them alone for awhile. Not only was it because his feelings for Jane made him empathize with his sister's behaviour this morning, but he played fair, and would have considered it to be too cruel to deny her what she had specifically come down for, and since Gideon appeared to be equally as eager to have a few moments alone with her, he rose to his feet, telling Gideon that he would meet him at the stables in a little while. "I shall not keep you over long, but I need to speak to Salmon." Then bending to kiss Elizabeth's forehead, his eyes laughing down into hers, said affectionately, "Don't pack all your trappings, will you?" Upon her smile and shake of the head, he left the dining room, closing the door quietly behind him.

Gideon, still sitting at his ease and lovingly observing her efforts to make him believe that this was her habitual morning custom, asked concernedly, "My darling, is your arm causing you any discomfort?"

Casting a quick glance from her arm to his face she shook her head. "No," she assured him. "Truly," she nodded, "it is much better."

"I am greatly relieved to hear it," he smiled, "because I could not help but wonder if you were feeling a little unwell because of it."

She looked at him, her heart beating rapidly and her eyes a little uncertain. "No. Why do you think that?" she managed.

"Well, you see, my darling" he told her in a deep voice, his eyes smiling at her in a way which made her hold her breath, "I cannot help but notice how you have not yet touched one of those *'delicious scones that only cook knows how to make!'*" He saw the colour flood her cheeks, but without giving her time to respond rose to his feet and walked round to her, assisting her to her feet by gently placing a hand under her arm. "My adorable, foolish little love," he said in a deep voice, his eyes looking down into hers with such love and warmth that she felt the breath still in her lungs. "Richard told me you did not come down to breakfast, but instead had a little something in your room." She bit her bottom lip. "But even if he had not told me," he smiled, "the look on all your faces was more than enough to do so." She lowered her head, the colour flooding her face, but lifting her chin with his forefinger, making her look up at him, asked unsteadily, "Why did you come down to breakfast this morning? Was it to see me?" he asked gently.

She nodded, managing a husky, "Yes."

"I see," he said softly. "Why was that?" he urged, taking hold of her waist with two firm hands.

"Why?" she asked breathlessly. He nodded. "Oh, Gideon!" she cried in a rush, the warmth of his hands and the look in his eyes rendering her acutely susceptible to him, "Don't you know? I had to see you! I couldn't wait. I love you so much!"

The only response she received to this was finding herself being ruthlessly pulled into his arms and thoroughly kissed, and although somewhere at the back of her mind she was conscious that her ribs could well crack from the pressure of his arms, she gave no more attention to this than she did to the quiet opening of the dining room door nor of Salmon's immediate and unobtrusive exit.

As it was impossible for Richard to show Gideon the whole of the Ferrers estate in one day, the area covering both Sussex and Kent, Elizabeth nevertheless did not expect them to return to the house until well into the afternoon, so after spending time with her aunt and telling her about the treat in store, she then bent her energies on the important task of her wardrobe. Susan, having already brushed and dusted the trunks which had been brought up by the footmen earlier, had, while waiting for her charge to join her, taken the opportunity to pack her own small amount of belongings, so when Elizabeth eventually entered her bedchamber, looking very much flushed, breathlessly apologizing for keeping her waiting, she merely smiled saying that there was plenty of time. Looking indulgently at her mistress, having a very shrewd idea of what she had been up to, prior to seeing her aunt, told her that there was nothing whatever to concern her because she had it all in hand, and that she need not worry because there would be more than enough silver paper in which to wrap her clothes. Four hours later, after much wavering and indecision, her trunks and bandboxes were filled, some, to Susan's dismay, to overflowing, but in answer to her gentle queries as to whether she would need this or that, had been told simply, "Well, you know Susan, there is no telling, and you can be sure that if I leave something behind it will be the very thing I shall need." As there was nothing she could say to contradict this most sensible theory, she began to return unwanted items to their drawers while Elizabeth dashed off a note to Jane before hurrying out into the gardens to speak to Phillips. By the time she had accomplished all the tasks she had set herself it was time to dress for dinner, arriving downstairs just a bare few minutes after Richard and Gideon had entered the sitting room, her colour rising as she remembered only too vividly how she had parted from him that morning. After enquiring if they had had a good day and being told they had, Richard then teased her about how long it had taken her to pack all her trappings, hoping that she had spared a thought for the poor nag who was expected to draw the carriage. She laughed and hunched a shoulder, but when Gideon forlornly asked in her ear as he escorted her into dinner, his eyes alight with amusement, "I take it you have you seen Phillips like you said you were going to? Now do, I beg of you," he urged, "tell me the worst; are you still in favour of the man with the rose, or have you reconciled yourself to my poor claims for your hand?" She looked up at him at this with so much love and mischief in her eyes that he had to strenuously resist his natural impulses, having instead to content himself with kissing her hand.

Aunt Clara, much in favour of her niece's trip into Wiltshire, talked at length to Gideon about it, ending by saying that she doubted she would see him in the morning before they departed, so she would charge him now with various messages for his parent's. He told her he would be honoured to carry them for her, then pleasing that old lady by offering her his escort to her bedchamber, wished her niece and nephew goodnight, but not before recommending Elizabeth to come and see her before she retired.

An hour later, standing in Gideon's arms at the foot of the stairs, she smiled mistily up at him, saying, a little shyly, "Do you think your parent's would have preferred seeing me first, before you asked me to marry you? They…they may not feel that …well…"

A kiss prevented her saying any more. "My darling," he said thickly, "my parent's know me well enough trust my judgement as well as my heart, and they, like me," he assured her lovingly, "will adore you."

As she liked being adored by Gideon, and even more so to being shown just how much, it was several minutes before she was able to catch her breath to say, "Tell me about Burroughs Croft."

"You will be seeing it yourself very soon," he pressed against her hair. "I am most eager to show it to you and telling you all about it; although" he smiled, moving his head to look down at her, "if I know my mother, she will want to show you everything herself."

"You love your home very much, don't you?" she said tenderly.

"Yes," he nodded, "very much." He smiled warmly down at her, gently rubbing her cheek with his forefinger. "It will be your home too, soon."

"Yes, I know," she smiled, "and I am most anxious for it to be so, but" a slight catch in her voice made her falter, "it's just that …"

"My darling," he said softly, knowing precisely what was in her mind as well as her heart, "I know how much Ferrers Court means to you, it has been your home all your life; you have known no other. I realize it is going to be a great upheaval for you to leave here, even though you leave it to go to the home of the man you love."

"You do understand!" she said lovingly, resting a hand against his cheek, this sad prospect being the only cloud on her horizon.

"My darling," he cried fervently, taking hold of her hand in a strong warm clasp, "of course I understand. Ferrers Court will always have a special place in your heart," wiping away a stray tear, "I have always known that." He smiled lovingly down at her. "I love my home just as much as you and Richard love Ferrers Court, indeed, it has been my home all my life; Aubrey and I were both born there, and I cannot imagine living anywhere other than at Burroughs Croft." He held her face between his hands, his eyes looking intensely down into her glistening ones. "My darling, whilst it is my dearest wish that one day you will grow to love it as much as I, I do not expect it to replace Ferrers Court in your heart, simply that it finds a home there too and lives contentedly side by side with it."

Something between a sigh and sob escaped her lips at this, and smiling up at him through unshed tears, telling him more than any words could how much she loved him, rendered it impossible for him to do anything other than comprehensively kiss her, feeling rather bereft when she eventually bid him a most reluctant goodnight. Had she have known what he meant to discuss with Richard when he rejoined him in the great hall after she had left him, she would not have closed her eyes all night from the sheer excitement of it, but she would have been extremely surprised to learn that Richard had confided much the same thing to Gideon the night before.

Much to Richard's amazement the whole party left Ferrers Court the following morning just after eleven o'clock, but having only an hour earlier seen two huge trunks, half a dozen bandboxes and a leather travelling case standing in the hall waiting to be stored inside the second coach, it would not have surprised him if they had not left until much later. Casting a bemused eye at Gideon, who had elected to ride beside the coach on his grey mare, Richard exclaimed, "What the deuce do they find to take?"

Gideon laughed, saying, not without a touch of pride, "You should have seen my mother when she used to go on a visit. She seldom does so now, my father not having been well, but he has more than once been obliged to turn back because she says she has forgotten something, and has long since become immune."

Having said goodbye to her aunt the night before had naturally been a little moving, but when the time finally came for Elizabeth to bid farewell to her brother she could not help but shed a tear. Gideon, who knew just how much brother and sister meant to one another, stepped outside to speak to Richard's grooms who would be accompanying them so that they could have a few minutes alone in which to say goodbye, but when, five minutes later, she emerged onto the front drive with her hand tucked under Richard's arm, it was clear from her glistening eyes that their parting had not been without its tears. It went without saying that Richard would miss her, but he knew that this visit into Wiltshire to see Gideon's home and meet his parent's would do her good, especially after all she had endured over recent months, and therefore attempted to raise her spirits by reminding her of all the treats in store at Burroughs Croft, to which she sniffed and nodded and said, looking tearfully up at him, "Yes, I know, and I am most truly looking forward to it, it's just that I am going to miss all of you!"

"You won't" he told her, "not when you've been there a day or two!" She nodded and blinked away a tear at this. "Let me look at you," Richard admonished, placing his hands on her shoulders and forcing her to look up at him, inspecting her face. "You'll do!" he laughed, after drying her cheeks with his handkerchief. "Can't have Gideon thinking you've changed your mind!"

She laughed, but the sight of Salmon coming up to them was enough to make her hiccup and sniff, bidding him an incoherent goodbye, to which he told her that that was enough of that, but by the time Richard handed her into the carriage she received his brotherly warning, delivered with an affectionate kiss on her cheek, not to get up to any of her tricks, with a watery smile. Then turning to Susan, who was sitting on the opposite seat with her hands folded primly on her lap, said "Take care of her, Susan."

"Yes My Lord, to be sure I will, My Lord," she said determinedly, looking forward to the journey far more than her charge appeared to be.

Her charge was certainly looking a little downcast, but this was not because she did not want to go, on the contrary, she would go anywhere with Gideon, but merely the inevitable result of just having said goodbye to those very dear to her, but when Gideon leaned inside the coach seconds after Richard and looked at her, asking in a deep voice if she were all right, her face lit up, causing her overseer to mentally nod her head, satisfied that things were progressing just as they ought.

Wearing a long drab driving coat down to his booted heels to protect his coat and breeches, he shook hands with Salmon then walked side by side with Richard to where his horse was waiting at the front of the first coach. "If you can," Richard nodded, "send me word with one of the grooms when they return to let me know what your parent's think about what we discussed last night. Personally, I'm all for it and I know Jane will be too."

"And Sir Arthur?" Gideon smiled, raising an eyebrow.

"I think you can leave Sir Arthur to his wife and Jane!" he grinned. "Having turned down two offers of marriage, I can't see her father putting up any objection. Are you going to mention this to m'sister, or are you going to wait until you have talked it over with your parent's? I can't see her saying no, in fact," he nodded, "it would mean a lot to her."

"Yes," he nodded, "I know it would, but I think I'll wait, not that I expect my parent's to be against it, especially my mother," he smiled, "but it depends on my father's health and whether or not he is up to travelling." Richard nodded his acceptance of this, and Gideon, having cast another quick eye over his mount, was just about to pull on his gloves, when Richard said "Gideon, I know that I don't have to…"

"No," he shook his head, smiling reassuringly down at him, "you don't. I know what it is you want to say, but there is not the least need. I shall take the greatest care of her, I promise you."

Richard nodded, gripped his hand then stood back as he mounted his grey mare and signalled to the grooms to move away, but it was not until the cavalcade was lost from sight did he and Salmon make their way back into the house.

Not until midway through the afternoon of the third day did the party finally arrive at Burroughs Croft, the journey of almost one hundred miles necessitating resting two nights on the road.   Elizabeth had no idea how Gideon had managed to acquire two rooms, one for himself and the other for her and Susan, a private parlour for their convenience as well as ensuring the comfort of the grooms and changing horses without prior arrangement at two different hostelries, but somehow they had been accommodated without any difficulty or argument. It was clear that these establishments catered for the quality, and Gideon, who certainly fell into that category, would still, surely, have had to bespeak rooms in advance, but there had been no time for such an arrangement and when she pointed this out to him as he was about to hand her into the coach for the last few miles, smiled, saying, a little guiltily "Well, you see my darling, I am well acquainted with Morton at *'the Red Lion'* ,and here," indicating *'The White Horse'* with a nod of his head, "the building and adjoining land forms part of my father estates.   I've known Clem since I was knee-high."   She smiled a tired acknowledgement up at him, whereupon he took hold of her hands and held them in his looking warmly down at her, a smile lighting his eyes as he read the unspoken question which suddenly entered her eyes. "Do not worry your head about paying the shot," he smiled, "there is no need. I have discussed everything with Richard."

She nodded. "I'm sorry, I ..."

"My poor darling, you *are* tired," he said softly.   "It won't be long now, I promise." Handing her carefully into the coach he then turned and assisted Susan into the plush interior, who, after thanking him and making herself comfortable, sat back against the squabs, her opinion of Gideon, always high, had increased considerably during the journey especially when she considered how his behaviour towards her charge during the whole long time they had been travelling had been impeccable.

Apart from kissing her cheek or taking hold of her hands, Gideon's behaviour towards Elizabeth had certainly been impeccable. He may have been called upon to exert every ounce of will-power at his command to refrain from taking her in his arms and kissing her, but to have done so out of the protection of her brother's home or, indeed, his own, at least until his ring was on her finger, would have been an unforgivable breach of trust.

Elizabeth, whilst longing to be in his arms again, had expected no less from him, and as she sat back against the squabs viewing unfamiliar yet beautiful scenery, contemplated her future with Gideon in blissful silence, extremely relieved that Susan could not read her mind. But it had been a long journey, the longest she had undertaken since her return home from her stay in town, and despite the comfort of the beds at both hostelries, Elizabeth was extremely tired, and by the time Gideon opened the door of the coach to assist her to alight, she had fallen asleep. Having let down the steps of the coach he helped Susan to descend, then stepping inside sat beside her, but sensing his presence, drowsily opened her eyes. "Gideon!"

"I told you you were tired," he told her softly, his eyes looking tenderly down at her. "We are finally home, my darling. Come," he smiled encouragingly, taking her gloved hand in his.

She remembered him telling her, 'Burroughs Croft is not a rambling Tudor house like Ferrers Court, but it is very beautiful, all the same'. He had spoken no less than truth. She found herself standing in front of a three storey red-bricked house comprising wings on either side of the prominent central edifice. Two long sash cord windows stood either side of the front door with two corresponding ones immediately above as well as two tiers over the portico, and these, together with the those in the wings, all reflecting the afternoon sun, gave off such a blaze of light that she blinked. She looked up at Gideon, who squeezed her hand, saying gently as he lightly brushed her lips, "Welcome to Burroughs Croft, my darling."

Before she could respond to this the big front door opened and a lady emerged dressed in the very height of fashion, tripping down the six stones steps without even holding on to the railings either side to support her dignity, and with no regard for her position as lady of the house she ran towards them with her damask skirts and lace front apron, floating behind her. Had Elizabeth been told that her future mamma-in-law had not long celebrated her fiftieth birthday, she would have been quite astonished, for the lady approaching looked to be no more than forty. She was a little taller than herself, slim and gracefully elegant in her movements, and her face, with its delicate bone structure and large luminous blue eyes, gave her an elfin-like quality which was really quite irresistible. Her thick blonde curls, becomingly arranged with ringlets entwined with amber coloured ribbon falling over one shoulder, made her look even younger, and her mouth, with its short upper lip and ready smile, stripped away any anxiety she may have had in meeting her.

"My mamma," Gideon whispered in her ear, smiling down at her. Releasing her hand he turned and strode towards her, shortening the distance between them, his eyes smiling warmly down into her jubilant face as he came up to her, taking hold of her hands and raising first one and then the other to his lips, before taking her into his arms and kissing her.

"Oh Gideon!" she cried at length, looking tenderly up at him. "My dear, dear son. You are home at last!"

"Yes, Mamma," he laughed, holding her tight. "I am home at last."

"How I have missed you!" she cried. "It is so good to see you again after so long. Let me look at you," holding him at arms length. "You haven't changed at all!" she shook her head, her eyes looking him over from head to foot. "A little thinner perhaps. But tell me," she urged, caressing his cheek with one slender white hand, "you are home to stay?"

"Yes, Mamma," he smiled, taking her hand and kissing its palm, "I am home to stay."

She hugged him again, barely reaching his shoulder, looking up into his smiling face with tears in her eyes, but then, as if recollecting herself, turned to Elizabeth, saying contritely, "Oh, my dear, you must forgive me, but it is so long since I have seen my son. You must be Elizabeth?" she smiled, taking her hands in her own and clasping them warmly.

"Yes. How do you do, Your Ladyship," Elizabeth smiled, bobbing a polite curtsey.

"Ladyship!" she exclaimed, her blue eyes widening. "No, no, my dear," she laughed kindly, patting her soft cheek, "please, do not call me that. My name is Sarah, but if you feel uncomfortable with it, for now at least, please, if you should not dislike it, call me mamma, which" she nodded practically, "is going to be the case very soon. But Gideon," she chided gently without a pause, looking up at him, "why didn't you tell me how beautiful my daughter to be is? Oh my dear!" she cried, turning back to Elizabeth's flushed face without giving him time to answer. "You must allow me to welcome you to Burroughs Croft."

"Thank you," Elizabeth laughed, taking an instant liking to this spontaneous and unaffected woman whom Gideon clearly adored. "It is a great pleasure to be here."

"Oh, but you must be exhausted after your journey!" she exclaimed, pulling Elizabeth's hand through her arm, without ceremony, "especially after having been so poorly!" She looked from Elizabeth to her son, who was standing beside her looking down at Elizabeth with such a look in his eyes that she knew instantly that at long last he had found the lady with whom he wanted to share the rest of his life. "Well," she nodded firmly, "we are going to take the greatest care of you, aren't we Gideon?"

"The very greatest care, Mamma" Gideon confirmed in a deep voice, smiling warmly down at Elizabeth.

She was about to reply to this when she saw Gideon turn his head in the direction of the house where a man had suddenly appeared on the top step looking in their way. Elizabeth did not need to be told that he was Gideon's father, the resemblance was instantly recognizable as was the love and respect she saw in his eyes, watching as he strode over to the steps, taking them in two.

It was good to be home and with his parent's again, and was greatly relieved to see that there appeared to be no deterioration in his father since they last met, and could only hope that now he was home he would be able to relieve him of most of his responsibilities.

"Gideon!" he nodded.

"How do you do, Sir" Gideon smiled, gripping the frail hand extended.

"Good to have you home, m'boy!" he expressed in a voice Gideon knew hid his true feelings.

"It's *good* to be home, Sir" he told him sincerely.

"I take it you have put aside your regimentals and are here to stay?" his father remarked, raising a humorous eyebrow, eyeing his son with unashamed pride.

"Yes, Sir," Gideon smiled warmly, "unless, of course, you intend to throw me out!"

Elizabeth, having walked steadily towards them with his mother's hand affectionately tucked under her arm with Susan following behind carrying her leather hand case, saw quite clearly the love which existed between the two men, but when she saw Sir Matthew grip Gideon's shoulder then embrace him and to see it returned with such heartfelt emotion, she felt a lump creep into her throat.

"How are you really, Father?" Gideon asked concerned.

"Don't look so worried, Gideon" he soothed, patting his arm reassuringly. "I admit I have been somewhat pulled of late, as you can see," he acknowledged, a little smile playing at the corner of his mouth, "but old Mawe tells me I'm fit for another twenty years ... ah," he broke off, his eyes telling Gideon they would talk later, "here are the ladies!"

At this Gideon turned and smiled, taking a step down and holding out his hand to Elizabeth, his strong fingers clasping hers. "Father, may I introduce Elizabeth Ferrers to you. Elizabeth, my father."

Since Gideon had entered her life aunt Clara had naturally told her about her acquaintance with Sir Matthew Neville, especially his marriage to the beautiful creature who had captured his heart upon first setting eyes on her. He was, according to aunt Clara, ten years older than the lady whom he had made his bride, but as she stood in front of him now, despite his frail health, there were still traces of the handsome man he must have been. Even though his dark hair was only slightly greying at the temples, he would not, unlike his son, be seen without his white tie wig with the hair rolled in curls over the ears with the tail at the back enclosed in a black silk bag. He was not quite so tall as Gideon, but even though his shoulders appeared to have shrunken slightly and even become a little bowed, he was still remarkably upright. He had a narrow forehead, now a little furrowed, but his eyes, a little paler than Gideon's, while sunken in his hollow and pallid thin cheeks, held the same qualities which she had come to know and love in his son, as did his mouth, because although his lips seemed to have been drawn in a little, it was easy to see they smiled just as easily, with that hint of determination and strength of purpose which was reflected in the rather gaunt jaw.

Elizabeth saw him transfer his cane into his left hand, extending his right into which she placed the tips of her fingers, dropping a small curtsey as he raised her hand to his lips. "Miss Ferrers," he inclined his head, his eyes smiling down into hers in a way that put her very much in mind of his son, "it is a very great pleasure to make your acquaintance and to welcome you to my home."

"You are most kind, Sir" she smiled. "But, indeed, the pleasure is mine," she cast a glance up at Gideon, whose eyes were fixed on her face in a way that made her blush adorably, a circumstance which was not lost on Sir Matthew. "Gideon has, of course, told me all about his home, but now, having seen it, I can understand why he loves it so."

He looked up at Gideon then back at her. "I can see my son is a most fortunate young man," he observed. "May I," he enquired, having no difficulty in understanding why his son had fallen in love her, "if you should not dislike it on so short an acquaintance, call you Elizabeth?"

"I should be delighted for you to do so, Sir" she told him sincerely, taking an instant liking to this man, whose courtesies reminded her so much of her father.

"Gideon," he said agreeably, turning to his son, "I shall, *without* your permission," he inclined his head, "take the liberty of escorting the lady who is shortly to become my daughter," his eyes smiling down into hers, "into the house; while you, my son" he bowed, "may accompany your mamma!"

"Yes, Sir," said his dutiful son, with becoming meekness.

Having rejoined his mother he took her hand and drew it through his arm, but instead of accompanying him up the steps she detained him a moment, looking up at him, chiding gently, "You know, Gideon, I ought to be very cross with you!"

"Ought you, Mamma?" he asked, kissing her cheek. "Why, what have I done?"

"There!" she exclaimed, unable to resist his smile. "You don't even know! Not *one* of your letters gave the slightest indication that Elizabeth is the most exquisite and captivating creature!" she scolded affectionately.

"Well," he reminded her, his eyes alight, "I only wrote two, Mamma."

"I will not allow that to be a reason!" she told him, patting his cheek.

"No, of course, not" he nodded meekly, taking hold of her hand. "I should, of course, have made that the first thing I told you about her."

"Yes, you should. Well," she sighed, "I shall have to forgive you I suppose," her eyes laughing up into his.

"Thank you, Mamma," he replied gravely.

"And before you ask," she smiled, "I like her very much."

"So do I," he smiled, kissing her hands. "But tell me honestly, Mamma," he said urgently, "did you mind my asking her to marry me before you had met her?"

She thought for a moment, her large blue eyes searching his face, saying "You know Gideon, it is not really proper for a mother to speak to her son on such matters, but you and I need not stand on ceremony. You are a man of nine and twenty and, or so I should suppose," she pointed out indulgently, "not be without experience in these matters."

"I have no recollection of ever asking anyone to marry me before, Mamma!" he said amusingly.

"Foolish boy!" she chided. "Of course you have not, but you know perfectly well what I mean!"

"Yes, Mamma," he smiled, "I think I do, but you have not answered my question."

"I was just about to," playfully tapping his hand, "before you interrupted me!"

"I'm sorry, Mamma," he said contritely, his eyes smiling.

"Were it Aubrey, then yes" she nodded, "I would mind, so would your father. I loved him the same as I love you, neither your father nor I favoured one of you more than the other, indeed" she nodded, "it would have been impossible to have done so, besides being quite wrong. You were both of you the most adorable children, but even now I shudder when I recall the mischief the two of you got up to, but you were always the sensible one, even as a child. Aubrey, well" she sighed, "you know as well as I how impulsive he could be, and the number of times you and your father have helped him out of one scrape or another is beyond counting. Yes," she nodded, upon seeing the frown which suddenly descended onto his forehead, "you don't like being reminded of it any more than you like to think I am comparing him to you, I have never done so, nor am I now," she told him firmly, "I am merely pointing out that where your father and I can rely totally upon your judgement in all things, especially when it comes to choosing your own bride, regrettably, we could not have done so with Aubrey. How much it cost your father to buy that young woman off whom he became entangled with, I dread to think! And she was not the first female with whom he embarked on a reckless affair which, as you well know, could have ended in scandal had it not been for your father's intervention or your own!" she remarked, sadly. "Then, of course, there were his gambling debts! My dear," she said softly, squeezing his hands, "I know how much you loved Aubrey, indeed, you were the best of friends as well as brothers', but you must acknowledge that he did have a tendency to go headlong into something without giving a moment's thought to what could result from it."

He nodded. "Yes, I know, but given time I am sure he would have settled down."

She took leave to doubt this, but kept it to herself saying instead, "So you see my dear, neither I nor your father had the least doubt when you wrote and told us you were offering for Elizabeth Ferrers' hand, because even if you had not been able to clear her brother's name, which, of course, we are both of us pleased you were able to do, there is nothing wrong with his sister, or his family, and, indeed," she added fairly, "apart from the fact that we have had some acquaintance with them over the years, I have always considered it to be grossly unfair to condemn every member of a family simply because one of them has behaved imprudently!"

"I did not realize you knew them," Gideon said, a slight inflexion of surprise in his voice.

"We were not intimately acquainted with them, you understand" she explained, "because, as you know, your father was not in politics as Viscount Easton was, but certainly we met them at any number of dinners and parties and such like, then of course, his sister, Clara Ferrers, who married Sir Thomas Winsetton, knew your father well, oh and by the way Gideon," she smiled deviating charmingly, "Elizabeth is very like her mamma!"

"You know," he smiled, "no one can sum up a case quite like you!"

"Yes, my dear," she scolded gently, "it is all very well for you to find it amusing, but what that poor boy must have gone through, and his sister too, well only consider what happened to the poor child!" she nodded. "Then her father, who, by the way," she digressed again, "was a most sincere and estimable man; it was all so very dreadful!"

"Yes, it was" he acknowledged. "Regrettably, I never knew her father, but from all I have learned of him he was held in the highest regard, and so is Richard."

"Well, my dear," she squeezed his hand, "I shall look forward to meeting this young man, indeed, he seems to think and behave just as he ought."

"Well," he smiled ruefully, "he is certainly an active young man, but I confess to having a deep and sincere liking for him and as for Elizabeth, she adores him, and he her."

"And who could not?" she demanded. "Such a delightful child! Your father has taken quite a liking to her, as I have."

"I am so glad you like her Mamma," he said fervently, "because if you did not…"

She placed her fingers over his lips. "Oh my darling!" she cried from the bottom of her heart, "how could we not like her? She really is most adorable!" he kissed her fingers then affectionately on the lips, before pulling her into his arms and holding her close. "You love her very much, don't you?" she said tenderly, moving a little away from him to look up into his face. "Yes," she nodded, "I know you do," she said astutely, "I can see it in your face; Elizabeth's too."

"Yes, Mamma" he nodded, relinquishing his hold on her, "I love her very much," he confessed unashamedly, "so much so," he told her whole-heartedly, "that I could not live without her!" She nodded her understanding of this, then allowed him to usher her carefully up the steps and into the house, following behind as she headed to the blue saloon to join Sir Matthew and Elizabeth.

"*Mr. Gideon, Sir!*" came a voice from the rear of the hall just as he dropped his discarded driving coat onto a chair before entering this impressive but comfortable apartment in his mother's wake. "I thought it was you who had pulled up. It *is* good to see you, Mr. Gideon!"

He turned and smiled at the man walking towards him. "Hello, Penny," he smiled, holding out his hand to the man who had grown old in his father's service. "How are you?"

"I'm well Sir, thank you," he nodded, gripping Gideon's hand, his old eyes lighting up. "And you, Sir?"

"Very well, thank you, Penny," he told him cheerfully.

"It *is* good to have you home again, Mr. Gideon," he cried, relieved.

"It's good to be home, Penny," he smiled.

Inclining his head towards the blue saloon, he said indulgently, "Been on the watch for you all the morning, has your mother."

"No!" he smiled, raising an eyebrow. "Has she really?"

"Yes Mr. Gideon Sir, she has! But as your father kept telling her, you know Sir," he nodded, "in that way he has when he speaks to your mother, that keep going to the window every time she hears something will not bring you home any the quicker!"

Gideon laughed, picturing his mother running to the window every few minutes and his father fondly chiding her, then, in his good-natured way, spent the next few minutes listening to him recalling a number of long forgotten incidents ending with the worrying time they had had when he was laid up. "Very anxious we all were, Mr. Gideon" he nodded. "I remember your poor mother, your father too," he nodded, "hardly able to rest or eat a morsel until they knew you were going to be all right. But you pulled through, Sir!" he nodded, carefully picking up his driving coat and placing it over his arm. "And the young lady, Sir?" he asked optimistically, indicating the blue saloon. "I take it my felicitations *are* in order?"

"They are, Penny," he smiled, having his hand shook again, "quite in order."

And so, ten minutes after his mother, he entered the blue saloon, apologizing for being so long. "Not at all, Gideon" his father dismissed. "I see you have been renewing your acquaintance with Penny."

"Yes, Sir" Gideon smiled. "I had no idea he remembered so much."

"You must know, my dear" Sir Matthew told Elizabeth, leaning forward a little in his seat, "that Penny has been here ever since he was a boy. So, if you wish to know anything about my son," casting a glance in Gideon's direction, "all you need do is ask him."

She laughed and turned a mischievous glance up at Gideon, thinking of Salmon, who, like Penny, could clearly tell stories about the young men they had watched over from childhood. "I shall remember that, Sir."

"You do that, my dear" Sir Matthew smiled, "because you must know that you will only receive a most favourable account of him from his mamma and I."

"Thank you, Sir" Gideon laughed, inclining his head.

"I *was*, Gideon" his father told him, the affection in his voice not lost on Elizabeth, "about to add that that is only because by the time you and Aubrey presented yourselves to your parent's, Penny had tended your cuts and bruises then bundled you upstairs to nurse in order to render you fit to be seen by your mamma and I without us being in the least aware of the mischief the two of you had been up to!"

Gideon burst out laughing at this, to which his mamma said affectionately, "Indeed, Gideon, I dread to think of the times poor Penny must have been obliged to tell fibs on your behalf! You know Elizabeth," she smiled, turning a proud eye upon her, "I never could make up my mind which one of them it was who broke the window in the rector's carriage when he came to call one day; and even now, I have no idea whether it was Gideon or Aubrey who let Farmer Drayton's pigs out of their sty!" Elizabeth laughed and glanced across at Gideon who was standing in front of the flower-filled fireplace looking at her. "Yes," his mother nodded, not unaware of the looks passing between them, "it is all very well for you to laugh," she admonished indulgently, twisting round to face her son, "but I swear that Farmer Drayton, to this day, has never forgotten it!"

"You know, Mamma," Gideon laughed, "much more of this and Elizabeth will be having the coaches put to again!"

"Nonsense!" declared his mamma, fondly patting Elizabeth's hand. "I am quite sure she would be very interested to learn what you were like as a boy! Wouldn't you, my dear?"

"I was rather hoping, Mamma," Gideon said unsteadily, "to gradually work up to confessing my offences during my early development."

Lady Neville, like her son, had not failed to notice that despite Elizabeth's efforts to the contrary, she was looking rather tired, but more importantly, she had not missed the looks which they exchanged between them and since she knew precisely how they were feeling and would, perhaps, like a few minutes alone, turned to Elizabeth, saying, in her irresistible way, "I daresay my dear, that you will find it most entertaining, not that I believe for one moment he can remember the half of it," she squeezed her fingers, "but something tells me you would like to be taken to your room in order to change or even, perhaps, rest before dinner."

"Thank you," Elizabeth smiled, not daring to look at Gideon, who clearly appreciated this charming and persuasive tactic as much as she. "I *am* just a little tired."

Taking her hand in her own, she walked her over to Gideon, laying it gently on his arm. "Gideon, why don't you escort Elizabeth upstairs to her room.

"Of course, Mamma, I shall be pleased to," her son smiled, raising an amused eyebrow. "Which room have you chosen for her?"

"Oh, yes! Well, you know Elizabeth, I did consider putting you in the corner room of the west wing, because you must know my dear it is such a beautiful room, but then I decided against it, thinking it would be far more comfortable for you to be in the main part of the house. Indeed, my dear" she smiled at Elizabeth, "you will like the pink room, although why it is called 'the pink room' I really cannot imagine," she shook her head, "because it has never been pink to my knowledge, however," she patted her hand, "it really is most delightful; I know you will love it so, especially as it receives the sun until well after midday! Now," she said decisively, gently shepherding them towards the door, "you will find Susan already waiting for you, and I shall be along directly to see you comfortably established as well as ensuring some refreshments are brought to you."

"You know, my dear," Sir Matthew said softly when the door had closed behind them, rising to his feet and taking his wife's hand in his, "you really are the same charming and romantic creature I married!" kissing her cheek.

"Oh Matthew!" she cried, her eyes sparkling. "Gideon loves her very much!"

"Yes, my dear" he nodded, "that is plain to see."

"You like her, then?"

"Very much," he smiled. "She is, I think" he said unhesitatingly, "as much in love with Gideon as he is with her."

"Oh yes!" she agreed. "It is undeniable."

"You know, Sarah," he said at length, "I think that when the time comes, we may safely leave Burroughs Croft in their hands; it will come to no harm through them."

Her eyes clouded a little. "No, I know," she acknowledged.

"You're thinking of Aubrey." She nodded. "So am I," he acknowledged. "You know Sarah, I never apportioned love to my sons' giving one more than the other, I loved them both the same. No one regrets Aubrey's tragic accident more than I, indeed, I would give all I possess to have him with us still, as I know you and Gideon would too, but there is no denying" he shook his head sadly, "that Aubrey, despite his taking ways, was as different to his brother as anyone could be."

"Yes, I know" she sighed, "but he and Gideon were always very close and he misses his brother, nor would he say anything to his disparagement."

"I know he would not," he agreed, "but whilst I admit that Aubrey, if he took notice of anyone it would be to his brother, you know as well as I," he reminded her sorrowfully, "that he abused Gideon's love for him as well as his generosity, not that he ever begrudged Aubrey either, but Gideon's loyalty and level-headedness, sadly, did not rub off onto his brother. You cannot deny, my dear," he said remorsefully, "that Aubrey, for all he was the eldest, was by no means reliable, in fact," he shook his head sadly, "he would have brought Burroughs Croft to its knees within a twelvemonth!" A statement she forlornly acknowledged to be the truth.

Unlike the solid heavy oak staircase she was used to, the one Gideon was now escorting her up positioned in the middle of the lofty hall, was an elegant structure with mahogany handrails on both sides and vertical barley sugar twists at regular distances between each one, gradually widening out as it rose gracefully towards the long window on the first landing, overlooking beautifully kept gardens at the rear of the house. Here, the stairway divided to the right and left into two corresponding flights as their direction reversed to the upper floor and as

Elizabeth looked up, she saw that the staircase repeated its pattern for another two flights. Not until they reached the first landing did either of them speak, and after looking through the window she raised her eyes to his, those brown depths intently watching her. "Well," he asked softly, "what do you think?"

"Oh, Gideon!" she cried breathlessly, "you were right when you said it was nothing like Ferrers Court, but it is all so very beautiful!"

"I *am* a little bias I know," he conceded, smiling down at her, "but I do love it so!"

"And with good cause. You have every right to be bias!" she told him truthfully.

"I am so happy you like it too," he breathed deeply.

"I do!" she told him fervently, laying a hand against his cheek. "Your parent's too," she nodded. Suddenly she bit her bottom lip, a gesture he was becoming used to and one which he found really quite irresistible. "I feel just a little silly now when I think how anxious I was at the thought of meeting them, but...Oh Gideon!" she smiled, "I do like them so very much."

"So do I," he smiled, taking hold of her hand, "but then, I am rather prejudiced."

"Your mother," she told him on a little laugh, "she is adorable!"

"Yes, she is" he nodded, drawing her hand through his arm before turning a little to the left and guiding her up the right hand staircase. "I have always thought so, my father too;" he told her, "he loves and adores her."

"Yes, I know," she smiled. "And they you."

"They made a very happy home and childhood for Aubrey and I," he told her fondly.

She looked up at him, her eyes suddenly mischievous, asking, "Tell me, were you really naughty as a child?"

He laughed down at her. "Oh, impossible! You would not believe the mischief Aubrey and I used to get up to."

"Ah," she nodded wisely, "then I think I had better take your father's advice and speak to Penny after all."

"Well, you can," he told her as though he was giving it some thought, "but I think I must warn you that he has always stood very much our friend."

"I see," she nodded. "No doubt you will do what Richard terms 'greasing him handsomely in the fist' to keep your secrets!"

He laughed and squeezed her hand. "You think I would have to?"

"Probably not," she conceded. "I have no doubt that Penny is to you what Salmon is to Richard!" An irrepressible gurgle of laughter left her lips as she thought of something. "Please, *do* tell me," she begged, "*was* it you who broke the rector's carriage window and let poor Farmer Drayton's pigs out, or your brother?"

"Well, as I remember," he smiled reminiscently, "it was Aubrey who broke the window with his catapult, which was immediately confiscated by Penny."

"And the pigs?" she queried.

"Actually," he confided, looking guiltily down at her, "it was both of us." She burst out laughing. "Aubrey opened the gate and I shooed them out. My father was right about Penny though;" he remarked, "he very often tidied the pair of us up as well as covered for us!"

"Ah," she nodded. "Then perhaps I should have the coaches put to after all!"

They had by now reached the landing which comprised the main body of upstairs rooms, and it was just as they were about to turn into the wide corridor on the right, when he told her, without any change whatsoever in his voice, "If you do, then I shall come after you and bring you back."

She stopped and looked up him. "Would you really?" she asked, curiosity tinged with exhilaration.

"Do you really think I would not?" he asked softly, his eyes glinting down into hers.

She held his look, a strange excitement spiralling through her, her breath stilling in her lungs, saying, hardly above a whisper, "Yes, I think you would."

He shook his head, a smile touching the corner of his lips. "No my darling," he told her in a deepening voice, "there is no 'think' about it."

"There ...there isn't?" she managed, blissfully drowning in those searing dark brown depths.

"No," he assured her. "Having waited all of my life for you," his voice deep and intense as he pulled her urgently into his arms, the force of her coming up against him causing her very expensive wide brimmed straw hat with its skilfully arranged flowers to slip off her head, being held loosely around her neck only by a wide and fragile gauze scarf, "I am never going to let you go."

A surge of excitement shuddered through her at this, saying huskily, "I don't ever want you to let me go."

A febrile glint entered his eyes and something resembling a deep throated groan left his lips, her trembling body in his arms doing nothing to help him contain his ever increasing need of her, but when she gently lowered his head and delicately touched his lips with her own, whatever control he had deserted him. Impatiently tearing the delicate gauze from around her neck with unsteady fingers, he threw it unceremoniously onto the floor, then bent his head and kissed her, an intensely passionate kiss which made her body convulse in his arms, causing him to press her more closely into him, and his kiss to deepen.

Lady Neville, who had a very good idea of what would happen between them, had no desire to intrude too soon on such an intimate moment, but when, after waiting at least twenty minutes, she decided the time was right to break up what was most probably a very passionate embrace, tripped lightly up the stairs

668

humming a tune as she went, and Gideon, releasing Elizabeth and looking ruefully down at her flushed face and heaving breast, smiled, saying hoarsely, "It may not be very subtle, but you must agree she plays fair!" but not by a word or gesture she did give any indication that she had seen Gideon hurriedly bend down to pick up Elizabeth's ravishing hat off the floor any more than she did their heightened colour.

It was at first a little strange to find herself waking up in a room that was not her own and in a house which was so different to Ferrers Court that the morning following her arrival, upon opening her eyes where nothing was in the least degree familiar, she felt just a little disoriented. But Lady Neville, apart from being an excellent hostess, knew from experience how strange everything would be to her son's future bride, and had therefore spared no effort to ensure her comfort, so much so that over the next few days Elizabeth found herself feeling quite at ease at Burroughs Croft, delighting in everything she saw, and growing more and more fond of her prospective parents-in-law.

Although Gideon had spent long periods of time with his father after being away from home for so long, he had never once neglected either his duty towards her as a guest or his own personal desire to be close to her. She had enjoyed being shown over the house and most of the gardens, which really were quite extensive, in his company, including the maze his grandfather had had created, laughingly assuring her upon being shown a doubtful face, that he knew his way in and out, telling her there was no fear of them ending up being unable to find the exit without requiring a search party to guide them out, unless of course, he had told her provocatively, they wanted to. As he had rightly predicted, his mother had assigned herself the role of guide-in-chief, showing her again, only in more detail, what she was convinced Gideon had left out. "Because it is useless to suppose that men have the same interest," she laughed, drawing Elizabeth's hand through her arm. It was during these pleasurable tours that she had learned from Sarah that there had been a house or some such thing on this site ever since the Nevilles came across the Channel with the Conqueror, or, at least, she deliberated, it was a very long time ago. It was evident from all she saw and heard that the Nevilles were indeed a most respected and wealthy family, used to moving in the first circles, but even though Sir Matthew and Lady Neville no longer adorned society as they were once used to due to his deterioration in health, they still maintained their house in town and was therefore not surprised to discover that there appeared to be a not a soul in society whom they did not know, including her parents, about whom Sarah was happy to tell her all she could. When asked if she missed entertaining or going to balls and such like, she smiled and shook her head, then tucking a confiding hand into her own, said, with delightful candour, "Well, you know my dear, I must confess that at first I did miss all that gadding about and not tumbling into bed until three or four o'clock in the morning, but now I never think about it at all. I am really most truly happy and contented here with Matthew."

She did not doubt this. She had often seen the looks which were exchanged between them, or some little show of affection one to the other, all of which told her more than any open declarations could have that they were still very much in love with one another. They also told her that Gideon was, in all respects, very much his father's son, not only inheriting his good judgment as well as the love he had for his home and family's long history, but his loyalty and devotion to what he believed in, besides being a deeply passionate and caring man, and one, moreover, who, having fallen in love would continue to remain so. His innate good manners and calm good sense were unquestionably his father's, but it was his mother from whom he had inherited his sense of humour and that irresistible charm and relaxed manner which not only put one instantly at ease, but had the power to make one do whatever he wished.

Elizabeth had, quite naturally, discussed her forthcoming wedding with Gideon's mother, and had tentatively mentioned that, were it at all possible, she would very much like the ceremony to take place in the church at Ferrers Court where all her family had been married, but realized that the journey into Sussex may well prove a little inconvenient for Sir Matthew. Upon being asked if she had spoken of this at all to Gideon, Elizabeth had told her yes, she had, and when Sarah enquired what his response was, she told her that all he had said was he did not care where they got married providing they did, and soon. Not unexpectedly her future mamma-in-law went into a peal of laughter which was so infectious that Elizabeth, who had found Gideon's response breathtakingly exciting rather than amusing, suddenly saw the humour of it and fell into laughter herself. Sarah, who really had taken to her future daughter-in-law for her own sake, was growing to feel nothing short of a traitoress as the days went by, because whilst she enjoyed these talks with Elizabeth about her forthcoming wedding and what plans she had in mind, she constantly had to remind herself that her husband and son had already sworn her to secrecy about the scheme he and her brother had drawn up between them regarding their marriage. But Elizabeth, as she had very quickly discovered, was intelligent as well as perceptive, and unless she wanted to generate suspicion in her mind she had therefore felt it prudent to put forward suggestions and ideas which hopefully would obviate this risk.

Matthew, having listened to Gideon's account of his participation in Richard Ferrers' affairs with profound interest, his quiet laughter at some of their exploits bringing a smile to Gideon's lips, had regarded it as perfectly natural that a strong friendship had grown up between them. As far as Richard's sister was concerned he had no difficulty in understanding why his son had fallen in love with her, indeed, he would have been astonished had he not have done so, and when Gideon had told him, "There is something else I would like to discuss with you Father, but as it is too late tonight, it will keep until the morning," he had instinctively known that his son wanted to discuss his forthcoming marriage, and when, midway through the following morning, he sat with Gideon in his library, the suggestion of a double wedding at Ferrers Court came as no real surprise. Matthew, who shrewdly suspected that not only was it the close attachment of brother and sister that had prompted the suggestion, but that both men were most eager to marry the ladies of their choice as quickly as possible, and, apparently, with the minimum of fuss. Upon hearing of the trials and tribulations which had beset Richard and his betrothed, as well as the lady's earnest desire to marry at the earliest opportunity as well as her complete lack of interest in making a name for herself in society by launching a successful career commencing with a magnificent wedding in town, he acknowledged that a private ceremony as the one described had a lot to recommend it. Since it appeared that Sir Arthur and Lady Trench would raise no opposition to such an arrangement and it seemed that Elizabeth too would very much like the wedding ceremony to take place at her home, there really was nothing to find against it. Whilst his acquaintance with Elizabeth was of very short duration, he had seen enough of her to be fairly certain that she was equally as keen to celebrate their marriage as his son, and would certainly have no arguments to put forward about being married alongside her brother, but when, in conclusion, Gideon outlined the intended means in bringing it about, it certainly made him raise an eyebrow, causing him to look long and hard at his son.

"And all of this, you say" his father commented at length, "within the space of only two weeks without Elizabeth being aware of it?"

"Yes, Sir" Gideon smiled ruefully.

"A romantic gesture, my son?" he said quietly, raising a questioning eyebrow.

"In a way Sir, yes" Gideon nodded, "but, indeed, it is much more than that." He saw his father raise another questioning eyebrow, and explained, "As I told you last night Sir, when I was sent into Sussex to discover the truth about Richard Ferrers, it was not with the intention of falling in love, and certainly not with his sister; but once having set eyes on her I knew instinctively that I had finally found the woman I had been searching for all my life. I shall ..." the remembrance, still acutely harrowing, rendered it necessary for him to pause momentarily, the raw pain in his voice not lost on his father, "I shall not easily forget the horror I felt when I saw her collapse to the floor at my feet with a ball in her shoulder and I thought I had lost her," he smiled a little sombrely across at his father. "I blame myself entirely for what happened to her," he said with self-reproach. "I should have done everything I could to have prevented it, or," he nodded, "at the very least, foresaw it. Richard too," he acknowledged, "feels himself to be equally responsible. Indeed, Father," he nodded, "she has endured much; especially the death of her father, brought about due to the unbearable harassment of Colonel Henderson. She has had to watch helpless while her home has been ransacked on many occasions as well as worrying over her brother who was being sought as a traitor, and whilst I know that none of us are immune from sadness and tragedies," he acknowledged, "I for one am resolved to making her as happy as I possibly can from now on. I know how much Ferrers Court and her brother means to her, and whilst she has never mentioned a double wedding, in fact I doubt it has even crossed her mind, both Richard and I know she would like it very much; and although Richard is most eager to place his ring on Jane's finger, it would mean an awful lot to him too, and it is for these reasons Sir," he said sincerely, "that we would like to do this for her; a surprise wedding gift from the brother who has a deep and sincere affection for her and from the man who loves and adores her more than life itself and cannot wait to make her his own!"

His father, who had listened to this in silence, eyed his son closely, not really surprised at the reasons for this rather unusual request; Gideon was, after all, his son, and he remembered only too well the lengths he himself had gone to to secure the heart of the woman he loved, and who now adorned his life. He nodded, his eyes smiling appreciatively across at his son. "Then who am I to cavil, if that is what you both want? My felicitations, Gideon," leaning across the narrow space separating their respective chairs, "on your *very* imminent nuptials!"

"Thank you, Sir," Gideon smiled, grasping his father's outstretched hand.

"You will, of course," he nodded, "have to speak to your mother, who, I have no doubt," he remarked amusingly, "will throw herself into these secret arrangements with zeal, and as for Elizabeth," he smiled, "unless I have misread that lively young lady's character, I would say that far from being displeased or disappointed in being deprived of the pleasure of arranging her own wedding, she will thoroughly delight in being taken by such a romantic surprise."

As far as travelling into Sussex was concerned, he assuaged his son's genuine concerns over his health and the length of the journey by informing him that although Dr. Mawe had strictly warned him against riding or even tooling the trap around the place, there was nothing whatever to prevent him from travelling into Sussex to attend his son's wedding in the comfort of the coach together with his mamma.

"You are sure you do not dislike it, Father?" Gideon asked earnestly. "I have no wish to …"

"What I *would* dislike, Gideon" his father interposed truthfully, "is to know that I had failed to support my son."

"You have never failed me in any way, Sir" Gideon assured him sincerely.

"I am pleased to say I fully reciprocate that sentiment," he returned with equal sincerity. "You know, Gideon," he told him with quiet candour, "I have never questioned your dealings or interfered in your affairs, indeed, I have never had cause to. You have long been of an age when you need neither my blessing nor approval for what you may choose to do, but I am both gratified and honoured that you still accord me the consideration of approaching me for my advice or endorsement."

"The honour is mine, Sir," he inclined his head, "and, with your permission, I shall continue to do so."

His father nodded. "You may, even though I know you do not stand in need of either."

"Thank you, Sir," Gideon smiled, "but I think this is one such occasion which has demonstrated I do."

"You know, Gideon" his father told him intuitively, "I take it for granted you are not without experience, indeed, it would be remarkable if a man of your age were, but since you have apparently conducted your liaisons with the discretion I would expect from you, I have no intention of discussing them, except to say that you know as well as I they merely satisfy a natural need which can be readily accommodated at any time while the connection continues, and nothing whatever to do with love. I know you have shared intimate moments with Elizabeth, that is only to be expected," he acknowledged, "but you have not gone beyond the line of what is acceptable but, I too," he smiled, "was once an ardent young man and know only too well what a torment it is to have to restrain one's very natural emotions when in the company of the lady who has captured your heart and upon whom you are about to bestow your name, and since it appears that Richard Ferrers is also suffering from the same malady as you obviously are, it would therefore be unpardonable of me to intensify his affliction, or yours too," he smiled, "by not giving you both my blessing and support." Pausing only long enough to swallow the medicine in a glass at his side, he looked across at his son, his eyes smiling appreciatively, saying, not a little perplexed "Of course, how you and your mamma intend to keep such a secret from Elizabeth, who is, as you know, most astute, especially when one considers the activity such arrangements will generate to ensure everything is attended to in time, I know not! I shall, of course, do everything possible to keep your plans and arrangements from her but, you may, Gideon," he warned, the smile in his eyes bringing a grin to his son's face, "be called upon to distract her from time to time. Should that eventuality arise," he raised a significant eyebrow, "I feel sure you will know precisely how to do it!"

"Yes, Sir" Gideon laughed, "I feel sure I will."

As expected, Sarah came to him immediately Gideon had left her, stating in ecstatic accents that it was the most romantic thing she had ever heard, and was looking forward to arranging everything for the happy day. Matthew had no doubt that she would thoroughly enjoy such a subterfuge, but had nevertheless deemed it prudent to caution her about not letting anything slip, but although she assured him that she would not breathe a word, she was nonetheless finding herself having to strenuously fight the temptation to tell Elizabeth the truth. She did not do so however, but although she set about making her arrangements to help bring about this happy event with enthusiasm, she could not deny that these covert activities were causing her some unnerving moments, because whilst it was an easy enough matter to smuggle correspondence in and out of the house between Burroughs Croft and Ferrers Court, the same could not be said for other and, in her opinion, far more practical matters.

To her relief, Susan, a most deft needlewoman, knew her young charge's measurements by heart as well as knowing precisely the kind of thing she liked, and upon discovering that she was to take part in such a romantic and secret endeavour, was ready and willing to sit up day and night if necessary in order to finish the gown she had been asked to fashion. So overcome was she that she even graciously permitted Sarah's own dresser, who had also taken to the adventure with equal gusto as Susan, to assist by making the under dress.   Sarah was even more relieved to discover from Gideon that he had received a letter from Richard advising that everything was progressing splendidly at The Court, but if he could contrive to keep his sister at Burroughs Croft for another week, for he felt sure that Gideon would know precisely how to persuade her to extend her stay, it would considerably assist his own plans.   "Ours to!" she told her son, "because there is no denying that being granted a little more time is most welcome. I can only guess at what you said to the child to account for her stay being extended, but she asked me not half an hour ago if it would cause me any inconvenience, as though it could!" she exclaimed. "I love the child dearly, indeed, I could not like her more than if she were my own daughter, but you know my dear," she commented practically, "this subterfuge is all very well, but how on earth can we keep it from her indefinitely?"

"I have every faith in you, Mamma," Gideon said confidently, kissing her cheek.

"Yes, I daresay!" she said with strong feeling, "but no fewer than three times has she entered her room to find me there; twice when I was consulting with Susan who had to hurriedly hide all her materials and such like out of sight, not that I am sure it fooled Elizabeth for one moment, and once when I was about to look through her wardrobe; I felt as guilty as though I was spying on her!"

He laughed. "And what did you say?"

"Well, my dear" she told him distractedly, "all I could think of was that I wondered if she had everything she required. And then," she told him, raising a hand to her forehead, "only yesterday afternoon, she saw me taking I don't know how many rolls of silk and satin and stuff out of my room."

His shoulders shook. "And what did you say to that?"

"Well, my dear" she told him truthfully, "I don't precisely remember what I did say, but she seemed to accept it perfectly well. Even so," she explained, "I have had to have Susan working on the dress in my own dressing room so the child won't catch sight of it!"

His sense of the ridiculous got the better of him and broke into laughter, exasperating his mamma to the point where she said, "Yes, it is all very well for you to laugh, but much more of this and I would not be at all surprised to discover that Elizabeth has decided not to become part of such an eccentric family after all, either that," she nodded firmly, "or I shall end up saying something which will set her thinking and bring all to ruin! Yes!" she nodded, "and that's another thing!"

"What is?" he smiled, holding out his hands to her.

"Her trunks!" she cried desperately, placing hers into them.

"Mamma," he shook his head, his shoulders shaking. "What pray, have her trunks to do with anything?"

"You would know perfectly well if you were a young lady, let me tell you!" she chided fondly. "Elizabeth, my dear" she said painstakingly, "arrived here with two trunks," trying desperately hard to resist his smile, "well, she will have to return home with three, because no matter which way you look at it, *that gown,*" she stressed "will have to go in another trunk to keep it from creasing. Now you know perfectly well," she said as firmly as she could, "that Elizabeth is by no means stupid, she will know something is amiss, if she does not already, when she sees three trunks being placed inside the second coach instead of two. Then," she added as a clincher, "there will be your trunk too, do not forget! Because although she fully expects you to remain at Ferrers Court a few days, such a short stay will not necessitate you taking a trunk!" As if he could no longer contain his amusement he burst out laughing, to which his mamma said, "Gideon my dear, you must see what a problem this ... oh, of course!" she cried, triumphantly, her eyes sparkling, "you will have to distract her!"

"Distract her?" he repeated, unsteadily.

"Yes, my dear" she nodded, "I am quite sure you will know just how to do that!" unconsciously echoing her husband's observation.

"Yes, Mamma" he laughed, "I know just how to distract her, but do you really believe it will be necessary?"

"I hope not, but you must see ..."

"Poor Mamma," he soothed, taking her in his arms and holding her close. "I am a brute to drop all of this onto you. Forgive me!"

"Foolish boy!" she said affectionately, kissing him fondly on the cheek. "As if I mind. Oh!" she cried suddenly, pressing a hand to her cheek.

"Another obstacle, Mamma?" he laughed.

"The wedding breakfast!" she gasped.

"Mamma," he said gently, "Richard has not ..."

"I know, but it is so very important," she assured him.

"Very probably," he dismissed amusingly, "but I have Richard's assurance that that is all being taken care of," a gleam suddenly entered his eyes which she had not seen before "even down to those *'delicious scones that only cook knows how to make'!"* he said as if to himself.

"Scones!" she uttered faintly, looking up into her son's face in bewilderment. "Yes, Mamma," he smiled reminiscently, "scones."

"Gideon," she said firmly, pulling herself together, "I hope I do not have to tell you that I love you very much, but when you are in this funning humour you are of no help to me whatsoever!"

"Funning?" he raised an eyebrow. "*I*, Mamma?"

"Elizabeth returns home the end of the week," she reminded him patiently, "and there is still so much to do, but if you cannot behave yourself I wish you will go away; go and talk to your papa or Billings or find Elizabeth."

"Anything you say, Mamma," he smiled, kissing her cheek.

Elizabeth may have been unaware of the subterfuge taking place all around her, but it had not escaped her notice that her future mamma-in-law was, over the last week or so, behaving in a manner she could only describe as conspiratorial, and although she could not begin to imagine what she was planning, because nothing would convince her otherwise, decided to ask Gideon if he had any idea. Having left his mamma to spend an hour or so with his father and Billings, he then went in search of her, not at all surprised to discover her sitting in a little recess in the maze with a thoughtful frown on her forehead, but upon setting eyes on him she smiled, the frown instantly disappearing, and as he sat down beside her and took her hand in his, asked amusingly, "What, my darling, has made you frown so?"

"I wasn't frowning," she asserted, smiling up at him. "I was thinking."

"And what could be serious enough to make you think so deeply?" he asked softly, rhythmically running his thumb up and down her palm. He knew her to be intelligent as well as astute, and although he was not altogether surprised to hear her mention his mamma's present behaviour, he had no wish to acquaint her with the surprise in store for her just yet, so raising a questioning eyebrow, said, with credible surprise, "Conspiratorial! Mamma?"

"Well, perhaps not that precisely," she conceded, "but I can't help feeling she is planning something."

"Planning something?" he repeated slowly.

"Yes," she nodded, her large blue eyes searching his face. "Do you perhaps have any notion what it could be?"

Having appeared to give this considerable thought, he shrugged, "I haven't the remotest guess." He saw her eyes narrow slightly, and deciding that this was one of those moments of distraction his father had spoken of was perfectly willing to take her mind off it in a way he knew would not only succeed but would afford him the utmost pleasure. From the moment his lips touched hers all thoughts of Sarah's odd behaviour were forgotten, in fact, it was some considerable time before she was able to give consideration to anything at all except the exquisite joy and exhilaration she was experiencing in the arms of the man who held her so tightly against him that she would not have been at all surprised to discover her ribs had cracked.

Sir Matthew, watching his wife's indefatigable contribution to their son's imminent nuptials with an indulgent eye, managed to capture her alone one afternoon while she was briefly resting in her sitting room between the numerous tasks she swore still needed to be attended to. "You know, my dear," he said gently, seating himself beside her and taking one slender hand in his, "I admire your efforts on our son's behalf, but I hope you will not be too exhausted to enjoy the outcome of all this frenetic activity."

She assured him it was no such thing, stating that when compared to the preparation of the wedding breakfast and all the bustle which must be taking place at Ferrers Court, then her contribution had been easy indeed.

"I am sure you are right, my dear," he nodded, "but if I have understood my son correctly, he would happily forgo what he calls all this rigmarole and marry her in a cabbage patch."

She sat bolt upright at this, her eyes widening in surprise. "Do you mean …?"

"No, no, my dear," he assured her, raising her hand to his lips, "it is simply that he is as eager to place his ring on Elizabeth's finger just as much as her brother is to place his on the lady who has captured his heart. From what Gideon has told me, I infer that not only would brother and sister like to be married from their home and that a double wedding is what they would both very much like, but that Miss Trench's parent's would neither welcome nor appreciate a cabbage patch wedding for their daughter!"

A delicious gurgle of laughter left her lips at this, looking up at her husband with her eyes so full of unalloyed joy, that she leaned her head against his shoulder and collapsed into uncontrollable laughter. "I know Gideon said he did not want an overly long betrothal," she managed at last, "but this has to be the shortest one ever I heard!"

He smiled, saying softly, "Yes, but then you see my dear, he loves her; and love you know" he reminded her softly, "is as impatient of convention as it is of time." He looked down at her in a way that had never failed to thrill her "He is, after all, his father's son, and his father, as I recall," he said warmly, "and which I am sure you do not need to be reminded of," tracing her cheek with his finger, "felt the same about you, and still do, my dear," lowering his head and kissing her.

CHAPTER THIRTY THREE

As it transpired, the need for Gideon to adopt diversionary tactics upon their departure was not necessary after all, much to his disappointment and his mother's relief, as by the time Elizabeth eventually descended the steps to be handed up into the coach, the luggage had already been bestowed into the one behind. She had received an affectionate goodbye from Sir Matthew, who, not by a word or gesture intimated what awaited her, told her warmly that he was extremely pleased to know that very soon he would be able to call her 'daughter', and looked forward with real pleasure to attending her wedding and welcoming her to her knew home. Sarah, despite the fact that she and Matthew would be arriving at Ferrers Court within the week, nevertheless told her tearfully as she folded her in a scented embrace, that she would miss her and longed for the day when she would be able to call Burroughs Croft her home, and looked forward to hearing of her wedding plans very soon. Having said goodbye to his father and mother, Gideon, having donned his drab driving coat, mounted his grey mare and escorted the cavalcade down the drive, turning round to wave a final hand in farewell just seconds before the party disappeared from their sight.

Had Elizabeth been told that she would come to look upon somewhere other than Ferrers Court with even a modicum of affection, she would never have believed them, but from the moment she had first stepped out of the coach three weeks ago to find herself standing before a house which was as different to her home as any could be, she had taken an instant liking to it, and as the days turned into weeks, this liking had gradually grown into real affection. Whether this was due wholly or in part to the fact that it was Gideon's home she was not entirely certain, but although Ferrers Court would always have a special place in her heart as no other could, she was nevertheless conscious of wanting to return to Burroughs Croft as soon as possible.

Every now and then she caught sight of Gideon's upright figure in the saddle, seemingly indefatigable as the miles sped by taking them nearer and nearer to Ferrers Court. During the relatively short time they had known one another, she had nevertheless acquired a storehouse of treasured memories, all of which were potent enough to bring a touch of colour to her cheeks. Every word, every look and every kiss were imprinted on her memory, and momentarily forgetting the book Sarah had given her with which to while away the journey, relived again all that had passed between them from the moment they had first met, until he had kissed her last night, closing her eyes on the recollection. It had been a beautiful day, from the moment she had opened her eyes the sun had never once disappeared behind a cloud, and by the time dinner had ended it was still pleasantly warm, the deep red and gold rays lowering on the horizon in a wonderful display of vibrant colour, bringing to life in a blaze of fire the red-bricked house as it lay in the path of the descending glow.   Having walked leisurely arm in arm with Gideon along the twisting paths of the flower beds leading to the rose garden and beyond in contented silence, they unhurriedly made their way to a small stone bridge beneath which a stream idly flowed, idyllically set at the side of a small copse just to the right where wildflowers grew in abundance. Upon arriving at the bridge they turned and looked back at the rear of the house, its warm sepia walls looking peacefully out across the landscape, and in that moment Elizabeth knew what it was about Burroughs Croft Gideon loved so much. She felt his fingers stir slightly as they covered her hand as it lay within his arm, telling her more than any words could what his home meant to him, and looking up at his profile saw the very real affection he had for the house he had known since he was born.   Looking down at her, he asked softly, "Tell me, will you enjoy being mistress of all this?"

"Oh yes!" she breathed contentedly.   "Very much," then laying the palm of her free hand against his cheek, said fervently, "but I hope it won't be for a very long time."

"Oh, why not?" he questioned, looking closely at her.

"Because," she smiled tenderly, "I have become much too fond of your parent's to want to step into their shoes too soon."

"Bless you for that!" kissing her fingers, his eyes warm as they rested on her. "Tell me," he asked softly, "when did I last tell you that I love you?"

"Mm" she pondered, "let me see," screwing up her face in an effort of memory, "oh yes, I believe it was this morning."

"As long ago as that?" he raised an eyebrow.   "Then it is time I told you again. I love you, Elizabeth Ferrers."

"And I love you, Gideon Neville," she breathed, her eyes darkening. "I like too, hearing you say you love me," she said warmly.

"And I like saying it," he told her in a deepening voice, "but more importantly," pulling her into his arms, "I like showing you." Which he proceeded to do most convincingly for some considerable time, in a way that was calculatingly constructed to leave no room in her mind for anything other than how he was making her feel.   So lost in these pleasurable reminiscences was she that something very close to a sob left her throat, causing Susan to instantly enquire if she were feeling unwell, but upon being assured that she was quite all right attempted to banish all such provocative thoughts from her mind, but it was so very difficult when all she had to do was glance through the window to see the cause of her recollections riding alongside the coach.

Had she have known it, by the time the tall twisted chimneys of Ferrers Court came into view midway through the afternoon of the third day, Matthew and Sarah had already embarked on their journey into Sussex.

Richard had not needed to hear his sister's animated account of how her stay had progressed, just one look at her face had been sufficient to inform him that her visit to Burroughs Croft had been a most enjoyable one.

Aunt Clara, who, upon being told of the plans her nephew and Gideon had in store, had raised an eyebrow in surprise, asking him if he had run quite mad. Upon being informed that he had not, and that he and Gideon had discussed it and were both in agreement, pursed her lips. At first, she had a number of arguments to put forward against it, not the least being that Elizabeth, who, she was certain, was no different to any other young woman, would much prefer to superintend her own nuptial arrangements rather than have them done for her, and as for her dress, then if she knew her niece, she would have something to say on the subject of one being chosen for her. Richard had listened patiently, neither arguing nor commenting on her objections, waiting until she had come to the end of her catalogue of arguments before explaining their reasons behind such an unusual arrangement. It may not have been quite what she had envisaged either of their weddings to be, but Richard's reasoning gradually won her over, nodding at length, "Well, now I think about it, it may work." She pursed her lips again before saying abruptly, "But have you considered what people will say?" He had told her that he had not and nor had he any intention of doing so, pointing out reasonably that no one, surely, ought to wonder at either of them preferring a private ceremony rather than a big to do in town in view of his recent affairs and the death of their father. Upon being asked what made him so confident that Sir Matthew and Lady Neville would accept such an arrangement for their son rather than a large society wedding in town, not to mention it being so hastily arranged without recourse to her niece, he had told her that he had every faith in Gideon, besides which, he had grinned, it appeared it was precisely the kind of thing his mother would enjoy, and as for his father, he trusted his son's judgement and therefore the only difficulty would be his health and the journey into Sussex. Since her nephew appeared to have all the answers to her objections, she threw down what she believed to be her trump card by pointing out that he had forgotten one small thing; Sir Arthur! For a more stiff rumped man she had told him tartly she had yet to meet, and would therefore own herself astonished if he agreed to go along with a double wedding in the church here at Ferrers Court rather than in town, besides which, he was just the kind of man to wonder why the ceremony was to take place in so short a time following their betrothal announcement, giving a very odd appearance. His eyes narrowed at this, stating firmly that his behaviour towards Jane had been irreproachable, indeed, he hoped it went without saying that he was not the type of man to behave so despicably, thereby tarnishing the reputation of a lady who meant more to him than life itself. As for the rest, having already turned down two very eligible offers for her hand, much to her father's annoyance, he felt reasonably certain that he would much prefer to accept this proposition rather than see his daughter lose yet another suitor. Since Richard's mind was clearly made up she could only hope for all their sakes that Sir Matthew and Lady Neville would not refuse to accept such an unusual arrangement, and upon receipt of Gideon's letter confirming that no objections had been raised, on the contrary, it had met with their full approval, Clara Winsetton had nothing to do but accept it, and set about assisting her nephew in ensuring that everything was attended to here at The Court. It was not that she disliked the scheme, indeed, she was more romantic than people realized, and knew perfectly well that both men were impatient to marry the ladies who had, apparently, taken their hearts by storm, it was simply that she would have much preferred to have arranged a magnificent ceremony in town for her niece and nephew, which, as Richard well knew, would have given her the opportunity to puff off such a dual accomplishment to all her acquaintance.

Miss Calne, whose aid had been enlisted to write cards of invitation and other small tasks, had eyed her mistress with a disapproving eye. Such goings on as this was not at all what she approved of, but since that redoubtable lady had not given her the opportunity to pour forth her list of objections, taking her participation for granted, set about the tasks in grumbling silence.

As Richard had rightly predicted, Sir Arthur's initial refusal to accept such a hastily got together affair, had been overborne by his wife and daughter; the first saying that whilst it held out every hope of attracting vulgar speculation, she feared if he withheld his consent it could well bring about an end to the betrothal and the Ferrers family, as he well knew, were as wealthy as any he cared to mention; and the second, that she for one was looking forward to a double wedding and it mattered not to her if it took place this very afternoon, tomorrow or next week, and if her father refused to give his approval and demanded the betrothal be brought to an end, then she would go and live with Aunt Matty and never marry at all! This uncharacteristic ultimatum from his daughter considerably surprised him, but only a moment's thought gave him pause; if there was one thing above all others he disliked it was gossip, and should the news spread that the betrothal had been brought to an end, because he could not fool himself into believing it would not, then there was no denying that his daughter, with two refusals at her back, could well be shunned by future prospective suitors. It was therefore in a mood of resignation tinged with belligerence that he gave his consent, stating "Very well, do as you will, since it appears I am no longer master in my own home!" closing the door to his book room with a snap and sinking into a chair with a copy of The London Gazette, issuing strict orders that he was not to be disturbed.

Clara Winsetton, in company with Mrs. Finch the housekeeper, was secretly enjoying superintending the preparation of the guest rooms as well as instructing cook and the three girls brought in from the village whom she had called upon to assist her, in what precisely was required to present a wedding breakfast.   Phillips, having been left in no doubt as to what this formidable lady wanted, set about his task in preparing various blooms with enthusiasm, instructing his underlings in no uncertain terms that it was for Miss Elizabeth, and therefore he expected his orders to be carried out.

As for Reverend Parton, he could not have been asked to perform a better or happier task than to marry His Lordship to Miss Trench alongside his sister and the Major in the family church where every member had been married for centuries, informing Richard that it would not only be a great honour but a real pleasure.   Upon being asked if he had any objection to Gideon staying under the parsonage roof the night before the wedding, "Because you know, Parton," Richard had laughed, "the poor fellow cannot remain here and he must sleep somewhere!" he had given his full approval, stating that it would be a pleasure to accommodate the man who had saved His Lordship from climbing the Scaffold.

Michael received Richard's request to act as sponsor to both men with enthusiasm, writing back saying that nothing would give him greater pleasure than to assist at the wedding of his friend and Gideon, necessitating Aunt Clara to give orders that yet another guest room was to be made ready.

In response to Richard's letter, Pritchard immediately set in progress the necessary course of action to prepare 'The Little House', a modest four bed roomed Queen Anne House that formed part of the Ferrers estate which fell in the county of Kent, about ten miles from the Sussex border and close enough to Rye for them to board the packet to France.   The establishment, which had been a favourite of his mother's, had not been used since before his father's death, and because of his own recent difficulties he had not set eyes on the place in over two years, and therefore had had to rely on Jennings to keep an eye on the place, an old retainer of the family living comfortably in the lodge, but he knew Elizabeth loved the house and would therefore enjoy spending her wedding night there.

He also knew that she loved Salmon, as he did, and since he could not escort his sister down the aisle being a groom himself, he could think of no one more fitted than this loyal and faithful stalwart to stand in their father's place. The old eyes filled with tears, causing him to hurriedly remove his handkerchief from his pocket, vigorously blowing his nose, saying somewhat thickly, "Well, yes, but Master Richard," apparently exempt from addressing him as My Lord, "is there no …"

"No, there is not!" Richard told him firmly, gripping his shoulder. "And even if there were," he told him truthfully, "it wouldn't matter! It would make us both very happy, so I'm not taking no for an answer!"

"Well Sir," he sniffed, "if that's what you would like, I'd pleased to, indeed, Sir," he nodded, "I'd be proud to." He was deeply touched by this, and although he would miss her being at The Court, he had to admit that he could think of no finer man or better husband for Miss Elizabeth than the Major, but as he watched the hectic preparations going ahead for the happy day, he could not prevent the odd tear from appearing in his eyes. He had watched over her since the day she was born; seeing her grow from a mischievous imp whom he had scolded and admonished, into a beautiful young lady on the point of being married and leaving her home, and although it would be an ordeal to say goodbye to her, he wanted her to be happy and he had no doubt she would be with the Major. Clara Winsetton, who was herself thinking along similar lines, had, more than once, to sternly prevent her feelings from over spilling, concluding that if she as well as Salmon succumbed to emotion then they would fall terribly behind hand.

But by the time Elizabeth arrived home everything seemed to be well on the way to being sorted or solved; the flowers to decorate the hall and great hall had been chosen, all the best linen had been cleaned and pressed and her late ladyship's best tableware and glasses had been unearthed and thoroughly cleaned and polished and Sir Matthew and Lady Neville were expected the day after tomorrow. It seemed then that all that remained was for Gideon to tell his betrothed of the plans which had been going forward without her knowledge, and although Clara Winsetton had believed Elizabeth would much prefer to tend to her own wedding arrangements, it had not taken her long to review this belief, eventually coming to the conclusion that, like Sir Matthew, had no doubt that her niece would relish such a surprise. Even so, she still maintained that her gown, the bride's most important consideration, may well pose a dilemma, but since it was too late to remedy it, she could only hope that Susan had managed to fashion something which Elizabeth would find to her taste. Having been informed in a quiet aside by Susan that Lady Neville had placed the dress in one of her own trunks, she told her that under no circumstances must the luggage be taken out of the coach until she had her niece comfortably settled in the sitting room, all they wanted was for her to catch sight of it and she would instantly demand to know where it had come from, and then, she told Susan firmly, the fat would be in the fire! "Get the footmen to take it to my room, where you will unpack it." She knew Susan was a deft and clever needlewoman and one with an eye for style, besides knowing precisely the kind of thing her niece liked, but she still wanted to cast an approving eye over it, not that she doubted for one moment that it would not be anything other than perfect. Managing to get Gideon to herself on the way to the sitting room, she nodded in the direction of Elizabeth walking ahead of them with Richard, saying tartly, "Well, Gideon," not quite able to hide the smile in her eyes, "t'would seem that you and my nephew between you have managed to turn the whole household in a bustle of late!" She twitched her shawl. "No doubt your father and mother think the two of you have run quite mad!"

"Let us just say," he laughed, pulling her arm through his, "that they were quite prepared to overlook it as a possibility in the name of love."

"I daresay," she nodded, "but your mother must have had a deal on her hands trying to keep Elizabeth from discovering what was afoot!"

Upon being told of the unnerving moments his mother had experienced and Elizabeth's conviction that she was being conspiratorial, she laughed, telling him that she did not envy her in trying to fool Elizabeth, because she was by far too intelligent, a statement to which he fully agreed.

It was as obvious to her as it was to Richard that Elizabeth had enjoyed her stay at Gideon's home, but even though she listened with keen interest to her niece relating the good time she had had, she decided the time was fast approaching when they should leave her alone in order for Gideon to tell her the news. She was just on the point of requesting her nephew's escort upstairs to her bedchamber, when the mention of the maze at Burroughs Croft held her attention, in fact so impressed was she that she went so far as to suggest to Richard he might consider having one created here at The Court, to which he raised an accusing but laughing eyebrow at Gideon, "Now, see what you have done!" Upon being asked by his sister if Jane was coming tonight, he said yes, whereupon she rose to her feet saying she had promised Jane some seeds for her mamma, and she would go and get them from Phillips before she went to her room to change.

Gideon needed no persuading to accompany her, and as he rose to his feet to open the door for her, cast a quick glance at Richard, whose raised eyebrow and crooked smile were sufficient for him to nod his head.

After leaving the house via the back door, they traversed the lily pond and walked through the gate just to the left of the stables towards the rear of the gardens, when she instinctively put her hand through Gideon's arm. By now it was almost half past four, and although the last few days had not been as pleasantly warm as they had been, in fact it had turned a little humid, leaving her dreading the thought that a storm was brewing, it was not too uncomfortable. Having cast aside her hat, which, said her aunt, no one would think cost a pretty penny the way she unceremoniously flung it onto the seat beside her, her dark hair shone in the sun's rays, a wayward spiral falling carelessly over her shoulder, her eyes smiling up at him as she pointed out various things which reminded her of Burroughs Croft. The man beside her felt his heart race, but managing to restrain his natural impulses for the moment guided her towards a seat he remembered seeing just out of view round the bend in the path, and as she was perfectly happy to linger awhile before seeing Phillips, sat down beside him, making no protest when he gently held her in his arms. She could feel his heart thudding as he held her tighter and pressed his lips into the soft skin of her neck, closing her eyes on a pleasurable sigh as she clung to him, agonizingly conscious that she longed for a far more intimate contact, yearning for the day when they could be together always.

"Do you know how much I love you?" he told her hoarsely, brushing his lips through her hair.

"Yes," she breathed, hardly above a whisper. "I know."

Easing himself a little away from her he cupped her face in his hands, looking intensely down into her glowing face, asking, not very steadily, "Tell me, truly, are you still in favour of a short betrothal?"

"Yes," she managed huskily, "a *very* short betrothal. My darling!" she cried from the bottom of her heart, "I love you so much; I long only for the day when I become your wife."

A deep sigh racked his body at this, and after thoroughly kissing her, said, a little ruefully, "What if I told you that we are to be married in three days time?"

"Oh, how wonderful that would be!" she breathed blissfully, "but it is quite impossible," she shook her head. "My darling, you can have no notion of what it entails; all the arrangements and…"

"What would you say," he interposed with a kiss, "if I told you that it is not only possible, but actually going to happen; and that I am very much aware of what it all entails and the arrangements which have to be made?" He looked lovingly down into her slightly puzzled face, his slightly trembling thumb caressing her parted lips. "I am afraid my darling," he confessed softly, "that your brother and I are guilty of practising deceit, in fact," he smiled contritely, "not only us, but my parent's, Aunt Clara, Susan, Salmon and a string of other people too!"

She shook her head, a little bewildered, a strange sensation invading the pit of her stomach. "You mean …?"

"I mean, my darling," he told her urgently, holding her close against him, "that in three days time, you and I and Richard and Jane, are going to be married, here, side by side, in the church, by Reverend Parton." He felt her tremble in his arms and heard something between a sob and choke leave her lips, and cradling her closely against him with her head resting comfortingly on his shoulder told her how it had all come about. "So you see, my darling," he said earnestly, when he had finished, raising her chin with his forefinger in order for her to look up at him, "unless you want to jilt me at the alter on Friday as well as break my heart, there is really nothing else for you to do but say, 'Yes Gideon, my darling, I will marry you on Friday!'"

Her large blue eyes swam with unshed tears, but at this they rolled down her cheeks, resisting her every effort to stem the flow, until she finally gave up trying.

"My darling," Gideon urged, "please tell me these are tears of joy," wiping them away with a trembling forefinger, "and not …"

She shook her head, smiling mistily up at him, laying a hand against his face. "Yes Gideon, my darling," she repeated, almost reverently, "I will marry you on Friday."

A deep raw sigh of relief ripped from his throat at this, his eyes burning as he kissed the palm of her hand before pulling her roughly against him, holding her so tight that she could hardly breathe. "I can't tell you how…"

"You don't have to," she soothed against his neck, "I know, because I feel precisely the same." Easing herself away from him, she looked lovingly up into his face, saying softly, "My poor darling, did you really believe I would say no?"

"I confess that for one horrifying moment I did think …" he got no further, deciding no words were in the least necessary, kissing her with such ruthless need that, for the moment at least, all the questions she wanted to ask him were relegated to the back of her mind.

Having taken their time to walk back to the house, her errand to see Phillips completely forgotten, she had learned of the hive of activity which had taken place in the two households over the last two and a half weeks, and could only marvel that everything had been organized in time. She had not been at all certain whether to laugh or cry when she knew she was going to be married alongside her brother, which was in itself a wonderful joy, but to know that Salmon, who had looked after them both for as long as she could remember, would walk her down the aisle, caused her to swallow a lump in her throat. She loved him dearly, and there was no one she would rather give her away in her father's stead, after all, he had stood in place of her father during his political absences, protecting and shielding her from all manner of harm, and knowing that he would be there beside her caused a stray tear to stream down her face. She realized what hard work it must have been for everyone in bringing about this double wedding, and without her knowing anything about it. She was pleased that they were going to stay the first two nights at 'The Little House', it had been a long time since she had been there, but it was the thought of Gideon's mamma, a woman so far removed from being surreptitious or scheming, striving to arrange everything with Susan without her getting wind of it, that made her laugh quietly to herself. "Your poor mamma!" she cried. "What a task she must have had! Only think; trying to prepare a wedding gown without the bride's knowledge."

"Yes, I know" he laughed, "she told me of her narrow escapes when you came across her carrying bundles of stuff, and discovering her in your room."

"I told you she was behaving conspiratorial," she accused laughingly, "only you said it was no such thing, and then" she told him as firmly as she could, "you tried to take my mind off it."

"Ah, yes" he nodded "I did, didn't I. In fact," he confessed, "my parent's were right when they said I may have to adopt diversionary tactics, and you must admit," he told her, coming to a halt and putting his arms around her, "it was a most enjoyable distraction!" proving his point admirably by kissing her.

Neither Sir Matthew nor her aunt had erred in their assumption in that Elizabeth would relish such a surprise rather than complain at having others arrange such a special day for her.   It was the most wonderful wedding gift she could have received from the two men she loved most in the world, and even though she knew that Richard was equally as eager to marry Jane as she was to marry Gideon, and Jane herself was looking forward to their marriage being celebrated with the same impatience, it was something she would cherish for the rest of her days.   To be married alongside the brother she loved and adored in their own church, meant more to her than any magnificent ceremony in town ever could, and more to this was knowing that he was having *'The Little House'* made ready for her and Gideon; the thought bringing tears to her eyes especially as she knew that no gift she could possibly give him could conceivably equal that which he had given her.   As for Gideon, it was certainly a romantic gesture, and one, surely, no woman in her right mind would not be thrilled at, but it also confirmed how much he loved her and how ready he was to demonstrate that love as soon as possible in public as well as private, as keen as she was to demonstrate hers to him.

At no point did she have any qualms about her gown, as not only was Susan an exceptional needlewoman, but one of impeccable taste, and the creation she saw hanging up in her aunt's bedchamber was not only exquisitely beautiful but precisely what she would have chosen. No words could adequately convey her thanks or gratitude, especially when she considered how little time she had had available to produce such a magnificent dress.   The stiff bodice, fashioned in oyster coloured Italian silk, had a low square neck, around the edge of which had been sewn a narrow border of gold threaded lace. The sleeves were tight fitting to the elbows from where a double fall of the same gold lace had been sewn. The overskirt, in the same oyster coloured silk, opened out at the front, exposing a silk underskirt of cream delicately embroidered with pink and gold thread, which, when worn over the rectangular hoops would flatten the skirt back and front. Aunt Clara, who, after inspecting it closely, gave it her full approval, said tartly that no one could sew or create something as beautiful nor in so short a time as Susan, but then, had she known it, Susan had been fired with the love of romance, and just knowing that she had been included in the secret had spurred her on, making her determined to show off her young mistress to her best advantage in front of the Major.   Upon being asked if she would be prepared to leave Ferrers Court for Burroughs Croft, Susan, who was already overwhelmed at the prospect of accompanying her young mistress to Paris on honeymoon, had known no hesitation in saying that she was ready to accompany her anywhere.

Aunt Clara, keeping a close eye on the two pairs of love birds, could find nothing improper with their behaviour one to the other, although if she had have been asked whether it was Richard or Gideon who was clearly struggling to restrain their emotions she would have been hard put to say. She had been young herself, yes, and in love, because no matter what people may say she had truly loved Sir Thomas, but where in her young day it was considered almost indecent for a couple to flaunt their feelings in public, she saw nothing untoward in the speaking glances both men cast in the direction of the ladies who had captured their hearts.

The arrival of Sir Matthew and Lady Neville, just before midday twenty four hours before the wedding ceremony, caused Richard and Gideon to exchange amusing glances one with the other, reinforcing his statement that his mother never travelled with just the bare minimum, the entourage pulling up outside the front door of Ferrers Court being adequate proof of this. In the second coach was a mound of luggage, and in the third sat his mamma's dresser, his father's valet, and Penny, whom he knew would not only attend him at The Parsonage to night and tomorrow but would accompany him to Paris in place of a valet. Having warmly greeted his father he then turned a laughing eye to his mamma, enquiring if she had come to stay for a week or a month, to which she tenderly kissed him, saying fondly, "Well my dear, one never knows when one may need something which has been left behind," before affectionately embracing her future daughter-in-law. They were given a warm welcome by Richard, and Aunt Clara, having stepped outside to greet them, told Sarah in her forthright way that she swore she had not changed a bit in thirty years, to which that unaffected lady slid an arm through the older and arthritic one, telling her that she looked forward to a comfortable gossip with her.

With the arrival of Jane not half an hour after Sir Matthew and Lady Neville with the news that her parent's, who had kindly accepted the invitation to dine, would come later, the ladies retired to Aunt Clara's room to spend a happy hour or so in discussing all the things that gentlemen were not in the least interested in, or so she assured the two younger ladies. As the hall and great hall, where the wedding breakfast was to take place, were currently under siege by an army of servants who were busily employed in displaying the fruit and flowers which had been brought up to the house in several cases, the gentlemen took refuge in Richard's book room with the decanter, where Michael and the Reverend Parton joined them only minutes later.

Elizabeth, no less than Aunt Clara, was still finding it hard to believe that Sir Arthur and Lady Trench had given their approval to so hastily arranged a marriage; but whatever it was that had persuaded them to accept it, when they finally sat down to dinner that evening, nothing could be detected in their faces except their smiling consent and support. As far as Gideon was concerned, being constantly in the company of the woman he loved for several days and nights prior to his stay at The Parsonage tonight had put a great strain on his self-restraint, because although he knew Elizabeth would not repulse his kisses, he was honest enough to admit that loving her the way he did the touch of her lips alone, however pleasurable, would not assuage the growing need he had for her. Although she had accepted this unspoken need with equanimity, it was clear from the look in her eyes as they focused on him across the dinner table that she felt exactly the same, and was just as eager as himself to see his ring on her finger in order to bring about such a joyous coming together.

Sarah too, had caught the speaking glances they cast at one another as well as those exchanged by Richard and Jane, and Sir Matthew, who was in full approval of his son's marriage, had no difficulty in understanding the aching need of these four young people, after all, he had felt the same towards Sarah, still did in fact, and saw no reason to deprive either couple a few moments alone before they parted for the night.   Lady Trench however, was not so accommodating or indulgent.   She may have no regrets about a connection with the Ferrers family, but nevertheless she was still far from happy about such a hastily arranged wedding, and had accepted it purely from very practical reasons and no other, but she was certainly not going to permit her daughter to have so much as a second alone with Richard until his ring was on her finger tomorrow.   In order to ensure this she took hold of her daughter's arm and propelled her irresistibly out of the house towards their waiting carriage, and as she and Sir Arthur thanked him for his hospitality Richard could do no more than accord his betrothed's hand a punctilious kiss, making no effort to return to the house until the coach had disappeared from view.

Half an hour later, Reverend Parton's trap had been brought round to the front of the house with Gideon's trunk bestowed safely in the back, and Penny, who had told him he would wait for him outside, left Gideon to say goodnight to Richard and his parent's, his mother telling him affectionately that she was very happy for both of them.   "I know, Mamma," he smiled, holding her close.   "And I am very happy too."

Over his mother's head he saw Elizabeth standing just by the door to the great hall, but Sarah, sensing her presence, patted her son's cheek and told him she would see him in the morning, whereupon she smiled at Elizabeth, saying warmly, "I will leave you to say goodnight to Gideon, my dear," whereupon she floated away out of sight.

"You know," he told her in a deep voice, after raising her hands to his lips, "I have the very strong feeling that tonight is going to prove to be the longest one I have yet spent."

"For me too," she said softly, smiling lovingly up at him.

Taking the third finger of her left hand in his strong fingers, he reverently kissed it, saying thickly, "Tomorrow, I place my ring on this finger, when you, Elizabeth Ferrers, become Elizabeth Neville," whereupon he glanced at the clock then back at her, his eyes burning into her own, "and this time tomorrow night, you will be mine completely."

She trembled at the thought, but was given no time to respond as he took her in his arms and kissed her, feeling quite bereft when he eventually released her. "Until tomorrow, my darling" he said warmly. She watched him stride out of the house and heard him say something to Reverend Parton and Penny, but made no move to leave the hall until she could no longer hear the sound of the trap's wheels on the drive.

Considering Elizabeth had barely closed her eyes all night, she was feeling remarkably invigorated and wide awake when Susan brought in her cup of chocolate just after half past seven. Her overseer, after drawing back the curtains, took one look at her and knew perfectly well that she had lain awake during the nocturnal hours thinking about what lay ahead of her, but when she charged her with this, was told that she had had all the sleep she needed. Sarah, taking a look in on her just as she was sipping her chocolate, thought precisely the same thing, but instead of scolding her about it as Susan had done, looked indulgently upon it, as she could remember only too well how she had felt the night before her own wedding. Waiting only until they were alone, she eyed Elizabeth affectionately, saying softly, "You know my dear, I really am most pleased about this marriage, so is Sir Matthew."

"Oh Sarah!" she cried, sitting up and hugging her knees. "I only want to make Gideon happy!"

"You already do, my dear" she said warmly, embracing her.

Elizabeth eagerly returned the embrace, before confessing, "I am most dreadfully ashamed to think that I have not yet thanked you properly for all you have done; the dress and everything! Oh, Sarah, it is so beautiful!"

"I am so glad you like it," she smiled. "Poor Susan," she laughed kindly, "told me she would sit up day and night to finish it," then going on to spend the next ten minutes laughingly recalling the unnerving moments when she thought everything would be revealed, but bringing her visit to an end after a quick glance at the clock, saying there was much to do before ten o'clock, kissed her cheek and left her in the hands of Susan.

It had seemed at first that Sir Arthur and Lady Trench were going to withhold their consent in letting Jane leave for the church from Ferrers Court rather than The Manor but, in the end, they relented and, at half past nine, their coach pulled up outside the front door, whereupon Jane tripped inside, Richard having made sure he was already at the church in order that he would not see her. Lady Trench, after giving last minute instructions to her daughter, nodded to the coachman to take her to the church while Sir Arthur followed Jane inside, in much need of the stimulant handed to him by Salmon. But after all the comings and goings and the advice from Aunt Clara and a last minute hug from Sarah, Jane and Elizabeth were able to spend the last ten or fifteen minutes alone together, laughing and talking and standing side by side in front of the mirror taking a last minute look at their reflections.   Jane was looking particularly lovely in an ivory coloured silk dress with an underskirt of the palest pink embroidered with cream and blue flowers and matching ribbons threaded through her chestnut curls.   Although both ladies were very much in favour of the rectangular hoops which were becoming the rage, although theirs were by nowhere near as wide as some of them, they did unfortunately render sitting side by side in the coach a little difficult, so with Elizabeth and Salmon on one seat and Jane and her father on the opposite one, they made the short drive from the house to the church.

Sitting proudly beside her with her hand tucked in his arm, Salmon, in his Sunday best, had recourse to his handkerchief but, by the time they entered the church, he had somehow managed to overcome his emotions to walk his young mistress down the aisle to the man whom he knew could be entrusted to take care of her.   As she walked slowly down the aisle beside Jane, approaching the two men who were standing waiting for them, their heads turned in their direction, she was totally unaware of the fact that the church was full to capacity with all the guests her aunt had invited, friends of long-standing from old county families who had known her family for many years.   Although Michael was looking really quite handsome in his regimentals, and Richard was splendidly attired in pale blue silk, it was only Gideon his sister had eyes for and all she would ever be able to recollect with any accuracy of her wedding day.

His coat was fashioned in pale dove grey silk, with deep cuffs edged in the same silver thread as along the edges, which were curved back at the sides, revealing his waistcoat of cream silk, heavily embroidered with silks of blue, silver and grey.   His breeches were of the same dove grey as his coat, tied at the knee with silver buttons, with cream stockings covering his shapely legs.   Although it was the current fashion to wear a wig, apart from when he was in regimentals, it was something he seldom wore, but as it was quite acceptable in polite circles to have one's own hair dressed to look like a wig, it was in deference to his father that he had had his hair dressed in this way, tied in the nape of his neck by the diamond chip clip bow.   Glinting in the heavy fall of lace at his throat was the diamond pin he always wore, and on the little finger of his left hand was the gold and opal signet ring given him by his father now he was heir to his title and dignities since Aubrey's death.

Since both ladies were looking exceptionally beautiful, fully deserving of attention, neither gentleman it seemed had eyes other than for the one he was about to make his wife, and as Elizabeth placed her hand in Gideon's, it could well have been only the two of them standing there at the alter, as neither of them seemed to be aware of anyone else.   The only responses she heard were Gideon's, strong and unfaltering, and when she made her own, although her voice may have quavered once or twice, her commitment was equally as heartfelt, and when he eventually placed his ring on her finger, the finger he had reverently kissed the night before, she felt a tear sting her eye, but the warm smile of recognition she saw in his eyes brought a smile to her own lips, causing Aunt Clara to hastily search for her handkerchief.   Upon being told by a beaming Reverend Parton that they may kiss the brides, both men were more than happy to do precisely that, having to reluctantly recollect themselves when they felt the response of the lady they had just made their own.

It was certainly a happy day at Ferrers Court, without doubt Salmon could not recall the house being filled with so many people since before the death of her late ladyship, but if brother and sister felt the loss of not having their parent's here to witness such a happy event as their double wedding, it was something they only shared between themselves; indeed, no one looking at them, with the exception of Gideon, would ever have suspected how acutely they felt it.   Elizabeth was pleased to have a little time alone with Richard during the wedding breakfast, and if no words could express the love and devotion one had for the other, the warm embrace they shared most certainly did.

She would never quite be able to remember what she had said or to whom, or, indeed, if she had eaten anything from the array of dishes laid out on the table, but before she realized it it was time to change her gown, and in company with Jane, her aunt and Sarah, Susan having already gone on ahead to 'The Little House' with Penny, she entered her room for what would be the last time.   Not unnaturally, it was a little emotional for her, but the thought of what lay ahead helped to temper any sadness she felt, and after carefully removing the string of pearls from her hair which her mother had left her, stepped out of her wedding dress and into the one already laid out on her bed.

Jane, who did not mind in the least about not going away on honeymoon, perfectly happy to remain at Ferrers Court with her husband while Sir Matthew and Sarah were their guests for the remainder of the week, could not prevent the tears from forming in her eyes as she hugged her dearest friend goodbye. Elizabeth may want nothing more than to be alone with Gideon, but she had known that saying farewell would be extremely painful, and although she managed to check the tears as she said goodbye to Aunt Clara and Sir Matthew and Sarah, when it came to Salmon and her brother they ran freely down her cheeks. Salmon's, "There Mistress, that's enough of that! You get in that coach like a good girl!" just how he had spoken to her as a child, proved almost too much, but it was Richard's crooked smile and glistening eyes that undid her, and as she walked into his outstretched arms, clung to him as the tears fell without restraint. He held her close for several minutes, saying something into her ear which no one else could here, and Gideon, having changed into a blue coat, riding breeches and top boots, a mode of dress he much preferred, wanted nothing more than to take her in his arms and comfort her, watched as brother and sister said farewell, making no move until Richard nodded to him, whereupon he strode over to them and gently took Elizabeth's arm. After shaking Richard's hand, he assisted her into the coach, then following a word with his father and a kiss for his mother, joined Elizabeth in the plush interior, the horses springing to immediately the door was closed behind him. Without saying a word he wrapped her in his arms and held her close, content to let her cry over what was a very natural reaction to such an emotional farewell to those whom she had known all her life and dearly loved but, gradually, the tears subsided, and tilting her chin he gently wiped away her tears with his finger. "Better?" he asked gently.

She nodded. "Yes, thank you. I …I'm sorry, I don't know what you must be thinking …"

"Don't be sorry," he said softly, "there is no need; I do understand. As for what I'm thinking," he smiled disarmingly down at her, "I would much prefer to show you than tell you, but that will keep until later. For now," he said warmly, "I shall just have to content myself with kissing you." Which he did to the satisfaction of both of them for several minutes. The last thing she remembered after his lips released her own was asking him if he had slept well and seemed to recall him amusingly recounting his stay at The Parsonage, saying that despite the Reverend's open-handed generosity, the bed had been somewhat uncomfortable and doubted he had closed his eyes for more than half and hour in total. But it had been an eventful and emotional day and, coupled with having lain awake most of the night, it was not long before she felt her eyelids slowly begin to close, helped by the gentle and rhythmic swaying of the coach and Gideon's strong arms holding her close against him, it was therefore not long before sleep claimed her. Upon discovering she had fallen asleep, Gideon moved her more comfortably against him and held her closer, then kissing the top of her head, lay back against the squabs, recalling the last time she had fallen asleep in his arms, but knew, with a thud of his heart, that next time she did he would be with her throughout the night, and there beside her in the morning.

The sensation of her rousing in his arms and the sight of her drowsy eyes looking up at him nearly two hours after, were hardly conducive to self-restraint, but managing to contain the desire to make love to her there and then, contented himself with kissing the tip of her nose, asking gently if she had enjoyed her sleep. As they were by now turning in through the gates of 'The Little House' she drowsily smiled and said, "Yes, I'm so sorry, I did not mean to," her attention suddenly caught by the darkening sky to see that the storm, which had been threatening for several days was beginning to break. It was by now just turned half past six, and the sound of thunder which could be heard and the flashes of lightning clearly visible in the distance, lighting up the ever darkening sky, made it seem much later, and was enough to tell them that it would be right overhead in a little while. Ever since she was seven years old when she had disobeyed Salmon and gone out in search of a puppy with Richard and had been forced to take shelter, she had always been afraid of storms, and hoped that this one would hold off until they reached *'The Little House'* and was therefore more than a little relieved to eventually leave the coach and step inside the house, where Jennings and his wife, delighted to have been asked to cook for the young couple, with Penny and Susan immediately behind, smiling a greeting, was a most welcome sight. A fire had been lit in the front parlour ready for them, laughingly telling Jennings that it was like old times when she used to come here with her mamma while her father was in town on political business. This recollection immediately opened the floodgates to his memory, causing him to recount in detail a list of long forgotten instances that he told her he would never forget, no, not if he lived for ever he, would not! His good lady, taking one look at him, knew he would be gossiping all night if she did not intervene and immediately told him he was embarrassing Miss Elizabeth, and that he would do much better giving her a hand in the kitchen. Gideon may want to take his adored wife in his arms, but his ready sense of the ridiculous overcame him as he called to mind one other occasion when he had been prevented from doing so. His shoulders shook as he watched Jennings being forcibly evicted from the parlour by his strong minded spouse, muttering that he had meant to do no such thing as the door closed behind them.

"I am afraid there is no escape from those who have known us since childhood," he laughed, finally folding her in his arms.

"Poor Jennings," she smiled, snuggling her cheek against his chest, "he will no doubt receive the sharp end of her tongue."

"I wouldn't be surprised," he laughed, "a very determined woman is Mrs. Jennings!"

It seemed he was destined, for the moment at least, not to kiss her, because his lips had barely touched hers when a soft tap was heard on the parlour door, and raising his head looked a little ruefully down into her laughing eyes. "What wager would you lay on this being Penny?"

And so, indeed, it proved. Penny had known instinctively that the young couple would like a little time alone before dinner, but Mrs. Jennings was a most formidable woman and would not take it kindly if her dinner was ruined, besides which, she not only held full sway over the kitchen as well as her husband but, from the looks of it, everyone else as well.

But no matter what the circumstances, one did have to dress for dinner, and it came as no surprise to Gideon, after following Penny up the stairs, to find himself being ushered into large bedroom opposite to the one of his bride, comprising an adjacent dressing room where his clothes for the evening had already been laid out. As he waited for Penny to open the door he cast an amusing glance across the square landing at Elizabeth, who found the door to her room suddenly opened by Susan, informing her that everything was ready.

694

Mrs. Jennings may bully her husband and everyone else within her orbit, but she certainly knew how to dress a dinner, to which Gideon did full justice and Elizabeth found herself spoiled for choice, having forgotten just what an excellent cook she was. Penny, who had delegated to himself the task of serving them, believed in the time honoured tradition of gentlemen partaking of a glass of something after dinner when the ladies had departed, but as he knew perfectly well that Gideon had no taste for port, he prepared the tray with the decanter of cognac and a glass while he escorted Elizabeth to the foot of the stairs. After raising her hands to his lips, he told her softly that he would join her directly, but he could not offend poor Penny's sensibilities by forgoing such a custom. Despite the fact that her colour was a little high, there was nothing in her face to suggest that she was either dreading or mentally bracing herself for what Miss Calne would have shuddered over, looking lovingly up into his face before turning on her heel to climb the stairs without a backward glance, knowing that he was still standing there watching her.

As Susan proved herself to be quite overcome, not only because of all the events of the day as well as the prospect of accompanying Elizabeth on honeymoon, but because the storm was now gathering momentum and the sound of the wind whistling fiercely outside put her a little on edge, it took her far longer than usual to help prepare her charge for bed. Having helped her undress then pulled her nightgown over her head, she began to extract the pins from her hair, but so unsteady were her usually calm fingers that Elizabeth rose to her feet and took hold of her hands in her own, clamping down on her own fears, telling her that the storm would soon be over. Another clap of thunder made her drop the brush, and Elizabeth, becoming rather nervous herself, after picking it up smiled, suggesting kindly that she could manage perfectly well, and she should go to bed. This however, Susan adamantly refused to do but, another, and far more violent thunder clap, startled her, so without giving her time to argue Elizabeth hugged her and kissed her on the cheek, shepherding her towards the door and telling her she would ring for her in the morning when she was ready for her. Susan, torn between her duty and her fear of storms, deliberated for a moment or two but another flash of lightning decided the issue and nodded her head, then after taking one last look at her beautiful young mistress, wished her goodnight and made a hasty exit.

By the time Elizabeth heard Gideon's tap on the door ten minutes later, the storm was directly overhead and the rain, which had begun some little time ago, could now be heard lashing against the window pane by the sheer force of the wind, the curtains billowing out a little and the candles flickering in their holders. It was just as he closed the door behind him that a flash of lightning lit up the sky illuminating the room through the curtains whilst at the same time a mighty burst of thunder exploded right above the house, making her jump. Having discarded the clothes he had been wearing for a nightshirt, over which he wore a burgundy brocade dressing down which accentuated his height and excellent physique, the diamond clip in the nape of his neck having been replaced by his habitual black bow, there was no denying he presented a very handsome figure, but the look she threw at him, rather than one of breathless admiration at the sight of him, was one of heartfelt relief that he was here. She had made a praiseworthy attempt to put on a brave face in front of Susan, but Gideon, who was not so easily fooled, especially as this was a particularly severe storm coming as it did after weeks of hot weather followed by several days of sultry and uncomfortable heat, knew precisely what she feeling.

"Frightened, my darling?" he asked gently.

"A little," she confessed, taking comfort from his strong arms as he wrapped them around her.

"I won't let it hurt you," he told her softly. "I won't let anything hurt you ever again."

"Don't you mind them?" she asked curiously.

"No," he soothed, holding her tighter. "I have bivouacked too many times in conditions like this to take any notice of them."

"It must have been dreadfully uncomfortable," she managed, tensing as another clap of thunder burst right over head.

"One becomes accustomed," he told her softly, the warmth of his body against her own beginning to seep deliciously through her nightgown.

"I suppose one must," she conceded, the unsteadiness in her voice having nothing whatever to do with the storm raging outside. He had held her many times, but her corset as well as the stiff bodice of her gown had always formed a barrier between them, but the fine material of her nightdress offered no such protection from an experience which, whilst totally new to her, was nevertheless an intensely arousing one. But although the unfamiliar sensations which were beginning to invade her were giving her immense pleasure they also had the effect of making her feel suddenly a little shy, filling her with the inexplicable need to say something. "I …I thought Jane looked very beautiful today, …did not you?" she faltered.

He knew this attack of nervousness had nothing to do with the storm or with the fact that she did not love him, and was deeply moved by it. He knew perfectly well that she loved and needed him as much as he did her, but knew too that despite the passionate embraces they had exchanged, she was wholly inexperienced when it came to making love. He had ached to feel her soft pliant body next to his own without any barriers between them but, at no time, had it been his intention to rush her into making love and, as he too had once been young and inexperienced, attempted to set her at ease, so gently easing himself away from her to look down into her slightly flushed face said, in perfect truth. "Yes, I did. So too did Richard, and who could blame him. Although," he pointed out without a tremor, "I must confess there *was* a woman I saw, other than Jane, who particularly caught my eye. You may know the lady to whom I refer," he said conversationally, "an awe-inspiring dowager wearing a wig at least a foot high off her head with towering feathers."

"You mean Mrs. Lavering?" she laughed a little shakily, informing him huskily, "She's a bosom friend of Aunt Clara's."

"But how fortunate," he sighed relieved, easing her awkwardness, "because you know," he told her, with all the air of one who had been given renewed hope, "I had begun to think that any chance of striking up an acquaintanceship with her was lost to me for ever."

Having discovered early on that his drollery was just as stimulating as his kisses and equally as irresistible, right now it had the effect of gradually demolishing her shyness. "I must tell Aunt Clara you wish an introduction."

He seemed to give this due consideration, saying at length, "I am sure she would not hesitate to bring one about," he told her gravely, his eyes alight with amusement and something else she had no difficulty in defining, "but, I think, on second thoughts," he mused, gently bringing his hands to rest either side of her waist, "it might perhaps be as well for me to wait awhile,"

"Oh, why is that?" she asked a little breathlessly, becoming increasingly aware of how hard she was finding it to resist the look in his eyes and how much she liked the feel of his hands on her body.

"Well, you know" he acknowledged ruefully, kissing her forehead, his eyes looking warmly down at her, feeling the rigidity slowly leave her, "it may well be that the lady, Mrs. Lavering I think you said," he raised an enquiring eyebrow, "will not take it kindly should she ever discover that she was not the only one who caught my attention."

The warmth of his hands were beginning to spread deliciously through her, melting away the last residues of shyness, and instinctively wrapped her arms around his neck. "She wasn't?"

"No," he shook his head, "in fact," he told her, his voice deepening, "the other lady to whom I refer was actually walking down the aisle towards her bridegroom standing at the alter impatiently awaiting her,"

"Impatiently?" she repeated huskily, feeling herself being gently pressed into his body.

"Mm" he nodded, lowering his head to brush her lips with his own. "I have it on excellent authority that the groom, who found it impossible to take his eyes off so beautiful and adorable a creature, indeed, has been quite unable to do so all day," kissing her a little more intensely, "is also very much in love with her, in fact," he kissed her again, this time a little more passionately, "he loves her more than life itself. I am also reliably informed, on the same excellent authority," he

697

smiled, his voice a caress, "that not only has the bridegroom been unable to keep his eyes off her, but has also found it well nigh impossible to refrain from taking her in his arms and kissing her. Indeed," he sighed melancholically, "it is only now that the poor fellow has been able to do so. I only hope," pulling her even closer against him, "that the lady takes pity on him and puts him out of his agony."

She trembled in his arms. "I too," she whispered against his lips, "have it on excellent authority that the lady has every intention of doing so and, what is more," she assured him, in a voice that sent a shudder coursing through him, "she too loves her bridegroom more than life and, whilst all of this is very new to her, she wants him to make love to her, so very much."

An agonized groan ripped from his throat at this, and kissed her with such ruthless need that the storm raging outside was completely forgotten, and as his kiss deepened she experienced such a breath-taking sensation of pleasure spiralling through her that she thought her legs would give way under her.

But as his need of her grew his lips and hands began to make increasingly more ardent demands of her mouth and body, demands to which she eagerly responded, until eventually he could no longer hold his emotions in check and began to pull the ribbons which fastened her night gown down to her waist with tremulous fingers until the front opened, exposing part of her seductively responsive naked body. As he gently slid the garment a little off her shoulders he heard her sharp intake of breath as it fell softly to the floor, his own rasping from his throat as he looked at the beautiful and malleable body trembling with need in front of him. The gentle caresses of his hands and mouth were almost reverent, but her response was sufficient to evoke a groaning cry of need from deep within his throat, his desperate need of a closer contact causing him to effortlessly pick her up in his arms and carry her over to the bed, laying her gently down and taking his place beside her, setting in train a devastatingly impassioned assault on her body and senses which she gave herself up to completely.

Somewhere on the periphery of her consciousness was the vague recollection of how she had always been a little dispirited to know that upon her marriage she would be leaving behind everything that was safe and familiar, to begin life again in a house that was alien and strange and where the servants were all unknown to one. But Sir Matthew and Sarah had opened their arms as well as their hearts to her as had their son, and knowing that she would be going to Burroughs Croft, not just as Gideon's bride but as the woman he loved, intensified her responses to his lovemaking. Her refusal of those most obliging offers were now totally justified, and as for Richard and her father, both of whom had suffered as a result of the machinations of men who had neither loyalty nor commitment, had, in a way they could not have foreseen, given her the most precious gift of all. But as the tempest raged all around them, all she knew was that she was where she wanted to be, in Gideon's arms, and just the joy and pleasure of knowing he loved her and was now demonstrating that love as effectively as the weather outside was sweeping all before it, all she knew with any certainty was that this was one storm she was in no hurry to see the end of.

Are you an Author?

Do you want to see your book in print?

Please look at the UKUnpublished website:
www.ukunpublished.co.uk

Let the World Share Your Imagination